The Free Frenchman

NOVELS

Game in Heaven with Tussy Marx
The Junkers
Monk Dawson
The Professor's Daughter
The Upstart
Polonaise
A Married Man
The Villa Golitsyn

NONFICTION

Alive: The Story of the Andes Survivors
The Train Robbers

The Free Frenchman
Piers Paul Read

Random House   New York

Library of Congress Cataloging-in-Publication Data

Read, Piers Paul, 1941–
The free Frenchman.

I. Title.
PR6068.E25F74 1986   823'.914   86-20419
ISBN 0-394-55887-1

Manufactured in the United States of America
24689753
First Edition

Design by Bernard Klein

The camp showed me that a man's real enemies are not ranged against him along the borders of a hostile country; they are often among his own people, indeed, within his own mind. The worst enemies are hate, and greed, and cruelty. The real enemy is within.

Pierre d'Harcourt, *The Real Enemy*

PART
ONE

A

1
————

A T the Convent of the Sacred Heart in Valenciennes in 1890 there were two pupils called Alice Ravanel and Françoise Bart, each ten years old, who had become locked together in one of those absorbing friendships formed by girls of that age. The nuns, who as a general rule discouraged such "particular friendships," made an exception in this case because each seemed to benefit from the influence of the other. Alice was strong, sensible and pretty; Françoise timid, devious and plain.

Both came from established families among the industrialists of northern France, though here again Alice had an advantage over her friend; for while her father and her uncles prospered in the manufacture of steel, the more modest projects of Monsieur Bart always lost money, and the capital he had inherited had dwindled with the passing of time.

When Alice and Françoise left school, Françoise still lived in a large house on the outskirts of Valenciennes, a mile or so from the larger house of Alice Ravanel. But some of the young men who were looking for wives had heard the rumors of the Barts' misfortunes, and though Françoise's mother, who knew quite well how these rumors would affect her daughter's prospects, did all she could to keep a semblance of prosperity, the cunning bourgeois of the Nord were not to be deceived.

If Françoise had been unusually pretty or exceptionally amusing, some young man might have gone against his better judgment and asked to ask for her hand; but while Alice Ravanel grew into a tall young woman with a graceful body, even features and a soft voice to match the gentle expression in her eyes, Françoise Bart had lank brown hair, a long, bony nose, and a smile which exposed the gums above her protruding teeth. Her only attractive feature was her long legs, but anyone who stopped to admire them was soon put off by her nasal, high-pitched voice and a collection of irritating mannerisms. She would laugh, for example, at anything anyone said, whether it was meant as a joke or not, and go back on an opinion within a minute of stating it simply to agree with another's point of view.

This lack of any substance in Françoise Bart undoubtedly had its roots in her childhood—in the weak character of her father, perhaps, which in its turn may have come from the father's fear of his father. Whatever the cause, the effect was sad. Not only was Françoise ignored by the eligible young men; she was also disliked by their sisters—not hated, for it was impossible to hate her, but despised and thus discounted when it came to giving a party or having a dance.

The one exception was her childhood friend, Alice Ravanel. Cynics say that pretty girls like plain companions because the contrast makes them seem prettier still, but if this had ever been the case with Alice, it was no longer so when at eighteen she set about the social life that was to take her so far from Valenciennes. For just as there are young men whose talents are so apparent that they are immediately advanced in their careers, so there are girls who are picked out by an unofficial caucus of powerful old ladies to go further than might otherwise be allowed. Alice, whose destiny was presumed to be that of the wife of a northern industrialist like her father, was noticed and then promoted by the mothers on the fringe of a smarter set—not just because she was rich and pretty, but because her manner was admirably modest and her demeanor more dignified than that of many a daughter of a duke.

This reserve, so tantalizing in a graceful girl, came from Alice's piety, for both at the convent and in her home she had been brought up to a strict observance of the Catholic religion. Though a capitalist, her father was a conscientious man who lived by the encyclical *Rerum Novarum,* and her mother was a devotee of Our Lady of Lourdes. Her brother Charles was already in a seminary training to be a priest, and Alice herself never went to bed at night without reciting a decade of the rosary.

In Alice, as in her parents, piety was combined with common sense. To the disappointment of some of the nuns, she never for a moment considered becoming a nun herself, but knew that her calling was to marriage and to family life. She had, at times, thought that Françoise might enter a convent, until it became quite clear that Françoise was incapable of such fixity of purpose. Then she thought that Françoise

might marry one of her brothers, but Charles was to be a priest and
the other two were not so holy that they would marry a girl who was
poor and plain.

Alice did what she could to introduce Françoise to her other friends,
but when invitations came to balls in Paris and to house parties in
different country houses, it became out of the question to take Françoise with her. Whenever Alice returned to Valenciennes, she made
sure that she saw her friend, but within a space of a single year, between
the ages of seventeen and eighteen, the two girls had moved into
different constellations.

In September 1899, Alice Ravanel became engaged to a young
cavalry officer called Edmond de Roujay. Some of the dowagers
thought that she could have done better, for the de Roujays were an
old but undistinguished family from Provence. Her parents, however,
who mistrusted the higher aristocracy, were pleased that she had chosen
such a decent young man. Their only regret was that his family home
was so far away in the south of France.

When Françoise Bart was told of her friend's engagement, she burst
into tears—tears of happiness, tears of envy, tears of chagrin. She was
only nineteen, too young to despair of making a match herself; but
her father's affairs were going no better, her mother had had to dismiss
some of the servants, no one courted her, no one asked her to visit.
The life of an impoverished spinster seemed her certain fate.

Alice, always optimistic where Françoise was concerned, hoped she
might meet a suitor among Edmond's fellow officers at her wedding.
When, at the reception, she drank champagne from the outer rim of
her glass and made her wish, it was not for herself but for her friend
—that she might find a husband and be happily married. But nature
is cruel, and the dashing young subalterns had no more reason to be
drawn to Françoise Bart than had the ambitious young businessmen of
Valenciennes.

Alice left on her honeymoon in Italy. Françoise returned to her dark
home and its atmosphere of despair. Alice sent her a postcard from
Venice, a second from Ravenna, a third from Rome, then a long letter
describing her husband's home in Provence. "It is a lovely old house
shaded by chestnut trees. There are the ruins of an old monastery on
the top of the hill. Edmond's parents are so kind. They have bought
me a mare to go riding through the vineyards by the river."

Françoise wrote back dull letters in large handwriting with all the gossip about other people's lives, and a certain bravado about her own. "Who can say that there's no social life in Valenciennes? We're going to a civic reception at the Hôtel de Ville on the 14th of July!"

Alice never had an account of this reception, at least not from her old friend. Edmond de Roujay's regiment was sent to Morocco in August, and Alice accompanied her husband to Tangier. It took time for letters to reach her, and it was not until September that she heard of Françoise's scandalous marriage. She had met a schoolteacher at the Hôtel de Ville and was married to him before the mayor a month later.

The scandal, for Alice's mother, who gave her the news in a letter, was not so much that the schoolteacher, Michel Bonnet, was young, poor and the son of a postman, but that he was a radical, an atheist and almost certainly a Freemason. "The poor Barts. It must be the last straw. May God give them strength to bear this humiliation."

For Alice the scandal was a challenge. She was expecting a child, and so was filled with a natural happiness which she took at the time to be the grace of God. She wrote at once to Françoise a letter of quiet congratulation.

In the eighth month of her pregnancy, Alice de Roujay returned from Morocco to the Domaine de Saint Théodore, Edmond de Roujay's home in Provence. Edmond was not able to accompany her; she was alone with her parents-in-law. The ecstasy of the early months had been dampened by the discomfort of these last weeks of her pregnancy. Despite the winter weather, her body felt hot and heavy. She slept badly at night and had intermittent cramps in her belly, all of which drew her mind away from the plight of Françoise Bart.

The de Roujays had lived at Saint Théodore only since the restoration of the Bourbons in 1815, but had owned small properties in Provence for five hundred years before that. They traced their ancestors back to a Jean de Roujay who had accompanied Saint Louis on crusade, and upon his return to France he had settled in that part of the Rhône Valley between Avignon and the Alps known as the Comtat Venaissin. It was ruled at that time by the counts of Toulouse, but after the defeat of the Albigensian heretics whom he had championed, Raymond of Toulouse was dispossessed and the Comtat Venaissin passed to the Pope.

In the fourteenth century, Pope Clement V fled from Rome and took up residence in Avignon, and so it was in the papal army and administration that the de Roujays of the time made their careers. It was a time when no rigid definition of nationality limited the scope of a soldier or a diplomat; it was only in later centuries that the de Roujays were drawn by the growing power of the France into the service of the French kings. Even so, they often served under different flags. One de Roujay fought for the French at the battle of Fontenoy; another served in the Dutch army; a third fought with the Americans at Yorktown; a fourth, an émigré, fought with the English against the revolutionary armies of France.

It was this de Roujay who returned to France under an amnesty, and after the restoration was rewarded for his loyalty to the Bourbons with the means to buy the Domaine de Saint Théodore, which until the Revolution had belonged to an order of monks. The monastic buildings at the top of the hill had fallen into disrepair and had been plundered by the villagers for materials to build their cottages and barns. Edmond's great-grandfather had therefore built a new house and outbuildings at the bottom of the hill, which sheltered it from the mistral. The ruins of the monastery had been shored up to provide the more mundane buildings of the estate—the wine cellars, barns, stables and cottages. No one had ever worked out quite what was what, but the barrel vaulting of the wine cellars had almost certainly been the roof of the crypt, while two of the cottages had been built within the outer stone shell of what had once been the monks' refectory. Several horses were stabled in the ruins of the chapter house, and two sides of the fold yard bore traces of a cloister.

Hidden from these outbuildings by the steep wooded hill, the house at its foot was solid and square, with pastel yellow walls. There were three rows of windows: glazed doors on the ground floor opening onto a graveled terrace, rectangular windows on the upper floor, and small openings into the attics under the deep eaves of the tiled roof. Each window had a pair of mauve shutters which were closed against the sun in summer, and blue cast-iron railings enclosed a modest garden of rough grass with graveled paths beneath two rows of chestnut trees.

On February 2, 1901, Edmond returned from North Africa, and two days later Alice gave birth to a boy. Three weeks after that her parents came from Valenciennes for the boy's baptism. He was called Bertrand. Here again, the joy and fuss about the baby made Alice think of little else and it was only well into her mother's stay, when all other topics had been exhausted, that she heard the latest news of the Barts. The father's company had crashed. They had had to sell their house and move temporarily to their holiday villa at Bray-Dunes near Dunkirk.

"And Françoise?" asked Alice.

"They left Valenciennes and went to Montpellier," said Madame Ravanel with pursed lips. "It's sad for Madame Bart to lose her daughter, but on the whole it's for the best."

Alice was about to ask more, but little Bertrand gurgled and once again the joys and anxieties of nursing a newborn child filled her mind. It was not until many months later, when the baby was weaned and was looked after for much of the time by a girl from the village of Pévier, that the empty hours led Alice to think again of her friend. Montpellier, after all, was not so far from Saint Théodore.

There followed an exchange of letters in which the two young women expressed a longing to see each other, but both seemed confused as to how this could be done. Edmond had returned to Morocco, and Alice was at first embarrassed to ask her parents-in-law if she could have a friend to stay. When she eventually suggested it, they not only allowed it but seemed delighted that Alice should find some distraction. But then, to her embarrassment, she received a note from Françoise to say that her husband had forbidden her to come to Saint Théodore, and inviting her instead to Montpellier.

It was possible, by taking an early train from Mézac, to reach Montpellier in time for lunch, and by taking another train in the late afternoon, to be back at Saint Théodore by ten at night. Alice therefore decided that she would go. Marthe, the nursemaid, was told to take charge of the baby, and the old de Roujays were delighted to lend Alice their car and driver. They understood that this was an errand of mercy, but they also knew that life at Saint Théodore could be monotonous for a girl of her age, and noticed that their daughter-in-law revived in spirit as she discussed the kind of costume she should wear for this trip to town.

Alice chose a yellow skirt and a white blouse, the papal colors, but when she reached the street in Montpellier where Françoise lived and climbed the stairs of the shabby tenement toward her flat, she began to regret the elegance of her attire.

The door to the apartment was opened by Françoise herself, and it occurred to Alice as she entered that perhaps there was no housemaid to help her. The apartment was small; the living room had books stacked on the floor. She took all this in before she turned to study the face of her friend, but when she did so, it seemed just the same. They embraced. Françoise laughed. She laughed again—that nervous laugh—as she apologized for the simplicity of her dwelling. "But as you know, we had so little money. Papa had nothing to give us, and Michel has only his salary."

"And schoolteachers are so badly paid," said Alice.

"Well, yes, but he's not a schoolteacher anymore."

"What does he do?"

Françoise laughed. "He's still a teacher, but at the university."

"I didn't know."

"In Valenciennes he was writing his thesis. As soon as he presented it, they not only gave him his degree but offered him a post." She laughed again. "That's why we came here."

No sooner had she said this than both women heard the sound of a key in the door, at which Alice straightened her skirt and Françoise's expression changed. A look of fascinated fear came into her eyes. "That's . . . that's . . ." she began. She went toward the small hallway, then turned to Alice. "That's him," she whispered.

Alice had not expected to meet Michel Bonnet, but had hoped that perhaps she would, for one cannot have a friend and not be curious to see the man she has married. She was prepared for the worst, but not for what occurred. As she sat there with a certain serenity, there walked into the room a short, swarthy man who instead of greeting her ignored her and crossed to the desk to remove the contents of his Gladstone bag.

Alice de Roujay was taken aback. Though free of vanity, she had become used to drawing all eyes upon her person, even in a crowded room; but Michel Bonnet behaved as if he genuinely had not noticed her sitting in the chair by the window. It was only when Françoise followed him in, and laughed, and then cleared her throat, that he turned, a book in his hand, and said sharply, "What is it?"

"Michel . . . I . . . this is Alice de Roujay."

He turned and looked where she pointed. "Alice de Roujay?"

Alice nodded. "Good day."

"Good day." While she had pronounced the two words as a greeting, he spoke them abruptly as if taking leave of her, and having said them turned back to the desk, picked up a book, turned, and without looking at either woman left the room.

Françoise sidled up to Alice. "You mustn't pay any attention," she said. "You see, he's always *thinking*."

"Thinking?" asked Alice, shocked by a discourtesy she had never met before.

"They say he'll be a professor very soon. You should see some of the letters he gets. He's tremendously admired. But, of course, he's not fond of talking . . . I mean, unless it's about his work."

"Doesn't he talk to you?"

"Not really."

There was a smell of cooking. Françoise looked uneasily over her shoulder. "We must have lunch," she said. "You see, usually . . . I mean, I thought, today . . . a Tuesday . . ." She laughed.

They moved through from the sitting room into a small dining room, where Michel Bonnet already sat at the head of the table. He was reading a book, and when Alice sat next to him he continued to read but began moving his finger to and from along the text, as if prepared for an interruption.

Alice said nothing. She was baffled, not just by his rudeness but by the way in which he seemed quite unaware that he was being rude. So absorbed was he in what he was reading that while Françoise was in the kitchen fetching the food, Alice was able to study him as if he were an animal at the zoo.

He was young, not yet thirty, but his face seemed prematurely old, with wrinkles around his eyes and stains on his cheeks the color of tea. His face had more expression than was usual for a man of his age, as if he had lived more fully, or lived through more, but the expression itself was hard to read—a blend of petulance and determination, unself-consciousness and inner absorption. He was unlike anyone Alice had ever seen before, and in a sense fitted the diabolic role he had been given; only unlike the devil, Michel Bonnet seemed indifferent to the condition of Alice de Roujay's soul. While his wife was in the kitchen, he did not look up from his book. The only sign that he was aware of Alice's presence was the finger he kept on the line of text.

The meat was undercooked, the beans were hard, and the gravy was greasy; but since Françoise, like Alice, had not been brought up to cook for herself, it amazed Alice that she could lay anything on the table at all. Michel Bonnet appeared not to notice the quality of what was put before him, but scowled because he could not cut the meat on his plate, or eat it, without putting down his book and using both hands. Even when he stopped reading, however, he appeared to be listening to his own thoughts, not the stilted chat of the two women; and when the meat was cut, and he had only to chew it, his eye moved slowly from his plate to the pepper pot, from the pepper pot to the two tawdry candlesticks in the center of the table, until finally they settled on the bodice of Alice de Roujay's blouse.

In a less innocent age, or in a less innocent person, it might have been thought that the manner in which his glance lingered there reflected an admiration for the pleasant proportions of Alice de Roujay's bosom. But Alice sensed at once that it was not her natural qualities which had caught his attention but the artificial elegance of her jacket and blouse, for there was something about the color and texture of what she wore, the impracticality of the fine materials and bright colors, the evidence of many hours of nimble-fingered labor on garments that would soon smudge with the dirt of life, which contrasted forcibly with the sensible but dowdy clothes worn by Françoise and Michel Bonnet.

Suddenly he raised his eyes from the matching cloth-covered buttons of her bodice and said, "Dreyfus, then? Innocent or guilty?"

He spoke with a certain relish, because already at this time it was apparent even to the diehard anti-Dreyfusards that the wretched man who had been twice convicted of spying for the Germans was probably innocent. It was a view that the Ravanel family had taken from the start, but that the de Roujays, particularly Edmond's father, still could not contemplate except in a half-sleeping, half-waking nightmare.

Alice had always accepted her father's judgment that Dreyfus was innocent, but now, when faced with the question by Michel Bonnet, expressed with all the taunting mockery of the radical atheist who has caught the Christian conservative on the wrong foot, she found a spirit of rebellion rise within her and so said, "Only God knows the truth about *that*."

"God, eh?" asked Michel Bonnet. "Then why doesn't he tell us?"

"I'm sure he would," said Alice, "if those who judge the man would only look into their hearts."

"Their hearts but not their heads? Why? No brains?"

Alice blushed. "Their souls, I should have said."

"Where are their souls?"

"Where?"

"Yes. The soul. Where is it? In the head? The breast? The big toe?"

"Our soul," said Alice, remembering her catechism, "has no material existence."

"No ears?"

"No."

"Then how can it hear God?"

"It was a figure of speech."

"Could Joan of Arc have heard her voices if she had been deaf?"

"Yes."

"And would Bernadette have had her vision at Lourdes if she had been blind?"

Alice hesitated. "Not in the same way."

"She had to have eyes?"

"Yes."

"So one cannot see the Virgin without eyes, but one can hear God without ears."

"Yes."

"And without a brain?"

Alice was now confused. "Everyone has a brain."

"But half-wits?" asked Michel Bonnet in an exasperated tone of voice. "Does God speak to half-wits?"

"Of course," said Alice.

He laughed. "Well there, at least, we agree."

Alice thought it more dignified to make no rejoinder to this last remark. Her face had gone pink with a species of holy exhilaration at this conversational martyrdom, the words of the skeptic striking her like the stones thrown at Saint Stephen. It was only Françoise who suffered at this exchange between her husband and her friend. She looked from one to the other like a nervous animal, and for fear of leaving them alone she hesitated before taking their empty plates to the kitchen. Only when she saw that her husband had gone back to his book did she leave the room.

No sooner had she done so, however, than Alice, flushed with her own courage, leaned forward and said, "You have your convictions, Monsieur Bonnet. You could at least respect the convictions of others."

The swarthy academic put his finger on the word where he had been interrupted. "Respect?" he asked.

"Tolerate . . ."

"It was a Pope who said that error has no rights—and I agree!"

He went back to his book. When Françoise returned, she and Alice made stilted conversation, but it was impossible to enjoy the easy chat of old friends in his presence. When they went through to the living room to drink coffee, he followed and sat reading in an armchair. It was only when he had finished his coffee that he went to the desk and prepared to leave for the university. He filled his Gladstone bag with books and papers, kissed his wife on her forehead like a father kissing a child, and then left the room without looking at Alice. A moment later, however, as if remembering that there had been a guest at lunch, he put his head back through the door and said, "Goodbye." Before Alice could reply, he was gone.

Alice proposed to help Françoise wash the dishes, but Françoise, who knew quite well that Alice had never washed a dish in her life, refused to allow it and suggested instead a walk through the town. "You see, we could have a maid," she said to Alice as they came down the stairs and walked past the concierge, "but Michel disapproves of domestic servants."

"Disapproves?"

"He says a man should clear up his own mess."

·"I didn't notice him doing much himself."

"Or have a wife to do it for him."

"So you're his servant!"

"In a way I am, yes." She gave one of her nervous whinnies.

"But it's intolerable, Françoise."

"Is it? Oh dear, but you see . . . I mean, you're so good at everything. It would be awful if *you* had to cook and clean, but there's nothing much else that I could do, or really want to do."

"Even so . . ."

"And though I'm not very good at cooking either, I do seem to cope with Michel when so many other people . . ."

"Can't abide him?" It was Alice who finished the sentence.

They came into the street. "He is very rude, I know," said Françoise, "but he doesn't really mean to be impolite. He just isn't used to company, you see, and his mother spoiled him. And then he is very clever, really he is. He's very young to be taken on at the university."

"I daresay."

"You have to make some allowances."

"For genius?"

"Yes."

"Perhaps."

They walked in the Jardin du Champ de Mars. "Do you like Montpellier?" asked Alice.

Françoise looked furtively at the people around them, as if trying to guess what her answer should be. "Well, yes, I mean . . ."

"It's very pretty," said Alice.

"And it's full of intelligent people."

"I suppose it is," said Alice doubtfully. "Have you made any friends?"

"Friends?" Françoise repeated the word as if she did not quite know what it meant.

"Are there wives of other teachers whom you see from time to time?"

"Not really."

"Do you go out to dinner?"

"Oh, no."

"What about your husband's colleagues?"

"He says they are all mediocre."

"So you see no one?"

"I see Michel."

They sat down on a bench. "Your life sounds so empty," said Alice.

"Oh, but it isn't, really."

"Aren't you lonely?"

"I have Michel."

"He isn't cruel to you?"

"Oh, no. At least, he doesn't mean to be."

"He seems to despise religion."

"Yes, he does."

"He wouldn't marry in a church?"

"No."

"But that's . . ." She was about to say "a mortal sin," but desisted.

"It makes me a Jezebel, doesn't it?" said Françoise, laughing, but whether from mirth or nervousness it was impossible to tell.

"Do you ever go to mass?"

"Sometimes."

"Doesn't he mind?"

"He doesn't notice."

"And when you have a child?"

"Ah . . ."

This was a sound, not a word, but a sound so filled with inchoate meaning that Alice stopped and turned to look into her friend's face.

"Won't you have a child?" she asked.

Françoise laughed. She looked afraid. "Michel doesn't want one."

"Why not?"

"It would disturb his work."

"But if God sends you one?"

"Sometimes he doesn't."

"But don't you . . . I mean . . ."

"Of course."

"Then . . ."

"There are things you can do."

"But Françoise, that is . . . that is a terrible sin."

Françoise laughed. "Worse than not marrying in a church?"

"Oh much, much worse."

Françoise shrugged her shoulders and laughed. "I told you, I am a Jezebel."

On the train back to Mézac, Alice de Roujay kept a book open on her lap but could not bring herself to read the words on the page. She had been confused by her visit to Françoise. The picture of her plain friend in dowdy clothes standing in the sun in the Jardin du Champ de Mars, presenting herself as a Jezebel, refused to be labeled in a conventional way. Certainly she was a Jezebel, a woman who had rejected both the disciplines and the teaching of the Church to live in sterile union with a man who denied God, but Alice's image of Jezebel had always been of a beautiful, sinuous woman with huge eyes, long eyelashes, painted lips and a sensuous smile. To see Françoise as a victim of the lusts of her flesh was absurd; to see her as a victim of her husband's lusts was equally improbable.

If it was not lust, then what was it? In her mind she went through the other six deadly sins, but none of them seemed to describe Françoise's transgression. Yet it was impossible to suggest that her friend was not in a state of sin, or did not know she had done wrong. There had been an admission of guilt—an almost shameless admission of guilt —in the look she had given Alice when she had told her that there were things you could do to avoid having a child—a look suggesting some sort of triumph that Michel wanted her for herself alone, not as a means to an end.

This was what confounded Alice—that her wretched friend was not wretched at all, that though denied a child, and obliged by a barbarous husband to lead the life of a skivvy, she was indisputably happy— happier, at any rate, than she had ever been in Valenciennes.

Alice returned to the Domaine de Saint Théodore with great relief, pleased not just to see her baby again, but to return to a life which at times might seem monotonous, but which was stable and secure. The space and light of the large rooms, the solidity of the furniture, the respect shown by the servants and the punctuality of the meals seemed somehow to prove that it was all in accordance with God's transcendental design, just as the poverty and disorder of the flat in Montpellier was in some way the result of a life of sin.

Alice did not forsake Françoise. She prayed for her vehemently every night, and from time to time wrote her letters to which from time to time Françoise replied. But it was a frustrating correspondence, for it was impossible for Alice to say what she thought of Michel Bonnet, yet she did not see how Françoise could ever be saved without breaking her liaison with such a monstrous man. She made allusions to the possibility of such a rupture in one or two of her letters, but far from seeing her husband's iniquity, Françoise in her answers seemed subject to a growing thrall. It was quite apparent that she had no life besides her life with him, and so had little to say which did not concern his work or his career. Moreover, she described his progress with a certain conceit, for the postman's son soon established a considerable reputation and was rapidly promoted to the post of Professor in the Faculty of History at Montpellier. The hours of scholarship bore fruit in books, and Alice, to her involuntary annoyance, sometimes stumbled upon admiring reviews in newspapers and magazines.

Since Françoise could not be redeemed by post, Alice relied upon the power of prayer, and in her nightly invocations to Our Lady of Lourdes she at first placed Françoise high on her list. But as the months passed these invocations became increasingly automatic and the more urgent needs of those still closer than Françoise pushed her childhood friend further and further down the list. Alice's own life began to fill up as she left Saint Théodore to live with Edmond in different postings in France itself and in the vast French empire, first with one, then two, then three young children whose different needs came first. It was not until the birth of the third—a daughter, Dominique—that she seemed to bring Françoise to the Virgin's attention, for it was then that Françoise told her she was expecting a child.

When Alice de Roujay heard of her friend's pregnancy, she took it to be a miracle like that of Saint Elizabeth or the Virgin herself. The truth, however, was more prosaic. In Montpellier the Bonnets had moved into a larger apartment, and the professor, now more secure in his success, had come to find his wife's obsessive attentions irksome and claustrophobic. He himself hired a cook and a maid to introduce some variety among those who attended to him, but this only left Françoise with more time and energy to devote to her husband. It was not that she ever spoke to him unless he spoke to her, or even remained in a room when she sensed that he would rather be alone, but he knew that she was always there, lurking at the end of the corridor, lifeless until he snapped at her or ordered her to perform some menial chore.

At first he thought she should have friends, but realized at once that no one of any intelligence would befriend her. She would almost certainly fill the house with tawdry examples of imbecilic gentility. He therefore fell back upon a child as a means to divert her oppressive devotion. He told her to take measures to conceive in just the same way as he had told her to arrange to move to the new flat. Françoise obeyed with no particular enthusiasm, for as Alice de Roujay had realized, she had felt flattered by her husband's initial desire to have her all to himself.

The baby was a girl and was named Madeleine because, said Michel Bonnet, "the whore was the only sympathetic woman among those who hung around Christ." She was pretty and healthy and established her own domain at the opposite end of the flat from her father's study. The professor showed no interest in his daughter whatsoever, but used her as he had planned in order to get rid of his wife when her presence became oppressive. "Go and see to your child," he would say when he saw her doglike eyes watching him from the corner of the room, and she would obediently remove herself to the nursery, though only from obedience, not because she wanted to be with her baby.

Madeleine Bonnet was born only a month or two after Alice de Roujay's youngest child, Dominique, but though the two families were geographically close when the de Roujays were at Saint Théodore, the ideological chasm between them remained as wide as ever. Alice could not contemplate subjecting herself for a second time to the insults she had received from Michel Bonnet on her visit, and Françoise never accepted—or seemed to want to accept—the invitations to visit Saint Théodore which Alice de Roujay issued from time to time. Thus the two daughters of these two childhood friends might never have met at all had it not been for two separate factors: the heat of the summer in Languedoc and the outbreak of war.

In summer Montpellier became intolerably hot, and those who were able to left for the mountains or the sea. Michel Bonnet himself was indifferent to the soaring temperature in July and August; he closed the shutters to keep out the sun and got down to the work he could never find the time to complete during the term. During the first summer after the birth of Madeleine, the professor assumed that Françoise would remain with him and be content with day trips to the seaside or walks on the Promenade du Peyrou. By Madeleine's second summer, however, he had learned that even in a large flat and with a reverential wife, it is hard to escape from the sounds and demands of a spirited child. When Françoise timidly suggested that she and Madeleine might join her parents at Bray-Dunes on the Channel near Dunkirk, Michel Bonnet was quick to agree.

This arrangement continued until 1914, when Bray-Dunes was threatened by the advance of the German army. It was then that it occurred to Françoise to take up Alice de Roujay's invitation, issued so many years before, to spend some weeks of the summer at Saint Théodore. She suggested it timidly to her husband, who at first replied with an angry tirade against such arrogant, posturing snobs as the de

Roujays, who, if given the chance, would put their heel back on the neck of the French people as they had under the *ancien régime*. Already his initial indifference to his four-year-old daughter had been eroded by an odd and envious affection, and he was determined to protect her from all unenlightened influence. But he also prized the peace of his solitary August, and so finally relented. Worse than the thought of the corruption of his wife and daughter by a priest-ridden, royalist household was their presence in the flat throughout the long summer vacation.

The first visit to Saint Théodore was a success. Because of the war there were no men about, and Alice de Roujay was glad of a companion. Both she and Françoise were older, and were superficially changed. Alice now wore her hair in a bun, and Françoise laughed less frequently. Beneath these changes, however, were the same two girls from Valenciennes, and their pecking order was reestablished. The old de Roujays were dead; Alice was now the chatelaine, and with Edmond and most of the workers away at the front there was much to do. Not only did Françoise make an amenable aide-de-camp, but her daughter, Madeleine, could play with Dominique.

Madeleine Bonnet was just four years old when she first came to Saint Théodore, a compact little girl with dark skin, straight black hair and large brown eyes. Alice saw at once that physically she resembled her father, and it soon became apparent that in character she was like him too. She was fierce, stubborn and silent—reasonable in her demands, but merciless if they were not met. She was not at all intimidated by the grandeur of Saint Théodore but at once took a delight in its space and freedom, running up and down the corridors on her plump little legs, delighted that she could go so far with no one to escort her. Sometimes she would play hide-and-seek with Dominique, squeezing behind the heavy pieces of furniture in the gloomy dining room which Alice de Roujay had brought as part of her dowry. They made better hiding places than the few older and more elegant pieces which were all that remained from the house's original inventory after the younger sons and daughters of earlier generations had exercised their rights of inheritance.

On other occasions Madeleine chose to hide behind the faded pink curtains in the drawing room, where portraits of earlier de Roujays looked down on her but never gave her away. She also liked to crawl behind the huge globe in the library, where some hanging scrolls from the Yuan dynasty, which Edmond de Roujay's father had brought back from a tour of duty in Tonkin, seemed to act as a protective talisman.

Once, when hiding upstairs, she slipped into Alice de Roujay's bedroom and disappeared beneath her huge four-poster bed. She waited behind the dark blue hangings, peering out at the upholstered prie-dieu which faced a large ebony crucifix on the wall. Then her eye lit upon a group of silver-framed photographs beside the ivory brushes on the dressing table, and curiosity lured her from beneath the bed to look at the severe faces which peered through the frames from the past. One was that of a young man in uniform; three were of the children as babies; and behind them, colored with the brown tint of a nineteenth-century daguerreotype, was the picture of two little girls.

"That's your mother and me," said a voice behind her.

Madeleine turned and saw Alice de Roujay.

"We were older than you are now," she said, "and we were already the best of friends." She smiled and took Madeleine's hand. "Now come downstairs, if you please. I don't like you children to play in here."

Françoise Bonnet, who at the time the daguerreotype had been taken had followed her friend in everything she did, now attended on her daughter like a housemaid under threat of dismissal. The child allowed her mother to dress and undress her, and to serve her meals, in the manner of the Sun King at the *grande levée*. Alice noticed this, and saw it at once as the dominating trait from her father's character. But this very strength of character made Madeleine a suitable companion for the wistful Dominique. The complementary qualities in the two mothers were in the daughters reversed. As the only daughter, Dominique was a solitary child who for want of a companion in the immediate family had made friends with animals: a pet rabbit, a pony, her father's gun dog and the three cats on the farm. She used to weep when her brothers went shooting, and once when they returned she stole the dead snipe from the game larder and gave them a Christian burial under one of the chestnut trees.

Bertrand and Louis, the two boys, ignored their sister not just because she was so much younger but also because she was a girl. During the term these two spirited adolescents were held in check by the Jesuits in Mézac, but during the holidays, especially in those years when their father was away at the war, they went about their manly pursuits without a man to guide them. Bertrand, being the eldest, and by nature more sober than Louis, exercised some caution and responsibility when it came to horses and guns, but once in the house he would descend to the level of his younger brother and bicker and bark to their mother's distraction.

Their disputes were not quarrels, but hotheaded arguments about politics and history. By and large the de Roujay family fell into two camps, with Bertrand, who was both physically and temperamentally like his mother, taking a more liberal stance on the issues of the day, while Louis, who had inherited not just his father's fair hair and blue eyes but also his traditional loyalties, was a royalist disciple of Charles Maurras. Thus they differed not just on public issues, but also on private matters with a political tinge. Louis insisted that the de Roujays were *nobles,* Bertrand that they were merely *notables.* To Louis, Saint Théodore was a *château,* while to Bertrand it was merely a *mas.* Sometimes the brothers would become so genuinely incensed that Bertrand's face would tighten and pale patches would appear at his temples as in a scathing tone of voice he would demolish the baroque edifice of his brother's argument; while Louis, stung like a bull by the taunts of Bertrand's more logical mind, would bellow insults and denunciations at the degenerate democrats who sapped the lifeblood of the nation.

All this was watched with astonishment by little Madeleine Bonnet, who outside Saint Théodore knew no family life. She looked on with the serious mien of an Indian from the Amazon, and the two boys pretended to tremble at her stern expression. The brown eyes under the black fringe seemed to be judging the two boisterous adolescents, and judging them severely. Sometimes they dared to tease her, but they were never able to make her cry.

Madeleine's presence in her house offered Alice an opportunity to do more than just pray for her salvation. She made no deliberate attempt to convert her, but hoped that the atmosphere of her pious household would influence the impressionable child. Like Françoise, her mother, Madeleine fell in with the Catholic practices of life at Saint

Théodore, standing mutely as grace was said before meals, and following them obediently to mass on Sunday. She did not go to communion because she was not baptized, but Alice could hope that the mere presence of the Eucharist would draw the young soul toward faith in God. While she recognized the characteristics in Madeleine which she had inherited from her father, there seemed no reason why they should lead to the same obstinate rejection of religion.

If Alice de Roujay took no more concrete steps to convert little Madeleine Bonnet, it was because there were other more pressing needs at that time. Her husband, Edmond, was in the trenches. Twice he had been wounded; twice he had come back to Saint Théodore to convalesce; twice he had returned to the front. His Croix de Guerre, his rising rank, the esteem and affection of his friends did not console her for her fears that he too would be slaughtered along with all the rest.

As the war progressed, a new and more terrible threat menaced Alice. Bertrand, born in 1901, would become eligible for conscription in 1918. To her it seemed impossible that this gangling child, whose voice had just broken, and whose mustache was no more than a smudge of down on his upper lip, should soon join the grown men in the trenches. She prayed morning and night, and when Bertrand's conscription was only weeks away, she retired whenever she could to kneel on the prie-dieu in her bedroom. On October 1, Bertrand entered the barracks at Coustiers. On October 3, Prince Max of Baden, the new Chancellor of Germany, asked President Wilson for an armistice. On November 11, while Bertrand was still in Coustiers, the armistice was signed. The war was over; peace had come to Europe. To Alice de Roujay the timing was not fortuitous but came as a result of her personal appeal to Mary, the Mother of God.

By the summer of 1919, when Françoise and Madeleine Bonnet could have returned to the Barts' villa at Bray-Dunes, their summer visits to Saint Théodore had become a fixture on the de Roujays' calendar and Alice de Roujay insisted that they return. She was still euphoric after the victory and could not see—or would not see—that even at Saint Théodore things were not the same.

Two workers on the estate had not returned; and while it was easy to find replacements from among the unemployed, there was nowhere to house them because the widows and children of the dead men remained in their homes. Another worker had returned, but without his left leg, and had to be paid a full wage even though there was little he could do in the vines or on the farm.

Edmond de Roujay himself had come back with none of the panache of a conquering hero. The war itself had come to him as a shock and a disappointment, because he belonged to a generation which had been brought up with German governesses, and he had learned in his youth not just to speak the German language but to love Bach, Mozart, Goethe, Heine and the baroque churches of Bavaria.

Alice, on the other hand, coming from a family in northern France which had commercial contacts in England, had learned to speak English from an English nanny, and though she was always prepared to obey her husband when he issued a direct command, she did not think it her duty to ask for his opinion on a matter when it was likely to be different from hers. When Bertrand was ten she had taken advantage of Edmond's absence on a tour of duty in Senegal to hire a Scottish nanny. Edmond had only realized what she had done when he had returned from Dakar and met Miss Ferguson in a corridor at Saint Théodore, but he had acquiesced to this *fait accompli* both to please his wife and in deference to the growing antipathy toward the Germans that was felt throughout France at that time.

He had fought his former friends without enthusiasm and now returned like one of the defeated. There was no swagger in his gait; his easy charm had gone. He was irritable and bewildered, and spent most of the day shut away in the library, as if avoiding the company of his family. Bertrand was at Saint Cyr that summer, but Louis, who had suffered from his father's absence during his adolescence, hung around the closed door of the library like a boisterous puppy waiting to be taken for a walk.

When Edmond appeared, however, he dodged his son and on the pretext of business went instead to see the men working on the vines. If he wanted company, it was theirs; he spent many hours in particular with the man with one leg. The women all seemed to exasperate him —the cook, the housemaids, the English governess, Françoise and even his wife. The more blithe Alice was, the more insistent that everything was "back to normal," the more Edmond de Roujay snapped at her, or shut himself away in the library. He struggled to be civil, and at times would succeed, but then suddenly a chance remark by Alice or one of Françoise's inane laughs would so irritate him that he would throw down his knife and fork and leave the dining room in the middle of lunch or dinner.

This condition was to pass, but by the summer of 1920, the second summer after the war, when Françoise and Madeleine Bonnet arrived as usual to spend August at Saint Théodore, it had changed not just the atmosphere but Alice's mood. The whole nation was suffering from disappointment and confusion that the fruits of victory had turned out to be so sour, and the de Roujays had had to face certain tedious and intractable problems about the management of their estate. Alice de Roujay could not bring herself to ask Our Lady of Lourdes to evict the war widows from their cottages or to raise the market price of wine, but it detracted from her spiritual serenity to have to consider these vexed questions with a husband who seemed not to care.

Alice had noticed the summer before that Edmond de Roujay was irritated by Françoise Bonnet, and, ignoring the evidence that he was also irritated by the other women of the household, she had begun to see her lame duck as a possible scapegoat. When Françoise arrived, she herself began to feel exasperated by Françoise's obsequious appreciation of everything Alice said or did. She was embarrassed by her admirer now that things were not going well. Nor did their daughters get on as well as they had the year before; in the mysterious way in which girls of ten or so decide these things, they had suddenly discovered that they had nothing in common. While Dominique continued to pick dandelion leaves for her pet rabbits, Madeleine remained in her room reading books she had borrowed from the library. At table she ignored Dominique's little sallies about nature and listened instead to the incessant arguments about politics and history between Louis, who was on holiday, and Bertrand, who was on leave.

Madeleine's fierceness, which had seemed so amusing in a four-year-old, was less endearing in the girl of ten. It came across more as moodiness, and the contemptuous manner in which she sometimes addressed her mother shocked the servants who overheard it. "An only child is always spoiled," said Marthe, Bertrand's nursemaid, who was now the de Roujay's cook. Alice agreed. Moreover, she recognized in the voice used by the daughter to bully the mother the same tone she had heard in the father in Montpellier so many years before.

This added to Alice's annoyance, for among the justifications for irritating her husband by having Françoise Bonnet to stay was the salvation of the soul of little Madeleine. Every evening Alice came to the bedroom which Madeleine shared with Dominique to kneel with the two girls at their bedside and lead them in their prayers. Dominique, who was normally left to say her prayers on her own, sensed that this was for the benefit of her friend, and knelt to say her Hail Mary and her Hail Holy Queen with an exaggerated piety.

Madeleine joined in with a bad grace. She never said prayers at home; at most her mother would make the sign of the cross on her forehead when she came to kiss her good night. To kneel on the bare boards and say prayers she did not know all the while subject to a strange, cloying, purposeful look from Alice de Roujay, was an unpleasant ordeal which spoiled the weeks she spent at Saint Théodore. She was well aware of her father's views on religion, and she put up with the nightly ritual only out of politeness, and from an imprecise understanding that it was the price she had to pay for her summer holidays.

About halfway through August of 1920, Alice de Roujay's brother Charles came to stay. He was already at this time a monsignor, the secretary to Cardinal Guturiez at the Curia in Rome. He often stopped off to visit his sister on his way between Paris and Rome, but never before had a visit coincided with that of Françoise and Madeleine. Whenever he came to Saint Théodore, certain traditions were observed. The parish priest at Pévier was asked to dinner, and Monsignor Ravanel was asked to say mass and preach the sermon on Sunday in the parish church. The curé was flattered by the presence of this dignitary from Rome, Charles Ravanel enjoyed addressing himself to the simple people of the Provençal countryside, and the congregation at Pévier liked a change.

That summer weekend, on Saturday night, Monsignor Ravanel, Dominique's Uncle Charles, came to his niece's bedroom to lead the little girls in a decade of a rosary. Dominique was delighted. Madeleine was afraid. She had never before seen a priest at such close quarters, and despite the pretty purple trimmings on the monsignor's cassock she felt an involuntary disgust in the overbearing presence of this tall, dark-haired man kneeling at her bedside, intoning monotonous, meaningless and interminable prayers in an unnatural and affected tone of voice.

In the presence of her uncle, Dominique put on an air of exaggerated piety, her hands clasped together, her eyes raised lovingly to the crucifix on the wall. Madeleine saw this and scoffed within. When the prayers were finished she got into bed and faced the wall. When the priest stooped to kiss her good night, he gave off a sweet smell which revolted her.

The next morning Madeleine overslept. Françoise came in to wake her. "Quick, my darling. We're all waiting."

"For what?"

"To go to mass."

Madeleine leaped out of bed, and while dressing saw the neat impression of Dominique's body on her bed. Why had she not woken her? She ran to the musty bathroom to wash her face, then down the stairs to the hall, where the de Roujay family had already assembled to leave for the parish church.

"Come along, Madeleine," said Alice de Roujay.

"I haven't had breakfast," said Madeleine.

"We never have breakfast before communion."

"I don't go to communion."

"We have breakfast afterward all the same."

Françoise now came into the hall. "Ah, there you are," she said. Madeleine stood still on the stairs. "I'm not coming."

"Oh yes, darling, you must," said Françoise Bonnet to her daughter.

"No."

"Everyone at Saint Théodore goes to mass on a Sunday," said Alice de Roujay in a severe tone of voice.

"Then I'll leave. I'll go home."

"Madeleine . . ." her mother said in a cringing, plaintive tone of voice.

"Papa says it's all a lot of nonsense, a bag of mumbo-jumbo for silly old women and her . . . her . . ." She tried to recall the word whose meaning she did not know, then remembered it and blurted out, "Hermaphrodites!"

For a long moment everyone in the hall and the ten-year-old girl on the stairs stood silent and still. Then Alice de Roujay turned to her wretched friend and said, "Françoise!" in the tone of an exasperated sergeant-major, while Françoise herself merely looked at her daughter and cried, "Madeleine . . ." as a moan of defeat and despair.

There was then a second long moment of silent paralysis—the outraged Alice de Roujay turning to the mother, the mother already cowed by the child. Then Bertrand de Roujay, the elder son, stepped forward with a smile, saying, "Let's go for a ride, little girl." He was tall and strong, and before Madeleine could say a word he had picked her up and had placed her on his shoulders. "I think Madeleine is worth a mass, don't you, Uncle Charles?" he said to Monsignor Ravanel.

"Most certainly," said the priest.

"But you'll miss mass," said Alice de Roujay.

"I'll go to Saint Giles at twelve," said Bertrand.

"Your uncle's sermon . . ."

"He tried it out on me last night," said Bertrand as he moved toward the front door. "And I warn you, Mother, he makes the devil out to be rather a charming fellow."

"He could hardly tempt us," said Monsignor Ravanel, turning to follow his nephew, "if he didn't have something to be said for him."

"Miss Ferguson always called Louis 'a little devil,' " said Edmond de Roujay, pronouncing the English phrase badly while following his brother-in-law toward the entrance to the house, "which to her, I think, had quite an attractive connotation, because she was always extremely fond of him."

"Ah, Miss Ferguson," said Louis. "What has happened to her, I wonder?" And with a dreamy look on his face as he remembered his Scottish governess, he left the house along with the others.

Before lunch that Sunday, Alice de Roujay took Françoise, her friend, by the arm and led her to one of the chairs beneath the chestnut trees in the garden. Her brow was smooth; it was the smooth brow of a woman who has composed herself, and has willed it to be smooth.

"We must ask ourselves," Alice said to Françoise, when the two of them were seated in the shade, "whether or not we are being fair to our two daughters by throwing them together at this impressionable age when each is being raised with quite different . . . values."

Françoise laughed—one of her old imbecilic laughs.

"It is not so much that I fear for Dominique's faith," Alice went on, "for I know that it is strong. It is rather that I think it is hard on Madeleine to be taught one thing at home and another here."

"Ah, yes, well, her father . . ."

"Her father. Yes. That's the point. She is certainly under his influence. That's only natural. I had expected it, but not, I must admit, the extent—the *depths*—to which his . . . ideas were already rooted in her mind."

"They are very close, the two of them."

"It is strange, isn't it?"

"Why?"

"Well, girls usually take after their mother."

Françoise laughed—a pathetic laugh, a braying lament over her own inimitable worthlessness.

Alice coughed and looked at her hands. "He is a man of strong convictions, I know, and perhaps it is only to be expected that Madeleine should be influenced by them."

Françoise nodded. "She is."

"I don't blame her; I don't blame you. But I think for her sake, as well as for ours, that she should not, perhaps . . ." Alice faltered. She did not want it to seem that she was turning her friend and her daughter out of her house.

"We could go to the sea," said Françoise.

"Your parents still have their house?"

"Yes."

"Was it damaged in the war?"

"Miraculously, no."

"Fortuitously."

"Fortuitously."

"So you could go there?"

"Yes."

"Excellent." Alice stood. "I shall go and ask Edmond about trains."

Françoise sniffed, then laughed. Alice did not want to look at her; she did not want to see any tears. She took her by the arm and led her back toward the house. "How are your parents?" she asked. "Your father had troubles, I know. My parents, too. If they hadn't had the factory in Saint Etienne, they would have lost everything behind the enemy lines. But they survived, and we survived, and there's still your villa at Bray-Dunes. You know that North Sea air will do Madeleine good. It's so hot here. You must come again, of course, some other time. We'll write, won't we? We mustn't lose touch."

2

Madeleine was not given any reason for the change of plan that summer, but she understood well enough that it had something to do with her outburst on the stairs. No one alluded to it, and all the de Roujays behaved as if they were sorry to see her leave; but already, at ten, she could detect a courtesy that was insincere, and knew that among her hosts only Bertrand and Louis were sad, and even their sadness was a slight, insignificant emotion which hardly lasted beyond the moment when they said goodbye.

Bray-Dunes was an ordeal for both mother and daughter. The journey itself, even two years after the end of the war, was through devastated towns and gouged countryside. The sea, the beach, the villa were unchanged, but the different members of the Bart family were all damaged within: her grandfather shell-shocked by his failure in business, her grandmother defeated by her disappointment.

Cousins and friends came and went, but none were as much fun as Bertrand or Louis de Roujay, and the seaside life was banal beside the rural routine at the Domaine de Saint Théodore. Madeleine was past the age of buckets and spades, and riding donkeys along the beach was a poor exchange for cantering through the vines on the de Roujays' horses. Nor did she know the donkeys—they were anonymous as well as slow—whereas as far back as she could remember she had followed the birth, death, purchase and sale of all the animals at Saint Théodore. Children do not respect the legal ownership of things, but appropriate what is around them as their own. To Madeleine the horses, vines, olive trees, cypresses, chestnuts, mauve shutters, red tiles and yellow walls, the smell of rosemary, pine needles and baked gravel, were things that had been hers, and now were hers no more.

But she did not repent. Neither that summer, nor during the summers which followed, when to escape from the heat in Montpellier they went back to Bray-Dunes for want of anywhere else to go, did she wish that she had held back those words spoken on the stairs. She felt a pang when the train stopped at Mézac and they did not alight; she watched the horizon as they traveled north, thinking of Saint Théodore over the rim of the scrub hills; she remembered small scenes from earlier summers, even the final scene and Alice de Roujay's expression of horror, Bertrand's smile, their ride through the vines—

but she did not want to relive the scene with a different ending, for to do so would have been to break a much stronger bond than that which held her to Saint Théodore.

Madeleine loved her father, not just with the ordinary affection that a girl of that age feels for her papa, but with the obsessive identification which came from several factors: her likeness to him, her contempt for her mother, her solitary nature, her maturity, and as an inevitable response to his obsession with her. Michel Bonnet had not wanted a child, and for the first years of her life he had hardly noticed her, never venturing down the corridor to her little nursery at the other end. He did not see her at meals—she was fed in the kitchen—and even on Sundays when she sat with her parents at lunch, he hardly noticed the child because he was reading a book or an academic review.

It was only when Madeleine was eight or nine years old and started to make rational conversation that Michel Bonnet remarked, with some satisfaction, upon her likeness to him. At her birth he had assumed that since she was a girl she would turn out like her mother, and it now came as a pleasant surprise to find his own swarthy, pockmarked face reflected in that of a lovely nymph. More satisfying still was her precocious intelligence, evident first in the awed admiration of her teachers at the lycée, then later in the professor's own appreciation of her intellectual aptitude.

Of course, the child had seen the way the father was esteemed, and like the primitive Indian whom she resembled at the age of five, had ascribed to books the magical powers which assured her father's ascendancy. She assumed, and announced, at this age that she would grow up to be a man; when later she had to acknowledge that her sex would not change, she remained determined to avoid the empty servility of women.

The equal education at the lycée in Montpellier encouraged the development of her powers. When she was twelve she began to eat with her parents in the evening, and for the first time in his married life Michel Bonnet put his book aside. As Françoise came and went with the food and dirty dishes, father and daughter would discuss history, philosophy, politics and religion. After supper he would lead her to his study and lend her books with passages marked on the subjects they had covered while they were eating. Madeleine would retire with the books down the long corridor while her father went to his desk and her mother remained in the living room to sew, to darn and sometimes, surreptitiously, to read *Le Petet Echo de la Mode* or a romantic novella.

This private tuition by her eminent father had its effect upon Madeleine's schoolwork. She was not just top of her class; her essays were passed around by those teachers who retained some curiosity in the subjects they taught. Of course, her precociousness estranged her classmates, but since Madeleine was solitary and self-contained anyway, she did not suffer from this alienation from those who might otherwise have been her friends. She shared none of their adolescent preoccupations; she was bored by their limited intellects. She often smiled; she sometimes laughed; she never giggled. Seeing this granddaughter at sixteen lying on the beach at Bray-Dunes, and noticing for the first time that she had the body of a woman, Françoise's mother, remarked, "Madeleine has all the luck; she has skipped adolescence."

The destiny of this daughter of two awkward, reclusive parents would inevitably have been that of some sort bluestocking—a teacher, a writer or an academic—had it not been for the unexpected beauty of her appearance. By the time she was sixteen the little Amazonian Indian had grown into a tall, brown-skinned girl with the same straight black hair and fringe. The only feature she had inherited from her mother was Françoise's long legs; otherwise she had her father's features, which in the stocky man were undersized and undistinguished but in the girl were set in perfect proportion in her face, and his coloring. From him too she had inherited a deep-timbered voice which spoke only to the point, and large brown eyes which stared with a guarded curiosity at anyone who spoke to her.

No one could ascribe Madeleine's smile. Her father grimaced when amused, and her mother only whinnied. Madeleine's normal expression was earnest, even severe, which made her smile, when it came, double its effect. It was slight at the lips but ample in the eyes; it came as if reluctantly, and so flattered all the more whoever had induced it.

Because her beauty was unexpected, and because beauty of body was not a quality admired in her immediate family, Madeleine had no trace of coquetry in her manner. If she looked at herself in a mirror, as all do now and then, it was to wonder rather than to admire. She had no guidance on growing up from her mother, who cringed in the corner of her life; thus her first menstruation came as a disagreeable surprise.

With no older sister, and no girls who were friends to whisper the secrets of breeding, she had grown up with only a hazy idea of how children were conceived and born. She knew about love from novels, and pondered on phrases and scenes in *Le Rouge et le Noir* and *Les Liaisons dangereuses* without quite understanding what they were meant to depict.

Her father was no help. He thought that Aristotle and Descartes gave an adequate preparation for life. He was also alarmed by his daughter's development into a woman, and like many men of outstanding intellect was unable to analyze the small slice of real life which lay under his nose. Some unconscious voice told him that her growing breasts and hips might one day lead her to leave him—she who was the only creature for whom he cared. When Madeleine first put on a pair of silk stockings and some high-heeled shoes, he lost control of that exasperated rage which always bubbled just below the thin crust of his character. She had done so only from convention; she could not, at eighteen, still dress as a child. All the same, it enraged her father, who, had he not himself been a little afraid of her, would have refused to let her go out.

Madeleine herself was of two minds about her own appearance. If she intercepted a look of lust from a man in the street, she blushed with rage and humiliation; yet if a fellow student befriended her in the lecture hall she knew quite well that part of his motive was her pretty face. With no Christian upbringing to suggest shame in the flesh, she carried her body with a natural ease; there was no rounding of the shoulders to hide her bosom, no fiddling with split ends to hide her eyes. She began to dress well. She liked good materials and subtle colors, and since her father gave her the money he had always denied his wife, she started to buy clothes from the better shops or order them from a good dressmaker.

Madeleine wanted to study at the Sorbonne in Paris—Montpellier now felt too small—but the alternating fits of rage and despair which the prospect induced in her father led her to resign herself to staying at home. Her mother, too, though she dared not intervene, was horrified at the prospect of being left without Madeleine to humor the professor. She therefore persuaded him that to keep their daughter in Montpellier they should move from the dark apartment in the old town to a house with a garden on the Avenue d'Assas.

This change, and the influx of intelligent fellow students from the
rest of France, made Madeleine's years of study more agreeable than
she had anticipated. As Professor Bonnet's daughter she immediately
enjoyed some prestige; the envious contemporaries from the lycée
disappeared from her life—only now and then did she catch a glimpse
of them in the street—and were replaced by agreeable young men and
women whose fathers were lawyers in Paris or diplomats abroad.

Her father allowed her to invite these friends to the house on the
Avenue d'Assas, and this, to the students, was a signal advantage of
being her friend. Françoise provided food and drink, and many mis-
took her for the cook. The professor smiled benignly before retreating
into his study. If there was one disappointment in Madeleine's under-
graduate life, it was that in concourse with students rather than school-
fellows, her academic ability was less marked. She was no fool, but
apparently no genius either.

This reappraisal might have disappointed her more had she not had
that second string to her bow, her beauty and charm. Solitary in her
phony adolescence, she now flourished in the company of her university friends. She swam, played tennis, went for picnics in the foothills
of the Cévennes. By her third year she formed part of a smart and
serious set of young men and women who discussed Plato and Boethius
as they danced together, and as they lay on the beach drinking cold
white wine argued vigorously about socialism, Fascism and Freud.

Inevitably, one after the other, the young men in this set, and others
who aspired to join it, intimated to Madeleine, with a word or a look
or an embrace on the dance floor, that their friendliness had turned to
love. She always accepted the avowals with a dignified reserve. The
honor was acknowledged but the love was never returned. One or two
of these suitors came closer than others—she had allowed herself to be
kissed on two or three occasions—but however eloquent the young
men might be in arguing the evils of "repression," none had been
permitted to go further; for though Madeleine had had an entirely
secular upbringing, and so was free of that prejudice in favor of
chastity, she nevertheless felt involuntarily disgusted when one or two
of her less timorous suitors moved their hands to caress her breasts or
touch her buttocks.

She now knew what sexual intercourse involved, and the thought of it appalled her. She had always wrinkled up her nose when touching on the subject of reproduction in biology; that men and women should behave in the same ignoble way as dogs and rats seemed to her incredible. Her dream of love was vague, but the embrace of the lover was always noble, comforting, protective and chaste. A medical student, Michel le Fresne, who was the expert in their circle on both Freud and Marx, diagnosed in Madeleine an unresolved Oedipus complex. "Unconsciously," he explained to his friends, "she is still in love with her father, just as her father is in love with her. Her rival—her mother—is defeated and enslaved. Madeleine holds court in the Avenue d'Assas. The passion cannot be consummated—it is blocked by taboo—but it demands a total fidelity. Madeleine is a dedicated virgin; she is in thrall to her Yahweh-Papa just as a nun might be to her Jesus-God."

"You only say that," said another in their group, a graduate student of law, Pierre Moreau, "because she won't go to bed with you."

"You try," said le Fresne with a laugh. "You won't get any further than I did."

"I'm not in her league," said Pierre. "None of us are. But one day, you'll see, the right man will come along, and poof!" He snapped his fingers. "She'll be away."

Michel le Fresne had come much nearer than he had realized to capturing the prize of Madeleine Bonnet. Of all the young men in their set, he was the most eligible—not because he was handsome or rich or came from a distinguished family, but because he had double the energy and ambition of the others, which, taken with his humor and intelligence, usually enabled him to have his way. He was already at this age a large man with thick brown hair and a dappled pink-and-white complexion which had it not been for his height, weight and deep voice might have given him an effeminate appearance. When, at times, Madeleine had thought that she would have to choose a lover from among the young men she knew, Michel was always the most likely candidate, for besides his ambition to do well, he was also the most outspoken idealist among them, outraged by the poverty and squalor to which the poor in France were condemned to live. "It doesn't matter how skilled I become as a physician," he would say, "if the working classes are trapped in conditions which breed disease."

Le Fresne was an atheist and a materialist, for as Flaubert put it, "You can't probe for faith with a scalpel," and he argued vehemently for political solutions to these social problems. Madeleine was impressed by his stamina during the interminable wrangles about state ownership and minimum wages, but when he made a pass at her he did so with an abruptness and a crudity which might have been consistent with his materialist ideals but disqualified him at once as an embodiment of her imaginary lover.

If Michel had behaved with greater delicacy and had courted her over a longer period of time, the outcome might have been different, because she was intrigued by him. But le Fresne, who wished to head a hospital before he was forty, was impatient to get on with his life, and so soon after his rejection by Madeleine he took up with the daughter of an olive-oil king called Nellie Planchet who for all her sour manner was plump and pretty and had a father who could further his career.

The Planchet family were Huguenots who had taken refuge in the Cévennes after the revocation of the Edict of Nantes but had moved cautiously south as from generation to generation the toleration of Protestants increased: first to a small village between Montpellier and Nîmes; then to Nîmes itself, where a first fortune was made; and finally to the city of Coustiers, where they were established as millionaires.

The original house near Montpellier remained in their hands and was lent to Nellie to entertain her friends. Since there were stables, tennis courts and a swimming pool, as well as servants to serve food and drink, it was not a facility which the group ignored, and most weekends in the early summer they would go out with their friends to enjoy the hospitality of the absent Planchets.

One Saturday morning in July of 1931, Madeleine was picked up by Michel le Fresne in a small Renault which he had borrowed—it seemed permanently—from the Planchets to go out to this private country club.

"Where's Pierre?" she asked.

"He's already out there with a friend."

"What friend?"

"Someone he knew at the école normale."

"A lawyer?"

"A civil servant."

They drove out toward Sommières, then at Fontmagne turned up into the hills. Madeleine always felt a little awkward when alone with Michel. His attitude toward her seemed to vacillate between the abruptness of a rejected admirer and the hovering attentiveness of a man with unfinished business, while she remained somewhat startled that he had so swiftly transferred to Nellie Planchet the feelings he had professed to have for her.

"It is sad to think," said Michel, "that our student days have come to an end."

"But you've a long way to go before you qualify."

"But not in Montpellier."

"Won't you be sad to leave us?"

Michel shook his head. "No. It's very pleasant here, but it's time to take life more seriously."

"Where will you go?"

"To the Institut Pasteur in Paris."

Madeleine hesitated for a moment, then asked, "And Nellie?"

He sucked the inside of his cheek. "What do you think?"

"She'll miss you."

"Perhaps she'd better come with me."

"As your wife?"

He shrugged his shoulders. "Why not?"

"Have you asked her?"

"No."

"Do you mean to?"

"Do you think I should?" asked le Fresne.

"Do you love her?"

He gave a slight snort—half a laugh, half a shrug of his shoulders. "She suits me."

"She's certainly very pretty, and . . ." She stopped.

"And rich?"

"Yes."

"I know, and that . . . well, it could be useful but it could also be a bore."

"How?"

"I want to make my own way."

"Yes." She hesitated for a moment, then asked, "Would she follow you—I mean, to the slums?"

He gave the same snort a second time. "I'm sure she would, in her Chanel dress."

"Are you sure you don't want her because of that?" She looked at Michel just as he drove the car through the gates of the Planchets' villa.

"Because of what? All this?" He glanced at the house as he stopped the car on the gravel. "I don't know. How can one be sure of anything?"

As they got out of the car they heard Nellie shout Michel's name. They turned and saw two figures on horseback cantering toward them across the fields. The sun was behind them. Madeleine raised her eyes to watch as they came closer. She thought at first that the man with Nellie must be Pierre, but then remembered that Pierre could not ride. She watched him as they grew closer; he was dark and thin, no one she had met there before. Then, when the steaming horses and puffing human beings came up to them, she looked up at the man and her heart faltered, because she felt at once that she knew him either from a memory or a dream.

They were not introduced, because Nellie thought it vulgar to assume that the friends who came to the villa did not know each other already, but at lunch Madeleine was seated next to Pierre's friend, who had changed out of his riding breeches into a summer suit. Alone among the group, he wore a tie, which made her realize that he was older than she had imagined. At first he did not talk to her but instead listened as Michel argued with Pierre about politics—in particular about the American proposal for a moratorium on the payment of German reparations.

"It is insulting," said Michel, "for Hoover to make such a suggestion. He may be President of the United States, but he is not yet President of France."

"That I accept," said Pierre.

"So what right does he have to postpone the reparations? It's a matter between us and the Boches."

"It's in nobody's interest to bankrupt Germany," said Pierre.

"Particularly not the Americans, who have lent them so much money."

"They're not just thinking of their own loans."

"That's what it looks like to me."

"And if the Americans cancel our debts to them?"

"They'll damn well have to. The two go together."

Pierre's friend listened without comment. Occasionally, Madeleine noticed, Michel glanced in his direction as if afraid that he might be making a fool of himself, but the older man merely listened politely as if both had an equally valid point of view.

Then Nellie turned to the newcomer. "What do you think?" she asked him. "You're in the government, aren't you? You must know what it's all about."

"It's a complicated question," Pierre's friend replied in a quiet voice which courteously declined to be drawn into the argument.

"It bores me to death," said Nellie, "but it irritates me when the Americans behave as if they won the war, when we did all the fighting."

He turned toward Madeleine. "What do you think?" he asked.

She hesitated. She had been about to put a forkful of food into her mouth, but the question, which she knew he had posed just to make conversation, seemed to demand a moment of earnest reflection. "I don't know," she said. "Everyone seems to agree that the Germans were to blame for the last war, and so should pay reparations, but they also say that we should disarm, and trust the Germans to do the same."

"Are those inconsistent positions?"

She looked at him. He had a kind face. "You can't trust someone and punish him at the same time," she said, "if the culprit doesn't accept that the punishment is due him."

"And this culprit does not?"

"No. So the punishment will lead to resentment, and the resentment to revenge."

"At the hands of Herr Hitler?"

"Yes."

"Blum seems to think that he is losing support."

"Blum isn't always right."

They went deeper into the political issues of the day, each seeming to tread carefully as if unwilling to contradict the other, but then moving with more confidence as they discovered that they shared a broadly liberal point of view. Madeleine was relieved that the civil servant from the Ministry of the Interior was less conservative than was suggested by his appearance, and that he spoke with none of the condescension that was so often shown by men when discussing politics with women.

He spoke well—wittily, succinctly—and was always apparently curious about her opinion. For a moment she thought he was too smooth—that he was getting on well with her from a practiced Parisian politeness that was insincere—but then, when lunch was over and they moved out to drink coffee under the parasols on the terrace, she found that she wanted to continue to talk to him, and was pleased that he came and sat on a chair at her side. When tennis was proposed, Pierre begged off, so it was inevitable that Madeleine should be teamed with his friend. She went to put on her tennis clothes in a spare room, and felt an odd tingling in her body as she changed her skirt for a pair of white shorts which uncovered her long brown legs.

He did not look at her legs—not, at any rate, with a look that she intercepted. He smiled only into her eyes, and then only with a courteous friendliness. He was an excellent player, something he concealed through the first set but then asserted in the second and subse-. quent sets, to Michel's growing chagrin. Every point they won infuriated him; he could not conceal his annoyance or restrain the exasperation he felt toward Nellie, who, if she had wanted to, could have beaten any of the other three, but had the tact not to play better than Michel even though that appeared to be what he wanted.

The game created a complicity among the victors. Madeleine was delighted that they had won and exchanged a secret smile with her partner when he winked at Michel's pink-faced fury. They returned to the terrace, where a manservant in a white tunic brought them glasses of iced lemon juice and later, at five, after they had changed, tea in the English style.

Shortly afterward, Pierre prepared to return to Montpellier. "Will you give Madeleine a lift?" asked Michel. "I think I'll go back later."

"Of course," said Pierre. He turned to his friend who had driven him out to the Planchets. "That's all right, isn't it?"

"I'd be delighted."

They took their leave, and Madeleine climbed into the back seat of the open car.

As they drove back to Montpellier the noise of the rushing air made it impossible to hear what the two men said when they talked together. Quite soon she gave up the effort and leaned back in the seat thinking of nothing in particular but feeling a novel sense of contentment. When they reached the Avenue d'Assas and stopped outside her house, she leaned forward to ask Pierre, as she often did, to lunch the next day.

Pierre looked at his friend.

"You too, of course," said Madeleine.

"I should love to," he said.

"Good," said Pierre. "We'll come at twelve." He moved forward to let her get out.

"Don't worry," she said. "I can climb out." She jumped over the side of the car onto the pavement and turned to say goodbye.

"You know, it's terribly silly," her tennis partner said to her, "but we weren't introduced, so I don't really know your name."

"Madeleine," she said. "I'm Madeleine Bonnet."

"And I'm Bertrand de Roujay."

He held out his hand, and as she took it in hers their eyes met and they both blushed, not because they had touched but because at that moment they realized who they were.

Chapter 2

1

*T*HE friendship between Bertrand de Roujay and Pierre Moreau, which had brought Bertrand to Montpellier, had been formed when they were fellow students at the école normale in Paris. It had always been considered an incongruous friendship, because Bertrand came from an unbroken line of conservative Catholics and Pierre from a family of Sephardic Jews.

Each candidly acknowledged that he liked the other not despite his background but because of it. For Bertrand, Pierre could only be a Jew. Although a secular upbringing and a liberal education, symbolized by his grandfather's change of name to Moreau, had freed him from any complexes and prejudices from the past, he possessed a cosmopolitan quickness which Bertrand had never found among his fellow gentiles in the officer corps, as well as the patience, modesty and self-depreciating humor which generations of oppression had instilled in his race.

Pierre had a similar attitude toward Bertrand. Part of what he liked about him was that he came from the midst of the hereditary enemy —not the northern industrialists on his mother's side of the family, but the crusading de Roujays who had slaughtered Muslims, burned Cathars and persecuted Jews. The great value of their friendship to both young men was that it symbolized a real reconciliation between the two hitherto antipathetic tribes within the French nation; for just as Pierre had escaped from the constrictions of Judaism to become a secular citizen of the French Republic, so Bertrand, though he still went to mass, had abjured the militant and exclusive Catholicism which had been followed by his family since the Middle Ages. Indeed, the affection he felt for Pierre seemed in some sense to atone for all those sins against the Jews perpetrated by his ancestors.

When they had first met, they had spoken cautiously when treating the issues affecting their respective religions, but gradually, as if testing the strength of the ice, they had ventured out over deeper water. Bertrand had dared to laugh at Pierre's thrifty instincts as a throwback to the parsimony of a moneylender; Pierre had felt he could ridicule the Catholics in Marseilles who had built a huge gold crown for the immense statue of the Virgin looking out over the Vieux Port from the Basilica of Notre Dame de la Garde.

Since Bertrand's mother had not only contributed a large sum of money to this pious exercise but had also been part of the crowd at the statue's coronation, Pierre's ridicule was indeed a test of friendship, but a test it passed with no difficulty. It was not just that Bertrand felt fond enough of the other man to take his criticism; it was also that at this time he was reacting against his mother's oppressive piety and could step outside the religion he practiced to criticize many of its pious excesses.

As a result, Bertrand had often come into conflict with his parents, and also with his younger brother, Louis, who accused him of an infatuation with "the Israelites." But in fact, Pierre Moreau was Bertrand's only Jewish friend, and there was nothing about him, other than his origins, which distinguished him from any other intelligent young Frenchman studying law. He was small and dark, but so were many natives of Provence and Languedoc. He was pleasant-looking, but too lean and too modest to seem attractive to women on sight alone. In this respect he had been right to recognize that he was not in Madeleine's "league."

Bertrand not only was older, taller and more obviously handsome than his friend, but after five years in the army had the bearing of a man who is used to command. It was this quality which together with his agile intellect had enabled him to enter and then rise in the French civil service, but outside the Ministry his life was less sure. When he came to see Pierre in Montpellier he was already thirty, and the fact that at this age he had never been close enough to a girl to consider making her his wife was evidence that he was not as competent and self-possessed in his emotional and social life as he was in the sphere of his career.

It was not just Bertrand's skepticism but also his idealism—his fervent, almost naive belief in the Fraternity that went with Liberty and Equality—that had estranged him from the circle of army officers and landowners within which his brother Louis moved and had married. In Paris, Bertrand hovered around several different milieux but had settled in none. He retained some friends from his army days, but had others from among the *normaliens* like Pierre, whose cultural interests Alice de Roujay would undoubtedly have thought profane. Bertrand went to the open lectures given by atheistic philosophers, and to the exhibitions of Surrealist painters. He remained anchored to his Catholic faith, but drifted away from it on a long line; and this mental truancy was matched by fleeting affairs with women of progressive views and emancipated behavior.

It was not that Bertrand wanted to avoid marriage; quite the contrary, he saw it as a welcome and necessary step toward maturity. But in finding a wife his choice was restricted by the way in which he was neither wholly controlled by nor wholly freed from his parents' prejudices. It was quite out of the question to take to Saint Théodore any of the bohemian women he knew in Paris, let alone present them to his parents as a possible wife; yet the decent Catholic girls from good families whom his mother presented to him from time to time exasperated him by their limited outlook and intelligence.

He was also loath to lead them into sin, for like many men from a Catholic culture, Bertrand found it difficult to combine respect and desire for the same woman. For his fleeting liaisons in Paris he had always chosen women who had already "fallen," and he was delighted and horrified in equal measure by their transports of sexual rapture. The concept of purity inculcated by the Jesuits had confused his reaction to sexual desire, and because purity was associated with girls of his religion, he only found himself attracted to non-Catholic women.

It was undoubtedly the knowledge that Nellie Planchet came from a Protestant family which led him to feel an immediate twinge of physical attraction when he was first introduced to her by Pierre Moreau.

"Do you ride?" she had asked him in an offhand manner belied by the flirtatious look in her eye.

"Yes," said Bertrand, "but I haven't brought any breeches."

"You can borrow my father's," she said, leading him up the stairs while Pierre went through to the living room. She took him into a bedroom and opened a wardrobe. "Help yourself. I'll meet you downstairs."

As they cantered over the raked ground between the olive trees that had been the foundation of the Planchets' first fortune, Nellie called, "What are you doing here?"

"I came to see Pierre."

"Where do you live?"

"In Paris."

"Are you a Parisian?"

"No."

"I thought not. You ride too well."

"Thank you."

"None of the others can. They're so middle-class."

"You should teach them."

"Can't be bothered." She sighed and slowed her horse so that they could walk side by side.

"I am a Provencal," said Bertrand.

"How do you know Pierre? You're not a Jew, are you?"

"No. A Catholic."

"Papa prefers Jews."

"And you?"

She shrugged her shoulders. "I don't really care."

"Would you marry a Jew?"

"If I liked him."

"But not a Catholic?"

She turned and gave Bertrand a sultry look. "I'd have to like him a lot," she said, and then kicked her heels into her horse's sides and cantered ahead toward a copse of pine trees.

Bertrand followed, his eyes on the beige of her breeches drawn tight over her buttocks and thighs. Like a satyr he set off in pursuit of her, but as the horses came clear of the trees they saw the house and, realizing that they were headed for home, broke into a gallop which only slowed as they reached the small Renault drawn up in front of the house.

No sooner had Bertrand set eyes upon the tall, dark girl who stood by the car than he forgot his hostess. It was not that he was more strongly attracted to Madeleine than he was to Nellie, but that he felt an immediate sympathy for her, a sympathy which grew as he talked to her over lunch. He did not notice her body, and he admired her eyes not just because they were big and brown but because they

complemented her comments on reparations or Léon Blum with an
earnest, pensive expression. What immediately appealed to him was
not so much her soft voice and lovely features as her intelligence and
sincerity—qualities which might equally have attracted him in another
man—and the fact that she did not flirt with her eyelashes or use her
body to impress him.

When, as they played tennis, he noticed that she had strong, long
legs, it was only to admire them with the detachment he might have
shown when studying any other aspect of natural excellence in, say,
a racehorse or a gundog. The long length of brown flesh which ran
from her knee to the hem of her shorts did not affect him as did the
pink, plump, almost flabby thighs of Nellie Planchet on the other side
of the net. But because Bertrand thought that crude desire was ignoble,
he kept his eyes off the daughter of the olive-oil millionaire and moved
still closer to his companionable partner.

In the car on the way back to Montpellier he wanted to find out
more about her from Pierre, but since she was sitting behind them on
the backseat he had to restrain his curiosity. By the time they entered
the suburbs of the city, however, he had decided to ask Pierre to
arrange for him to meet her again. When, instead, Madeleine asked
him to lunch, it came to him as no surprise, because from the very start
he had sensed the straightforward way in which she had cooperated
with his overtures of friendship; and when he asked her name and
discovered that she was the daughter of his mother's childhood friend,
he felt neither astonishment nor curiosity, because already he felt he
had formed a bond with her that had nothing to do with the past.

Nevertheless, when Bertrand returned with Pierre to the Avenue
d'Assas for lunch the next day he went through the pretense of pleasure
and amazement at this fortuitous reunion of childhood acquaintances.
He made no mention of that last day at Saint Théodore so many years
before, because he had forgotten it; indeed, he had forgotten almost
everything about the Bonnets except Françoise's inane laugh, which he
recognized as soon as he set foot through the door. What curiosity he
felt was not about these fossils from his mother's past, but about the
home and family of the eminent scholar Professor Bonnet.

Françoise, who opened the door, seemed quite overwhelmed to see
Bertrand. "Alice's boy," she mumbled; then, laughing, "Alice's boy,
here in our house!" Behind her, however, came Madeleine, who firmly

pushed her mother aside and took charge of her guests, leading them through the hall into the book-lined living room, apologizing with a smile that the hospitality they could offer was not on a par with the Planchets'.

Professor Bonnet sat by the window in a wicker chair. He turned as Bertrand approached and greeted him gruffly when Madeleine presented him. Bertrand, who supposed this to be his usual manner, took no offense. Pierre and Bertrand were not the only guests—there were three or four other students, and an academic from Bordeaux—but it became quite apparent that for the two women of the household Bertrand was the guest of honor. Madeleine, for example, kept glancing at his plate and glass as if to see that they were filled, then looking away toward the window as if she could not care less whether they were or not. Her precise and confident presence at her parents' table soon became a blushing, self-conscious one. She took part in the conversation, as she always did, but then would suddenly lose interest and in full flow rise from the table to remove a glass or a plate which could well have remained longer.

Madeleine's clothes were also different, not just from the casual costume that she had worn the day before, but from the simple but elegant skirts and blouses that she usually put on for Sunday lunch. She had chosen what was almost a party dress with a pink, embroidered bodice upon which she had pinned a small posy of wildflowers. The effect of this costume was a little absurd; it might have suited her dark complexion to have dressed as a gypsy but not as a Tyrolean peasant. In the middle of lunch it suddenly seemed that Madeleine herself had realized this; rising on the pretext of helping her mother, she left the room and returned a moment later from the kitchen with the posy of wildflowers gone.

Bertrand, for whose benefit she had prepared her appearance, failed to notice her halfhearted coquetry, just as he failed to remark on her father's brusqueness or her mother's confusion. The sun shone in through the window. The food was good. The students were cheerful. Pierre was benign. All this was reason enough for his contentment, and for most of the lunch he sought no other explanation for his sense of exhilaration. It was only after the cheese, when Madeleine looked at his plate as if to see if he wanted more, and then raised her eyes to his —raised them reluctantly, and in an instant, without words, inquired not whether he wanted more cheese but whether he felt doomed as she did—that Bertrand realized that he was probably, indeed certainly, in love.

Paris was a long way from Montpellier, but Montpellier was a charming city in which to pay court to a girl. Bertrand returned there a fortnight later, ostensibly to visit Pierre, and with the obtuse timidity that can come over a man in love, did nothing himself to arrange a meeting with the girl he had really come to see. Certainly when he had telephoned from Paris he had said to Pierre, "Have you seen Madeleine Bonnet?" But he had not asked him to arrange a meeting. So wrapped up was he in his love for her that he would almost rather have walked the streets of Montpellier dreaming of her than risk disillusion by meeting her face to face.

Though he suffered a twinge of sadness as he saw his friendship for both Bertrand and Madeleine superseded by their passion for one another, Pierre understood what was expected of him by his friend. When he ran into Madeleine in the middle of the week he told her that Bertrand was coming back to Montpellier, and suggested meeting for a drink on the Place de la Comédie at around six on Saturday evening.

Madeleine had looked perplexed, knitting her brow as if wondering if some other engagement might prevent her coming, or as if considering the amount of work she had to do for her examinations. It was a pretense, and Pierre knew it—not the sham of coquetry, but a protective mechanism of the mind which has put all its eggs in one basket and dare not look to see if they are broken.

This time Madeleine was wiser in what she wore and appeared on the Place de la Comédie in almost casual attire. It was not that much thought had not gone into her costume, for despite her serious mind she had pondered, chewing her pen, for the past three days over just how she should present herself. She might feel disdain for the animality of sexual attraction, but the instinct to look her best was strong; so too was the subtler and conflicting instinct not to seem to try too hard.

She therefore washed her hair the night before, and that evening put on a blue skirt and yellow blouse—clothes that were clean and simple, not grand or new. There was no embroidered bodice, no posy of wildflowers. Nothing she had done to her appearance gave her away, and she approached the men at their table on the pavement with the casual air of a student on her way home from the university.

Bertrand was deceived; Pierre was not, for nothing could disguise what nature had done to Madeleine, pumping the blood faster through her veins, giving a beautiful hue and texture to her sallow skin and a clarity and luminosity to her large brown eyes. It is only those subject to instinct who do not notice its contrivance. Bertrand stood, shook hands and drew up a chair, quite oblivious to the details of her appearance, only delighted and relieved that the Madeleine standing before him matched the Madeleine of his inflamed imagination.

For a time the three friends chatted together, a group among many other groups at the pavement café. The sun set. The light faded.

"I hope you're free to have supper with us?" Bertrand said to Madeleine.

She looked at her watch. "Yes, why not?"

"You say 'us,' " said Pierre, "but I must go back and do some work."

"But that's absurd," said Bertrand. "You can't work on a Saturday night."

"It's all very well for you civil servants," said Pierre. "When you leave your office, your work's done. But those of us who are still studying . . ."

This too was pretense, and they all knew it, but it was the necessary nicety of courtship. The three stood, Pierre left, and as soon as he was gone he was forgotten. Bertrand and Madeleine walked back into the old town to a restaurant on the Rue de l'Herberie.

"Do you remember," she asked, as they waited for their food to be brought to their table, "when we rode together through the vines?"

He shook his head. "No. When was that?"

"My last day at Saint Théodore."

"I only remember you at table," said Bertrand. "Very serious, with straight black hair."

Madeleine laughed and shook her head so that the same black hair swayed to and fro. "I was terrified of you and Louis. I didn't know any older boys."

"Why did you never come back?" he asked.

"Why? I don't know. We went to the north after that." She wrinkled her nose. "Awful holidays by the sea."

"You must come again now," he said. "It's not so far from here."

"I think that our mothers must have quarreled," she said. "They used to be such good friends, but now . . . they haven't seen each other for years."

"I can't imagine that our fathers were ever close friends."

"Ah, no. Chalk and cheese." She laughed.

"That generation took their political differences too seriously," said Bertrand.

"The Dreyfus affair still enrages my father," said Madeleine.

"Mine prefers not to talk about it."

They laughed again. "I'm so glad all that's changed," said Madeleine.

"Yes," said Bertrand. "I can't conceive of anyone of our generation —the postwar generation—making friends and enemies according to people's political opinions."

"I disagree with many of my friends on many things," said Madeleine, "and they're still my friends."

"Would *we* agree?" asked Bertrand.

"On what?"

He shrugged his shoulders. "The issues of the day."

She laughed. "I doubt it."

"Does that matter?"

"Of course not, unless . . ." Her face became serious.

"What?"

She blushed. "No, I mean only that . . . well, it would be hard to like a Fascist."

"I'm not a Fascist."

"I know."

"But I do think that politics are important."

"So do I."

He took on an intent expression. "I didn't become a civil servant just because it was a safe job. I really do believe that the power of the state is now so great that it becomes a moral duty to make sure that it is used to good ends."

Madeleine said nothing, but her eyes encouraged him to go on, to risk appearing naive or idiotic by revealing his private ambitions.

"The older generation," Bertrand said, "made such a terrible mess of things. I don't just mean the war, but the complete failure to reconcile the different groups within the nation: the workers and the managers, the Catholics with the non-Catholics, the indigenous French with immigrants like the Jews."

"But who's to blame?" asked Madeleine.

"They were all to blame. They fed off each other's prejudices. So many of them still do—Catholics who see a conspiracy among Freemasons, Freemasons who see a conspiracy among Catholics, Communists who see nothing in capitalism but exploitation, capitalists who see nothing in socialism but legalized theft. Of course, in all these phobias there's an element of truth, but if only each would look at the other's ideas with an open mind, and recognize above all that we have common interests as Frenchmen which transcend our interests as Jews, Catholics, Communists, capitalists."

"Of course," she said, her eyes alive with admiration. "And our generation could do it."

"We can and we must. It's our duty not just to France but to the whole human race."

Bertrand spoke with such fervor and conviction that to Madeleine his face across the table became like that on the bust of a Roman hero she had seen in a museum. As he talked she found she felt both elated by his unselfish ambitions and relieved that he had not revealed himself to be a reactionary bigot. Perhaps in some inner chamber of her brain there was a whisper of skepticism—a whisper not from Madeleine but from Professor Bonnet, who would have scoffed at his naïveté, or from Michel le Fresne, who would have dismissed Bertrand's solutions as high-minded platitudes. But Madeleine was not her father, nor was she arguing with Michel le Fresne. She was already falling in love with Bertrand, and so instinctively held back from subjecting what he said to rigorous intellectual scrutiny. She listened, smiled, admired. There were no pauses, no silences, but the words and the ideas they expressed were not the purpose of their presence there in the restaurant, just as it was not for the food that they sat at table. They ate and drank without noticing the food or the wine, and it was only when they came out of the restaurant and walked towards the Place Castellane that they came to the true point of their presence in one another's company. Bertrand took Madeleine's arm. She inclined her body toward his. They walked in this way up the Rue Saint Firmin, past the Palais de Justice and down by the side of the Promenade du Peyrou. They stopped under one of the arches which carries water to the Château d'Eau. Bertrand turned to face Madeleine, put his other arm around her and kissed her gently on the lips. She trembled and clung to him. Their pact was formed.

Bertrand went to mass at eight the next morning at the gaunt Cathedral of Saint Pierre. He hardly followed the ceremony, because his mind was filled with the events of the night before: the whispered declarations of love, the repeated proof of the worth of their words by the impress of lips upon lips.

He went through the motions of kneeling, standing and singing the Credo all from habit. His only prayer was a brief one, inspired by the sight of the semifortified porch of the church. He thanked God that he did not live in an era of religious intolerance, when whole communities had been slaughtered for their faith in doctrines which were now obscure. But even this prayer was not divorced from his feelings, for in going to mass so early to get this obligation out of the way, he remembered that Madeleine was not a Catholic, and that in other eras their love would have been forbidden.

He returned with fresh bread for breakfast in Pierre's flat on the Rue de la Petite Loge. Pierre only awoke as he entered, and came into the kitchen in his dressing gown while Bertrand heated water in a saucepan to make coffee.

"You were up early," said Pierre.

"I went to mass."

"Even after a late night . . ."

"Especially after a late night."

"I hope you had nothing to confess."

Bertrand turned and smiled. "We say 'Deo gratias' as well as 'Confiteor.'"

"You had reason to be grateful?" asked Pierre, sitting at the kitchen table.

"Ah, yes."

Pierre scrutinized his friend. "Yes, you have the look of a well-fed cat."

"Thank you," said Bertrand, watching the water in the pan.

"The evidence all points to a successful evening."

"I can't deny that it went well."

Pierre's expression became serious. "I'm delighted for your sake, Bertrand, but you must take care."

"Why?"

"She's a serious girl."

"I know."

"She's not as grown-up as she seems."

"How do you mean?"

"She hasn't been around much."

"I realize that." The water boiled, and he poured it into the coffee-pot.

"She's an only child. She lives at home. And . . . well, Montpellier isn't Paris."

"That's part of what makes her so charming."

"Of course. But one is easily deceived by her intelligence into thinking that she knows what she is doing."

"What is she doing?" Bertrand asked with a smile.

"Falling in love, I daresay," said Pierre. "But what to you might be an adventure—"

"It's not an adventure," Bertrand interrupted.

"No, I'm sorry, but—"

"I'm almost sure," said Bertrand, "that I shall ask her to marry me."

Pierre blanched. "Are you serious?"

"Completely."

"You don't waste time."

"I don't have much time."

"Even so . . ."

"Don't you approve?"

"Listen, Bertrand," said Pierre, speaking slowly, choosing his words with care, "you are both . . . each of you . . . two of the people I like best in the world, but . . . well, you hardly know each other."

"I love her."

"You come from such different backgrounds."

"Our mothers were childhood friends."

"You've only met her twice."

"Three times."

Pierre sighed. "Do you feel you know her?"

"Yes."

"You see, she seems young and innocent, and she is, but she's also very *strong*."

"I don't want a weak wife."

"Of course you don't, but . . ."

"I feel sure I'm meant to marry her."

"And what does she feel?"

Bertrand shrugged his shoulders. "I don't know. I think she likes me, and, as you say, she's a serious girl."

"Take care," said Pierre.

"Of what?" asked Bertrand.

"A *coup de foudre.*"

"Why?"

"It's usually followed by a storm."

At midday Pierre and Bertrand went once again to Sunday lunch at the Bonnets' house on the Avenue d'Assas. For Professor Bonnet and the other guests it was a lunch like any other, but to Pierre, who knew, and to Françoise Bonnet, who guessed, it was a lunch which betrayed the lovers; for Madeleine, despite her natural reserve and the presence of her parents and friends, hovered around Bertrand as if no one else were in the room, and Bertrand, even when addressing others, kept glancing at Madeleine as if he had only to lose sight of her and she would disappear.

After lunch Madeleine left with Pierre and Bertrand, and once again Pierre withdrew with the excuse that he had work to do. Bertrand and Madeleine made only a faint pretense of wanting him to stay. When he had gone they immediately embraced, and then walked together across the old town to the Musée Fabre, where, hand in hand, they looked at the collection of paintings.

Bertrand adopted a mildly pedagogic manner with the younger girl as he explained what he knew about Courbet or Delacroix, while she, who knew more, remained silent until they stopped in front of a self-portrait by Berthe Morisot.

"That's charming, don't you think?" he said.

"It's too pretty."

"Perhaps she was pretty."

"It's the painting that's too pretty," said Madeleine, "not Berthe Morisot. It's too decorative. It isn't real."

Bertrand looked perplexed. "Do you think that is better?" he asked, pointing to a portrait of a woman by van Dongen.

"Yes."

"Why?"

"It's by a man. He depicts life as he sees it, not as he would like it to be."

"Couldn't a woman do the same?"

She frowned. "In theory, yes." She looked more closely at the van Dongen. "But in practice they can't escape from their subjective condition."

"What do you mean, their subjective condition?"

"Nature imposes psychological as well as physical constraints," said Madeleine. "Women, because they are weak, depend on men. Men use them to bear their children and keep their home. It's therefore inevitable that a woman's horizon should be limited to the hearth; that she should feel no curiosity about life outside; that her analytic powers should atrophy; and that her paintings should not be statements or investigations, but decorations to hang on the walls."

"You're very hard on your own sex," said Bertrand, taking her arm.

"Oh, I daresay things will change," she said, turning and smiling at him as if she had suddenly remembered that she was in love.

They came out of the Musée Fabre and sat at the same café on the Place de la Comédie where they had met as mere acquaintances the day before.

"When is your train?" asked Madeleine.

"At seven."

"When will you come again?"

"Soon."

"How soon?"

"How soon do you want me?"

"I don't want you to go."

"Yesterday, under the aqueduct . . ." said Bertrand. "Do you remember what I said?"

She blushed. "Of course."

"The thing is . . ." He leaned on the table. A waiter who came to take their order saw that there was no point.

"What?" she asked, her face open and fragile.

"I have to be in Paris. I can come on weekends. We can meet like this. But I know already . . ."

"Know?" she whispered.

"I would like to marry you."

"Ah."

"I don't expect an answer. I haven't given you much time."

"Time doesn't matter."

"Do you love me?"

"Of course."

"And might you marry me?"

"Yes."

"Soon?"

"Whenever you like."

2

Later in their lives both Bertrand and Madeleine were to wonder how they could have made up their minds to marry in so short a time. In retrospect it seemed extraordinary to make a lifelong commitment after a single kiss. Had they belonged to an older generation they would undoubtedly have discussed the advantages and disadvantages of such a match with interested members of the family. Had they been truly emancipated they would probably have lived together before making any irrevocable decision. But, though they thought themselves modern, both of them belonged rather to a transitional generation which showed neither the social practicality of their fathers and grand-fathers nor the sexual realism of the present. They were also subject to the particular limitations of their own temperaments and upbring-ing. Like his uncle on his mother's side who ran Ravanel Frères in Valenciennes, Bertrand was decisive and sure of his own judgments. Already, before he had met Madeleine, he had decided that it was time he was married. He knew the kind of girl he wanted to marry; now he had found her. There seemed no reason to procrastinate.

He also believed in love. Everyone of his generation believed in love, and like most of his friends Bertrand was impatient to feel it. Since caution and calculation were incompatible with the condition, he could not permit himself to show them without immediately sug-gesting that he was not in love.

Madeleine was caught in the same dilemma, for despite her intelligence, and the skeptical influence of her father, she was as romantic as any other girl her age. She liked sentimental films like René Clair's *Sous les Toits de Paris,* and the higher class of romantic fiction, which she would keep hidden from her father in her room. Since she despised her mother and had no close friends of the same sex, some of these novels had assumed a certain authority in teaching her about matters of the heart, and it so happened that at the time of Bertrand's first visit to Montpellier she was reading a recently published novel by Paul Bourget called *The Relapse.*

It was the story of a young man called Pierre who meets a girl called Cilette in the south of France, and, since his car breaks down in Lyons, is given a lift in her car to Paris. The journey lasts only a day, but as they reach the outskirts of the capital he asks her, "If, later, when you are sure of me, when you know me through and through, with my faults but also certain qualities such as honor and loyalty which I hope I have, would you think it extraordinary if I came to ask you: Cilette, how about founding a home together?"

Cilette makes no answer, but on their arrival in Paris introduces Pierre to her mother, who, upon hearing his name, turns away. Unknown to the two young people, Pierre's father, Camille Therade, is Cilette's mother's onetime lover, a lover who first seduced her and then betrayed her with another woman. The remorseful ex-mistress now dreads her daughter marrying the son of this "Don Juan," and dreads too meeting the father again, for as the author tells the reader, "When a woman has only known one amorous adventure, she keeps a memory, sometimes unconscious, sometimes all too vivid, of these unique experiences, and she both dreads and longs for the presence of him through whom she experienced these feelings when the chance arises of meeting him again."

A few days later Pierre proposes to Cilette, and Cilette accepts him. The couple have not yet kissed. Upon returning to her parents' house, Cilette finds Pierre's father paying court to her mother. The mother faints; the lover leaves. The "relapse" is averted, but such is the daughter's repugnance that she decides she cannot marry Pierre and writes him to say so. When he is told why she has made this decision, he agrees that it is the right one. The marriage between two children of an adulterous couple is out of the question. Pierre sets out across the Atlantic in his airplane and is drowned, while Cilette dedicates her life to "the evangelization of the Red zone around Paris."

The novel, which Madeleine finished between Bertrand's two visits, deeply affected her. The gallant young Pierre Therade was not unlike the gallant young Bertrand de Roujay. Both were Catholics; both were principled and straight. Certainly there were aspects of the novel which Madeleine found a little absurd. If she were to discover that her mother had once had an affair with Bertrand's father, she would not break off her engagement to dedicate her life to converting Communist workers to Catholicism! But the immediate and honorable declarations of love by the two young men—the fictional and the real—impressed her young mind, and when Bertrand proposed marriage so soon after meeting her, it did not seem to her unduly hasty to accept him. Cilette, after all, accepted Pierre before she had even been kissed!

Madeleine therefore returned home from the station, where she had gone to see Bertrand off on the night train to Paris, filled with that intoxication which we all feel when our lives become like a fairy story; and as if to confirm that she had behaved in a proper way she reread *The Relapse* at a sitting, pondering on the phrase "sensations of a supreme intensity in the arms of a man," the mere memory of which had made Cilette's mother behave in such a scandalous way.

On the following weekend Bertrand once again took the night train from Paris, but rather than stay on it as far as Montpellier he alighted at Mézac, where a car had been sent to fetch him. He reached Saint Théodore in time for breakfast, and while he sat drinking coffee with his parents he told them that he was going to marry Madeleine Bonnet.

His mother turned white. She opened her mouth, then closed it again, and finally, without saying anything at all, got to her feet and left the room. Bertrand remained with his father, who looked nervously toward the door through which his wife had departed, then stroked his chin as if to check whether the morning's shave had been close enough and said: "You should have let us have a look at her first, you know."

"I know. I'm sorry," said Bertrand.

"Is she like the mother?" asked Edmond de Roujay.

"Not at all."

"Like the father, then?"

Bertrand smiled. "You'll adore her, Father. She's very pretty."

"I'm sure I will," said the colonel, "and you're thirty, after all. That's old enough for you to decide for yourself who you're going to marry. It's just that it's come as a shock to your mother." He stroked his chin again and glanced at the newspaper on the table beside the fire, as if looking for a topic to change the subject.

For a moment Bertrand felt a twinge of chagrin at his father's lack of interest, and the chagrin was tinged with jealousy because he remembered how delighted Edmond had been when Louis became engaged to Hélène de Sourcy. It was almost as if he had picked her himself, because Edmond, though he had not lost the esteem he felt for the pious and intelligent wife whom he had chosen partly because she possessed qualities he lacked, was naturally drawn to jollier and simpler women.

It was because Bertrand took after his mother that Edmond de Roujay had always conceded that she had greater rights over his elder son. This was the reason why he now distanced himself from the present crisis, and why, with an uneasy look at Bertrand, he advised his son to go after his mother and placate her.

Bertrand took this advice and, after gulping down what was left of his coffee, went up the cold stone stairs with his stomach tingling with dread at the thought of a quarrel with his mother; for even at the age of thirty, he was terrified of her self-righteous rage, and he was astonished at his own stupidity in not preparing the ground more carefully before telling her that he meant to marry Madeleine.

He knocked on her door.

"Come in."

Her tone of voice terrified him. He opened the door, and as he did so his mother rose from where she had been kneeling at her prie-dieu. "Come in," she said again.

Bertrand closed the door and came farther into the room. "Mother, I'm sorry . . ." he began, then stopped as his eye saw the photograph of his mother and Françoise Bart as children, which had been taken from its frame, torn in two and thrown on the floor. Alice de Roujay followed the direction of his eyes and with a quick, angry gesture swooped down to pick up the two halves of the daguerreotype and put them down on her dresser. "How could you, Bertrand?" she said. "How could you decide something like this without a word, not a word . . ."

"I'm sorry. It was so sudden . . ."

"So sudden? Yes. So sudden. And why? How can you decide

something like that in a flash?" She snapped her fingers. "And that wicked, stubborn little girl. What has she done to bewitch you? Did she seduce you? Is she pregnant? Is that why you are marrying her?"

Bertrand blushed. "Of course not, Mother."

"I can think of no other explanation—a girl of no background, with neither treasure in heaven nor treasure on earth . . ."

"You don't know her, Mother."

"Of course I know her. I know her better than you. Her mother's an imbecile and her father's an evil oaf."

"She is neither her father nor her mother."

"Nonsense. All children are one or the other, or a bit of both."

"If you met her, Mother . . ."

"I did meet her. She used to come here every year. She was stubborn and rude. I remember her only too well."

"She has changed, Mother."

"People don't change."

Now Bertrand became angry. "For God's sake, Mother, how can you say that? Didn't Christ come on earth to make people change?"

"He can change people, perhaps, but not those who don't believe in him."

"She is enchanting, Mother."

"She certainly seems to have enchanted you."

"She is good."

"How do you know?"

"One can tell."

"Does she even believe in God?"

He hesitated. "I don't know."

"You don't know? You decide to marry a girl before you know what she believes?"

"I'm in love with her."

"Bewitched by her!"

"She knows of my beliefs."

"Well, that's something!" said Alice ironically. "And the children?"

"What about them?"

"Will they be baptized?"

"Of course."

"And brought up as Catholics?"

"Yes."

"Has she agreed?"

"We haven't discussed it."

"Perhaps you should."

"When you meet her, Mother, you'll realize that she isn't the sort to make a fuss about that sort of thing."

"Very well," said Alice. She gave a deep sigh as she regained some control of her temper. "There's only one thing I ask, as a favor to me."

"Of course."

"Talk to your Uncle Charles."

"All right."

"And listen to what he says."

"I always do."

Bertrand left Saint Théodore early the next morning, and reached the Cathedral of Langeais in time to hear his uncle, who had recently been installed as bishop, celebrate high mass.

Charles Ravanel was well suited to this particular episcopal throne, for while Langeais was an ancient city whose buildings and battlements had hardly changed since the sixteenth century, it included within its diocese the more modern cities in the plain below. In the same way, its new bishop, who had the austere and elegant demeanor of a medieval prelate, possessed the vigor and practicality of an industrialist. His years in the Vatican had given a suave veneer to his matter-of-fact manner, and because, as a secular cleric, he had taken no vow of poverty, he could take advantage of his private income from Ravanel Frères to live in the style of an earlier era.

When he received his nephew after mass in the library—a beautiful room with carved bookcases and a decorated ceiling—a manservant brought in a silver tray with port in a cut-glass decanter and served the two men with an apéritif before bowing to the bishop and leaving the room.

"So you're to marry?" said the bishop to Bertrand.

"Yes."

"The daughter of Françoise Bart."

"You knew her?"

"Of course. Your mother rather hoped that I might marry her, but providence had other plans." He raised his eyes to the painting of a dove depicting the Holy Ghost on the ceiling.

"If my mother wanted you to marry Françoise," said Bertrand, "why is she so opposed to my marrying her daughter?"

"I don't think for a moment that she's opposed to your marrying this girl because she's the daughter of Françoise Bart."

"She didn't seem pleased."

"Parents rarely are. You see, you children carry the invisible burden of their expectations, which are often, in their turn, the fruit of their own disappointments."

"Is Mamma disappointed?"

"No, no, I don't think so. I was talking generally. She might have hoped, perhaps, for a vocation in the family, but that was not to be. It is not in our hands, after all." Again he raised his eyes to the ceiling.

Bertrand frowned. "One doesn't become a priest to please one's mother."

"Indeed not, indeed not. But you must respect her piety. Her faith is all-important to her—as indeed it is to me."

"I know," said Bertrand, still with a wrinkled brow, "but in this day and age, she can't expect me to confine my affections to girls who are Catholic."

"In this day and age." The bishop repeated the phrase in a tone of distaste. "No, well, perhaps you're right, dear boy, but I don't think it is simply a matter of what she expects. It's more a matter of what she fears."

"What she fears?"

"For your soul."

Bertrand shook his head. "I bitterly regret not introducing her to Madeleine first," he said, "because if she met her—if you met her— you would realize that she could not possibly endanger my soul."

"Of course, of course," said his Uncle Charles. "I am sure she is enchanting, but when in love . . . you are in love, aren't you?"

"Of course."

"Of course. And love is a wonderful thing, but it is just in such moments of intoxication that we should listen to the teaching of the Church."

"By all means."

"Who in her holy wisdom forbids a Catholic to marry someone outside the Church."

"Forbids it?"

"Forbids it as a general rule, but in certain circumstances grants a dispensation."

"Do you think . . . I mean, would it be possible . . ."

"For you to qualify for a dispensation? Certainly. I'm sure—sure, that is, if the young lady agrees to meet certain conditions."

"I'm sure she'll agree to anything."

"You see, only this year the Holy Father in his encyclical on holy matrimony warned us of the danger to the life of the soul of those who rashly contract mixed marriages."

"This isn't a rash decision, Uncle."

"Have you known her long?"

Bertrand blushed. "No."

"It was love at first sight?"

"More or less."

The bishop sighed. "And can you be sure, Bertrand, that it is . . . the right sort of love?"

"Absolutely sure."

"You feel a strong attraction . . ."

"But that's just the point, Uncle Charles. I don't feel that kind of attraction—lust, you would call it—which I confess I have felt for other women. It was simply because my affection for her was so pure that I knew at once that she was meant to be my wife."

The bishop rose to take the decanter of port from the tray and fill his nephew's glass. "My dear Bertrand, you're not a child anymore. You have always been sensible, and I do not want to suggest for a moment that I think you have lost your head like some romantic adolescent."

"Thank you."

"But just because you are so sensible, you must see that, like your mother, I am a little surprised that you should choose to marry . . . should fall in love with the daughter of a notorious atheist."

"Madeleine is not her father."

"But she is an atheist."

"I daresay."

"Haven't you asked her about her attitude toward religion?"

"Not really, no. Perhaps I should have done so, but somehow, if you're in love, it's difficult to . . . negotiate."

"Of course."

"You can't say 'I love you, I want to marry you, but only if you accept this or change that.' "

"I know."

"You love the whole person just as she is. Even the things that you might otherwise dislike about her become endearing."

"I can imagine."

"The truth is, Uncle, that although I believe in God and love God, and would never abandon my faith in the Church, it is partly because she is *not* a Catholic that I am drawn to her."

"You see marriage as a mission?"

"Yes. Perhaps that's it."

"You would want to convert her?"

"Of course."

"And don't fear that it is she who might convert you?"

"No."

The bishop sat down again. "My dear boy, I know you well, and I trust you completely, but if I am to help you obtain the necessary dispensation, we must comply with canon law."

"Of course."

"Madeleine must agree to be instructed in the Catholic faith before you marry."

"Yes."

"And she must promise that any children born of your marriage will be brought up in the Catholic faith."

"I'm sure she will agree to both."

"She lives in Montpellier, is that right?"

"Yes."

"Well, there are several good priests there whom she could talk to, but the one I would recommend is a young Dominican called Father Antoine Dubec. I hardly know him myself—I have met him only once —but he is young and unusual. Quite different, I think, from what she might expect in a Catholic priest."

"I'll ask her to meet him."

"Good. And I, in turn, will speak to your mother and will do what I can to allay her fears about the danger to your soul."

After lunch Bertrand was driven from Langeais to Coustiers in the bishop's black limousine. There he caught the night train to Paris. He went from the Gare de Lyon to his apartment on the Rue de Médicis, where he took a bath and changed his clothes before going to work at the ministry.

He suffered all day at the thought of how far he was from Madeleine, and how many days he had to endure before the next weekend when he could once again go to Montpellier. When he returned to his apartment in the evening he picked up his telephone and was eventually connected to Madeleine in her home on the Avenue d'Assas.

"I told my parents," he said.

"What did they say?"

"My mother asked me to speak to my uncle."

"What did he say?"

"That everything would be fine."

She said nothing. The line crackled.

"I miss you abominably," said Bertrand.

"I miss you."

"The weekend seems so far away."

"I know."

"Could you come to Paris?"

"When?"

"Tomorrow."

She hesitated, then said, "All right."

"I'll meet you at the station."

"Very well."

He had spoken without thinking, but now as he told her which train to catch it seemed both an obvious and an extraordinary thing to have suggested. Each longed to see the other; he could not leave Paris. But as he put down the receiver he realized that she had not asked where she would stay, and he had not brought up that aspect of their arrangements. He sat back and looked around at the living room of his elegant apartment, which looked out over the Rue de Médicis onto the Luxembourg Gardens. It was comfortable and elegantly furnished, but there was only a single bedroom.

Throughout the next day at work he dithered about whether or not to book a room at a hotel, but in the end did nothing. He went to meet her that evening at the Gare de Lyon a little nervous that she would think that he had asked her to Paris simply to seduce her.

All at once, as he saw her climb down from the train, he realized that his apprehension was absurd, that already there was trust between them that was beyond suspicions of this kind. She smiled and embraced him with a shy friendliness that contained within it a complete confidence in his good intentions, and the delight he felt at the sight of her —her brown skin glowing beside the wan faces of the dour Parisians —had more in it of astonishment and wonder than of male sexual desire.

They went back to his apartment with her suitcase, and he asked if she would mind staying there for the night. "You can have my bed," he said in a comradely tone of voice, "and I'll sleep here." He patted the sofa, causing small particles of dust to rise and reflect the light in a shaft of the evening sun.

"No," said Madeleine. "I'll sleep on the sofa. You take the bed."

She looked around his living room with a sober curiosity, as if the furniture and pictures might give Bertrand a quite different character from that of the man she had known in Montpellier. Apparently reassured, she turned back and smiled at Bertrand, saying, "It's very nice."

"When we're married," he said, "we'll need a larger place."

"Won't this do?" she asked.

"For a family?" He laughed. "No, it's really a bachelor apartment."

They went out into the street and because it was such a fine evening crossed over into the Luxembourg Gardens.

"Was it easy to get away?" he asked.

"I lied," said Madeleine. "I told them I was going to spend the night with Nellie Planchet."

"Have you told them . . . that we're to marry?"

She blushed. "My mother."

"Not your father?"

"Not yet. I wanted . . ." She hesitated.

"What?"

"To be sure that you were sure."

"I've told my parents."

"What did they say?"

"My mother was a little upset."

Madeleine blushed again, a blush that might have been of either embarrassment or anger. "I thought she might be."

"She is obsessed with the Catholic Church."

"And I am not a Catholic."

"That is what worries her. So I went to see my uncle, who thought it would be fine, and promised to reassure my mother, although he did explain that to get a dispensation you would have to be instructed by a priest." He looked anxiously at Madeleine; she said nothing. "And promise that the children will be raised as Catholics."

"Is that what you want?" she asked.

"Yes . . . that is . . . would you mind?"

Madeleine stopped as if she could not walk and think deeply at the same time. "I don't know. I don't think so. It's very hard to imagine a child growing up with quite different beliefs, but then I never thought I would fall in love with a Catholic." She turned toward Bertrand. "And I do love you, and I love you altogether for what you are, so my answer is no, I don't mind. I can't mind because it was always understood that you would be what you are."

He took her hand. They walked on. "My uncle knows of a young priest in Montpellier. Would you talk to him sometime?"

"I will if you want me to."

He sighed. "You know, Madeleine, I love you so much, and so entirely, that all these rules and regulations seem tiresome, but I suppose it is irresponsible to marry without considering one another's beliefs."

"I have no beliefs."

"None at all?"

She shrugged her shoulders. "Decency and common sense. Are those beliefs?"

"Yes, I think so. But what about an afterlife?"

She shrugged her shoulders. "I neither believe in it nor disbelieve in it. I don't see how one can know. To me your God in heaven, the Virgin Mary and the Communion of Saints are like ghosts or goblins. I recognize that many sincere and intelligent people believe in them. I know some even claim to have seen them, like Bernadette at Lourdes. But other equally sincere and intelligent people do not believe in them, and I myself have no opinion one way or the other."

"But can you marry a man who does believe?"

"In ghosts and goblins?" She laughed. "Yes, if I love him."

They had dinner together in a restaurant on the Boulevard Saint Germain and afterward walked back arm in arm to the apartment on the Rue de Médicis. The wine in their blood and the warm night air in their lungs combined with their emotions to make their bodies move together without their minds' intent. They kissed as they closed the door to the apartment; they kissed again as they came into the living room, then sat and embraced once again on the sofa. Hands clutched, caressed and strayed until, through half-closed eyes, Bertrand remembered his resolution.

"We must take care," he said, drawing back.

"We're going to marry," she murmured.

"I know," he said, "but we should wait."

She sat up and straightened her skirt. She said nothing, but she sighed, and that sigh, together with the ambiguity of the smile which followed it, and the trace of impatience in the movement of her lips, suggested to Bertrand that she thought his honor an ass—or if not an ass a phantom as insubstantial as the ghosts, goblins and saints in heaven.

Madeleine returned to Montpellier the next morning. She and Bertrand were agreed that it would be foolhardy to risk her parents' anger by her staying away for more than a single night. For Madeleine, however, the long journey had been worthwhile. If she had expected a more significant and irrevocable initiation into adulthood, alone with her lover in his apartment, she was not consciously disappointed that it had not occurred, for Bertrand's honorable reserve, like his riding breeches or his Catholic beliefs, was a necessary accouterment of the chivalrous knight who had galloped into her limited life and was to carry her away. And despite its chaste outcome, the very fact that she had spent the night in Bertrand's apartment—that they had seen each other in their nightclothes, and had sat together at the breakfast table—had given some substance to their decision to live their lives together. She was still sufficiently in the shadow of her childhood to feel an exhilarating sense of defiance and liberation in doing what her parents would consider wrong; the night in Paris, like the decision to marry, was both the proof and the fruit of her maturity.

Deceiving her parents was one thing; defying them would be another. She dreaded telling her father that she was to marry Bertrand, and hoped that her mother had prepared the ground. But as soon as she entered her home on the Avenue d'Assas and was kissed absentmindedly by the professor, one could tell that he knew nothing of what she had decided.

The three of them ate supper alone, and she chose this moment to break the news to her father, hoping that the presence of her mother might provide some support.

"Papa," she said.

"What is it?" he asked, his eyes still on the print of a review which he had sneaked onto the table.

"Can I tell you something?"

"Of course."

"I want to get married."

Françoise laughed. The professor raised his eyes but kept his finger on the page. "To de Roujay?" he asked.

"Yes."

"You'll be unhappy."

"I love him."

"I don't doubt that."

"And he loves me."

"I don't doubt that either."

"Then why will we be unhappy?"

"A leopard can't change its spots."

"What spots?"

"The spots of the *ancien régime.*"

"He's not like that, Papa. He has an open mind."

"Blood is thicker than water."

"You don't know him."

"Perhaps not."

There was a short pause. Professor Bonnet looked back at his magazine.

"Do you forbid it?" asked Madeleine.

"No."

"Will you give me away?"

"Before a priest?"

She blushed. "For the sake of his parents."

"Of course," he said acidly. "One must respect superstitions."

"Sometimes, Papa, you seem more intolerant than they are."

He smiled malignly and, looking up from his review again, was about to make some rejoinder when he saw the angry, affectionate eyes of his daughter, the lower lids stemming the release of two tears, and with a strong and unusual effort of will he checked not just the words he was about to utter but the thought which provoked them. Instead he smiled and said, "You are no longer a child, Madeleine. I accept anyone you choose."

"You'll come to my wedding?"

"Of course. In my robes as grand master of the lodge!" He laughed, and Madeleine laughed too. She rose from the table and went to kiss her father, and after him her mother, who until then she had ignored, but who was also laughing, though whether from mirth, relief or confusion it was, as always, impossible to tell.

On the following Saturday morning, Madeleine met Bertrand off the night train from Paris and took him from the station to her parents' house on the Avenue d'Assas. There Françoise embraced him, and then sent him alone into Michel Bonnet's study.

The professor rose from his desk. "Come in and sit down," he said, as if Bertrand were a student who had come for a tutorial.

Bertrand did as he was told. "I should perhaps have asked your permission . . ." he began.

"No formalities," said Bonnet, waving his hand and seating himself once again. "Madeleine has made her choice. I accept it."

"I shall try—"

"All I have to say is this," the professor interrupted. "She has no money, and I have only my salary and what I earn with my pen, so if you were expecting a dowry of any kind, you will be disappointed."

"There's no question of that."

"Good. The only other comment I have to make is about Madeleine herself. She has always been, and remains, the person I love best in the world. If I lose her now, too bad, but it had to happen sooner or later."

"I promise you—" Bertrand began again, but got no further.

"My affection, however," said Michel Bonnet, interrupting him again, "has not blinded me to her faults."

"I cannot conceive of them," said Bertrand.

"That is the point. You are in love with her?"

"Most certainly."

"So you are in no position to form an objective assessment of her qualities." Bonnet reached behind his desk to take a book from the shelf. "Have you read Schopenhauer on women?" He opened a copy of *Studies in Pessimism* and read from it, again as if Bertrand were one of his students. " 'With young girls Nature seems to have in view what in the language of drama is called a striking effect: as for a few years she dowers them with a wealth of beauty and is lavish in her gift of charm, at the expense of all the rest of this life; so that during those years they may capture the fantasy of some man to such a degree that he is hurried away into undertaking the honorable care of them, in some form or other, as long as they live—a step for which there would not appear to be any sufficient warranty if reason alone directed his thoughts.' " He closed the book and put it down on his desk.

"I have never assumed," said Bertrand, "that all my thoughts should be directed by reason."

"No," said the professor, "I thought not."

"Only that they should be reasonable."

"I do not see the difference."

"It could be reasonable to believe that reason has its limits."

"I think that is where we would differ."

"You cannot think it unreasonable for me to love Madeleine."

"No."

"To want to share my life with her."

"No, but I'm her father."

"And I want to be her husband."

"And you shall be," said Bonnet. "No one seeks to prevent it."

The two men left the study in time for lunch, and it was a reward for both to see Madeleine's delight as she perceived that they had reached an amicable understanding. She ran to her father, hugged him and kissed him, then went to Bertrand and with greater reserve merely looped her arm through his and stood smiling at his side.

That afternoon Bertrand took Madeleine to see Antoine Dubec, the Dominican friar recommended by his uncle. He had telephoned from Paris to make the appointment, and now entered the ancient building on the Rue des Augustins with a certain unease, for he sensed Madeleine's aversion to everything smelling of candlewax and incense. He also knew that she considered the Dominican Order, which had been founded to fight the heresy of the Cathars in Languedoc and had run the infamous Inquisition, to be the secret police of the Catholic

Church. As they were shown into a large room, with high windows looking out over the street, he wondered why his uncle had not chosen some pious monk who might have impressed Madeleine with his holiness and simplicity.

They sat down on two hard leather armchairs. Over the mantel there was a crucifix, and on the walls dark paintings of Saint Dominic, Saint Thomas Aquinas and other heroes of the order.

"No portrait of Torquemada," Madeleine whispered to Bertrand.

"Perhaps they aren't so proud of him."

"Saint Dominic killed many more Cathars in France than Torquemada burned heretics in Spain."

"It wasn't Saint Dominic," said Bertrand. "It was Simon de Montfort."

Madeleine was about to say something more when the door opened and a Dominican friar entered the room. He was young, as the bishop had promised, but also rough in appearance, with a thick neck, tousled hair and scraped patches of skin on his ill-shaven chin. He scowled rather than smiled as he shook hands with Bertrand, but turned with more warmth toward Madeleine.

"I congratulate you, mademoiselle," he said, "but you also have my sympathy. It cannot be easy for the daughter of Professor Bonnet to marry the nephew of the bishop of Langeais."

"You know of my father?" asked Madeleine.

"I not only know of him," said the friar, "I used to sneak into his lectures at the university. I needed some antidote to our Catholic view of history, and your father, one has to concede, provides it in masterly fashion."

Madeleine flourished under this praise of her father. "Did you study history?" she asked.

"No. Theology." He spoke in a rough, rasping voice with a Marseilles accent. "But the two are interconnected."

"Indeed," said Bertrand. "Madeleine was wondering why you have no portrait of Torquemada."

Antoine laughed. "Why not indeed? Then it would be a regular rogues' gallery."

"Are you ashamed of him, then?" asked Madeleine with a trace of impudence in her smile.

"Am I, or are we? I cannot answer for the whole order."

"Then you . . ."

"I have to concede," said Antoine, "that his attitude toward the Jews was much the same as Herr Hitler's."

"And Saint Dominic?"

"More complicated, but not without some moral responsibility for the terrible massacres of the Cathars."

Madeleine looked with a trace of triumph at Bertrand.

"One should be cautious, surely," said Bertrand to the Dominican, "of judging other eras by the lights of our own."

"I disagree," said Antoine bluntly. "The issues are essentially the same, and the Church must recognize that her enemies now are merely following the example of her intolerance over the centuries."

Again Madeleine glanced at Bertrand with an air of triumph.

"Perhaps you're right," Bertrand said in the tone his mother had used to call a truce in a dispute when he had argued with his brother, Louis. "Luckily, this has nothing to do with marriage."

"Don't be too sure," said the Dominican in a somewhat insolent tone of voice. "The article of canon law which forbids marriage between a Catholic and a non-Catholic almost certainly dates from the time of Saint Dominic, and in a sense it reflects the intolerance of that time." He turned to Madeleine and in a gentler tone of voice said, "I apologize in advance for subjecting you to this course of instruction. It is really an insult to the integrity of your conscience, but"—he shrugged his shoulders—"we have our bureaucracy, our rules and regulations."

"I understand," said Madeleine.

"If you could find the time to call in here for an hour or so, half a dozen times?"

"Of course."

"Shall we say Monday at the same time?"

"Fine."

"I'm afraid I shall be in Paris," said Bertrand.

"That doesn't matter," said Antoine. "Indeed, it's better that I should see her alone."

3

When Bertrand and Madeleine had left, Dubec returned to his room, where for a time he tried to work, then to pray, but he had been sufficiently distracted by their short visit to find that his prayers degenerated into formless rumination. He got up off his knees and went to his desk to study the letter from the bishop of Langeais which had arrived two days before. It was a simple request in his own hand to instruct the girl his nephew was to marry.

Antoine had once met the bishop; he had come to lunch with the Dominicans at Montpellier, and during that lunch Antoine had put some provocative questions to him on the attitude of the Church toward social reform. He had been rebuked afterward by his fellow friars for his insolent tone, and after a fierce examination of his conscience he had had to acknowledge, and later confess, that he had taken against Monsignor Ravanel for his chauffeur, his limousine, his well-cut, purple-trimmed frock coat, his charm, his elegance, his fastidiousness—all of which had seemed to embody what he most disliked about the hierarchy of the Church.

Antoine could hardly believe that the bishop remembered their exchange from the year before, but if he did not, then why, in all Montpellier, had he been chosen to instruct Mademoiselle Bonnet? Was the bishop patronizing him by showing this mark of trust? The idea had enraged him, and his first impulse had been to ask his superiors if he might refuse. He did not imagine that he would like the bishop's nephew, and when he saw Bertrand de Roujay he found this prediction confirmed. He was the same type as his uncle; indeed, he might have been the prelate, just as the bishop might have been the civil servant. They were both men who could afford to cut their coat according to their cloth, because circumstance had given them bales of the finest materials. Both had the complacent mien of men who served others only when they had first served themselves, whereas Antoine felt a sense of personal mission to preach that Christ was for the poor, the imprisoned, the sick, the lame—not the well-fed, well-dressed scions of the French bourgeoisie.

This sympathy was not without cause. Antoine himself came from the gutters of Marseilles, and had it not been for the Catholic Church —indeed, the Dominican Order—he might well have been a pimp instead of a friar, shepherding his whores around the Place de l'Opéra. His mother was unmarried and lived alone. She had been one of ten children of a stevedore who as a girl of eighteen had gone to work as a cleaner at the Hospital of the Hôtel Dieu, where a middle-aged surgeon had seduced her.

When it was discovered that she was pregnant, her father had thrown her out. Her seducer offered to end the pregnancy, but from piety Antoine's mother declined. She went to lodge in a refuge for girls in her predicament that was run by nuns, and when the child was born found a small flat in one of the seamy streets along the Vieux Port. She never married. She never had another lover. She was plain and pious, and each Friday she went to clean the Dominican church on the Rue Edmond Rostand to expiate her pathetic sin.

In time, and in return, the friars took care of her son. They supervised his education, and after his baccalauréat, accepted him into the order. They did not encourage him to become one of their number —it was clear from the start that he would be rebellious, disruptive, stubborn—but his determination from adolescence onward to become a friar convinced the superior that he had a real vocation.

Dubec had been sent to study at Montpellier, where he played truant from his proper courses in theology to attend the lectures of Professor Bonnet, and if he had not written back to the bishop to refer Bertrand's fiancée to some other priest, it was because Monsignor Ravanel had added a postscript: "She is the daughter of Professor Bonnet."

Antoine had been fascinated by Bonnet because he so vigorously attacked the role of the Catholic church in history. To him the Popes, crusaders and inquisitors had given a divine sanction to bigotry, oppression and torture. The propaganda practiced by Goebbels—the art of the audacious lie—was in the tradition of the Christian missions which had followed in the wake of the crusaders and conquistadors preaching meekness, forgiveness and brotherly love to those they had enslaved.

But it was not just in America, Africa and Asia that the Catholic religion had been used by the imperialist powers to emasculate the indigenous population. In Languedoc itself it had been the ideology of the French and Norman invaders, who with unparalleled brutality at the beginning of the thirteenth century had first conquered and then destroyed the gentle and tolerant civilization which had flourished

south of the Loire. To the Languedocians of that period, the French
had been as barbarous as the Fascists seemed today. The Holy Inquisition was its secret police, and Protestantism, like the Cathar heresy, was
the ideology of the resistance. "And this resistance has always continued," the professor had declaimed in the ampitheater of the university. "Look at the way in which the people of Toulouse treated the
corpse of Montmorency, beheaded by Richelieu! Like the relics of a
saint! And the same spirit of revolt is reborn with the great Revolution
of 1789, and lasts through the centuries to the radicals, socialists and
anticlericals of today!"

The effect of Bonnet's lectures on the young Dominican had been
to throw his energetic mind into confusion. By temperament he was
a rebel, but his faith in God was strong, and his devotion to the
Dominicans who had raised him and befriended him was not to be
shaken. It seemed impossible, however, to deny their historical crimes.
He was not impressed by the fine distinction between the Dominican
inquisitor who had discovered the heretic and the secular law which
had burned him. Rather, he became convinced that the wrong they had
done in the past must be undone in the present. To God, as Saint Peter
wrote, "one day is like a thousand years and a thousand years is like
a day." The misconceptions of the Middle Ages could quite properly
be put right in the twentieth century.

Antoine was young, and was still under the discipline of his superior, but already within the Church there was a certain unease, an
awareness that the working classes were disaffected from Catholicism
and were giving their loyalties instead to the atheists on the left. Thus
the young friar Antoine, who despite the genes of the bourgeois
surgeon had the bearing of a stevedore, was given considerable freedom
to pursue his own concept of his vocation, and if at times this led to
a stir—as with his insolent questions to the bishop of Langeais—some
thought it all to the good.

Despite his youthful constitution, Antoine Dubec was untouched by
temptations of the flesh. Either from the power of the Grace of God
or from a fanatical *pudeur,* inculcated perhaps by his mother, who had
suffered so much for her moment of weakness, he had been able to
master his nascent sexual desires and now channeled all his energies into
his sense of mission. When he first saw Madeleine Bonnet, he took note

of her beauty, but that was all. He did not want to endear himself to her. He did not even want to convert her—at least not to the Catholic Church of her father's lectures, nor to the smug club to which Bertrand de Roujay and Monsignor Ravanel belonged. All he wanted to do was to convince her, while instructing her, that the Catholic Church need not be, and would not be, all that it had been in the past; that she should not judge it now by Torquemada or Thomas Aquinas, but by radical priests like Antoine Dubec.

"When I think of what was done by our Church in the name of Christ," he said to Madeleine on her first visit, "I feel quite ashamed. But we must live today, and listen to what God says to us now. And what he has to say, what he wants us to do, may be at odds with everything that has been done in the past. There's no doubt in my mind, for example, that the hatred felt and fostered by us Catholics for the so-called heretics and infidels—Jews, Muslims, Cathars, Protestants—was a worse sin than the heresies themselves, if, indeed, heresy can be considered a sin. If you love your neighbor, you must respect his point of view. The good Samaritan, after all, was not a Jew; he was, from the Jew's point of view, a heretic."

"So it doesn't really matter that I'm not a Catholic?"

"No. We used to believe that outside the Church there was no salvation, but I don't think even the Pope would suggest that God speaks to man only through Popes and prelates. It is here"—he pointed to his heart—"that God speaks to each one of the creatures he has created."

Madeleine looked at the food stains on the friar's habit.

"It is in your heart that you will meet him," Antoine went on. "It is there that you will get to know him, seeing a side of him perhaps that I have missed, just as I may see God in a quite different way than Bertrand, your fiancé."

"Yes," said Madeleine. "I think you do."

On her second visit, a week later, Madeleine and Antoine talked about marriage. He had given her a copy of the Pope's recent encyclical on the subject, parts of which, she told him, she found difficult to accept. "He says, for example, that the primary purpose of marriage is the procreation of children."

"Yes."

"But that is not why I want to marry Bertrand, nor, I think, why he wants to marry me. We are marrying because we love one another, not because we want to breed."

"Of course," said Antoine.

"The Pope seems to begrudge the joy of love, and to justify it only through having children."

"Yes," said Antoine. "Pope Pius is a grand old man, but he belongs to the past. There are good things in his encyclical, but I wouldn't want you to take it entirely seriously. You see, the Church's attitude toward marriage has been colored by the ideas of two brilliant but unusual men, Saint Paul and Saint Augustine, who today, thanks to Freud, we can see were seriously disturbed by sexual neuroses."

"But does that mean," asked Madeleine, "that all the Pope says about the evils of concupiscence no longer applies?"

Antoine looked somewhat confused. "In marriage," he said, "as in everything else, the command to love is supreme. If we obey that command, everything else will follow."

"I'm quite sure that I love Bertrand," said Madeleine, "but I am not sure that I feel"—here she pointed to a passage in the encyclical with just the same gesture her father used to mark a line of text—"that I should *submit* to him."

"Remember," said Antoine with a laugh, "that the Pope was born in 1857."

"I was brought up to believe that men and women are equal."

"And so they are," said Antoine. " 'Man and Woman he created them.' "

"Yet didn't Saint Paul write that wives should obey their husbands?"

"Yes."

"A symptom of his sexual neurosis?" she asked with a smile.

"More a sign of the times he lived in, like, 'Slaves, obey your masters.' "

"Would Bertrand agree with what you say?"

"I'm sure he would if he thought about it."

"And the bishop of Langeais?"

"I'm not sure."

"Yet he sent me to you?"

"Yes."

"So I can assume that what you say has his blessing?"

"Indeed."

In the midst of Madeleine's instruction, Bertrand took a week's leave from the ministry in Paris and came in a car to drive her from Montpellier to Saint Théodore to stay with his parents.

The meeting between Madeleine and his mother, which had made Bertrand so apprehensive that he had hardly slept the night before, went so well that it might have been rehearsed beforehand. As the car drew up on the gravel, Alice glided out of the house and opened the door to the passenger seat, and no sooner was her future daughter-in-law standing beside her than she kissed her on both cheeks and said, "Madeleine, my dear! How you've grown!" as if she were returning as usual for the summer holidays.

Equally determined that this visit should go well, Madeleine concealed her suspicions behind a fixed smile and walked arm in arm with her future mother-in-law into the house. In the hall she stopped, overwhelmed by strong recollections. She looked up at the staircase where she had stood, defiant, as a child, and for a moment it seemed as if something should be said by one of the two women to ratify the peace which each had made in her own mind. But Alice, following Madeleine's glance and sensing her faltering step, took a firmer grip on her arm and said, "You must come and see Edmond." She led her into the drawing room, where the old soldier rose from the sofa and betrayed at once, in the twinkle of his eye, that whatever else he might feel about Madeleine, he appreciated the appearance of a pretty girl.

As Bertrand followed them in he realized that his mother had made an unusual effort for the occasion. There were three vases filled with flowers, and as she talked to Madeleine, sitting next to her on the sofa, she kept hold of her hand, clutching it tightly every now and then to emphasize a point.

"Do you like flowers, my dear?" she asked.

"I like them, yes."

"Now that Dominique has gone, I have no one to advise me about the garden. These men, you know, only care about the vines, and all their dreadful machines."

"We've got a garden now in Montpellier," said Madeleine. "Before, we lived in an apartment."

"Of course, of course. Well, if one lives in a city . . . I mean, Bertrand lives in a tiny apartment."

"Yes, I know," said Madeleine, and too hastily added, "He's described it to me."

"Will you live there when you marry?" asked Edmond de Roujay.

"Too small," said Bertrand.

"No room for a child," said Alice.

"There's no hurry," said Madeleine.

"Let's wait and see," said Bertrand quickly.

"One must be prepared," said his mother.

In the course of the eight days that they remained at Saint Théodore, Louis came over with his wife and their two small children to inspect Bertrand's bride-to-be.

In the years since Madeleine had last seen him, Louis had grown still less like his older brother. Where Bertrand had the grave air of a serious-minded man, Louis remained an overgrown schoolboy. He loved practical jokes, and played them continually on everyone around him. Certainly he could be serious—he was a captain in the army— but now, off duty, his plump round face always wobbled on the verge of laughter, just as it had when he was a child.

Hélène, his pretty, vapid wife, was his permanently appreciative audience. She had discovered the delights of marriage not just in bed, but also in the bathroom, where, to her delight, her husband would fart as he lay in the tub up to his chin and explode the bubbles with a lighted match as they rose to the surface of the water.

Louis was shorter than Bertrand, with a fair complexion, and while Bertrand was more methodical and efficient, Louis gave the impression of more energy—always jumping up and down, tickling his wife, throwing his children in the air, juggling with oranges from the fruit bowl on the sideboard, untying the strings of the cook's apron as she served lunch. "For goodness sake, Louis, be your age," Alice de Roujay kept shouting at her twenty-seven-year-old son. She was the least amused by his antics.

When he came face to face with Madeleine in the garden of Saint Théodore, Louis went through a whole routine. "No, I can't believe it . . . it can't be true . . . little Madeleine . . . no . . . it's someone different. Yet she's the same . . . it is . . . it's you . . . but look

. . . no . . . so . . . Bertrand, you rogue . . . such . . . Madeleine!"

She bestowed on him one of her rare smiles. He took her hand and kissed it with an affectation of old-fashioned courtesy, then ("But this is absurd!") hugged her like a bear, lifting her feet well off the ground. "But are you really going to marry Bertrand?" he asked.

"So it seems."

"Do you know what you're doing?"

"I think so."

"Has anyone told you about him? His . . . er . . . ? No? You know he's not quite . . . well, he's *special,* you know. Not as others are. You realize that?"

Madeleine laughed. "That's why I'm marrying him."

"Of course, of course. Good . . . well, so long as you know."

"Know what?"

"You *don't* know?"

"Tell me," she whispered.

"He's completely mad," he whispered back.

"He seems sane to me."

"That's a facade."

"What are the symptoms of his madness?"

"He takes life seriously."

"Ah, yes, that's bad."

"Has he . . ."

"What?"

"No fits?"

"Not yet."

"You may not recognize them."

"Perhaps . . ." She hesitated.

"Go on."

"I'm not sure I should."

"I'm his brother."

"That's true."

"Tell me."

"He did do something strange."

"What?"

"He asked me to be his wife."

"Ah, that," said Louis, no longer whispering, "that is the first sane thing he's done in his whole life."

Louis and his family departed on Sunday afternoon, and on Monday, Bertrand's uncle, the bishop, came to lunch. At first his episcopal attire provoked a reflex mistrust in the Freemason's daughter, but her discussions with Dubec had done much to demystify the papist priesthood, and in a short time she was talking to him with an easy familiarity.

"Now what did you think of Antoine Dubec?" he asked, breathing in through his teeth as he spoke.

"I liked him."

"He clearly thought you were splendid. He has given you a clean bill of health, as it were. The dispensation is assured."

"We can marry in October?" asked Bertrand.

"Certainly, certainly."

"And will you marry us, Uncle?"

"I should be honored to. But where?"

"In Montpellier?"

"Of course. The home of the bride. I must write to the bishop for permission."

"Will he give it?"

"Of course, of course, a mere formality."

"Will he lend us the cathedral?"

"I'm sure he will if we want it, but it's such a gloomy church, don't you think?" Monsignor Ravanel turned to Madeleine.

"It *is* a little dark."

"I'm sorry," said the bishop, his eyes raised to the ceiling as he addressed Saint Peter, the patron of the cathedral at Montpellier, "but since we only marry once, we're entitled to a cheerful church." He turned back to Madeleine. "We can do better, can't we? Saint Roch, perhaps, or Saint Ravy, or even the Pénitents Blancs."

"Have you thought about the wedding trip?" asked Edmond de Roujay. "More important to get that right, I always say."

"We thought we'd go to Italy," Bertrand began.

"Too hot," said Edmond. "Much too hot. I always recommend Deauville. Comfortable hotels, bracing air, nothing to do. In fact, dear boy, I'll make you a gift of it. A week—no, ten days—no, two weeks in Deauville."

The next day Bertrand and Madeleine drove to the Carmelite convent in Mézac where Dominique was now a nun. It was an encounter which Madeleine anticipated with the greatest unease, for while she could almost understand the vocation of a friar or a bishop, she found the decision of her childhood friend to shut herself away from the world quite incomprehensible. Though a priest was already an oddity, she could see the value of a clerical life for a fastidious bachelor like Bertrand's Uncle Charles, or for a young man like Antoine who liked the sound of his own voice. But for a girl of her own age to live behind the high walls of an enclosed convent, to rise at four in the morning, pray for six hours a day, keep almost permanent silence, have no heating, eat no meat and sit only on a stool, seemed to her not just odd but morbidly perverse, a case of the sinister irrationality of religion that her father had always condemned. It seemed impossible to her that the gentle, cheerful companion of her youth should have chosen such self-immolation unless as a result of some mental collapse.

When Madeleine was shown into the visiting room of the convent, with Bertrand behind her, she expected to see a drawn face behind the grille, pale from a life of mortification. Instead, beneath the cowl she saw the rosy cheeks of a larger but otherwise identical Dominique, who giggled as soon as she saw her and said, "My goodness, I wish I could kiss you."

"Dear Dominique," said Madeleine in the tone of a visitor to someone dying of an incurable disease, "I've thought about you so often."

"It was so clever of Bertrand to find you again," said Dominique, "and bring you back into our lives."

"It was luck," said Bertrand.

"Or providence," said Dominique. "God's always up to something."

"Does he arrange marriages in heaven, then?" asked Madeleine.

"Oh I think so, don't you? His first miracle was at a wedding, after all."

"Will you come to ours?" asked Bertrand.

"In spirit."

"You can't leave?" asked Madeleine. "Not even for a day?"

"They don't lock the door," said Dominique, "but I've made a vow and I'd like to keep it."

"It's a pity."

"I'm very happy."

"It's hard to imagine."

"Oh, there are bad moments," said Dominique, "but then there may be in marriage too."

"I find that hard to imagine too," said Madeleine, turning and smiling at Bertrand.

"Papa sends his love," said Bertrand to Dominique.

"Don't say it in such a mournful voice," said Dominique. She leaned forward on her stool toward Madeleine. "Whenever Bertrand and Louis visit me, they try to make me feel guilty for coming here, but I know quite well that Papa's very cheerful."

"How can you know?" asked Bertrand.

"Because I pray for him, and anyway, Maman says he's perfectly all right."

"She doesn't want to upset you."

"Nonsense." She turned again to Madeleine. "Tell me honestly, how did he strike you?"

Remembering the sparkle in the colonel's eye when she first returned to Saint Théodore, Madeleine felt obliged to answer, "Quite cheerful, really."

"There you are," said Dominique to her brother. "And now that he's got a second daughter-in-law as pretty as the first, he must be in heaven."

"In heaven?" asked Bertrand.

Dominique giggled into her sleeve. "Well, his idea of heaven."

"Are you here forever?" asked Madeleine.

"I hope so. I take my final vows next year."

"But how can you know?" asked Madeleine. "You might change."

"You know, don't you, about Bertrand?"

"But that's different. That's love."

"Oh, this is love, too, I promise you. It's really just the same."

As they drove back to Saint Théodore, Madeleine shook her head and said to Bertrand, "I really don't understand it. She seemed so happy, quite as happy as we are, yet the place was like a prison, and she means to live there until she dies."

"Perhaps she's afraid of life," said Bertrand.

"Why should she be?"

He shrugged his shoulders. "She was so happy at Saint Théodore, so protected, that it's possible that she couldn't face the real world and chose the convent as a way of escape."

"But you lived there too."

"I know, but Louis and I were forced out of the cocoon into the army. Besides, the outside world, once you get to know it, isn't such a bad place."

They reached Saint Théodore and drove into the courtyard through the rusty gates.

"You love it here, don't you?" she said.

"Yes."

"Will we live here one day, do you think?"

A slight frown came onto Bertrand's forehead as he stopped the car. "I hope so. It depends."

"On what?"

"Well . . ." He looked down as he removed the keys from the ignition. "I think Louis would like to live here too."

"But you're the elder son."

"I know, but Papa . . ." He stopped, as if he did not want to pursue the thought.

"Do you think he prefers Louis?"

"They're more alike."

She nodded. "Yes."

"Would you like to live here?" he asked.

"Yes," she said, taking his hand and moving closer. "But I don't really mind where I live, as long as it's with you."

That night, before she went to sleep, Madeleine opened the shutters of the spare room where she was sleeping. The cool evening air smelled of rosemary, pine needles and dew. She drew it into her lungs and felt an overwhelming sense of well-being. All the strands of beauty were tied together; the view of the chestnut trees and the vines beyond, lit by the pale white light of the full moon, was enhanced for her by cherished memories of youth. The air, with its delicious and evocative scent, cooled her long body, as if touching her skin under her night-dress.

Her thoughts turned to Bertrand, asleep at the other end of the house, and if she did not long for him to be beside her, it was because she felt him to be already present in the peeling parapet and the tiles on the floor. The touch of the air on her body was the messenger of his gentle hands, which, when the time came, would envelope and caress her in the same way. She awaited that moment with no apprehension, for here at Saint Théodore all conscious thoughts of what love involved were placed in abeyance. Her mind seemed to acknowledge the preeminence of her emotions, and her emotions at that moment were attuned to the pleasant anticipation of her body.

Chapter 3

*T*HERE was a waiter at the Grand Hotel in Deauville who was considered an expert on the intimate experiences of the honeymoon couples at the hotel. It had become a tradition that when breakfast was ordered by a young couple on the first morning, Simon would go up with the tray, or if they came down to have breakfast in the dining room, would serve at their table. Though holding no rank in the hierarchy of the staff, he had worked at the Grand since his demobilization after the Great War, longer than the manager or the headwaiter. Regular visitors to the hotel asked after him by name; his skill of blending familiarity with respect endeared him to the more aristocratic guests, who so often sensed a sneer in those who served them, while the more recently enriched (for no one poor came to the Grand), intimidated by the splendor of the establishment, were reassured by his slight seediness. His white shirt was never quite clean, his black bow tie was frayed at the edges, and there were shiny patches on the elbows of his black jacket.

Old Simon was popular with the staff as well as the guests, not only because he got away with a dirty shirt and scruffy jacket, but because he kept them amused with his comments on the sexual antics of the clientele—especially his judgments on the wedding nights of the newlywed couples, which he delivered as he returned through the flapping doors of the kitchen. "A fiasco!" he might say. "She was almost in tears. Her eyes never left the telephone. She wanted to ring her mother. And the husband was reading the paper!"

Simon had established certain patterns of evidence which told whether things had gone badly or well. A disappointed bridegroom, for example, gave a stingy tip or none at all; and a girl whose eyes avoided his as he came in with the tray in the morning had clearly been pained and humiliated by what she had endured the night before.

The condition of the sheets and blankets was another important clue. If they were still neatly tucked in, it was a sign to Simon that little had happened; if they were disturbed in a certain way, it proved that there had been an unpleasant struggle. It was only if they were still languorously wrapped around the legs of the bride that he would report that things had gone well. "If she shows a little bit of leg," he would say, "you can be sure she's had a good time."

"And did she?"

"Up to the thigh."

"Was it nice?"

"Superb! And the smell! Like a brothel! Oh, they had a good time, all right. They'll keep themselves happy for at least six months."

In October 1931, a young couple came to the hotel straight from their wedding in the south of France. It was late in the season, and because of the economic depression there was little custom anyway. The staff was bored, so no sooner had the husband signed the register than the bellboy scuttled off to the kitchen to announce to old Simon that a honeymoon couple had arrived.

The bride and groom went to their room, but came down at six for a drink in the bar of the hotel. They then went on into the enormous dining room, both apparently unawed by either its emptiness or its grandeur. The husband ordered the food and wine with a certain authority, which made Simon suspect that he had been an officer in the army. Experienced as he was in manipulating those he served, he saw at once that he should not try to fool this particular young gentleman, who, quite exceptionally, was not trying to impress his bride. Nor did the girl look at her husband with the kind of cloying meekness that was common in women at such a moment in their lives; indeed, as he returned with the plates soiled with *pâté de grive,* Simon sent a young waiter to check with reception that the couple on table twenty-three were indeed the promised newlyweds.

Confirmation came, and Simon returned with the next course: sole for the girl, pheasant for her husband. He was followed by the furtive looks of his younger colleagues, whose curiosity was heightened by the beauty of the bride. If this had been high season and the hotel had been full, she might not have dazzled the young waiters in the same way, because her face, with its sallow skin and even features, was somewhat too determined to conform to their vulgar taste in simpering women, and her figure, though upright and elegant, lacked the exaggerated bust and buttocks which provoked their wolf whistles on their days off.

Moreover, the young wife was simply dressed, and her dark hair fell straight to her shoulders, whereas most of the women at the other tables wore long dresses and had their hair arranged in elaborate coiffures. Thus, though prettier and more elegant than the others, she seemed somehow out of place—a student among dowagers—which only accentuated her youth and titillated the waiters' lascivious curiosity.

Her husband wore a dark blue double-breasted suit with a paisley tie, while most of the other men in the hotel dining room had changed into a dinner jacket. He seemed unconcerned at this breach of etiquette; indeed, rather than showing signs of awe at the luxury of his surroundings, he seemed instead somewhat impatient with the slow ceremonial of the dining room. He talked to his wife; she talked back; they smiled at one another across the table, and at one point he leaned forward to take hold of her hand and squeeze it; but he ate his food with methodical dispatch, and once his plate was cleared looked toward Simon to have it taken away.

"Quick, quick," said Simon to a younger waiter. "Clear table twenty-three." Then he went through to the kitchen: "Quick, quick, the sorbets for twenty-three."

"Tell them to take their time," said one of his friends among the chefs.

"They want to get on," said Simon. "There are other appetites, you know."

He winked and returned to the dining room, but he was unconvinced by his own innuendo, for the impatience shown by the man was not that of a husband eager to get his wife to bed, but that of an officer—or, for that matter, a headwaiter—who was habitually efficient and wanted to finish what he had started as quickly as he could. The husband was a type Simon recognized not just from his experiences during the war, but from twelve years of observation at the Grand Hotel. "He's the kind of man," he told the sommelier, as they both stood by the sideboard next to the swinging doors, "who thinks that life's so short that you have to get everything over and done with as quickly as you can so as to pack more in."

"It makes sense," said the sommelier.

"Not on your wedding night."

"Perhaps they've done it already."

"I don't think so."

"She doesn't look nervous."

"Look at the bread crumbled all around the plate. She's still fiddling with it. She's nervous, all right, but she doesn't want him to know."

"Perhaps he's nervous too."

The couple rose from their table. Simon watched them as they left the dining room and crossed the foyer to the entrance of the hotel as if contemplating a walk on the promenade. They seemed to decide against it, turned, and went up to their room.

The next morning a warm wet wind blew in from the west. The honeymoon couple had left no instructions for breakfast, but at a quarter past eight the husband rang the kitchen to ask for it to be brought to their room. He added a request for a morning paper.

As usual, Simon was chosen to take up the tray. When he knocked on the door there was a sharp command to come in. He entered and, while apparently looking for somewhere to place the tray, made a quick, flickering survey of the large bedroom. The wife was still in bed. The husband, wearing a dressing gown, was standing by the window looking out to sea. He turned toward Simon, who, still holding the tray, looked toward the wife as if she might want it beside her. She smiled and pointed to the table and two chairs by the window.

"Put it there, please," she said.

Simon nodded, noticing the swell of her brown-skinned breast through the loose bodice of her white nightdress. She caught his eye but frowned rather than blushed, and instead of covering the bare skin turned to fatten the pillows before pulling herself straight in anticipation of breakfast in bed.

Simon put the tray on the table. The husband came toward him from the window, and Simon, anticipating a tip, turned to meet him. But rather than reaching into the pocket of his dressing gown for a coin, he snatched the newspaper and started to read it as he returned to the window. Simon coughed. The husband turned and seemed to realize from the old man's stance, practiced over so many years, that he should tip him.

"Wait a minute," he said, crossing to the wardrobe to take a coin from his jacket pocket. He gave it to the waiter and then said, "You aren't Simon, are you?"

"Yes, monsieur, yes, indeed."

"My father told me to look out for you."

"Your father?"

"Colonel de Roujay."

For a moment Simon was confused, for Edmond de Roujay, the colonel of his regiment, had been small and stout, with a bluff manner, whereas before him was a tall, wiry man who looked nothing like him at all.

"You are the son of Colonel de Roujay?" he asked.

"Yes. I'm Bertrand de Roujay."

"Well, welcome, sir, welcome to the hotel." He clasped the hands of the younger de Roujay, and tears came into his eyes, because for all the cynicism, the waiter's jacket remained only a dust sheet over the breastplate of the old soldier. The Great War had been for him, as for so many others, the most vivid moment of his life, and his affection for his old commander remained almost the strongest emotion still felt by his dry heart.

"This is my wife," said Bertrand de Roujay.

"Of course, of course." The waiter crossed to the bed and clasped the delicate hand of Bertrand's bride, who smiled weakly and looked impatiently toward the breakfast tray.

"And how is your father?" asked Simon. "And Madame Alice? It's so long since they've been here."

"They say they can't afford it," said Bertrand with a smile, leaning over the breakfast tray and pouring some coffee into a cup. "But it was the only place for our wedding trip." He crossed and gave the cup to his wife. "To tell the truth, we'd thought of going to Italy."

"Naturally . . ."

"But he insisted, and he told us to look out for you." He smiled as he led the old waiter to the door.

"Well," asked the sommelier as Simon returned to the kitchen, "how did it go?"

"Yes," asked his friend among the chefs, surrounded by an inquisitive cluster of scullery boys, "what do you think happened?"

Simon frowned. "He's the son of my colonel," he said. "The son of Colonel de Roujay."

"A flanking action? A frontal assault? Or did he shoot his bolt too soon? How did she look? What about the sheets? And the smell?"

"I don't know, I don't know," said Simon. "Anyway, he's the son of my colonel, Colonel de Roujay, so he's entitled to some privacy, after all. . . ." He shuffled off, scowling, for the first time a little ashamed of the prurient curiosity that heretofore he had always encouraged, and a little afraid at the same time that things had not gone quite as well as he would have hoped for the son of his commanding officer.

However long a couple are engaged, the first days of marriage invariably bring surprises, and in Deauville Bertrand and Madeleine learned things about one another that neither had known before. It surprised Bertrand, for example, that though Madeleine was neat in appearance, she was otherwise untidy, leaving her clothes scattered around the room, the clean muddled with the dirty.

Madeleine, in her turn, had not realized that Bertrand had an addiction—not to alcohol or cocaine but to news. On the first morning she had noticed the alacrity with which he had seized *Le Figaro* from the breakfast tray, and had felt somewhat offended that he read it in silence while he drank his coffee.

After breakfast he had dressed and gone down to the lobby while Madeleine took a bath. She found him later in the reading room of the hotel, half hidden by his *Echo de Paris.* When she suggested a walk on the beach, she saw him hesitate, and then reluctantly lay down the paper. He was attentive and cheerful as they strolled along the front, but when they returned he picked up a copy of *Le Matin* and took it up to their room.

It was warm enough to play tennis in the afternoon, but as soon as they got back to the hotel Bertrand asked impatiently for the evening papers from Paris.

"But you read all the news this morning," said Madeleine.

"So much is going on," said Bertrand, "not just here but in Germany and in England."

"You don't have to know every detail." She spoke with a slight pout.

"It's important for my work to keep up with events."

"But you're on holiday."

"Of course." He laid aside his paper and looked at his bride, who smiled at her small triumph. But it was short-lived, because instead of reading a political commentary, he delivered one, giving Madeleine his views on the League of Nations, the recession, Herriot, Blum, von Papen, Brüning, Chamberlain and Churchill, until she wished he would pick up the paper again but dared not say so.

She could see as their holiday proceeded that her husband was bored, and that he was ashamed to be bored and so tried to conceal it. She suggested that he might like to read one of the novels she had brought with her, and watched him struggle for a while with *The Brothers Karamazov*.

"I used to read fiction," Bertrand said finally, laying it aside. "It's working at the ministry that makes me so impatient with works of imagination."

"Why?"

"Our minds are trained to deal with facts, not fantasies."

"That seems shortsighted."

"Why?"

"I should have thought that politics in particular has as much to do with fantasy as fact."

Both were relieved when they returned to Paris and began a normal life together in Bertrand's apartment on the Rue de Médicis. Bertrand went back to work at the ministry, while Madeleine started a course of graduate studies at the Sorbonne.

In the evenings and on weekends, away from the artificial luxury of the Grand Hotel, they could enjoy the delightful novelty of being lovers quite alone in their own home. Here again there were further surprises. It quickly became apparent, for example, that Madeleine had never in her life had to consider, let alone practice, those domestic arts which at that time were still thought the natural accomplishments of women. The slavish Françoise Bart had not only run the household for husband and daughter, cooking and cleaning, or arranging for others to do so in her place; she had also provided for her daughter an unobtrusive room service quite as all-embracing as that of the Grand Hotel. As she described it to Bertrand, Madeleine had only to step out of her dirty clothes at night, leaving them scattered on the floor, to find them washed, pressed, aired and put away in her chest of drawers on the following evening.

Bertrand had always intended to employ a cook, but it was impossible while they continued to live in his bachelor apartment. The maid who came every weekday was used to caring for a single and fastidious man, and a month after Bertrand's marriage she became so exasperated at finding the apartment always in a mess that she gave notice. Bertrand thought it Madeleine's responsibility to find another maid, while Madeleine—since it was his apartment—thought it was up to him. It led to their first quarrel.

"You think, don't you," she said, "that your work is more important than my studies."

"It feeds us."

" 'Man does not live by bread alone,' " she mocked.

"It was your fault that Lise left," he said, "so you should find someone else."

"It was your fault that you hired such an idle girl in the first place."

"She did me fine for five years."

"Because she had nothing to do."

"Just because I didn't leave my clothes scattered all over the bedroom—"

"So I'm meant to tidy up for the maid, am I? That's why you married me, perhaps? To save on a housekeeper!"

Bertrand had not realized that Madeleine had such a quick temper —quick, that is, to come, but not so quick to go. In this instance she was not mollified until a new maid had been found who at double the wage picked up Madeleine's dirty clothes and laundered them in her own home.

Such quarrels were rare. There were many more occasions when the newly married couple were happy in one another's company, either alone in the evening or out with friends. Bertrand was inordinately proud of Madeleine, because she was younger, prettier and above all more intelligent than most of the other wives. More exceptional still, she was not afraid to join in every kind of conversation, while the other women, often as intelligent as their husbands, left arguments about history and politics to the men.

Certainly there was some reshuffling of Bertrand's circle now that he was married. With an unerring instinct, Madeleine took against the bohemian ladies with whom Bertrand had had brief affairs. At the other extreme, she found many of his army friends intolerably dull.

She liked best of all the sharp minds of his fellow civil servants—partly, no doubt, because they respected her not just as Bertrand's wife but as Professor Bonnet's daughter.

She was also appreciated as such at the Sorbonne, and was sufficiently encouraged by the esteem of her teachers to see in her studies more than a pastime while Bertrand was at the ministry; yet it was only after two months of marriage that she realized how difficult it would be to pursue them if she was to find that she was pregnant.

From a mixture of innocence and embarrassment, neither Bertrand nor Madeleine had raised the question of a child. Madeleine, who had learned so late in life how babies were conceived, had only the most imprecise notions of how conception could be impeded. From reading the Pope's encyclical on marriage, she knew that to Catholics contraception was a sin, but since she did not know exactly what was involved, she had no view on its morality herself.

"And if you don't want to have a child," she had asked Antoine, "what can you do that isn't a sin?"

The friar had blushed. "Well, the Pope would say that you should abstain."

Here again, at the time the word "abstain" meant little. Now she understood what it involved, and it was a comment on this aspect of her married life that she did not find the Pope's suggestion absurd. She loved Bertrand—she had no doubt about that—but her attitude toward his body was less straightforward. She was drawn to it more by fascination than by desire. She thought his muscular torso, with the black hair growing between his flat breasts, rather bizarre. When she saw him naked, she looked with a kind of mesmerized horror at his lean buttocks and legs, and when he approached her to make love she looked upon his phallus as an angry worm that had to be placated by her ministrations.

She could not quite make out what Bertrand experienced as he lay over her. It often seemed as if he too saw his penis as a creature apart, with its own demands that periodically had to be appeased. Although he embraced her with murmurs about beauty and love, he seemed to perform the act in much the same way as he did his exercises in the morning, and afterward looked breathless and glum.

"You don't seem very happy," she said to him one night after they had made love.

"Coitus induces melancholy," he said with a smile.

"Then why do people do it?"

"They like it." He leaned over and kissed her.

"Tell me," she said, leaning on her elbow, her brown breasts bare above the white sheet, "have you thought about when we should have a child?"

He looked at her and smiled. "When the good God sends us one, I suppose."

"I was thinking," said Madeleine, "that it would be much more sensible if the good God sent us one a little later on."

"Why?"

"Well, for one thing, there's this apartment."

"I'm looking for a larger one."

"There's also my thesis."

"Of course." He spoke with a touch of irony, as if he did not take it seriously.

She frowned. "I can hardly go to the Sorbonne with a baby at the breast."

"It could drink in wisdom with its mother's milk."

She did not smile. "Do you want a child?"

He shrugged his shoulders. "Of course. If it comes."

"And if it doesn't?"

"I'm in no hurry."

"Then can we postpone it?"

"How?"

"There are ways."

He frowned. "They are immoral."

"Only for a Catholic."

"I am a Catholic."

"There are ways even for a Catholic."

"What ways?"

"There are certain moments when it is less likely . . ."

"Yes."

"And to be sure . . ."

"What?"

"There's abstinence."

He laughed. "Oh yes, abstinence."

"It's approved by the Pope."

He laughed again. "Who told you that?"

"Antoine Dubec."

"It's all very well for a celibate priest to talk about abstinence," he said, "but how am I to keep my hands off you—" he caressed her shoulders and breasts—"always there, in front of my eyes."

"But men aren't animals."

"Oh, yes, they are."

"I could sleep on the sofa," Madeleine said.

"Are you serious?"

"I don't want a child," she said firmly. "Not yet."

Bertrand pulled himself up, leaned against the headboard and sighed. "I don't understand," he said.

"I married to be with you."

"But . . ." He sighed again. "Don't you ever want children?"

"Of course. When I've written my thesis."

"You'd rather write a thesis than have a child?"

"No," she said. "I want both. First the thesis, then the child."

Bertrand shook his head. "Life can't be planned like that."

"Why not?"

"Some things must be left to providence."

"That's a word with no meaning."

For a while Bertrand was silent. It was past the time when they usually switched off the light and went to sleep. "Why," he asked eventually, "is this thesis so important to you?"

"It interests me."

"Of course. But one thesis more or less."

"I want to be more than a brood mare."

"You would never be that."

"I want to be someone myself before I give life to another."

"But you are someone. You're my wife."

"And you're my husband, but you're also a civil servant."

"That's different."

"Because you're a man?"

"Yes."

"I don't agree."

Bertrand had turned a little pale; the bones wobbled under the skin of his cheeks. "I'm sorry," he said quietly, though what he was sorry about was not clear; nor did Madeleine bother to find out, because suddenly she felt she had argued enough, so she pulled the sheets and blankets up to her chin, turned away from her husband and closed her eyes.

Bertrand sat for a while staring straight ahead at his half-raised knee under the bedclothes. Then he got out of bed to put on his pajamas, because he could never sleep naked, opened the window, switched off the light and returned to sleep by the side of his wife.

The next morning Bertrand left for his office with a perplexed expression on his face, but after talking to a Jesuit during his lunch hour, he returned home that evening in a more conciliatory frame of mind.

"If you don't want a baby just yet," he said to Madeleine as he mixed her a cocktail, "don't have one. There are ways and means of putting it off, some of which are allowed to Catholics and some of which are not. But since you aren't a Catholic, there's no real reason why you should be bound by our rules."

She came toward him, took her drink and smiled. "Quite soon," she said, "when I've finished my thesis, I'll have a child, I promise." She kissed him sweetly. "What would you like? A boy or a girl?"

"A boy."

"Egoist!"

"A son first, don't you think?" He sipped his drink.

"That we have to leave to providence."

Later that week Madeleine went to a doctor to ask for advice about how to avoid conception. She mentioned in passing that she had been feeling sick for some days. Alerted, the doctor took a sample of her urine before giving her a diaphragm.

Four days later he called her back to his office and told her that it was too late. "You are already expecting a baby, Madame de Roujay," he said. "The appliance I gave you can go into a drawer until next time around."

Madeleine returned home dejected. The trap which she had seen in front of her, and which she had tried at the last moment to avoid, had already closed on her. The freedom which she had envisaged in marrying Bertrand was to be replaced by the constrictions of motherhood. Certainly, once the child was born, she could hire a nanny to look after it, a cook to feed it and a maid to keep their home clean, but the thought of these servants did not make her feel free. She felt too young to play the role of the mistress of a bourgeois establishment. She even disliked being called "madame."

She stood in the hallway looking at herself in the ornate mirror on the wall. Though early in the afternoon, it was dark because there was no window to the outside but there was light enough for her to see her figure reflected in the glass. She turned; there was no sign of a swelling stomach. Only the slight sickness and a prickly feeling in her nipples suggested that there was another life in her body.

The doctor had told her to rest. She went to the bedroom and lay down. The apartment was silent; there was only the muffled sound of traffic from the street below. She looked with a mental disgust, which matched the nausea she felt in her belly, at the alien furniture, covers and hangings of Bertrand's bedroom. The little pagoda of liberty had turned into a place of house arrest.

Why had she not been to the doctor before? She thought with enmity first of her mother, whose weakness and timidity had left her in such ignorance of the elementary facts about her own body, then with equal resentment of her husband, who was so much older and so much more methodical, yet who had used her body for his own purposes without first considering the consequences to her life. But then was he not himself a victim of the crude custom of families like the de Roujays to whom marriage was not the love of two autonomous individuals but a contrivance to continue the line? How could he be held responsible for adopting such an attitude when his church, too, for all its talk of the spirit, imposed on marriage a biological justification?

She fell asleep and was only waked by the sound of a key in the door. She jumped off the bed, ashamed of being caught lazing during the day. Then she remembered why she had been resting, and with a flushed face went to greet Bertrand in the hall.

"What is it?" he asked, seeing her sleepy eyes and blotched red cheeks.

She went over to kiss him, but instead of putting her lips to his mouth, hid her face in his breast and cried.

"What is it?" he asked again in a gentle, solicitous voice.

"I'm going to have a baby," she said, her cheek half on the smooth cotton of his shirt, half on the scratchy cloth of his lapel.

"A baby?" he said. "Well, that's wonderful, my darling. I'm delighted."

She sobbed again, and Bertrand hugged her, taking her tears to be tears of joy.

In the third month the nausea ceased, but the bulge became pronounced in Madeleine's belly. By then they had moved from the Rue de Médicis to a larger apartment near the Champs Elysées on the Rue Marbeuf. It had none of the charm of their first home, but there were separate quarters for a cook, a maid and—when the time came—a nanny, as well as a second bathroom and two extra bedrooms in the main area of the apartment itself.

It was more expensive to rent, and for the first time in their married life Bertrand betrayed some unease about the cost of what they had undertaken. "Our running expenses now take most of my salary," he said.

"But you have other money, don't you?"

"Yes, but everything has been hit by the recession. The vines make a loss, and my shares in my uncles' company pay a very low dividend."

"Could you sell them?"

He frowned. "It would be disloyal, and they wouldn't fetch much."

"You could reinvest the money in something like the Bayonne bonds."

"They'd be a very dubious investment," said Bertrand. "And anyway, I don't like to profit from speculation."

"Why not?"

"So many people have no money and no work."

Madeleine sniffed. To her the source of money was as remote and uninteresting as the source of food that the cook brought from the kitchen, but she suspected Bertrand of a puritan outlook which had nothing to do with sound economics. However, his reference to the unemployed silenced her for a time, because it enlisted in his defense her own sympathies with the political left.

By instinct a Radical like her father, Madeleine had befriended a Socialist group at the Sorbonne and had come to share their point of view. Bertrand, who was by nature an uncommitted conservative, had always realized that Madeleine's opinions were not the same as his own, but felt an involuntary annoyance that instead of drawing closer to his outlook, his wife was moving further away. Politics was not just Bertrand's profession, it was also his passion, and it seemed implicitly insulting that she should not acknowledge his greater knowledge and experience by sharing his views.

His irritation at the influence of her left-wing friends went with his resentment of her life as a student, for though she was invariably at home when he returned from the ministry, and though she accompanied him dutifully to official dinners or parties given by his friends, she did so with an air of obligation, as if wearing a dress that she had not chosen but that he expected her to wear.

On weekends, too, when he was free to spend his time with her, Madeleine would turn down a shopping expedition or a walk in the Bois de Boulogne, saying that she had to work on her thesis, leaving him with the choice of setting off alone, or joining up with friends who would think it odd that she did not accompany him.

Their differences came to a head over the elections of May 1932. Having flirted for a time with the idea of voting for a Left Republican like Tardieu or Flandin, Bertrand in the end chose the Popular Democrats. Madeleine, who as a woman had no vote, announced one Saturday morning at breakfast that she was going to work for a Socialist candidate whom she had met at dinner with her old friends from Montpellier, Michel and Nellie le Fresne.

Bertrand frowned. "I'd rather you didn't," he said.

"Why not?"

"It might compromise me at the ministry."

"Nonsense. I'm sure half of them are Socialist."

"Not at my level."

"What you really mean is that you feel embarrassed that I don't share your political opinions."

"No."

"You should be proud to have a wife who has opinions of her own. You're the only one among your friends who does."

"I am, I am, but I don't see why you should actually campaign—"

"I think it's important."

"I thought you were busy with your studies."

"There are moments to stop studying history and make it instead."

"Handing out pamphlets isn't making history."

"On the contrary, that is just how history is made—ordinary people taking the trouble to promote their views."

"Has it ever occurred to you that the Socialists are wrong?"

"Has it ever occurred to you that they might be right?"

"No. Their schemes are pie-in-the-sky. How can we nationalize the oil companies, the insurance companies, the armaments manufacturers, when there is no money in the Treasury?"

"Raise taxes."

"But the economy is already shrinking. If you cut demand by raising taxes, it will shrink still further, and drive more people out of work. No, what we have to do now is cut government expenditure, not squander people's hard-earned money on ideological extravagance."

He turned to Madeleine. She had stopped listening; indeed, at the very moment he glanced at her, she yawned.

They were a popular young couple: intelligent, amusing, good-looking, well dressed. They rarely spent an evening alone together, for when they were not dining out or entertaining others, they would go to the theater or the cinema with their friends. They never quarreled in public, and in private no more than most other couples, but their differences were well known, and it amused their circle to have Bertrand and Madeleine take different sides in an argument.

Madeleine usually had the best of these dinner-party disputes, not because the other guests were Socialists themselves, but because the husbands thought it chivalrous to come to the support of Bertrand's young wife while their wives invariably kept quiet. Pierre Moreau, for example, who came to stay from time to time, would argue in favor of disarmament when Bertrand knew that he had misgivings. Even Louis de Roujay, who when passing through also took advantage of the spare room of the flat on the Rue Marbeuf, would abandon his own reactionary opinions and argue against his brother like a knight errant defending an innocent girl from the intellectual bullying of her brutal husband.

It was Bertrand's misfortune that his maturity and seriousness, together with his concise, sometimes impatient manner of speech, gave him an air of invulnerability which almost obliged anyone else to weigh in against him on Madeleine's side. Moreover, since he liked to analyze through argument, and could hardly fence with those who always agreed, Bertrand was happy to be contradicted by his male friends. If he was less happy when Madeleine disagreed with him, it was because she seemed to invest her conflicting opinions with an emotional defiance; and when she recruited his friends to support her, it was as if she had in some sense turned them against him. He was more vulnerable than he seemed, and his sense of isolation was exacerbated by the victory of the Radicals and Socialists in the May elections. It seemed that most of France agreed with Madeleine.

The baby grew in her womb, and changes came over Madeleine's body which she detested. Her delicate breasts grew into huge blue-veined gourds. The tiny pink nipples became big and brown. The expanding sack of fluid pushed down on her bowels and bladder and stretched the skin of her stomach.

May turned into June, and June into July. It became hot. She could not leave Paris because of the baby. With a tacit understanding that was never put into words, Bertrand and Madeleine no longer made love, as if nature, having achieved her purpose, had withdrawn the instinct to do so. She waited—puffing, sweating, cross. Her mother came from Montpellier and irritated everyone. She hovered around Madeleine, never leaving her alone, plying her with plaintive requests to eat, rest or drink more milk. When she was not attending to Madeleine, she would go into the kitchen and exasperate Hortense, the cook, by offering to help in a manner which implicitly criticized the way things were done.

Bertrand was as irritated as Madeleine and Hortense by Françoise Bonnet's presence in the apartment, but he appreciated her good intentions and was appalled by the contemptuous tone in which Madeleine spoke to her. He had to beg her to be more polite to her mother. "You treat her worse than you treat the servants," he said, to which Madeleine replied that he should mind his own business before bursting into tears and sobbing into her pillow, "Oh, why can't you leave me alone."

It was a relief to everyone when the moment came for Madeleine to go to the hospital. Bertrand, who had only an imprecise understanding of how it was known that the time had come, was given the news at his office, and on his way home went to the hospital, where he was told that his wife was in labor and that there was nothing he could do.

He returned home, dined with his mother-in-law, and then telephoned the hospital for news. Madeleine was still in labor. He smoked
a cigarette, played a Brahms quintet on the gramophone, then telephoned again. The doctor spoke to him. "I would go to bed, Monsieur
de Roujay. It looks as if it won't be delivered today."

The child was born at seven the next morning after twenty-two hours
of labor. Bertrand looked in at nine carrying a bunch of flowers and
was shocked by Madeleine's appearance. Her face was pale and drawn,
her eyes red and dazed.

"My poor darling," he said.

She forced herself to smile. "Have you seen it?" she asked.

"What?"

"The baby."

"No."

"It's a girl."

"I'm delighted."

"You wanted a boy."

"It doesn't matter."

"It's a pity all the same."

"Next time . . ."

She looked away and lay back on her pillows. A nurse entered the
room carrying a bundle. When Bertrand stood and peered at the little
old face of his sleeping daughter, his heart sank because she looked so
ugly.

They called their daughter Albertine, which, when she could talk, she
pronounced "Titine," and Titine became the nickname used by all. As
soon as Madeleine felt well enough to travel, she was taken south to
Saint Théodore. There she fed her baby at the breast, but when they
returned to Paris at the end of the summer, she was shifted to a bottle
so that the English nanny, Miss Spinks, could feed her while Madeleine
was at the Sorbonne.

Life returned to normal. The only changes were those effected by
the needs of the child. The nanny, cook and housemaid bustled around
the flat, a hundred times more obedient to its wails and burps than they
were to the instructions of their employers. The three women bickered
among themselves about which of them was principally in charge, but

they were canny enough never to make trouble for Bertrand or Madeleine, who otherwise were happy to leave them alone.

It was apparent to these women—in particular to Hortense, the cook—that Madeleine was not, as she put it, "one of nature's mothers." When, on weekends, the nanny had a day off, Madeleine would call on Hortense or the maid, Maude, to change the baby's nappies or burp it, and she was quick to accept Hortense's offer to have Titine to sleep in her room.

If anything, the servants remarked, the father seemed more drawn to the child than the mother. "Of course, he's older," they said, as if that explained it. Every evening, when he returned from the ministry, Bertrand would go straight to the baby's room, where Titine, who had been put to bed, would be waiting for his good-night kiss, gripping the bars of her cot.

For the first few months of her life, Bertrand had felt afraid to touch the mysterious newborn creature, but eventually he had felt sure enough to pick her up, hold her, then hug her, and finally throw her up and down in the air until her gurgling giggles brought Hortense, alarmed, to see what was happening to her Titine.

Madeleine was happy to see this bond formed between her husband and her child, for it alleviated the small spasm of bad conscience at her own distraction from her baby's well-being. It was not that she felt ashamed at the feebleness of her own maternal instinct, for maternal instinct, like instinct of any kind, was something she thought appropriate to the less evolved of the species, like Hortense, the cook, or Maude, the maid, but she noticed that Bertrand was confused because she did not behave with the baby in the way he had expected. He was proud that she had given birth to the child, and felt all the conventional affection of a husband for a young mother, but he could not quite comprehend why she left so readily each morning, and seemed in no hurry to return at night.

However, now that she had shed her burden, Madeleine's body returned to its slender shape and they made love again. They were married, after all. And Madeleine, with the doctor's appliance firmly in place, sometimes seemed to enjoy it.

2

The personal contentment of the de Roujays which followed the birth of their daughter was marred only by a growing public anxiety about the world into which she had been born. Both her parents were obsessively preoccupied by political events, which seemed to be leading toward chaos. The great victory of the Radicals and Socialists in May of 1932, and the coalition they then formed to rule the country, should have led to a period of stable government, but the worldwide recession which now affected France and the obstinate demands of Germany for parity with the other European nations made it difficult for any government to succeed.

It was a time when many saw politics in moral terms and easily became indignant toward those with different opinions. Bertrand may have dithered between the center and the right, but he was convinced that France must stand up against Germany, and must buttress her stance with effective armaments. He was not an obdurate nationalist who sought revenge for what France had suffered in the war, but he feared that any concession to Germany over the terms of the Treaty of Versailles would only encourage those nationalistic Germans who asked for them. He therefore resented the pressure put on the French government by the British and Americans to meet the German demands, and he was thrown into moods of irritable despair when Madeleine put forward the views of the Socialist leader, Léon Blum, that France should disarm whether or not the Germans agreed to do the same.

There were many nuances to the attitudes taken by the de Roujays and their friends following the elections in May. Pierre Moreau, for example, who mistrusted the Germans as much as Bertrand, thought that a deal should be made with the Junker government of von Papen in Berlin to check the growing popularity of the Nazis. Michel le Fresne, on the other hand, despite his Socialist stance, appeared at times to prefer Hitler to von Papen, because "at least he represents a body of popular opinion, whereas von Papen represents nothing at all."

Louis de Roujay thought Hitler a joke. "He's completely gaga," he said. "He foams at the mouth. If only they would make him Chancellor of Germany! He'd ruin the country in a week."

"Even a fool can drive a tank," said Bertrand.

"He couldn't even make the trains run on time. Mussolini at least does that, and saves on the national laundry bill by dressing everyone in black shirts."

"I think you underestimate the danger," said Bertrand.

"We're ready for them, my dear fellow. I've seen the Maginot Line. It's impregnable. All we'll have to do, if there's a war, is sit in a deck chair and pull the trigger with our toes."

In January 1933, Hitler took office as Chancellor of Germany. The reaction in France was calm. Two days after the inauguration, Bertrand and Madeleine went to the cinema, where the goose-stepping storm troopers on the newsreels provoked no boos or catcalls from the audience, and only one or two giggles and guffaws. No one seemed afraid, because Hitler bore no resemblance to the Prussian Junkers who had threatened France during the last war. It seemed astonishing, not frightening, that the Germans could be ruled by such a clown.

Moreover, Hitler's advent put France in a good light. The new prime minister, Daladier, seemed so reasonable in comparison that no one could doubt that his policies would prevail. Even Bertrand respected Daladier, who was a Provençal like himself. The only misfortune was that Daladier's majority in the National Assembly was not as secure as it seemed. Bertrand had grave misgivings about the loyalty to the government of Madeleine's friends, the Socialists, for before the election they had drawn up a "minimum program" which included the nationalization of major industries and the introduction of a forty-hour work week—policies which the Radicals, like Daladier, had declared quite impractical in the present state of economic recession.

Until midway through 1933 the coalition held together. In July, however, the Socialists denounced the government at their annual congress and as a result split in two. The right-wing minority condemned the pacifist and internationalist approach of the majority as inimical to the interests of France, and formed a neo-Socialist party of their own. One of these rebels, Adrien Marquet, was reported to have said that Léon Blum, with his oriental mind, could not appreciate the French point of view.

"But this is appalling," said Madeleine, reading the report over breakfast in Le Petit Parisien. "He's as anti-Semitic as Hitler."

"Is it anti-Semitic," asked Bertrand, "to suggest that a Jew like Blum might have a different outlook than a native Frenchman?"

"Aren't Jews native Frenchmen?"

"They're Frenchmen, of course, but they're hardly indigenous Frenchmen."

"I don't see how Pierre is any less French than you are."

"It's not a question of being *less* French," said Bertrand irritably. "It's a question of what you think it means to be French."

"What does that mean?"

"Well, clearly to a peasant from the Auvergne—"

"Like Laval?"

"To a peasant from Burgundy, then, whose family has farmed the land for hundreds of years, it means something different than it does to the Jew whose family immigrated one or two generations ago."

Madeleine had grown pink in the face, but attempted to control her anger. "Even the Franks were immigrants at one time," she said.

"You know quite well what I mean," said Bertrand.

"I don't think I do," she said coldly.

"All I'm suggesting is that a man—an ordinary Frenchman—who has lived in one tribe, speaking one language, on one piece of land for a thousand years will have a different attitude toward that tribe, and that piece of land, than another Frenchman whose tribe, if you like, has wandered all over the world and has found itself fragmented in several different nations. Of course a Jew can be a Frenchman, just as a Jew can be a German, a Pole or a Russian. But he is likely to be a different kind of Frenchman to the Frenchman who is *just* a French-man, because the Jewish Frenchman is also a Jew, and as such he will have something in common with his fellow Jew in another country. It is therefore only to be expected that men like Marx, Trotsky or Léon Blum will have a different attitude toward international affairs than men like Marquet, Déat or, if you like, Laval."

Madeleine listened in silence to this little speech, delivered by Bertrand in the tone of a teacher with an obtuse pupil. When he had finished, however, she looked at him with a severe look—the same look she had given him at Saint Théodore as a child—and said, "I knew that your family was anti-Semitic, but I always assumed that you were different."

"I am not anti-Semitic," said Bertrand quietly.

"You may not know it, but you are."

"If I were anti-Semitic—" Bertrand began.

"You wouldn't have a Jewish friend like Pierre?" She gave him a mocking smile. "Dear Pierre. How useful he is. He not only finds you a wife, he provides you with an alibi as well."

Throughout that summer, some of which was spent at Saint Théodore, there was an undertow of enmity between Bertrand and Madeleine whenever political questions arose. Louis and his family joined them during the second half of August, and in the easygoing atmosphere of his own home Louis forgot his chivalrous support of Madeleine's views and instead voiced his own. Since these came straight from the polemical royalist paper *L'Action Française*—he quoted Léon Daudet with delight when he referred to Blum as "a circumcised hermaphrodite" —they could only antagonize his sister-in-law. But rather than argue with Louis, she listened quietly to his extreme opinions and then darted quick looks of triumph at Bertrand across the table.

In September they returned to Paris and resumed their metropolitan life. In the middle of October the Germans left the League of Nations and withdrew from the Disarmament Conference in Geneva. The government's attempts to placate the Germans had failed. There seemed nothing now to keep them from arming themselves to the teeth. Ignored by the Americans, abandoned by the English, rebuffed by the Italians, dismissed by the Poles, France now seemed vulnerable and isolated.

Exasperated by this turn of events abroad, Bertrand could not help venting his frustration upon Madeleine, whose Socialist friends, in his opinion, had brought things to this state of affairs. Then, ten days after the debacle in Geneva, the Socialists withdrew their support from Daladier's government, which consequently fell. This threw Bertrand into yet deeper gloom. The chaos abroad had come home. Here again he blamed the Socialists, and by extension Madeleine, and there were nasty arguments between them—not shouting arguments but clipped, hissing exchanges about whether or not it was reasonable to expect a six percent cut in the salaries of civil servants, the issue upon which the government had been defeated.

"I'm prepared to take the cut," said Bertrand.

"Of course, because your stocks and shares would bounce up on the Bourse by far more than you'd lose on your salary."

"That's not the point."

"It *is* the point to the wretched little clerks and postmen who have to feed their families on what they earn."

"Daladier was our last chance of stable government."

"Then he should have come up with a sensible budget."

After Daladier, another Radical, Sarraut, formed a government which Bertrand predicted would last only a month. It fell after three weeks. In November a third Radical, Chautemps, met with more success. He put forward a budget similar to that which had brought down Daladier and Sarraut, but by now Blum's Socialists were alarmed at the precarious state of the French economy, so when the time came to take a vote they walked out of the Chamber of Deputies and left Chautemps's coalition intact.

When Bertrand and his colleagues at the Ministry of the Interior dispersed for Christmas they were agreed that France had overcome the immediate political crisis and could look forward to a period of stable government. It was not until they returned after the New Year that the name Stavisky first appeared in the newspaper headlines.

Like Dreyfus, whose case had divided their parents' generation, Stavisky was a man of no inherent interest or distinction. The son of a Jewish dentist from Kiev, he had emerged from a world of gigolos, drug dealers, hoodlums and petty crooks as a police informer and self-styled financier. In 1930 he gained control of the municipal pawnshop in Bayonne, and proceeded to issue unsecured bonds in its name —backed by two letters of recommendation from a Radical minister, Albert Dalimier. The fraud came to light in November 1933, but it was not until the end of December that a warrant was issued for Stavisky's arrest. The police went to collect him at Claridge's on Christmas Day, but Stavisky had been tipped off and was gone.

It was now that the "Stavisky affair" was picked up by Charles Maurras and Léon Daudet, the right-wing polemicists on *L' Action Française*. Both were the sworn enemies of republican democracy and advocates of the restoration of a king. Few of their readers—Louis de Roujay was one of them—took their royalism seriously, but many, like Bertrand, were delighted by their denunciations of corruption and fraud. He therefore read them whenever he could, though because of Madeleine, never when at home.

In the first weeks of January, however, even those like Madeleine who loathed what she called "a reactionary rag" were obliged to read it, because *L' Action Française* seemed to have uncovered evidence of graft in the Council of Ministers itself. On January 3 it published the two letters from Dalimier vouching for the Bayonne bonds—and suggested, in its commentary, that the letters had been written in return for large contributions to Radical Party funds.

With the apparently incontrovertible evidence of Dalimier's letters, the rest of the press took up the hue and cry, but *L' Action Française* was always a stage ahead. "Down with the thieves!" said its headline on January 7. "Dalimier is not alone. We can see behind him a crowd of other ministers and influential members of Parliament, all of whom have in one way or another favored the adventurer's racket, especially instructing the police to leave him alone. . . . There is no law and no justice in a country where the magistrates and the police are the accomplices of criminals. The honest people of France . . . are forced to take the law into their own hands!"

On January 8 it was announced that the police had found Stavisky in a chalet near Chamonix, but that before they could arrest him he had shot himself in the head. The news redoubled the public outrage, for no one believed in the suicide. Rather, it was assumed that the Sûreté Générale, as the tool of the corrupt politicians—the "marching wing of the Masonic lodges," as *L' Action Française* put it—had no sooner found Stavisky than it had murdered him to prevent any compromising revelations.

The opposition demanded a parliamentary inquiry. The prime minister, Chautemps, refused. He thought the Stavisky affair was a minor scandal which would soon be forgotten, but his own furtive manner, as well as the established links between some of his ministers and Stavisky, led to a relentless campaign against his government. Not just the right-wing newspapers but those on the left became convinced that the Sûreté had either murdered Stavisky or persuaded him to kill himself.

As the month proceeded it became clear that whether innocent or guilty of complicity in his frauds, Chautemps and his cabinet would never brush off the mud of Stavisky. The scandal now blocked the government's more serious measures, and Chautemps thought it better to resign.

The president, Lebrun, recalled Daladier, the honest man from the Midi of whom Bertrand approved. But Daladier appointed old and

ineffective politicians to serve under him, and the only official to be
purged as a result of his taking office was the prefect of the Paris police,
Chiappe.

Chiappe's dismissal was the last straw for the right wing, because
he alone was thought sympathetic to their point of view—at least his
police were always easier on right-wing demonstrators than they were
on those who agitated for the left. His dismissal therefore seemed like
a preliminary measure for a dictatorial suppression of all right-wing
dissent. The various organizations that felt themselves threatened—the
royalist Camelots du Roi, the Croix de Feu, the ex-servicemen's
associations, as well as small groups like the Jeunesses Patriotes and the
Solidarité Française—all called for a demonstration in front of the
National Assembly in Paris on the evening of February 6, 1934, to
coincide with a vote of confidence in the Chamber of Deputies.

At four that afternoon, Madeleine telephoned Bertrand at the ministry to say that Louis had turned up at their apartment with a young
cousin of the de Roujays, asking if they could stay the night.

"Which cousin?" asked Bertrand.

"Raymond something or other. A long name."

"Blaise de la Vallée?"

"Yes."

"What on earth is he doing in Paris?"

"He's come with Louis."

"Are they on leave?"

"Apparently."

"It's a funny day to come to Paris."

"Not for them."

"Is that why they're here?"

"I imagine so."

Bertrand sighed. "We can't turn them out."

Madeleine said nothing.

"You'd better move Titine in with Hortense and let Raymond sleep
in her room."

"All right." She sounded clipped and cross. "He seems slightly
mad," she said.

"He is."

Bertrand put down the receiver. He sat for a moment biting the nail
of his thumb and staring out the window. He wondered whether it

could be coincidence that Louis and Raymond had come to Paris on the day of the demonstration; then, realizing that this was impossible and that they had come expressly to join in the riot, he suddenly felt angry that they meant to use his home as a base, because Louis knew quite well that Madeleine was behind the government, while he was its paid servant.

Certainly the new minister of the interior, Eugène Frot, was playing some sort of double game; only the evening before Bertrand had heard him speak scornfully of Daladier and suggest to the Nationalist Kerillis that the time had come for men like them to "take the situation in hand." But even if his minister hoped to make political gains from the day's disorder, it did not excuse one of his officials from aiding and abetting those helping to create it. If it were to become known, it would irreparably harm Bertrand's reputation among his colleagues for sound judgment and impartiality.

He was also incensed that Louis had brought their cousin, because of all the Blaise de la Vallées, Raymond was the most ridiculous. They were the children of his father's sister, whose husband, a Breton land-owner, had so mismanaged his estates that they had to retreat into their only surviving property, a tumbledown farmhouse, and live off the mother's pin money. Their family went back to the time of Charle-magne, which made the de Roujays seem parvenus beside them, but their political opinions had scarcely evolved with the centuries, and they now all adhered to a quixotic royalism which enabled them to blame their penury on the corruption of republican politicians, and dream, at the same time, of a new restoration, not just of a king, but of their fortunes.

Bertrand left his office at six. A line of police stood in front of the ministry. "I don't advise you to walk, monsieur," the inspector said. "They're already pulling up the paving stones."

"They're after the deputies," said Bertrand, "not the civil servants."

"Perhaps so," said the inspector, "but how are they to know which is which?"

Bertrand passed through the cordon. In any case, there was no question of finding a taxi. He either had to retreat into the ministry and remain there for the night, or walk home across the Champs Elysées. He decided to walk, but to do so he had to change his usual route, because the police had cordoned off the Avenue de Marigny to block off the approaches to the Elysée Palace. Bertrand was therefore obliged to take the narrower Rue de Cirque and follow the Avenue Matignon to the Rond Point des Champs Elysées, which was already thick with people walking toward the rallying point at the statue of Clemenceau. For the most part the demonstrators seemed to be sober, serious ex-servicemen, though every now and then he recognized the crazed look of a royalist fanatic like his cousin.

When Bertrand entered the apartment on the Rue Marbeuf he found Madeleine sitting in the drawing room with Louis and Raymond Blaise de la Vallée. Both officers were wearing civilian clothes. He glanced first at Madeleine, who scowled and pursed her lips, then at Louis, who rose to greet him.

"I say, Bertrand, old boy," he said, "I hope this isn't a most terrible imposition."

"Of course not," said Bertrand, who was too fond of his brother to show his irritation.

"We should have telephoned," said Louis, "but the fact is that we only decided to come at the last minute, and it is, as it were, a rather unofficial visit."

"Aren't you on leave?"

"Not exactly."

"Won't you be missed?"

"Luckily the colonel's a good sort. He's looking the other way. But there'll be hell to pay if it ever gets out that we came up to Paris to join in a riot."

"Will there be a riot?" asked Bertrand.

"A revolution!" said Raymond, stepping forward to shake hands with his older cousin. "We'll drive this rabble from power and bring in a government of honest men."

He had the soft, pink complexion of a girl. His cheeks wobbled as he spoke.

"You had better take care," said Bertrand.

"We're not afraid," said Raymond.

"They have set up machine guns on the steps of the Assembly."

"How typical," said Louis. "That's their idea of democracy. To shoot the voters."

"We're not afraid of machine guns," said Raymond. "We've faced them before."

"At Verdun?" asked Bertrand sarcastically. "Or were you at the Marne?"

The young man blushed. "I didn't mean me personally."

"The ex-servicemen," said Louis.

"I daresay," said Bertrand. "But not machine guns fired by their fellow countrymen."

"A bullet is a bullet," said Raymond.

Bertrand sat down. "And what is this riot meant to achieve?"

"A change of government," said Louis.

"A change to what? There is always the same majority."

"There won't be when we've thrown the gangsters in the Seine," said Raymond, his fierce threats coming from plump, angelic lips.

"And then?" asked Bertrand.

"A king!"

Bertrand looked at his brother; Louis avoided his eyes.

"If you'll excuse me," said Madeleine, her face pale, her voice breathless, "I must go and see to Titine." She stood and left the room.

"What are we meant to do?" Louis asked Bertrand. "Sit back and let the gangsters get away with it?"

"With what?"

"Their corruption, their evasion, their lies."

"It should be possible," said Bertrand, "to pick out the weeds without burning the whole crop."

"It's a crop of weeds," said Louis.

"And if you throw all the deputies in the Seine?" asked Bertrand. "What then?"

Louis shrugged his shoulders. "A directorate of some kind."

"And what about the rest of France? The southwest, for example? Would they accept your coup d'état in Toulouse?"

"In time."

"After a civil war?"

"A civil war?" Louis laughed. "You take things too far, Bertrand. All we want to do is teach the government a lesson, to show them that they can't lie and cheat and steal and get away with it just because they are deputies and ministers."

"Well, if that's all you have in mind," said Bertrand, "that's fine. But take care. Remember the machine guns on the steps of the Assembly."

. . .

Madeleine reappeared for supper, which was served at seven. Louis, who seemed chastened by her silent rage, attempted to enlist her support for the demonstration planned for that night. "No one believes that Stavisky killed himself," he said. "Not even the Socialists."

"They're supporting the government," said Bertrand.

"Under protest."

"Under protest, yes," said Madeleine, "but they're supporting it all the same to avoid playing into the hands of Fascists like you."

"We are not Fascists," said Raymond, turning pink with outrage.

"No one trusts this government," said Louis.

"And you take advantage of that," said Madeleine, "to throw the country into chaos."

"To save the country from chaos."

"How can a riot do that?"

"By bringing back the king!" said Raymond.

"Don't be absurd," said Madeleine, turning with a look of contempt on the young cousin of the two de Roujays. "This isn't the age of kings. Your king would be just another dictator like Mussolini, Salazar or Hitler."

"Madame de Roujay," said Raymond, getting to his feet, "it is quite impossible for me to enjoy your hospitality if you insult Monsieur le Duc de Guise by comparing him to—"

"Shut up and sit down," said Louis.

Raymond sat down.

"Blood is thicker than water," said Bertrand.

"Your blood," said Madeleine, "not mine."

After supper the three men went down into the street. Bertrand did not mean to join in the demonstration, but he was curious to see what would happen, and also thought he might exercise some restraint on his younger brother and cousin.

It was a warm evening. Louis and Raymond were wearing tweed jackets and raincoats as if they were country gentlemen on a visit to Paris, but to Bertrand they were so clearly officers in mufti that even in the dark their civilian clothes were no disguise. He himself still wore a dark suit from the office, and on top of that a light raincoat. Most of the men in the crowd who now walked down the Champs Elysées in large numbers were respectably dressed. If there was to be a revolution, it would be a revolution of the well-to-do.

No sooner had the three of them joined the crowd in the Place de la Concorde than they ceased to be individuals and became at once part of a huge human mass, bulging and quivering like a glob of bacteria under a microscope as it moved toward the Chamber of Deputies on the other side of the Seine.

Raymond, having been subdued by Madeleine's contempt for his opinions at supper, now took heart from the jostling bodies in the crowd, and like them began to shout, "Down with the thieves! Down with Daladier! Long live Chiappe!" He pressed forward through the throng; Louis and Bertrand followed.

It was dark. Most of the lamps had been smashed. As they came nearer to the Concorde bridge, Bertrand saw that many of the demonstrators were carrying iron railings or walking sticks with razor blades spliced into the ends. Every now and then he stumbled into the shallow pits where cobbles had been torn from the ground to be thrown at the police. To his left he could see the floodlit obelisk in the middle of the square, and beyond that the glow of a fire. "It's a bus," said a man who had come from that direction. "Someone has set it on fire."

"There's been some shooting," said another.

"Any dead?" asked Raymond.

"I don't know."

Suddenly Bertrand sensed that they were approaching the front line. A young man came staggering back with blood pouring from a gash in his head. Others, with improvised bandages swathed around their heads, were returning to the fray.

"This looks dangerous," he said to Louis.

"Yes," said Louis. There was a gleam in his eye.

They reached an improvised barricade made with chairs from the Tuileries Gardens, and suddenly, through a gap in the ranks of shouting men, Bertrand caught sight of the line of police and mounted guards drawn up across the Concorde bridge. No sooner had he seen them than they moved forward, and the men around him, after hurling a last cobblestone or fragment of railing, fell back, but such was the pressure of the crowd behind that it was impossible to avoid the mounted police who in a moment were among them. Bertrand ducked and dodged to escape their slashing sticks, and perhaps because he had nothing in his hands he avoided their blows. Raymond, however, had picked up a long piece of cast-iron railing, and just as he was about to hurl it like a javelin at one of the guards, he was hit over the head by another. He staggered and fell. A man behind him stepped forward and slashed at the horse with his walking stick. The rider reined in the wretched beast, and seeing others with a variety of weapons approach him, wheeled around and retreated.

Louis helped Raymond to his feet. Though blood poured down from his scalp, he seemed quite unaffected by the blow. "The pigs," he said. "They won't stop me as easily as that." He took a handkerchief from his pocket to staunch the flow of blood.

"Let's get back," said Bertrand.

"Never," said Raymond.

At this moment a solid and well-organized phalanx of demonstrators moved toward the front line and swept up the victims of the first assault. Bertrand, who had been prepared to abandon his brother and cousin if they were fool enough to stay on, found that he was carried on against his will toward the retreating line of police.

"It's the boys of Solidarité Française," shouted Raymond. "Bravo! On to the Chamber! Throw the guards in the river!" And these fresh recruits, recognizing the blood on his cheeks as a sign of rank, took up his chant and followed.

"This is madness," said Bertrand to Louis.

"Of course," said Louis, "but it's fun."

Hurling every kind of projectile, the crowd now advanced in the gloom toward the bridge. As they came closer to the police line, Bertrand could see the faces of the guardians of law and order—tired, frightened and stained with sweat and blood. He noticed a group fumble with some piece of machinery, and for a moment was caught by a spasm of panic as he imagined that they had brought forward the machine gun from the steps of the Chamber on the other side of the river. To his relief, however, he saw that it was only the nozzle of a fire hose, and a moment later he was knocked to the ground by Louis, who, standing in front of him, had taken the full force of the jet of water.

"Sorry, old chap," said Louis as the two brothers struggled among the kicking legs of the other demonstrators to get to their feet. "My

God, I'm soaked." He spoke as if he had been thrown into a swimming pool at a boisterous party.

"For God's sake, let's leave," said Bertrand, but just then he and Louis were both carried forward again by a sudden surge of the crowd as the front line, led by Raymond, rushed at the police with the fire hose. When the de Roujays caught up, Raymond and his friends had captured the nozzle and had turned it upon the retreating police.

"Into the river," they shouted. "The guards into the river!"

Having cleared a path with the jet of water, they rushed forward for a final assault on the line of police across the bridge. Bertrand ran behind Louis, Louis behind Raymond. They were within yards of the police, who, their backs to a line of Black Marias drawn up across the bridge, now turned to face the charge. Bertrand could see their fear, and the fingers of one gendarme fumbling at the buckle of his holster.

"Stop," he shouted to Louis. "They're going to shoot."

"On to the Chamber!" shouted Raymond.

"Down with the thieves!" shouted Louis.

There was a crack, then three more. Raymond faltered, then fell. Louis caught him before he hit the cobbles. Bertrand came to his other side. His raincoat was torn at the shoulder, and almost at once Bertrand saw blood gurgle through the layers of rent gabardine.

"He's hit," said Louis.

To their left there was a shriek. A youth clutched his eye and fell dead.

"Louis," said Raymond, clutching the lapel of his cousin's coat. "Are we there, Louis? Have we crossed the bridge?"

"More or less," said Louis. He looked up. The line was falling back. He turned to Bertrand. "We've got to get him out of here."

Without a word, Bertrand took hold of his cousin under the shoulders and with one sweep lifted him. Then, while Louis forced a way through the crowd, shouting, "Stand aside, stand aside, a wounded man, a wounded man," he staggered back with him across the Place de la Concorde.

Raymond, pale but conscious, smiled with a mixture of pain and exaltation. At long last they reached the pavement on the edge of the square, where a makeshift first-aid post had been set up by an ex-servicemen's association. There, by the light of an oil lamp, an orderly cut away some of the clothes which obscured the wound and taped on a dressing to staunch the flow of blood. "Better get him to a hospital," he said. "I can't do much for him here."

"Call an ambulance," someone shouted.

"No," said Louis with all the authority of an officer. He turned to Bertrand. "The police will check the hospitals. We'll have to take him back to your apartment."

Some youths from the Jeunesses Patriotes had commandeered a taxi and offered it to Louis as a makeshift ambulance. Bertrand and Louis lifted Raymond onto the backseat, and were driven slowly through the crowd up the Champs Elysées to the Rond Point, then more rapidly, as the crowd thinned, toward the Rue Marbeuf. The taxi stopped outside the apartment. At first they tried to hold Raymond between them, his arms around their necks, but as they lifted his left arm he shrieked with pain, so this time Louis picked him up. Bertrand held open the doors, and they sneaked past the concierge and carried Raymond into the elevator and up to the third floor.

Madeleine came from her bedroom as they entered. She looked dismayed when she saw the wounded man. "What on earth has happened?"

"An accident," said Bertrand.

"Where can I put him?" asked Louis.

Remembering that Raymond was to sleep in the baby's room, Madeleine led the way down the corridor and opened the door to let Louis pass. He laid his pallid cousin on the small bed, then stood for a moment to recover his breath while Madeleine, stock-still, stared in horror at the wet black hole at the shoulder of the beige raincoat. Bertrand came in behind her.

"What happened?" she asked again.

"The police lost their heads. They opened fire."

"And he was shot?"

"Yes."

"But he should be in a hospital."

Bertrand led her out of Titine's room and back down the corridor to the drawing room. "He can't go to a hospital," he said. "The police would find him. He'd be cashiered."

"But what else can we do?"

"Get a doctor to come here."

Louis now joined them. "Do you know a doctor?"

"Yes, of course," said Madeleine, "Dr. Laffont."

Bertrand shook his head. "I don't think we can trust him."

"A Freemason?" asked Louis.

Bertrand shrugged his shoulders. "I don't know. But he is obliged by law to report a gunshot wound."

"You haven't a friend who is a doctor?"

"No."

"There's Michel," said Madeleine.

Bertrand frowned. "Yes. At the Institut Pasteur."

"Would he come?" asked Louis.

"Yes."

"And could you trust him?"

"He's a Socialist, almost a Communist, these days."

"So he might report it?"

"He won't," said Madeleine, "if I ask him not to."

It took three-quarters of an hour for Michel le Fresne to reach the Rue Marbeuf through the blocked streets. He came into the de Roujays' apartment with a black bag of instruments and a look of professional anxiety on his florid face. He followed Madeleine into the child's room.

"The idiot," he said as he took the makeshift dressing from the wound.

"Long live the king," murmured Raymond.

"He should go to a hospital," said Michel.

"He can't," said Bertrand, who stood in the doorway behind his wife.

"Then I'll have to try to find the bullet, but I can't do that here."

He gave Raymond an injection of morphine, then told Bertrand and Louis to carry him to the dining-room table. There, while his instruments were sterilized in boiling water in the kitchen, the three men removed most of the young royalist's clothes.

"It's not so bad," said Michel as he probed at the wound with his tweezers. "Be brave, young man."

"Long live the king," said Raymond again, and passed out.

"So much the better," said Michel, seeing that he had fainted. He probed deeper into the wound and finally pulled out the bullet. "There we are," he said. "He's very lucky. An inch to the left and it would have hit his lung."

It took Michel half an hour more to clean and dress the wound. Then Raymond was carried back to Louis's bed in the spare room and, dressed in his own pajamas, left to sleep.

Michel le Fresne was given a glass of whiskey in the drawing room. "Who is the young man?" he asked Bertrand.

"A cousin."

"How did he get shot?"

"On the Place de la Concorde."

"I thought as much."

"If he's found out, he'll be chucked out of the army."

"All to the good," said Madeleine.

"He has no money."

"So?"

"There's nothing else he could do."

"The army's not there to provide employment for the aristocracy," said Madeleine.

"But it is," said Michel with a laugh. "If only they did as much for the working class." He finished his glass. "I must get back. I shall look in tomorrow morning."

"We are very grateful," said Bertrand.

"The time will come when you can return the favor," said Michel.

"Will he be all right?" asked Louis.

"Yes. The only risk is of infection, but if we keep an eye on things, all should be well."

Michel rose to go. Bertrand stood too, but Madeleine directed a look at him to suggest that he leave it to her to see Michel to the door.

"Is he safe?" asked Louis when she and Michel had left the room.

"He's an old friend of Madeleine's," said Bertrand. "He won't want to make trouble for her or for me."

"But if he's a Communist . . ."

"They're used to conspiracy."

"That's true."

Madeleine returned to the drawing room.

"Well?" asked Bertrand.

"He won't say a thing."

"Good."

"But another time," she said, "when you want to play revolution, don't count on him to get you out of trouble." She turned and left the room.

When Bertrand followed her to bed twenty minutes later she was either asleep or pretending to be, curled up under the blankets and facing the wall. Bertrand washed and changed into his pajamas, then went to open the window and stood for a moment listening to the faint roar of riot which still came from the direction of the Place de la Concorde.

He joined his wife in bed, but instead of turning on his side and shutting his eyes he lay on his back for a while as the many incoherent thoughts which passed through his mind combined with his fatigue and enervation to induce a mood of overwhelming despair. There was chaos in the Assembly, chaos in the streets and chaos in his home. The two people he loved most in the world—his brother and his wife— not only despised one another's opinions, but also felt contempt for his own moderate views. If three members of the same family could not hold together, what hope was there for France?

The next morning Hortense, the cook, brought Madeleine her break-fast in bed, while Bertrand and Louis took theirs at the dining-room table.

"I must get back to Nancy," said Louis, "and cover up for Raymond."

"What will you say?"

Louis shrugged his shoulders. "I'll think of something."

"We'll hold on to Raymond."

"I'll move him as soon as I can."

Once Louis had left, Bertrand returned to the bedroom, where Madeleine lay reading the morning paper. "Fourteen killed," she said. "Over a thousand injured."

"It's insane."

"Really, Bertrand," she said, her face still angry, "to be part of a Fascist conspiracy, and to drag Michel into it . . ."

"There is no Fascist conspiracy."

"They want to bring down the government."

"Yes."

"By riots in the street."

"Perhaps. But there's no Hitler waiting in the wings."

She said nothing, but raised the newspaper to shut out her view of her husband.

"I'm afraid Raymond will have to stay here for a while," he said.

The newspaper crashed down onto the bedclothes. "And am I to look after him?"

"Hortense will look after him."

She snorted.

"I must go to the ministry," he said.

"Go, and leave me to clean up the mess."

Bertrand walked to his office by way of the Place de la Concorde, and was alarmed to see new bands of demonstrators forming around the debris of the night before.

At the ministry it was thought that the government would not survive. It was said that Daladier had lost control, that he did not know what to do.

Bertrand went to report to an undersecretary that it looked as if the riots might start again. "I know, I know," said the undersecretary irritably, "but what are we to do? We've rung the prefect half a dozen times. He won't even take the minister's calls. The police are exhausted and demoralized. They don't see why they should suffer for Daladier."

In the early afternoon news reached the ministry from the Elysée Palace that Daladier had resigned, and that Gaston Doumergue, elder statesman and former President of France, had been asked to form a government of national unity.

Bertrand telephoned Madeleine to give her the news.

"They always fall back on the old men," she said in her flat voice.

"How is our young man?" asked Bertrand.

"He's all right. He sounds delirious, but then he always did. Michel came by. He says he'll be fine."

Bertrand left the ministry at six and before returning home walked down to the Rue de Rivoli to see for himself whether the change in government had brought calm to the streets. He was appalled by what he saw. All the windows of the shops had been smashed, and the goods they had displayed had been looted: silk dressing gowns stolen from Sulka, cameras removed from the Kodak store. All the streetlights had been broken, so the arcades were dark. There were no police to be seen, only gangs of delinquent youths from the grimmer parts of Paris scuttling up and down to see what pickings were still to be had.

Bertrand followed this trail of devastation up the Rue Cambon to the Boulevard de Capucines. The windows of the Trois Quartiers department store had been smashed, and next to it a newspaper kiosk had been set on fire. At the Madeleine he saw a disconsolate detachment of police who did nothing but supervise the comings and goings of ambulances and Black Marias.

He turned back into the Rue Royale and walked toward home. Here the street was crowded, not with the well-dressed demonstrators of the night before, but with the sinister hoodlums of the Paris underworld, whose shifty, envious faces took on grimaces of perversity and evil in the obscure light of the half-lit streets.

Bertrand reached home at eight, tired and dejected. The concierge peeped out through her window as he passed. "Ah, Monsieur de Roujay. What a mess!"

"Indeed, madame."

The elevator carried him to the third floor, and as he raised his key to the door of his apartment he was struck by the fragile inadequacy of the polished wood as a protection against the anarchy and chaos he had witnessed in the street below. For the first time the idea entered his head that perhaps they should leave Paris.

The smell of disinfectant which met his nostrils as he entered the apartment reminded him of his wounded cousin lying in the spare room. He took off his coat and went into the drawing room. Madeleine sat at her desk. She turned, saw that it was him, and stood without smiling, as if meeting an obligation to attend to him. Her face was drawn; she looked anxious, almost old.

"You're late," she said.

"I made a detour," he said. "There's still trouble in the streets."

"Why?" she asked. "They've got what they wanted, haven't they?"

"Trouble of a different kind." He poured himself a drink. "There's looting around Saint Honoré. The police have lost control."

"So much for the discipline of the Camelots du Roi."

"It's not them."

"Who, then?"

"All the dregs of Paris."

"Your friends stirred them up."

"I know." He sighed and sat down in an armchair. She sat on the sofa opposite him.

"How's the patient?" he asked.

"There's no infection."

"Has he eaten anything?"

"Oh, yes. Hortense has been fattening him up."

"I'm sorry. It must seem like a madhouse."

"In spite of his opinions," said Madeleine, "one can't deny that your cousin has a certain charm."

"The charm of a Don Quixote?"

"He was certainly tilting at windmills last night."

"You didn't know, did you, when you married me, that I had cousins like that?"

"No."

"I should have warned you."

"I didn't marry you for your cousins."

"But it hasn't turned out quite as you expected, has it?"

"What?"

"Our marriage."

"No," she said, shaking her head and looking down so that her black hair fell like a screen to hide her tears.

"Have I disappointed you?" Bertrand asked gently.

She sniffed. "No, not you, but somehow . . . I don't know . . . this whole life . . . I feel trapped, suffocated."

"What would you like to do?"

"I don't know, I don't know." She sobbed out loud.

Bertrand crossed to comfort her. "How would it be," he asked, sitting down next to her, "if we left Paris and went to live in the country?"

She sniffed and looked up. "Leave Paris?" she asked. "How? Where?"

"Sooner or later," he said, taking hold of her hand, "they'll offer me a subprefecture."

"That would be better—yes, to get out, to breathe. But where would they send you?"

"They need someone in Mézac."

"Mézac? But that's near Saint Théodore."

"Normally," said Bertrand, his voice becoming excited, "they won't send anyone to his hometown, but Mézac and Saint Théodore are in different departments, so it's just possible that I could be sent there."

"But your career?" Madeleine asked. "Would it help your career? I don't want you to end up in a backwater just because of me."

"It would be a backwater for an older man, but at my age a post like Mézac would be a step up the ladder."

"It would be wonderful, Bertrand. I could finish my studies at Coustiers. Pierre's there now, and Michel has applied for a job at the hospital. And we'd be near to your parents and mine, and Titine would love the freedom of Saint Théodore." She turned, put her arms around his neck and kissed him. It was the first such spontaneous embrace for some time.

Chapter 4

1

*B*ERTRAND and Madeleine left Paris that autumn when he took up his appointment as subprefect of Mézac, in the department of Basse-Provence, and moved into a large, somewhat gloomy apartment on the third floor of the Renaissance mansion that housed the subprefecture. The apartment appealed to Bertrand, because some of his childhood had been spent in similar quarters which his mother had rented during the Great War so that Bertrand and Louis could be educated by the Jesuits in Mézac. Madeleine, however, disliked it from the start. The dining room and drawing room both looked out across a narrow street at the back of the subprefecture toward another mansion which blocked out the light, and were decorated in the bureaucratic taste of the Ministry of the Interior.

Bertrand brought some furniture from Saint Théodore, and for a time they talked about redecorating some of the rooms, but neither of them cared enough to see it through. Madeleine's life came to center upon the university at the larger city of Coustiers, while Bertrand was drawn toward his childhood home at Saint Théodore. On most week-days, Madeleine would drive to Coustiers in the car that Bertrand had bought for her, leaving Titine with the nanny, Miss Spinks, who had come with them from Paris. It meant that she spent many hours on the road, but she adored her little blue Renault, which symbolized her independence. She kept it in a mess with pencils, coins and lipsticks scattered on the floor, and she drove it fast, overtaking the tractors and horse-drawn carts which still were the principal traffic on the local roads, with a complete disregard for anything that might be going in the opposite direction.

Bertrand, who might have returned home for lunch had his wife been there, preferred to go to a restaurant with his colleagues rather than eat alone with Titine and Miss Spinks. He saw Madeleine in the evenings, but they were rarely alone together, because either one of them would be occupied by work or they would hurriedly change to go out to some gala or reception that the subprefect and his wife were expected to attend.

Of course, the social and cultural life of Mézac was not the same as that of Paris. At a dinner party in the capital, Madeleine might have found herself next to a writer whose book she admired or an actor she had seen on the stage. At dinner with the prefect in Coustiers, she was more likely to find herself conversing with the inspector of roads and bridges, or the director of the municipal abattoir. Moreover, Bertrand's official position made it necessary for her to treat such fellow guests with all the courtesy and charm she could muster, for not only was it appropriate in the subprefect's wife, but it was also the only way to disarm the suspicions of the Radical bourgeois of the district, who, knowing the de Roujay family, expected in Bertrand all the arrogance and disdain of the Catholic gentry. It was worse still in Mézac itself, where Madeleine, still in her twenties, had herself to receive the prominent citizens of the smaller city. Because she was both pretty and sensible, her youth did not act as a disadvantage, and the bourgeois shopkeepers on the town council who might otherwise have been suspicious of a de Roujay were reassured to find by his side the daughter of the celebrated Radical Michel Bonnet.

Without doubt this had formed part of the calculations of Bertrand's superiors when they had decided to send him to Mézac. The more perceptive among those who ran the French civil service wanted to heal the fissure between left and right, for a divided nation was weak and the power of Germany grew more menacing each day. Much of Europe now looked to France as its guarantor and protector. It was time for the nation to close ranks.

The only company in which Bertrand and Madeleine could feel at ease was that of what Bertrand called "the Montpellier gang" because its members had been Madeleine's friends at the university. A year or two before the de Roujays had returned to Provence, Pierre Moreau had been appointed an examining magistrate in Coustiers, and soon after Bertrand's appointment as subprefect, Michel le Fresne had been made a registrar at the teaching hospital in the same city. There Nellie le

Fresne bought a large, modern villa near her parents' home and kept open house in the same way as she had in the house outside Montpellier.

Nellie was quite happy to spend her money like this, and Michel, though now known to be a Communist, liked to extend a grand hospitality which only his wife's fortune enabled him to afford. Both he and Nellie were unchanged. Now a mother of three children, Nellie remained the same sour and sultry girl who had gone riding with Bertrand on that memorable day. Michel was the same ambitious and determined idealist whom some admired and others found insufferable. His height, thick hair and deep voice, together with his enthusiasm, sense of humor and air of sincerity, invariably made him attractive to women.

Perhaps because of this, Bertrand had mixed feelings about Michel le Fresne. The two got on well when they were together, because both were interested in politics and Michel's left-wing line made him a better sparring partner for Bertrand than Pierre, for example, who by and large agreed with his point of view. Also, Bertrand thought it useful to have some contact with the left, for particularly after the elections of May 1936, when the Communists increased their representation in the Chamber of Deputies from ten to seventy-two, and a Popular Front government was formed under the Socialist Léon Blum, it could hamper a career in public service to be too exclusively identified with the right. Wenkler, the prefect in Coustiers, once commended Bertrand for "keeping in with men like le Fresne."

On the other hand, it was irritating to hear Michel champion the proletariat while drinking his wife's champagne. He also had that slightly superior manner so common in doctors, as if his greater knowledge of the liver and bowels gave him a deeper insight into life itself. He liked to imply that if only a revolution would provide him with the scalpel of state power he could cure the body politic as easily as he could the body of an individual.

The practical advantages of friendship with the le Fresnes overcame any doubts. Madeleine and Nellie got on well. They had been close friends in Montpellier and became closer still. One of Nellie's children was a girl of the same age as Titine, so when on occasion Madeleine brought her daughter with her to Coustiers, she could leave her for the day at the le Fresnes' villa. Indeed, the villa became the de Roujays' base at Coustiers, and often if they went there to see a film or have dinner with the le Fresnes they would stay the night in the comfortable spare room with its view down over the city toward the hills.

If Bertrand and Madeleine, or Michel and Nellie, had been free to choose a favorite from among those they knew to be their close friends, none might have chosen one of the others; but marriage imposes compromises on those who are engaged in it, and the de Roujays were for the le Fresnes as suitable companions as the le Fresnes were for the de Roujays. Both families were well off, so there was no embarrassment at going to the better restaurants in the city, or staying at expensive hotels when they went on holiday together.

Individually each might have preferred Pierre, for example, but it was about this time that he married a wife whom Nellie and Madeleine found "mousy and dull" and who, in her turn, was terrified by the two confident, well-educated women and regarded dinner at the Villa Acacia as an ordeal. Nor was Pierre himself "good in a group," as Madeleine put it. "Dear Pierre," she would say. "He's really a man for a tête-à-tête." She would sometimes meet him for lunch, whereas Bertrand, trapped in Mézac at midday, would hardly see him at all.

On weekends and on holidays, Bertrand, Madeleine and Titine would always go to Saint Théodore, which, far more than the apartment above the subprefecture, they all regarded as home. The little girl flourished in the space of the large house set amid its vines, enjoying her freedom to run around in the garden or roam from room to room. For a while she missed Hortense, the cook from Paris, but with the fickleness of the young she soon transferred her affections to old Marthe and became the darling not just of the women who worked in the house, but also of the men who worked on the vines.

Madeleine was also happy at Saint Théodore, not just for the sake of her husband and daughter, but because in her too the house provoked memories and feelings which enhanced her sense of well-being. The man she had married, after all, was not the civil servant in a dark suit who returned each evening with his briefcase, but the chivalrous cavalier who had whisked her from the stairs and had ridden off with her in the sunlight between the vines to the river.

There were also practical advantages to the well-run household at Saint Théodore. Though all the de Roujays insisted that she should regard Saint Théodore as her home, Madeleine checked in and out of it as if the house were a hotel with a creche as well as a bedroom and restaurant. Both Bertrand and his parents were quite happy that she should do so. None of them seemed to want anything changed.

For Bertrand in particular this return to his unchanged childhood home gave him a sense of profound reassurance in a disintegrating world. As a child he had derived a great sense of security and ascendancy from the Domaine de Saint Théodore—from the thick stone walls and the warm kitchen when he was small; from the small kingdom of the garden and the vineyards when he grew older; and from the respect and deference accorded to him as the son of the house as he became a man. The very confidence which made him such an able administrator came in part from the soil and substance of Saint Théodore.

There was another factor which, just below the level of conscious will, drew him back to his home. This was the question of inheritance. French law does not accord any particular rights to the eldest son; indeed, it states that the greater part of the parents' property must be shared equally by the children of a marriage, so that if one wants the house and land he must compensate his brothers and sisters with money.

In the case of the de Roujays there was no danger that the Domaine de Saint Théodore would not go intact to the next generation, because Edmond de Roujay had had the luck, or the foresight, to marry the daughter of a northern industrialist. Though Alice de Roujay was not infinitely rich, she had sufficient capital to enable the son who took on Saint Théodore to buy out his brother.

It was probable, because it was usual, that this son would be the elder, but ever since childhood Bertrand had recognized that however fond his father was of him, he felt for Louis the instinctive affection that like feels for like. He knew that Edmond respected his opinions and enjoyed his company, but he noticed that his father never laughed in his presence as he did with Louis, and that there were times when he seemed almost afraid of him—afraid that Bertrand would criticize his management of the estate, or scoff at his wild opinions on the political events of the day. He saw his father's face light up when Louis returned on leave, and as he watched the two of them set off arm in arm to shoot snipe, he could not suppress a sour pang of jealousy and sadness.

Bertrand loved his brother—he would have risked his life for him —but he did not love him so much that he was prepared to forgo what he saw as his right to Saint Théodore. He knew that his father, seeing himself in Louis, would therefore see Louis at Saint Théodore, but he also knew that Edmond de Roujay was a straightforward man who would not deny his elder son his presumptive inheritance without good cause.

The good cause could only be that in the eyes of his father Bertrand showed no interest in Saint Théodore and was rarely there; thus, behind the decision to move to Mézac was not just a desire to get out of Paris and arrange a more congenial life for his family, but also a half-acknowledged intention to take possession in some sense of what would one day be his. In this he had the unspoken support of his mother. If Edmond saw himself in Louis, she recognized in Bertrand all the best qualities of her own family given elegance and charm by a patrician bearing and name. She loved her son not with the passion of a Jocasta, but with the contentment of a prudent banker who sees a long-term investment produce its anticipated return. Just as Edmond had been conscious of what Alice Ravanel would bring to a marriage, so Alice had been aware of just what she had purchased with her dowry. The sturdy structure of Ravanel steel had required a baroque embellishment of de Roujay stucco. Bertrand was the building complete.

His marriage to Madeleine had been her only disappointment, but with the same practical bent she had accepted this setback as an accomplished fact whose true purpose was known only to God. She saw their return to Provence as undoubtedly a development in God's plan for her family. If she had doubts about living with Madeleine under the same roof, she suppressed them for Bertrand's sake; and as time passed she had discovered that in many ways it was easier to get on with a daughter-in-law with whom she had nothing in common. Though she disapproved in principle of the way Madeleine left Titine to the care of others, she not only loved the laughter of the toddling child echoing down the corridors of her large house, but also saw a chance to nurture a tender soul and teach Titine the prayers she had failed to teach her mother.

On some weekends, Bertrand and Madeleine would invite their friends from Coustiers out to Saint Théodore, which always led to a certain

awkwardness because of the presence of the elder de Roujays. Age had
not made them more open-minded, and of the inner circle of their son's
friends one was a Marxist, another a Huguenot, a third a Jew. Whenever such friends came out to Sunday lunch, Alice and Edmond de
Roujay tried to behave well, but they could not entirely conceal the
distaste they felt for the company of such people, and they tended to
talk to them as if at the same time they were inwardly holding their
noses.

Moreover, it was at these lunches that Madeleine—who otherwise
left the running of the household to Marthe and her mother-in-law
—made decisions which went against all the customs and habits established by the two old women. There was, for example, a fine Sèvres
service which was never used. Instead, the de Roujays always ate off
undistinguished dishes of modern design. The Sèvres was kept for
"occasions" which never came. The same was true of the cutlery. There
was a set of silver forks and knives from the eighteenth century,
engraved with the de Roujay coat of arms, which were always kept
locked away in a wooden box, and a beautiful lace tablecloth of a
slightly later period which was kept in reserve for weddings and
christenings. But though Madeleine was certainly no snob, it seemed
to her absurd that this fine porcelain and silver should never be used.
She wanted the de Roujay family, as it were, to put its best foot
forward. They might not be olive-oil millionaires like the Planchets,
but no amount of money could buy an eighteenth-century service
marked with one's family's coat of arms.

Thus whenever the Montpellier gang came to lunch, Madeleine
would tell Marthe to bring out the best plates and the silver. Marthe
would bustle off to Alice de Roujay, asking her if these instructions
were to be obeyed, and Alice, with a sigh, would say, "Yes, Marthe,
but please take care"; then, angry at this defeat on territory she thought
her own, she would, on seeing Bertrand, drop a sarcastic remark about
the "grand habits of your distinguished friends."

Bertrand was caught between the two women, who never confronted one another on issues of this kind. On the one hand he saw
Madeleine's point of view—that it was absurd to have beautiful china
and never use it—but on the other he shared his mother's fidelity to
the custom that the Sèvres, like the tablecloth, was only to be used for
"occasions" like christenings or weddings. He himself had no particular
opinion one way or the other, but by nature he was conservative and

hated to see old customs changed. Yet he also recognized that if Madeleine was to be happy at Saint Théodore, she had to be allowed to entertain her friends in a style she thought fit, and if this meant using the best silver and china then they must use it. He put this to his mother, and with bad grace she gave in.

At the end of the summer of 1936, Bertrand, Madeleine and Titine returned to Saint Théodore from a holiday in Italy. Since they had not seen the le Fresnes or the Moreaus for some time, they asked them out to Sunday lunch. It was an ill-considered invitation, because the political events of that summer had not been such as to endear the old de Roujays to their daughter-in-law's left-wing friends—or, for that matter, the progressives among the Montpellier gang to Catholic conservatives like the old de Roujays.

What had upset both parties, and made their tolerance wear thin, was the outbreak of a civil war in Spain. Already, by the autumn, there had been massacres and atrocities on both sides. To Madeleine and the le Fresnes the rising itself was a crime; to Edmond and Alice de Roujay the Republican government in Madrid was a claque of demons whose majority did nothing to legitimize its crimes.

Most painful of all for Alice de Roujay were the stories she read almost daily of attacks by the Republicans upon nuns and priests. Between July and September, eleven bishops and seven thousand priests had been murdered, and often their churches and monasteries were burned to the ground. The bishop of Jaén had been killed with his sister before a mocking crowd outside Madrid. The bishops of Guadix and Almería had been forced to wash the deck of a prison ship before being murdered near Málaga. A nun was shot because she refused to marry one of the militiamen who sacked her convent; other nuns were raped before their execution. In Cervera, rosary beads were forced down the ears of monks until they perforated their eardrums; in Ciempozuelos, a priest was forced into a corral of fighting bulls, and after he had been gored into unconsciousness, one of his ears was cut off and held up in honor of the Republican matadors. The parish priest of Torrijos, who had told his tormentors that he wanted to suffer for Christ, was stripped, scourged and crowned with thorns. "Blaspheme and we will forgive you," his captors said. "It is I who forgive and bless you," he replied as he was dragged to his execution.

To the old de Roujays, events in Spain were following the same pattern as events in Russia in 1917. The Spanish Republicans themselves seemed to model themselves on the Soviets; the self-appointed units of secret police proudly called themselves "chekas." To Edmond and Alice this was the inevitable outcome whenever facile idealists or unscrupulous opportunists tried to overturn the established order. Though Bertrand had tried to persuade them that the French government under Léon Blum did not contemplate anything more radical than an increase in wages and a forty-hour week, it was inevitable that these events in Spain should fill them with alarm and foreboding, and lead them to look more severely on those who espoused the cause of the murderers of priests.

Madeleine and her friends from Coustiers interpreted the same events in an opposite way—so precisely opposite that it was as if their moral view were a print taken from the old de Roujays' negative. To them Franco was a Fascist usurper without even the popular following of a Hitler or a Mussolini. Instead Franco had used Moroccan soldiers to overturn the democratic government of the Spanish Republic. If his revolt led to extreme measures by the Republicans, so much the better, and if priests and nuns were murdered, it was only to be expected after the centuries of collusion between the Church and the ruling classes.

If there had been no open argument about events in Spain within the family, it was partly because Madeleine had been away for most of the summer—first with her parents in Montpellier, then with Bertrand in Italy—but also because Madeleine and the older de Roujays treated each other with such courtesy and reserve that they avoided political conflict of any kind. As always, each side complained to Bertrand about the attitude of the other, and Bertrand—with Spain as with the Sèvres service—could see the justice of both points of view, though he himself shared neither. It was not that he was undecided as to where his sympathies lay—he was a determined democrat and against any military usurpation of power—but he considered the gravity of the conflict in Spain to be the fault not of either left or right, but of the passionate and fanatical Spanish temperament; and though aware of the polarization of opinion not just in France but within his own family, he was confident that French affairs would never come to a similar pass because there was a sufficient number of Frenchmen of sound judgment and common sense—Frenchmen like Bertrand de Roujay.

It was still warm enough to eat out, and when Bertrand, Titine and the old de Roujays returned from mass, they found the table under the chestnut trees covered by the old white tablecloth with lace edges which Madeleine had taken from the linen chest.

"But it's for christenings," muttered Alice de Roujay.

Bertrand blushed, because he knew how precious the old tablecloth was to his mother, but in defense of his wife he said, "Still, it does look wonderful, Maman."

"Yes," his mother said sadly, "but it would look more wonderful still if it were for the christening of another child."

Marthe came out of the house holding a tray piled with the best cutlery and glasses. Behind her came another woman from the village —a cousin of Marthe's—who was brought in to help when needed.

"Monsieur Louis telephoned," said Marthe.

"Louis?" asked Alice de Roujay.

"He was in Coustiers. He said he would be here for lunch."

"And Hélène?"

"No, only Monsieur Louis." She continued across the gravel toward the table. Bertrand could see that she was furious; she hated it when Madeleine told her what to do.

"Did she say Louis was coming?" asked Edmond.

"Yes, my dear," said Alice. "Evidently he was in Coustiers."

"Excellent," said the old colonel. He turned to Bertrand. "We can see what he thinks about the new machinery."

"Yes," said Bertrand. "I'm sure he'll approve." As they had walked back from church he had put a plan to his father for modernizing the plant that they used to make wine.

"I hope he'll like Madeleine's friends," said Alice.

"They're my friends too," said Bertrand.

"Yes, of course, dear," she replied in a skeptical tone of voice. "But you know Louis is so unpredictable. You never know what he may say."

Louis was tactless from the moment he arrived. "Ah, a christening!" he said, seeing the white linen tablecloth fringed with lace. "Madeleine, you minx, you've had a baby on the sly."

"No, Louis," said Alice sadly. "It's not a christening."

"So what are we celebrating? The fall of Madrid?"

"There's no celebration," said Bertrand. "We just thought we'd impress our friends from Coustiers."

"But I didn't think you mixed with dukes and duchesses."

"We don't," said Madeleine. "They're people I know from Montpellier."

"Marxists! Intellectuals! My God, I hope you don't mind my being here."

"Of course not," said Madeleine.

"I'll try not to embarrass you. Should I change out of my uniform?"

"Don't be absurd."

"I thought you didn't approve of the officer corps."

"As long as you're not planning a coup d'état," said Madeleine with a sour smile.

"I swear to you," said Louis, his hand held to his breast, "that I am loyal to the Republic."

"Good."

"Long live the king!" he shouted, laughing, clapping his sister-in-law on the back. "The army is full of royalist republicans," he said. "It's the famous logic of the French."

They sat down on the garden benches under the chestnut trees drinking cold vermouth from small glasses. The three men talked about the vineyards and Bertrand's plans to invest in new machinery.

"It will cost a lot of money," said Louis.

"I'm prepared to find that myself," said Bertrand.

"I don't see how you can make it back."

"We won't need so many men."

"It seems a pity to throw them out of work."

"We can't afford to be sentimental."

Louis sighed. "Progress. How I hate it. Have you ordered the machinery?"

"I'm getting quotations from a German company, Ludwig and Kummerly."

"German? Don't we make equipment of the same sort?"

"Not of the same standard."

"I don't like buying off the Boches," said Edmond.

"Trade is the best antidote to war," said Bertrand.

"Maybe," said Louis. "It still sticks in the gullet."

This brief conversation about family business appeared to put Louis in a bad mood. Fond though he was of Bertrand, he could not suppress an instinctive envy which matched that which his older brother felt for him. It irked him that Bertrand should make decisions of this kind about the vineyard at Saint Théodore and invest his own money in their implementation, as if the property already were or certainly would be his. He therefore frowned and turned away, at the very moment an open blue car approached the house along the drive. "Ah, your guests," he said in a sarcastic tone. "As always, the champions of the proletariat travel in style."

Bertrand rose to greet his friends as they got out of the elegant new car which Michel le Fresne had bought with his wife's money, but as he walked toward them across the gravel he saw them through his father's and his brother's eyes and was filled with dismay. Not only was the car itself a provocation when owned by a Marxist, but also Nellie le Fresne was too well dressed. She looked as if she had walked straight out of the showroom of a Parisian fashion house. Her clothes were informal—appropriate to the occasion—but too bright, too new, too clean. Michel himself was also too elegant, though in the somewhat uncomfortable manner of a man who is himself indifferent to what he wears but puts on whatever his wife chooses for him.

By the standards of Saint Théodore, where a certain shabbiness was de rigueur, the le Fresnes seemed vulgar and out of place. The Moreaus, who were with them, were equally so, not for what they wore but for who they were. Pierre had brought his wife, a quiet, timid girl named Bérénice, whom Bertrand had thought charming when he had met her in Coustiers, but now, through his brother's eyes, he found her conspicuously "Israelite" in her appearance, with black hair, brown eyes and sallow skin.

Though Bertrand did not share his brother's views on Jews, a certain measure of anti-Semitism was so common to his class, and went back over so many generations, that he felt at once that Bérénice was out of place. All the same, he welcomed her with a reflexive politeness, then turned to Pierre and the le Fresnes. "Well done. You've timed it perfectly."

"Michel was sure we'd be early," said Nellie.

"Not as fast as it looks?" asked Bertrand, looking at the new Citroën.

"I'm breaking it in."

"It looks superb," said Bertrand.

"It's a symbol of the revolution," said Michel.

"How?"

"It's the first car in the world with front-wheel drive. Instead of being steered parasitically from up front, the wheels which do the work seize the direction of the motorcar for themselves."

Bertrand laughed. "It's as good an excuse as any to buy a new car," he said.

Madeleine came out of the house and led her guests toward Edmond and Louis de Roujay. "You know Bertrand's father and brother, don't you? Ah no, Bérénice hasn't met them. Edmond?" She led Pierre's shy bride and presented her to her father-in-law. "Edmond, this is Madame Moreau."

The colonel shook her hand with a disciplined politeness, saying, "Give us something to drink, Bertrand."

"Allow me," said Louis, inclining his head in what might have been mock courtesy or the real thing. "I am only the younger son, of course, but even a younger son can pour the drinks." He took the bottle of vermouth from the tray and began to fill the small glasses in a manner which in itself had a trace of irony.

"How is the army?" asked Pierre, who had met Louis before and had got on with him well.

"The army?" Louis replied. "Well, it's still there, though as you may imagine it's a little bizarre to be a soldier in a nation governed by pacifists."

Pierre blushed. "They're not altogether pacifists," he said.

"Has Monsieur Blum changed his mind, then?"

"I think the war in Spain has obliged him to modify his position."

"It has obliged us all, I think," said Edmond de Roujay, just as Alice came out of the house to join the party. She too looked askance at Bérénice Moreau.

They sat down at table. "Take care," said Louis to Bérénice in a tone of perfect courtesy. "I fear that the pâté may be made with pork."

Bérénice blushed. "It doesn't matter."

"But the vegetables, I think, are ritually clean."

"It really doesn't matter." She darted a look of anguish at Pierre, but he was caught in conversation with Alice.

"Are you sure? I would hate to feel that we were corrupting you."

"My parents are strict about that sort of thing," she said, "but I am not."

"I have to admit," said Louis in a conspiratorial tone, "that I'm a little easygoing about eating fish on Friday. I simply cannot believe that I will be damned for eating a beefsteak instead of a trout."

She smiled.

"On the other hand," he went on, "you never know. We may all get a nasty surprise on the other side of the grave. Perhaps I'll be met by an avenging angel saying, 'Louis de Roujay, thou art not circumcised. Thou shalt not enter the kingdom of heaven.' "

"I'm sure you wouldn't be damned for that," said Bérénice, blushing and confused.

"Then for what?"

"Something serious."

"What is serious?"

"Well . . . killing someone."

"But I kill people all the time. It's my job."

"Only in wars, surely."

"Oh, there's always some little trouble in Africa which means shooting the occasional black. But don't worry, we never kill people in metropolitan France. We leave that to the police."

Now Michel le Fresne leaned over and said to Louis, "You aren't tempted to deal with internal enemies?"

"Not as yet."

"But in the future?"

"Unfortunately I have come without my crystal ball."

"Then I will look into mine," said Michel, cupping his wineglass with his hands and peering over the rim.

"What do you see?" asked Berenice.

"I see blood."

"That's the wine, you fool," said Nellie.

"I see a putsch."

"Does it succeed?" asked Louis.

"No, it fails."

"And then?"

"The army collapses. The people rise. There is a revolution."

"Can you read the street signs?" asked Louis.

"Why?"

"To know if we are in France or Spain."

Michel looked into his glass again. "Ah, wait a minute, yes, the street signs . . . they're in French but . . . what's this . . . a *mannekenpiss!* My God, it's Belgium!"

They all laughed, because until then their banter had been good-humored; Michel was adept at being a Marxist among millionaires, and Louis too had been bred to put courtesy before conviction. It was the older man, Edmond de Roujay, who lost control and said, "And do you see any murdered priests?"

Michel looked up and smiled awkwardly. "My vision is blurred," he said.

"Yes," said the colonel. "By damned ideology."

"By the dregs of the wine," said Michel.

"I thought it was blood," said Louis with a sneer.

"For a Catholic, I think, they are the same thing," said Michel, a sharpness entering his tone of voice.

"Certainly both play a role in our religion," said Louis.

"An essential role, I think," said Michel. "The Church thrives on the blood of its martyrs."

"Yes," said Louis. "And the Party on the blood of its victims."

"Every dog has his day."

"And thank God for Franco!" said Edmond de Roujay, scarlet in the face. "Who knows just what to do with mad dogs in his part of the world."

Michel put down his knife and turned toward Madeleine. "Must I put up with this?" he asked.

"With what?" she asked. She had missed what had been said.

"I don't like to eat with Fascists," said Michel.

"I don't understand."

Bertrand by now had gathered what was taking place. "Let's keep off politics," he said.

"By all means," said Michel, "but I'm afraid I have lost my appetite, so if you don't mind I shall wait in the car." He stood and left the table.

"For God's sake, Michel, don't be a fool," Nellie shouted after him.

"I apologize, madame," said Edmond de Roujay. "I fear that I went too far."

"Don't worry," she said in her lazy voice. "He'll come back when he's hungry." And sure enough, when the roast lamb was brought from the kitchen, Michel le Fresne, who in the open car could not fail to catch its aroma, returned and without a word resumed his seat at the table. The incident, however, had caused great embarrassment, and for the rest of lunch they made only halting and stilted conversation. The only two smiling faces were those of Louis, who had engineered the dispute, and Nellie le Fresne, who had observed what had happened with the callous amusement of a Roman matron watching gladiators in the amphitheater.

While her guests remained at Saint Théodore, Madeleine continued to behave with a controlled graciousness, but she could not conceal from Bertrand the rage she had suppressed for the sake of convention, and once the le Fresnes and Moreaus had left, she turned on him and gave vent to her anger with all the eloquence of a scene well rehearsed in her mind.

"It's quite intolerable," she said, "to have my friends insulted by your family."

"They were hardly insulted. . . ." Bertrand led her away from the house into the vineyard so that their quarrel would not be overheard.

"It takes a lot to make Michel leave the table!"

"On the contrary. He loves to play the martyr."

"He was genuinely upset."

"Not so upset that he did without the *gigot.*"

"Now you insult him! And when you think what he did for your cousin in Paris!"

"Papa didn't know about that."

"Even so."

"At his age, something like the war in Spain—"

"At his age, at his age! Well, I've had enough of living under the same roof as a gaga old reactionary."

From the sound of her voice, Bertrand could tell that she was about to start sobbing. "Madeleine," he said in a conciliatory tone of voice.

"I've had enough."

He stretched out his arm to put it around her shoulder and comfort her, but she shook him off. "Leave me alone," she said, the tears trickling down her face.

He walked apart, offended in his turn that his gesture of reconciliation had been rebuffed. "It was a pity," he said, "that Louis happened to be there."

"He provokes on purpose."

"He always has. He doesn't mean it maliciously. We always argued like that when we were children."

"You're no longer children."

"We revert when we're at home."

"If it's his home, then it can't be mine."

"He's rarely here."

"I want a home of my own."

Bertrand sighed. "You have a home in Mézac."

"Do you call that gloomy apartment a home? I want a house, a proper house, like the le Fresnes'."

"But you're always in Coustiers."

"I want a house in Coustiers."

"You may have forgotten," Bertrand said coldly, "that I am the subprefect of Mézac."

"You could work there from Coustiers."

"That's out of the question."

"Why?"

"The prefect would never allow it."

"If it was *my* house, he couldn't object."

"We can't afford to run three establishments."

"Why three?"

"A house in Coustiers, the apartment in Mézac and Saint Théodore?"

"But the ministry pays for the apartment in Mézac, and your parents pay for Saint Théodore."

"I also contribute to the expenses of Saint Théodore."

"What expenses?"

"I have committed myself to modernizing the wine machinery."

Madeleine's tears stopped. She was furious. "So I am to do without a house of my own so that you can spend your money on the damned vines?" She looked at the bunch of black grapes ripening for the harvest.

Bertrand frowned, and a hard look came onto his face. This morning everything had seemed so clear and straightforward. Saint Théodore was to be his home; therefore it seemed only sensible that he should spend his capital on putting its production on a sound footing so that the profits from the vineyard could sustain the estate in future years. Now these plans were to be frustrated because Michel le Fresne had been upset by something his father had said at lunch.

"I don't understand you," he said.

"And I don't understand you," she said angrily.

"You've changed."

"I've changed? And what about you? What happened to the idealist who was going to dedicate his life to bettering the condition of the people of France?"

"I haven't lost those ideals."

"But charity begins at home, does it, by buying German machinery and sacking half your men?"

"You don't understand—"

"I understand only too well!"

Bertrand was silent, his face pale, the skin drawn tightly over the bones. He felt baffled and angry. What had he done to provoke such bitter recrimination? Why was Madeleine so determined to sabotage his plans for Saint Théodore? It could only be because she did not share his vision of their future; because she had never committed herself to him as a wife should commit herself to her husband. For the first time since he had married, a certain resentment against Madeleine came to the surface of his mind, as all those contrary qualities which in courtship had seemed to complement his own—and were, in a sense, what had led him to want to marry her—now appeared as destructive and disloyal.

He turned to look at her as if something in her appearance would give a clue to her behavior. Her tears had stopped. She was scowling down at the earth on the track. Yet even with this ugly expression on her face, he was astonished and soothed by her beauty. Not for a moment did he wish that someone else was walking there beside him, or that he was walking alone.

"Listen," he said to her, his voice as conciliatory as his dignity would allow. "I can see that it's difficult living half in Mézac, half here, while your life is in Coustiers, but you agreed—we both agreed—to live in this way when we left Paris. To some extent, when you've made your bed, you must sleep in it."

"And what about Titine?" she asked angrily, her own thoughts exploding with a rejoinder that had nothing to do with what he had said.

"Titine?"

"Shut up in that gloomy apartment with that ogre Mabel Spinks, hardly seeing her mother or her father, and with no friends . . ."

Bertrand opened his mouth to point out that it was Madeleine who had chosen to study in Coustiers, but realizing that this would only open up the old argument about her academic career, he merely said, "She has her little friends from her school."

"Shopkeepers' children!" said Madeleine.

"I don't think she minds."

"But I do. They contaminate her with their petit bourgeois values."

"And who would be her friends in Coustiers?"

"The children of people at the university, and of our own friends —our real friends."

"I have to confess," said Bertrand in an exasperated tone of voice, "that it had never occurred to me to move for the sake of a five-year-old's social life."

"No, I am sure it hadn't," said Madeleine, "because you never think of anyone but yourself."

"In which case," said Bertrand, finally losing his temper, "you can appreciate that I would rather walk by myself."

"Good," she said. "So would I. I loathe these bloody vines."

They parted, both enraged, Bertrand to walk toward the river, Madeleine to return to the house. What Bertrand had forgotten—the ructions of the day had driven it out of his mind—was that he had arranged to meet the area representative of Ludwig and Kummerly, the German manufacturers of vinicultural equipment, at Saint Théodore at six that evening.

This salesman, Oskar Lutze, had driven out from Coustiers that Sunday evening because Bertrand had told him that he would be in Mézac during the week. He had reached Pévier half an hour early, and had waited there until ten to six. When he reached Saint Théodore, however, he could find no one to impress with his punctuality. He went first to the back door, then to the front, and since no one answered when he knocked on either, he seated himself on one of the chairs under the chestnut trees.

Lutze was a pale young man with lank hair who gave the impression that nothing about him fitted together—neither his clothes, shoes, legs, torso nor the expression on his face. He was a Rhinelander whose father had left his mother soon after the birth of this scrambled son. The mother had taken up with the local butcher, who, since his wife owned the business, could not marry her, but had moved to and fro between the two houses. The young Oskar had loathed his mother's lover, and had had to bury his head under his pillow to shut out the sounds when the butcher spent the night. The only person to befriend him was the parish priest, who happened to have a passion for France. It was this patient man who had not only taught Oskar to speak the French language, but had inspired him with an enthusiasm for history and a lasting curiosity about their neighbors across the Rhine.

Like Antoine Dubec, the Dominican, Oskar Lutze had felt drawn toward the institution which did much to make up for the inadequacy of his family life; but in his later adolescence he was lured away from the Church by the more dramatic and alluring Hitler Youth. The fanatic nationalism which he had learned in its camps and at its rallies had poisoned his affection for the French, but because of his fluency in the French language he had been hired by Ludwig and Kummerly of Trier to sell the company's products in France.

This visit to Saint Théodore was his first without the tutelage of a senior salesman, but he had been thoroughly briefed before he left Trier and knew enough about the de Roujays to be in awe of their name. Like many Nazis, Oskar Lutze was both a populist and a snob who held together the conflicting facets of his disjointed personality by playing imaginary roles which enhanced the quality of his life.

In Trier, wearing a brown shirt, he was a member of the master race. In France, however, he had cast himself in the role of a handsome and courteous aristocrat. His blanched body and wide Teutonic face were transformed in his fantasy to the elegant form and sensitive features of an urbane entry in the *Almanach de Gotha* who was visiting various domaines in the south of France not as a salesman but as a guest. On his journey from Germany he had begun to imagine the beautiful women who would receive him and then inevitably fall in love with this debonair stranger.

So vivid was this fantasy that when he saw a young woman walking toward him across the garden, he felt no discomfiture to be found lounging on a chair, but rose to greet her with a suave smile on his lips.

"My dear madame . . ." he began.

"Who are you?" said the woman, who was indeed as beautiful as he imagined her.

"Madame la Comtesse," he murmured, taking her hand and stooping to kiss it.

She snatched it away. "What are you doing here?"

She seemed angry, but this did not upset him; her disdain was just right. As soon as she knew, all would be well. "I was just passing," he said.

"This is private property."

He smiled. "Of course, but Monsieur de Roujay—"

"Which Monsieur de Roujay?"

"Monsieur Bertrand—"

"What about him?"

"He invited me—"

"Invited you?" She seemed incredulous.

"That is to say, we had an appointment."

"For what?"

Now reality had to intrude. "To discuss business." He took out his card, and with a modest click of the heels to denote his transition from French count to German salesman, he presented it to Madeleine de Roujay.

"Oskar Lutze? Ludwig and Kummerly? What is this?"

"Vinicultural machinery, madame."

"That!"

At last she seemed to understand. He smiled as he anticipated her change of expression. "Monsieur de Roujay, I believe—"

She went pale. "But you have no business here," she said in a loud and furious tone of voice. "This is the house, not the estate office."

"But there was no one—"

"Go, please. Leave at once."

"But—" He backed away.

"Up the hill. Find the bailiff. You have no business to be here." And with all the venom of a woman who saw in this wretched German not just a vulgar intruder but the man who would frustrate her newly made plans to have a house in Coustiers, she shooed him away like a pig that had strayed from the farm into the garden.

In the meantime, Bertrand had walked on alone as far as the river. While his rage persisted, he was conscious of nothing else, and of the thudding of his heart in his ears. But gradually his anger had subsided and was followed not by remorse but by dismay. His last words to Madeleine—"I would rather walk alone"—echoed in his mind and appalled him. He listened to them as if they had been spoken by someone else. Their parting seemed to signify far more than a decision to stroll in different directions. Would she take it to mean that he would rather live alone? That their marriage should end?

In panic he suddenly realized how easy it would be for Madeleine to withdraw from his life, either to return with Titine to Montpellier or live on her own in Coustiers. He would be alone with his parents at Saint Théodore, and the past six years would have counted for nothing. Was that what he wanted? Decidedly not. He loved Saint Théodore, and he loved his mother and father, but they were all things apart—things that had given him life—whereas Madeleine and Titine were part of that life itself.

He turned back toward the house. Perhaps, he thought, there was some justice in her complaints. Perhaps it was just because she loved him that she resented the place and the people that had nothing to do with her life with him. Certainly nothing at Saint Théodore bore the imprint of her personality. His parents had been accommodating, but only in the way they would accommodate a guest. He too had treated her as a visitor who had come for a long stay.

He hurried up the track. She would have her house in Coustiers, and to pay for it he would abandon the idea of investing in the vines. If this meant that he would have less claim to inherit the property from his father, that was the price he would have to pay to preserve his marriage.

He walked quickly through the gate into the garden, imagining that at this very moment Madeleine was packing her suitcase to leave him. Yet even as he rushed toward her, he wondered how best to present his change of mind, because even though he had come to acknowledge her grievance, he still felt a sense of grievance himself that she was not as receptive as a wife should be to the interests and aspirations of her husband.

Before he found Madeleine, however, he ran into his father in the hallway of the house.

"Ah, Bertrand," said Edmond de Roujay. "Everyone's been looking for you."

"I went for a walk."

"There's a young Boche come to see you."

Bertrand hit his forehead with the palm of his hand. "I'd completely forgotten."

"He went up to the farm to find Claude, but Claude said he knew nothing about it and sent him down here again."

"Where is he now?"

"He's waiting in the library."

Bertrand glanced at the passage leading to the library, then at the stairs. "I'll see him in a moment," he said to his father, turning away from him to run up the stairs.

Madeleine lay on their bed reading a novel. She did not look up when he came into the room.

"I'm sorry," he said, standing at the door. "You are quite right. We must have a proper home of our own. We'll get a house in Coustiers."

"What about the vines?"

"They can wait."

"The salesman's downstairs."

"I know. He'll be disappointed, but it can't be helped."

"Are you sure?"

"Yes." He glanced at her face to see if she was mollified. She was not looking at him, but instead was studying the split end of a hair from her head. "I must go down." He left her to run down the stairs to the library.

The young German was standing with his back to the door studying a map of France. He turned as Bertrand came into the room. His anger and humiliation were well hidden.

"I'm so sorry," said Bertrand.

"It doesn't matter. I am in no hurry."

Bertrand shook him warmly by the hand. "I had no idea it was so late."

"It is a lovely evening."

"Yes, indeed. You must come and see the vines. And I trust you will stay to dinner." The invitation came out without reflection, as the only expedient to make up for his rudeness, and to give him time before adding to it the disappointment of a canceled order.

"I should be delighted," said the young German, nodding with an affected graciousness.

"Excellent. My parents will be pleased." Bertrand opened the door and guided him out of the room. "As you can imagine, we are rather isolated here, so the arrival of a guest is quite an excitement. . . ."

2

If Madeleine de Roujay did not have her way about a house in Coustiers, it was not because Bertrand changed his mind yet again, but because he was told by the prefect, Wenkler, that the subprefect of Mézac must live there.

"Your parents' place is one thing," said the austere Alsatian. "We can overlook the time you spend there because it is their home, not yours. But if you or your wife sets up a separate establishment in Coustiers, it will look to the citizens of Mézac as if you consider yourselves too good for their city."

"Who could be too good for Mézac?" asked Bertrand with a smile.

Wenkler laughed. "Don't think I don't appreciate your dilemma, de Roujay. The provinces are the provinces, but there we are, it's part of our job, and our wives, I am afraid, have to put up with it too."

Madeleine accepted this setback with good grace. Her demands had been made in the heat of the moment, after the terrible lunch, and by the time Bertrand broke the news to her that they could not move to Coustiers, she had recalled all the advantages of keeping a distance between her personal life and her domestic responsibilities. Not only were there her studies at the university, but she had also become involved in organizing support for the Republican cause in the Spanish Civil War. After the fall of Málaga to the Nationalists in February of 1937, the first refugees had disembarked from their feluccas on the Mediterranean coast near the mouth of the Rhône. Many of them had

made their way to Coustiers, and Michel le Fresne had asked Madeleine
to join a committee to find them work and lodging.

Though Michel was only just thirty, his success had smoothed the
rough surface of the impatient student of their Montpellier days. His
ability had been acknowledged not just as a physician, but also as an
administrator. He was practical, decisive and extraordinarily energetic,
yet had a charm and good humor which invariably won over those
who disagreed with him. His superiors in the hospital were reassured
by the subtle mixture of deference and familiarity with which Michel
treated them, and they never forgot that he was the son-in-law of
Emile Planchet, who had furnished the hospital with many of its grants
and endowments.

It was also because of this link with Emile Planchet that Michel's
membership in the Communist Party was not seen as a threat, and
when Léon Blum formed his National Front government with Communist support, it was considered an actual advantage. Indeed, the
enemies Michel inevitably made among the junior doctors who resented his rapid rise would whisper that le Fresne had joined the Party
only after the election of '36, when he saw that things were going their
way.

To Madeleine, Michel's Marxism could not be opportunistic because
it conformed exactly to his scientific outlook. She had been brought
up to respect knowledge, as against intuition or superstition, and felt
the same veneration for the white coat of the surgeon and the smell
of carbolic acid as her mother-in-law did for a priest's vestments and
the aroma of incense. She also felt, because of their long friendship,
that she understood Michel better than others. Only those who saw the
surface scoffed at the Marxist living in luxury off his wife's private
income. She knew how he suffered from the dilemma presented by the
impetuous choice of his youth. He would have been much happier
dressing in shabby clothes instead of the smart suits which Nellie
bought for him and the manservant laid out for him to wear each day.
She felt that while Bertrand's idealism had become mired in the kind
of economic sophistry whereby it benefits the poor to lower their
wages, Michel's principles were sincere. He had no private practice, but
sacrificed the leisure he might have spent with his wife and children
to work at free clinics in the working-class suburbs of Coustiers.

This devotion to the cause of the working class seemed to Madeleine quite consistent with Michel's scientific attitude toward life. Workers were somehow more real than members of the middle class, and their cause consequently more true. Under Michel's tuition, she was increasingly inclined to accept that a proletarian revolution was both inevitable and good. In Spain it was quite apparent that only the Communists, with their ruthlessness and discipline, could defeat the Fascists; and a leader of the Communists in Coustiers like Georges Auget, whom Madeleine met through Michel, had a decency and a simplicity that came only from the trials and sufferings of a proletarian past.

The pomposity and affectation of her bourgeois friends were now odious to her. She longed for a greater simplicity in her own style of life, and saw in this simplicity the kind of personal liberation that Michel insisted would come with the revolution. He directed her to passages by Engels on the exploitation of women in marriage and family life, and Madeleine came to see in the constraints imposed upon her by her role as a wife, mother and daughter-in-law the burden of class oppression.

Bertrand was resigned to Madeleine's political opinions, and her inexorable move to the left. She was still young, after all, and her idealism did credit to her heart, if not her head. He looked on with a benign, almost paternal tolerance as she threw herself into political activities which he knew, from the police reports, were organized and directed by the Communists. Both he and Nellie were amused by their spouses' efforts to undermine the capitalist system within which both of them lived so well. Implicit in this tolerance, however, was a certain condescension. Like Nellie, Bertrand was confident that his own political conservatism was both economically sound and morally correct, but he recognized that it went with his wealth, and that those from a different background could not necessarily be expected to share his point of view.

This mild disdain for the social origins of their respective spouses formed a bond between Bertrand and Nellie. He was amused by her sardonic comments on her husband's "hobby," and at the same time was somewhat contemptuous of the way in which Michel professed convictions so utterly at odds with his way of life. This implicit ridicule enabled him to avoid the kind of disputes over political issues which might otherwise have made the friendship between the two couples impossible.

Only rarely did Bertrand's tolerance give way to his old resentment against Madeleine that she did not share his values or political convictions. It was usually when he was tired, and when some setback at the subprefecture had induced a mood of self-pity. One evening, for example, after he had worked a full day at his office, then driven to Coustiers to dine with Madeleine and the le Fresnes, then had driven back to Mézac with Madeleine, reaching home at one in the morning, he had come to bed to find her deep in an article in a magazine of Marxist thought called *Coustiers Prolétarien*.

"I don't know how you can stomach that rubbish," he said.

"To each his own kind of rubbish," she said, glancing at the crucifix before which Bertrand had just said some perfunctory prayers.

"Do you really believe in a classless society?" he asked.

"Do you really believe in heaven?"

"That doesn't answer my question."

"I think it's worth a try."

"They haven't done very well in Moscow."

"They've made a start."

"At a cost."

"What cost?"

"Famine, massacres . . ."

She looked him squarely in the eye. "There have always been famine and massacres, but before they served no purpose."

"Whereas now they will lead to paradise?"

"Not paradise, no, but a better life for the poor whom you Christians call blessed but leave to rot in their slums."

"That's not true."

"Oh, I grant you the odd nursing sister or Curé d'Ars, but most of you talk about loving your neighbor as you plunder the colonies and speculate on the Bourse."

"And if we sold all our stocks and shares and gave the money to the poor, what would be the result? A few full stomachs for a day or a week, then a total collapse of the world economy and empty stomachs for all forever."

"Nonsense. The state would invest—"

"With what?"

"Its revenues."

"Raised how?"

"Through taxation."

"How can you tax people who have given all they have to the poor?"

"Through profits, then, on its own enterprises."

"So the state becomes the capitalist?"

"Yes."

"And that's all right?"

"Yes."

"Why?"

"The state is the people."

"The state is *not* the people," said Bertrand. "The state is an oligarchy of politicians and civil servants quite as selfish and ruthless as any capitalist."

"They act in the interests of the people," Madeleine retorted.

"They act in the interest of their cronies like Stavisky."

"While capitalists, I suppose, are only out to help the poor?" She laughed with a forced derision.

"A capitalist works for profits because without profits his enterprise goes under. But there are many capitalists like my uncles in Valenciennes who are quite as sensitive to the needs of their workers as the Communist commissars are to theirs."

"Ah," she said in a mocking tone of voice. "We always come back to the same argument: the exemplary nature of the Ravanels and the de Roujays!"

"At least they don't murder their opponents."

"Like Franco!"

"That's entirely different."

"Of course it's different. He's blessed by your Church, and as a result he'll go to heaven, along with all the Ravanels and the de Roujays, in the bishop of Langeais's limousine!"

As the Nationalists under Franco advanced in Spain, more men and women with Republican sympathies fled to France. Madeleine spent more of her time helping these refugees obtain work and lodging, and papers to legitimize their residence in France. As the wife of the subprefect of Mézac, she could hardly involve herself in the more controversial work of raising money for the International Brigade. That was undertaken by Michel le Fresne, who confided to his friends that but for instructions from the Central Committee of the Party to remain at his post at the hospital in Coustiers he would himself have enlisted in its ranks.

Madeleine did not resent the restrictions imposed upon her political activities by her husband's position. Quite the contrary, she found it particularly useful when badgering lesser officials on behalf of her wretched Spaniards. On occasions she would even bypass the bureaucracy and go straight to Bertrand to settle some question of a work permit or decree of naturalization. Partly to prove to his wife that he had a conscience, Bertrand always did what he could to help.

The greatest difficulty facing Madeleine and her committee was not the immediate housing of those refugees who reached Coustiers or Mézac, because makeshift camps had been made out of redundant army barracks and *colonies de vacances,* but the implementation of the next stage, which was to move the families out of the camps and integrate them into the local community. It was here that they came up against not just the shortage of housing but also the enmity of the local population, who feared that the Spaniards would take their jobs. They had also to overcome the pedantry and mistrust of the government officials, who, despite the sympathy of Blum and his ministers for the Republican cause, were invariably antipathetic toward the refugees.

At the end of June 1937, when the school term came to an end, Titine and Miss Spinks moved to Saint Théodore. Bertrand went out whenever he could, but Madeleine, though her term had also ended, remained mostly in Coustiers. At times Bertrand felt angry that Titine saw so little of her mother and that he dined alone so often when his work kept him in Mézac, but she seemed so happy working for the Spanish refugees that it seemed churlish to suggest that she should abandon it simply to sit at table in the flat above the subprefecture, or come out to Saint Théodore to take Titine for a ride by the river.

There was also a better atmosphere at Saint Théodore when Madeleine was not there. His father and mother were more at ease without her, and when Louis was staying the two brothers could argue about politics as they had done as boys without the severe eye of Madeleine judging them from across the table. Bertrand also discovered that he liked having his daughter to himself. Marthe and Miss Spinks saw to her practical needs and were ready at any point to take her off his hands, but when he chose to go riding with her or swimming in the river, her laughing eyes were on him alone and there was no rival for her affectionate attention.

In the middle of July, Madeleine came out for the weekend. It was so hot that no one went out of the house between eleven in the morning and four in the afternoon, but on Saturday evening Bertrand and Madeleine took advantage of the cooler evening air to escape from the rest of the family and walk in the woods behind the house.

They were both in an amiable mood, for as with most married couples, the bad patches were interspersed with good ones. Absence had made both hearts grow fonder. Bertrand was obliged to recognize once again that Madeleine had flourished with a certain measure of independence—her eyes were as bright and her skin as fresh as when he had first met her—and she was undoubtedly grateful that her husband made no fuss about her protracted absences in Coustiers.

"Do you mind if we go by the farm?" Bertrand asked.

"No. Why?"

"I want to see Claude."

"Will he be sober?"

"I doubt it."

They came out of the woods and entered the large yard of ramshackle buildings which had been built on the ruins of the medieval monastery. Bertrand went to the bailiff's house, built in the shell of the original refectory, and after knocking at the door was let in.

Waiting for her husband, Madeleine sauntered over to the four other cottages which had been made from the monks' cells. Three of them had curtains covering the windows. The fourth, though not derelict, seemed empty.

"Who lives here?" she asked Bertrand when he returned.

"No one at present."

"Is it for a worker?"

"We don't really need another man." He glanced at her uneasily, as if she might attack him for throwing a man out of work.

Instead, Madeleine took his arm again and said, "Do you think it would be possible—would your father consider it, do you think—to lease it to a family of refugees?"

Bertrand frowned. "Lease it? And give them a job?"

"No. I mean, that would be wonderful if you needed a man, but for the time being all most of them need is to get out of the camps and have a roof over their heads."

"But what would they live on?"

"We have funds enough to feed them."

They walked down the hill toward the house.

"I don't see why not," said Bertrand. "I'll have to talk to my father."

"Of course."

"He may not like the idea of a Bolshevik at his back door."

"They aren't all Bolsheviks, and even those who are are so wretched that they couldn't frighten anyone."

"All right. I'll try."

Bertrand waited until Madeleine had returned to Coustiers before approaching his parents on the question of the cottage.

"But what kind of people are they?" asked Alice de Roujay. "Won't they murder us in our beds?"

"I'm sure they won't, Maman. It's far more likely that Claude will get alcoholic poisoning and go berserk with a scythe."

"Won't we need the cottage for a man?" asked Edmond.

"Only for the harvest, and then the Spaniards can help. We can make it a condition."

His mother still looked dismayed. "But how are we to know that they won't be the murderers of priests?"

"We can't be certain," said Bertrand, "but I think it unlikely. The fanatics are almost certainly still fighting in Spain."

She sighed. "Oh dear, oh dear. Do you really think we must?"

"Here are people without homes—" said Bertrand.

"Through their own damned fault," his father interrupted.

"Maybe so, but are we not told that we must love and forgive our enemies?"

"Yes, Edmond," said Alice. "We must set an example. Think how it will seem to Madeleine if we refuse." She glanced at Bertrand, because, like most mothers, she knew more about his marriage than he supposed.

The family sent by Madeleine a week later were named Astran. In all there were five, but the eldest son remained in Spain, fighting in the ranks of the Republican army, and the father would no doubt have done the same had he not been wounded in the leg at the siege of Málaga. He was a dark, taciturn man whose brooding eyes were hard to read; it was impossible to tell whether he was grateful for the cottage or considered it too mean a dwelling. Only when Bertrand told him that the rooms had once been monks' cells did a sour smile come to the man's rough, dark-skinned face.

His wife was friendlier toward her benefactors. She spoke no French but repeatedly thanked Bertrand in her own language, and when presented to Alice knelt and kissed her hand beneath the contemptuous gaze of her husband and eldest daughter.

This girl, Lucía, was apparently married, but her husband, like her brother, had remained in Spain. Her manner suggested that she wished she had done the same; less controlled than her father, she seemed to glower with contempt for Bertrand and his parents. She was pretty, a wild Carmen who as soon as she got out of the little Renault in which Madeleine had brought her to Saint Théodore made Bertrand feel uneasy. Though susceptible to the beauty of women, he almost always required in them a conventional elegance to which he could ascribe his feelings. This Spanish girl was dirty, hot and dressed almost in rags, and yet the sight of her unsettled him.

Tagging along beside Lucía was the fourth member of the family, a boy of around thirteen, and it was clear from the way Lucía tried to avoid standing beside him that she felt humiliated to find herself back in the fold of the family. Sensing this, the younger brother kept teasing her as if she were not a married woman in her twenties but a girl of around his age. She edged away, muttering to him in Spanish and occasionally swatting him like a fly.

The Astrans had few belongings. The cottage was furnished with a table and chairs and two beds, but when it became apparent that it was insufficient for a family of four, Bertrand returned to his parents' house and went with his mother to the attics, which were filled with sturdy pieces of furniture brought from Valenciennes when she married.

"They might like this," said Alice de Roujay, pointing to a chest of drawers. "It's perfectly good. I don't know why it was brought up here."

"There's no room for it downstairs."

She sighed. "Don't you need anything else in Mézac?"

"No. We have enough."

"It's rather good for the cottage," she said, looking wistfully at the chest of drawers, "but still, in for a penny, in for a pound. . . . We'll get Claude and some of the men to take it up there."

She went farther into the attic. This charitable venture aroused her enthusiasm. Her neighbors had been astonished that she and Edmond had agreed to house these Spanish Bolsheviks, but the curé had preached a sermon the Sunday before commending those who had the courage and magnanimity to live out their faith "with audacity, and take risks as fishers of men."

It was therefore a slight anticlimax when, once the Astrans were installed, the de Roujays barely saw them. Even Claude, the bailiff, and the other workers who lived side by side with the Spaniards, and had at first been angry that they were to be housed in the empty cottage, reported that the family kept discreetly to themselves. The wife would walk to the village to do her shopping, and the wounded husband would sometimes hobble along with her and drink a glass of wine at the bar. The married daughter, Lucía, soon moved away to take a job in Mézac, and it was chiefly the mischievous thirteen-year-old boy who, scampering around the property, made their presence noticed at all.

By the winter of 1937 it became apparent that the war in Spain would continue for some time, that the Republicans might lose, and that the Popular Front government in France, which was sympathetic to the Spanish refugees, might itself fall and be replaced by a coalition of the center and right. It therefore became important for Madeleine and her committee to obtain French nationality for the Spaniards under their protection. For this Bertrand's position as subprefect became increasingly useful, and though he used his influence sparingly, it was invariably effective when he brought it into play.

Among those whose papers he supervised himself were the Astrans'. One Thursday afternoon in early December, some documents which they had to sign appeared on his desk, and rather than post them to Saint Théodore he put them in his briefcase to deliver in person the next day.

At seven he left his office and went up to the apartment above his office. Madeleine was not there—she had been in Coustiers all week—but Titine was waiting with her nanny, and he read her a story before sending her to bed.

He ate supper alone, and afterward went to the drawing room to work on some papers he had brought up from his office. As he took them out of his briefcase he noticed the documents on the Astrans' naturalization, and seeing the address of their daughter, Lucía, he remembered that she no longer lived at Saint Théodore but was working now in Mézac.

He knew the street where she lived—a ten-minute walk away near the vegetable market—so he decided he would deliver the documents before going to work the next day. Better yet, since it was an agreeable evening, he would saunter over there at once while smoking a cigarette and hand them to the concierge.

He remembered the angry, attractive Lucía and was curious to know what she had made of herself in Mézac. When he came to the dark and dingy building where she lived, he realized that of course she must have little money and would be living in the cheapest of dwellings. The door to the tenement was open; he walked in, rapped on the window of the concierge's door, and when a thick-necked man looked out, asked for Lucía Astran.

"In a maid's room at the top," said the man, who then immediately shut the window before Bertrand had time to hand him the envelope he held ready in his hand.

He was about to knock again but then thought that he might as well call on her if she was at home and have her sign the paper then and there so that he could take it back to his office the next morning.

He walked up the stairs holding the letter, and at the top came to a small landing from which corridors branched off in two directions. He turned to the left and went down a narrow tunnel with dirty green walls lit by a naked bulb. The first door he passed was ajar, but from the smell he knew that it was the lavatory. The next had a name written in Arabic on a card. So too the third. He came to a corner where the corridor branched yet again. Set into the wall was a brass tap which dripped into a small cast-iron basin.

Again he turned left, and after studying one or two names in semiliterate handwriting he came to one which had the name of Lucía Rodríguez de Astran. Light shone from its rim. He knocked. There was a silence, then a rustle of movement. Finally a voice asked in Spanish, "Who's there?"

"Señora Rodríguez," he said, "it is Bertrand de Roujay."

There was another pause, then the sound of feet on the floor, a key in the lock, and the door was opened. The light was behind her head, and he could not see her features, but was immediately conscious of the sweet aroma of cheap soap.

"Come in," she said.

He entered a small room which a sloping roof made smaller still for a man of his height. He stood for a moment, confused by his confinement, for there was nowhere he could walk to and nowhere to sit but on the bed.

"I have brought some papers for you to sign," he said awkwardly.

She nodded. Her face showed little expression. He could not tell if she was irritated, embarrassed or indifferent to his intrusion.

"Please sit down." She pointed to the bed.

He sat on the edge. "I thought I would take your parents papers to Saint Théodore tomorrow, but I did not know if you would be there."

"No."

She took the papers and sat opposite him on a small stool. She wore a blouse and a skirt, but had bare legs and feet. "I do not really understand this," she said, speaking slowly and carefully in a guttural French.

"You don't have to," said Bertrand. "Not, that is, if you trust me."

She looked up at him and shrugged her shoulders as if to say that she had no alternative.

"Or my wife," Bertrand added, recognizing that she hardly knew him.

She put the papers down on the bed. "May I offer you something?" she asked.

"Not really."

"I have some coffee."

"Only if it's no trouble." He had no wish to drink anything, but the pathos of her offer of hospitality made it impossible to refuse.

She stood and went to a corner of the room, where there was a small electric ring. She leaned over to take a jug of water from behind a curtain and poured some of it into a cooking pan, which she set upon the electric ring. She did all this with grace and dignity, as if her garret were a handsome and spacious apartment.

"How are you getting on in Mézac?" asked Bertrand.

She shrugged her shoulders. "I have a job."

"Doing what?"

"Cleaning."

"What did you do in Spain?"

"I was a student."

"Where?"

"Madrid."

"What subject?"

"Political economy."

"Did you take your degree?"

"Yes. Then I married." She shrugged her shoulders and watched the water in the pan.

"And your husband?"

"He is a worker."

"Like your father."

"Yes." She turned and looked at him with an expression of aggressive pride, as if workers were a family of far greater distinction than the de Roujays or even the Bourbons.

"What was his work?"

"Now it is killing Fascists," she said.

When the water came to a boil she poured it into a pot into which she had already put two spoonfuls of coffee. She stirred it with the spoon and then, while waiting for it to mull, prepared two cups with saucers and spoons. Bertrand watched all these movements, because they were performed with delicacy and care, as if Lucía had long looked forward to serving someone in this way.

"Have you made some friends in Mézac?" he asked.

"A few. I don't like . . ." She stopped, confused.

"The French?"

"They despise us." She handed him a cup of coffee and held out a bowl of sugar. As he took a cube, he noticed the fine black hairs on the skin of her wrist.

"They're afraid," he said. "There is already so much unemployment."

She nodded, and taking her own cup of coffee she sat down at the head of the bed, her knee raised, one foot on the mattress to hold her back against the wall.

"Wouldn't you be better off at Saint Théodore?" he asked.

"There's no work."

"We could find some for you."

She shook her head. "I can't live with my parents," she said. "They treat me like a child."

"Yes."

"Then I behave like a child. I start to quarrel with my brother."

"I can understand." He drank his coffee, then, since there was nowhere to put the cup near at hand, leaned forward to set it down on the bedside table next to Lucia. As he did so, his face came close to hers. She looked at him with a mixed expression of alarm and excitement, a look which at once made the empty cup seem but a pretext for his proximity, and Bertrand, who until that moment had not thought of an untoward gesture, found himself held by his nearness to her body. His eyes looked into hers, but he sensed the strength of her shoulders and the mounds of her breasts under her blouse. Their two bodies were inches apart. His heart beat in his ears. All at once he felt the enormity of what he envisaged, and might at that point have drawn back, had he not seen in her eyes such an anguish and longing that he took hold of her and clasped her and made love to her as she wept with mixed ecstasy and shame.

In the weeks which followed it was as if two different people took possession of Bertrand de Roujay—one a radiant creature from the animal kingdom whose verve and high spirits proclaimed the triumph and delight of the successful lover, the other a baffled, cowering, conscience-stricken sinner who had jeopardized the happiness of his family and at the same time consigned his soul to hell.

The two did not coexist; the one stepped out as the other stepped in. Deep in his mind, formed by the Jesuits in Mézac, there was a real fear of hell, but equally awful and more immediate was the danger of scandal and divorce. Bertrand, the guilty adulterer, lay in bed with his wife, confident that she could not know what he had done, but terrified of what she would suffer if she did. The sight of Titine, too, filled him with remorse, and when he returned home each evening after visiting Lucía, he embraced her with all the more fervor.

No guilt or anxiety, however, could repress the joy which possessed him when the cowering sinner stepped out of his skin and the triumphant male returned, to anticipate or to remember making love with Lucía. These bouts in her garret, snatched from a busy day, were more than sessions of pleasure. They were lessons which taught him what he had never known before about the power of human sexuality and the paradoxical nature of women.

He knew, for example, that Lucía dearly loved her husband and loathed betraying him, and that each time he came to see her she was violated not by his impetuosity but by her own intense desires. The most graphic instance of the perversity of her passion came one evening when Bertrand found her on her bed with blotched eyes, clutching a telegram informing her that her husband had been killed.

For a time she wailed in words he could not understand, while he tried to comfort her with phrases of conventional solace. Then, from respect for her grief, he rose to leave her alone, but she clung to him and, with her eyes closed, drew him down over her body. The sobs of sorrow became the gasps of desire, and she made love to him with a frenzy he had never known before.

Now Bertrand's work, his family and the political events which would otherwise have preoccupied him were all forgotten for his dark-skinned Spaniard. He became obsessed by her body, for while Madeleine had never lost a sense of privacy, Lucía was obedient to the maxim of Montaigne that a woman should shed her modesty with her clothes. She was happy to let Bertrand use her body as he pleased. Her pleasure induced his pleasure, and his pleasure induced hers, and she altered not just his qualities as a lover by reproaching him for his briskness and laughing at his modesty, but also, in some sense, his qualities as a man. The fastidious, somewhat snobbish subprefect of Mézac came to welcome the sight of the grim green walls of the corridor which led to her room and the smell of the lavatory at the top of the stairs. He loved the cramped, tatty room, the pot on the electric ring. Her cheap skirts and blouses were more beautiful to him than a whole wardrobe of fashionable dresses, and her dingy underclothes, her vests and petticoats, took on the power of holy relics to inspire an irrational devotion.

But he did not love Lucía, and he took it that she did not love him. Each felt gratitude toward the other, and there was even an amused affection when, for example, lying in bed together, Bertrand tried to teach her to speak better French. They evolved certain private words, they had little quarrels, but it was always understood that he only saw her to sleep with her, and that when he no longer wished to do so, he would not see her at all.

Because he did not love her, Bertrand's reinvigorated sexuality was not confined to Lucía, but like a wild beast prowled at large. Suddenly he became aware of the women who worked at the subprefecture—not just the younger secretaries, some of whom had pretty faces or figures, but also the older women, whom as they walked to and fro or leaned over their desks he saw only as white haunches astride hirsute orifices. If he did not pounce on them, it was only because there were others present, and because none of them was sufficiently desirable to remain in his mind once she had left the room.

More problematic were the women whom he met in the course of his social life, women who were not only more attractive but also more plausible as sexual partners. There was not one of them whom he did not imagine naked beneath him, not so much from desire as from curiosity to know how each would behave as a lover. All social conventions—games, dances, even conversation—now seemed to him mere ersatz copulation. Tennis, chatting and flirting were the tame evasions of those with no stomach for the real thing.

He understood the reasons for these evasions, for though crazed at times by his newfound lust he was sane enough to acknowledge that the stability of the family, and therefore of society at large, depended upon a long-lasting bond between the mother and father of a child. This was why he concealed his liaison with Lucía not just from Madeleine, but from everyone else as well. But having seen that he could get away with one, it was inevitable that in time he should consider another—inevitable that the curiosity which each woman aroused in him should on some occasion demand to be satisfied.

With most women in society, as with most women in his office, the desire and curiosity rarely outlasted their presence in the room. There was one, however, whose image nagged at him with an augmenting persistence. This was Nellie le Fresne. He could never look at her now without remembering how he had been drawn to her on the first day he had met her, as he had ridden behind her through her father's olive groves.

She was older now and had born three children, but despite her heavier figure and her fuller face she retained her sullen sexuality, that sour, taunting manner which seemed to defy Bertrand, or any other man, to draw the compliant girl from the matter-of-fact matron. While Madeleine was harassed and preoccupied by her pursuits outside the home, Nellie showed no interest in anything but luxury, comfort and love.

Yet the idea of seducing her scandalized Bertrand's residual sense of honor. Not only was she Madeleine's closest friend, but her husband, Michel, was supposedly a friend of his, and in the code of honour of a Provençal it was worse to cuckold a comrade than it was to deceive one's wife. But it was not easy to shake her off. He saw her all the time and often alone. There were many occasions when Bertrand arrived at the Villa Acacia, after a day's work at Mézac, to find that Michel was still at the hospital and Madeleine at the university.

At first this had irritated Bertrand, who had himself taken the trouble to leave his office promptly, but later he came to enjoy these moments alone with Nellie in her home. She exuded a certain serenity, and the hospitality she provided seemed to spring from the patient solicitude of her feminine nature. Bertrand, who had little of such care from his own wife, was particularly susceptible to the small ministrations she provided. As soon as he came through the door Nellie would greet him with her matter-of-fact smile, then would send for the servants to bring him tea or pastis or whatever he demanded, and while he washed his hands in the cloakroom (where there was always a clean white towel) she would move through to the sitting room and wait there in one of the deep armchairs facing the door, as if impatient to hear his news of the day.

Bertrand would come in and sit opposite while the manservant, in his white tunic, would bring in not just the tea or the pastis, but always, if it was tea, a plate of petits fours or, if it was pastis, a variety of carefully prepared hors d'oeuvres.

Before his affair with Lucía, Bertrand had accepted this solicitude as no more than an expression of courtesy, but when he came to regard all social niceties as sexual shadow-acting, it was inevitable that he should be enticed by this hospitality and contemplate gestures that would make the shadow-acting real. Yet the more the idea pressed upon his imagination, the more appalled he became at the monstrousness of what he envisaged. It was one thing for an erotic adventure to evolve into a friendship, quite another for a friendship to change,

after so many years, into a love affair. Nellie would certainly think
him mad if he suggested it—mad, disgusting, depraved—and since she
had such a sharp, sardonic manner, he quailed in anticipation of the
contempt she would level at him were he to cross the room from one
armchair to the other and bridge the chasm which separates the con-
vivial from the carnal in the bond between man and woman.

And yet there was something in her manner which drew him nearer
and nearer to the edge. With Michel and Madeleine, they chatted about
this and that, played cards together, or went to the cinema; they dined
out with others—always the four of them, two couples, old friends.
He took to studying her minutely, like a scientist with his eye to the
microscope, for evidence to suggest some attraction to him, but there
was none—not a glance, not a gesture, not a blush, not the flutter of
an eyelid—only the solicitude, the pleasure in his company, the nod
of recognition when he came into the room. Without doubt she
looked upon him as nothing more than a friend, and to try to change
that would ruin the friendship not just between him and Nellie, but
between him and Michel too, for she would consider it her duty to
tell her husband and he in his turn might tell Madeleine, if only to
prove his point about the decadence and hypocrisy of Catholic capitalists, and Madeleine . . .

Bertrand trembled at the thought of how Madeleine would react
to the knowledge of his infidelity. The idealist is intolerant of imper-
fection, and he had never heard her speak of unfaithful husbands
without the greatest disdain. How could she understand how he felt?
Her own innocence and inexperience, and her indifference to sexual
feelings, would make lust seem foul and inexcusable. It would quite
undermine not just her trust in him but the image of the courtly knight
that had first won her heart in Montpellier. She would certainly
divorce him; he would be faced once again with a life without either
a wife or a child.

The clarity with which Bertrand saw the dreadful consequences of
attempting to seduce Nellie le Fresne did not diminish his longing to
sleep with her. Not only when he was with her, but both at home with
Madeleine and with his colleagues at work images of Nellie passed in
and out of his mind: not the Nellie he knew—elegant, sour, witty,
assured—but Nellie as he had never known her—naked, gasping,

obscene. It reached a point where he ran to Lucía to relieve the lust aroused by this image of Nellie, but while her attentions sated his physical appetite, his mind remained a flame, and he would lie beside the hot-blooded, dark-skinned Spaniard imagining the cool white limbs of the olive-oil princess.

In April 1938, the government fell. The Popular Front disintegrated and the Radicals under Daladier formed a coalition with the parties to their right. On the Friday which followed this political reversal, the de Roujays and the le Fresnes were dining at Bessier's in Coustiers— the two Socialists gloomy, the two Conservatives doing what they could to conceal their satisfaction.

As they were sipping their coffee at the end of dinner, a friend of Bertrand's from his army days, Philippe de Gateny, who had been dining with two or three other couples at the back of the restaurant, passed their table and stopped to greet him. Bertrand introduced him to Madeleine and the le Fresnes, whereupon Philippe de Gateny invited them all to a party at his house. "Something to celebrate, eh? We can get things shipshape at last."

"Of course," said Bertrand. "We'll see you later on."

De Gateny left the restaurant, whereupon Madeleine looked furiously at her husband and said, "You have charming friends!"

"He's not so bad," said Bertrand.

"Not my type," said Michel.

"Is he the de Gateny who married Ariane de Bedoit?" asked Nellie.

"Yes," said Bertrand. "Do you know her?"

"No, but I've heard about her chintz curtains."

"Now is your chance to see them."

"I have no intention whatsoever," said Madeleine fiercely, "of celebrating the fall of the Popular Front with a gang of reactionary officers."

"Oh, don't be so prim," said Bertrand. "You depend on reactionaries like that to keep Hitler on the other side of the Rhine."

"One depends upon the plumber to keep the shit in the sewer," said Michel, "but one doesn't go to his party."

"It's not the same thing," said Bertrand.

"I'd love to see their house," said Nellie.

"You'd dine with Goering," said Michel, "just to see the color of his curtains."

"There's more to life than politics," said Nellie.

Bertrand called for the bill. "What do you want to do?" he asked Madeleine.

"Anything but go to that party."

"Come back to the villa," said Michel.

"I'm sick of the villa," said Nellie. "I'm stuck there all day."

"Let's look in at the party," said Bertrand. "We needn't stay long."

"Yes," said Nellie.

"You go," said Michel. "I'd rather go home and read a book."

"So would I," said Madeleine, yawning.

"What fun!" said Nellie. "We can all sit around reading Marx."

"Go with Bertrand to the party, then," said Michel, "and I'll take Madeleine back to the villa."

Nellie glanced at Bertrand, Bertrand at his wife.

"Go ahead," said Madeleine. "Don't let me stop you."

"All right," said Bertrand. "We'll go for half an hour and then join you back at the villa."

Bertrand and Nellie dropped Michel and Madeleine at the villa and then drove back toward Coustiers until they reached the gates of the de Gatenys' house.

"I drive past these gates every day," said Nellie to Bertrand. "I always wanted to know what it was like inside."

She said this in her usual matter-of-fact tone of voice, as if this curiosity explained and excused going out with Bertrand alone, but the very fact that she felt it necessary to excuse and explain this excursion was the first intimation to Bertrand that she recognized its other potentialities. They turned in through the gates and parked their car behind half a dozen others in the driveway.

"Good heavens," said Nellie. "It's a real party. I should have changed."

"They hadn't changed," said Bertrand.

"That's true." She opened the door to the car. "Anyway, we're only here to see the curtains."

They were met at the entrance by a maid, who took their coats, and by a manservant holding a tray of glasses, some filled with whiskey, others with champagne. Bertrand took one of the former, Nellie one of the latter, and together they pushed forward into the crowded drawing room.

"Ah, Roujay!" shouted Philippe de Gateny, extracting himself from the throng and coming toward his newly arrived guests. "You've made it. Well done." He took the arm of a woman who stood near him. "Ariane. Come here a minute. Come and meet Bertrand de Roujay."

A younger, smartly dressed woman turned and was introduced to Bertrand. "And Madame de Roujay," her husband said, pointing to Nellie.

"No," said Bertrand. "She wasn't feeling well. This is Nellie le Fresne."

"Of course," said Ariane de Gateny. "Don't you live up the road?"

"That's right."

"I've always wanted to meet you. How very nice."

They were dragged forward and introduced to a group of the de Gatenys' friends, some of whom were acquaintances of Bertrand, others of Nellie. Coustiers was a large town, but there were no circles among the upper classes which did not touch at some point on their circumference.

They drank; their glasses were refilled. They emptied them again. "Come and dance," said Ariane de Gateny to Bertrand. "We've made a nightclub in the children's nursery."

Bertrand went with his hostess along the corridor of their modern house. He could not understand why Nellie had wanted to see inside; it seemed to be decorated in no particular style at all. They reached a large room which was dimly lit with colored lights. Jazz blared from the gramophone, and five or six couples were dancing furiously. They moved onto the floor and were picked up by the rhythm. Bertrand was too drunk to be self-conscious. He cavorted along with all the others, watching Ariane de Gateny's wobbling bosom and vacuous smile.

The music stopped. They left the dance floor and went back along the corridor to the throng in the drawing room. There Ariane drifted away and Bertrand went in search of Nellie, whom he found sitting back on a sofa, chatting to two men who by their manner were certainly officers in the army.

"Do you want to go?" she asked Bertrand.

"After a dance."

"Is there dancing?"

"In the nursery."

With a smile at the two other men Nellie lifted herself off the sofa

and followed Bertrand back down the corridor. Once again there was
fast music on the turntable. They danced, Nellie moving in time to
the Negro rhythm with the same efficiency and formality that she
applied to everything else. She looked into his eyes with no particular
expression in her own.

The music changed and became slow. Now convention allowed him
to put his arm around her waist and hold one hand in his. It also
allowed them to move together in time to the music, and specified no
distance that they should be apart. Nor, in the colored gloom, could
anyone see what parts of their bodies were touching.

Inch by inch he moved closer, waiting for the moment when Nellie
would recognize that his touch had gone beyond convention and resist
him. But the moment did not come. His edging body met no resistance,
but rather encountered a reciprocal movement in hers. First came the
moment when her breast touched his chest, a mere brush which might
have been ascribed to the crowd; then the time when her bosom was
clearly and deliberately held to his, its softness a pleasure to him, his
strength a pleasure to her. Encouraged by this, they moved closer still,
his hand squeezing her hand, his cheek touching her cheek, until his
nose was nuzzling her neck and his legs became entwined with hers.

It was only at a break in the music, when they were obliged to stand
apart, that he looked into her face and saw in her downturned smile
that she understood quite well what was going on.

They danced a little longer and then left the floor, because somewhere in the back of his mind Bertrand was afraid that those who knew
they were not man and wife would notice their manner of dancing.
They walked along the corridor, still holding hands, both their bodies
aching.

"Should we go back?" he asked.

"I want to see upstairs," she whispered. She let go of his hand and
started up the steps.

Bertrand hesitated for a moment and then followed, climbing
around the other guests who sat chatting and drinking in their path.

There was a maid at the top of the stairs. "Do you want your coat,
madame?" she asked.

"No," said Nellie. She went to the door of the de Gatenys' bedroom,
knowing that Bertrand was behind her.

"There's your chintz," he said, standing close enough to sniff the scent of her hair and looking in over her shoulder through the open door at the ornate decoration of the room.

"Yes," she said. "Too much of it."

She turned away and continued down the landing. Bertrand followed. She looked in at another bedroom. "Too fussy," she said.

At the end of the landing they came to a corridor, and at the end of the corridor was a small guest bedroom with a plain double bed.

"That's better," she said.

"No chintz," said Bertrand.

"But good taste. I like that blue." She pointed to the curtains and went in as if to examine the fabric. Bertrand followed and stood behind her, once again inhaling the scent of her hair.

She felt the material. "Not bad, don't you think?" She turned, her face up against his.

"Not bad," said Bertrand.

Their lips touched. He held her and kissed her. Her lips were soft, like marshmallows.

"You'd better shut the door," she whispered.

He crossed the room, shut the door and turned the key in the lock. They kissed again, and his hands moved over her body. "Nellie," he whispered.

"Shush." Her eyes had changed. The scorn had gone.

They kissed again. Her clothes and hair became disheveled. He felt under her skirt the taut silk that encased her legs, then higher to the warm soft flesh that bulged out at the tops of her stockings.

They moved toward the bed. "I've always wanted . . ."

"Always," she murmured, lying back and drawing him toward her.

He moved over her, and with his fingers burrowing in silk and lace he uncovered parts of her body he had never seen before. As he did so he kissed them softly with his lips. Her breathing grew heavy. She clutched at him. Her blouse was unbuttoned, her huge white breasts exposed, but the sight of what he had touched only a moment before, and their difference from the breasts of the childless Lucía, suddenly made Bertrand remember that Nellie was a mother of three children by another man. He stopped, paralyzed. The thought had brought home to him the enormity of what they were doing.

"What is it?" asked Nellie, sitting up on the bed. "Is someone coming?"

"No."

"You locked the door, didn't you?"

"Yes."

"Good." She looked back into his face, smiled, put her arm around his neck. "Come along, then."

"We can't."

"Why not?"

"Think of the children."

"They won't know."

"And Michel and Madeleine."

"They won't know either."

"They would sense it."

"Nonsense." She smiled and gave another tug at his neck. "Come on," she whispered in his ear.

"I can't."

"Don't be silly."

"It risks too much."

"It risks nothing." She was beginning to sound impatient.

"If they knew."

"If they knew," she mimicked. "They won't know."

"We couldn't hide it."

"Of course we could."

"We see too much of one another."

"Don't be absurd."

"They would sense it." He gently took hold of her hands on his neck and broke them apart.

"*You* haven't sensed it," she said in exasperation.

"Sensed what?"

"What *they've* been up to."

"What have they been up to?"

She smiled and put her arms around his neck again. "My poor little Bertrand. You really haven't a clue."

"About what?"

"They've been screwing for months, my darling idiot, perhaps even for years."

"When?"

"When? All the time. All those committee meetings, all those seminars, all those emergencies at the hospital."

"I don't believe it."

She shrugged her shoulders. "Please yourself."

"She wouldn't."

"That, no doubt, is what she says about you."

"She's incapable of it."

"And you?"

"I'm different."

"We're all the same," said Nellie. "Two arms, two legs and . . . all the rest."

Bertrand had turned white. "Then now . . ."

"Of course. They don't want us to hurry back."

"In your bed?"

"In the spare room."

"How do you know?"

"Michel told me."

"Why?"

"He hates deceit."

"He didn't tell me."

"Ah, no. His principles have their limits."

"What a swine."

"What a swine," she repeated mockingly. "And what are you doing with his wife?"

He turned and looked at her, half undressed. "I don't know."

"I suppose you're no longer in the mood," she said.

He shook his head. "I'm sorry."

"Another time." She started to button up her blouse.

"I can't believe it."

"Let's go and look," she said. "Perhaps they're still at it."

"The tart!"

"Oh yes," she said, again in a tone of amused mockery. "All women who like sex are tarts, and all men who like sex are jolly good fellows."

He scowled. "Come on."

They left the room, collected their coats and went down the stairs. Neither of the de Gatenys was to be seen, and their guests lolled around on the floor. Only the manservant seemed to be sober; he opened the door as they left and closed it behind them.

Like thieves they left the car at the entrance to the le Fresnes' villa and crept up the drive into the garden.

"No lights in the bedroom," said Bertrand.

"One can do it in the dark," said Nellie.

They walked across the lawn to the glass-paned door to the drawing room. Lights were on behind the curtains, but only a gap of a few inches remained open between them.

"You won't be able to see much," whispered Nellie.

But Bertrand saw enough. Madeleine lay on the sofa, her head on the lap of Michel le Fresne. Both were reading. She held her book in her two hands; his was propped against her bosom, while his hand gently stroked her hair. Then, as Bertrand watched, Madeleine put her finger on the page of the book to mark her place and looked up to ask Michel a question. He answered. She smiled, and for a moment looked on into his eyes. Then she returned to her book with a sigh, and it was that sigh, and that look, which convinced Bertrand that everything Nellie had said was true.

Nellie went into the villa, and by the time she had removed her coat and had crossed the hall to the drawing room, Madeleine had sat up on the sofa and Michel had crossed to his desk.

Nellie came to the doorway and stood for a moment watching the studied nonchalance of their postures. "Too late, I'm afraid," she said.

Michel frowned. "Too late for what?"

"He saw you through the window."

"Who?"

"Bertrand."

Both Michel and Madeleine looked toward the window and saw the gap in the curtain.

"Where is he?" asked Madeleine.

"Gone."

Michel stood and came toward his wife. "But why? We were just reading."

"Yes," said Nellie, "with her head in your crotch."

"You're drunk," said Michel.

"And so was he. Perhaps in the morning he'll think it was all a hallucination."

"Why was he looking through the window?" asked Madeleine.

"To see if you were at it."

"But why should he suppose . . ."

"I told him."

"You fool," said Michel.

"I thought you believed in frankness," she said mockingly.

Madeleine had turned pale. "Has he gone back to Mézac?"

"I don't know."

Madeleine looked at Michel. "What should we do?"

"Leave him."

"I'd better go."

"Tomorrow."

She seemed to accept what he said and sat down.

"It had to come out anyway," said Michel.

The two women said nothing.

Madeleine went to bed in the spare room of the Villa Acacia. At two in the morning Michel joined her. "I couldn't sleep," he said.

"But Nellie . . ."

"She's snoring like a sow." He got in beside her.

"But when she wakes up . . ."

"I shall leave her."

"You don't have to because of me."

"I'd leave her anyway."

At nine the next morning Madeleine telephoned the apartment in Mézac. There was no reply. Then she rang Saint Théodore, where Edmond de Roujay answered the telephone. "Madeleine! Where are you? Are you coming out?"

"Perhaps," she said. "Could I speak to Bertrand?"

"He's just appeared. I'll go and get him."

Bertrand spoke in a gruff voice. "What do you want?"

"To talk to you."

"Then talk."

"Not on the telephone."

"Very well. Go to the apartment in Mézac this afternoon. I'll meet you there at three."

"May I speak to Titine?"

"Not now. Later."

Madeleine reached the apartment before Bertrand at one of the rare moments of the day when the sun shone into the drawing room that had never been hers. She looked around, seeing one or two of her books, and here and there a picture or gramophone record that they had bought together, but there was little of her in the somber apartment, just as there was little of her in her marriage with Bertrand.

She tried to recall why she had married him, to recreate, even for a moment, her love for the man on a horse. She could only just remember it, like a story she had been told as a child. She sat on the edge of the bed, which like all the other furniture had come from Saint Théodore. In her mind, Bertrand was just another period piece which had been lent by Edmond and Alice de Roujay. She could still admire him in a way, as she might admire an Empire desk; certainly she did not hate him. But she felt as detached from him as she did from the walnut-framed cheval mirror in which she caught a reflection of her own melancholy face. Like the furniture, Bertrand was not her style, whereas Michel, that huge, noble and modern man who lived for others and held her in his strong arms close to his chest, enveloping her in his smell of sweat and cigarettes. . . .

Almost by the way, she remembered how Michel had once made a pass at her when they were students in Montpellier, and how she had turned him down. But he, like Bertrand, was a different man at that distance in time, just as she was a different woman. Now she saw herself smile in the looking glass as she realized that she would be able to live with him—that the subterfuge and separations would now end. Never before had she dared to imagine that this might happen, but she had always known that if Bertrand ever discovered she had slept with another man, their marriage would be over. Until now she had felt afraid and ashamed of what sadness would come in the aftermath of exposure, but now the thought of living with Michel induced such joy that it diluted the misery she had caused to herself and others to the faintest trace of a bitter taste.

The door to the apartment opened and shut, and she heard Bertrand's footsteps in the hall. She was not afraid of this encounter, for beyond it lay her liberation.

He seemed tired and ill as he stood for a moment in the doorway, looking at Madeleine sitting on the edge of the bed. "Not here," he said. "Come into the drawing room."

She stood and followed him, recognizing with relief from his tone of voice that he was confining his feelings within the persona of a government official.

He sat down in an armchair, indicating to Madeleine that she should sit on the sofa opposite. "I want a divorce," he said.

"Yes."

"Also, for my parents' sake, I would like the marriage annulled."

"Whatever you like."

"You must find yourself a lawyer."

"Yes. Michel . . ." She blushed. "I can arrange it."

"We can discuss the divorce through the lawyers, but you should know that I shall claim the custody of Titine."

"Yes."

"Will you dispute it?"

"No. She will be better off with you, but I would like to see her sometimes."

"Of course. There will also be the question of the separation of property, but the lawyers can settle that. You have a key to this apartment. Take what you like, but if possible during the day when I am not here."

"Of course."

"If there is anything of yours at Saint Théodore—"

"There's nothing."

"Good." He paused, struggling to put certain distasteful thoughts into words. "I would not want you to think," he began, "that the fault for this is all yours."

"No."

"You don't?"

"I don't think it is a matter of faults—that's to say, faults in the sense of errors and misdeeds."

He looked annoyed. "Then what?"

"We change."

"Yes." He still had a frown on his face, as if he did not agree but did not want to argue with her. "I think you should know that I also have been unfaithful to you."

She looked at him, surprised, and without thinking said, "Poor Bertrand."

This seemed to irritate him. "Most wives would feel jealousy, not pity."

"But you must have suffered," she said, "and anyway . . ." She stopped before finishing the sentence.

"You're no longer my wife? No. Good. That's true." He got to his feet. "I think we've said all we need say."

"Yes." She stood and followed him in silence down the hall and out of the apartment.

"The car . . ." she began as they stood together on the street.

"Keep it."

"Thank you."

"And if you need money, ask your lawyers to let me know."

"I have enough."

They stood as if there must be something else they should discuss, but neither could think of it.

"Bertrand . . ." she began.

"What?"

"I am sorry." She did not mean to apologize for what she had done, and he knew from her tone that she only meant that she was sorry that marriages in life were not like marriages in fairy stories.

"I'm sorry too," he said in a voice of great sadness. Then he turned and held out his hand to her as if caught in the role of a civil servant on official business, and she, in a reflex response, took it. In this way, on the pavement behind the subprefecture, they shook hands and parted.

PART
TWO

Chapter 5

1

WHEN France declared war on Germany in September 1939, Bertrand de Roujay applied for a transfer from the subprefecture of Mézac to active service in the army. He already held the rank of captain in the reserve, but because of his position in the administration his application was refused.

Nine months later, as the German columns approached Paris, Bertrand tried again. There was now a new minister of the interior, Georges Mandel, and a new commander-in-chief, General Weygand. He went to Paris to lobby his superiors, but half the staff at the ministry had already fled to Bordeaux. Over the packing cases, the harassed official who remained in charge told him that only with a specific request from the War Office could he take it upon himself to allow Bertrand to leave Mézac; but at the War Office he was told that the request could be issued only once he had obtained his release from the Ministry of the Interior. He spent several days hanging around Fouquet's on the Champs Elysées and the Brasserie Lorraine on the Place des Ternes in search of officials and staff officers who might be able to help him. In the end he obtained an interview with Mandel himself. It lasted half a minute and he was ordered to stay at his post.

Bertrand returned to Mézac on the night train. When he stepped down onto the platform at six the next morning the sun was already warming the hazy air of Provence. He was saluted by the porters and ticket collectors, who at this time of crisis liked to think that they were serving the nation, and that their determined subprefect was the man in command.

A car was waiting to meet him. The driver was an old soldier from the Great War. He took on a self-important expression as he set off from the station, and drove the black Citroën through the gates of the ancient city as if a minute saved on the journey to the subprefecture might hamper the German advance. He did not know what Bertrand had been up to in Paris, but like all the minor employees at the subprefecture he assumed it was a mission of some importance.

The senior officials who arrived that morning to find their chief already at his desk were less impressed than the driver. They knew that despite his commanding manner, Bertrand de Roujay had been passed over for promotion, remaining a subprefect in the little city of Mézac when he should now have been a prefect in another department or high in the ministry in Paris.

Those who had known him since his first appointment blamed this setback on his divorce, which had changed him overnight from a confident and decisive administrator into a melancholy man who only went through the motions of his job. Those who had been recruited more recently onto the staff found this hypothesis hard to believe, because the shock of the Munich crisis, when Daladier and Chamberlain had abandoned Czechoslovakia to the Germans, had induced de Roujay to escape from his mood of pessimistic paralysis into one of vigorous activity. However, the more he asserted his administrative talents—as he had done, for example, when enforcing Daladier's dissolution of the Communist Party in September 1939—the more confined the arrondissement of Mézac became, and by the outbreak of war it was clear to everyone that de Roujay was ready for a change.

It was for this reason that his colleagues in the subprefecture were somewhat cynical about his visit to Paris. His assistant, Julien Devaux, had let it slip that he had gone there to lobby for a transfer to the army, not so much from disloyalty to Bertrand as to impress the others with his inside knowledge.

"Oh, it's easy enough to play the hero," an older official, André Pidner, had said, "but if we all went to fight, who would run the country?"

Pidner disliked Bertrand not only because he resented his subordination to a younger man, but also because to Pidner a practicing Catholic from a prominent local family was inevitably a reactionary, and possibly even a member of the secret society of right-wing fanatics, the Cagoulards. He was constantly irritated by the easy way in which Bertrand would lounge back in his large, ornate office in the subprefecture as if he were the eldest son of the sovereign prince who had once ruled the city of Mézac.

Upon his return from Paris, for example, when he summoned Devaux to give an account of what had happened in his absence, Bertrand sat well back in his chair, with his legs crossed, like an off-duty officer in the mess. Despite this casual pose, however, his eyes never left those of his subordinate, for he had learned to read between the lines of Devaux's reports. His assistant's weakness was that he pretended to be straightforward when he was not, so that whenever his clear blue eyes looked down or away, Bertrand was alerted to some distortion or omission introduced by Devaux to protect his friends.

"And the case against the Burzios?" he asked when Devaux had finished.

"It's in the hands of the examining magistrate."

"How far have they got?"

"Not very far."

"Is it Inspector Guillot who has come up with the evidence?"

"Yes."

"Strong?"

Devaux shrugged his shoulders.

"They've probably paid him off," said Bertrand.

"I don't think so."

"Do you trust Guillot?"

"He knows that world."

"And we don't? I know." Bertrand stood—he was thinner than before, too thin for his clothes—and went toward the window. "Of course, we need men like Guillot, but we must never let them call the tune. In the end, that's the principal difference between them and us."

"Them?"

"The Nazis. We may use men like Guillot, but they *are* men like Guillot."

A green light filtered into the square through the foliage of the plane trees. Bertrand saw a man buy a packet of cigarettes at a café next to the church. A woman tilted a carriage to raise the front wheels onto the pavement. None of that would change when the Germans reached Mézac.

"How was Paris?" asked Devaux from behind him.

"Chaos."

"You were lucky to get out in time."

"Yes."

"It all seems impossible."

"War makes the impossible possible."

"They wouldn't let you fight?"

"No. Anyway, it's too late."

"Someone ought to pay."

"Whom do you suggest?"

"The politicians."

Bertrand returned to his desk and stood behind the chair. "It was the generals who wanted the Maginot Line."

"Then the generals."

"We're all responsible." He pushed his chair toward the desk, as if blaming the piece of furniture for the past years of a sedentary life, and began to walk up and down the room.

"It's the malaise and corruption of French society," said Devaux, as if he were quoting from *L'Action Française*.

"Couldn't a corrupt Republic have spent its money on tanks and dive bombers instead of concrete bunkers?"

"I suppose so."

"We listened to the wrong advice," said Bertrand. "We chose a defensive strategy when it was out of date. Was that a sign of decadence?"

Devaux looked confused. "In a sense, perhaps."

"Marshal Pétain supported that strategy. So did men like my father. All the old soldiers who'd seen the slaughter in the last war were behind the idea of the Maginot Line. Do they exemplify the decadence of France?"

"Clearly not."

"The irony of the whole affair is that though our defeat is essentially a technical matter, it has led to a collapse in morale. I met people in Paris who now seem to believe that the Germans are a master race."

Bertrand and his assistant ate lunch together in a restaurant on the square. It was disagreeably hot, too hot for either to think profoundly about the catastrophe that had befallen their country, and when they had finished they parted until their office reopened. Bertrand went back to his apartment, where he found himself alone. Miss Spinks had returned to England the year before, and Titine was now a weekly boarder at the Convent of the Assumption in Carpentras. An old lady, Anna, who had been his mother's maid when he was a boy, still came in to cook and clean for him, making his coffee in the morning and then, after he had gone to his office, washing and ironing his clothes and cooking a dish that he had only to heat up if he wanted to dine at home that evening. Now, as he returned for a brief siesta, he saw the signs of her presence: the table set with one place, a knife, a fork, a soup spoon and a wineglass on an old raffia mat.

Because the windows opened onto narrow streets on that side of the building, the apartment was dark and cool—a coolness augmented by the floors of red polished tiles, a darkness enhanced by the somber pieces of oak and rosewood furniture which had come from Saint Théodore. Bertrand went to his bedroom. The suitcase which the driver from the subprefecture had delivered had been unpacked by Anna; only the books and magazines which he had bought in Paris remained in a neat pile on the chaise longue at the end of his bed.

He removed his shoes, jacket and tie, lay down on the large bed and closed his eyes. He had hardly slept on the train; his body was exhausted, but his mind raced so fast that there was no question of sleep. After only a moment of attempted repose, he got up and went in his stockinged feet to the hall, picked up the telephone and dialed a number. It rang for a while and then was answered by the slightly guttural voice of Lucía.

"Were you asleep?" he asked.

"Dozing."

"Can I come around?"

"Yes."

He put down the telephone and returned to his bedroom. The word "yes" had been spoken, as it always was, as if it might as easily have been "no," though throughout the two years and more that Bertrand had asked the question of the same girl—sometimes twice a week, sometimes not for many months—the answer given had always been the same. Whenever he rang she said yes, yet he never visited her without ringing first. He passed it off as courtesy, but it was also a way of reminding her that he had no rights over her, and that, concomitantly, she had none over him.

Lucía now lived close at hand. Decisive and efficient in his private as well as his public life, Bertrand had arranged for all those upon whom he paid regular visits, such as his barber, dentist and mistress, to be within walking distance of the subprefecture. His present journey was no longer than any of the others, but it took him outside the walls of the old city, across the boulevard that had been laid out over the filled-in moat, and up a street leading out of the town to a small block of modern apartments.

It was one of those buildings which seemed at first to have been built by the municipality for the poor, but instead of the official notices and unofficial graffiti which mark such buildings, it had instead a few wilting geraniums planted near the entrance and a title, "The Cedars," to establish its status as a privately owned condominium. Since those who lived in it were scarcely richer than those who lived in the municipal block, it was not in a better state of repair, and as always, rather than risk taking the elevator, Bertrand walked up the stairs to the fourth floor. He stopped at one of the three doors on the landing, a blue door with peeling paintwork, and instead of ringing the bell knocked once, and then again.

The door was immediately opened by Lucía, as if she had been waiting for this particular sequence of sounds. She closed it quickly behind Bertrand while he, without a word or gesture of greeting, squeezed past her in the narrow foyer to enter the small living room. It was stuffy, noisy and hot, with low ceilings and coarse-plastered white walls. There was a double bed in the corner of the room, piled with cushions to make it pass as a sofa, and on the walls were two large framed posters for exhibitions of modern art, one of Miró, the other of Braque. To the left there was a wardrobe, the open door showing a chaos of clothes within; opposite it a doorway which led to a small galley kitchen. The only other furniture was a table and four chairs. A smell of dead cigarettes rose from a half-filled ashtray.

Lucía followed Bertrand into the room. She had altered little in the years since he had first met her. Her skin was still soft and brown, and her thick black hair remained down to her shoulders, cut in a fringe over her eyes. In these alone there was some change; they were large and brown as before, but their expression had exchanged some of their defiance for a look of patient melancholy. She also stooped a little, as if the burden of her life was on her shoulders, and when she turned to kiss Bertrand with lips that tasted of tobacco she had to rise on her toes to put her arms around his neck.

"You're not in uniform," she said with a faint smile on her lips.

"No. Anyway, it's too late."

Now she bit her lower lip and looked anxious. "What's going to happen?"

"I don't know."

"Will they come here?"

Bertrand shrugged his shoulders. "If they can get to Paris, why not Mézac?"

Lucía covered her face with her hands and went to sit on the bed.

"Everyone is so demoralized," said Bertrand.

"It's horrible."

He thought that she might be weeping, and for a moment his preoccupation descended from the fate of France to the plight of an individual who had already lost a home and a husband. "Don't worry," he said. "I can protect you."

He crossed to the divan and took her hand with the awkwardness he always showed when making any gesture of affection. She clung to him, her head over his shoulder to hide her tears. The heat had made them both sweat, but while his white body gave off the scent of soap and cologne, hers oozed the rich aroma which always provoked in him the same blend of disgust and desire. He felt her flesh under her thin dress, and then when it was off, and he too had removed his clothes, he felt her naked limbs like clamps on his body. They made love, the sounds mixing with the noise of traffic which rose from the street through the open window. Then Lucía went to wash in the bathroom, for she had no wish to get pregnant by a man who would never marry her.

Bertrand lit a cigarette. There was never an occasion when he made love to Lucía and did not regret it afterward. Once sated, his desire left him only with a sense of disgust. It was not so much that he was troubled by his conscience; it was more the irrationality of the act of love which marred the image he had of himself as a man who was lucid, controlled and aloof.

In most cases love elevates a man's instincts to the sublime, but Bertrand had long since decided that he did not and could not love this woman, who embodied the opposite of everything he respected. She was an atheist, a Communist, poor, malodorous and untidy. She also reminded him of the most miserable moments of his life. To visit her, moreover, was a risk, only a little less risky than Lucía coming to him. If, for example, the subprefect should get stuck in the elevator of The Cedars, and the police or fire brigade had to be called to rescue him, Inspector Guillot would ensure that some sneering story would appear in a Socialist or Radical paper. It was not a crime to have a mistress in Provence, but it would harm his reputation among the respectable middle class and would embarrass his uncle, the bishop of Langeais.

He suspected, too, that Lucía felt an equal contempt for him, for when she returned from the bathroom she sat sluttishly on a chair near the door as if waiting for him to leave. He too, after all, embodied everything she despised: the state, bureaucracy, capitalism, aristocracy and the Church. Often it seemed as if all they had in common was the irrational drive which brought them together, for though he would often leave The Cedars determined not to return, and would keep this resolve for a week or even a month, the time would always come when he would remember some detail of their last encounter—a garment, a smell, a surface of skin or a sound from her parted lips—and without consciously acknowledging his motive he would visit her.

He looked at his watch. There was not enough time to go back to his own apartment before returning to the office. His eyes went around the room as if looking for a newspaper or a magazine. Lucía, who still sat on a wooden chair with her legs apart, a wet patch from the douche on her dressing gown, saw that he meant to stay. "Do you want a drink?" she asked.

"That would be nice."

"What?"

"What is there?"

"Water."

"What else?"

"I could squeeze some lemons."

"Only if it's not too much trouble."

She went into the little kitchen. Bertrand picked up a clandestine copy of *L'Humanité*, now two days old. When Lucía returned with a jug of fresh lemon juice and two glasses he threw the paper down on the floor, saying, "They have a nerve."

"Who?"

"Your Communist friends."

"Why?"

"Writing such lies at a time like this."

For a moment she said nothing. She filled a glass with lemonade and gave it to him.

"It's despicable," he said, taking the glass.

"What did you expect?"

"What did I expect? Anything, almost anything, but not to see Stalin hand in hand with Hitler."

"He had no choice."

"That's always the excuse of those who cut and run."

"If France and Britain had been prepared for a treaty . . ."

A look of angry mockery came onto Bertrand's face. "But I thought socialism was an ideal, a value?"

"It is."

"Then what's all this talk of *raison d'état*?"

"They must protect the revolution where it is established." She spoke slowly and without conviction, as if reluctant to be drawn into a fight.

"By making a deal with Fascists?"

"If necessary."

"And by sharing the spoils of war?"

"I don't expect you to understand." A little strength came into her voice.

"Why? Am I too stupid?"

"You're blinkered."

"How?"

"By your class attitudes."

"Whereas you have none?"

"I come from the working class."

"Which has no class attitudes?"

"Whose attitudes are correct."

"Correct?"

"Progressive."

"Progressive for whom?"

"For everyone."

"Especially the Poles!"

"If you don't understand, then you're a fool!"

Their arguments of this kind always ended in abuse, for inevitably they took place when they were both in that mood of involuntary repugnance and confused regret which followed their sexual encounters, and though politics was the only interest they had in common, their temperamental approach to the issues of the day followed not only their ideological prejudices but also their national character. Being French, Bertrand analyzed each question with the logic of his countrymen, while Lucía, being Spanish, invested her convictions with an intense emotion that was easily provoked into anger by his sarcasm. She was not stupid—she had her university degree—and at times could match his mind trained at the école normale, but it was hard to marshal arguments to defend convictions which she herself had not chosen but had adopted partly from her father and partly from the wretched husband who had been killed in the civil war.

Bertrand knew from police reports that Lucía herself no longer belonged to the Communist Party, and that it was from loyalty to her dead husband that she still stuck to the Party line. Thus her arguments were not only made with disproportionate passion, but were also hampered by her difficulties with the French language, which so frustrated her that she invariably lost control and ended up abusing her lover in her native tongue—a jumble of sounds of which Bertrand could only distinguish words like *beato, asquerosa,* and *hijo de puta.*

When she broke down in this way, Bertrand would sit back in his chair with an amused smile, as if her vehemence proved not just that he was right, but that women in general were incapable of reasoned argument. It was his revenge on her allure; yet despite the smile his own face was pale, and there was a wobbling beneath the skin at his jaw as he clenched and unclenched his teeth, for his own diatribe against the Communists was not as dispassionate as he pretended.

When Bertrand got back to his office there was a message that he was to ring the prefect, Charrier, who in 1938 had replaced Wenkler.

"Have you heard?" asked Charrier.

"What?"

"The Italians have declared war."

"How typical."

"Yes. Our new Caesar waits until it's all over, and then moves in."

"Will there be problems on that front?"

"I doubt it, but we must be prepared. I've called a meeting here tomorrow."

"Good."

"We'll meet at ten, but I'd like a word with you first."

"At what time?"

"Come at nine."

As Bertrand put the telephone down, Devaux came into the office. "Any news?" he asked.

"The Italians have declared war."

He gave a snort of contempt. "To share the spoils."

"I daresay."

"What do we do?"

"I don't know. We'll see. There's a meeting at the prefecture tomorrow, but we should be ready."

"For what?"

"For the fight."

Devaux looked confused. "Of course," he said.

"Call Guillot," said de Roujay, "and get him over here; then try to get hold of Colonel Bax."

Inspector Guillot came within half an hour. He was a swarthy, thickset man with heavy arms and shoulders who at first, in plainclothes, might have been taken for a butcher or grocer, but after a second look could be seen to be something more. For example, he had a technique which he used on suspects to great effect of staring at them without any expression in his eyes. This, together with the physical menace of his heavy arms and thick torso, cowed the culprits of Mézac. There had been occasions in the past when Guillot had gone too far in his interrogations. It had earned him a rebuke from his superiors, but also a reputation which encouraged his prisoners to tell all.

Although the chief of the Sûreté in Mézac, and so technically under the authority of the subprefect, Guillot's power as a policeman came from his connections in the larger city of Coustiers, where he had lived as a child. Both Mézac and Coustiers had been Roman cities, and still showed the ruins of temples, amphitheaters and citadels from almost every period of European history. Both were inhabited by the descendants of Phoenicians, Greeks, Romans, Gauls, Vandals, Goths, Normans and Moors; but while the population of Mézac had hardly changed since the French Revolution, Coustiers, because of its greater proximity to the sea, had attracted a more recent influx of immigrants from

North Africa, Sardinia and Corsica. It was the Corsicans in particular, who dominated the criminal classes in Coustiers, especially the two rival gangs, the Burzios and the Jacopozzis.

Because Guillot was a native of Coustiers and was himself of Corsican origin, it had always been thought inappropriate that he should head the Sûreté in the city, but the commissaire, Mercier, was a weak man, competent at administration but quite out of his depth when it came to back-street intrigues. He was therefore quite content to leave the criminal underworld to Guillot, conceding quite correctly that "nothing happens in either Coustiers or Mézac without Guillot knowing about it."

Until 1939 the power of the Burzios and the Jacopozzis had not stretched as far as Mézac, principally because there was no Corsican community in which it could thrive, but because of the shortages and rationing which followed the outbreak of war, a black market had started everywhere and both the Burzios and the Jacopozzis had made tentative attempts to extend their operations to the smaller city. Bertrand had been determined to prevent them, and had pressed the police to be vigilant. Sure enough, it was soon discovered that stocks of gasoline were being filched from government depots and sold by the Burzios to private buyers.

What had made Bertrand uneasy was that this evidence had been presented by Guillot, who he knew was the Burzios' friend. For some time he had suspected that the inspector used his knowledge of the underworld in Mézac and Coustiers not to enforce justice but to dominate and manipulate the two cities. It was hard to prove that Guillot was corrupt, because he lived modestly with a wife and children in one of the suburbs of Mézac. If he took bribes from the Burzios, it was largely in kind: free food in certain restaurants, free drinks in certain bars, and a pick of the whores in their brothels around the Place de l'Opéra. There were no weekly bundles of notes, no checks paid into his bank; but if Guillot was short of money, he almost certainly took an occasional fifty francs from the till of one of the Burzios' establishments, and if Guillot required an arrest or a conviction to confirm his reputation as an efficient policeman, Bruno Burzio would arrange for some wretch to be found with a packet of heroin or with the Beretta used in a recent shooting.

One of Bertrand's ambitions was to outwit Guillot—not simply to dismiss him, but to see him sent to jail. Charrier knew of this objective and approved of it, but doubted that Bertrand would achieve it. Guillot had friends among the politicians in Paris, Radical deputies who relied on his links with the Burzios to deliver votes at elections in both Coustiers and Mézac. Moreover, Guillot also held a stick: he had something on almost everyone who had a string to pull in the two cities. If in recent months Bertrand himself had let up on his campaign against Guillot, it was partly because of the war, but also because he suspected that Guillot knew of his liaison with Lucía.

Now, for example, when Bertrand asked for a report on the refugees in the city, Guillot said, "But Monsieur de Roujay, you know as much about that as I do."

"How do you mean?"

"The refugees from Spain, at any rate."

"What makes you think that?" asked Bertrand.

Guillot smiled. "Isn't Madame de Roujay on the Committee for Refugees?"

"First of all, Guillot, I am no longer married to Madame de Roujay."

"Of course. Divorced."

"Annulled."

"Ah, annulled." Guillot nodded like a peasant who cannot grasp an abstruse nuance.

"And secondly, it's not the Spanish refugees I'm talking about, but the recent refugees from the war."

"There are lots of them."

"How many?"

"It's difficult to say who are refugees and who are just visitors."

"How many new residents, do you estimate, since the war began?"

"Eight or nine thousand."

"Where do they live?"

"Here, there and everywhere."

"Are they still using the holiday camp?"

"Yes. We'd just got rid of the Jews and the Spaniards when the Belgians turned up."

"Aren't there some Frenchmen?"

"I suppose."

"Have you any view as to whether any might constitute a fifth column?"

Guillot shrugged his shoulders. "I doubt it. Mézac, after all, isn't on the front line."

"Not now, but it may be. The Italians have declared war."

"Ah, the Italians. Then . . ."

"What?"

"There are one or two Italians."

"Fascists?"

"Nonpolitical." Guillot smiled again.

"I'm going to Coustiers tomorrow. The prefect will want to know how we propose to defend Mézac."

"But surely," said Guillot, "if we have to defend Mézac, there won't be much left of the rest of France."

"Possibly not," said Bertrand, "and that's why, if it comes to it, we must be prepared."

"But if the rest of France has fallen," said Guillot, "how can Mézac hold out?"

"It's not a question of holding out," said Bertrand. "It's a question of fighting to the last man—from the roofs, the streets, from here, behind this desk."

Now Guillot resumed his manner of servile sarcasm. "You must forgive me, Monsieur de Roujay, but I never went to Saint Cyr and so do not grasp the strategic significance of your desk."

"I'm not talking about strategy, Guillot. I'm talking about honor, the honor of France."

"Ah," said Guillot. "Honor. Of course. I hadn't thought of that."

Guillot left Bertrand feeling irritable and foolish because the policeman, who could conceive of nothing worse than pain or death, and nothing better than a whore or a hot meal, could by mere intonation make a word like "honor" sound absurd. To Bertrand they meant something intangible but real. The war he wanted to fight was not just for the defense of French territory or French citizens, but for the values embodied in the nation he thought the finest in the world. Guillot annoyed him not only because he scoffed at such transcendental values, but because he spoiled Bertrand's image of his own country.

Pidner, who was the next to come into his office, did the same.

Guillot could be dismissed as a Corsican, but Pidner was entirely French and equally repugnant. He had a bent body, greasy receding hair and a shifty way of never looking Bertrand in the eye, for his obsequious manner was always at variance with his resentful feelings; he had never mastered Guillot's knack of expressing nothing at all.

Bertrand was quite aware of his subordinate's envy and resentment. Pidner exemplified to him the dregs of the French Revolution—the mean-minded man who tried to use the egalitarian ideal to annul his own mediocrity. He was an atheist because Citizen Pidner would not bend his knee to anyone, prince, prelate or Christ on the cross. His deference to Bertrand, who had the power to frustrate his career, was in his own mind a cunning ruse, an ironic pretense, for neither to others nor to himself would he acknowledge that merit made Bertrand the subprefect of Mézac. Rather, it must have been his family connections, friends from Saint Cyr, or colleagues who had been with him at the école normale who had ensured de Roujay's promotion. For Pidner, nobody did better than Pidner unless as a result of some secret conspiracy of the privileged. This was the sort of thing said by Catholics about Freemasons, and Pidner was a member of his local lodge.

"Listen, Pidner," Bertrand said to him. "There's a meeting with the prefect in the morning. I want the statistics on supplies, a reassessment of the position we would be in if the war were to be fought here in Mézac."

"Here in Mézac?"

"As you may have heard," said Bertrand sarcastically, "the Italians have declared war and the Germans are approaching Paris."

"But if they come as far as Mézac, the war will be over."

"Our duty is to plan for any eventuality."

"Of course." Pidner looked at the pen he held in his hand.

"Imagine, for example, that we are cut off from Coustiers or Marseilles, or even from the surrounding countryside. What provisions are there in the city itself?"

"We've always assumed—"

"Assume nothing. We must plan as if the last ditch were here in this room."

"Very well, monsieur," said Pidner, twisting his neck in an attempt to hide the skeptical expression on his face.

"Go now. Bring me what you can by six."

Pidner shuffled off, whereupon Devaux entered the office to tell Bertrand that Colonel Bax was waiting to see him.

Bax was an elderly man, almost certainly drawn from the reserve. "Ah, Roujay," he said as he came in. "A great pleasure, even in this moment of distress." He sat down on a chair without waiting to be invited. "I knew your father, dear boy. Served under him the last time around. An excellent officer. If only there were more of his kind today."

"It's very good of you to come," said Bertrand. "The prefect has called a meeting in Coustiers tomorrow, and I wanted to go fully briefed about what plans you may have for the defense of Mézac."

The colonel looked dumbfounded. "The defense of Mézac?"

"Now that the Italians have entered the war—"

"But they won't get to Mézac!"

"The Germans have reached Rouen."

"Ah, the Germans. They're a different kettle of fish." Colonel Bax gave a nervous twist to his mustache.

"It *is* possible, isn't it, that the Germans may come down the Rhône Valley both to relieve the Italians and to seize Marseilles?"

"Yes," said the colonel, still with a baffled air. "But I have to admit that so far as I know there are no contingency plans to hold a line at Mézac. You see, the only strategic significance of the city is the railway junction and marshaling yards, and there, as you know, we have three antiaircraft guns, two of which are in working order though without ammunition, but that has been requested. Now if the Germans were to reach Mézac itself, the railway would lose most of its strategic significance because the lines of supply would be short."

"It's not the railways I'm concerned with," said Bertrand, "but the city itself."

"I fear that their tanks and Stukas would make short work of our medieval walls."

"There are no outer defenses?"

"Only the Maginot Line."

"Shouldn't we draw up some sort of contingency plan?"

The colonel sighed. "In theory, perhaps, but in practice it would be futile."

"Why?"

"Look what they did to Rotterdam. A city ceases to be a city. It becomes rubble. No, Roujay. Plan, if you like, but if the Germans reach Mézac it will be all over anyway."

Toward seven that evening, Bertrand returned to his apartment carrying the various reports that he had asked for earlier in the afternoon. Now, suddenly, he was hit by fatigue. He put the papers down on the desk in the living room, poured himself a glass of Lillet, then returned to glance at the folder on top of the pile, Pidner's assessment of supply. He read the first paragraph. The man's skepticism was apparent in every line.

Bertrand put it back on the desk. He felt tired and sticky. He would have liked to go straight to bed, but partly because he felt obliged to read the reports he had commissioned and partly because he was by nature a man of routine, he went instead to take a bath. He filled the deep, old-fashioned tub and lay back with the water touching his chin. The apartment was quite silent; it was the moment which others imagined he must find testing, when three or four hours of solitude lay before him, but which in fact he valued above any other moment of the day.

When he had first separated from Madeleine, Bertrand had received invitations from his friends which, though couched in a social formula such as an invitation to dinner or to the opera, always seemed to include an introduction to an eligible woman. It had always surprised him that it was assumed that a man who had so recently suffered and failed in one marriage would be impatient to begin another. For a while he had accepted these invitations, but as time passed the falsity of such occasions—the empty conversation and forced bonhomie that went on as all waited in vain for Cupid's arrow—depressed and exasperated him.

It became worse after the annulment, when the more pious and respectable mothers in Mézac suddenly realized that an unmarried daughter might make a match with the handsome subprefect. He was then asked into a circle which he had not known since his youth— families like the de Sourcy cousins of Hélène de Roujay, whose political opinions seemed to come from the days of General Boulanger. He suffered in their company, because the conversation invariably turned to politics and he was obliged to listen to views which caricatured his own. He was embarrassed by their contempt for anyone who was not of their stock or did not share their point of view: Jews, foreigners, Socialists, freethinkers. They were people from whom he had been protected by his marriage, and seeing them now made him miss Madeleine, a spasm of regret which was the most disagreeable of all.

He therefore began to make excuses—usually pressure of work—which annoyed the matrons of Mézac and finally gave him a reputation of being odd. "He only cares about his work," said one. "I begin to see the wife's point of view," said another. "He should have been a priest," said a third. It was generally considered "unnatural" that Bertrand should spend so much time alone. "A good man needs a good woman" was an adage which seemed to come up whenever Bertrand was discussed in such circles; nor did these pious ladies hesitate to speculate about how the subprefect might satisfy his sexual desires.

None of them knew about Lucía. She never came to Bertrand's apartment, nor were they ever seen together in a café or a restaurant. Bertrand confined her in his life as in his mind. Even now, as he washed her scent from his body, he could exclude her from his thoughts not only because he was preoccupied with the fate of France, but also because her image destroyed his peace of mind. He kept away from the issue of Lucía in the same way that the jaw avoids chewing on a rotten tooth, because his Catholic conscience could not wholly accept the way he made use of her as and when he liked.

When he was dressed again, Bertrand went into the large tiled kitchen and lit the gas under the pan of soup that Anna had prepared for him. He broke two pieces of bread from the baguette on the dresser, then went to the larder and took out a plate of cold meat and a bowl of bean salad. When the soup was hot he took his supper on a tray to the place already laid in the dining room. He returned to the living room for Pidner's report, then sat at the table to read it while he ate.

2

The driver, Albert, was waiting outside in the black Citroën at six the next morning to take Bertrand to the station. The early start was a familiar routine, and from long experience the old chauffeur kept quiet on the short drive to the station.

The concourse was already crowded with bewildered travelers, refugees off the night trains from the north. Bertrand noticed two of Guillot's men standing at the barrier—watching, no doubt, for likely-looking spies. He bought three morning papers and then found his reserved place in a first-class compartment of the train, which, even though it had started at Perpignan, was packed tight with doleful, bleary-eyed passengers.

Bertrand read the news from the front with a horrified fascination. The counteroffensive on the Somme had collapsed. There seemed nothing to stop the Germans' reaching Paris. He turned aside from the newspapers and looked out for a moment at the vines and fruit trees beside the railway line. He had not had breakfast, and for a moment considered fighting his way along the corridor to the dining car, but then decided against it, calculating that he would have time for some coffee when he reached Coustiers.

He opened his leather bag and took out the reports which he had read the night before. They were all brief—time had been short—and dealt with the questions within their competence; yet, by the manner in which the facts were presented, they all were implicitly skeptical of the idea that the administration should prepare to fight the war in the streets of Mézac. Bertrand himself dithered between rage at the cowardice of men like Pidner and a growing suspicion that his idea of a last stand was indeed absurd.

At Coustiers, Bertrand went to the station buffet and ordered some breakfast. As he dipped his brioche into the large cup of white coffee, he made up his mind to present his ideas in a more tentative tone than he had envisaged, and by the time he climbed the steps of the huge nineteenth-century prefecture, this intention had been modified still further. He decided that he would wait to see what others had to say.

As Bertrand entered the prefect's office, Marcel Charrier rose to meet him. A man approaching sixty, with a solid body and thick white hair, he was always courteous with his subordinates; even his secretaries were treated with tact and consideration. Those who took this kindliness as a sign of weakness soon discovered that Charrier's charm was a ploy. He had complete confidence in his own judgment, and though he always listened to what others had to say, the conclusions he presented as a synthesis of the various views were always markedly similar to the opinion he had held before discussion began. Nor, once Charrier had made a decision, did anyone dare cross him, because one mild reproach, one sigh, one scowl, was worse than the sarcasm or abuse which other prefects used to keep their subordinates in order.

Between Marcel Charrier and Bertrand de Roujay there was that particular affinity which can exist between an older and a younger man of similar disposition. The one played the role of a father, the other that of a son, more happily than they did with their blood relations. Bertrand was fond of his own father, but he found in Charrier qualities which he respected and which his father did not possess—a combination of perception, detachment and mental agility which enabled him to consider each question from every point of view.

Charrier came from a background quite different from Bertrand's. His father had been a Radical deputy, a fierce supporter of Ferry's laws against the Church, but he had inherited none of his father's vituperative anticlericalism; indeed, the father's success, which had brought the son to Paris, meant that he had been brought up among the very people whom the father affected to despise. As a result he was neutral in the quarrel between left and right and between Church and state, and one of the reasons for his support of Bertrand was his conviction that fair-minded Catholics from conservative circles should be brought into the administration of the secular republic whenever possible.

"Was the train crowded?" he asked Bertrand as he pointed to a chair by his desk.

"Packed."

"It's going to get worse. We will have to revise our estimates."

"Yes," said Bertrand, waiting until his superior was seated and then sitting himself. "We have drawn up a report—"

"Good, but let's wait before we go into that. Tell me first, how was Paris?"

"I saw Mandel."

"So I gather."

"He wouldn't let me go."

"Well, I'm sorry for your sake, but not for ours, and to be quite honest with you, I think that the way things are going now, you'll be of more use here than at the front."

"I know."

"Whenever an army collapses, the government invariably collapses as well."

"Hasn't it been strengthened by the reshuffle?"

"I'm sure that's what Reynaud meant to do, but I suspect that it will have the opposite effect. First he brings in Marshal Pétain, now General de Gaulle—two men with quite opposite points of view. If Reynaud had more weight himself, it would be one thing, but he's too insubstantial to lead his own team. He's a politician whom events have proved right, but he's a politician all the same. If Reynaud and Pétain differ, how can we be sure that it will be Reynaud who will prevail?"

"Differ over what?"

"There's talk of asking for an armistice."

"That's impossible," said Bertrand.

"Weygand evidently considers that the military position is hopeless."

"But there are divisions in reserve. It has only just started."

"There are already a hundred thousand casualties."

"And forty million Frenchmen."

Charrier looked toward the window. "It's very difficult," he said. "If Pétain were Reynaud or Reynaud were Pétain . . ." He mused for a moment, then went on, "The English are lucky with Churchill. Like Reynaud, he is a politician whom events have proved right, but he is also a man with the blood of Marlborough in his veins. He embodies the triumphant history of his people, whereas Reynaud . . ." Charrier shrugged his shoulders. "He doesn't really embody anything at all."

"But Pétain . . ."

"The marshal, yes, he has the weight, but does he have the spirit?"

"I can't believe that Pétain will surrender."

"He's always hated loss of life."

"Unnecessary loss of life."

"What is necessary and what is unnecessary?"

"It is necessary to fight to the finish."

"Perhaps, perhaps, but there are those who think that discretion is the better part of valor."

"Yes, the cowards!"

Charrier had his elbows on his desk, and now started to drum the fingers of his two hands together, keeping his eyes on them as he spoke. "You must remember what we suffered in the last war."

"That's just the point. To have suffered all that, and now to lose in a month all that we gained."

"Perhaps," said Charrier again, clasping his hands together and looking away. "In any case, the decision is not ours; we are not the government. Our duty, it seems to me, is to be prepared not just for any decision the government may make, but for a possible disintegration at the center."

"I agree."

"But not, perhaps, in the way you envisage."

Bertrand blushed. From the way Charrier looked at him when he said this, he sensed that his superior had been told of the reports he had commissioned in Mézac. "I thought we should be ready," he said.

"Yes," said Charrier, "but we must be careful not to alarm the population."

"Of course."

"And if it is thought that we expect the Germans or Italians here in Coustiers or in Mézac . . ."

"News travels fast," said Bertrand bitterly.

"Your people are not discreet."

"I know."

"For example, it's generally known why you went to Paris."

"I'm sorry."

"Your man Devaux . . ."

"I shouldn't have told him."

"Perhaps you should have an assistant who can hold his tongue?"

"It's sometimes useful."

"How?"

"I can control rumor."

Charrier shrugged his shoulders. "As long as you know what you're doing. I just thought you ought to know that your trip to Paris and your plans for the defense of Mézac have annoyed some of the people here. It makes their own inactivity seem like cowardice."

"I'm sorry."

"You needn't apologize. But bear in mind that if it becomes known that the civilian administration has taken such matters into its own hands, it suggests first of all that we have given up all hope of being defended by the army."

"I hadn't thought of that."

"And it also suggests the imminent arrival of the Stukas and panzers in Basse-Provence, which would certainly clear our department of troublesome refugees, but will lead to complaints from our colleagues in Marseilles."

"Of course. It was stupid."

"Our duty, Bertrand, is to deal with Frenchmen as they are, not with Frenchmen as we would like them to be. We face defeat. Of that I am certain. We cannot hope to alter this, but we can mitigate the effects of the defeat on the civilian population. Above all, we must keep order when, as I predict, the government falls apart."

In the meeting which followed, Bertrand said little. His affection for Charrier and the lucidity of his argument stymied the indignation he felt as he listened to the discussion of rationing, refugees and the budgetary estimates for the next quarter. It seemed absurd to be sitting in a room with the sun shining through the windows, making plans for the rest of the year, when at the next meeting a gauleiter might be sitting in Charrier's chair.

He looked around at the faces of his fellow subprefects. None seemed to share his frustration. Quite the contrary; they appeared reassured that the prefect was carrying on as before. Every now and then one would look uneasily in Bertrand's direction as if afraid he might say something to disrupt the calm conduct of their deliberations. He had never been close to his colleagues, who, because they themselves amounted to little more than was given to them by their official positions, resented not only Bertrand's position and friendship with Charrier, but also his social standing among the more aristocratic families in the department. The story spread by Devaux that Bertrand had gone to Paris to try to get a commission in the army had driven them to deflect the implicit slur on their own courage by discounting Bertrand as an irresponsible prima donna who neglected his professional duties in pursuit of a more glamorous role. When Charrier brought the meeting to a close with a sober address of the kind he had delivered to Bertrand before the meeting, ending with the words "Gentlemen, return to your posts," they all glanced at Bertrand with a certain complacency, and then looked away again because none of them wanted to join him for lunch.

Bertrand was in any case disinclined to waste his time with men he considered second-rate, and had arranged to have lunch with Pierre Moreau, who remained an examining magistrate in Coustiers. He walked out of the prefecture and down the Avenue de la République to the Palais de Justice, where he found his friend waiting in the huge concourse outside the courts. The two men, both dressed in light gray suits and carrying leather briefcases, walked on down the Rue de la République to a street off the Place de la Croix. There Pierre led the way into a small restaurant with a marble floor, white tablecloths and long windows looking out into a quiet courtyard.

While the waiters, who knew both men and the positions they held, ministered to them with particular discretion, the examining magistrate and the subprefect took on that relaxed manner which only exists between very old friends. They talked at once about the war, and Bertrand spilled out all the frustration that he had felt since it had started. "Think of Danton," he said to Pierre in a subdued voice. " '*De l'audace, et encore de l'audace, et toujours de l'audace.*' And what do we have now? *De la prudence, et encore de la prudence, et toujours de la prudence.* No wonder we're losing the war."

"But you've become prudent," said Pierre, "quoting Danton in a whisper."

"I've just had a rebuke from Charrier for spreading alarm and despondency."

"What had you said?"

"That we should prepare to fight in the streets."

"Of Mézac?"

"Yes.

Pierre laughed. "Read a little history, Bertrand. The citizens of Mézac never fight."

"Then they can start."

"You don't understand your own people. They've had so many different regimes over the centuries—the Greeks, the Romans, the counts of Toulouse, the Popes in Avignon, the French in Paris. So what if they wake up tomorrow and find that they're governed by the Germans in Berlin?"

"Then they deserve to be governed from Berlin."

"I wasn't suggesting that we're not getting what we deserve."

"You were always a cynic."

"And you a romantic. We who know you from the old days,

Bertrand, are not taken in by your bureaucratic *gravitas*." Pierre picked up the menu; his eager, amused face ran up and down the list of dishes. "It's important to eat well while we can," he said, "and to drink some decent wine before it's looted by the Wehrmacht." He called the waiter and ordered.

"Have you heard that we have a case against the Burzios?" asked Bertrand.

"Yes," said Pierre, "and I advise you to take care."

"Why?"

"As I understand it, your only witnesses are the Jacopozzis' men."

"How well do you know the Jacopozzis?"

"I had a case involving one of them a year ago."

"What are they like?"

Pierre shrugged his shoulders. "They're like the Burzios."

"Better or worse?"

Pierre emptied his glass of wine. "None of these gangs is better or worse than another. Some are younger, some older, some on the way up, some on the way down. Ethically speaking, they are equally good, bad or indifferent."

"Bad."

"If you like."

"Don't you think so?"

"My dear Bertrand, it is my job to prosecute criminals, and so it is convenient to assume that they are bad, and for that reason I don't ask too many questions—questions of conscience, that is. Still, it sometimes occurs to me that these Corsicans who come to France to plunder and exploit the natives bear a remarkable resemblance to those Frenchmen who do the same sort of thing in Africa and Asia."

"But that's different."

"It's on a different scale."

"You're taking your impartiality a little far."

"Oh, I'm not impartial when it comes to the rough justice of the state. All I want to suggest is that there's little to choose between gangsters like the Burzios and delinquents like the Jacopozzis, so if your only witnesses come from the Jacopozzis, it's highly likely that you're being used by them, or even by the Burzios."

"The Burzios?"

"Who has the evidence?"

"Guillot."

"As I thought."

"I don't trust him."

"Did you know that the grandfather of your Inspector Guillot was a certain Antonio Guillone who came from the same village in Corsica as the Burzios?"

Bertrand frowned. "It shouldn't be so easy to change one's name."

"Appellation contrôlée?"

"Yes."

"Easily said for a *premier cru* like a de Roujay. I myself have always been exceptionally grateful for my grandfather's metamorphosis from Halévy to Moreau."

"I'm sorry. I'd forgotten."

"Don't apologize. I quite understand how annoying it must be to have these Corsicans and Jews posing as sons of Saint Louis."

"It's not at all annoying."

"But you must see it from our point of view. At the lycée a boy called Halévy is a yid, while a boy called Moreau—however sallow his skin or crooked his nose—can usually pass himself off as a native Provençal. For example, my sister Isabelle never suffered from anti-Semitism until she went to university, because she hardly knew what a Jew was, let alone that she was one. Of course, later in life it's different. No one is taken in at the Palais de Justice."

They ate for a while in silence.

"Tell me more about the Jacopozzis," said Bertrand.

"They're fairly new."

"From Corsica?"

"Yes, but they were in Marseilles for a while with the Guerinis. Then, when Surleau took over last year, they moved here."

"Who's the boss?"

"There are two brothers. The older one is called Stefano, and the younger one Emmanuele or Jaco. He makes all the noise."

"What are their rackets?"

"The same as the Burzios—whores, drugs, protection—but they take more risks than the Burzios. They've got less to lose."

"At least they're not friends of Guillot's."

"Not that we know of. Not yet."

Bertrand sighed. "There seems as little to be done about the enemy within as the enemy without."

Pierre laughed. "To clean up Coustiers, Bertrand, you must first change human nature."

"You're very pessimistic for a magistrate."

"If we reformed the human race, I wouldn't have a job."

Besides the sympathy which Bertrand felt for Pierre—a sympathy which had begun when they were students together—there was another reason which led him to seek his company, a reason which, since he barely acknowledged it himself, always took time to emerge in the course of their conversation. It was that Pierre was the only person who remained both his friend and Madeleine's. So sour had been his feelings at the time of the divorce that Bertrand had obliged all his other friends to choose between the two. Only Pierre had been licensed to continue his acquaintance with them both; and since Bertrand now rarely communicated with Madeleine—and then only by letter concerning practical matters like the dates for the visits of Titine—he relied upon Pierre to fill him in on the details of her new life.

Pierre had always admired Madeleine, and had thought Bertrand fortunate to have married such an exceptional woman. When the two had divorced, he had seen much more clearly than either of them just what had happened and why. If he had not intervened, it was because he knew that nothing could be done to avert the catastrophe; all he hoped was that he could preserve the friendship of both. Until now he had succeeded, but it was hard. He sensed, for example, that like so many separated spouses, Bertrand asked after Madeleine in the hope that he might hear that she was unhappy in her new life. But if Pierre told such a story, whether or not it was true, it might then get back to Madeleine, who in her turn would feel that she had been betrayed.

The solution to this dilemma was always to sound noncommittal when Bertrand asked after his wife. Now, for example, as they sat at lunch, he described the quarrels among her friends between those who supported the Nazi-Soviet pact and those who denounced it. "It's difficult for her," he said, "because I'm sure she feels the same as you and I, but others take the Party line and she feels she has to support it."

"Does she know that I went to Paris?"

"Yes."

"Does she know why?"

"Yes."

"What did she say?"

"I think she was worried."

"Not about me."

"About Titine."

"She should have worried about her before."

"I think you're a little unfair."

"She abandoned her."

"I don't think she thought of it like that."

"How else?"

"Just of leaving her where she would be better off."

When Bertrand got back to Mézac he had a radio installed in his office so that he could follow events from hour to hour. While listening to the reports from the front, he also searched the morning's newspapers for some item which would allow him to hope that the cataclysm could be averted. However, the rumors were rather that some ministers wanted to surrender. The Germans were in Rouen, Elbeuf and the outskirts of Paris. He then had a few fragmented conversations on the telephone with his friends in the Ministry of the Interior who were making their way from the capital to Bordeaux. Apparently there had been a meeting of the Council of Ministers at the Château de Cangé on the Cher. Weygand had told the government that the military position was hopeless and that an armistice was therefore inevitable. Reynaud himself wanted to form a redoubt in Brittany, and Mandel and Dautry were behind him. Pétain, however, supported Weygand. "I am of the same opinion as the military commanders," he said, "who alone are in a position to judge."

On Friday the news came through that the Germans had entered Paris. Everyone in Mézac looked baffled, the officials in the subprefecture as much as the people in the street. To Bertrand the thought of Nazi storm troopers marching down the Champs Elysées induced anger rather than despair. His respect for Charrier wrestled with his exasperation. Over and over he stalked up to the large, shiny map of France which hung on a wall in his office. It was one with geographical elevations, showing the lowlands in a pale green and the highlands in beige and brown. It seemed obvious to Bertrand from this coloring that the redoubt should not be in Brittany but in Provence. The Alps to the east and the Cévennes to the west formed a natural line of defense against the German tanks, while the ports of Marseilles and

Toulon kept open the lines of communication not only to the large French territories in North Africa, with their divisions of colonial troops, but also to British and eventually American reinforcements through the strait of Gibraltar and the Suez Canal.

This absolute determination to fight on came not so much from a fanatic patriotism as from an identification of his own fate with that of France. Bertrand was almost forty, and the life which had begun so gloriously when he graduated with Pierre from the école normale now seemed becalmed in mediocrity. The pessimistic resignation of the French people to their defeat by the Germans was like his own moods of melancholy which followed his divorce; but just as he, by an effort of will, had recovered his own ambition and determination, so could the French rise and resist the barbarous invader.

3

At six that evening Bertrand left the subprefecture and collected the Panhard which he kept in a garage near his flat.

The drive to Saint Théodore on a Friday evening was always the happiest moment of the week, and even now, in the midst of the disaster that had befallen France, he looked at the landscape in the yellow light—the mixture of rocky sparseness and colorful fecundity that was particular to that part of Provence—with the same delight that had inspired him in earlier times. It was warm enough to drive with the windows open, and the currents of dry, scented air tousled his hair. He had made the journey so frequently, as a child and as a man, that he could brake, accelerate and turn the steering wheel without consciously considering what he was doing.

It was nearly nine at night when he turned off the Route Nationale and drove through Pévier. A mile or two beyond the village he turned through the arched entrance to the Domaine de Saint Théodore, whose rusty gates had not been closed for many years. He left his car outside the coach house and walked to the back door. Passing through a back pantry, he came into the large, low kitchen where Marthe stood by the stove.

"Ah, Monsieur Bertrand," she said when she saw him. "Quick, quick, they've already started."

There was no other form of greeting, for Marthe, who had looked after Bertrand as a baby, always covered the slight confusion she felt when she saw him as a man by treating him as if he were still seven years old. She loved Bertrand as much as she would have loved a child of her own, but thought it improper for a servant to show this affection, and so covered it up with a crotchety brusqueness. She always chided him for being late for dinner on weekends, and Bertrand, though mildly irritated that she did not seem to appreciate that a man in his position could never predict when he could get away, responded as a child, saying, "I'm sorry, Marthe," and scuttled through the kitchen into the dining room, where his parents and daughter sat at table.

The large room was lit only by two candles burning on the table and the remaining evening light that came in through the windows. His father, Edmond, who sat facing the door to the kitchen, saw Bertrand first, and while wiping his mustache with his napkin, got to his feet.

"Well done," he said, as he always did, as if the journey from Mézac was a delicate army maneuver.

Titine, now nearly eight, turned and, seeing her father, dropped her spoon with a clatter, pushed back her chair and rushed to meet him.

"Papa, Papa," she said as she hurled herself at him, trusting him, as always, to catch her in his arms and carry her as he continued toward the table.

Only his mother, Alice, who sat with her back to the door, neither turned to greet Bertrand nor got to her feet, but waited as he came up behind her, disentangled his daughter's arms from around his neck and stooped to give her a kiss.

"I'm sorry I'm late," he said.

"Don't apologize, my dear. We know you're busy."

Bertrand now went to embrace his father, then took his place at table between his parents and opposite his daughter. Marthe came in from the kitchen with a tureen filled with soup, some of which she ladled into Bertrand's plate, then shuffled around to the colonel to finish it off.

"I'm glad you got back from Paris," the older man said as he sucked the soup out of his spoon.

"Yes," said Bertrand. "Just in time."

"But they wouldn't let you fight?"

"No."

"Thank God," said his mother.

"No news from Louis?" Bertrand asked her.

"None."

"But that's no reason to suppose that he's dead," said the colonel, his brow contracting into an irritated frown. "First of all, the post is disrupted; secondly, the telegraph lines to the front are reserved for military communications; and thirdly, Louis has almost certainly had other things to think about than writing to his mother."

"Not so busy," said Alice de Roujay, "that he couldn't send a postcard to his wife."

"Hélène hasn't heard?" asked Bertrand.

"Not for a month."

"And the censor?" said the colonel. "If every officer sent a postcard to his wife, you could piece together the disposition of the whole French army."

Alice de Roujay merely shrugged her shoulders.

The colonel turned to his son. "Your mother, you know, prays to God to keep an eye on Louis, and then worries herself to death about whether he's dead or alive. What kind of faith is that, I ask you?"

He looked away. So did Alice de Roujay. In retirement they spent most of their time together, and were irritated not only by certain mannerisms but by one another's habits of thought. The colonel was now over seventy. He had grown slim and bony, with close-cropped gray hair; Alice, who was ten years younger, remained dark and heavy and now seemed taller than her husband.

"Papa," asked Titine, "are you going to fight the Germans?"

"They won't let me," said Bertrand.

"His work in Mézac is too important," said Alice de Roujay.

"Everyone in Mézac relies upon your Papa," said the colonel.

"Everyone in Mézac," said Bertrand to his father, "relies upon me to do nothing."

"What could you do?"

"Prepare to fight."

"That's up to the army."

"And if the army collapses?"

The colonel shrugged his shoulders. "Without an army, there isn't a nation."

Bertrand frowned. He was about to make some rejoinder when Marthe came in from the kitchen to clear away the soup plates and serve the next course, smoked pork and cabbage. He therefore turned to his daughter and asked, "How's school?"

"Mélanie has measles," she said.

"I hope you don't catch them," said Bertrand.

"She's had them, thank God," said Alice.

"Only three more weeks," said Titine.

"Until what?" asked Bertrand.

"The holidays, silly."

"Already . . ." Bertrand frowned.

"Are we going away?" asked the little girl. "Are we going away to the mountains?"

Bertrand glanced at his mother. Both physically and temperamentally he resembled her so closely that he could often anticipate her thoughts and feelings. Now, however, she said nothing, so he turned back to his daughter. "We'll see, Titine," he said. "It all depends on the war."

When they had finished supper, the two older de Roujays went to the drawing room while Bertrand took his daughter to bed. She was already wearing her nightdress and dressing gown—dining with the grown-ups was a privilege given only when her father was expected from Mézac—so he had simply to see that she brushed her teeth and said her prayers, then read to her rhymes from *Struwwelpeter*.

"Is Hitler like that?" the child asked, pointing to the wicked scissor man.

"A little."

"And will he come and cut off my thumbs?"

"Of course not," said Bertrand. "You mustn't be afraid."

"But Hitler doesn't like children."

"Everyone likes children."

"He doesn't like Jewish or African children."

"How do you know?"

"Sister Annunziata told us."

"Then the Great Agrippa will dip him in ink," said Bertrand, " 'because they set up such a roar, and teased the harmless black-amoor.' "

She smiled, and stretched up her arms to hug him. "Good night, Papa."

"Good night."

"I love it when you're here."

"So do I."

"When will I see Maman?"

"In the holidays."

Titine looked perplexed.

"Don't you want to?" asked Bertrand.

She didn't reply, but clutched a rag doll in her arm, put her thumb into her mouth and closed her eyes. Bertrand kissed her again on her cheek, then switched off the light and left her.

He went back down the wide stone steps to the hall, and from there into the drawing room, where Alice de Roujay was pouring camomile tea into large Luneville cups. "Would you rather have coffee?" she asked.

"No."

"Marthe can easily make some."

"No. It keeps me awake."

Bertrand took a cup of camomile tea and sat on one of the frail old chairs, to one side of the fireplace. His mother sat on the sofa opposite him, and his father, farther away, was trying to read a newspaper by the dim light of an electric lamp.

"You should have stronger bulbs," said Bertrand to his father, but Edmond de Roujay either did not hear or more probably ignored it, for every time Bertrand came to Saint Théodore he said the same thing.

"We're not millionaires," said his mother with a smile.

Bertrand smiled too, because his mother was more than a millionaire in French francs, but was as frugal as her husband, and like him saw no need for bright lights. She took her embroidery out of a round wicker box, then put on an old pair of spectacles to thread a needle.

"Would you like me to do that?" asked Bertrand as he watched her battle against the dim light and her own poor eyesight.

"No, thank you," she replied sharply, and a moment later pierced the eye of the needle with the thread. "What's your news from Paris?"

"Much the same as you see in the papers," said Bertrand. "What is yours from London?"

She glanced over her sewing and gave her son a conspiratorial smile, for Bertrand was alluding to her habit of listening to the BBC on an old radio on her bedside table. "They're relieved to have saved so many of their men from Dunkirk."

"They're lucky to have the Channel."

"Yes. It's like a moat."

"Better than a Maginot Line." He glanced toward his father, but the colonel appeared not to have heard.

"They seem to think that we will ask for an armistice."

Bertrand shook his head. "It seems impossible . . . after only a month."

"The English are worried about the fleet."

"With some reason."

They talked quietly, not to conceal what they were saying from Edmond de Roujay, but to avoid obliging him to join in.

"Have you thought," Alice now asked her son, "of what is to become of Titine during the holidays?" She did not look at Bertrand when she said this, but kept her eyes on her stitching fingers.

"Can't she stay here?" he asked.

"Of course. This is her home. She must stay here. My only worry is"—and here her voice became hard—"that *others* may feel that they have right to take her elsewhere."

Bertrand was always ill at ease when he spoke about Madeleine with his mother, for however much he may have felt that he had suffered at her hands, his resentment was nothing compared to the cold enmity felt by the pious Alice de Roujay for her former daughter-in-law. It was not just that Alice, like any mother, had sided with and suffered for her son; it was also that Madeleine had become the butt of all those hatreds and antagonisms she had formerly repressed for the sake of her soul.

"The fact is, Maman," said Bertrand, "that others have whatever rights they have, and there is nothing we can do about it."

"But it is intolerable that a child of that age should be allowed into an adulterous household, and come under the influence of that atheist."

"All the same, she's her mother."

"A true mother would not have deserted her daughter."

"The court allowed her a month in the summer."

"It's evil."

"We can't bring up Titine as a stranger to her mother."

"You should marry again, Bertrand. Find a decent girl who would be a mother to her."

Bertrand sighed, for even though he was now almost forty years old, his mother could rile him by a simple remark of this kind. At times she seemed to know him so well that she could read any of the thoughts which came into his head; yet she continued to speak of his marrying a "decent girl" as if the choice of Madeleine nine years before had been an aberration. It vexed him that she should be so obtuse, yet he could never bring himself to tell her outright that he would never marry the kind of pious simpleton that his mother had in mind, and he was appalled to think that she might ever know about his affair with Lucía.

"It's not a moment to get married," he said.

"No," she said. "Perhaps not."

"And if I were to marry again, it might not be to the kind of girl you have in mind."

She kept her bespectacled eyes on her sewing. "I can't imagine that you'd make the same mistake twice."

Bertrand lit a cigarette, and as always the smell of tobacco evoked the taste of nicotine on Lucía's lips.

"It's well known," he said with a laugh, "that divorced men marry replicas of their first wives."

"You are not divorced," said Alice firmly.

"I know, I know."

"The marriage was never a marriage." She spoke in a tone of triumph, as if the annulment had been proof that God shared her point of view.

"Of course, but all the same, it wouldn't necessarily be a good thing for Titine," he said.

"What?" asked his mother.

"If I got married again."

His mother said nothing.

"She's settled here. You give her a home."

"But we are old."

"Better old grandparents here at Saint Théodore than some young stepmother in an apartment in Mézac who finds her a nuisance."

Alice broke the piece of thread with her teeth. "A decent girl wouldn't find her a nuisance."

"Well, you'll have to find me one."

On the chair opposite Bertrand, Edmond de Roujay had finished the article he had been reading. He leaned forward and, having heard the last exchange, said to Bertrand, "Don't be in a hurry, dear boy. These ladies can't bear to see a man single."

"It's not that at all," said Alice.

"The little girl's happy here, isn't she?"

"She seems so," said Bertrand.

"My mother always used to say," said Edmond, "that you should never marry unless you have to."

"If everyone took her advice," said Alice, "the human race would be extinct."

Her husband laughed. "It's too late to argue," he said. "I'm for bed."

"I'm coming," his wife said. She put her embroidery away.

"Don't forget to turn out the lights," said Edmond to his son, as he always did.

"I won't."

"Good night, then." The colonel left the room.

Alice de Roujay stooped to kiss her son. "Sleep well."

"Yes."

Bertrand watched her leave the room, then picked up the magazine that his father had left on the table—*Le Bulletin du Diocèse de Langeais* —but since there was little in it to interest him, and in any case the light was too dim, he soon followed his parents and climbed the wide staircase to sleep in the room which had been his since he was a child.

He awoke late. The slatted shutters kept the sunlight out of his room, but he could tell from the strength of the yellow beams which hit the wooden floor that it must already be after nine.

The room had a particular smell and the bed a particular shape which always held him in a semiconscious trance between waking and rising. It had taken him a moment to know where he was, and then another to remember whether it would be his sister Dominique who would come and bounce on his bed or his daughter Titine. For a moment he even imagined that Madeleine lay next to him on the bed, for she had breathed so quietly that often only her warmth told him that she was there.

Now, however, as the chaotic jumble of dreams and memories became organized in his mind, he realized that the warmth against his back came from the bolster which at some moment in the night he had pushed off his body. He raised himself on an elbow and looked at his watch. It was twenty minutes past nine. He rose, went to the window and pushed back the shutters. The last wisps of cool air wafted around his face as he looked out over the rough turf of the garden to the meadows, olive trees and vines beyond. He could hear a tractor from behind the house, and a clatter of trashcan lids from outside the kitchen.

He turned back into the bedroom and crossed to the dressing table to brush his hair. He peered for a moment at the face he saw in the mirror. The bright light from the windows showed new crevices around his mouth and eyes, and tufts of graying hair like the badger bristle of his shaving brush. He turned away from his own reflection to look for his dressing gown and slippers in the painted wardrobe which had been brought to his room when he married. He kept some clothes at Saint Théodore—the dressing gown, a tweed jacket, some corduroy trousers and an old-fashioned double-breasted suit which he wore when asked to dine with neighbors, or at the fête at Pévier on the 14th of July. One or two dresses which Madeleine had kept for the same reason remained hanging in the wardrobe next to his suit. She had never returned to collect them.

On the landing he could smell coffee, and on the stairs he was met by his daughter, who like a puppy came up from the hall to kiss him, then turned and accompanied him down again. "At last, Papa. I thought you'd sleep till lunchtime, but Grand'mere said I wasn't to wake you because you were very tired because you work so hard."

She took hold of one end of his dressing-gown cord and led him like a pet dog into the kitchen. There Marthe stood by the stove in her blue dress and gray apron, as unchanging as the brown china coffeepot which she took to fill the bowl on the table.

Bertrand sat at the only place which remained. Titine sat down beside him, and in a moment, as if sensing that Bertrand was there, his father came to join him. Breakfast at Saint Théodore had always been a moment when the de Roujay family would begin those discussions which often ran on into the middle of the morning—provoked, on most occasions, by some item of news in the morning newspaper, or an article in a magazine.

The newspaper which lay on the table showed the first pictures of the Germans in Paris. For a moment Bertrand fell into a mood of such rage and despair that he turned to remonstrate with his father, who with Louis had always advocated the defensive strategy which events had shown to be wrong, but he saw at once in the old man's eyes that he too was aghast at what had befallen France. Politics had ceased to be a game. Moreover, the presence of Titine, chattering excitedly to her father, and the need to protect her from the fear they all felt at the thought of the German triumph, prevented any serious discussion.

"They say Churchill was in France," said Edmond de Roujay. "He met Reynaud in Tours."

"What can he do?"

"Send the RAF."

"And leave Britain defenseless?"

The colonel shrugged his shoulders. "If they'd sent more planes in the first place . . ."

"A lot of things should have been done in the first place," said Bertrand.

His father turned away. Even less than Bertrand did he wish to analyze the reasons for France's defeat.

"Hurry up, Papa," said Titine, tugging at the cord of his dressing gown. "It's so lovely outside. We mustn't waste the day."

When he was dressed, Bertrand went with his father and daughter to inspect some newly planted vines. Two years before, Edmond de Roujay had dismissed Claude, the bailiff, not only because he judged him idle and dishonest, but also because he wanted to manage his estate himself. Running a vineyard, however, had turned out to be more difficult than commanding a regiment, and Edmond had come to rely on the advice of the Spaniard Astran, who remained housed in one of the cottages with his wife and son.

Astran no longer limped from his wounded leg, but he remained a taciturn man whose brooding eyes were hard to read. His knowledge of vines came from his father's smallholding in the Andalusian hills. He himself had moved into the city of Málaga as a young man to work on the railways; it was his work as a trade unionist which had led him into the Communist Party and, at the time of the civil war, into the ranks of the Republican army.

He had never found a job near Saint Théodore, and so to keep himself occupied he had started to help with the vines. It had soon become apparent that whatever else he might have learned as an industrial worker, he had never unlearned the skills of a peasant with a half hectare of vines. He could tell from the look of a leaf whether the soil was acid or alkaline, and at a glance could diagnose the first signs of the different pests which could blight the harvest of a whole year.

Astran was working on the new vines as the three of them approached. Bertrand greeted Astran, but he was always ill at ease in his presence, because he did not know if the Spaniard knew or suspected that he slept with his daughter. Lucía always insisted that her father knew nothing, and Astran himself gave nothing away. He hid his expression under his dark brow; his eyes seemed to stare at the soil. It was as if his disappointment and disillusion had killed his concern for anything other than the leaf he held in his hand.

"They're growing," he said to the colonel.

"They've taken root?"

"Yes."

"Excellent."

Bertrand looked at the tawny neck of Astran as the man looked at his boots. It would have been difficult to believe that the soft skin of Lucía's neck came from this man, had not his eyes and nose reminded him of her.

"Bad news from the north," Bertrand said to Astran.

"Yes."

"You should be safe here."

Astran said nothing.

"You're a French citizen, after all."

"Yes." Astran had once, and only once, thanked Bertrand for using his influence to obtain papers for his family. Thereafter it became impossible to tell whether he felt beholden to the de Roujays for what they had done, or whether he resented his dependence on them and loathed them as examples of the class he had fought to destroy.

"If things get worse," said Bertrand, "Lucía shouldn't stay in Mézac. She should come out here."

At the mention of his daughter's name, Astran made a quick movement with his head—a movement which was almost a gesture, a gesture which was almost a word, but a word which could have meant many things. "She'll make up her own mind," he said.

"I daresay."

There was an awkward pause. Then Edmond said, "We'd better get on," and set off with Bertrand and Titine toward the house. The child ran ahead to fetch her school books while Bertrand went to wait for her in the library. He stood for a while in the cool, dark room, studying the odd collection of books on the tall mahogany shelves: vellum-bound editions of Madame de Sevigné or the Duc de Saint Simon, side by side with military memoirs of the Franco-Prussian War and more modern novels by Bourget, Gyp and Mauriac.

On the wall there was a portrait of Bertrand's grandfather, the staunch anti-Dreyfusard, in military uniform. By the window there was an Empire desk, and next to it a radio housed in a large cabinet veneered in walnut. Titine came in, and father and daughter sat down side by side on a fat sofa with frayed covers of beige damask. Titine's dark little face looked earnestly at him as he looked through the exercise books at the work she had done: short dictations in a neat, precise hand, and the same precision in the rows of figures in mathematics.

At the age of seven, Titine had already begun to show the same strengths and weaknesses as her father. When he looked at her and she smiled up into his face, it was as if he were a boy again smiling at himself in a mirror, for in shape, size and physiognomy she took after her father. There was no trace of Madeleine. Only at rare moments, and in a certain light, did she suddenly take on some mannerism of her mother's which carried Bertrand back beyond their marriage to the days when the little friend of his sister, Madeleine Bonnet, had come with her mother to stay.

They had been warned that Bertrand's Uncle Charles, the bishop, was expected for lunch, and at ten to twelve Titine saw a sleek black episcopal limousine approach up the drive. Bertrand, who was fond of his Uncle Charles, went to the door to meet him, and as always his uncle embraced him with the same huge hug that he had given him as a child.

Charles Ravanel was now over sixty years of age, but a life of measured mortification had left him strong and alert. He remained a tall man with thick black hair no more gray than Bertrand's and was dressed in the same elegant, old-fashioned black frock coat, with a gold crucifix hanging at his chest beneath his clerical collar.

"My dear Bertrand," he said. "I hoped you might be here. It's such a pleasure." Then he walked on into the house, saying in the loud voice that filled the cathedral of Langeais, "Ah, Théodore, how pleasant you have made it here." He met his sister in the hall and kissed her with the same warmth that he had shown her husband and son. "I'm sure you are partly responsible, my dear," he went on, "but I sense a certain peace, a holy tranquillity, which I can only ascribe to the influence of its patron saint."

Alice de Roujay smiled and led her brother into the drawing room, saying to Bertrand, "Pour your uncle a drink."

"Now tell me," the bishop asked his sister, "what news of Louis?"

"None."

He sighed and shrugged his shoulders. "He is in the hands of God."

"As is France," said Alice.

"The government is a little disappointed in our French saints," said Bertrand, referring to the solemn invocation by Reynaud and his ministers the month before at the Basilica of the Sacré Coeur in Paris.

"But it was ridiculous," said Edmond de Roujay. "All those Radicals, Socialists and freethinkers who have been persecuting the Church for decades expecting Saint Geneviève to stop the German tanks."

"Who do we invoke to stop the Italians?" Bertrand asked with a smile.

"Oh, we can deal with them on our own," said Edmond.

"It is all unbelievable, unbelievable," said the bishop. "I happen to know that the Holy Father is mortified. Only a week ago he received Monsieur François-Poncet and had to confess that there was nothing, nothing, he could do to stop the Italians from declaring war. The Duce won't listen to him. They say he won't even read his letters!"

"Then His Holiness should denounce him," said Bertrand.

"Of course, of course, but he cannot seem to take sides."

"Why not?"

"Ah, it's simple for us to say that. But think of what he must consider: the Church in Italy, the Church in Germany, all the faithful in Poland and Bohemia. He cannot provoke persecution with noble rhetoric that would do nothing to alter the course of the war."

Bertrand shrugged his shoulders. "Then the vicar of Christ becomes a spectator."

"Some think we deserve our defeat," said Alice de Roujay.

"Deserve it? How?" asked Edmond de Roujay.

"France is now so depraved . . ."

"Certainly, certainly . . ." said the bishop.

"But France all the same!" expostulated the colonel.

"Are the Nazis less depraved?" asked Bertrand in a calmer tone of voice.

"No," said the bishop. "They are just depraved in a different way."

"Neither better nor worse?"

"In a struggle between two different varieties of depravity," said Charles Ravanel, "perhaps the just man should stay neutral."

"The curé thinks," said Alice, "that we are being punished for our sins."

"Our sins?" asked Edmond. "You mean the sins of the damned Jews and Freemasons."

"Of course, of course . . ." murmured the bishop.

"It's not the fault of France that it's been run by a bunch of crooks."

"Take heart, take heart," said the bishop. "The Lord works in a mysterious way his wonders to perform. Who knows? Perhaps this disaster has been sent by the Lord to chastise us, and change us all into better men."

"Under the Nazis?" asked Bertrand.

"No, no," said the bishop, "but perhaps, God willing, under Marshal Pétain."

At lunch the presence of Titine enabled the adults to keep off the war as a subject of conversation, and the little girl, used by the grown-ups in this way, flourished under their attention. Afterward, however, she ran off to the kitchen while the older de Roujays went to take coffee at the table and chairs under the chestnut trees. There, in a quieter and graver tone of voice, the bishop gave a serious exposition of his views on the war.

"It's undeniably true," he said, "that the war is lost. Whether it is lost because of Freemasonry, freethinking, socialism, pacifism or simply strategic misjudgment by the high command is of interest solely to historians. The only question to be asked and answered now, surely, is what can be salvaged from the wreck."

"I don't accept," said Bertrand, "that France is a wreck."

"Accept the facts, dear boy. The army is defeated. We are at the mercy of the Germans."

"We still have the fleet," interposed Edmond.

"And the colonies," said Bertrand.

"The fleet, the colonies, yes, so a few of us could continue the war with the English—if, that is, the English continue the war, which I doubt! But what use would that be to those left in France? It would only antagonize the Germans and lead them to treat us in the same way as they have treated the Poles. No, if Reynaud were to be replaced by someone who had always regarded them with more understanding . . ."

"Laval?" asked Edmond.

"No, someone who was above party politics."

"The Marshal," said Bertrand.

"Precisely. If the Marshal, who stands for all that is best in France, indeed who *is* France, were to ask for an honorable armistice, isn't it possible that Hitler would respond?"

"But what about the English?" asked Bertrand.

"The English, you know," said the bishop, "the perfidious English, would do the same to us if they were in the same predicament."

"I've never been happy with an English alliance," said Edmond de Roujay. "I've always thought they were very expensive allies."

"But they stand for democracy and freedom," said Bertrand.

"And profit—their profit," said his father.

"Certainly in Rome," said the bishop, who had spent ten years in the Curia, "there is little sympathy with the English."

"But no one can want Hitler to win the war!" said Bertrand.

"Hitler *has* won the war," said the bishop. "May God forgive me, but not even Saint Geneviève can save us now."

"The English don't think so," said Bertrand.

"Oh, that's what they say, but I wouldn't be surprised if at this very minute they are negotiating with the Germans. What else can they do? The Russians are neutralized by an alliance. The Americans show no signs of coming to their help. That Channel of theirs can hold off the

Germans for a time, but in the end they'll have to sue for peace."

"We should reach some understanding with the Spaniards and Italians," said Edmond. "I've always liked Laval's idea of some sort of alliance between the Mediterranean states. The English have no business there."

"The Marshal got on well with Franco," said Charles Ravanel. "And I'm sure some sort of support could be gained from Mussolini as well."

Bertrand had turned pale. Over the years there had frequently been arguments of this kind with his father, uncle or brother—invariably the other members of his family had expressed a conservative point of view—but now, when opinions led to policies which affected the destiny of France, he could hardly restrain a sense of disgust.

"But I cannot understand," he said to his uncle, "how you as a priest can propose any kind of compromise with a man like Hitler."

"My dear Bertrand," said the prelate, who when earnest dropped his baroque style of speech, "if I was the abbot of La Trappe, or St. Simeon Stylites on top of his pillar, I would remain aloof from the mundane quarrels between states which, *sub specie aeternitatis,* are just the snarling and scrapping of different beasts. But I am a bishop, not a monk. I must think of the good people of Langeais. The army is defeated. The vandals are at the gates. Should I mount the battlements, like Gregory the Great in Rome? And even he came to terms with the barbarian invaders. Remember, Bertrand, the Germans are not the murderers of priests and nuns. Among the invaders there are men who are as Christian as you and me. Remember, too, that the Germans conquered us before, only seventy years ago. Thiers made terms with them then. The Marshal could do the same now."

The bishop left at four that afternoon, and Bertrand, depressed by their conversation, retired to the library to listen to the news. What he heard depressed him further. The Germans continued their inexorable advance into France; the Maginot Line was outflanked; Normandy was overrun. In Bordeaux the Council of Ministers was in session, and it was thought that an armistice had been suggested but that no decision had been taken.

Abroad, the Soviet armies had marched into Lithuania, Latvia and Estonia, and this last item of news angered Bertrand as much as any of the others. Like hyenas, the Soviets were feeding off the corpses left by the marauding wolves. He loathed them more than the Nazis, because while the Nazis never pretended to be other than what they were, the Communists preached the freedom and equality of man while conquering sovereign nations and seducing other men's wives.

It was a result of his training as a civil servant that Bertrand could conceal his strongest feelings. At supper that night he neither argued with his father nor even alluded to their differences on the terrible questions of the war. Edmond, too, seemed chastened and confused by his own thoughts and feelings. Like Bertrand, he had no desire to add to his sufferings by quarreling with his son. As a result they hardly spoke at all, for they were beyond the pretense that they could show interest in the farm or vineyard. Only Titine enforced some semblance of cheerfulness and normality, though even she sensed that things were not normal, and retreated with an instinctive discretion to pass her time with Marthe in the kitchen.

What held the de Roujays in one another's company for the rest of the weekend was not just the meals they took together, but the two radios—the large cabinet in the library, and the smaller receiver made of black plastic on Alice de Roujay's bedside table. At ten that night they all assembled to listen to the news from Bordeaux; at eight the next morning, before leaving for mass, they met again for the same reason. Little had changed overnight; the plight of the army deteriorated by the hour. Reynaud had sent a telegram to Roosevelt, imploring him to bring America into the war. "If not, you will see France sink like a drowning man and disappear with one last look toward the land of Liberty, whence she awaits salvation."

They were there again at midday. Now there were rumors that Reynaud wanted the French army to surrender while his government continued the war from abroad. Weygand had refused to bring dishonor on the flag, and Pétain had refused to leave France. The three de Roujays listened to the transmission, and then once again parted without exchanging a word.

After lunch that Sunday, Bertrand returned to Mézac. He ate supper alone in his flat, listening yet again to the news. Roosevelt had replied to Reynaud: America would do what she could to help the democracies, but "I know you will not interpret this declaration as implying military intervention. Only Congress can enter into such an engagement."

At nine, Bertrand tuned in to the BBC. The British cabinet had proposed an indissoluble union between Britain and France for the pursuit of the war against the Axis powers. At ten the same news came from Bordeaux. Reynaud, it seemed, supported the idea of a union, but many of his ministers opposed it.

A few minutes before midnight the telephone rang. It was Pierre Moreau in Coustiers.

"Were you in bed?"

"No."

"Have you heard?"

"What?"

"Reynaud has fallen. A friend rang from Bordeaux. Pétain has taken over."

This news was given in more detail over the radio the next day. General Weygand had been made minister of national defense, Admiral Darlan minister of the marine. Léon Blum had approved the presence of two Socialist ministers in the new coalition.

At his office at the subprefecture, Bertrand was telephoned by Charrier. "It's for the best," he said.

For a moment Bertrand said nothing; then an unconscious caution prompted him to agree. "I'm sure you're right."

"He's asked for an armistice," said Charrier.

This time he did not hesitate. "Let's hope for the best," he said.

To Devaux, Bertrand repeated what the prefect had said—"it's for the best"—and this phrase went around the subprefecture as the approved point of view.

At noon, Bertrand, Pidner, Devaux and most of the others who worked at the subprefecture, including Bertrand's driver, Albert, stood around the radio in his office to listen to the first broadcast of Marshal Pétain as president of the Council of Ministers.

"Frenchmen," he said. "Summoned by the President of the Republic, I assume from today the leadership of the government of France. It is with a sad heart that I tell you today that we must stop fighting. I have this night approached the enemy and asked him if he is prepared to negotiate with us, as between soldiers, and after the battle has been fought with all honor, to find means of putting an end to hostilities.

"Let all Frenchmen gather loyally during this hard trial in support of the government over which I preside, and let them put aside their anguish and retain only their faith in the destiny of our motherland."

Bertrand looked at the faces of those around him. They were all pale and still. Albert, the driver, stood at attention, his eyes fixed on the middle distance, tears running down his cheeks. The instinct which had prompted Bertrand to agree with Charrier now led him to sigh and say, "Well, that's it. It's over." Devaux and some of the other officials took up the same refrain, investing their sighs and the tone of voice with which they repeated the phrase with varying degrees of relief and exasperation. Only Pidner, the Freemason, said nothing but scuttled furtively back to his desk, looking anywhere but at his colleagues lest they would see the expression of fear in his face.

His unease, and Bertrand's caution, were both given substance later in the day when they heard that Georges Mandel, who twenty-four hours before had been the minister of the interior, had been arrested in Bordeaux. This confirmed to Bertrand what he had realized from studying the list of ministerial appointments—that the soldiers now in command would be less tolerant of dissent and indiscipline than the men they had succeeded. Already Albert, when he came for instructions for the following day, had brushed away his tears and carried himself with a new zest. "We should have had the Marshal years ago," he said.

That evening Bertrand went to dinner with those cousins of Louis's wife Hélène who persistently tried to match him with their unmarried daughter. They had three sons in the army, and could not hide their delight that hostilities were to end. "It was the only thing to do," said the host. "And with the Marshal in charge, it gives us a chance to clean up the country."

The next morning, in his office, on a faint and crackling line, Bertrand heard the voice of his brother, Louis. "I'm in Nevers," he said. "This whole war is insane. We killed a dozen Boches. Then we were captured, but they had so many prisoners they let half of us go."

"Thank God you're alive," said Bertrand.

"Tell Hélène, will you?" said Louis. "And the old folks."

Bertrand immediately rang his sister-in-law in Coustiers, but was told by her maid that she had gone with her children to Saint Théodore. Rather than telephone his home, Bertrand decided that he would give the news to his family in person. He left his office early, but before leaving Mézac returned to his apartment to telephone Pierre. "Are you alone?" he asked him.

"Yes."

"Take care."

"Of what?"

"Of what you say."

"Already . . ."

"Yes. And our conversation last week at lunch . . ."

"What about it?"

"Keep it to yourself."

"Of course."

Bertrand rang off, picked up his car keys from the marble-topped table in the hall and left to fetch the Panhard.

He reached Saint Théodore soon after five. The news that Louis was safe made Hélène burst into tears. She had become more placid as she had grown older, and without Louis's effervescent presence she went flat, like a disconnected battery. Alice de Roujay did not cry, but went to her bedroom, where she fell to her knees on the well-worn prie-dieu placed before a crucifix between the two windows. After a moment of prayer to the Virgin of Lourdes, she was disturbed by a knock on the door.

"Come in," she said, turning as Bertrand entered the room.

Bertrand saw his mother on her knees. "I'm sorry," he said.

"No, come in."

"The BBC . . ." he began.

"Is it time?"

"More or less."

She stood, went to the radio by her large four-poster bed and switched it on. As she waited for it to warm up, she smiled at her son. "So he's safe," she said.

"Yes."

"For him it's over."

She bent over the radio. A voice came through the whistles, whines and crackles, saying: "This is the French Service of the BBC. We now broadcast an appeal by General Charles de Gaulle."

"Who is de Gaulle?" asked Alice de Roujay.

"He was undersecretary for war under Reynaud."

"And now?"

Bertrand shrugged his shoulders. "Now he's nothing."

An abrupt, haughty voice came over the air. "The leaders who for many years have been at the head of the French armies have formed a government. This government, alleging that our armies have been defeated, has started negotiations with the enemy to stop the war.

"Indeed, we have been, we are, overwhelmed by the mechanical forces of the enemy both on the ground and in the air. It is the quantity of tanks and airplanes as well as the tactics of the Germans which, much more than their numbers, have surprised our leaders and led them to the situation in which they are today.

"But has the last word been said? Has all hope gone? Is defeat final? No!

"Believe me, a man who knows what has brought this about, when I say that France is not lost. The same methods which have defeated us may well one day bring us victory. For France does not stand alone. She is not alone. She has a huge empire behind her. She can make a solid bloc with the British Empire, which has command of the seas and continues the struggle. She can, like England, make limitless use of the huge industrial resources of the United States.

"This war is not confined to the unhappy territory of our land. This war is not determined by the outcome of the battle of France. This war is a world war. All the mistakes, all the delays, all the sufferings do not alter the fact that there is, in the world, all that is necessary to destroy our enemies one day. Overwhelmed today by mechanized forces, we can conquer in the future by superior mechanized forces. The fate of the world depends on it.

"I, General de Gaulle, at present in London, invite French officers and soldiers who are in British territory or who may find themselves there, either with or without their arms, to get in touch with me. Whatever may happen, the flame of French resistance must not and shall not be extinguished."

The transmission came to an end. Alice de Roujay looked at her son. "Yes," she said, "for Louis it is over, but for you, Bertrand, I am afraid it is just beginning."

4

On Monday, July 1, the government of Marshal Pétain arrived in the spa town of Vichy, which, until the Germans left Paris, was to be the administrative capital of France. The Marshal himself, together with the Ministry of Foreign Affairs, moved into the Hôtel du Parc, while the Ministry of National Defense went to the Hôtel Thermal and the ministries of Justice and Finance to the Carlton.

Already it had been made clear that the new government, led by a marshal and including several senior officers from the army and navy, expected a greater measure of discipline among those they governed than had existed before. The armistice in particular was to be accepted by all. Those who refused were insubordinate, while those who rallied to General de Gaulle were guilty of treason.

Though few among the French had heard de Gaulle's first broadcast, word spread of his appeal and its scorn for those leaders who had taken advantage of a defeat, which they themselves had largely brought about, in order to seize power, and in the first few days of that week in the beginning of July, Bertrand overheard some grumbles in Mézac about the speed and ease with which Pétain and his ministers had resigned themselves to coexistence with the deadly enemies of the week before.

On Thursday, however, news reached France which seemed to justify *post facto* the Marshal's shifting loyalty. A British fleet under Admiral Sir James Somerville had trapped the Atlantic squadron of the French fleet off the North African coast near Mers-el-Kebir. Admiral Gensoul had been sent an ultimatum either to surrender or scuttle his fleet to prevent it from falling into the hands of the Germans. He had refused to do either, and at three minutes to five in the afternoon the British ships had opened fire at point-blank range, sinking or disabling most of the ships and leaving over twelve hundred French dead.

When it received this news, the government in Vichy reacted "with stupefaction," and on the 5th and 6th of July made two air raids on Gibraltar in symbolic retaliation, dropping their bombs into the sea. It stopped short of declaring war on its former ally, but the perfidious attack at Mers-el-Kebir made it easier for Pierre Laval and his political allies to persuade the National Assembly, reconvened in Vichy, to vote for its own demise and, with pedantic legality, transfer full executive and legislative power to a single man, Marshal Pétain.

The government also introduced further measures against those who wished to continue the war. Already directives had been issued to arrest anyone who was suspected of leaving the country to join de Gaulle, and by the end of the month legislation had been passed depriving all those who did so of their French citizenship, and imposing the death penalty on any member of the armed forces who left France to fight abroad. De Gaulle himself was ordered to return from London to face a court-martial, and when he failed to appear he was tried in absentia and condemned to death by the Military Tribunal of Clermont Ferrand.

Soon after the incident at Mers-el-Kebir, Louis de Roujay returned to Saint Théodore. Bertrand came out for the weekend to greet his brother, sunburned and exhausted after the campaign, and on Sunday went with the rest of his family to the parish church, where on the orders of the new government the curé recited a Te Deum to give thanks to God for the end of the war. They then walked back on the well-known path to the house and ate Sunday lunch, hardly able to believe that the family had emerged intact from the disasters of the previous weeks.

This happiness did not inhibit their arguments at table, for Louis, whose men were now prisoners of the Germans and who was himself still to hear whether he would be demobilized or would be kept on to serve in the armistice army, insisted that the cause of their defeat lay with the weakness and corruption of the Third Republic. "You can't blame the men," he said. "They fought, when they had the chance, with extraordinary courage on a personal level, but however brave you are, when you are faced with Stukas and flame-throwers . . ."

"But why," asked Bertrand, "did our men not have their own dive bombers and flamethrowers?"

"Because the politicians denied them to the army. They were all Socialists, pacifists, Freemasons and Jews who since the days of Dreyfus have had a pathological hatred of the army, and so voted against the estimates in the Chamber."

"But it was the army," said Bertrand irritably, "and you yourself,

Louis, who dismissed the ideas of General de Gaulle and insisted on a defensive strategy around the Maginot Line."

"Yes, and the Maginot Line held its sector, but how could we know that both the Belgians and the English would let us down in the north?"

"They didn't let us down," said Bertrand.

"Listen," said Louis. "The English had nine months to build up their expeditionary force. What did they send to the Continent in those nine months? Ten divisions! Against the Germans' one hundred and thirty. And the celebrated RAF—where were their fighters when the Stukas were hammering us from the sky?"

"It has always been my opinion," said Edmond de Roujay in his ageing, quavering voice, "that the English were never serious about involving themselves once again in a war for the defense of France."

"How can you say that, Papa?" said Bertrand. "When they lost so many men on French soil in the last war?"

"But that's precisely my point," said the colonel. "They bled, just as we bled, but for what? Their real interests are not here on the Continent, but in India, Africa and America. And their chief rivals were never Germany or the Bolsheviks, but Italy and France—yes, France!" His voice rose a tone. "Doesn't Mers-el-Kebir prove it? They're after our colonial possessions in Africa and the Middle East!"

"Then why," asked Bertrand, "are they supporting de Gaulle?"

"De Gaulle," said Louis in a derisive tone of voice. "His only value is as a puppet—especially as he has the nose of Monsieur Punch."

"Yes," said Edmond. "He is a disappointed man whose promotion was delayed because of his impossible personality, and who hoped to outflank his superiors by writing books and meddling in politics. Well, Reynaud may have had his uses for him, and I daresay Churchill does too, but as far as France is concerned, he is a traitorous mutineer."

"I don't agree," said Bertrand coldly. "He is a patriot."

"It's easy enough to be a patriot," said Louis, "when you're safe with your wife and children on the other side of the Channel."

"He may well be a patriot, according to his own lights," said Edmond, "but is he President of France? Is he even president of the Council of Ministers? No. He is the former junior minister of war in a government that has fallen from power. He has no legal authority whatsoever to carry on the war."

"In my opinion," said Louis, "he has gone slightly mad. The sound of his name has gone to his head."

"Not at all," said Bertrand. "He is—he always was—a man who looked ahead. He saw what kind of war we would have to fight against the Germans, and begged us to prepare for it. He was ignored."

"Oh, he wasn't the only one," said Louis.

"Now he recognizes that we have lost a battle, but that the war will go on and in the end will be won."

"That's fantasy."

"Not at all," said Bertrand again. "The Germans have won the first round because they always intended to attack us and so were better prepared. We were not, that's clear. But if the English can stave off an invasion and organize the resources not just of their empire but of the United States as well, in the end the Germans will lose, and when that happens France will be there among the victors."

"You're dreaming," said Louis, tossing his head back with an arrogant laugh. "You're dreaming the dreams of a man who has never seen action."

Bertrand turned pale. "Wars are won by intelligence," he said, "not by imbecilic bravado."

Louis laughed, delighted to have riled his brother. "You may be right," he said. "In five years, ten years, Germany may be defeated. But what will happen to France in the meanwhile? Must the country be destroyed like Poland on a promise of a share in the spoils of victory?"

"All this is beside the point," said Edmond, pink in the face with exasperation. "The question is not whether we should fight on or come to an arrangement. The question is one of authority. Who decides? What is the chain of command?"

Bertrand looked perplexed. "Ideally the government should decide—" he began.

"And it has decided. A democratic government. A republican government, led by our most distinguished citizen, Marshal Pétain, which has listened to the advice of its commanders in the field. It has decided. The war must cease. It has issued its orders. De Gaulle disobeys."

"There are moments," said Bertrand, "when one must disobey."

"But who does he think he is," asked Edmond, "to defy Marshal Pétain and the government of France?"

During this argument among the men, Alice de Roujay said nothing. Even when her sons were boys and had harangued one another across the breakfast table, she had never joined in, because she saw discussions of this kind as a male pursuit, like shooting, smoking or serving in the army. Despite this silence, however, she had opinions of her own. She read the newspapers and listened to the bulletins on the radio as assiduously as the others, but she kept her opinions to herself, and even when asked to express them by Edmond did so reluctantly because she had been brought up to believe that a wife should never contradict her husband, and the conclusions she arrived at were invariably the opposite of his.

Knowing this, Edmond rarely asked for her views on politics or military affairs; nor did Louis, who knew that she would side against him, and Bertrand, over the years, had learned not to appeal to her for help against his father and brother because he saw that it upset her to disagree with Edmond. Yet her silence at their discussion that Sunday was quite as powerful as her arguments might have been, because all three recognized the practicality of her Ravanel mind and knew what she would have said had she spoken.

That evening, after supper, Louis and Edmond went out into the garden to smoke a cigarette in the cool evening air, while Bertrand followed his mother up the stairs to her bedroom to listen once again to the BBC and hear what comment de Gaulle would make on the British attack at Mers-el-Kebir.

The general spoke of his grief and anger at the news, but asked his listeners "to consider the whole affair from the point of view that matters in the end—that is to say, the point of view of ultimate victory and deliverance of our country. . . . By viewing the whole tragedy in its true light, but at the same time doing everything possible to prevent it from resulting in mortal strife between French and British, all men of foresight on both sides of the Channel are also running true to form, the form of the patriot. Come what may, our two great peoples are still linked together. Either they will both succumb, or they will triumph side by side."

When it was over, they both sat in silence until Bertrand said quietly, "You know, don't you, that I must join him."

His mother sighed. "Yes."

"Do you think I am right?"

"I don't know. There's so much you could do here."

"Not for much longer. I am suspect already."

"Even so, here at home . . ."

"You'll have Louis."

"But Titine . . ."

"Titine, yes. She will suffer." He stood and looked away from his mother out of the window toward the vines. "I have thought of that —I have thought of it a thousand times—but will she suffer less growing up under the Nazis?"

"Pétain is not Hitler."

He turned to face her again. "I know, Maman, I know. But he's an old man. Laval will follow and ape the dictators. Titine will be taken and shaped in that mold." He sat and took hold of his mother's hands. "You know, a week ago I thought how awful it would be if in ten years' time Titine were to ask me, 'Why did you let it happen?' But now I realize that it will be worse, far worse, if she does not ask that question, but accepts what they teach her."

"You don't think," asked Alice tentatively, "that it is God's intention to punish us?"

"No."

"Your Uncle Charles . . ."

"I know. But to me that hypothesis is absurd, because however weak and decadent our Republic may be, it was never an evil regime like the Nazi government of Germany."

"Perhaps not."

"So why should God punish us rather than them?"

She shook her head. "I don't know."

"The Lord helps those who help themselves, Maman. It is a question of will—the will of the French to survive as a nation, the will of individual French men and women. And I have that will, not just from a sentimental attachment to the tricolor and the 'Marseillaise,' but from a considered certainty that the values embodied in France are of unique value to the human race."

"Yes."

"To preserve them we must fight for them."

"Yes."

"You see, Maman, I would rather die fighting for the real France, even though it would make Titine an orphan, than live safely with her in a department of the Reich—for then, in ten years, she might ask herself: 'Why did my father die?' And in asking that question she would keep alive in her mind the idea of liberty and a love of France."

As subprefect of Mézac, Bertrand was informed of what measures were being prepared against the Gaullists well before they were made public. He therefore knew that his own departure would not be easy to arrange. He would need an exit visa from France, a transit visa through Spain and a visa to enter Portugal; yet if it became known that he was applying for any one of these he would immediately become suspect himself. To allay suspicion he would have to convince his colleagues that the man who a few weeks before had planned a redoubt in Mézac had now rallied to Pétain and the armistice. He therefore called a meeting of Bax, Guillot, Devaux and Pidner to discuss preemptive measures against possible defectors, during which he not only repeated Charrier's directives that it was essential for public order that they strictly enforce the policies of Vichy, but also advanced the arguments of his father and brother that perhaps the essential enemy of France had been Britain all along.

The massacre of Mers-el-Kebir made it easier to lend conviction to his change of heart. Certainly to Edmond and Louis de Roujay it had proved beyond doubt that the British meant to take advantage of France's defeat on the Continent to plunder her colonial possessions in Africa and the Middle East, and Bertrand put forward this point of view as his own.

"I don't understand you," his assistant, Devaux, said to him at lunch. "A month ago you wanted to fight to the finish. Now you seem to have done a complete about-face."

Bertrand looked at the menu as if his mind were only half on their conversation. "We are civil servants, Julien. Our job is to administer the policies of the government of the day."

"Even so . . ."

"When Reynaud was in power, the policy was to resist. Now, with Pétain, we must acknowledge our defeat."

"But you must have some convictions yourself," said Julien.

Bertrand shrugged his shoulders. "Of course. Even a civil servant keeps an eye open for his own interests, and they seem well enough protected by Pétain."

Devaux forced a smile, for he was obliged to recognize that the government taking shape in Vichy was tailor-made for families like the de Roujays.

"So you aren't tempted to go to London?"

"No," said Bertrand. He leaned forward and lowered his voice. "Strictly between you and me, if it had looked as if Hitler meant to treat us as he treated Poland, I might have tried to take my daughter to Algiers."

"Not to England?"

"No. The *entente cordiale* was always an uneasy alliance whose only purpose was to contain Germany. Having failed to do that, what interests does it serve?" He looked at Devaux for an answer.

Devaux looked back at Bertrand, studying him quizzically as if trying to judge whether he was bluffing, but so earnest was the expression on the subprefect's face that Devaux was convinced, and word went around the subprefecture that Bertrand de Roujay was loyal to Pétain.

Besides his mother, Bertrand told only Pierre that he planned to leave for London. He told him not just because he trusted him, but because he needed his help in making his escape. On August 4 he would begin his holiday. He would take it with Titine in the Pyrenees, staying in Céret with the Moreaus. Before leaving he would fake an authorization from Charrier for an exit visa, and under cover of the family holiday would obtain visas at the Spanish and Portuguese consulates in Perpignan.

Pierre thought he was mad. "You take all this trouble to go to London, and as soon as you're there a bomb will drop on your hotel and that's that."

"You are a true pessimist," said Bertrand.

"My father fought in the last war," said Pierre. "He said the secret of survival was to keep your head down."

"A true Pétainist."

"He worships the Marshal for just that reason."

"And you?"

"I hate the old fraud, but I still want to keep my head down."

"There may be risks in coming to the Pyrenees."

Pierre shrugged his shoulders. "What could they prove?"

"Nothing, but it would be a mark against your name."

"One among many."

"You'll take Titine back to Madeleine?"

"Of course. But you must tell Madeleine what you are doing."

Bertrand frowned and fingered the ribbed side of the glass of pastis on the table of the café in Coustiers where they had met for a drink. "Do you think I can trust her?"

"Of course."

"Will she tell Michel?"

"I suppose so."

"And can I trust him?"

"Yes." Pierre sounded less certain.

On Wednesday, July 10, the day the National Assembly in Vichy transferred its powers to Marshal Pétain, Madeleine Bonnet returned from teaching at the Lycée René le Bon in Coustiers to her apartment in the Rue Turgot. At a kiosk at the corner she bought a copy of the latest edition of *Coustiers Soir;* this purchase of an evening paper was the only departure from a routine which had hardly changed since the outbreak of war. She had no father, son or husband at the front; the position of Michel le Fresne as a physician at the hospital had saved him from active service in this "scrap between Fascists and imperialists," just as it had saved him from discomfiture when Daladier had proscribed the Communists the year before.

Madeleine glanced at the headlines as she stood in the elevator which carried her up to the seventh floor, then tucked the newspaper under her arm as she let herself into the apartment with her key. When she had closed the door she went straight to the kitchen to get rid of the asparagus she had bought on the way home. She moved back along the corridor to deposit her bag in her small study, then went to the living room, with its wide view over the rooftops of the city, to sit in one of the soft beige armchairs and read the news in more detail.

She studied the terms of the transfer of power with mixed feelings. Her old liberal instincts were affronted by the advent of a dictatorship, but Michel had taught her to temper these instincts with a scientific detachment. Did it matter, after all, whether France was governed by a gaggle of bourgeois geese in a National Assembly or by a single bourgeois gander called a marshal of France? The lines of demarcation in the class struggle would remain the same.

She kicked off her shoes and lay back in the armchair to consider how this new state of affairs would affect her life in Coustiers with Michel. Though neutral in the imperialistic struggle between Germany, France and Britain, she had been unable to suppress a sense of relief when the armistice was declared and it became clear that the Germans would not be coming to Coustiers. She disliked Pétain, and Laval even more, but she preferred them both to Hitler and Goering. One could assume that they would serve just as well as the Nazis to exacerbate the contradictions inherent in French capitalism—though to be sure of that she would have to consult Michel, who was better than she was at dialectic, and could often see through the superficial meaning of events to their true scientific significance.

She looked at her watch, wondering when he would return. Whereas Bertrand had always been fastidiously punctual, Michel was unpredictable, sometimes kept by an emergency at the hospital or, by his own admission, by the demands of an affair with some girl on the staff.

From the start of their life together, each had agreed that the other should be free, and that their only obligation should be to tell one another the truth. At first Madeleine had found it hard when Michel had confessed making love with other women. Because she felt no impulse to have other lovers herself, she could not understand his promiscuous passions. But they had discussed the matter openly and had agreed that it was almost certainly an evolutionary difference between the sexes that a man found it natural to prowl at large and have physical encounters of no emotional weight, while women by instinct preferred to stay with a single man. It was, as Michel put it, a "contradiction in the relationship between the sexes" which would undoubtedly be resolved when socialism abolished the family, because the fidelity of the wife, so admired in bourgeois society, was in reality merely the expression of her economic dependence upon a man.

Since Engels had written along these lines, Madeleine was obliged to agree, and she dismissed any anguish she felt when Michel described his sexual adventures as a residue of her bourgeois past. She had agreed that they should not marry, but should live together as free individuals, and had chosen not to call herself either Madeleine de Roujay or Madeleine le Fresne, but to return to the use of her maiden name.

In her own mind, and in the perception of her friends, Madeleine was happy. Only the incorrigibly snobbish could have thought that she had lost anything by giving up her position as the wife of the sub-prefect of Mézac and future chatelaine of the Domaine de Saint Théodore. Certainly she was poorer—and Michel was poorer because he had been divorced by his rich wife—but neither of them was needy. Michel drew a salary from the hospital, and Madeleine was paid by the Ministry of Education. Michel had also trimmed his principles to take some private patients at a clinic in Coustiers, and Nellie made no claims on him for the support of their children.

Again it was as much Madeleine's choice as Michel's that they lived in a modern apartment with modern furnishings. After Saint Théodore she had had enough of ancient period pieces, and the clean lines of their beige sofa and beechwood tables and chairs seemed to match the progressive ideology to which they were both committed. Their plates and wineglasses came from Sweden; the desk and chair in Michel's study had been designed by a graduate from the Bauhaus school in Weimar.

As part of their progressive and functional approach to life, Madeleine now wore plain, straightforward clothes, and since she eschewed makeup of any kind, she made the least of the natural beauty which had been so remarkable in her youth. Still, she was not plain, for however seriously she took life, nothing could diminish the beauty of her face and figure. Both might have lost the softness of the girl, but her eyes and the skin of her brow and cheeks still shone with a mellow luminosity.

She stood and put on the shoes she had kicked off. The expression on her face, which had always been serious, had now become almost stern—the result, perhaps, of political activism or of working as a teacher of history in a school. She went out of the living room and back to the gleaming, functional kitchen to see what the cook had prepared for their supper. This arrangement, which was the same as that arrived at by Bertrand in Mézac, was a compromise between Michel's insistence that they not have servants and her wish to avoid the drudgery of housework. Often Michel came back with comrades whose proletarian origins, while assuring their credentials as Communists, had left them with a somewhat conventional attitude toward the role of women in the home. Michel himself, though a champion in conversation of the rights of women, could not bring himself to put

on an apron or wash the dishes; therefore Madeleine always served the
food and cleared up afterward.

Now she saw that a filet of beef was ready to be put in the oven,
and that the vegetables, cheese and stewed fruit were prepared on the
kitchen table. She washed the asparagus, placed it ready in a pan, and
went back to her study to correct the exercise books of her students
that she had brought home.

She sat down at her desk, on which stood a rack of reference books
and three framed photographs: one of Michel, one of her father, a third
of Titine. If there had been a fourth of Pierre Moreau, it would have
made a little shrine to those she loved most in the world. Michel's
photograph was the largest and most prominent. It had been taken
when he was sailing; there was a grin on his face and his hair was
tousled in the wind. Titine's was a school photograph; she too was
smiling but with childish embarrassment. Only Professor Bonnet in the
smallest photograph, looked severe.

As she glanced at them now, before taking up a red pencil to mark
the exercise books, Madeleine felt, as always, a twinge of regret that
she saw so little of her father and daughter. But the size of the
photographs reflected the relative weight of her affections for each of
the three. She had never regretted the decision she had made more than
two years before to sacrifice her daughter for her lover; indeed, even
the thought that in a week's time, on August 4, she would have Titine
on her hands for half of the summer holidays caused her to frown and
chew the end of her red pencil. During the last two summers, while
Michel had gone sailing with some friends from the hospital—and
quite possibly with some nurse too—she and Titine stayed with her
parents in a house the Bonnets now owned in the mountains, but this
arrangement had been upset by the quarrel she had had with her father
over the Nazi-Soviet pact.

Certainly several friends had avoided them when it became known
that she and Michel defended the Party line on Molotov's agreement
with Ribbentrop, but it had astonished her that her father, who
normally judged the political developments of the present with the
same dispassion as he did the historical events of the past, should have
reacted to Michel's defense of Stalin over Sunday lunch with such fury
that he had left the table and shut himself away in his study.

They had not seen him since, and though Madeleine had written to her mother and had received letters in return, there were no invitations to return to the Avenue d'Assas, nor, as yet, to spend the summer at their house in the mountains.

In pondering over this quarrel between Michel and her father, Madeleine had been obliged to acknowledge that her father had never seemed to like Michel, and had been patently irritated by the divorce. This had puzzled her, since he had always predicted that her marriage to Bertrand would end in this way, and Michel—with his open, rational, Comtian approach to life—should have appealed to the professor more than Bertrand had. Yet on many occasions Michel Bonnet had let drop remarks which suggested that he missed his superstitious son-in-law, and that Madeleine had made a mistake. She never asked him outright what he thought of Michel; consciously she told herself that it would serve no purpose to bring his reservations into the open.

It struck her that perhaps her father, despite his freethinking, was rather conventional, and was confused that she had chosen to live with a man without marrying him. "I think he sees you as the seducer of his innocent daughter," she said with a laugh to Michel when discussing the professor's dislike of him. "And of course he was always wildly jealous of my boyfriends."

"And who first proposed that theory?" asked Michel.

"Was it you?"

"Yes. In Montpellier, ten years ago."

Shortly after seven, Madeleine heard the front door open and the sound of men's voices in the vestibule. She left her study to find that Michel had returned with Georges Auget, the Communist trade unionist who was one of the underground leaders in Coustiers.

Michel had also changed over the past two years. He remained tall and vigorous, but his clothes were scruffier than they had been when Nellie had chosen them for him, and he had taken to smoking a pipe, which he held always in his hand, waving the stem like a conductor's baton to emphasize a point in conversation. As always upon his return to the apartment, the complexity of holding his hat, keys, pipe and briefcase at the same time left him in confusion, so as always Madeleine took his briefcase and held it for him while he put his keys back into his pocket.

"Ah, Madeleine, good," he said, kissing her fondly on the cheeks.

"Here I am again," said Georges Auget, who often came for supper, since his own family were in hiding in the north.

"I am always delighted," said Madeleine. "I bought some asparagus just in case." She shook his hand and smiled with sincerity, for she was fond of the small, stocky Communist, who was one of the few among Michel's friends who did not fancy himself a Party intellectual.

"I hope you bought plenty," said Michel, "because Pierre said that he might drop in."

"With Bérénice?"

"No. It's because she's away."

"There'll be enough."

"Like good Communists," said Georges with a smile, "we can share what there is."

Madeleine followed the men into the living room.

"It seems to me," said Michel, apparently continuing a conversation, "that the Party can only benefit from the defeat. The bourgeois army has shown itself to be a sham. All those posturing officers in their fine uniforms capitulated or turned tail. All the arms and fortifications, paid for by taxation, were shown to be useless."

"Yes, that's true," said Georges, "but it was the Nazis who defeated them, so the workers might now look to Fascists like Doriot or Déat."

"Perhaps, perhaps." Michel poured Georges a drink, offered one to Madeleine, then poured one for himself. "It all depends upon the attitude of the Germans. After all, a Doriot or a Déat—"

He was interrupted by the doorbell.

"That must be Pierre," said Madeleine, rising and going to the hall. She opened the door and embraced her dearest friend. "What a pleasant surprise."

"But weren't you expecting me?"

"I am always expecting you," she said. "At least I always hope . . ."

"I promise I won't eat much."

"Don't be silly."

"We should all probably get used to living on less," Pierre said as he entered the living room.

"Must we tighten our belts?" asked Michel, rising to greet him.

"I think so, don't you?" He shook hands with Michel, and then with Georges, whom he had met before.

"I don't see why," said Michel.

"Because the English will impose a blockade."

"Oh, the English," said Michel in a dismissive tone of voice.

"The Continent will be cut off from the granaries of America."

"Do you really think the English will go on fighting?" asked Madeleine.

"Under Churchill, yes."

"Believe me," said Michel, "they'll throw in the sponge within a month."

"I doubt it," said Pierre.

"Their army is nothing."

"They don't need an army if their air force and navy can beat off the Germans."

"But what interest have they in fighting on?" asked Madeleine.

"It wouldn't surprise me at all," said Michel, "if perfidious Albion comes to some arrangement with Herr Hitler."

They went on talking about the war over supper, which the two Communists ate with relish, while Pierre merely picked at his food as if he was indeed preparing his stomach for leaner times to come. He also seemed to Madeleine to be on edge. Normally his cynical neutrality between left and right made him an excellent guest to have with Michel's Communist friends. He could prompt with wit their earnest conversation, just as a competent pianist can accompany any song. This evening, however, the apparent satisfaction of the two Party members that Stalin's ally was now master of France appeared to irritate him, and while as always he said nothing contentious, he reminded them how Hitler had treated his own Communists and Jews.

"I don't think he will behave in the same way toward Communists and Jews in France," said Michel.

"Why not?"

"Because the man is cunning, and there is always a purpose behind what he does. In Germany, we Communists were his rivals and you Jews were the scapegoats for Germany's misfortunes. But now the Germans are no longer unfortunate, so the need for a scapegoat disappears, and the Communists, far from being his enemies, are his allies against Anglo-Saxon imperialism."

"I think you take our position too far," said Georges diffidently.

"In what way?" asked Michel.

"The pact between Moscow and Berlin is, I should have thought, merely a means to buy time while the Soviets strengthen their armed forces."

"Certainly, but the stronger those forces become, the stronger the reason for avoiding a war."

"But if you read *Mein Kampf* . . ." said Pierre.

"The mad dreams of a psychotic adolescent," said Michel. "God forbid that we should all be held responsible for the mistakes of our youth." And with this he glanced at Madeleine, who, knowing that he was referring to their flawed first marriages, smiled and inclined her head as a gesture that she agreed.

When supper was finished, Michel, filling his pipe, led Georges back into the living room; Pierre stayed behind, on the pretext of helping Madeleine clear the table. "I have spoken with Bertrand," he said to her quietly. "He would like to see you."

She stopped, holding the tray, and looked at him in surprise. "To see me? Why?"

"To discuss Titine, and the holidays."

"But he knows my dates."

"The war has made it necessary to change things."

She frowned and turned to take the tray into the kitchen. Pierre followed, carrying the bowl of stewed fruit.

"Couldn't he telephone?"

"He thought not."

Madeleine had rarely seen Bertrand since they had parted outside the subprefecture in Mézac two years before, and though she'd had frequent brusque exchanges on the telephone over those years, she was always reluctant to meet him face to face. It irritated her now that Bertrand had sent the only friend they still had in common to arrange a meeting, because she loved and respected Pierre and had no wish to seem cruel or unreasonable in his eyes.

"How is he?" she asked, as if the question might soften Pierre's perception of her attitude toward her former husband.

"He is . . . agitated."

"Of course."

"The defeat has unsettled him."

"It is a pity they wouldn't let him fight."

"I know."

"He's been subprefect in Mézac for too long."

"Yes." Pierre said this sadly.

"Is that my fault?"

"How could it be?"

"He lost some of his drive after the divorce."

"Perhaps. But that might just have been middle age."

She smiled, because Pierre would never criticize her or even allow her to criticize herself.

"I think," he said, speaking carefully, "that you should meet him this once."

"Why?"

"I can't say more."

She sighed. "All right. I'll go."

She saw her former husband sitting at a table on the pavement outside the Café Colbert, a figure at once strange and familiar, as if a photograph from an album had come to life; and before he had spoken to her or even seen her, she was irritated by him and felt in an instant all the emotions which had led her to leave him. He was dressed fastidiously in a dark, well-pressed suit, as if to inform those who did not know that he was a government official, and was reading one newspaper but had two others waiting on the table. His air of authority, which so impressed minor officials at the subprefecture or the ticket collectors at the railway station, struck her as the same self-importance which had so disillusioned her as, over the years, it had grown up under the old skin of earnest, benevolent idealism and had finally replaced it altogether.

How could I ever have been taken in? she asked herself as she approached him. As he turned and recognized her, and she saw a brief look of sadness on his face give way to the expression of a long-suffering official with a tiresome petitioner, she realized that this meeting was as disagreeable to him as it was to her.

He stood, and with a cold courtesy pulled out a chair for her. "Is all well?" he asked.

"Yes. And you?"

"As well as can be expected."

"Of course."

She allowed him to order her a glass of lemonade, but did not sit

back in her chair. Instead she leaned forward and said, "I understand
that you want to change the dates for my having Titine?"

"Yes. If it's possible."

"Of course, though I don't know as yet what I'm going to do with
her."

"Aren't you going to the mountains?"

She frowned. "I don't think so. Not this year."

"I wanted to take her to the Pyrenees."

"When?"

"Next week. On the first of August."

"Very well."

"We are going to Céret with the Moreaus."

"I see." She felt a pang of jealousy that he had poached Pierre.

"They will bring her back to Coustiers on the fifteenth."

"And you?"

He hesitated, then said in a low voice, "I am going on."

"On? Where?"

"Through Spain to Lisbon."

"To Lisbon?"

"And then to London."

She looked at him for a moment as if he had said something in a
language she did not understand. Then a smile came onto her face and
she laughed—a harsh laugh, almost like a fit of coughing—which
ended with a nasal, derisive, "Of course. I should have known."

"It will mean that for some time to come . . ."

"You won't be there to take care of Titine."

"Precisely. But I would hope that we could agree that she should
remain at the convent in Carpentras, and continue to regard Saint
Théodore as her home."

She laughed again. "Yes, yes, of course. She belongs there—and
you, of course, belong in London."

"I'm glad you think so," he said coldly, sensing the derision in her
tone of voice, "but I wish you would speak more quietly."

"Only last night," she went on, ignoring his admonition, "we were
wondering who, if anyone, would rally to that apotheosis of petit
bourgeois nationalism, and we could think of no one, except perhaps
a few soldiers who found themselves in England and didn't want to
return to their nagging wives."

"I didn't expect you to approve."

"But now, of course, I realize that the bourgeois who can't stomach Pétain can always swallow de Gaulle."

Bertrand had turned pale. "Keep your ridicule for those who appreciate it," he said in a hissing voice.

"But really, Bertrand, you must see that it is not just ridiculous but also a little sad. I know you are bored. I know you are disappointed. I know that Mézac turned out to be a dead end as far as your career is concerned. But really, to go off tilting at windmills . . ."

"It is better than doing nothing."

"Don't try to persuade me that your heroic gesture is going to alter the course of history."

"I won't try to persuade you of anything."

"He represents nothing—no one—your posturing general. He only exists thanks to Churchill; he only speaks through the BBC."

"Have you heard him?"

"Yes. He's a pompous little man crazed with his own self-importance."

"Whatever else he may be, he is not little."

"All right," said Madeleine. "He is large. But you can't measure a man's significance by his size."

"Because Lenin was small?" asked Bertrand contemptuously.

"He was small, yes," said Madeleine sharply, "but Lenin had history on his side."

After parting from Madeleine, Bertrand went to the prefecture to see Charrier, who had recently returned from Vichy. He greeted Bertrand with an unusual warmth and informality, and immediately gave an account of his visit to the capital of the unoccupied zone of France.

"There is a real consolidation of power by the right," Charrier said. "They try to present themselves as a government of national unity, but only Belin comes from the left, and he has no real influence."

"Who does?"

"Laval, Alibert, Darlan . . . But the truth is that the old man has strong ideas of his own. There's already talk of a new order, even a national revolution."

"A revolution from above?"

"Yes, and that means, inevitably, a purge of the civil service. It is already beginning. Heads will roll from the undersecretaries in Vichy down to village schoolmasters."

"Including the corps of prefects?"

"Indeed. The prefects above all will be scrutinized. The subprefects too. Which is why I wanted to talk to you—quite informally, of course—because, given my background, it is unlikely that I will survive, whereas you have all the qualities to endear you to the new regime."

"Thank you," said Bertrand with an ironic inclination of the head.

"They asked about you at Vichy, and of course I gave you a discreet recommendation. They might have been suspicious if I had pushed you too hard."

"What qualifies me as a man of the new order?"

"Your class. Your background. Your religion."

"The Marshal is not notably pious."

"No, but he approves of the Church, and the Church approves of him."

"My divorce would count against me."

"Not at all. Bonnet is one of their *bêtes noires,* and the fact that you obtained an annulment counts in your favor."

"Why?"

"It proves you take religion seriously."

"It means that my mother and my uncle take religion seriously."

"Your uncle. You see, there is your trump card. An uncle who is not just a bishop, but a bishop who has preached in favor of the armistice and the new regime."

"I don't necessarily subscribe to my uncle's views."

"I know that, but they don't, and that's all I wanted to tell you. That you could soon find yourself promoted to a position of considerable influence."

"Thank you."

"All you need to do is tread carefully over the next few months."

"Of course."

Charrier rose to see him to the door. "All this is off the record, of course. I only thought I'd tell you in case . . . well, in case you had other plans."

The two men shook hands. As Bertrand departed, Charrier summoned his secretary to come into his office. Bertrand went toward the door of the antechamber, then stopped, turned and looked back at the secretary's desk, realizing that this was his opportunity to take a sheet of the prefect's stationery, which he would need to forge an authorization for an exit visa. Charrier's words, his subtle promises of preferment, remained fresh in his mind, and Bertrand accepted that they might well be true, but however high he might rise under Pétain, however certain it was that his ambition would be realized, he was not tempted now to reverse his decision to join de Gaulle in London. The choice had come from conscience, not calculation, and while the promise of power, like opium, can induce an ersatz ecstasy, the certainty of righteousness, like physical vigor, can induce an equal and more lasting elation.

He therefore returned to the secretary's desk, and with his heart thudding in his ears he opened two drawers before finding blank sheets of stationery with the letterhead of the prefecture. He took two sheets and quickly stamped them with the prefect's rubber seal, which lay on the secretary's desk. Then he left her office, and once in the corridor outside he put the raw material of his forgery into his briefcase.

The forgery itself was easy to effect with a typewriter from the subprefecture and a thousand documents from which to copy Charrier's signature. On the Friday before his departure, Bertrand applied for an exit visa, which, because of his own position and Charrier's authorization, was issued to him at once. He then returned to his apartment, where his suitcases had been packed by Anna for a holiday in the Pyrenees: short-sleeved shirts, bathing trunks, climbing boots. He looked sadly at his army uniform and the dark suits and white shirts that he would need in London but would have to leave behind.

After supper he rang Lucía. As always she was there when he telephoned, and as always she invited him to come around. He walked toward her apartment through the streets of Mézac, a stroll which gave him time to smoke a cigarette, whose stub, as so often before, he buried in the bed of withered geraniums at the entrance to The Cedars.

Lucía had been reading; he could see an open book beside her on the bed. She greeted him as she always did, as if he had seen her that morning; her manner was always unaffected by the amount of time he had stayed away.

While he sat on a chair, she went into the little kitchen and came out with coffee that she had prepared while he was on his way.

"Well?" he asked as he sipped the coffee.

"Well?" she mimicked him.

She sat on the bed. She never began the sequence of movements and gestures that led them to make love, and now, when it became evident that Bertrand had come for another purpose, she showed neither disappointment nor surprise. They drank their coffee in silence, and only when he had drained his cup did he tell her that he was going away.

"Where?"

"I can't tell you."

"For how long?"

"I don't know."

"And Titine?" It was the first time she had ever referred to Bertrand's daughter by name.

"She stays."

"Without a father?"

"She has grandparents."

"Yes."

"You too . . . you must be ready to go to Saint Théodore."

"But the war is over."

"Even so. You may not be safe."

"I am a French citizen."

"I know." He sounded doubtful.

"Won't that protect me?"

"They are talking of revoking the naturalization of some categories."

"*Hijos de putas.*"

"At Saint Théodore they can protect you, and if necessary hide you."

"When will you come back?"

"I don't know."

"Soon?"

"I don't know."

"Shall I wait for you?"

"Wait?"

She shrugged her shoulders and looked down.

Bertrand frowned. "You are free. You have always been free."

She turned away from him, and the sound of the word "free" hung in the air without any of its usual allure.

"If you need money . . ."

"No." She shook her head.

"Or help. I shall leave you the name of a friend, a magistrate in Coustiers."

She nodded.

"He will help you if he can."

"And if he can't?"

"Go to Saint Théodore."

The next morning, Bertrand went to confess his sins in the Jesuit church next to the school he had attended as a child. Like a soldier on the eve of battle, he did not want to start his venture in a state of sin. Such was his trust in the secrecy of the confessional that he confided in the priest his decision to leave France and join de Gaulle. The Jesuit said nothing to deter him. He then confessed his sins with Lucía, and with a confidence which came from his chaste visit the night before, and the knowledge that circumstance would now bolster his purpose of amendment, he felt able to assure his confessor that he would never sleep with her again.

Packed and shriven, he drove to Saint Théodore to fetch Titine. She was fidgety with excitement, and although they were not to leave until the next morning, she had her suitcase ready in the hall.

After supper that night Bertrand went with his mother to her bedroom to listen to the BBC.

"You are off tomorrow?" she asked when it was finished.

"Yes."

"Are you ready?"

"Yes."

"What about money?"

"I have my twenty-five thousand francs. One is not allowed to take more."

"Will that be enough?"

"To take me to Lisbon? Yes. And then, I daresay, the English will help me."

Alice de Roujay turned and went to a drawer in her dressing table. From it she took an envelope and a long leather belt. She gave them to Bertrand; his wrist bent under the weight.

"I have sewn in some gold napoleons," she said. "You may need them."

"Thank you."

"The letter is for London. When you get there, take it to Barings Bank. It holds sterling deposits in our name, and this letter will authorize you to draw on them."

"Thank you."

She smiled. "I don't want you to starve."

"I shall only use what I need."

"Of course."

They walked toward the door.

"And don't worry about Titine," she said.

"No. We all realize how happy she is here."

His mother hesitated at the door. "You spoke to *her?*"

"Madeleine? Yes."

"She won't try to take her away?"

"No."

She turned to leave the room, then stopped again. "There is one other thing."

"What?"

"I think you should tell your father."

"It will upset him."

"It will upset him more if he feels that you do not trust him."

"Very well."

He found his father sitting alone in the garden. A newspaper lay on his knee—the light was now too dim to read—and he sat silently in the cool, scented air gazing toward the vines and the river. Bertrand came and sat down next to him.

"It's odd, isn't it," said Edmond de Roujay, "that the world is in turmoil, yet here there is such peace."

"Yes."

"We have been lucky," said the old colonel. "I was so afraid that this one would turn out like the last."

"It isn't over yet, Papa."

"No. That's true. Others fight on."

"And I too must fight on, I am afraid, Papa."

His father nodded. "I thought you might."

"I am going to London."

"Yes." He nodded again, his gaze still on the silhouettes of trees against the sky. "Through Spain and Portugal?"

"Yes."

"That's why . . . the Pyrenees . . . I wondered."

"I'm sorry."

"No, no. You're doing what you think is right. One must always do that."

"But you think it wrong."

"Yes, but . . . one can't always agree."

"No."

"If you need a place to stay in Lisbon, I recommend the Avenida Palace. The manager there may remember me."

"Thank you."

"But take care. No heroics."

"I promise."

"There's Titine . . . and your mother." Now he turned to Bertrand, tears in his bleary old eyes. "And there's Louis, too, and there's me. We all want to see you return."

<hr>

5

They reached the small Pyrenean town of Céret on the Sunday evening —the Moreaus by car, the de Roujays by train—and moved into the rooms that Bertrand had reserved in the Hotel Bellevue. With Bertrand and Titine were Pierre, his wife, Bérénice, his five-year-old son, Thomas, whom they called Turco because he was plump and dark and had the imperious manner of a pasha, and Pierre's younger sister, Isabelle. The Moreaus registered under their own name; Bertrand and Titine registered under the name Mornay.

It was an odd assortment of different ages, but it was in Bertrand's interest to cover his escape with a family group of this kind. He was also reassured that Titine would not feel abandoned when he left her in this large party of his closest friends. He knew that she loved Pierre as much as any man after her father, and that she found in Bérénice the kind of patient, maternal serenity that was absent in both her mother and her grandmother. She also loved little Turco, with his dark, curly ringlets, and felt an admiring passion for Pierre's sister, Isabelle, who was halfway in age between the two generations but always seemed happy in the company of Titine.

Isabelle Moreau was twenty-two. She had graduated from the university of Aix-en-Provence, passing the *agrégation,* and had just completed her first year teaching in the same lycée in Coustiers as Madeleine. Her appearance, like Pierre's, was more Italian than Levantine, and while Bérénice, Pierre's wife, had both the appearance and attitudes of a Jewish mother—she might have been Sarah in modern dress —Isabelle appeared unconscious of or indifferent to her racial origins, and even became irritated when the question of her Jewishness arose.

She was exceptionally pretty, with the same fine features as her brother. She also had his sharp sense of humor, and without any need for a magistrate's *gravitas,* used it freely to mock her elders. Being the youngest in the family—what is commonly called an "afterthought" —she was also a little spoiled, and this, together with her precocious intelligence, made her on occasion seem gauche, a girl with adult mannerisms who still had the mind of a child. She had few friends of her own, and still lived at home, at once clinging to her aging parents and tormenting them, so that they had begged Pierre to take her with him on his holiday.

On Monday morning the six of them squeezed into the Moreaus' Citroën and set off up into the mountains. Seven miles outside the town, beyond the village of Amélie, they stopped, and while Pierre set off on foot with his wife and sister and the children, Bertrand took the wheel of the car and drove off down the narrow road toward Perpignan.

He reached the Spanish consulate at eleven, but had to wait an hour before reaching the desk, where a plump, grumpy official met him with a look of dislike and distrust.

"I would like a visa," said Bertrand.

"For travel when?"

"At once."

The suspicion increased. "The purpose of your visit?"

"Transit."

"To Lisbon?"

"Yes."

The suspicions were confirmed. "You have business in Lisbon?"

"Yes. The export of wine."

"Wine." The official repeated the word with contempt for the frailty of the excuse, but he took a form and copied out Bertrand's name and address in Mézac. Then he stopped and said, "You have a visa to enter Portugal, of course?"

"No."

"Ah, then I cannot issue a transit visa for Spain." He sat back with a grunt and a smile.

"Why not?"

"No transit visas can be issued until the applicant has a visa for the country of final destination."

Bertrand contained his exasperation; an official himself, he knew how fruitless it was to rail against official procedures.

"Can you tell me the address of the Portuguese consulate?"

"No, monsieur. This is not an information bureau."

Bertrand turned to go; then he remembered the application form with his name and address. "Should I take that with me?" he asked.

"No. We shall keep it here until you return . . . if you return." A mocking smile came onto the man's face as he carefully laid the form to one side.

Bertrand left the consulate and went out into the street. No one was there to observe him. The Portuguese consulate would undoubtedly be closed for lunch. He went to the post office to study the telephone directory and find its address, and discovered to his horror that there was nothing in Perpignan under the entry of Portugal or Portuguese. He turned to the directory of Carcassonne. There was nothing there either. It was not until he searched in the Toulouse directory that he found what he was after.

He walked back to the car. It was impossible now to drive to Toulouse before the offices closed for the day. If he took a train he might get there in time, but then he could not get back to Céret. He could telephone the hotel, but his absence might be noticed. All the same, he had to take the risk. He thought it possible, even likely, that the official at the Spanish consulate was even now giving his name to the local Sûreté.

A train left at twenty to two. He parked the car at the station and sat back in the corner seat of a first-class compartment, exhausted

already by the nervous stress of the morning. He slept, then awoke
with a start, imagining Guillot leering above him. It was the ticket
inspector. He showed his ticket and sat back again. The train was
drawing into Narbonne.

In a car he could have driven faster; in a train he was powerless to
make haste. He knew from the timetable that if the train was on time
he should reach the consulate before it closed, but it was already
running ten minutes late and the chances were that it would not make
up the time. The whistle blew; the train drew slowly out of the station.
Bertrand shut his eyes again, afraid that the other passengers in the
compartment would notice his agitation. The excitement of subterfuge
which he had felt in Mézac had evaporated; he now felt wretched, and
longed to be with Titine and the Moreaus in the mountains. He was
as angry with himself as he would have been with an inefficient
subordinate for not foreseeing the need to get a Portuguese visa in
France. Why had he assumed he could get one in Spain? And what
if the Portuguese demanded proof that he was a bona fide businessman?
If they refused him a visa, he would be finished. He could not return
to Mézac, because sooner or later it would emerge that he had forged
the authorization for an exit visa from France. He could only go on,
perhaps over the mountains as an illegal immigrant, which would
mean, if he was caught—he could speak no Spanish—imprisonment
in the camp of Miranda de Ebro.

The train arrived in Toulouse half an hour late. Outside the station
there was a long queue for taxis. Bertrand ran out into the street,
walked over the bridge across the Canal du Midi toward the center
of the city, and eventually found a cab on the Rue de Bayard, which
delivered him to the Portuguese consulate ten minutes before it closed.

Here too there was a crowd of applicants, and it was forty-five
minutes before he reached the desk. He repeated his request in a tone
of resigned despair, for no one could believe that this middle-aged man
in a short-sleeved shirt, grimy, disheveled and sweating, was a government official on his way to negotiate export quotas in Lisbon. But his
luck had turned, for if the official at the Spanish consulate in Perpignan
had had sympathies in one direction, the small, swarthy Portuguese
who now received his application had sympathies in the other. The
look he directed at Bertrand did indeed suggest that he saw through
the pretext for his journey, but also that he was ready to help him

achieve his end. "Please return tomorrow morning," he said. "Your visa will be ready."

Bertrand now had to find somewhere to spend the night, and knowing well how travelers without luggage always arouse suspicions, he returned to the station to buy a suitcase. With it he went into a small hotel in a side street off the Rue de Bayard. The young porter offered to take the case from him, but because its lightness would reveal that it was empty Bertrand refused his offer and so suffered that look of contempt which porters direct at those they think are trying to save a tip.

From the hotel he telephoned Céret. It took him half an hour to get through; eventually he spoke to Pierre and told him that he would not be back that night but would hope to see them the next day.

"Don't hurry," said Pierre in a loud and cheerful tone of voice. "The whole holiday lies ahead, after all."

Bertrand went out into the street and ate some supper in a small restaurant near his hotel. It was cooler now, but he had nothing to wear except his short-sleeved shirt. He wished he had bought a jacket before the shops closed, and for a second time that day he castigated himself for his lack of foresight. Clearly a clandestine life demanded more precise and detailed planning than he had anticipated. All the insignificant aspects of everyday life, which until now had been part of a well-established routine, would have to be foreseen and considered.

He bought an evening paper and returned to the hotel. He went to his room, read the paper, washed and went to bed in his underclothes. The room overlooked the street. It was noisy, and the streetlights shone through the curtains. He lay on one side, then turned onto the other. Thoughts raced through his mind; as he slept they merged with his flickering dreams until the noise or the light or the strangeness of the room made him wake again, whereupon the dreams became semi-conscious thoughts again—not the noble and heroic sentiments which inspired him during the day, but splintered images of squalor, wretchedness and fear.

At seven the next morning he found a barber to shave him, and afterward ate breakfast in a café. The streets were cool, but already he could feel the heat of the sun. He dithered about whether or not to buy a jacket, and decided in the end that it might make him appear a more convincing businessman if he was respectably dressed when he returned to the consulate. On the Rue de Rémusat the proprietor of a haberdashery was raising the shutters. Bertrand followed him into his shop and bought a blue linen jacket, a shirt and a tie. Back at his hotel he changed into these new clothes, came down to the foyer and paid his bill. From the hotel he went to the station, deposited his suitcase at the baggage claim, then took a cab to the Portuguese consulate.

His visa was ready, as had been promised. With his passport in his pocket, Bertrand returned to the station. A train was just leaving for Perpignan, and he ran across the concourse to catch it. He climbed into a coach with a minute to spare and found a corner seat in a first-class compartment. Still breathing heavily, he looked out the window; the train was moving. He sighed, pleased with his luck, but there was no sense of movement, and when he looked out the window once again he realized that it was not his train that was moving but the other train that was drawing into the platform. As it stopped, he saw through the two windows the thick, familiar face of Inspector Guillot.

Their eyes met. Guillot's were without expression. Bertrand tried to look away but could not, and at that very moment his own train started to move out of the station. Apparently without haste, Guillot rose from his seat, and Bertrand lost sight of him as he left his compartment. Bertrand was now seized with panic. He ran out into the corridor and looked out the window onto the platform. Guillot would have to run back down the platform the length of four coaches and pass through two barriers before reaching this train, but it was moving out only at the pace of a walking man. Gradually it moved faster. Bertrand leaned out as far as he could and twisted his body to see if Guillot had caught it, but there was no sign of him, and soon the smooth platform disappeared from under the train.

He returned to his seat. Had it been Guillot, or had his fears invested a man like Guillot with the identity of the police inspector? He considered the procedures which would have followed either the discovery of his forgery in Mézac or a report from the Spaniard in Perpignan. In both instances, the case would certainly have been referred to Guillot in Mézac, and if this had happened it was likely that Guillot himself would want to make the arrest, because of his dislike of Bertrand.

What would Guillot do now that he had missed his quarry in Toulouse? He would telephone the Sûreté in Perpignan to meet the train, or at least have the Spanish consulate watched. Bertrand therefore decided to get off the train at Narbonne, and there, rather than leave the station, he waited for an express from Marseilles to Barcelona. He arrived at Perpignan three hours after the train on which he had been seen by Guillot, and again, instead of leaving the station, caught a local train toward the Spanish frontier at Port Bou, alighting at Elne and there taking a taxi the twenty miles or so to Céret.

He found the holiday-makers in high spirits. Only Pierre and Bérénice darted anxious looks across the table. After supper, while the women took Turco up to bed, the two men went out to smoke on the terrace of the hotel. There Bertrand explained what had happened, and apologized for abandoning Pierre's car outside the station at Perpignan.

"The car doesn't matter," said Pierre. "I can take a bus down tomorrow. The question we must consider is what you should do now."

"I'll have to enter Spain without a visa."

"That would be madness. You'd be sure to be caught."

"They'll be watching the consulate."

"For you, yes, but what if *I* take your passport?"

"Too risky. Guillot knows you."

Pierre thought for a moment, then said, "But he doesn't know Isabelle."

"I couldn't let her take the risk."

"What risk? Even if they find out afterward, she can always play the innocent."

Bertrand shook his head. "I've involved you all enough already."

"I'm still an examining magistrate," said Pierre. "Guillot wouldn't dare touch my sister."

Bertrand hesitated. "But even with a Spanish visa, they'd be waiting at Le Perthus and Cerbère."

"Then cross somewhere else. They can't be everywhere."

Again Bertrand hesitated.

"It's too late to turn back," said Pierre.

"All right. But do we tell Isabelle that she's running the risk of being an accessory to treason?"

"Yes. Explain everything. I think she'll rise to the occasion."

· · ·

Pierre knew his sister well, for as they told her about Bertrand's plan to go to London and what they wanted her to do to help him, her eyes grew wide, her face went pink, and every now and then she wriggled and grew straight in her chair. Finally she said, "Well, what an adventure," as if mocking her own excitement.

"Will you do it?" asked Pierre. "Will you go to the consulate?"

"Of course. Of course I will."

"But never tell anyone what you have done," said Pierre.

"No." She put her finger to her pursed lips and smiled a smile of pride and delight.

While Pierre and Isabelle took the bus to Perpignan, Bertrand went with Bérénice, Titine and Turco for another picnic in the mountains. He lay by a stream in the sun watching his daughter build a dam for Turco, wondering if this would be the last time he would see her as a child, for the war was likely to be a long one and it might be some years before he would return to France.

Lying beside him, Bérénice said little. She was a woman who thought it wrong to pry into the affairs of men. She had prepared a good lunch, which Bertrand ate with the appetite of a condemned man who relishes each morsel, as if its taste might be among his last sensations on earth. It was not that Bertrand expected to die, but he knew that this peaceful day on holiday with his child was the last of its kind in his life. The die was cast. Tomorrow he would be either in Spain or in prison; both would mean the end of the life he had led until now.

They got back to the hotel at four in the afternoon. Pierre and Isabelle had not returned. He sat on one of the wooden chairs on the terrace drinking tea and reading a paper. At five he heard the sound of a car and saw the Citroën draw up beside the hotel. Pierre and Isabelle got out and waved to him, and he knew at once from Isabelle's beaming face that their trip had been a success.

The next morning after breakfast he left them, embracing each in turn until finally he came to Titine. He took her up in his arms and held her for some moments with her head clutched to his face as if storing up memories of how she felt and smelled to last him in his exile. She knew that he was going away, but not where. "Don't be long, Papa," she said.

"Be good while I'm gone. I'll come back when I can," he replied, with only his apprehension containing his tears.

"I'm always good," she said with a laugh.

"And take care of Turco."

"I will."

He kissed her again and went toward the door. He turned for a last glance and saw that already she was chatting gaily with Isabelle and the little boy.

"She'll be all right," said Pierre.

"I know."

They drove west to Amélie, then north through Vinca to Saint Paul de Fenouillet. There they turned west again on the main road through Quillan and Foix.

"This will use up all your fuel," said Bertrand.

"You can bring us some from London."

They ate lunch in a small restaurant in Saint Girons, and then drove on through Castillon and Saint Béat to the frontier at Fos.

"Here we are," said Pierre when they reached the striped barrier across the road. "Off you go on your crusade."

"Take care of things until I get back," said Bertrand.

"Of course."

"Thank you for everything."

Pierre shook his head. "Don't thank me. You don't need to thank a friend."

They embraced, then Bertrand got out of the car. For a moment he stood quite still, inhaling the mountain air as if it might be his last breath as a free man. Finally he walked toward the customs barrier carrying his suitcase. He handed his passport to the French official, determined that fear not show in his eyes. The officer studied his exit visa, then looked up at Bertrand. Their eyes met. The man looked down again and stamped his passport. Bertrand walked on to the Spanish post. There the guard opened his passport and studied first his photograph, then his visa. Bertrand turned and saw that Pierre was waiting. The guard stamped his passport. Bertrand took it, then waved to Pierre, who waved back, and Bertrand walked into Spain.

Chapter 6

1

STANDING on the banks of the Tagus estuary at the westernmost extremity of the continent of Europe, and so at the greatest distance from Hitler's armies, Lisbon in 1940 was filled with every kind of fugitive and refugee, not just from the conquered nations but from the conquering one too. Thus, the Avenida Palace Hotel, standing next to the Central Station by the Rossio, had under its roof both anti-Fascist Germans and agents of the Gestapo, as well as spies under various guises from every nation involved in the war.

When Bertrand de Roujay arrived in the city from Spain, he went straight from the station to the foyer of this grand hotel. The receptionist sighed at his ignorance when he asked for a room, and explained that all the space in the hotel had been reserved for many months in advance, but when Bertrand made himself known to the manager as the son of Edmond de Roujay, he was given the benefit of an unexpected vacancy. A young Austrian woman, a political refugee, had been found hanging from her curtain rail that morning.

Innocent of the real reason for his good fortune, Bertrand was taken up to the fifth floor and shown into a large, dark room which looked across a small courtyard to the station. It was hot outside, but the gloom made the room cool, and he was grateful to find himself at last with a bed, bathroom and wardrobe in which to hang his clothes.

Later that same day he took a taxi from the hotel to the British consulate in the Rua de São Domingos. There he asked for a visa to enter England, and when asked for the purpose of his visit said firmly, "To fight for France under General de Gaulle."

At this a frown came onto the face of the sandy-haired Englishman and his hand holding a pen stopped in midair.

"Ah," he said. "I'm afraid you've come to the wrong place."

"Isn't this the British consulate?"

"Yes, but we have a special department for political refugees."

Bertrand, who had not thought of himself as a refugee, nonetheless took the address given to him by the young man. He found a taxi outside the consulate and was driven farther west to the suburb of Belém. There, in a wide street above the Hieronymite convent, the cab drew up in front of a modern villa surrounded by a high fence. The bell was not at the door but at the garden gate. A moment after Bertrand had pressed it, a thick-set, polite young Englishman came out of the house to open it. He wore a light linen suit and looked as if he might play rugby for Oxford or Cambridge.

Bertrand was expected—the sandy-haired man at the consulate must have telephoned ahead—and was led straight through a cool hall with a polished marble floor into a comfortable drawing room furnished with elegant artifacts from the Portuguese past, where a thinner man, about ten years older than Bertrand, rose from a sofa to greet him. "Please come in," he said courteously, guiding Bertrand toward a chair.

"Thank you," Bertrand replied.

"I wasn't told your name."

"Captain de Roujay," said the muscular young man who hovered at the door.

"Yes. Bertrand de Roujay," said Bertrand.

"Good. My name is Trent, Martin Trent, and this is Dickie Fry."

Bertrand de Roujay nodded to both Englishmen and said, with an odd formality, "I am delighted to meet you."

"You speak excellent English."

"I had a Scottish nanny."

"Indeed. Then I should say you speak excellent Scots."

The three laughed mirthlessly. Trent glanced at Fry, who took a seat at the edge of the room. "You would like to go to London?"

"Yes."

"To join General de Gaulle?"

"Yes."

"Well, of course we are delighted, and we would like to do everything we can to help, but I wonder if you would mind . . ." Trent hesitated, as if embarrassed. "Well, I'm sure you will understand if we ask you some questions first."

"Of course," said Bertrand, sitting back in his chair as if these questions were a formality.

"When did you arrive in Lisbon?" asked Trent.

"Last night."

"From . . ."

"Madrid."

"Were you there long?"

"One night."

"Before that?"

"Lérida."

"Where did you cross the frontier?"

"Fos."

"You had a transit visa?"

"Yes."

"From the Spanish consulate?"

"In Perpignan. It wasn't easy."

"And a Portuguese visa?"

"From Toulouse."

"And an exit visa from France?" He watched carefully for Bertrand's reaction to this last question.

"Yes."

"Was that easy to obtain?"

"For a man in my position it was not difficult."

"Your position?"

"I was subprefect of Mézac."

"I see." Trent paused. He seemed nonplussed. "You were a subprefect?"

"Yes."

"Yet you left France . . ."

"Certainly."

"That's most impressive."

"It is only natural," said Bertrand, "to want to fight for one's country."

"Of course, and we would like to encourage you, Captain de Roujay, but as an ex-officer and a government official, you will appreciate that we will have to make certain inquiries."

"Of course."

"We have to make sure that you are who you say you are."

"I understand."

"Where are you staying in Lisbon?"

"At the Avenida Palace."

Trent looked surprised. "You managed to get a room there?"

"Yes."

"Had you reserved it?"

"No."

"You were very lucky."

"I know."

Trent got to his feet and came around his desk to shake Bertrand by the hand. "We shall be in touch with you there. In the meantime, I hope you enjoy your stay in Lisbon."

"Thank you," said Bertrand. He went toward the door, then turned back to Trent. "You will understand, I hope, that I did not come here as a tourist. I am eager to reach England as soon as possible."

"Of course. I quite understand." And still with the amiable, distracted manner of a university tutor, Trent led the Frenchman to the door.

Bertrand left the villa in a rage. Of all the unforeseen disasters that had dogged him since he had left Mézac, this English standoffishness was the most difficult to bear, for despite an uneventful journey across Spain, he felt that he had risked much to reach Lisbon and had imagined, if not a hero's welcome from the English, at least some enthusiasm for the choice he had made.

He returned to his room in the Avenida Palace and counted his money. He had already used most of his foreign allowance of twenty-five thousand francs. He therefore took his penknife to his belt, cut out the first of the gold napoleons, went out to a bank on the Rossio and changed it into escudos. Then he went into a travel agency on the Rua da Carmo to inquire about passage to Britain. Here he was met with the same incredulity that he had encountered when he had first arrived at the Avenida Palace. All British boats had been requisitioned by the British government, and all berths on neutral ships were booked for every sailing scheduled for the rest of the year. So too were the seats on all planes leaving Lisbon. For the private traveler, it seemed, the only way out of Portugal was back into Spain.

Bertrand knew no one in Lisbon, and in the days which followed, as he waited to be summoned by Trent, he spent his time exploring the city—first the fashionable streets and squares near his hotel, the Rossio and the Figueira where the Lisboans gathered for their evening *passeata,* then the narrow, medieval streets of the Alfama. Sometimes he would climb up to the ramparts of the Castillo de São Jorge and sit under the pine trees looking out over the city toward the docks, longing for the day when one of the ships standing there would take him to England. On other occasions he would stroll through the Botanical Gardens, or the Parque de Edward VII, remembering his saunters in similar parks in France from the Promenade du Peyrou in Montpellier to the Jardin des Plantes in Coustiers.

His favorite spot, however, became the small Praca de Allegria just off the Avenida da Liberdade, which had a small playground in the middle where children like Titine would play in the late-afternoon sun. There was also the bust of a man called Alfredo Keil—composer, painter and poet—who for want of any other became Bertrand's companion. Though he had no knowledge of Keil's music, painting or poetry, or indeed of anything about the man whose memorial stood in the park, Bertrand imagined him a man of many accomplishments and would confide to him his frustrations and misfortunes.

Of course, Bertrand could have made friends of flesh and blood rather than marble—several Frenchmen were staying at the Avenida Palace—but he knew that conversation with a compatriot would be dangerous. Any of them might denounce him to the embassy, and the embassy to the Portuguese secret police. Though Portugal was neutral and had ancient ties with England, it was governed by a dictator, Salazar, who was unlikely to feel much sympathy for Gaullist volunteers.

On the Saturday of his second weekend in Lisbon, Bertrand came down to have dinner in his hotel, only to find that the restaurant was full. Rather than return to his room and eat alone, he asked the porter to reserve a table at a restaurant in the city. The man tried first Montanha, then Martinho, but both were also full. Tavares, however, promised a table, and Bertrand therefore left the hotel and walked up toward the Bairro Alto.

When he reached the restaurant it too was full, and the embarrassed headwaiter asked if, in these exceptional circumstances, he would consider sharing a table with another man. By now hungry, Bertrand agreed, and was placed opposite a younger man whom he saw at once was not Portuguese. Suspecting at first that the man was German, Bertrand merely nodded as he sat down and made no attempt to engage him in conversation. Every now and then he glanced at his companion's reflection in the mirrors set into the ornate walls of the restaurant and noted his vigorous, handsome features and strong, curly hair. It was only when he heard him speak to the waiter in unmistakably American English that Bertrand realized he was a citizen of the United States.

Bertrand felt no instinctive affection for Americans, who ever since the time of the Dawes Plan had undermined France's policy of containing Germany, and with their isolationism had encouraged French appeasement. That evening in Tavares, however, he had little reason to feel fond of his fellow Europeans, whether German, Italian, French or English; indeed, an American was perhaps the only kind of companion he could reasonably trust. He therefore leaned across the table and asked the man in English where he came from.

The young man thrust his hand across the table and shook Bertrand by the hand. "Lowell, Massachusetts," he said. "My name is Harry Jackson."

"Bertrand de Roujay."

"Good to meet you, Bertrand. I guess you're a Frenchman."

"I am indeed."

"I am a great admirer of your country, sir, and I regard it as a tragedy that your army was defeated in that way."

Bertrand shrugged his shoulders as if he himself was indifferent. "The fortunes of war."

"Sure, but from the nation that gave us Napoleon!" Harry Jackson shook his head in incredulity.

"A little disappointing," said Bertrand.

"Well, we sure weren't much help."

"Are you here on business or on holiday?"

"Business. Carpenter Engineering. How about you?"

"I am a civil servant," said Bertrand, "here to negotiate wine quotas with the Portuguese government."

"Wine? For the Portuguese? Isn't that a case of coals to Newcastle?"

"We like to think that some of our wine is of superior quality."

"Of course." Jackson laughed. "That's what we feel about our machine tools."

"You sell machine tools?"

"I don't sell them, I install them. I'm waiting to set some up in a factory in Braga, but because of this damned war they haven't arrived." He laughed again. "If you ask me, they've been diverted to Britain, but no one wants to admit it, so they just say they're on their way and leave me to cool my heels until they turn up."

They continued to talk as they dined. The American was open and affable, ignoring Bertrand's shy reserve and treating him at once as an old friend. He had chosen a Portuguese speciality, pork with mussels, which he found inedible, and with a cheerful insouciance he pushed it aside and asked the waiter to bring him a steak instead. He laughed enthusiastically at this culinary fiasco, and as he did so his nostrils flared, giving him, despite his white skin, a slightly negroid look. His laugh was engaging, his conversation intelligent and amusing, but from the start Bertrand sensed that there was something incongruous in the American's manner. He seemed young and yet old, naive and yet knowing, and it soon occurred to Bertrand that Harry's machine tools were perhaps as fictitious as his own quotas of French wine.

They finished their dinner at more or less the same time. Harry offered Bertrand a glass of port with his coffee, and Bertrand offered Harry one of his cigars. When they left the restaurant Harry suggested a nightcap in the Bairro Alto. Grateful for some company after so many days alone, Bertrand agreed. They walked into the narrow streets and passed small bars, restaurants and nightclubs, some of them promising fado, the plaintive song of the Portuguese.

"Are you married?" asked Harry.

"Divorced. And you?"

"Single." Harry laughed. "I guess I like women too much to settle for one."

"It is sometimes a woman who settles for you."

"*C'est toujours la femme qui décide,*" said Harry.

"You speak French?"

"Sure." He answered as if this was no great accomplishment, but it was an added incongruity in an engineer from Massachusetts.

"And Portuguese?"

"No. An impossible language." Harry turned toward Bertrand and smiled. "I know only the necessary phrases. *Quanto custa, menina? Muito caro, menina. Obrigado, menina.*"

They stopped at a bar, a room open to the street, with a few tables and chairs and a primitive counter with a few dusty bottles on shelves behind it.

"Last night, for example," said Harry, lowering his voice but with a lively look in his eyes, "I met a young lady in this same little bar who for the cost of a bottle of wine . . ." He winked and led Bertrand through the door.

They sat down at a table, and the proprietor brought them two glasses of port. A small boy scurried out into the street. A moment later a girl came to the door. She was dark—perhaps gypsy—and greeted Harry with an amused effrontery.

"Haven't you got a friend?" Harry asked her, pointing at Bertrand. *"Una amiga* for my *amigo?"*

She turned to Bertrand and raised her dark eyebrows as if considering which friend would suit him.

"No," said Bertrand, smiling and shaking his head.

The girl shrugged her shoulders and sat down at the table.

"Why not?" asked Harry. "They're perfectly safe."

"I'm tired."

"Oh come on."

Bertrand searched for a convincing excuse. "Perhaps if I were ten years younger . . ."

"Please yourself," said Harry, stretching out to stroke the girl's shoulder. "But I always think that a man should sample the local product, particularly if it's a bargain."

Bertrand returned to his hotel alone, and the next morning went to mass at the Se Patriarchal. The atmosphere of the austere cathedral, first a church, then a mosque, then a church again, and rebuilt many times after the earthquakes that had shaken Lisbon, calmed Bertrand's impatient state of mind. *Sub specie aeternitatis,* it did not seem to matter whether he reached England sooner or later as long as what he was doing was right. After reciting from habit an Our Father and a Hail Mary, his thoughts meandered around the problems he faced in his life, directing toward God a request here, an apology there, like the peasant who prays for rain on a particular day, or an invalid who asks for relief from his pain. It assuaged his anxiety about Titine and his mother to invoke the protection of Mary, the Mother of God; and he asked God the Father, who he assumed took more interest in men's affairs, to assist in his attempt to fight in the war.

He had no doubt whatsoever that right was on his side. If Christian knights in the twelfth century had died to rid Spain and Portugal of the Moors and return the cathedral in which he knelt from the worship of Allah to the worship of Christ, surely it behooved him to risk his life to rid Europe of these more terrible hordes of new barbarians who in time might make both mosque and church into a temple for the worship of the state.

After mass he returned to the Avenida Palace, and as if in answer to his prayer he was given a note that had been delivered from the British embassy. He took it into the dining room and read it as he waited for his breakfast. It was from Trent, asking him to come to lunch at the villa in Belém. It seemed that at last some decision had been made. He put the note down on the white tablecloth, and as he did so felt a hand on his shoulder. It was Harry Jackson, fresh and vigorous despite the dissipation of the night before.

"Good news, I trust," he said, looking down at the embossed coat-of-arms on the letter.

"Only if no news is good news," Bertrand replied, picking up the letter and putting it into his pocket.

"How about a day at the beach?" asked Harry.

"I'd like to, but I have an engagement for lunch."

"Then come along to Cascais in the afternoon. You can find me on the beach there."

"With a girl?"

Harry chuckled. "You never know."

At twelve, Bertrand returned to the villa in Belém and was met once again by Fry, the rugby Blue, with a polite and noncommital expression on his face. He was led into the drawing room, and this time Trent rose to greet him with a greater affability than he had shown on their first meeting.

"De Roujay," he said. "How good of you to come." He took Bertrand by the arm and instead of guiding him to the chair facing his desk led him to a sofa by the window. "I am sorry we have kept you waiting all this time, but as you can imagine things are pretty chaotic, and with everything in code, communications take twice as long as they should." He sat down with Bertrand on the sofa but turned at an angle to face him. "This message, for example . . ." He waved a telegram in his hand but did not show it to Bertrand. "It includes, among other things, a message from some friends in France saying 'The fruit is fresh,' which is, of course, a coded message, but that did not prevent our people in England from encoding it yet again, which meant decoding it here." He shrugged his shoulders in affected exasperation.

"*À la guerre, comme à la guerre,*" said Bertrand.

"Indeed." Trent placed the telegram in a folder which he held in his other hand. "Now I have to confess to you that while you have been waiting we have not been altogether idle. You will appreciate that we had to check on your credentials, as it were."

Bertrand blushed. "Of course."

"One of the easiest ways for the enemy to put agents into England is to send them to us as volunteers."

"Of course," Bertrand said again, not liking to admit that it had never occurred to him that he might be taken for a German spy.

"Now this message, 'The fruit is fresh,' is from our people in France, and it means that Bertrand de Roujay, the subprefect of Mézac, has indeed left France and is thought to be a genuine Gaullist."

"Good."

"And you are Bertrand de Roujay?"

"Of course."

"How can we be sure?"

"I have my passport."

Trent smiled. "I'm afraid forgeries are so simple these days."

Bertrand was flummoxed. "You could ask . . ."

"Who?"

"Well, anyone in Mézac."

"As you can imagine, that wouldn't be easy."

"No, of course."

"There isn't anyone in Portugal who could vouch for you?"

"No. I know no one."

"Or in England?"

"Yes, of course. My nanny. Miss Ferguson."

"Do you know where she lives?"

"In Scotland. Saint Andrews."

Trent glanced at Fry. Fry noted down the name of Miss Ferguson.
"And the Blacketts," said Bertrand.

"Who are they?"

"A family I stayed with to learn English."

"Where do they live?"

"Outside Cheltenham. He is a doctor."

"Do you think they would remember you?"

"I am sure."

Trent's manner did not change. It was impossible to tell what he
thought. "Come in to lunch," he said, leading Bertrand back across the
hall into the dining room, "and tell me once again about your escape."

"Of course."

"You see, from our point of view it seems too well arranged."

Bertrand laughed. He remembered the dreadful day in Toulouse,
and Guillot's expressionless face through the two panes of glass. "It
wasn't as easy as it seems," he said as he sat down at table between the
two Englishmen.

"I daresay," said Trent. "Did anyone help you?"

"Yes. A friend. Pierre Moreau. He is an examining magistrate in
Coustiers. He came with me and my daughter to Céret near the border
as if we were going on holiday."

"You have a daughter?"

"Yes. Albertine."

"I thought—I don't know why—that you weren't married."

"I am divorced."

"May we know the name of your former wife?"

"Madeleine Bonnet."

"Bonnet . . ."

"Her father is Michel Bonnet."

"The historian?"

"Yes."

"Ah." For the first time Trent betrayed an emotion. "So you are
the son-in-law of Michel Bonnet?"

"I *was* the son-in-law of Michel Bonnet."

"Of course." Trent hesitated. He turned toward Fry, but said nothing, then back to Bertrand. "Did Bonnet know that you were going
to London?"

"No."

"Did your wife?"

"Yes."

"And this man Moreau?"

"Yes."

"Anyone else?"

"My parents. Moreau's wife and sister."

"But no one outside those two families?"

"No."

"You weren't part of a circle of any kind?"

"How do you mean?"

"A circle of people who want to fight on."

"No. One has to concede, I am afraid, that most people wanted the fighting to stop."

"Why were you different?"

Bertrand hesitated. "I heard the broadcast of General de Gaulle. Like him, I think that the war is not over."

"Yes." Trent sounded dubious. He paused while the manservant, wearing a white tunic, offered Bertrand a dish of roast veal and vegetables; then, as he helped himself, he said, "To be quite frank, one must concede that for France, from a military point of view, the war *is* over."

"I am sure that thousands of my compatriots will rally to General de Gaulle."

Trent glanced at Fry, then, with an apologetic smile, turned back to Bertrand. "I am afraid that of the French in England, only one in six has answered his appeal."

Bertrand turned pale. "I can't believe it."

Trent looked embarrassed. "It is an . . . unfortunate statistic, but you must bear in mind that many of the men who were stranded in England after Dunkirk were naturally anxious for their wives and families in France."

"It is a time to sacrifice sentiment," said Bertrand.

"Perhaps," said Trent. "Yet if I were a Frenchman, I am not sure that I wouldn't agree with Marshal Pétain that the armistice makes the best of a bad lot. It seems to me that France has always done well from defeats in the past, and who knows—when this war ends another Talleyrand may deliver you from the clutches of Herr Hitler more efficaciously than General de Gaulle."

"Only at the cost of liberty and democracy in France!" said Bertrand.

"Are they so important?" Trent raised his face with an ironic smile.

"You, an Englishman, ask that?"

"Oh, we English like democracy, all right—for ourselves—but we don't insist upon it for everyone else. I'm a historian, you see, like your former father-in-law, Professor Bonnet, when I'm not helping out with a war, and I'm obliged to acknowledge that there are civilized countries which manage quite well without liberty or democracy."

Bertrand felt an angry exasperation rise within him. "Do you include France among them?" he asked.

"Well," said Trent, in the amiable voice of an absentminded tutor in an Oxford college, "France is an interesting case, because terms like 'the rights of man' or 'liberty, equality and fraternity' were coined by French thinkers. But when you come down to it there's been very little liberty in the course of your history—and democracy, what, only for the past seventy years or so?"

"All the more reason," said Bertrand coldly, "to fight for it now."

"Perhaps," said Trent dubiously, "but when you see how contented most of the Portuguese seem to be living under Salazar, and the Italians, from what I hear, under their Duce, and when you remember how France flourished under Louis XIV and Napoleon, one is obliged to consider the possibility that perhaps Latin nations, on the whole, work better under an authoritarian regime."

"One can consider the possibility," said Bertrand, struggling to contain his rage. "One can even accept it. But the point at issue in this war is not democracy in France, but the right of the French to choose democracy or dictatorship without the coercive presence of the German army."

"Of course, of course," said Trent in a soothing tone of voice. "I was merely arguing . . . academically, you must understand, and to convince young Fry here, our devil's advocate, that your commitment to the war is sincere."

"I see." Bertrand blushed, embarrassed that he had been so easily provoked.

"Have you considered," asked Fry, "how France is to be liberated?"

"By an invasion."

"An invasion, yes. But who will invade?"

"The Free French."

"All seven thousand of them, against a hundred and fifty German divisions?"

Bertrand hesitated, realizing how quixotic his words must sound. "The English too," he said, "and perhaps the Americans."

"It seems to me," said Trent cautiously, "that the Free French movement is likely to remain a diplomatic notion rather than a military or political reality."

For a moment Bertrand was silent. Then he looked up at his host. "Are you suggesting that it would be a waste of time for me to go to London?"

"Not at all." Trent smiled. "Quite the contrary. What I would like to suggest is that perhaps the best way for a man with your knowledge and experience to pursue the war against the Germans is not by offering your services to General de Gaulle, but by offering them to us."

"I don't understand."

"If, as you say, it is the British armed forces which will one day liberate France, then it is the British intelligence service which will have to prepare the ground."

"Of course."

"We already have our networks, and we intend to extend them throughout France, initially to gather intelligence and assist our agents, subsequently to plan sabotage, and finally, at the time of an invasion, to put those plans into effect. What we should like to suggest to you, Captain de Roujay, is that when you get to London you join the British Secret Service and help us put these plans into effect."

At last Bertrand understood. "You want me to work for you, and not for the Free French?"

"Only because by doing so you would be more useful to France."

"And also," said Fry from Bertrand's other side, "it would make it much easier to transport you to England."

"It is not that we want to delay you," said Trent. "If you want to join the Free French, we will of course issue a visa, but you will have to make your own travel arrangements, and that might mean a wait of weeks, even months. But if you were already engaged as a member of our armed forces, then of course you would have priority and could leave in a matter of days."

. . .

Once again Bertrand left the suburban villa, and walked down toward the Tagus to catch a train to Cascais, seething with anger against the British. Now at last he could see why his father had always disliked them—their deviousness disguised as common sense! For how long had they been planning to recruit him into their own Secret Service? And how deep did their schemes go? Had they genuinely suspected that he was a German spy? Or had that been a pretext to keep him waiting for weeks in order to soften him up until he was desperate to get away? Was it true that so few of the French in England had rallied to de Gaulle? Or had they invented that statistic to demoralize him? Or had they themselves made it true by discouraging volunteers with the same arguments that they had used on him?

He bought a second-class ticket to Cascais and sat brooding on the train as it ran along the edge of the Tagus estuary toward Estoril. He was glad to get out of the hot, damp city, which already seemed to have infected him with its pessimistic *sandade,* but he wished it had been for more than an afternoon's outing. Both his time and his money were being frittered away for nothing. In London other Frenchmen would secure the leading posts under General de Gaulle. If he waited six months or a year it would be too late. Could he pretend, perhaps, to agree with what Trent proposed, and then, once in London, defect to General de Gaulle? Impossible. The English would intern him if he double-crossed them—Mers-el-Kebir had shown how ruthless they could be—and de Gaulle would not want a man whose presence angered his hosts.

The train reached Estoril and drew up at the station between the casino and the beach. Bertrand glanced at the crowds of bathers on the sand happily splashing at the edge of the Atlantic Ocean. In the summer sun the sea looked benign, but he glowered at it as if it were a moat barring him from the fortress of his destiny.

The train started again. What depressed him more than the practical difficulties facing him was the smug logic of Trent's argument. How could Free France be anything more than an idea, a symbol? What resources could they muster in the struggle against Germany except those poached from the British, who themselves were critically short of everything necessary for the prosecution of the war? What could they spare for the French? Only enough to keep the symbol alive, never enough to give it substance or make it strong; for in their own minds the English were undoubtedly convinced that theirs was the only substantive force which could be brought into play against the Germans. In which case perhaps he should accept their argument and agree to serve in their Secret Service.

Again Bertrand remembered Louis and his father scoffing at de Gaulle, saying that he was Churchill's puppet. How much more would they despise him if he placed himself under English orders and wore an English uniform, and how right they would be to do so. The war was not just against Germany, nor to extirpate Nazi ideology. Nor was it for an abstract liberty or an ethereal notion of the rights of man. The war was for France—not an area of earth or a group of people categorized by the language they spoke or the place where they were born, but for France as a unique set of values and ideals which lived or died in each individual citizen. How could he fight for England when he was not just French but part of France?

By the time he reached Cascais, his mind was made up. He would decline Trent's offer and either bribe the captain of a ship to take him to England, make his way by Morocco to Senegal, or return to France in disguise and find a fishing boat in Brittany that would take him across the Channel.

On the beach, Bertrand found Harry, who took him to change in a cabin he had rented for the day. The two men swam, and just as the decision he had made had lightened Bertrand's mind, so the cold seawater refreshed his body. Later that evening, when they ate supper on the vine-covered terrace of a small restaurant overlooking the sea, he chatted cheerfully to Harry about his life in France. They sat at a table covered with blue oilcloth and shared a bottle of *vinho verde*, which, after the first course of olives and cheese, they found to be empty, and so they ordered another.

"Beginning to enjoy yourself?" asked Harry.

"It looks as if I'll be here for some time," said Bertrand, his tipsiness eroding his discretion, "so I might as well get used to an easier pace of life."

"You can't get back to France?"

"I don't want to go back to France."

"Where do you want to go?"

"To England."

"Why England?"

"Business," said Bertrand evasively.

"If you want my advice, don't make the journey. If you aren't torpedoed by a U-boat or shot down by a Messerschmitt on the way, you'll be done in by a bomb when you get there."

"There are pressing personal reasons."

"Cherchez la femme?"

"She's called Marianne."

"And she's in London?"

"For the duration."

"Then you'd better get there."

"It's not that easy."

"Won't the British give you a visa?"

"They'll give me a visa, yes, but . . ." He hesitated, then looked at the American and said, "Do you like the English?"

"Not altogether."

"They're very pleased with themselves, aren't they?"

"Superior, yes."

"They sneer at us French for our poor showing against the Germans, but without the Channel what would have happened to them?"

"London would have fallen within a week."

"Precisely."

"Chamberlain brought back as head of the government, or Halifax . . ."

"An armistice."

"Almost certainly."

"A government in Edinburgh . . ."

"Or Manchester."

"So they have no right to take credit for what amounts to a piece of luck."

"None at all."

Sitting there across the table, Harry looked so open, decent and friendly that Bertrand, desperate to discuss his predicament with another man, leaned forward and said, "It isn't a girl, Harry."

"I thought it might not be."

"Marianne is France. I want to join de Gaulle."

"You're a brave man."

"Wouldn't you do the same for America?"

"Yes," said Harry earnestly. "Yes, I think I would."

"But the English want me to work for them."

"Do they?" Harry gave an inward smile which Bertrand was too intoxicated to notice.

"But I don't want to work for them."

"Why not?"

"I don't trust them."

"Nor would I."

"But they say that if I don't, there's no knowing when I can get from Lisbon to London."

"A little bit of pressure?"

"Yes."

"Polite blackmail?"

"Yes."

"They're very good at that."

If Bertrand had drunk no *vinho verde*, he might have remarked upon the lack of any surprise in the American as he heard these revelations while eating grilled fish and fried potatoes. Yet that strange blend of youth and age, naiveté and sagacity, flickered on in Harry's face until, in a nonchalant way, he said, "Had you thought of going to Britain by way of America?"

"By America? No."

"There are planes out of Lisbon all the time, and once in New York you shouldn't find it too difficult to get back across the Atlantic to England."

"But I'd need a visa for the United States."

"That wouldn't be difficult."

"And the planes must be full."

"A seat can be arranged."

Bertrand laughed. "And the British could go to hell." His spirits hovered, afraid to rise. "Are you sure I could get a visa to go to New York?"

"Certain."

"Won't I need a sponsor?"

"I'll act as your sponsor."

"You hardly know me."

"I know you well enough."

Now, despite the wine, Bertrand suddenly understood that Harry had dropped the pretense that he was waiting in Lisbon to install machine tools, and the realization made him suspicious. He asked, almost ungraciously, "What do you want in return?"

Harry seemed neither surprised nor offended by the question. "Nothing," he answered. "At least nothing now. You see, we aren't in the war, but we know which side we want to win."

"Of course."

"And we're interested, very interested, in what follows."

"Yes."

"Don't take this wrong, Bertrand, but I think this time around, just like the last time, we Americans will have to come in to clean up the mess. To do that we'll need friends in the European countries, so if a little help now leads to a little friendship in the future, I guess we'd consider it a fair return."

Harry Jackson dropped Bertrand at the Avenida Palace at midnight, and for the first time since he had arrived in Lisbon he slept well. After breakfast he set off in high spirits for the villa in Belém to deliver his reply to Trent's proposals.

"I am very sorry," he said once they were seated in the drawing room, "but I have decided to stick to my original intention to put myself at the disposal of General de Gaulle."

"Ah," said Trent. "A pity. But I respect your choice."

"I trust that you will allow me to enter England to do so?"

"Of course, of course. A visa is easy. It's getting there that is the problem."

"I have made my own arrangements."

"That's very clever." Trent peered at him, as if looking over a pair of spectacles.

"I mean to travel via New York."

"By New York?" Trent glanced at Fry, who sat on the arm of an armchair, then at Bertrand again. "I shouldn't have thought you'd find it any easier to find a seat on a plane to New York."

"I think one can be found."

"By Mr. Jackson, perhaps?"

Bertrand blushed. "You know Jackson?"

"Yes, indeed. We are, as it were, in the same line of business."

"Machine tools?" For the first time since he had met him, Bertrand now smiled at Trent.

"Is that what it is these days?" Trent paused, glanced again at Fry, then back to Bertrand. "Do you have your passport with you?"

"Yes."

"If you'll go with Fry now, he'll take you to the consulate for a visa."

"Now?"

"I think you've wasted enough time already."

Bertrand got to his feet. "But when could I leave?"

"Unless you very much want to see New York, you could sail tonight for England."

"Tonight?"

"As luck would have it, there's a spare berth on the *Bonaventure*. It would be a little absurd, wouldn't it, to go to London by way of America? And we can't possibly allow ourselves to be outdone by your friend Mr. Jackson."

2

The headquarters of the Free French, which had first been housed in Saint Stephen's House on the Embankment, had by the time Bertrand de Roujay reached London moved to a large, modern building in Carlton Gardens. One set of windows looked out over the back of the Reform Club on Pall Mall, and another faced the more elegant house which had once belonged to Lord Kitchener.

When Bertrand arrived from Euston Station he was met at the door by a young lieutenant in the uniform of the Chasseurs Alpins. He was taken at once to an office on the first floor, where a captain in the same regiment, Jean Etlin, whom Bertrand had known at Saint Cyr, embraced him warmly and congratulated him on his escape from France. "Thank God you've arrived at last," he said. "We've been expecting you for weeks."

After a short wait in Etlin's office, Bertrand was taken up to the third-floor office of Geoffroy de Courcel, the private secretary of

General de Gaulle, and a moment later was shown into the office of de Gaulle himself.

Though he had once seen a photograph of the general in a newspaper, Bertrand was nonetheless astonished to see rise from the seat at his desk an immensely tall man with a large nose, large, protruding ears and a head that seemed disproportionately small for his body. As he came forward to greet Bertrand, his small gray eyes looked aside, as if he were too shy to look his visitor in the face. As he extended his hand, Bertrand noticed the nicotine stains on the general's fingers, and when he smiled the same yellow stains on his large, irregular teeth.

"De Roujay?" de Gaulle asked.

"Bertrand de Roujay, at your service, General." Bertrand saluted, and then shook hands.

"Well done. Come and sit down." De Gaulle returned to his desk. "Were you held up in Lisbon?"

"Yes, General."

"By the English?"

"Yes."

"You are not the first." He pointed to a chair, and both men sat down. "You came from Mézac?"

"Yes."

"Where you were subprefect?"

"Yes. And a captain in the reserve."

"Consider yourself placed on active duty."

"Thank you, General."

"But your civilian experience will be invaluable to us." The general lit a cigarette.

"I am here to help in any way I can."

"What signs of resistance in Mézac?"

"Very few."

"No anger?"

"Relief."

De Gaulle nodded. "I feared as much. But that will change." He drew in the smoke from his cigarette. "They tell me that your mother is a Ravanel."

"Yes."

"From Valenciennes?"

"Yes."

De Gaulle nodded. "They will have a bad time, under the Germans, in the Nord."

"It may provoke a revolt," said Bertrand.

"Certainly." The general nodded. "Whereas in the south they have yet to suffer."

They talked further, but when de Gaulle had finished his cigarette he stood up to signify that the interview was at an end. "Much has still to be done here," he said as Bertrand took his leave."

"I am sure."

"We shall need all our wits about us to survive." He held out his hand to say goodbye. Bertrand shook it, saluted once again, turned and left the room.

There was a sense of some confusion at 4 Carlton Gardens, but despite this Bertrand felt elated to have reached his goal and to be at last among Frenchmen committed to continuing the war. He was immediately taken in hand by his friend from Saint Cyr, Jean Etlin.

"Nothing is organized as we would like it to be," Etlin said, leading Bertrand back to his office, "but as you can imagine, we are entirely dependent upon the English, and they have had their hands full keeping Fritz on the other side of the Channel."

"Of course."

"At first our funds came chiefly from the French in England, who sent in their savings and their jewelry, even their wedding rings. But now we have money from the English, and we have been able to form not just fighting units but a civilian administration as well."

"Is it true," asked Bertrand, "that only one in six of our men in Britain wanted to stay on and fight?"

"Yes," said Etlin, "I am afraid it is. But don't be too quick to condemn them. Most had families in France and wanted to go back to protect them."

"Didn't you?" asked Bertrand.

Etlin laughed. "My wife can look after herself," he said. "She's more than a match for Fritz." The two men sat down. "Also, the English did nothing to encourage them to stay. We were told—we officers—that if we remained over here we would have to serve as privates in the British army."

"Why?"

Etlin shrugged his shoulders. "I don't know. Perhaps lesser men than Churchill had a smaller vision of what France can still do in the war."

"What can we do?"

Etlin laughed. "First, find somewhere for you to stay. If you like you can billet with me and a couple of others in what they call a 'mansion flat' on the Fulham Road."

"Have you room?"

"Yes, but I warn you, it is far from being a mansion."

The apartment was large and dingy, with seven or eight rooms opening off a dark corridor. The occupants were all officers who were used to having either their wives or their batmen to cook and clean for them, and they had made it so untidy that even the char lady who came every day had little effect on the squalor.

In early September, Etlin left headquarters at Carlton Gardens to join the Free French Secret Service run by Colonel Passy in Saint James's Square, while Bertrand, who took the code name Montrouge, was appointed as liaison between the military and civilian departments of the Free French forces.

It was a difficult post to hold, because there was no established hierarchy, as there had been in the civil service in France. There was de Gaulle, whose authority was accepted by all, but who was often abroad, and below him an assortment of eccentrics, idealists and adventurers whose courage was equaled only by their rivalry and conceit. The purely military aspects of the movement were simple to envisage, because there were at their disposal certain units of the French armed forces which could be organized, equipped and used in conjunction with their English allies. The political objectives were more complex and intractable, particularly since there remained many Frenchmen in London who would not accept de Gaulle as the leader of the French in exile. Moreover, though the British themselves supported de Gaulle, they still had contacts with Marshal Pétain, who was recognized as French head of state by almost every leader of the nations of the world, including Roosevelt, Stalin and the Pope.

From France itself there was silence. A few individuals like Bertrand trickled out to join de Gaulle, and some colonial governors like Catroux in Indochina and Legentilhomme in Somalia came out in his favor; but when a mixed force of British and Free French forces attempted to take Dakar on the coast of West Africa on September 23, they were beaten off by Frenchmen loyal to Pétain. The British press blamed this fiasco on the Gaullists in London, and that autumn it seemed to Bertrand that all the cynical predictions of Martin Trent had proved true.

At the end of September, Etlin and a young lieutenant called Alain de Chabanais found a small house in Peel Street in Kensington. They invited Bertrand to join them there, and the three moved in with a Polish corporal to cook for them.

The cost of living in this pretty little house was more than it had been for sharing the mansion flat, but Bertrand quickly discovered that he was much better off than most of his fellow officers, for not only did he have his salary as a captain but there remained half a dozen gold napoleons sewn into his belt. He also discovered when he went to Barings Bank that the letter from his mother was sufficient to give him access to the sterling account of Ravanel Frères, which the firm had kept in the City of London to finance its British trade. He was therefore able to commission a tailor in Savile Row to make him not just a uniform, but also some suits which were more elegant than anything he had ever owned in France.

Despite his perfidious treatment by Trent and Fry in Lisbon, Bertrand took an immediate liking to the English for the cheerful way in which they put up with the privations caused by the war, and for their patent determination to defeat the Germans, which compared well to the lethargy of the people of Mézac. By the time he had established himself in Peel Street, the Battle of Britain had been won and it was no longer likely that the Germans would be able to cross the Channel; but as the German fighters retreated from the skies, German bombers began almost nightly raids on London. Bertrand himself felt oddly exhilarated to hear for the first time the sound of the war that had eluded him for so long. He knew each night that a bomb might fall on the house in Peel Street, yet during the raids he never went down to the Anderson shelter in the garden but lay awake on his bed listening to the thudding of the bombs as if it were the rumble of thunder.

Etlin and de Chabanais also ignored the sirens; all three Frenchmen were resigned to the destiny which awaited them. Etlin, in particular, had a sardonic attitude toward life, which sometimes seemed to include a cynicism about the outcome of the war itself. He was an Alsatian, a professional army officer who had been part of the French expeditionary force in Norway that had been stranded in England after the Germans had driven them out. He had rallied to de Gaulle the day after his appeal. At first Bertrand could not believe that simple patriotism had inspired this gesture in such a cynical man. He suspected that perhaps an unhappy marriage awaited him in France.

Nor could he quite fathom the bizarre friendship between the older career officer, Etlin, and Alain de Chabanais, the young lieutenant fresh from Saint Cyr. They came from quite different backgrounds—Etlin from the Strasbourg middle class, Alain from a minor branch of an old French family. Their values, tastes and temperaments seemed ill matched; it was as if each was drawn to the other because of opposite qualities. For a time Bertrand thought that there was a homosexual attraction between them, but if this was so both were unconscious of it. Etlin, Bertrand soon discovered, was a systematic seducer of all the eager young French girls who worked as secretaries at Carlton Gardens, whereas Alain was an earnest Catholic. He confided in Bertrand that before the outbreak of the war he had been torn between marriage and a monastery. On his bedside table in the house in Peel Street lay an open leather wallet with framed photographs of his parents, his sister and a second cousin who since adolescence had inspired in him a pure and chaste affection, while on the wall above the bed there hung a large crucifix.

There were qualities in Alain de Chabanais which reminded Bertrand of his own cousin, Raymond Blaise de la Vallée—he had the same delicate, almost feminine appearance—but he had none of the pose and buffoonery which had led the young Breton into the Place de la Concorde. Though at times he seemed naive in his expectations of human nature, his judgments, delivered in a grave and gentle manner, were often wise for a man of his age, and the thought which preceded them was unusually profound.

One day in the middle of October, Bertrand was crossing Saint James's Street after lunch at Prunier's with the French jurist René Cassin when he found himself face to face with a familiar figure in a crumpled brown suit whom he recognized at once as Martin Trent. His first reaction, and that of Trent too, was to pretend not to have seen the other man, but then both realized that it was too late and so were obliged to greet one another. Bertrand introduced Trent to his companion, but as Cassin was in a hurry he soon took his leave.

"Have you settled in all right?" Trent asked Bertrand with a timid, apologetic smile.

"Yes, thank you."

"I hope there are no hard feelings about Lisbon?"

"In your position," said Bertrand in a tone of cold magnanimity, "I am sure I would have done the same."

"It's very decent of you to say so." Trent glanced down toward Saint James's Palace. "Are you on your way back to Carlton Gardens?"

"Yes."

"Then I'll walk with you, if I may."

The two men set off toward Pall Mall.

"Are you getting on all right with General Spears?" asked Trent, referring to Churchill's representative with the Free French.

"Yes. He seems well disposed toward us."

"He is, indeed he is. He has been since he first met de Gaulle last June. So are we all. But it's hard just now. So little is happening in France."

"I am afraid," said Bertrand, "that most Frenchmen will wait to see which way the wind is blowing."

"I know, and who can blame them? But the wind is turning, don't you think? Well, perhaps not turning, but it no longer blows quite so strongly against us."

"We all admire the courage of the Londoners."

"They're plucky, aren't they? I think the cabinet were very worried about how they would react to the bombing."

"I wish the French had shown such spirit."

"But it's different, quite different. And it will change. We must be patient."

They turned out of Pall Mall and came into Carlton Gardens. "We must keep in touch," said Trent.

"Certainly."

"You must come to lunch at my club."

"I would like that."

They shook hands and were about to part when a thought struck Trent and he turned back to Bertrand. "You don't shoot, do you?"

"Shoot what?"

"Grouse, pheasants, that sort of thing?"

"I used to shoot snipe in Provence."

"Would you like to come to Yorkshire this weekend?"

"I'd be delighted."

"My brother has a place up there. He'd be pleased to have you. I'll write you a note to tell you how to get there."

Bertrand took a train from Kings Cross, and after three hours steaming over flat, foggy landscape reached York. There he changed to a smaller train that took him northeast of the city on a branch line.

He was the only passenger to get out at the small station of Gilling, and at first it appeared there was no one there to meet him. As he handed in his ticket, however, he heard the scrape of tires upon gravel as a car came abruptly to a halt outside, and a moment later a fair-haired girl wearing a tweed suit appeared at the entrance to the station. Her delicate face was pink from some sudden excitement or exertion, and on seeing him it broke into a friendly smile.

"Captain de Roujay?"

"Yes."

"I'm Jenny Trent. I'm sorry I'm late."

They shook hands; then she turned to an old chauffeur who appeared behind her. "Take his case, will you, Gower?" she said in a cheerful but imperious tone of voice.

"Of course, Miss Jenny, I was just about to," the old man muttered.

"And I'll drive again, if you don't mind."

"I do mind, miss, but I'm sure that won't make much difference," the chauffeur muttered again as if speaking to himself, not the girl.

She led Bertrand out of the station toward a large gray car. "I'm only a learner, you see," she said, "so Gower has to come along. Why don't you sit with me in the front. He can go in the back."

They set off with the girl behind the wheel, Bertrand in the passenger seat next to her and the chauffeur, looking pained and ill at ease, on the comfortable seat behind the glass partition.

"Gower hates me driving," said Jenny as the car lurched forward. "He doesn't really think gentlemen should drive themselves, and as for a lady!" She raised her eyes to heaven, and the car swung out of the station yard, cutting in front of a horse and cart. "But the one good thing about this war is that it gives us women a chance at last." She turned and smiled at Bertrand. "Actually, I would have learned anyway, but Father would never have let me drive the Humber."

It was still foggy, but Jenny Trent drove as if the roads were clear. They became narrower as they left the plain and rose into the hills, but she turned each corner as if confident that nothing was coming in the other direction, and when she met a car or lorry would mutter "Damn" under her breath and jerk the Humber up onto the shoulder while continuing to converse with her guest.

"You're with General de Gaulle, aren't you?"

"Yes."

"Uncle Martin is mad about the French." She spoke as if this predilection were an eccentricity.

"It was very good of him to ask me to stay."

"It was a brain wave, really, because lots of the men couldn't get leave and Father hates to waste a gun, especially since this is likely to be the last shoot for a long time."

"I hope I won't disappoint him."

"You must be a good shot, mustn't you, if you're in the army?"

"It doesn't necessarily follow."

"Well, I'm sure it won't matter if you don't hit anything, because we all think you're frightfully brave."

"Why brave?"

"Uncle Martin said that if you'd been caught leaving France you might have been shot."

"I don't think they would have shot me."

"Or the Spanish might have put you in jail."

"That was a possibility."

"You know, Father used to adore Franco. Of course, he denies it now, but I can remember quite well that he used to say that he was just what the Spanish needed."

"We're all entitled to change our minds."

"Yes, I suppose we are, but he might at least own up to it, instead of denying that he ever stuck up for him." She laughed and swung the car through some park gates. "Here we are," she said. "Ascombe Abbey."

It was an immense mansion, about four times the size of Saint Théodore, built of yellowish limestone and looking out over cast-iron railings onto undulating grassland, with woods barely visible in the distance through the mist. Some military vehicles were parked in front of the imposing entrance, and after lurching to the left as they approached it Jenny Trent drove the Humber through an arch into a courtyard at the back.

"We've moved back into the main bit," she said as she stopped the car and pulled up the brake. "First we thought we'd have to move out altogether because they were going to evacuate some boys' schools from Bradford. Then they changed their minds and said it was going to be a regimental headquarters. But now they only use the ballroom for giving lectures, so we can use the rest of the house."

She got out of the car, and Bertrand followed. "How did I do?" she asked the chauffeur, who came around the back of the car carrying Bertrand's suitcase.

"An improvement, Miss Jenny," said the old man. "But I wish you wouldn't drive so fast."

"Don't be so cautious, Gower. We'll never win this war if we don't take a few risks." She turned to Bertrand. "Come and meet the others."

The others were her father, mother, uncle, brother and a friend of the brother, who were all sitting silently in a large, comfortable book-lined room reading newspapers and magazines as if in a dentist's waiting room.

Martin Trent, dressed in a crumpled tweed suit, stood up when he saw Bertrand and came to the door to greet him. "Ah, de Roujay. You've survived the journey. Well done."

"That's not very flattering," said Jenny to her uncle, "when you know perfectly well I fetched him."

"I wasn't thinking of the last bit, my dear. I'm sure that was the safest." He gave Bertrand a conspiratorial smile and led him into the room.

A frail lady, Jenny's mother, shook his hand and greeted him weakly. So did her bluff husband, Martin Trent's older brother, the baronet, Sir Geoffrey Trent. "Always delighted when Martin asks his friends," he said, looking back at the newspaper he had left on his chair.

He introduced his son, Percy, and his son's friend, Eddie Macleish. Bertrand, who had been warned by Etlin that the English often seemed cold only because they were inhibited, took their languid handshakes and drawled greetings as the usual way in which young men of that kind introduced themselves. Percy offered Bertrand a drink and went himself to pour him a glass of sherry, but the friend returned to the magazine he had been reading as if even its advertisements were more interesting than the conversation of a Frenchman.

"Where can Captain de Roujay sleep?" Martin asked uneasily.

"Mary?" said Sir Geoffrey to his wife in a tone of military command. "Where should he go?"

"Oh dear, I don't know," said the etiolated woman, turning toward her daughter with an expression of dismay.

"The blue room," said Jenny emphatically. She turned to Bertrand and said, "Come on. I'll show you the way."

Bertrand found it difficult to tell whether the Trents were rich landowners or indigent gentry, for while the house was furnished with dark furniture from past centuries and there were large and gloomy paintings on the wall, there were also cracks in the masonry and the rooms did not seem to have been painted for many years. It was hard to draw any conclusions from the family's personal appearance, since the men were all dressed in crumpled tweeds that seemed to be the uniform of their class, the mother wore a dress as drab as anything that Bertrand had seen on an English woman, and Jenny, who now led him up the stairs, wore a skirt and blouse that might have come out of a chest of old clothes.

His room had a fine Jacobean bed, but the faded curtains which Jenny closed as they came in were threadbare, and once the dim dusk had been shut out, the only light came from a single bulb hanging beneath a shriveled lampshade in the center of the ceiling. Though the weather was cold, the room was not heated; in the corner, by the fireplace, was a small electric fire which Jenny pointed out to him as she left, saying that he could switch it on "if you feel you need it."

She also showed him the bathroom, which was a long walk down the passage. "If I were you," she said, "I'd have a bath now before someone pinches all the hot water. Oh, and by the way, don't bother to change for dinner. Father may, but Percy and Eddie won't, so I wouldn't bother unless you want to."

Bertrand took the girl's advice on every point and came down to dinner to find both Geoffrey and Martin Trent in moth-eaten smoking jackets and black ties. The young men, however, remained in their crumpled tweeds. "No damned point changing," said Percy pointedly to his sister, "when you can't have a bath."

"No one stopped you," she said.

"No hot water."

"A cold bath would make a man of you."

"Oh, for God's sake put a sock in it," said Percy. Though both in their early twenties, the two of them seemed quickly to resort to childish bickering.

Jenny had changed into a blue silk dress which reminded Bertrand of what he had realized as soon as he had seen her at the station—that she was one of the prettiest girls he had seen since he had come to England. Her blond hair fell to her shoulders and softened still further the delicate features of her face. She was young, not more than twenty-three or twenty-four, but had the assertive and confident manner of a favorite younger child. Her mother, apparently paralyzed by her diffidence and shyness, seemed to allow her daughter to make all the arrangements, while Sir Geoffrey, who bullied every other member of the family, seemed a slave to the whim of his only daughter.

The brother, Percy Trent, though handsome, was stolid in mind as well as appearance; his wits moved at half the pace of his sister's. He teased her and bickered with her, but it was quickly clear to Bertrand that whether because he recognized her greater intelligence or because he conceded her greater influence with their father, he invariably gave her her own way. The only two members of the party who might have been a match for Jenny were her Uncle Martin and her brother's friend, Eddie Macleish; but her uncle seemed cowed in the presence of his older brother, and her brother's friend seemed to remain in that cynical phase of youth which says little but merely observes with a cold and dismissive eye.

At dinner there was evidence either that the Trents were poor or that the shortages caused by the war were greater than Bertrand had realized. The soup, served by a decrepit old woman, seemed little more than the water in which she had cooked the mince and turnips.

"I understand," said Bertrand to Sir Geoffrey, remembering the legs of lamb spiced with rosemary and the glistening brown skin of the roast chickens which he had eaten in France, "that English agriculture has been depressed over the past few years."

"Scandalously neglected," his host replied.

"Quite true," said Martin. "But I think they've learned their lesson."

"Do you know," said Sir Geoffrey to his brother, "I had a chap from the Ministry of Agriculture last week? He wants me to drain that marsh at the bottom of the hill and plow it up for potatoes."

"No more duck if you do," said Percy.

"You can't tell them that, though," said Sir Geoffrey. "Not when there's a war on."

"Do you shoot duck in your country?" Mary Trent asked Bertrand with the anguished relief of a woman who has at last found something to say to her guest.

"Sometimes, yes. Duck and snipe."

"Where is that?" asked Percy.

"In Provence. Near the Rhône."

Percy turned to his uncle. "Is that near Monte Carlo?"

Martin Trent looked embarrassed. "Not really, no."

The brother's friend now looked at Bertrand and asked, "And do you shoot those . . . what are they called?" He turned to Percy and made a flapping motion with his left hand.

"Frogs?"

The two young men guffawed.

"No, you clod," said Eddie Macleish. "What are those big pink birds?"

"Flamingoes," said Martin Trent.

"That's right," said the brother's friend. "Flamingoes."

"In the Camargue, it's true, there are flamingoes," said Bertrand, "but we don't shoot them. At least not as far as I know."

"I should think not," said Jenny. "All this shooting is dreadful, and I shall be jolly glad when you run out of cartridges and can't get any more."

When the cook came in with the pudding it was confirmed in Bertrand's mind that the food shortages in the provinces were clearly more severe than anyone in London appreciated, for she presented a bowl filled with milk-sodden slices of white bread. Bertrand took a modest helping of this horrible concoction and, mustering all his self-control, swallowed the few spoonfuls on his plate before washing them down at once with the wine that remained in his glass.

Yet once again he was obliged to admire the spirit of the English, not just of the cook in improvising such a pudding but also of the Trents, who, to his astonishment, took several spoonfuls of the sludge and ate it with apparent enjoyment. Indeed, his host, having taken only a taste, turned to the cook as she was leaving the dining room and actually congratulated her on the pudding.

Yet at breakfast the next morning, in the same dining room, several silver dishes were set out on the hotplate on the sideboard, one containing sausages, another fried eggs and a third rashers of precious bacon, which in London was not just rationed but difficult to find.

Since he had spent half the night shivering under heavy but threadbare blankets, the electric fire giving off an impotent glow like a mocking hobgoblin, Bertrand ate what was offered in greedy silence, sitting between Martin and Geoffrey Trent, both of whom read newspapers.

The shoot that morning was a fiasco. The fog had not lifted, and though Sir Geoffrey had judged that they could see enough to proceed, the pheasants had only to fly high to disappear into the mist, the sound of their cackle and fluttering wings mocking the sportsmen from the white obscurity.

Bertrand was the least disappointed. He had never before been part of a formal shoot of this kind, with herds of beaters marching through the woods to rouse the birds, tame from the gamekeepers' feeding, but had only sauntered over his own lands at Saint Théodore, taking potshots at birds that were genuinely wild. That morning he was aware that he had inadvertently committed various breaches of etiquette, either by standing too close to the next man or by shooting before it was time, and sensed that as a result he had been made the scapegoat for all that had gone wrong. His fellow sportsmen avoided him; only Martin Trent would talk to him, and he, by his very attentiveness, confirmed to Bertrand that he had no other friends.

They had lunch on trestle tables laid out in a barn—carrots, sprouts and shepherd's pie, with Jenny, her mother and the wives and sisters of the neighbors who formed part of the shoot, who had walked over from Ascombe Abbey. Though she wore gum boots and a mackintosh, Jenny looked fresh and pretty. She made a point of coming with her piled plate to sit next to Bertrand at the trestle table. "Well," she asked, "how many of those poor birds did you slaughter?"

"Almost none, I am afraid," said Bertrand. "I think I rather let the side down, if that's the right expression."

"The weather let the side down," said Jenny cheerfully. "I think Father's going to call it a day."

"Call it a day?"

"Cancel the shoot. Give up this afternoon."

As she had predicted, the shoot was called off and the despondent sportsmen set off toward the house.

"Are you feeling energetic?" Jenny asked Bertrand.

"Yes, more or less."

"There's a rather pretty walk to the abbey ruins," she said. "Would you like to see it?"

"Yes, certainly I would."

"Percy," she shouted to her brother, who was walking with his friend a few paces ahead. "What about showing the abbey to Captain de Roujay?"

The two youths stopped and turned. "Rather you than me, old girl."

"Lazybones."

"I've seen it once too often," Percy said. "I'm sick to death of the damned place."

"What about you?" Jennie looked pertly at Eddie Macleish.

"Another time," he said abruptly, turning away as he spoke and resuming his walk toward the house.

"Come on, then," she said to Bertrand. "We'll go on our own."

They followed a track up the side of a hill.

"Who is your brother's friend?" asked Bertrand.

"Eddie? He's known Percy since prep school, and now they're both in the Guards."

"And you?"

"I'm just about to join the Auxiliary Territorial Service. If you'd come next week you'd have found me in uniform."

"And before the war? What did you do?"

"Nothing much. I went to Vienna for a while, then I came back and came out."

"Came out?"

"You go to parties, meet people. You know the sort of thing."

"Yes."

"It's just a marriage market, really."

"But you didn't buy a husband?"

She blushed. "No. All the men were such bores."

"All of them?"

"All the ones I met. Father says it's because I'm fussy, but really, they were all so jolly predictable. The only good thing about the war is that it's got us all out of a rut."

"Into the ATS?"

"It's better than the Land Army, which is where I would have ended up if I hadn't joined the ATS."

"Where will you be stationed?"

"Catterick, to start with, but Uncle Martin says that if I learn how to drive he'll get me transferred to London."

"You aren't afraid of the bombs?"

She shook her head. "No. Perhaps I should be, but I'm not." She led him through a gate and into a wood where water dripped on them from the leaves of the trees. "Mother is, though. She wants me to stay up here."

"That's understandable. I wouldn't want my daughter to be in London just now."

"Is she in France?"

"Yes. With her grandparents in Provence."

"What about your wife?"

"I am divorced."

"Oh. I'm sorry."

"It happened some time ago."

They came to the far side of the wood, passed through another gate and began to walk down a steep grass bank.

"It's such a bore," said Jenny. "If it weren't for the fog you'd get a lovely view of the abbey from here."

"Are we near it?"

"It's just there," she said, pointing directly ahead, "but we can't see it."

Then slowly, through the blank whiteness of the mist, shapes emerged which slowly revealed themselves as the soaring pillars, arches and buttresses of the ruined church.

"It's very beautiful," said Bertrand when they had reached it. He stood in the middle of the nave, watching two crows hop on the sill of the empty rose window.

"Isn't it?" said Jenny, her eyes on the face of her guest.

"Was it destroyed by Henry VIII?"

"He took the monks' land and sent them packing. Then the locals pinched the stone and the lead off the roof to build their houses."

They strolled toward the cloisters, the only two people visiting the ruin.

"Are you a Catholic?" Jenny asked.

"Yes."

"Then you probably think that it was an awful thing for Henry VIII to do, but the truth is that if he hadn't taken the monks' land and sold it off to the *nouveaux riches* Trents, we wouldn't have had Ascombe Abbey."

"Don't worry," said Bertrand with a laugh. "My home is also built on land which once belonged to a monastery."

"So it happened in France too?"

"During the Revolution."

"And is there a ruined abbey?"

"Not quite like this. We use what's left of our monastery as cottages and farm buildings."

"I don't think Father could get away with it if he tried to do that here."

"It's more beautiful like this," said Bertrand, waving his hand toward the elegant arches of the cloister.

"That's what Uncle Martin says. He thinks that if the monks had kept it they'd have ruined it."

"What did your uncle do before the war?"

"He was what we call a don at Oxford."

"So he knows all about the Middle Ages?"

"He should." She stood silently for a moment, her breath condensing in the cold air. Then a slight frown came onto her forehead. "But if you're a Catholic," she said, "how can you be divorced?"

"The marriage was annulled."

"What does that mean?"

"That the Church judges that the marriage was not a marriage in the first place."

"Even though you had a child?"

"Yes."

"How odd."

"What?"

"Well, to live with someone, thinking you're married, and then find out later that you weren't married after all."

"Yes. It was odd."

As they walked back toward the house, Bertrand described Saint Théodore to Jenny—the house, the wooded hill which rose behind it, the garden under the chestnut trees and the vines which ran down to the river. "It's much smaller than your house," he said, "and everything is on a smaller scale. When we go shooting, for example, we don't organize it like a military campaign as you did this morning. We simply set out with a couple of dogs and a gun under our arms, and hope to see some snipe, but if we don't no one minds much."

"You sound as if you love it there."

"Oh, I do," he said, contrasting in his memory the sunlit October days at Saint Théodore with this soggy afternoon in Yorkshire.

"Do you miss it?"

"Yes."

"And your daughter?"

"Yes," he replied, and then looked down to the ground to hide the misery which he felt when he thought of Titine.

They walked for some time without talking, but it was not an empty silence. Bertrand's thoughts remained at Saint Théodore, which suddenly he missed with a particular acuteness. In London he had the company of his French friends, and the life he led in the city was unlike anything he had known in Provence, but here in Yorkshire, despite the dismal climate, there were many things which reminded him of Saint Théodore, and so exacerbated the misery he felt in exile.

Jenny walked silently at his side. Bertrand assumed that she did not know what thoughts were passing through his mind; his expression was of melancholy sagacity, as if he were pondering the condition of man or the grand strategy of the war. Certainly, he thought to himself, a girl of her age could not imagine that a middle-aged army officer could be as wretched in exile as any ten-year-old boy at boarding school. But when, after walking in silence, he looked up at her, she returned a smile of such gentle sympathy that impulsively he held out his hand and took hold of hers.

"It must be very hard," she said, moving her hand to hold his more comfortably.

"Yes," he said, "but for others it must be much harder." And he too took a firmer grip, and they remained walking hand in hand until they came within sight of the house.

It had never occurred to Bertrand that he could inspire affection in a girl so much younger than he was, and as he lay in a tepid bath before changing for dinner, he did not let his thoughts run beyond the sympathy Jenny had shown as they had walked back to the house, pondering on her sweet nature that had taken pity on an exiled Frenchman.

It was only when Jenny came into the library that evening and sought him out with her eyes that he realized that she found his age no obstacle. His first reaction was a sense of relief that at least one person in the household seemed to like him, and his second a reflex conceit that a man of his age could attract a younger woman. It was in this way that love crept up on him, for if it had confronted him at once, he would undoubtedly have avoided it; ever since his divorce he had mistrusted love and had decided that he would never succumb to it again.

His exile in England, however, had made him vulnerable. He thought he was in control of his physical desires, but his resolution to lead a celibate life had been undermined by the sudden withdrawal of the solace and affection which had emanated from his mother and daughter in France. He had braced himself to live without Lucía, but he had not realized that the human appetite for chaste affection—for the hugs and kisses which Titine used to give him when he came to Saint Théodore—was equally acute and demanding; it was the promise in Jenny's eyes not just of sexual love but of feminine fondness which so rapidly and effectively overwhelmed him.

She sat next to Bertrand at dinner, and though at times she was obliged to talk to her brother's friend, Eddie, on her other side, just as he, for the sake of politeness, had to talk to his hostess, Mary Trent, she turned whenever she could to talk to him or to look at him with a reassuring smile.

After dinner there was a call for volunteers to go to a dance at the village hall to raise money for defense bonds. "You really ought to go," Martin Trent said to Bertrand. "It will give you an interesting insight into English rural life."

Bertrand therefore set out in the Humber with the three younger

Trents, and once they had arrived at their destination followed them into a long wooden hut which was brightly lit with hurricane lamps and heated to the temperature of a Turkish bath by a large cast-iron stove. There was a strong, sweet smell of sweat from the heavy bodies cavorting on the wooden floor to the sound of a piano, accordion and drums. The bright, bucolic faces lit up with friendly recognition as the Trents entered, and Bertrand saw that Jenny was immediately engaged in conversation with a rough-looking youth who might have been a farmhand or poacher.

Percy introduced Bertrand to one or two farmers and their wives, who, once they had been told that he was a Frenchman, looked at him with an amused suspicion. When Bertrand began to talk to them in English, they reacted with unconcealed amazement, as if a baboon had suddenly spoken. They answered cautiously, but here communication ceased, because their accents were so strong that Bertrand, whose ear was attuned only to the King's English, could not make head or tail of what they were saying. He asked the farmers to repeat themselves two or three times over, and then, when he still did not understand, gave up the attempt and merely nodded at every remark—all of which went to confirm the farmers' conviction that all foreigners, including Frenchmen, were fools.

Percy and Eddie went off to dance with two of the farmers' daughters. Bertrand stood watching the spectacle of the two suave young gentlemen with the plump girls in their arms. He noted that Jenny too was dancing with her poacher, and would himself have asked someone to dance had he known the complicated steps of the Gay Gordons and the Veleta.

When these came to an end, several strong young men placed a line of chairs down the center of the hall, each facing in an alternate direction.

"You can join in this," said Jenny, who was suddenly beside him.

"What is it?"

"Musical chairs."

"What do I do?"

"The men dance around the chairs. The women sit against the wall. When the music stops you have to grab a girl, find a chair and sit on it with the girl on your knee."

"And if not?"

"You're out."

"Is that all?"

She gave a mischievous grin. "Not quite. You have to kiss the girl who lands on your knee."

The music started. Everyone trooped around the chairs. When the music stopped, Bertrand grabbed a hand, then a chair, and all at once found a fat middle-aged woman on his lap. He immediately gave her a smacking kiss on her cheek, which gave rise to a chorus of giggles and cheers, for though all the ladies had received a kiss, only one had been kissed by a Frenchman.

The music started again. By entering into the spirit of the game, Bertrand had earned more friendly glances, and when the music stopped and he again sought a girl he found two or three ladies at hand. He snatched without choosing, sat on a chair and then found that he had kissed a scurvy old woman who rewarded him with a toothless, coquettish grin.

The music restarted; the survivors continued the round. Bertrand became determined to do well; the honor of France was at stake. The music stopped. He grabbed a hand and darted in front of an agile farmer to beat him to one of the few remaining chairs. A younger girl as plump as his first settled her fat thighs on his knees and shrieked with laughter as he kissed her.

The music started again, and Bertrand and three other men circled the three remaining chairs like tigers stalking their prey. As the music stopped, Bertrand grabbed a girl and rushed for a chair, and no sooner was he on it than he found Jenny on his knee. She turned his face to hers; both were breathless. He hesitated, because the look in her eyes as she waited was not jovial but determined and earnest. He moved to kiss her cheek just as she moved her head too, and they found instead that it was their lips that touched. This hesitation, this more intimate kiss, and the way in which it lasted for a moment longer than the raucous bussing of the other couples was noticed by the circle of happy spectators, who cheered, whistled, laughed and applauded—all, that is, except for Jenny's brother and his friend.

At the next round Bertrand was out, but since the two men left in the ring were agile young men in their twenties, he felt that the honor of France had been saved, and the riotous swirl of farming folk clearly thought so too, because many a heavy, horny hand clapped him on the shoulder as they led him forward to refresh himself with sausage rolls, butterfly buns and a cup of tea.

The next morning at breakfast, Bertrand asked his host whether it would be possible to go to mass.

"We go to the village church," said Sir Geoffrey, "but I suppose that won't do for you."

"If it is not inconvenient," said Bertrand, "I would rather go to a Catholic church."

Sir Geoffrey looked down the table toward his wife. "You'd better ring the Elmsleys, Mary. They're papists, aren't they?"

"Yes, dear. I think they go to Thirsk."

"And we'd better tell Gower that he'll be needed."

"I can drive myself," said Bertrand, "if you could tell me which way to go."

"Very well," said Sir Geoffrey, making no attempt to hide his irritation. "Take the Humber, if you like. The rest of us can walk."

Martin Trent seemed embarrassed that his guest was proving a nuisance to his older brother. He did what he could to cover his confusion by bumbling on in an academic manner about the difference between the Catholic and Anglican religions. "Now so far as I know," he said to Bertrand, "there never was any attempt in France to bridge the gap between the Catholic and Protestant positions as there was in England. You see, there are some of us here who see the Church of England as the Catholic Church in England, and there are undoubtedly others who see themselves as the heirs to Luther and Calvin."

"Perhaps only the English," said Bertrand, "could manage such a compromise."

"I daresay," said Martin, "I daresay."

"Better than burning one another," said Sir Geoffrey.

"Undoubtedly," said Bertrand with a smile. "We French have never liked burning since the English burned Joan of Arc."

After lunch Jenny drove Bertrand to the station with Percy, her brother, as her instructor. Bertrand felt obliged to sit with him in the back of the car, and once they had reached the station Percy felt obliged to accompany him onto the platform.

"I'm sorry the shooting was so poor," Percy said without conviction. "You must come some other time."

"Thank you," said Bertrand.

Percy looked at his watch. "I bet the train's late. I'll go and find out." He walked down the platform toward the stationmaster's office.

"He's afraid he'll have me for another night," Bertrand said to Jenny with a smile.

"He's still very young," said Jenny as if her brother's youth explained his unfriendly behavior.

"He's older than you," said Bertrand.

"Only in years."

"Are you old enough," he asked, "to want to see me again?"

"Yes."

"It would be a pity, wouldn't it, if we only met while playing musical chairs?"

She blushed. "Yes."

"When will you come to London?"

"I don't know. Not for a while."

"Will you ring me when you do?"

"Yes."

"I shall write to your mother, of course, which will give you my address and telephone number."

"Will you remember who I am?"

"Of course."

"It may not be until after Christmas."

"It doesn't matter."

A train drew into the platform, and Percy hurried toward them shouting, "This is it."

"Thank you," said Bertrand to Jenny.

"For what?"

"For the weekend."

"Oh . . ." She shrugged her shoulders.

Percy opened the door to the train. "You'd better get in."

"Goodbye," said Bertrand. He held out his hand.

Jenny took it, sniffed and smiled. "Goodbye," she said. "Have a good journey."

"Don't forget to change at York," said Percy as he slammed the door.

The train started. Steam rose from beneath the coaches. Bertrand leaned out of the window and waved, and Jenny, while her brother walked toward the ticket barrier, stood and waved too until he passed out of sight.

3

In the weeks which followed, Bertrand did not forget the girl he had met in the north of England, but he was distracted from sentiment by political events, which seemed to favor the fortunes of the Free French. Tahiti and the islands of French Oceania came over to de Gaulle; so did New Caledonia. De Gaulle himself had progressed from the fiasco at Dakar to a tumultuous welcome in Douala in the Cameroons, which had been liberated in his name by an army captain, Philippe de Haute-cloque, who took the *nom de guerre* Leclerc. From there he had gone on to Fort Lamy in Chad, where once again he was welcomed by the governor and the local population.

In London the spirits of Bertrand and his friends had been raised by the arrival of General Catroux, the governor of French Indochina, who, having failed to enlist his colony in the Free French movement, had resigned and made his way to London. For some days after his arrival, rumors went around Carlton Gardens that Churchill had asked Catroux, as a higher-ranking officer than de Gaulle, to take over the leadership of the Free French, but that Catroux had refused.

Most significant of all, however, were events in France itself, for on October 24, Marshal Pétain had met Hitler at Montoire. There he had been photographed amicably shaking hands with the German Führer, and afterward had broadcast to the French nation that "it is in all honor and in order to maintain the unity of France . . . that I am today pursuing the path of collaboration." The traitors at Vichy had at last shown their true colors, and the moral standing of those who had defied them was thereby immeasurably increased.

Three days later in Brazzaville, de Gaulle issued a manifesto denouncing Pétain and established a Defense Council of the Empire, which gave him full powers as leader of the Free French until a

National Assembly was restored in a liberated France. The dissolution of the Third Republic was declared unconstitutional and the government of Marshal Pétain therefore illegal.

These events, however, were at best straws in the wind. The Gaullists still depended upon Britain, and Britain had barely the strength to stave off her own defeat. The Russians and Americans remained neutral as the Germans relentlessly bombed London. Saint James's Church in Piccadilly, which Bertrand passed every day as he got off the bus from Kensington, had been hit by a German bomb on October 15. The sight of its smoking ruins depressed him, and he was further demoralized by the bickering and intrigue that went on in Carlton Gardens whenever General de Gaulle was away.

In the general's absence, the senior officer was the Corsican Admiral Muselier. Like most of his colleagues, Bertrand disliked the posturing Corsican and acknowledged that Muselier seemed to dislike him, for despite the theoretical importance of Bertrand's job as the liaison between the political and military wings of the Free French movement, Muselier ignored Bertrand's office as a channel of communication.

Bertrand did not take this as a personal slight, because there was a general grudge against Admiral Muselier among the army officers, who resented his preference for his navy cronies; yet even his colleagues from the army seemed to treat Bertrand with a certain mistrust, as if his links with the civilian politicians made him suspect. The British had blamed the Dakar fiasco on loose tongues among the Free French, and the serving officers in turn ascribed undeniable indiscretions to the inexperience and lack of discipline of the civilian volunteers.

This rancorous atmosphere in Carlton Gardens infected the household in Peel Street as well. Etlin suddenly became reluctant to discuss his work with the Service de Renseignements in Saint James's Square. Bertrand, who thought of himself as one of the senior members of the Free French movement, felt humiliated when his questions were parried by Etlin as if he were one of the eighteen-year-old typists Etlin brought back for the night from time to time.

The visits of these girls in themselves annoyed Bertrand, for while many of them were pretty enough, it was irritating to be kept awake at night by the yelps and grunts which came through the walls of Etlin's bedroom, and to find strange girls in the kitchen when he came down to breakfast in the morning. More irritating still were the little dramas which occurred when, in due course, one girl was dropped in favor of another. Etlin's favorite way of getting rid of a tiresome mistress was to pretend that he was leaving London for some secret mission in France, and then to flee the city for a weekend in the country with his new conquest, leaving it to Bertrand and Alain to give equivocal answers to the anxious telephone calls, and sometimes to comfort the wretched women who, once they discovered that they were rejected, would come to weep on the shoulders of their unfaithful lover's friends.

Once, when the three men were dining alone, Bertrand complained to his friend about this tedious chore.

"Tell them to go away," said Etlin.

"It's not so easy when they're threatening to kill themselves."

"Poof," Etlin said. "They never kill themselves."

"Have you no remorse for making them suffer?"

"None, because before I make them suffer, I make them ecstatically happy." He lit a cigarette. "I assure you, Bertrand, they get the better part of the bargain; woman's pleasure *in extremis* is a thousand times greater than anything a man can ever feel."

"And is that why you sleep with so many women?" asked Bertrand. "To give the greatest happiness to the greatest number?"

Etlin laughed. "I'm not so altruistic," he said. "Like Montherlant, I eat a fruit. I like its taste. What is more natural than that I should try another and, if I like that, a third?"

"It may be natural," said Bertrand, "without being moral."

Etlin laughed again. "Certainly it may not be moral, but women don't care about morality."

"That's not true," said Alain de Chabanais, who until then had kept silent.

"But you're an innocent," said Etlin mockingly. "Where do you think I find my inexhaustible supply of willing girls? Not in the street, I assure you, but in the company of the girls themselves. Each one leads me to the next; I've yet to meet a woman who would not steal the lover of her best friend."

"You have a low opinion of them," said Alain.

"Like the serpent in the Garden of Eden," said Etlin. "My opinion is neither high nor low but waist-high." He laughed. "And they have the same opinion of themselves. Talk to a girl about Jesus, if you like, and note the bored expression on her face. Then change the subject to love and see her face light up."

Alain frowned but said nothing; he knew too little about women to disagree.

"I tell you, my Catholic friends," said Etlin, "there isn't a woman in the world who wouldn't rather be loved and then abandoned than not be loved at all."

Etlin's pursuit of women meant that he rarely dined with his two friends at Peel Street. As a result Bertrand and Alain frequently found themselves eating together in the evening on what their Polish cook had managed to make of their rations. Though their friendship lacked that attraction of opposites which drew Etlin and Alain together, the similarity of their backgrounds and religious convictions made for an easy companionship.

"The point about Etlin," said Alain one evening, "is that he has no faith in God, and so cannot accurately evaluate his own behavior."

"But does that make him innocent," asked Bertrand, "like a buck rabbit running among the does?"

"As far as I remember," said Alain, "from the theology I learned from the Jesuits, that depends upon whether he is vincibly or invincibly ignorant of the immorality of his acts."

"And if he is invincibly ignorant," asked Bertrand, "would that make the acts themselves innocent?"

"No, surely not. Good and evil have an objective existence. They are not just in the eye of the beholder."

"So even if Etlin is sincere . . ."

"It cannot be said to excuse him. Hitler, after all, may be sincere, but he is also undoubtedly evil."

"And Etlin, the seducer, is ready to die to defeat him."

"That's what is so difficult," said Alain, wrinkling his brow as if the problem had perplexed him for some time. "Etlin has great courage and charm, yet his Don Juanism somehow detracts from his authority."

"One respects him less," said Bertrand.

"And particularly now," said Alain, "when it seems so important that our leaders be upright men. I cannot help feeling that if Daladier had not had his marchioness and Reynaud his countess, France might not have collapsed in quite the way she did."

Bertrand smiled. "Do you think they sapped the strength of our statesmen?"

Alain remained serious. "Yes, I think they did in a way, with their interference and their intrigues."

Bertrand shook his head. "I fear that France would have fallen even if our leaders had been faithful husbands."

"Of course," said Alain. "I didn't quite mean that their infidelity was a direct cause of our defeat. It's rather that if he is to inspire a nation, a leader must be more than an able administrator or a cunning politician, because his authority will to some extent rest upon his probity."

"A man with a mistress does not necessarily take bribes," said Bertrand.

"It goes deeper than that. It is not enough to be reassured that a leader is incorruptible in that narrow sense. One must feel that his authority comes from above."

Bertrand smiled again. "The divine right of kings?"

"Yes," said Alain gravely. "Even in a democracy we look for the mark of divine approval, because in our hearts we know that a simple majority has no moral authority whatsoever—that it is capable, indeed, of greater wickedness than any individual tyrant."

"So they look for a man they can trust, and as often as not they would rather trust a man with a mistress than a man without one."

"Not in a moment of crisis," said Alain. "Would the French have followed Joan of Arc if she had not had her visions but had been the mistress of the king? Would we now follow de Gaulle if he had a countess or a marchioness in tow?"

"Probably not," said Bertrand.

"Because we know that his authority rests upon his probity, and his probity upon his keeping the Law of God, even the Sixth Commandment, for as Saint James says, if a man keeps the whole Law except for one small point at which he fails, he is still guilty of breaking it all."

On November 18, de Gaulle returned to London and some order was restored among the squabbling factions in Carlton Gardens. Muselier was put in his place and Bertrand was confirmed in his post. He still felt a sense of caution, almost mistrust, among many of his colleagues, however, which he ascribed to their envy—the same envy that had provoked men like Pidner in Mézac, for many of the Free French came from Radical or Socialist circles and disliked Bertrand's background and religion. They also envied him his qualifications and administrative experience, and even the money he drew each month from Barings Bank, which enabled him to wear his well-cut suits and lunch now and then at Prunier's and the Ritz.

As a result there were rumors, which Etlin passed back to Bertrand, that he was a reactionary who wished to see de Gaulle return to France as a Franco. It was even said that he had belonged to the secret society of right-wing fanatics, the Cagoulards, and Bertrand assumed that it was these unjust and unspoken charges which kept him from the center of power in the Free French movement.

In the middle of December, Bertrand received a letter from Jenny Trent saying that she was in London. He immediately telephoned the Mayfair number embossed on the top of the stationery, but there was no answer. He tried again from the house in Peel Street at seven that evening, and when Jenny answered the telephone they arranged to have dinner together the next day.

They met at the Ritz. Bertrand was there before her, and sat with a drink waiting for her. To his consternation he realized that he could not remember what she looked like; he knew that she had fair hair and an elegant figure, but however hard he tried he could not recall her face.

A woman came in, tall and blond, but as he rose from his chair he realized that she was too old to be Jenny. He sat down again and ordered another cocktail. His eyes never left the door, because it occurred to him that she too might have forgotten his face and, since he was in uniform, might fail to recognize him.

Then, as the waiter brought his second drink, he saw a girl come in from Piccadilly behind a boisterous group of men and women, and knew at once that it was her. She was younger and prettier than any of the other women, yet had the assurance in her bearing as she entered the hotel that she had shown when driving the Humber down Yorkshire's country lanes.

She saw him and came toward him at once. "Hello," she said in her mild, clipped voice.

Bertrand stood and offered her a chair. "I thought you might not recognize me."

"I knew it was you," she said. "I recognized the French uniform." She smiled with a trace of mockery as she sat down.

"I'm sorry," he said. "I had hoped to go home and change, but I couldn't get away."

"I love the uniform," she said.

"It has its advantages. You get better service." He called the waiter and ordered her a drink.

Jenny wore a simple, elegant dress which because of its simplicity made her seem almost a child. "What do people think?" Bertrand asked her. "That I'm your uncle?"

"No."

"Or perhaps that you've been assigned to show this wretched foreigner around London?"

"I'm sure you know your way around better than I do."

"Only a small part of the city. Kensington, where I live, and Saint James, where I work."

"Well, I don't know much outside Mayfair."

"Perhaps we can explore London together?"

"We may as well, while it's still standing."

They did not start their exploration that night but merely crossed Piccadilly from the Ritz to have dinner at the Berkeley Grill. Bertrand had chosen it because it was elegant yet respectable, the sort of place where an uncle might be expected to take his niece. But as the evening proceeded and the food and the wine entered his blood, he felt less and less avuncular toward her. All the affection and attraction that she had inspired in Yorkshire were reanimated now that he was with her in London. She too seemed patently delighted to see him. Every now and then the assurance she had shown when entering the Ritz would give way to a grin of childish delight, as if dining with Bertrand was an unexpected, grown-up treat. She kept glancing around the restaurant as if hoping she would be seen by people she knew.

"Father often comes here," she said, "and so does Uncle Martin."

"Will they be here this evening?"

"No. Don't worry. Father's in Yorkshire, and Uncle Martin is off on some deadly secret mission."

"And what would they say, your father and uncle, if they knew you were dining with me here in London?"

She shrugged her shoulders. "I don't know. Let's wait and see."

"And your brother?"

"He'd think I was showing off."

"And your brother's friend?"

She frowned. "It would be none of his business."

They were drinking their coffee when the sirens began their whining warning of an air raid. Some of the diners immediately rose and left the room. Bertrand called the waiter, who hurriedly brought him his bill.

"Do you want to go to a shelter?" he asked Jenny as the man scuttled off with his money.

"What do you usually do?"

"I don't usually bother."

"Then let's finish our coffee." But as she spoke with such nonchalance, the whole building shook from an explosion close to the hotel.

"We'd better go down," said Bertrand, standing and putting his napkin down on the table.

She looked alarmed. "Very well."

He took her by the hand and led her out of the restaurant into Piccadilly. There was a smell of smoke in the air and the sound of bells from fire engines and ambulances. The sky above Stratton Street was lit by flames.

"Better take shelter, sir," a warden said to Bertrand. "It looks like a heavy one."

They walked to the Underground at Green Park and went down the escalators into the station. There a crowd of people had already gathered, some, like Bertrand and Jenny, well-dressed men and women who had been caught by the raid, others more permanent residents who because of the bombing came to the station every night and had marked out a corner of the platform as their temporary abode. Everyone seemed in a jovial mood, and Bertrand, in his unfamiliar uniform, provoked a dozen friendly remarks.

Jenny, for whom this was the first taste of the Blitz, looked around at the mass of people with astonished excitement, clinging all the time to Bertrand's arm. Though he knew that perhaps she did so only because she was confused and afraid, the touch of her white hands on his khaki arm was the most poignant and pleasant thing that had happened to him since he had come to England.

A cry went up: "It's the all clear." Slowly the crowd shuffled by the permanent inhabitants of Green Park Station and made their way up into the street.

"I'll take you home," Bertrand said.

Jenny said nothing but leaned against him as they walked toward her parents' apartment. The side streets of Mayfair were now quiet, lit only by the fires started by the raid. The dark, the danger, the bizarre experience they had been through seemed to have formed a close bond between them, and as they walked they took hold of one another's hand, not to express the sympathy they had felt on the walk in Yorkshire but as the preliminary gesture in the ritual of love. Neither spoke, because from Jenny's manner, from the way in which she walked in unison with him and leaned against him with absolute trust, it was clear that words were superfluous to establish or analyze her state of mind.

But Bertrand, who had lived longer, was distracted by memories from wholehearted happiness. This walk arm in arm through the London streets reminded him of a similar stroll beneath the Promenade du Peyrou ten years before. Then the air had been dry and scented by pine and rosemary; now it was damp and dark, and smelled of bombs and burning buildings; but the gait was the same, and the love and the trust it represented.

They came to the door of the apartment block where Jenny was staying. "Come up," she said. "I can give you a drink, or make you a cup of tea."

"What will your mother say?"

"She's not there. No one's there."

It was an elegant, old-fashioned building with polished paneling and a slow old elevator. She smiled into his eyes as they stood waiting for it to reach the fourth floor. He kissed her lips.

The apartment too was elegant and old-fashioned, furnished sparsely like the suite in an Edwardian hotel, with a comfortable sofa and armchairs but only a few silver-framed photographs of Trents to give it a personal touch.

"What would you like?"

"Have you any whiskey?"

"Of course." She poured some into a glass. "It's malt. Father has a friend who distills it."

She held out the glass, but instead of taking it he took hold of her shoulders and drew her toward him.

"Let me put it down," she whispered.

She placed the glass on the table next to a photograph of herself on a pony as a child, then went to switch off the lights and close the door. Now the room was black; only a faint light shone in around the edges of the door from the hall. He could hardly see her as she came back to him across the room, and then kissed him with such a confident fervor that he wondered for a moment whom she had kissed before. But her kiss was more powerful than any doubts or misgivings; he enveloped her with his arms and shut out all thoughts of anything but the touch, scent and taste of the girl in his arms.

Under the cloth of her dress he felt the line of her spine and then the silk of her stockings. When he touched her body she nuzzled his neck, and rather than drawing back encouraged him to go on. Again a memory intruded—of when he had gone this far in his apartment in Paris on the Rue de Médicis, and of how his younger self had then been too honorable to continue.

Once again he drew back. "Perhaps . . ." he began.

She smiled and looked lovingly into his eyes. "Don't worry," she whispered. "It's quite safe."

"It wasn't just that," he said. He wanted to mention God and the law but merely said, "I'm so much older than you are."

"Don't be silly," she said. "We might both be killed tonight."

"I know."

"And then we'd never have done it."

That weekend Etlin and Alain de Chabanais both went to Ringway for parachute training, and the Polish corporal took advantage of their absence to take two days off and visit his brother in Lincoln. With the house to himself, Bertrand took Jenny back on Saturday night after dining with her in Soho and made love with her on his own bed.

"Can you stay the night?" he whispered in her ear as she lay drowsily in his arms.

"If you like." She shut her eyes and moved closer to him, her light body leaning against his heavier, hairier frame. He listened to her breathing as it settled into a regular rhythm and then, as she sank into sleep, became almost inaudible.

Bertrand himself could not sleep, partly because he was used to sleeping alone, partly because Jenny's presence in his bed set a series of thoughts moving through his mind. He felt overwhelmed by the joy of having this smooth, warm girl lying against him, a joy which went beyond the triumph of conquest or the satiation of lust. It was a nobler delight in the trust and love which his physical person seemed to provide. Her slender arm lay limp on his chest, a leg lay half entwined with his, and it was the immobility of her sleeping body that made him feel happier than he had in many years.

Once again, however, his bliss was marred by the memory that he had felt happy in this way before, first with Madeleine, then with Lucía, and this memory confused him, because by temperament he was not a man who could live in the present alone. His ecstasy was eroded by remorse—not just toward God, whose law he had broken, but also toward Geoffrey Trent, whose hospitality was now repaid by the seduction of his daughter.

He imagined how he would feel if, in a few years time, Titine were to sleep with a man like Etlin. It was the thought that he was behaving like Etlin which more than any other kept him awake that night, for if his possession of Jenny expressed only a transient desire for the pleasures her body gave him, he could hardly escape the censure that he and Alain had directed at their friend. But if it was not, if he was sincere, then undoubtedly he should marry her.

The thought of marrying Jenny both delighted and dismayed Bertrand. At a stroke it would change the seamy sin of fornication into a sacrament of the Church. The breach in the law would be annulled, the flow of God's grace restored. At the same time, however, he might fall once again for the same illusion which had led to so much suffering earlier in his life. How could either of them know whether the attraction and affinity which had seized them now, when he was a foreigner stranded in a strange country, and she a girl wrenched from the formal pattern of her life, would survive the war? How could they know whether in the ordinary circumstances of everyday life, which were sure one day to return, they would see one another in the same light and feel the same emotions?

He dozed and then slept, his body adjusting to the presence of Jenny. Some time later, at four in the morning, he was waked by the sound of the siren. With a shock he realized that Jenny was with him in the bed. The sirens had not waked her; she slept as soundly as before. He waited, and in a moment heard the drone of the bombers, then the distant thud of a bomb, then one closer, then one closer still.

She stirred, and her body, like his, was paralyzed for a moment as her mind failed to recognize the strange touch of another. Then she remembered, and stirred against him.

"Is it a raid?" she whispered.

"Yes." He paused. They both listened. "Are you afraid?" he asked.

"No." She moved closer to him in the warm bed, and the scent of the warm air beneath the blankets and the feel of her soft skin reawakened his sexual senses, and they made love again, the rhythm of their bodies unaffected by the sounds of explosions, as if the sheets were a shelter and ecstasy itself a magic protection.

She wore his dressing gown for breakfast the next morning and sat sipping coffee with the same nonchalance she might have shown had she been in her own home. There was no embarrassment, no complicit glee. She behaved as if being there with him was normal because it was natural, and had Bertrand not had the evidence of her virginity he might have mistaken her innocence for experience, and have assumed that she had breakfasted with lovers on many occasions before.

"You know," he said, his mouth half full of toast and marmalade, "you make me very happy."

She looked up and smiled. "Good," she said. "You seemed so sad in Yorkshire."

"Am I just a good cause, then?"

"War work?" She smiled. "Of course not."

"Do you love me?"

"Yes." The word tripped easily off her tongue.

"Will you always?" asked Bertrand.

"I daresay." Again she spoke with an innocent assurance, and just as she did so Bertrand heard the sound of a key in the front door.

"Who is it?" asked Jenny.

"I don't know."

"Is it your cook?"

"No. It must be Etlin and Alain."

Bertrand stood, and wearing only his pajamas went out to the hall, where he found his two companions shivering from the cold.

"Do I smell coffee?" asked Etlin. "Thank God. We've spent the night in the corridor of a crowded train." He patted Bertrand on the shoulder as he passed him to enter the kitchen.

"Etlin . . ." Bertrand began.

"We're famished," said Alain, also moving toward the kitchen. "I tell you, Bertrand, the journey was so awful it has wiped out the horror of jumping out of a plane."

Bertrand trailed after his two friends into the kitchen. "I have a guest," he said lamely.

"So we see," said Etlin, laughing as he saw Jenny.

She looked up and smiled without a trace of embarrassment.

"There was a raid last night," said Bertrand.

"Of course, of course," said Etlin in an amused tone, as if any explanation were superfluous. "And the buses and taxis disappeared from the streets."

"Just so." Bertrand smiled at Jenny. "This is Jean Etlin," he said to her, "whom we all call Etlin, never Jean." He turned to Alain, but saw on his face a look of astonishment, quickly followed by a blush of shame. "And this is Alain de Chabanais."

Alain nodded toward Jenny.

"Come and have some breakfast," said Bertrand.

"Willingly," said Etlin.

"Later," said Alain, who turned and left the room.

"I hope you were comfortable," Etlin said to Jenny with a smirk.

"Yes, thank you."

"Good. You used my room, I hope, or Alain's?"

"No," said Bertrand, frowning. "She slept in my room."

"Oh?" said Etlin in affected amazement.

"And I slept on the sofa."

"Of course." He laughed. "I should have realized that, because with Bertrand"—he turned to Jenny again—"it is courtesy above all." He filled his cup with coffee and hot milk.

"Doesn't your other friend want some breakfast?" Jenny asked Bertrand.

"Yes," said Bertrand. "He'll be down in a minute."

"Unless," said Etlin, "as the youngest of the Three French Bears, he thinks a little English Goldilocks has eaten all his porridge."

The raid the night before had been heavy, and as Bertrand and Jenny walked down toward Kensington they saw the smoldering ruins of the Carmelite church where Bertrand and Alain had gone to mass the Sunday before.

Remembering now what he had been doing at the moment the bomb had fallen, Bertrand felt a renewed and acute remorse. It was as if God had called the bomb down onto his own sanctuary to prevent it from falling on Bertrand as he sinned. Yet if he had sinned, so had Jenny, and it was he who had led her into it, because however willing she had been to sleep with him, he was the older and must bear the responsibility. He looked at her. She seemed so fresh, innocent and affectionate that it seemed impossible that she could have anything to do with the ugliness of evil.

"What are we going to do?" he asked in a voice made breathless by his agitation.

She smiled and said, "I'd better go home and change."

"Of course, but after that. Are you free?"

"Yes, quite free."

"Can we spend the day together?"

"Of course."

"The whole weekend?"

"If you like."

"I'd like to spend my life with you." He looked into her eyes. "I'd like to marry you."

She stopped laughing. "You don't have to."

"Please, please say that you will marry me."

She looked perplexed. "I love you."

"Enough?"

"Completely."

"Then marry me."

She hesitated. "I do love you," she said again.

"Am I too old?"

She clutched his hand. "It's not that."

He looked away as if she had asserted what she had just denied. "It was mad of me . . ."

"It's just that the war . . ."

"What?"

"It makes everything so uncertain."

"I'm not uncertain."

"How can you be so sure?"

"I don't know, but I am."

She looked away for a moment, as if something she might glimpse in the shop windows would help her to make up her mind. Then, turning to him again, she said, "You really do want to? You promise?"

"Yes."

"Then I will, of course I will. I'll marry you."

"Soon?"

"Whenever you like."

At eight the next morning, Bertrand went to mass with Alain at a small church in Notting Hill. They said nothing to one another as they walked through the dark, damp streets, either going to the church or on the way back to breakfast at Peel Street. Bertrand knew quite well how the presence of Jenny must have affected Alain, who, if he had hoped that there might be an innocent explanation, had his darker suspicions confirmed when Bertrand, because he was in a state of sin, did not take communion.

Only when they were sitting together at breakfast did Bertrand say, "Do you think I have lost my soul?"

"Why?"

"Because of the girl."

"It's none of my business."

Bertrand paused, then said, "We're going to get married."

Alain looked up from his cup of coffee with a candid, delighted expression in his eyes. "Then you love her?"

"Of course."

"That's wonderful." He put down his cup, sighed and smiled. "No, really, I have to confess that when I saw her there in your dressing gown I was rather taken aback, because everything you had said . . ."

"I know. And strictly speaking, I have behaved badly, because she is young, but at least I am sincere. I do love her. We are to marry."

Etlin was flabbergasted by Bertrand's news. "But you are mad," he said. "She's charming, of course, but how can you tie yourself down now, at the start of the war? Before you know it you'll have a squalling brat, and when the time comes to go back to France you won't want to go."

"Not at all," said Bertrand. "She understands that I'm here to fight in the war."

"That's what she says now, because she's excited by your uniform, but later—you'll see—they're all the same."

"You forget," said Bertrand irritably, "that I have been married before."

"That's true," said Etlin. "You have more experience than I do—both of marrying and unmarrying, after all."

Jenny wished to keep the news from her parents until she returned to Yorkshire at Christmas. "It will be easier," she said. "I can catch them in a jolly mood."

"They may forbid it," said Bertrand dejectedly.

"They can't," said Jenny. "I'm over twenty-one."

"Even so, they won't like it."

"They'll come around to it."

"They would probably rather you married your brother's friend," said Bertrand.

Jenny blushed. "Perhaps they would, but I'm not going to marry because they like the idea of Eddie's grouse moor in Scotland." She had a fierce, determined look on her face.

"What about a vineyard in the south of France?"

"Is that where we'll live?"

"After the war."

"After the war." She repeated the words with a certain relief, as if it were premature to speculate about what would happen in such a faraway, different world.

Bertrand, Etlin and Alain de Chabanais all celebrated Christmas with the family of a colonel in the Free French forces, Armand Gary. He had managed to escape with his wife and three children, and had rented a large house in Hampstead left vacant by a family that had fled to the United States. They all went to midnight mass at the French church in Leicester Square, then returned to eat oysters and goose. They returned for lunch on Christmas day, when they ate a turkey, and in the afternoon they exchanged gifts and sang carols around a Christmas tree.

Many of the Garys' guests were, like the three men from Peel Street, separated from their families in France, and even Etlin, who was so relieved to be rid of his wife, became melancholy as he thought of his son and daughter celebrating Christmas without him. Alain had a remote look in his eye, as if in his imagination he was with his brothers and sisters in their parents' castle in the Vendée. Bertrand, too, sat alone, thinking of Titine at Saint Théodore, hoping that if he could visualize clearly her opening her presents with her grandparents and cousins around her, she would feel his presence too and the strength of his affection from a thousand miles away.

Then his inner eye left his daughter and moved to the faces of his mother and father, then Louis, Hélène and Marthe, the cook. They all seemed real, yet remote—part of him, yet detached from him. He missed them acutely, yet the longing he felt was not like pain, something which impelled one to avoid it; rather, it was like a mellow color on the canvas of his present life in which Jenny was vivid in the center, and he thought with pleasure and pride of how, when the war was won, he would return to Saint Théodore with his English bride—and perhaps with a son as well. He imagined how his parents would approve of this girl, who, though not a Catholic, came from a good family. He felt sure that Pierre would like her, and he even imagined how Madeleine and perhaps Lucía would come to hear of his pretty young wife, for love is mixed with vanity, and vanity requires an imagined audience of the intrigued spectators of one's life.

Between Christmas and the New Year, before Jenny returned from Yorkshire, Bertrand was telephoned by Martin Trent and invited to lunch at his club.

At first Bertrand assumed that Trent had been delegated by his brother to put him off the idea of marriage, and he went to White's in Saint James's in an anxious but stubborn frame of mind. But as each drank a glass of sherry before going in to lunch, Martin Trent made no mention of his niece, and Bertrand felt a deeper dread that she had balked at breaking the news to her parents, and would return to London with a changed mind.

No clear reason for Martin Trent's desire to see him emerged while they ate lunch. When Trent said that he felt sorry for the Free French exiles in London, separated from their families over Christmas, it occurred to Bertrand that this lunch, like the invitation to shoot in Yorkshire, was a gesture of Anglo-French friendship. Certainly Trent seemed concerned for the well-being of the Gaullists; he asked Bertrand whether there was anything he thought the British could do to make their life easier.

Bertrand made some suggestions—suggestions, however, which he had already made to General Spears—and then, in an easier mood, chatted to Trent about life in the French community in London.

"It seems de Gaulle himself has established his authority," said Trent.

"Without doubt."

"You all like him?"

"We all respect him."

"No one wants Catroux to lead them?"

"No."

"Or Muselier?"

"God forbid."

"You don't like him?"

"No."

"Why not?"

"He's unstable. *Farouche.*"

"Ambitious?"

"Yes."

"Why did he come over, I wonder?"

"Pique. Evidently he quarreled with Darlan."

"Not a genuine Gaullist?"

Bertrand shrugged his shoulders. "He wants to fight the Germans, but when he arrived in London he had never even heard of de Gaulle."

It was only when they had returned to the leather armchairs in the smoking room of the club, and were drinking bad coffee from small cups, that Bertrand asked Trent if he had been to Yorkshire for Christmas.

"Yes. Always do, since I have no family of my own."

"Did you enjoy it?"

"Always the same."

"And how were the other Trents?"

"Fine." He smiled, then suddenly looked perplexed. "There was some sort of crisis."

"What about?"

"Something to do with you."

"And Jenny?"

"That's right. Yes. She told us all you were going to get married. Is it true?"

"I hope so."

"Are you sure?"

"Yes. Why? Wouldn't you advise it?"

"In principle, I'm always against it."

"And you've taken your own advice."

"Very much so."

"You won't take it amiss if I don't?"

"I won't, but I don't think that my brother was very pleased."

"Because of my age?"

"Age, religion, nationality—almost anything you can think of."

"Will he forbid it?"

Trent laughed. "He wouldn't dare."

"He seems a strong-willed man."

"Not beside Jenny. Nor is Mary. They'll both do anything she says."

Bertrand came away from White's still unable to understand why Trent had asked him to lunch, but on New Year's Day it became clear. On Churchill's orders, Admiral Muselier was arrested and imprisoned for treasonable contact with the government in Vichy. There appeared to be evidence that Muselier had told Darlan of the expedition to Dakar, and that more recently he had been plotting to return the submarine *Surcouf,* which the British had seized at the time of Mers-el-Kebir.

Carlton Gardens was in turmoil with rumors of every kind. First Bertrand was told that de Gaulle was so indignant at Muselier's arrest that he had threatened to break off all relations with the British, but then Churchill himself had given documents to the general which proved the admiral's treachery. De Gaulle had shown the documents to his own experts, who had quickly established that they were forged. Suspicion fell on two men whom General Spears had recommended to Colonel Passy to help with counterespionage at Saint James's Square. They were now arrested by the British, and Admiral Muselier was released, but the indignity suffered by this eminent Frenchman was taken by de Gaulle as an affront to the honor of France. He blamed the British—the forgers seemed to be their men—and ordered every British subject working in Carlton Gardens to be dismissed.

On January 10, Bertrand was telephoned by Etlin and asked to go over to Saint James's Square "to help deal with some of the aftermath of the Muselier affair." He spoke in a strangely constrained tone of voice which led Bertrand to believe that the matter was urgent. It was only a short walk from Carlton Gardens to Saint James's Square, so he set off at once. He had rarely been to the headquarters of the Service de Renseignements, which because of the danger of indiscretion among the less disciplined volunteers in Carlton Gardens was run as a separate and secret organization. It had also already established a somewhat sinister reputation, and even Etlin, who came down to meet him at the entrance, seemed in these surroundings to have a shifty and suspicious look on his face.

"What can I do to help?" asked Bertrand as he followed Etlin into the back of the building.

"They want to ask you some questions," said Etlin.

"Who?"

Etlin stopped in the corridor and said to Bertrand in a whisper, "Look, I know this is ridiculous, but some of the others need to be convinced."

"Convinced of what?"

"This business with Muselier has made them all jumpy."

"I don't understand."

"Some of them think that you're working for the British."

Bertrand went white. "But that's absurd."

"Of course," said Etlin, continuing along the passage to a small office at the rear. There they were met by a man in civilian clothes; he was about Bertrand's age and had a harsh and irritable expression. Two other men stood at the side of the room, one young and pale, with a cold, fanatical look in his eye, the other tall and muscular, with the close-cropped hair and swarthy face of a marine or Foreign Legionnaire.

"Sit down, if you please," said the first man, who himself sat at the desk.

Bertrand did as he suggested.

"My name is Lieutenant Rivière, and I have been ordered to review the security status of certain officers in our organization. I have been looking through your file, Captain de Roujay . . ." He looked down at the folder on his desk, then up at Bertrand. "I trust you have no objections?"

"Of course not."

"Do you wish Captain Etlin to be present?"

Bertrand turned to Etlin, who seemed confused. "There is no need," said Bertrand.

"Then I'll get back to my office," said Etlin. He started toward the door, then turned back to Bertrand. "I'll see you later."

"Of course."

When Etlin left the room, Bertrand turned back to Rivière. "What do you want to know?" he asked.

"We should like to know," said Rivière, speaking slowly, precisely and malevolently, "for how long you have been working for British Intelligence."

"That is an absurd question," said Bertrand dryly, "based upon an erroneous premise."

"Were you recruited in Lisbon by Major Trent, or were you already in touch with them in France?"

"In Lisbon I was asked by Mr. Trent if I would care to join the British Secret Service. I reported this when I arrived in England. You will see from my file that I refused."

Rivière looked down at the file. "I see that you said you refused."

"Yes."

"Then why did Trent arrange for your passage on the *Bonaventure* when other Frenchmen had to wait weeks, even months?"

"He kept me waiting for two weeks."

"Two weeks, and then he relented."

"Yes."

"Because you agreed to work for him."

"No."

"Why, then?"

"Because I was preparing to leave Lisbon for New York."

"For New York?"

"Yes. It seemed at the time that it would be quicker to come to London via New York."

"And how did you get a ticket for New York?"

"Through a man called Jackson."

"Who was Jackson?"

"An American."

"What kind of American?"

"He said he was a businessman, but I imagine that he was up to the same sort of thing as Trent."

"You didn't mention Jackson in your report."

"I didn't think he was important."

"Are you working for Jackson?"

"I am working for General de Gaulle. Even Trent . . ." He snorted, exasperated.

"What?"

"Even Trent did not ask me to spy on my own people. He wanted me for his own Secret Service."

"Perhaps."

"I am not the only Frenchman to have been approached by the British."

"But you're the only serving officer who retains a close contact with Trent."

"I had lunch with him last week."

Rivière looked down at the file. "You also went to stay with him at his brother's house in Yorkshire."

"Yes."

"And you have seen his niece from time to time."

"Yes."

"Was she your contact?"

"What do you mean?"

"Did she carry information from you to Martin Trent?"

"Don't be absurd."

"It would be a convenient cover."

"It is a purely personal friendship."

"That's what you say."

"Ask Etlin."

"We already have."

"Didn't he confirm it?"

"He confirmed that she'd been in your house, but he thought it out of character. Odd."

"I'm in love with her. We're going to be married."

Rivière looked up. "Congratulations," he said sarcastically.

The younger man with fanatical eyes now leaned forward and said into Bertrand's ear, "Can you prove to us, Captain de Roujay, that you are *not* working for Trent?"

Again Bertrand gave a snort of exasperation. "If I were working for Trent, would I marry his niece?"

The young man glanced at Rivière as if it was indeed unlikely. Rivière closed the file. "I have no further questions at present."

"What do I do now?" asked Bertrand.

"Return to your duties."

"I'm no use to anyone if you think I'm a spy."

"I shall make my report," said Rivière coldly, "and in due course you will know what has been decided."

After his interrogation by Rivière, Bertrand did not go to see Etlin but went out at once into Saint James's Square and walked toward Carlton Gardens in a mood of rage and despair. Now at last he understood why he had been cold-shouldered by his colleagues within the Free French organization: he was thought to be a stooge of MI6. That was why he had not been sent on any of de Gaulle's missions abroad, but had been kept in London in a spurious post of some prestige but no importance.

The thought that so many of his friends had mistrusted him made him hesitate before returning to Carlton Gardens. He therefore went into the garden in the middle of Saint James's Square. It was dead and dank at that time of year, but this small oasis of nature in the middle of the paved city seemed to offer some rest for his maddened mind, so he sat down on a damp bench to give time for his rage to subside.

The anger he felt as he sat there was not directed so much against those who mistrusted him as against himself for so stupidly assuming that he could befriend the Trents—even marry a Trent—yet still play a leading role among the Free French. He understood quite well how essential it was for the Free French movement to remain independent of the English and to be seen to be not just independent but even, at times, antagonistic toward their hosts and patrons; he remembered once again the gibes of his father and brother about de Gaulle, and he knew that many million Frenchmen shared their point of view. If, when the war ended, the Gaullists were seen as mere English mercenaries, the ancient rivalry and mistrust of the French for their ancestral enemies would count against them, and they would never succeed in their essential mission, which was to preserve and one day reestablish on its native soil the honor and integrity of France.

Bertrand therefore did not rail against the injustice of the suspicions he had inspired in Lieutenant Rivière, but only at that combination of naiveté and bad luck which now made it seem as if all the risks and sacrifices he had endured would be for nothing.

When he got back to his desk, Bertrand found a message to say that a Miss Trent had telephoned while he was out. He looked down at the note in gloom. He should have felt excitement, apprehension and delight now that Jenny had returned to London; instead, his spirits sank into a pool of sour bile, for often when love conflicts with ambition it comes out the worse, and certainly at this moment Bertrand saw in Jenny Trent the source of all his troubles.

He telephoned her at her father's flat.

"I'm back," she said cheerfully.

"Well done. What news?" He made an effort to sound pleased.

"It will cost you a decent lunch to hear it."

"The Ritz at one?"

"I'll be there."

Bertrand put down the telephone. From the tone of her voice he knew what her news would be—that she had persuaded her parents to agree to their marriage. He knew too, without any doubt, that if he could reestablish the trust of the Free French by breaking off his engagement to Jenny Trent he would do so that very day.

He could think of only one way to settle the matter once and for all. He picked up his telephone and rang de Courcel. "Would it be possible to see General de Gaulle?" he asked.

"Is it urgent?"

"Yes."

"Very well. Come up at twelve-thirty."

At twelve twenty-nine Bertrand presented himself at the general's office and was shown straight into the paneled room. De Gaulle sat at his desk. He looked up as de Courcel discreetly closed the door.

"Ah, de Roujay. Well?"

"General, I would like to marry."

"Are you married already?"

"No."

"Then what is there to stop you?"

"She is an English girl, the niece of Major Trent."

"Well?"

"He is an officer in British Intelligence."

"Report it to Passy."

"He is aware of it, General. I am already suspected of working for the English."

"And are you?" De Gaulle's squinting eyes now looked straight into his own.

"No, General."

"You give me your word?"

"I do."

"Very well, then, marry."

"Thank you, General."

"But remain a Frenchman!"

"Until I die!"

Jenny was at the Ritz before him. She rose from one of the chairs in the lobby, came toward him with a beaming smile and, scornful or oblivious of the people around them, put her arms around his neck and kissed him on the lips. "Well, we're engaged, aren't we?" she whispered, her mouth close to his ear.

"Are we?"

"Yes. It will be in the *Times* tomorrow."

"Did you have a hard time?"

"I fought them on the beaches, I fought them on the—"

"And they capitulated?"

"Of course. They had to. Right was on my side."

They were married in February. At first Jenny wanted the wedding to be in Yorkshire, for she had always imagined the reception in the ballroom at Ascombe Abbey, but since the ballroom was now a lecture hall for the King's Own Yorkshire Light Infantry, and since in deference to Bertrand's religious convictions the ceremony could not have been held in the old parish church of Ascombe but would have had to have been celebrated in the drab brick Catholic church in Thirsk, it was decided to have the wedding in London—the ceremony in the Brompton Oratory and the reception at the Hyde Park Hotel. Most of the Trents' friends were in London anyway, and it was easier to fill the benches on the bridegroom's side of the church with Bertrand's friends and colleagues from the Free French community. Among them was General de Gaulle himself, who was present with his wife not just as a gesture of cordiality toward the English, but also to show his complete faith in the loyalty and integrity of Bertrand de Roujay.

Chapter 7

1

CHRISTMAS at Saint Théodore had passed much as Bertrand had imagined it. Titine, who all through the autumn had felt a yearning for her absent father, was distracted from her sadness by the preparations for the festival, and on Christmas Day itself by the large pile of presents waiting for her under the tree. The biggest and best was a new bicycle with a card tied to the handlebars saying "From Papa." It had been found with great difficulty for Edmond de Roujay by a shopkeeper in Pévier who, now that Edmond was mayor of the village, was eager to do him a favor.

The previous mayor had been dismissed by the government in Vichy because he was a Socialist. He had been replaced by the most prominent member of the town council, the owner of the olive press, but this man had then been denounced by his predecessor as a Freemason and so was dismissed in his turn. The prefect had then turned to Edmond de Roujay, who, although the father of a Gaullist, was both in appearance and by conviction the closest he could find to a local Marshal Pétain.

Though reluctant to accept the post, Edmond had decided that it was his duty to do so. Once again, it was a time for Frenchmen to obey orders and put their scruples aside. There were aspects of the Marshal's "National Revolution" which he disliked, but by and large the policies of Vichy were those he himself had been advocating for many years. He thought it right that the civil service should be purged of Socialists and Freemasons; he was a little less certain about the disqualification of Jews. He had known many Israelites who had fought courageously for France in the Great War, and he found it difficult to distinguish between assimilated Jews like Bertrand's friend Moreau and an ordinary Frenchman. He was astonished when he heard that after the decrees of October, Moreau had been dismissed as an examining magistrate; he had always seemed so admirably suited to the post. He was equally amazed when the postman from Pévier, whom he had known for thirty years, came to him secretly to confess that three of his grandparents had been Jews and that he therefore might be subject to the new legislation.

Edmond de Roujay did not hesitate to advise the postman to keep this information to himself, nor to lose certain documents in the *mairie* which enabled the man to keep his job. He justified his action to himself on the grounds that Provence had a different tradition from the rest of France and the people in Vichy could not be expected to understand it; the Popes in Avignon had protected Jews, and Carpentras had one of the oldest synagogues in France. He also felt that he knew the mind of Marshal Pétain better than the bureaucrats in the prefecture. The kind of Jews the Marshal wanted out were men like Stavisky and Blum, not Bertrand's friend in Coustiers or the postman in Pévier.

It was the same when it came to the revision of all French naturalizations granted since 1927. It was a sensible decree, because Blum's government had made Frenchmen of all kinds of seditious riffraff from Germany and Spain; but when he saw on the list of those to be denaturalized in the commune of Pévier the names of the Astrans, he removed them because he knew quite well that they were decent, hardworking people.

These exceptions to the rule provoked doubts in the old man's mind, which he might have kept to himself had not Louis been such a strong supporter of the new regime. Without Bertrand to argue against him, it was Edmond who found himself supporting the contrary point of view. "If the Germans were honorable men," he said to his younger son, "which they were in the time of the Kaiser, then there might be some sense in collaboration. But those Nazis are ruffians. They are not to be trusted. They don't keep their word. Hitler will promise one thing one day and do another the next. You can't make a bargain with a man like that."

"Politics is the art of the possible, Papa. We were defeated in battle and so must try to recover by cunning what we lost by force of arms. That's what the Marshal and Laval are up to, and when you think of the fate of Poland and Czechoslovakia, they have already achieved a great deal."

. . .

Three days after Christmas, Louis drove Titine to her mother's apartment in Coustiers. Madeleine invited him to stay to lunch, for despite
the divorce and their political differences, the two still got on well
together, and Louis was always used as the go-between. When lunch
was over, Louis returned to Saint Théodore and Madeleine was left
alone with her daughter. This was not easy for either of them, because
the confines of the apartment and the sudden absence of her rambunc-
tious uncle lowered the spirits of the little girl, who was still too young
to hide her moods, while the presence of the child confused the mother,
who could not think how to amuse her. For a while Titine was
distracted by the neatly-wrapped presents under the small tree placed
on the sideboard in the drawing room, but since too many of them
were books they did not improve her mood. She followed her mother
into the kitchen, where Madeleine was preparing supper with food
Louis had brought from Saint Théodore, and tormented her with a
vivid description of her happy Christmas with the de Roujays.

Michel le Fresne returned at seven. As he stooped to kiss Titine, she
turned her face away. The kiss was only a formality, for Michel and
Titine did not like one another, and both had given up the pretense
that they did. There had been a time when Michel, in the usual way,
had tried to bribe her with dolls and chocolates, but like most children
in her position, Titine had seen through his ploy and had treated both
the gifts and the giver with contempt. As a result, Michel now ignored
the child, talking through her in a petulant voice about the arrangements Madeleine had made for his meals in her absence, for knowing
how bored Titine would be in the apartment and how irritable Michel
became when she was there, Madeleine had arranged to take her to
Montpellier for the New Year. Since the summer, when tempers had
run high, Professor Bonnet had relented and had withdrawn his ban
on his daughter's presence in his house.

The next morning, Madeleine and Titine were driven by Michel to
the station. He carried Titine's smart leather carry-all and Madeleine's
battered suitcase down the platform and saw them installed in their
seats; then, with the mixed expression of a man who is half glad and
half resentful that his wife is leaving him on his own, he turned away
to go back to the hospital.

As the train moved out of the station, Madeleine rummaged in the large cloth bag which she carried over her shoulder for a map and a guidebook to Provence. Since she did not live with Titine, she did not know quite how to treat her. She escaped from her confusion by behaving as if she had been put in charge of a class of one from the Lycée René le Bon, and seeing the week ahead as a job to be done, she started to explain to Titine the historical or geological significance of this or that town or range of hills that they passed in the course of their journey.

The role of pupil suited Titine too. All the childish love which expresses itself in enveloping hugs was expended on her father and, in his absence, on her grandmother and on old Marthe in the kitchen at Saint Théodore. She would have found it awkward and artificial if Madeleine had expected to be treated in this way. It was far easier for her to behave like a favorite pupil with a nice though sometimes distracted teacher who dressed oddly and wore men's shoes.

Titine felt the same about her Bonnet grandparents. She saw them infrequently, so they were not essential to her sense of well-being, but they were nevertheless reliable figures who reappeared year after year in a particular corner of her life. They had their own musty smell, which she recognized as soon as she came into their house in the Avenue d'Assas, and which seemed to emanate from both Françoise and Michel Bonnet as she embraced them. She then went at once into the living room with her grandmother, where, though there was no tree and no decorations, she found a third consignment of Christmas presents.

While she opened them, with Françoise laughing behind her, Professor Bonnet sat down in an armchair and Madeleine sat on the sofa beside him. She felt nervous in her father's presence, because although she had seen him since the summer when they had quarreled, she knew that their reconciliation was only a truce, and that he remained inwardly outraged by her attitude toward the war.

"Well?" he said gruffly. "Are you pleased to be a mother again for a few days?"

"Yes, of course."

"But she's a little de Roujay, isn't she?" said the professor malignly, looking over his spectacles at the child at the other end of the room.

"She grows more and more like Bertrand," said Madeleine.

"Let's hope she inherits his courage," said Bonnet with a swift, savage look at his daughter.

Madeleine blushed and said nothing for a moment. Then she looked timidly at her father and said, "Has everything been all right here?"

"What do you mean, all right?"

"You were afraid the government might move against you."

Bonnet laughed. "Yes. They made me take an oath that I didn't belong to any clandestine group or secret society. Since they knew quite well that the lodge had been dissolved, because they themselves had insisted on its dissolution, the oath was superfluous, so I could swear it in good conscience."

"Does that make your position secure?"

"For the time being. There are still some envious jackals who would like to see me thrown out, but luckily, my girl, I have something called a reputation which extends even to the Third Reich."

"Your views cannot be popular in Vichy."

"People respect notoriety as much as celebrity," said Professor Bonnet. "Anyway, Mireaux isn't a fool. If he throws out all the Radicals the universities will have to close down."

"You must take care."

"Yes, I must be cautious, but not so cautious that I do nothing at all." He darted another contemptuous look at his daughter.

Again she blushed. "What can you do?"

He hesitated, as if about to make some particular retort, then thought better of it and said vaguely, "Reconceive France."

She leaned forward. "I don't understand."

"Reconceive France," he repeated. "Decide what it means to be a nation. Is it a government? A network of ministries, prefectures, barracks and palaces of justice?"

"More an area," said Madeleine. "An area or a people or a language."

"Yes," said the professor with the air of a tutor with his pupil, "all those may help identify a particular nation, but they are not what constitute a nation, because large nations absorb smaller ones, irrespective of language, race or borders. A Burgundian or a Provençal becomes a Frenchman; an Austrian becomes a citizen of the Third Reich."

"So what defines a nation?" asked Madeleine.

"In the end," said Bonnet, tapping his forehead with the index finger of his right hand, "a nation is born here in the head. It is an idea in the mind of man—an idea formed, no doubt, by extraneous factors such as race, language and land, but an idea all the same, sometimes in the mind of only one or two men. There would be no Germany without Bismarck, no Italy without Mazzini and Cavour, and no United States without Jefferson and Washington."

"But France existed long before Germany, Italy or the United States."

"And that is what has thrown us off the track. We assume that because we are an old nation with our own language and natural frontiers like the Alps, the Pyrenees, the Rhine and the sea, France will exist without our having to think about it, but that's not so. France could very easily be absorbed into Germany, just as Burgundy and Provence were absorbed into France."

"But surely," said Madeleine gravely, "it is a question of power, not of will."

"No. Or only if the power affects the will, leading a defeated people to lose faith in their own identity and to sink into the lethargy of despair."

"I hate all nationalism," said Madeleine. "I wish we could all grow out of it."

"Into Communism?" asked the professor with a harsh laugh.

"Into some kind of transcendent fellow-feeling for the whole of mankind."

"If you think Communism is that," said Bonnet, "then you are deluding yourself, because it is not Communism that has absorbed nationalism, but Russian nationalism that uses Communism, just as Napoleon used the ideals of the Revolution to try to dominate the world."

Madeleine made no rejoinder. She remained, as before, a Marxist for whom the only true liberation would not be that of France but that of the proletariat. Yet she did not want to quarrel with her father, and so felt relieved when Titine ran across the room to show her mother her new presents.

There were some crisp, cold days around the New Year when Madeleine, devoting herself to her daughter for the short time she had her to herself, took her to the different churches and museums in Montpellier. What she found, however, was that Titine, who was not yet ten years old, was most interested in the streets, squares and public gardens as the backdrop to her mother's youth, and rather than ask questions about Simon de Montfort or the Huguenots, she wanted to know if Madeleine had played hopscotch on the Promenade du Peyrou, or whether she had met her school friends on the esplanade.

It also happened that Madeleine had reached that age when people become susceptible to nostalgia for the earlier years of their lives. She had not wandered around Montpellier in this way for some years, and every now and then the sight of a small corner of the city would provoke a memory of her youth. At the Musée Fabre, for example, she found herself searching for the self-portrait of Berthe Morisot and comparing it once again with the van Dongen.

"Which do you like best?" she asked Titine.

"Oh, *that* one," said the little girl, pointing to the Morisot.

"So did your father," said Madeleine.

"Did you come here with him?"

"Yes. Before we married."

"And which one did you like?"

"The other one."

"Because it is more like you?" She laughed and skipped away.

When they came out of the museum they walked down to the Place de la Comédie and ordered two cups of hot chocolate at the same café where Pierre had brought Bertrand to meet Madeleine. It was cold, so they sat inside behind the glass doors.

"Did you and Papa go to the same school?" asked Titine.

"No. He didn't live in Montpellier."

"Did you know him when he was a boy?"

"Yes. We used to go and stay at Saint Théodore."

"Did you always know you'd marry him?"

"No."

"Did he come and live here?"

"No. He came to visit Pierre."

"Were they friends?"

"Yes."

"And is that why you met him?"

"Yes."

"Did you remember him?"

She frowned as she thought back. "Yes, in a way. I think so."

"And what happened?" Titine's little face was alert with excited curiosity.

"He came to Montpellier. Pierre introduced us again, first in someone's house, then here in this café."

"Here?" Titine seemed incredulous that something so long ago could have happened in the same place.

"Outside on the pavement. It was summer."

"And then?"

Madeleine smiled. "We had dinner together and walked back to Grandmama and Grandpapa's house."

"Did he ask you to marry him?"

"Not that time."

"The next?"

"Yes. Or the time after. I can't remember."

"And you accepted."

"Yes."

The child sighed. For her the story ended there. Then she picked up her cup of hot chocolate and drank. As she sat straight again she looked out past Madeleine into the Place de la Comédie. "Look," she said, "there *is* Pierre."

Madeleine smiled. "It can't be. He's in Coustiers."

"It is him, I promise, and he's with Grandpapa."

Madeleine turned and looked out onto the square. Two men were walking away from the café who certainly, from behind, resembled Pierre Moreau and Michel Bonnet.

"Shall we go and say hello?" asked Titine.

"Wait," said Madeleine. "I'd better pay the bill." She called the waiter, wondering why, if it was her father, he had not told her that he was meeting her oldest friend.

The waiter came, and she paid for the hot chocolate, then followed Titine out into the Place de la Comédie. Titine ran on in the direction taken by the two men, but in a moment came back to say that she had lost them.

"But are you sure, darling, that it was Grandpapa and Pierre?"

"Absolutely sure."

During lunch with her parents in the house on the Avenue d'Assas, Madeleine turned to her father and said, "Titine thought she saw you in the Place de la Comédie."

"When was that?" he asked.

"This morning."

"You were with Pierre," said Titine.

"No, I was here all morning."

Françoise laughed.

"But I saw you, I'm sure I did," said Titine.

"Is Pierre in Montpellier?" Bonnet asked Madeleine.

"Not that I know of."

"You'd think he'd give us a ring if he was," said the professor.

"I'm sure he would," said Madeleine. "It couldn't have been him."

Michel Bonnet was a bad liar; Madeleine knew as soon as he had denied it that he had indeed been in the Place de la Comedie with Pierre, and this certainty immediately confused her, because she could think of no reason why her father should lie to her, or why her closest friend should come to Montpellier and meet her father, yet fail to come and see her.

She said nothing more on the subject to either Titine or to her parents, but when she saw the New Year in among the professor's students and friends at their house on the Avenue d'Assas, she was suddenly struck by a mood of terrible sadness, for the secrecy of the two men could only mean that in some way they did not trust her, and this mistrust was a worse personal calamity than anything that had yet happened to her since the start of the war.

Madeleine returned to Coustiers, and Titine went back to Saint Théodore. Term started at the Lycée René le Bon. She did not call Pierre, nor, she noticed, did he call her or turn up at their apartment in the way he had before. It was not until the middle of January that she bumped into him while shopping in her lunch hour on the Avenue de la République.

"Ah, Madeleine, where have you been?" he asked in a tone of exaggerated friendliness.

She could tell that he was embarrassed, and that he had put the question to her before she could put it to him. "And you?" she asked.

"Working . . . working hard. Now that I'm no longer a magistrate, but a publisher of children's books."

Madeleine blushed. It occurred to her that perhaps Pierre thought his old friends would be ashamed of him in his distress. "Is it hard?" she asked.

"Harder than dispensing justice."

"It's our fault," she said. "We should have asked you and Béré-nice . . ."

"To dinner?" He laughed. "No, we're all too harassed for that. But what about a quick drink now?"

She looked at her watch. "I have twenty minutes."

"And I have ten." He looked back over his shoulder at a bar on the corner of the street. "There, that will do."

"Tell me," she asked when they were seated at a table, Madeleine on the shiny plastic seat against the wall, Pierre on a bentwood chair opposite her, "were you in Montpellier at the New Year?"

"Montpellier?" He looked up at the ceiling as if running through an almanac in his mind. "No, I don't think so."

"It's hardly something you would forget," she said sharply.

"I travel around now selling my cousin's books. I was in Nîmes just after Christmas, but Montpellier . . . no."

She knew that he too was lying, and for a moment her anger gathered like blocked blood in her brain, but then instead of a burst of sarcasm or a bitter rebuke, tears came into her eyes and she found that she was crying. She leaned forward on the table to hide her face in her hands, but her sobbing was so unexpected that she could not control it.

For a moment Pierre watched with a hard look on his face, as if he knew why she was crying and felt that she had only herself to blame; but he could not sustain his indifference, and as her sobbing continued he stretched his hand across the table to clasp hers.

"Don't cry," he said.

"But why do you lie?" she said, sniffing. "You and Papa. Why?"

"Did you see us?"

"Titine did."

He smiled. "Ah, the sharp-eyed Titine."

"You were in the middle of the Place de la Comédie."

"A public place is often the best camouflage."

"But why the camouflage?"

"In case we were watched."

"Watched? Watched by whom?"

He shrugged his shoulders. "The police."

"But you're not criminals."

He said nothing.

She dried her eyes. "What are you up to, you and Papa?"

He stirred the sugar into his cup of coffee. "Nothing much," he said.

"Can't you tell me?"

He looked sadly into her eyes. "No."

"Don't you trust me?"

Again he said nothing.

"But Pierre," she said, "I'm his daughter, and your oldest, dearest friend."

"And a Communist."

"A Communist? Yes, but . . ."

"You accept the discipline of the Party."

Now she understood. "Is it because of that?"

"I respect your convictions," said Pierre, "and I recognize the value of a party which has first call on its members' loyalty, but you must realize, Madeleine, that there is a price to pay, and that price is the mistrust of those who love you."

"But I would never . . ." She hesitated.

"What?"

"Betray you."

"And Michel?"

She did not answer.

"A wife has no secrets from her husband."

"He isn't my husband," she said, "and anyway, he too is devoted to you."

"More than to the Party?"

She opened her mouth to answer but hesitated, then lowered her eyes to the table and said in a strange, low voice, "I don't know."

"Listen," said Pierre, "listen and then forget what I have said. Forget it before you leave this bar."

She nodded her assent.

"Six months ago I was a citizen and a magistrate of France. I had a safe salary and a cynicism that was safer still. When Bertrand left, I thought he was mad. I helped him not because I believed in what he was doing but because he was an old friend. They grilled me afterward—Guillot and his friends—but they could prove nothing. I went back to my job, prepared to live and let live—Pétain, Laval, anyone, as long as they left me alone.

"Then, in September, the Germans published their decrees against the Jews in the occupied zone—decrees in violation of the armistice and in contravention of the Geneva Convention. What was the reaction in Vichy? They objected not against the decrees, but against the Germans jumping the gun, because our noble National Revolutionaries in Vichy had their own decrees in mind—and in October, you will remember, they published them in the official gazette. No Jews were to hold public posts or positions of influence in the press and industry. And who is a Jew? Not just the man with three Jewish grandparents, which is the Nazi definition of a Jew. No, in Vichy a man with only two Jewish grandparents is defined as a Jew if he is married to a Jew, so they bring more into their net than do the Germans in the occupied zone.

"The very next day I was shown the door of the Palais de Justice. Charrier was apologetic, of course, but he's still prefect only by the skin of his teeth, so he didn't want to take risks by making exceptions or looking the other way. He told me that he too was frightened, because there are those who would denounce him if he did not see that justice is done. Justice!"

"It is horrible," said Madeleine.

Pierre shrugged his shoulders and leaned back in his chair. "It's horrible, but it could be worse. At least I have a job."

"Publishing? With your cousin?"

"It means I can travel, visiting bookshops and printers. The printers, in particular, are useful to know."

"Useful?"

Pierre leaned forward and said in a lowered voice, "We're planning to publish an underground newspaper."

"A newspaper?"

"I mean to fight back, Madeleine, not just against the Germans but against the collaborating traitors in Vichy."

"But how?"

"With words, because words sustain the spirit, and if that is ever broken, everything is finished."

"Yes."

"Your father is one of our group. The newspaper is to be called called *Fortitude,* and with it we will attack not just the occupation but the whole concept of collaboration."

Her eyes widened with excitement, but Madeleine said nothing.

"We'll distribute it among students here in Coustiers, as well as in Nîmes, Montpellier, Mézac, even Marseilles."

"It will be dangerous, Pierre," Madeleine said softly.

"It's more dangerous for me to do nothing, because it is they who have attacked me, and if a man does not do something to defend himself he loses his self-respect."

"Yes."

"I refuse to wait passively for a pogrom."

"No, you are right," she said, "and I promise that I shall forget everything you have told me."

"I would be grateful."

"I am grateful to you for trusting me."

He shrugged his shoulders and smiled. "It was a weakness, but after all, trust is one of the things we are fighting for."

The two friends parted, Madeleine to return to the lycée, Pierre to go back to the office of his cousin's publishing house, the Saint Barnabas Press, on the second floor of a seedy building on the Rue du Panier, which ran from the commercial district down to the old town.

Until 1922, the Saint Barnabas Press had been known as Gross and Bloch, but then the proprietor, Etienne Gross, the man who had married Pierre's aunt, had been given a subcontract to print Catholic prayer books and holy pictures. This had proved so profitable that he had changed the name of his company and entered the religious market.

It was a prudent thing to do, for in 1940, when Jews were banned from positions of influence over the young, it did not occur to those in power that the Saint Barnabas Press was a firm owned by Jews. Not only did the company publish many illustrated children's books with fair-haired heroes and heroines, but also several prayer books, holy pictures and even an illustrated Bible for children in which the child Jesus was portrayed as a fair-haired Aryan.

Maximilien Gross, Pierre's cousin, who had taken over the firm from his father, was not, however, a converted or even an assimilated Jew. Though not pious, he was Orthodox and kept the company only of his fellow Jews. He had always scorned and been scorned by his brilliant cousin Pierre, who had studied in Paris and Montpellier and had gentile friends like Bertrand de Roujay. To Maximilien, who was cautious and lazy, no good would come from this meteoric rise into the wider world, and when Pierre fell victim to the October decrees he could not suppress an involuntary *Schadenfreude*. When his mother had suggested that Max give poor Pierre a job, the *Schadenfreude* became glee. So strong was his desire to take revenge on his cousin for the shadow he had cast on him in boyhood that Max did not stop to wonder why a man of Pierre's age and ability would want to work for his dingy firm. All he saw was the chance to gloat over his misfortunes and treat the former examining magistrate as an office boy.

Pierre had borne his humiliation with what appeared at first to be extraordinary humility but later, it became clear, was indifference. After a month or so of learning the patterns and routines of the office, he began to come and go as he pleased. Maximilien at first reprimanded him, then remonstrated, then ranted and raved. Pierre paid no attention. Max stopped his salary. Again Pierre did not react but came as usual to the office. Since he did not work for the company, and now was not paid, Max could not understand why he came or what he did, but he noticed that Pierre seemed to be busy, and that others in the office went in and out of his room at the opposite end of the corridor.

One day he crept in while Pierre and a woman called Ginette were studying something on the desk. Max suddenly pushed between them and seized the sheet of paper in his hand. It was the proof of a page of *Fortitude*. He read a few words, then turned pale. "But this is criminal," he said.

"Yes," said Pierre, "and it is being published here in this office."

"But I shall be imprisoned, expropriated . . ."

"Almost certainly."

"I shall tell the police."

"Then you may not be imprisoned, but you will still be expropriated, because they will see at once that you are a Jew."

Still white in the face, Max staggered back to his own office; and from that day onward two businesses were run from the Saint Barnabas Press, one publishing prayer books and children's stories, the other seditious leaflets and a clandestine paper.

Though his family still thought that poor Pierre had gone to work for his cousin for want of any other employment, there had been others at the time of his dismissal who had been shrewd enough to recognize his talents and brave enough to offer him a job. The first of these was

Emile Planchet, the olive-oil king, whose daughter Nellie had been married to Michel le Fresne. Though no longer a disciple of Calvin or a believer in God at all, his instincts remained Huguenot, and this prompted him to help a man oppressed by the Catholics in power; so no sooner had he heard that Pierre had lost his job than he told Nellie to ask her friend to visit his office.

Nellie still lived in the Villa Acacia, overlooking Coustiers, with her children by Michel le Fresne, and Pierre—the "dear Pierre" of the prewar days—had remained her friend. But her natural propensity had never been to mix with the serious-minded, and once cut from her moorings both to her Communist husband and to her high-minded friends the de Roujays, she had moved into a more indulgent circle of the hedonistic rich. She had told her new friends, as she told herself, that her divorce was a liberation—that she was delighted to be rid of the Marxist bore who had lived off the capital he affected to despise. This was partly true, but there was also the harsher truth of nature, which is that a husband is a husband whatever his political views, and while Nellie had several suitors and many lovers, her mind, like her body, was too well used for her ever to marry again. The suitors were always after her money, and the lovers were usually drunk. She too was almost always drunk, and the effect of alcohol on her eyes and skin was to accelerate and exaggerate the depredations of age.

Every month or six weeks, when she felt sad and depressed, Nellie would telephone Pierre and he would come up to her villa. He never brought Bérénice, and Nellie never asked them to her parties. The limits to their friendship were understood by them both, but when they did meet they would talk for hours, and if on those occasions Pierre drank more than he was used to, Nellie le Fresne drank less.

Anyone seeing the sallow, earnest examining magistrate and the aging lush together would find it hard to divine what they had in common, and like so many friends in middle age there was little but the past. For Nellie, Pierre was her only link with the old Montpellier gang, and however much she told herself that she was glad to be rid of "that dull lot," they had played too large a part in her life to be altogether forgotten.

Before taking Pierre to see her father, Nellie met him in a café on the Avenue de la République. She then took him across the street to the Planchet building, which Pierre had passed a thousand times, but now entered for the first time. In principle his distaste for capitalist trusts, which he had considered quite as self-interested and con- spiratorial as both the Communists and the Freemasons, should have included Emile Planchet, but having eaten his food and drunk his wine since his days as a student, he had always felt a residual gratitude toward the fair-haired old man who came out from behind his desk and greeted him with unexpected warmth and sincerity.

"These laws against the Jews make me feel ashamed to be French," Emile Planchet said, showing Pierre and Nellie to two comfortable chairs, "but I have to confess, my dear Moreau, that I am a businessman, and a businessman sees advantage where others see only misfortune. As soon as I heard that you had been dismissed, I thought, 'There is a man I can use.'"

"You are exceptionally kind," said Pierre.

"Not kind. Shrewd, if you like." He laughed.

"Oh, admit it, Papa," said Nellie. "You can also be kind."

Her father smiled. "I like to think that kindness and shrewdness can sometimes go together. Certainly in the case of Monsieur Moreau." He turned to Pierre. "I have no particular post in mind, but I am certain that if you would consider joining our organization we would find something that would benefit us both."

"I am very grateful," said Pierre in a quiet voice which suggested by its tone that he was not going to accept the offer.

"Oh, do," said Nellie, "do work for Papa. You would have a salary and you would be safe."

Pierre looked at Nellie, then at her father. "I am afraid I cannot. I am sorry, but . . . I cannot."

"Ah," said Planchet, "someone has moved faster than I."

"No," said Pierre. "I intend to work for my cousin, Maximilien Gross."

Planchet looked curious. "I don't think I know him."

"No," said Pierre. "He has a small company which publishes chil- dren's books."

"Does that interest you?" asked Planchet.

"Not in itself, but you see, Monsieur Planchet, my real work will be with publications of a different kind."

"More adult, perhaps?"

"And controversial."

"Of course," said the old man. "I should have known."

"So if I came to work for you, I could compromise you and your company."

"That wouldn't worry me," said Planchet. "But it would certainly be less safe, because in a large company you can never be sure of everyone."

"My cousin's business is very suitable," said Pierre. "It is small, obscure, almost unknown, but it has contact with printers."

Emile Planchet stood up and went to the wide window of his office, which looked out over the roofs of the city toward his textile mills in the industrial suburbs and his warehouses beside the river. Finally he turned back to face Pierre and his daughter. "You will need money," he said simply.

"I daresay," said Pierre.

"Then let me provide it."

Pierre did not reply.

Emile Planchet returned from the window. "You will need money, Moreau, not just to buy your paper and printer's ink but to keep yourself and your associates alive."

"Certainly it would help."

"If things go as I predict," said Planchet, "the war will drag on and opposition will grow not just to the Germans but to Vichy as well."

"I hope you are right."

"I am sure I am right. But this opposition will need money. Everything needs money, and it will be hard to raise it. People will be poor. Only the peasants will be rich, and they will stay with Pétain to the end."

"It could be dangerous for you."

"It could if we are foolish, but who but us three need know? Nellie can act as intermediary. I see her from time to time; you see her from time to time. Neither of us would alter the usual routine."

"I would not want to put Nellie in danger," said Pierre.

"I know my daughter, Moreau." He turned toward her. "Don't underestimate her."

"Of course." Nellie looked at Pierre. "Just say how much you need and we will have it for you."

"It will be in trust," said Pierre.

"In trust?" asked Planchet.

"For the French people."

"In trust, if you like. I prefer to see it as an investment." Planchet gave a sly smile.

"But you should know . . ." Pierre hesitated.

"What?"

"You should know, I think, that my intentions in the longer term go beyond the printing of leaflets."

"They may go where they like," said Planchet.

"They may go all the way."

"We shall back you all the way."

"You are brave."

"And you?"

"I was forced into it."

"And so am I. I tell you, Moreau, this morning I was ashamed to be a Frenchman. Now I feel a little of my pride restored."

The group which formed around the underground newspaper *Fortitude,* and itself came to be known as Fortitude, included some former Freemasons proposed by Michel Bonnet. Among these was André Pidner, Bertrand de Roujay's subordinate in the subprefecture of Mézac. At first Pierre had been reluctant to accept him, because he remembered Bertrand's low opinion of the man, but since Mézac had no university, they had few other contacts in the city, and Pidner, though purged from the local administration, would unquestionably be useful in establishing a network.

Pierre therefore went to Mézac, where Pidner awaited him at the station. The two men had never met, but Pierre was to carry a copy of the *Revue des Deux Mondes* upside down, and Pidner promised to be wearing a yellow shirt and green tie. Since there were few passengers on the train, they quickly recognized one another. Pidner greeted "Monsieur Chalcot" as if he were a visiting businessman, while Pierre shook hands with "Monsieur Lambert" in the same manner. Since both of them were reasonably well known, this use of false names would have told anyone who had overheard them that they were up to no good, but none of Guillot's men was on duty at the station and the two men walked unnoticed to a bar on the boulevard which ran around the outside of the city.

It was a large café used by truck drivers who parked their vehicles overnight beneath the walls, but at eleven in the morning it was empty enough for the conspirators to find a table where they could talk without being overheard. Pierre outlined the plans he had drawn up with Michel Bonnet. What they wanted from Pidner, if he was up to it, was a network to distribute *Fortitude,* and in time safe houses for escaping English airmen or members of the group who were "burned."

Pidner demurred. He looked as seedy as before and had the same fawning manner, and the struggle within was between two conflicting but equally ignoble emotions—hatred and fear. "You see, Mézac is not a heroic town," he said. "We have no students as you do in Coustiers and Montpellier."

"But among your fellow Masons?"

"They are all very frightened. They mostly want to lie low."

"Is there no one in the subprefecture?"

Pidner shook his head. A greasy lock fell over his face, and he brushed it back. "No, they are frightened too. There was such an uproar after de Roujay left."

"I can imagine."

"They questioned us all. We were all under suspicion."

"Among the military, perhaps?"

Again Pidner shook his head; again a strand of greasy hair fell from his balding head; again he swept it back. "No. They all worship the Marshal."

Pierre bit his thumb to hide his irritation. "Is there nothing you can suggest?"

"The Socialists," said Pidner. "They're our best bet. Of course, Mézac hasn't much of a working class, but those there are have inclined toward the Socialists since the Nazi-Soviet pact."

"Can you make contact with them?"

"Yes," said Pidner. "I know one or two of the union leaders. I'll see what they have to say."

"There's another matter," said Pierre.

"What is that?"

"Arms."

Pidner turned pale. "What . . . what do you mean?"

"We must be ready to defend ourselves. We must be armed."

"But that is against the law."

"Of course," said Pierre.

Pidner swallowed. "I know nothing about arms."

"We don't need artillery," said Pierre. "Just a few revolvers."

Pidner vigorously shook his head, and again his hair fell over his face. "I don't know," he said. "I really don't know where you can find them."

"The barracks?"

"Impossible. How would you break in?"

"The police?"

"The same problem. No, I think we must recognize that perhaps we aren't the right type for that kind of thing."

"Then we must become the right type," said Pierre harshly.

"But no one has arms but soldiers, policemen and gangsters."

"And we can't get them from the soldiers or policemen?"

"No."

"That leaves the gangsters."

"What? Get guns from the *milieu*?"

"If there's no other way."

"The Burzios?"

"No. They're in with Guillot."

"Who, then?"

"The Jacopozzis."

"Do you know them?"

"Socially?" Pierre laughed.

"No, of course not. What I meant . . ."

"I had Jaco Jacopozzi in my office when he was subpoenaed last year."

"The Clermont case?"

"Exactly."

"But would he sell guns to you, of all people? An examining magistrate?"

"A former examining magistrate."

"Even so . . ."

"If the price is right, he'll sell anything."

"But where will we get the money?"

"I have the money."

"And you think he won't betray you?"

"Not while Guillot and the Burzios are on the other side."

. . .

From the dossier on the Clermont case Pierre knew that the territory of the Burzios was to the west of the river and that of the Jacopozzis to the east. The Burzios' whores hung around the Opéra; the Jacopozzis' stayed on the Quai du Fleuve. They had one side of the wide Avenue de la République each and only disputed the warren of small streets between the railway station and the Place de la Croix.

Accompanied by a friend of his sister, a young lawyer named Guy Serot, Pierre drove from his house at ten that night and parked his car near the Church of the Assumption. The two men then walked along the Quai du Fleuve to the Bar Fénelon, where the Jacopozzis were supposedly to be found. Serot was only in his late twenties, but he was strong and agile and could put on a convincing expression of menace. Pierre was aware that he himself was not a physically intimidating figure, and while he did not expect to have to defend himself against the Jacopozzis, he thought the presence of Serot might save him from ridicule.

As soon as they entered the bar he felt that their presence was unwelcome. The other customers bristled as the two blatant bourgeois trespassed upon their preserve. Pierre, however, was too determined to be deterred by their animosity. He went to the bar, ordered two glasses of beer, and then said to the barman, "Tell Jaco that I would like to see him."

"Jaco?" The barman looked blank.

"Monsieur Emmanuele Jacopozzi," said Pierre. "Tell him that Pierre Moreau would like a word with him."

The barman did not change his expression, but it was apparent that he was impressed that Pierre knew the full name of his boss. He sidled away, polishing a glass and muttering that he knew no one of that name, and disappeared through a door at the back of the bar.

Pierre and Guy stood without talking, like the sheriff and his deputy in a western movie, and in due course the barman returned and without saying a word nodded toward a door at the back of the room.

Pierre, followed by Guy, went through the door into a dark hallway. There they were met by two swarthy thugs who searched them both roughly and, when satisfied that they were not armed, opened a second door and showed them into a large, brightly lit room.

It could have been the living room of any peasant's house in Corsica —a peasant, that is, who had made money enough to buy tables and chairs of heavy, varnished wood and a sofa upholstered in thick velvet. On the aquamarine walls were framed photographs of the fortress at Calvi and the Cathedral of Ajaccio. In one corner of the room was a huge glass-fronted cupboard filled with ornate bowls, plates and silver dishes. Between it and the window was a small plinth on which stood a statue of the Virgin Mary.

Two men sat in two armchairs. One Pierre recognized as Jaco Jacopozzi; the other, who was older, he took to be his brother, Stefano, a heavy man with an expression of suspicion and stupidity on his fleshy, pockmarked face. Jaco, the younger brother, looked quite different, as tall as Stefano but thinner and more delicate, with quick, dark eyes and an arrogant snarl on his upper lip which could rapidly change into a smile.

As Pierre entered the room with his escort, neither of the Jacopozzi brothers rose from his seat, but Stefano lounged farther back in his armchair and laughed as if amused to see the mighty magistrate brought so low. Jaco smiled too, with the same derision, but his eyes remained alert, curious to know what had brought Pierre to their lair.

"Well, Monsieur le Juge," he began.

"Yes, Monsieur le Juge," repeated Stefano in a tone of heavy sarcasm.

"May I sit down?" asked Pierre. He spoke with assurance, as if it were natural for him to be there.

"Yes," said Jaco.

Pierre sat down on the sofa, Guy on one of the polished wooden chairs at the table.

"Before I start," said Pierre to Jaco, "I want you to tell me frankly —did I play fair in the Clermont case?"

Jaco hesitated, then said, "The cops never play fair."

"I wasn't a cop."

"As good as," said Stefano.

"I wasn't a cop," Pierre repeated.

"No," Jaco acknowledged.

"Did I play fair?"

"Maybe," said Jaco.

"I dismissed Guillot's evidence."

Jaco laughed. "You had to."

"No," said Pierre. "I did it to play fair."

·

Jaco shrugged his shoulders. "So what?"

"I'm not here to ask favors. I'm here to do business, but there would be no point starting if you think that I won't play fair."

"No, no, all right," said Jaco irritably. "You played fair."

"Good," said Pierre. He sat back in the huge sofa.

Jaco looked annoyed, as if he had already suffered some sort of defeat. "What do you want, then?" he asked Pierre.

"Guns," said Pierre.

Stefano guffawed. "You're joking."

"No," said Pierre.

"What makes you think—" Jaco began.

"Don't pretend to me," said Pierre sharply, "and I won't pretend to you. I know you have guns. I know you can get them. I want them. I can pay for them. There. That's all."

"And if we sell you guns, how do I know that you won't squeal?"

"To Guillot? Me? A Jew?"

Stefano guffawed again. "A yid, yes."

"I hate Guillot more than you do," said Pierre.

"Perhaps," said Jaco, "perhaps." He studied Pierre's face. "What guns do you want?"

"Revolvers. Later, perhaps, submachine guns."

"And what do you want them for?"

"To kill my wife's lover," said Pierre impassively.

"With submachine guns?"

"She has several lovers."

"Even so."

"Do you need to know why I want them?"

"Yeah," said Stefano.

"No," said Jaco. "Business is business."

"We can pay in dollars."

"Good."

"Fifty for each handgun with ammunition."

"That's too little."

"How much do you want?"

"At least a hundred."

"I could manage seventy-five."

"Eighty."

"Very well."

"When do you want them?"

"As soon as possible."

"And how many?"

"Six."

"How do we communicate?"

Pierre gave him a card of the Saint Barnabas Press. "Call me here at my office. Say: 'The proofs of Monte Cristo are ready for collection.' "

"And you'll send someone here?"

"Wherever you like."

"Here is as good a place as any. But don't send a heavy like him." He nodded toward Guy. "He'll attract attention. There'll be talk."

"I'll come myself."

"That's worse."

"Who, then?"

"Send a woman, a girl. There are girls in and out of here all the time. No one pays any attention to them."

"Very well." Pierre rose to go. "Secrecy is essential," he said.

"Of course." Jaco too got to his feet and accompanied Pierre toward the door "Goodbye, Monsieur le Juge," he said, shaking both Pierre and Guy by the hand. "It's strange, isn't it, what happens in a war?"

When the guns were ready, Pierre sent Isabelle to collect them. Of all those who now belonged to Fortitude, she was the girl he could trust most not merely to show the courage to enter the den of thieves and pimps at the Bar Fénelon, but also not to boast about it afterward.

Isabelle herself thought it quite proper that she should have been chosen for this task. It was she, after all, who by entering the Spanish consulate in Perpignan to fetch Bertrand de Roujay's visa had been the first of the Moreaus to defy the government in Vichy. This simple act had had a profound effect on her. The awe she had felt for Bertrand since her childhood was transformed by his escape into a dazzled idolization. The grateful kiss he had given her upon leaving Céret had put her into a trance which had been broken only by the rowdy importunity of Turco and Titine. By the time she had got back to Coustiers she had changed from a gauche, precocious girl whose adolescence seemed to have lingered into her twenties into an earnest and determined idealist. Long before Pierre had been dismissed from the magistracy as a Jew, Isabelle had urged him to follow Bertrand's example, and in the school where she taught, the Lycée René le Bon, she had risked dismissal by talking to the students against the regime.

First Madeleine Bonnet had warned her to take care; then the headmaster himself had spoken to her more formally, reminding her that her Jewish blood made her vulnerable to denunciation by other envious teachers. These warnings had taken effect not because they had frightened her, but because by that time Pierre had been dismissed as a magistrate and was already contemplating resistance. His first recruit was his sister, his second her friend Guy Serot.

Serot was only her friend and companion. Though twenty-four years old and exceptionally pretty, Isabelle had had no lovers, because no man had yet met her expectations. She looked for someone who would master her, but she was herself so able and outspoken that all her would-be suitors fell short. When Pierre complained that his sister was too choosy, Bérénice told him that she would fall in love only with either an older man whose seniority would overawe her or an artist who had convinced her of his genius. Since the older men she met in Coustiers were all married and the artists in the city mostly frauds, Isabelle seemed destined to be a spinster unless she could escape from the limited circles in which she had lived since she was a child. Before the war there had been talk of sending her to Paris, but the German occupation now made that impossible. She had been stuck in Coustiers among her family and friends until sent by Pierre to pick up the guns at the Bar Fénelon.

It was around seven in the evening of a late-autumn day and already dark when Isabelle walked down the Quai du Fleuve and saw for the first time the smartly dressed whores from the Jacopozzis' stable waiting for customers outside the bars. She herself was wearing her simplest dress, which may have reassured the prostitutes that she was not a free lance poaching on their preserve, but also made her seem younger than she was. Thus when she reached the Bar Fénelon, instead of blending inconspicuously with the company of tarts, pimps, thieves and strong-arm men, she was as patently out of place as Pierre and Guy had been two weeks before. Moreover, she faltered at the threshold of the smoke-filled bar like an angel at the entrance of hell, and only when she had filled her lungs with a last breath of fresh air and her mind with a renewed determination did she enter, cross to the bar and ask for Mr. Jaco Jacopozzi.

The barman had been told to expect a girl, and seeing at once that this must be the one, he led her through the dark vestibule behind the bar into the Jacopozzis' back room.

When the door was opened, Isabelle blinked in the bright light and then saw four or five men leaning over some papers on the dark polished table. What struck her at once was that while the men to the left and the men to the right were heavy and ugly, the one in the center was slender and handsome.

He looked up as she came in, glanced over her shoulder at the barman as if to question her presence, and then all at once seemed to realize who she must be and why she was there. He said one word—"Later"—which immediately dispersed the men around him. Only Stefano remained behind.

"Have you come for the proofs of Monte Cristo?" asked Jaco Jacopozzi awkwardly when he and his brother were alone with their visitor.

"Yes."

"Come and sit down."

The two Jacopozzis were patently confused by Isabelle's presence. Although it was Jaco who had suggested that a girl be used, he had envisaged the kind that he employed on the Quai. Here in his presence, however, was a girl of the other kind—for to the Jacopozzis, as to many Latins, all women were either saints or sluts. Since Isabelle was so obviously not a whore, she belonged in their minds with their mother, sister, cousins and nieces, not in the Bar Fénelon.

She was there, however, and they had no choice but to treat her with the courtesy they always showed to respectable women. She was invited to sit down and was offered a glass of lemonade. As she sipped it she watched Jaco's nervous, arrogant, handsome features as he made conversation about the cinema and the weather while Stefano looked on with a hanging jaw.

When Isabelle had finished the lemonade she took an envelope from her pocket. "I was asked to give you this," she said.

"Ah, yes, thank you." Jaco took the envelope and was about to open it to count the money when he remembered his manners and put it unopened into his pocket. "And we have a packet for you," he said.

He nodded to Stefano, who took a small canvas carryall from the
corner of the room.

"Thank you." Isabelle stood up and picked up the bag, almost
dropping it because it was heavy.

"Do you have a car?" asked Jaco.

"My brother is waiting at the Chamber of Commerce."

"It's too much for you to carry all that way."

"No, I promise you, I can manage."

She took a step toward the door which led to the bar.

"You'd better come out the back way," said Jaco.

He led her out by a door on the other side of the room and down
a passage which led out through the back of the building. As they
reached the street, Isabelle changed the bag from one hand to the other.

"Let me carry it," said Jaco.

"No," said Isabelle, but already he had taken it from her hands.

"Wait here," said Jaco to his older brother, who lurked in the dark
doorway. "I shall be back in a quarter of an hour."

Isabelle remained the principal liaison between Fortitude and the Jacopozzi brothers, because Coustiers, though a large city, shrank to the
size of a village when it came to gossip. If Jaco had been seen with
Pierre, or even a lawyer like Guy Serot, it might have posed a riddle
which Guillot in time would be asked to solve, but to be seen in a café
with a pretty girl aroused little attention. They therefore met a month
later and a month after that, but never again in the Bar Fénelon. On
the first occasion Isabelle asked Jaco if he could obtain paper and
printer's ink; on the second if he could do anything to help a student
who had been picked up by the police for sticking posters on the walls
of the Bourse.

Jaco did both. He filched the paper and ink from the wharves and
sprang the student from Coustiers jail. He was paid for what he did,
but he lingered at the meetings for longer than was necessary, and at
their third meeting—at a café on the Rue des Carmélites—he asked
Isabelle if she would meet him on an occasion when they had no
business to discuss. He asked in an arrogant, almost offhand manner,
his eagle eyes on the passersby, but his tone of voice was slightly
strained and breathless, and a moment after he had put the question,

as she hesitated over her reply, he darted a look in her direction as if afraid of how she might answer.

There was never any doubt as to what the answer would be, for even if Isabelle had not noticed with a feminine calculation that his nonchalance was all affected, she had unconsciously been enticing him to make such a request from the moment of their first meeting. Now she blushed as if confused and hesitated as if uncertain, but her confusion was the confusion of pleasure and excitement, and the hesitation came only from concern about her brother.

Misunderstanding the cause of her blush, Jaco Jacopozzi said quickly, "Naturally my sister will be with us. I thought we might all go to a film."

"And should I bring my mother?" asked Isabelle with a smile.

"Certainly," said Jaco, "if she would like to come."

When Isabelle passed on Jaco Jacopozzi's invitation, Pierre was first amused, then annoyed, then astonished at his luck, because he had realized very quickly that to mount a serious resistance, enthusiasm and idealism were not enough. They would need the skills of the back streets and the cunning of criminals, and here was a little warlord with a small army at his command courting his sister.

Of course, Pierre knew enough about Jaco to laugh at his foolishness in falling in love with Isabelle, but he did not know enough about women to imagine for a moment that she might love him in return. Isabelle was shrewd enough not to show her feelings; she sensed that if he had known them, Pierre would have abandoned the political advantage to keep her away from such an undesirable suitor. She therefore presented Jaco's proposals in a deadpan way and allowed Pierre to think, when she started to go out with the Corsican, that she did so for the sake of the movement.

The truth was, however, that Isabelle loved Jaco Jacopozzi quite as much as he loved her. From the first time she had met him in the back room of the Bar Fénelon she had seen him as another Corsican, Napoleon Bonaparte. Certainly he lacked the epaulettes, and his henchmen hardly resembled Bernadotte and Ney, but who could say that at the beginning, when they commanded the bedraggled rump of the Revolutionary army, Napoleon and his future marshals had not looked very much the same? When she told Jaco, on one of the first occasions when they dined alone together without Jaco's sister as a chaperon, that he reminded her of Napoleon, he smiled with the contentment of any Corsican who is likened to his great fellow countryman. Until that moment, it was true that Jaco would have been more flattered to be compared to Al Capone, but her culture was one of the reasons why Jaco respected Isabelle, and why, until the day they were married, he never did more than kiss her gently on the lips.

By the time the Moreaus realized that their daughter was engaged to a gangster, it was too late to do anything about it. It was not simply that they had lost control of Isabelle, but that a dramatic turn of events had made the alliance between *Fortitude* and the Jacopozzis more important than ever.

On June 22, 1941, Hitler invaded Russia. The Soviets thus became the allies of the British, and the Communists swung overnight from a tacit support for Pétain and the German occupation to widespread preparations for armed resistance.

Pierre and Michel Bonnet had mixed feelings about this change of heart among the Communists. On the one hand they still felt a contempt for their slavish obedience to Soviet interests; on the other they had to recognize that the Communist Party already possessed an experienced clandestine organization that would be invaluable in mounting an effective opposition to Vichy.

The danger this presented to the Fortitude group, however, was that it would be dominated and later absorbed by the larger and more ruthless Communist cadres. It was for this reason that the Jacopozzis suddenly became so important, for though their men had neither ideals of any kind nor loyalty to any political ideology, they were at least as experienced as the Communists in survival outside the law. The hoodlums therefore became their necessary allies, and it was principally for this reason that Pierre suppressed his misgivings and later that summer gave away his sister to Jaco Jacopozzi at the altar of the Church of Saint James in the little Corsican village of Pervaccio.

2

On the day the news reached Coustiers that the Germans had invaded Russia, Michel le Fresne returned from the hospital and greeted Madeleine with the words "At last!" They were spoken with emotion, even elation, and fortunately the surgeon did not wait to see what effect they had upon the woman to whom they were addressed but went on into the flat fumbling with his hat, pipe and bunch of keys.

Madeleine carried his briefcase to his study with a frown of irritation on her face. She remembered quite well what Michel seemed to have forgotten: that a year, even a month, even a week before, he had been a strong supporter of the Nazi-Soviet pact. God knew—or would have, had he existed—that she had always loathed it, and so had more right than Michel to say "At last," but what annoyed her now was not that he had upstaged her or stolen her lines, but that he showed such an astonishing disregard for everything he had said on the subject earlier.

She went back to her desk to finish correcting the exercise books she had brought back from the lycée, but even as she marked the books with a red pencil she was trying to make up her mind if it was amnesia or insincerity which had inspired his "At last," or whether he was now so much a Party man that he would not only accept any political line that was put out by the Central Committee but would obediently feel the requisite emotion.

With a certain indifference she found herself concluding that the last of these three possibilities was probably true—that Michel was prepared to feel any emotion because fundamentally he felt none. If this was so, it had grave implications for his feelings toward her, but such is the nature of a bond of long duration—in this case not a marriage, but in most respects just like one—that cataclysmic thoughts can enter the minds of one or other of the partners without in any way changing their outward routine. She continued to mark the test she had set her pupils, and when that was done she went to the kitchen to prepare supper.

This was always the worst moment of the day, because the raw materials of the evening meal, once prepared during the day by their cook, were now no longer to be found in the shops. Of course, Madeleine and Michel had their daily ration of nine ounces of bread, one ounce of meat, half an ounce of fat, half an ounce of sugar and a quarter of an ounce of cheese—but to rely on the ration alone would mean death by slow starvation. There was the black market, and though Madeleine had at first considered it ignoble to bribe butchers and grocers to give her more than her share, her good intentions did not survive the hard winter of 1940. Soon she too was smiling at the loathsome grocer and fawning on the butcher she despised, begging them obsequiously to take her money and keep something extra aside. It demoralized her to discover how dependent she was on food. When she saw Titine, she would ask her to bring food from the de Roujays at Saint Théodore, and Michel would filch medicines from the hospital which Madeleine would exchange for eggs and cheese. Once she burst into tears of joy when Michel returned with a leg of pork given to him by a grateful patient.

Despite these expedients, there were often days when the cupboard was bare. On that evening in June of 1941 she had only noodles, scraps of ham and dandelion leaves which she had bought at the market on her way home from school. This might have been enough for the two of them, but tonight it was their turn once again to entertain Georges Auget, who, since he remained an outlaw, had no ration card and so depended for his sustenance upon his comrades in the Party.

When he arrived soon after eight, he too said "At last," or words like them, but while Madeleine was again irritated by his anxious and excited face, she had to acknowledge that Georges at least had some excuse, because he had always seen the pact as a tactical feint to give the Soviets time to prepare for war.

The two men sat down at table. "I have to say," said Georges, "that though I see hard times ahead, I am glad that the gloves are off at last."

"Yes," said Michel, rubbing his hands together and looking anxiously to see what Madeleine was serving for supper. "I should say that now, at last, Hitler has bitten off more than he can chew."

She put the bowl of noodles on the table so that the two men could help themselves. Michel looked disappointed—they had had the same noodles the night before—but said nothing as he pushed the bowl toward Georges. The noodles were garnished with a few fragments of ham and some tinned peas, and Michel watched anxiously as Georges helped himself, for though the thought was never spoken—it was hardly formulated in his mind—he was always afraid that Georges might forget his mendicant status and take more than his share.

Innocent of his host's calculations, Georges helped himself to a third of the noodles and then pushed the bowl across the table to Michel.

"There can be little doubt about the final outcome," said Michel, raising the noodles to see if any pieces of ham were hiding beneath them. "However many divisions the Germans put into the field, they can hardly turn back the clock of history."

Georges looked less certain. "I like to think that the Red Army is a match for the Wehrmacht." He started to eat.

Michel took onto his plate two thirds of the noodles that were left; women, after all, consumed fewer calories than men. Madeleine then scraped what was left onto her own plate, noticing as she did so that there were no scraps of ham left among the peas. She glanced involuntarily at Michel's plate; he caught her glance and with an air of self-sacrifice offered to pass some of the fragments of ham onto her plate. When she refused his offer, Michel shrugged his shoulders, twirled some noodles onto his fork and with a small sigh of relief and satisfaction shoveled them into his mouth. What Madeleine had bought after queueing for hours the three gobbled up in minutes.

"What is important," said Georges, putting down his fork on his empty plate, "is that as many Germans as possible should be pinned down here in France to prevent them from being transferred to the Russian front."

"But that would lead to dreadful reprisals," said Madeleine.

"Yes," said Georges, "but that can't be helped. We must not just support our comrades in Russia, but take a lead in the resistance here in France."

"That won't be easy," said Madeleine.

"Why not?" asked Michel.

"Because there are those who will still hold the pact against us."

"Pah! Only the small fry."

"That's just why," said Georges, "we must make up for lost time through audacity, and show the French people that we are the only effective opposition to Vichy and the Germans."

Again Madeleine shook her head. "There are those who will never fall in behind us."

"We will be broadly based," said Georges Auget, looking carefully at Madeleine as he spoke, because he valued her assessment of how policies would appeal to those outside the Party. "We already have the National Front representing quite different strains of opinion."

"But controlled by us?" asked Michel.

"Of course."

"Who will you get to join it?" asked Madeleine.

"In the end, anyone who wants to defeat Hitler."

"The Gaullists?"

"Not as yet."

"The Fortitude group?"

"I don't regard it as significant."

"It is the only resistance we have seen so far."

"But it is confined to bourgeois, academic circles."

"Perhaps, but even so it will always have the prestige of being the first."

"We can find people of their kind when we want them."

Madeleine frowned; it annoyed her when either Georges or Michel dismissed all endeavor by those who were middle-class. "And who else?" she asked.

"A priest is always reassuring."

"You had better ask the bishop of Langeais," she said.

"We already have one in mind who claims to know you."

"A priest?"

"A friar. A Dominican named Antoine Dubec."

"Ah, yes."

"I didn't know you knew any friars," said Michel.

"It was a long time ago."

"He has been working in one of the mills at Braulhet," said Georges.

"As a priest?"

"At the machines."

"To wean the workers from Marx?" asked Michel.

"That may have been his original intention," said Georges, "but it is not quite how it has turned out."

"Don't tell me he has asked to join the Party?"

"No," said Georges Auget. "Not as yet."

The invasion of Russia by Hitler had a disturbing effect upon Louis de Roujay, who had been demobilized that spring. No place could be found for him in the army, limited by the armistice to a hundred thousand men, so he had come to live at Saint Théodore with Hélène and his three children.

For his parents, and for his niece Titine, Louis's presence was a gift from God, for his duties as mayor of Pévier left Edmond de Roujay with little time to see to the estate, and Titine flourished in the company of her wild cousins. Hélène, too, was happy to settle down in the pleasant house after moving from billet to billet; indeed, everyone was content but Louis de Roujay himself.

The simplest explanation was that he was bored. He was thirty-eight years old, at the height of his powers, yet now that the destiny of the world was being decided on the plains of central Europe he spent his days filling in potholes on the paths around the estate or studying the vines for signs of disease. He felt envious of those like his cousin Raymond Blaise de la Vallée who had been kept on in the army—even if it meant fighting Frenchmen in Syria—because they were at least involved in the drama of history, whereas Louis, in the prime of life, was stagnating offstage.

Yet if he had been in Syria, he might have faced Bertrand on the battlefield. He was haunted by the thought of his absent brother—missing him, envying him and resenting him all at the same time. Saint Théodore seemed empty without him—there was no one with whom he could argue—yet when he saw that his parents missed Bertrand too he became angry that for them his company was not enough. He could not escape the feeling that he was a usurper, because as he took charge of the vineyard and as Hélène settled into the house they inevitably took on the mantle of heirs; yet he imagined himself followed by the troubled look in his mother's eyes as if she were asking herself secretly, "But what will happen when Bertrand gets back?"

This involuntary usurpation troubled his conscience, for though he told himself that it was only for the sake of his family that he remained at Saint Théodore, he undoubtedly dreaded his brother's triumphant return. He was not the type to look into his unconscious and try to analyze his confused feelings for Bertrand but instead sought to explain them by their political differences. In his own mind his antagonism toward Bertrand came not from rivalry or envy, but from disgust at his treason. He had chosen to fight not just with the enemies of France, but now with the enemies of Christendom. The expedition to Dakar and the conquest of Syria were bad enough—outrageous attempts by French mercenaries to deliver their patrimony to the British—but to support the Bolsheviks in their war against Germany was to side with the devil himself.

For the year following the armistice the French had lived in relative peace, but after the invasion of Russia that summer, the war returned like a dormant disease and brought the start of further slaughter in France itself. The bacillus, however, had mutated from a conflict between the armies of different nations to a war between civilians of different convictions. On July 26, Max Dormoy, a former minister in Léon Blum's Popular Front government, was killed by a bomb in Montélimar, where he had been held under house arrest. On August 21, a midshipman in the German navy was assassinated in a Paris Métro station by a member of the Communist resistance. On August 27, a young Frenchman named Collette shot at two right-wing politicians, Laval and Déat, as they presented a banner to the first contingent of the Legion of French Volunteers in the fight against Bolshevism. On August 29, the Germans executed three Gaullist agents captured in the occupied zone.

All these events caused a ferment in the mind of Louis de Roujay. "I have to say," he said to his parents at dinner, "that those Gaullists only got what they deserved."

"But one of them might have been your brother," said Alice de Roujay.

"Even so," said Louis, "to wage war without authority is terrorism, and terrorism is murder."

"You oversimplify," said Alice quietly.

"What do you think, Papa?" said Louis to his father.

"I find everything confusing," Edmond said. "On the one hand the government in Vichy arrests and executes Frenchmen it finds spying for the Germans; on the other we see Déat and Laval giving banners to the Legion of Volunteers."

"It's mad," said Hélène, who hated political discussions.

"It's horrible," said Alice de Roujay, "to see Frenchmen parade in German uniforms."

"It is shocking, certainly," said Louis, "but they are fighting for their convictions."

"Evil convictions," said Alice.

"Is it evil to fight for Christian civilization?"

"For a pagan civilization!"

"No, listen, Maman," said Louis angrily. "I will grant you that the Nazis are not pious Catholics, but do they murder priests? Do they burn churches? No. Did the Wehrmacht plunder, pillage and rape when they conquered France? No. I was there. I was behind their lines. They were always disciplined and correct."

"And are they disciplined and correct in Poland and Czechoslovakia?" asked Alice.

"There, certainly, they behave in a different way, because they see the Slavs as a subordinate people—"

"By what right?" she interrupted.

"By the same right as we subject the Arabs and the British subject the Indians."

"It is not at all the same thing," said Alice. "The Slavs are white."

"Really, Maman," said Louis with a laugh, "you must be a very subtle theologian to judge the justness of a war by the color of people's skin."

"It is not simply that," said Alice. "The Nazis are cruel and totalitarian."

"And the Soviets?"

"The same!" said Edmond de Roujay. He turned to his wife, red in the face. "Like you, Alice, I dislike the sight of Frenchmen in German uniform, but the fact remains that if the Marshal, who embodies the legitimacy of France, permits them to fight on the Russian front, they are soldiers, and the Communist or the Gaullist who shoots a German sailor in the Paris Métro has no legitimacy whatsoever. He is a murderer, plain and simple, and should be treated as such."

From the well-protected house where Isabelle went to live with her husband, Jaco Jacopozzi, there was a clear view over the roofs of the old town of Coustiers to the bars and cafés on the Burzios' side of the river. Above them, at night, a line of lights marked the winding road which led up to the Esplanade de la Roseraie, where the Burzio family had its villa. It was to a villa like the Burzios' that Jaco Jacopozzi would have liked to bring his bride, but the Burzio family had been established in Coustiers for two generations, and had put down deep enough roots to move out of the narrow alleys into a pine-scented suburb. Whereas Jaco dared not live far from the enclave he controlled, the Burzios could move around as they pleased, for they had an understanding not only with policemen like Guillot but with the local politicians as well. Business was business, and for decades now the elected representatives of the people had exchanged their influence at the *mairie,* the prefecture and the Ministry of Justice for the money and muscle of the Burzios.

In the years between the two world wars, Bruno Burzio, the father, had become an accepted member of the commercial establishment in Coustiers. With the exception of Emile Planchet, most of the leading businessmen in the city, though they might not invite Bruno Burzio to their houses to meet their wives or elect him as president of the Chamber of Commerce, would shake him warmly by the hand if they met him in the street, and might even call at his villa on the Esplanade de la Roseraie if there was an intractable problem to be solved like a strike in one of their factories or on one of their wharves.

Invariably it had been Guillot who had acted as a broker between the different powers in the city, particularly when in the summer of 1941 he was promoted from his post as inspector in the Sûreté in Mézac to replace Mercier as commissaire in Coustiers. To Guillot, justice and legality could all be subsumed by order, and order was not an abstract ideal but a balancing of the powers that be. Since human nature was such that crime could never be suppressed altogether, it was best that it be controlled by men like the Burzios, and lest the Burzios become unmanageable, that there be a rival power in the underworld like the Jacopozzi family.

It was in this role as broker that Guillot went to see the Burzios in their villa on the Esplanade de la Roseraie. He knew that Bruno Burzio was a murderer—that he had killed a dozen men himself and had arranged the death of a dozen more—but to Guillot the deaths for which Bruno Burzio was responsible were a necessary and inevitable part of his responsibilities as *capo di mafia* in Coustiers, and were no more right or wrong than the execution by governments of enemies of the state. He therefore shook hands with the old man without any qualms, and followed him into the living room of the lavish villa.

"What brings you here, my good friend?" asked Bruno Burzio. "Is this a social visit, or is there business to attend to?"

"Business, Monsieur Burzio."

"As always, business." The old man sighed. "We're too busy to live, wouldn't you say?"

"The times make us busy," said Guillot.

"Yes," said Bruno Burzio. "So many laws, so many decrees, so many changes."

"There are changes," said Guillot, "which can act to our advantage."

The wrinkled face now looked curious. "How?"

"I was approached by the German consul here in Coustiers."

"What did he want?"

"He introduced me to a Herr Lutze, and after a brief conversation I concluded that it would be a good idea for Herr Lutze to meet you."

"Who is this Herr Lutze?"

"He used to be a salesman."

"And now?"

"He works for the Reich."

"Selling?"

"Buying."

"What?"

"Anything and everything."

"But what have I got to sell?" Bruno Burzio looked around at the grandiose furnishings of his villa.

"It would be best if he explained what he wanted."

"I am an old man," said Bruno Burzio, his cunning eyes retreating behind the loose skin of his heavy lids. "You had better take Andréas with you."

"Decisions may have to be made."

"Andréas can make them. He is my eldest, my first boy."

"Very well." Guillot sounded disappointed. He knew that Andréas would only act as a messenger.

"Where should he meet you?"

"Away from the city. Herr Lutze suggested Le Manoir de Valmagne."

Bruno Burzio laughed. "I hope he is paying."

"I am sure he will pay."

"And does he speak French?"

"Fluently."

Oskar Lutze, the salesman of agricultural machinery, had changed since his visit to Saint Théodore five years before. He had grown heavier in the body and sleeker in the face. His suit was better cut than the gray one he had worn on that wretched day when Madeleine de Roujay had been so rude to him and Bertrand de Roujay so polite, but he still wore it awkwardly, as if even now he were playing an ill-rehearsed role.

Le Manoir de Valmagne was a sumptuous restaurant in a country house halfway between Coustiers and Mézac. When Lutze had been a salesman he had dreamed of the day when he would be able to afford to eat there; now, as he arrived with the German consul, Herr Smucker, this dream had come true. If the guests he was to entertain were not the elegant aristocrats of his youthful fantasies but a policeman and a gangster from Coustiers, it did not inhibit him from brashly bullying the waiters as he ordered the food and sampled the wine.

"Gentlemen," he said to Guillot and his sallow companion, Andréas Burzio, "would it be premature to order champagne? Yes, let's wait until our dessert, but . . ." He turned to the sommelier. "Put a medium-sweet bottle of Krug on ice. You know. . . ." He turned back to his guests. "I was once in vinicultural machinery, so I picked up some knowledge of wine itself." He turned back to the waiter. "We'll start with a bottle of the 1936 Bâtard-Montrachet, and you must also open some of your Cambolle-Musigny."

"And you are our guests," said the other German, the consul, Herr Smucker, as if to reassure the two Frenchmen that they would not have to pay for these expensive choices.

"You are very kind," said Andréas Burzio with no expression of gratitude on his face.

"*Na, ja,*" said Lutze, noticing this lack of bonhomie, "let's get straight down to business while our heads are clear."

"We are at your disposal," said Guillot.

"The position is this," said Lutze. "The Führer and Marshal Pétain, as you know, reached an amicable arrangement at Montoire about relations between our two nations. Certain agreements were made about the cost of the occupation, exchange of assets, that kind of thing. But beyond these official agreements, Reichsmarschall Goering wishes to reach certain unofficial agreements at a local level."

"Agreements? For what?" asked Andréas Burzio.

Lutze held up his hand, counseling patience. "When one eats," he said, holding up a scallop on his fork, "the substantial nourishment goes into the mouth like that." He put the scallop into his mouth, chewed it and swallowed it. "But there is always the sauce, as it were, which escapes the fork." He took a piece of bread and wiped it around his plate. "That must be sopped up in another way." He put the piece of bread in his mouth, and as he ate it said, "As with food on the plate, so it is with the resources of nations."

"I do not understand," said Andréas.

"Let me explain," said Lutze. "The Reich is engaged in a life-and-death struggle with Bolshevism and international Jewry. The Reich needs resources. Above all it needs food. Now, we have certain agreements for the purchase and delivery of supplies from France on a government level, but we mean to supplement these by large-scale purchases on the black market. Already, in the occupied zone, we have founded companies for this purpose, but here in the south, where the black market operates in the back streets and alleyways of your cities, we need partners."

He paused, and they all sat back for a moment in silence. Then Andréas Burzio leaned forward. "You want us to buy food on the black market?"

"Not just food. Anything, everything—gold, paintings, jewelry. Coustiers is packed with Jews and refugees selling everything for nothing. You can buy, and then sell to us."

"At a profit?"

"Of course."

"You have funds?"

Lutze laughed. "Do you know how much your government is paying in reparations? Millions and millions of francs. Yes, my dear friends, we have funds."

Andréas Burzio glanced at Guillot, then back at Lutze. "I am sure it could be arranged," he said.

"Excellent," said Lutze. "We can work out the details on another occasion, but I can promise you, gentlemen, it will be profitable for all concerned."

Guillot came out of Le Manoir de Valmagne self-satisfied and slightly drunk. Only a flush on his cheeks suggested the amount of wine he had drunk at lunch; when he got into his car and gave directions to his driver his speech was not slurred, and there was nothing in his expression to suggest that after the cognac and a cigar he had another treat in mind to complete his indulgence.

The car took the road to Mézac. The driver, who knew it well, paid no regard to the speed limits as he passed through the villages on the way. Every gendarme between Coustiers and Mézac knew the number of the car and would take it that the commissaire was on police business. Their assumption was usually correct, because Guillot was rarely off-duty, using his home only as a place to sleep, and then only when it suited him. Because he was always suspicious, he was always at work—always checking up on his contacts, and appearing unexpectedly to impress on those who feared him that Guillot was always there.

The car reached the outskirts of Mézac and turned up a narrow street before stopping outside a yellow stuccoed block of flats. One of Guillot's men, in plainclothes, leaned against a wall at the entrance to a driveway next to a sign which read "The Cedars." When he saw the commissaire's car the man stepped forward and stooped to look in through the rear window.

"Is she there?" asked Guillot.

"Yes."

"Good." Guillot got out of the car. "Wait here."

Lucía Rodríguez de Astran sat on her bed darning a stocking. Beside her was an open novel which every now and then she read as a respite from her mending.

Her weekends were always solitary, because she had few friends. Many of the French Communists who had befriended her when she had first come to live in Mézac had dropped her when she had left the Party. The few who had not were now on the run. So too were her friends among the Spanish refugees—those who had not been interned or deported. For a time she too had expected to be arrested and had considered moving from Mézac to her parents' cottage in Saint Théodore. She had hesitated for a number of reasons—partly because she was reluctant to lose her independence, partly because she was afraid that her presence might compromise her parents, and partly because she had convinced herself that Bertrand de Roujay's influence was still strong enough to protect her. She remembered how he had mentioned a friend, an examining magistrate, who would take care of her, and she assumed that even now he was using his authority to prevent any administrative measures from being taken against her.

But perhaps the most forceful but least acknowledged reason for remaining in her flat in The Cedars, when everyone, including her kindly employers in the flower shop, had warned her that she should leave, was that The Cedars was where Bertrand had left her, and so it was to The Cedars that Bertrand would return. He had said he would come back, and just as before she had waited passively for his occasional visits, so now she waited passively for the day when the telephone would ring and she would hear his voice or simply see him standing at her door.

That afternoon, for example, when she heard a quiet knock as she lay on her bed she jumped up and glanced quickly in the mirror to tidy her hair and straighten the collar of her blouse in case, by some chance, it was him, but then she opened the door and saw instead the cold, gray eyes of a heavier, older man.

"Lucía Rodríguez de Astran?" he asked.

"Yes."

"Commissaire Guillot, Sûreté." He took a card from his pocket and held it up for a moment for her to see.

She stepped back into the hall, and Guillot walked into the single room of her flat. His eyes circled around the walls, noticing the posters advertising exhibitions of Braque and Miró and the double bed for the single girl. He saw too the open book, roll of wool, darning needle and woolen stockings. Then he looked at Lucía, who waited, standing, her legs bare, her feet in bedroom slippers. "I am here to serve a deportation order," he said.

"An order?"

"Yes. You are to be deported to Spain."

"But I am French."

"Your naturalization has been revoked."

"Why?"

"You are unworthy of France."

She looked at the window. "I have kept the law."

"You are a Communist."

"No, not in France."

"The Communist Party is international. Your husband died fighting for the Reds. You have bought clandestine newspapers published by the Communist Party and you have consorted with the enemies of France."

"That isn't true."

"You were the whore of the Gaullist de Roujay."

"He was not an enemy of France."

"He has been tried in his absence and condemned as a traitor."

"He is not an enemy of France," Lucía repeated.

"I am not here to argue with you," said Guillot. "I am here to take you into custody prior to your deportation to Spain."

She thought of her husband's fate at the hands of the Falange. "That would mean death," she said.

Guillot laughed. "What your own people do with you is no concern of ours."

"I shall appeal."

"To whom?"

"I have friends who will help me."

"What friends?"

"A magistrate." She looked at Guillot defiantly, but he only smiled.

"Monsieur Moreau, perhaps?"

"Yes."

Guillot laughed, a laugh like a cough. "He was sacked a year ago."

"Sacked? But why?"

"He's a yid. I suppose your boyfriend forgot to tell you that."

She hung her head and shook it.

"He's in no position to help you. He can hardly help himself."

"But I can't go back to Spain."

"You have no choice."

"I must wait here."

"For de Roujay?" He laughed again.

"I must."

"He'll never return."

"Please . . ." She now looked at him for the first time and saw his expressionless eyes.

"Pack a suitcase," he said.

"Please," she said again.

"It's time to go."

"There must be a way . . ." She meant nothing by what she said, but Guillot stopped and let his eyes run down her body to her bare legs.

"Of course," he said. "There's always a way."

She blushed but did not move. Guillot leaned forward and took hold of the material of her skirt. Her body stiffened, but still she did not move away. He lifted her skirt above her knee. "You could use that," he said.

She bit her lip. Tears came to her eyes. "And if I did?" she muttered.

He lifted the skirt higher still and stood for a moment staring at her pudenda with eyes empty even of lust; then he unbuttoned his trousers as if to urinate and pushed her back onto the bed.

When he had finished with her Guillot stood, fastened his trousers and said, "Let's go."

"But you said . . ."

"Nothing."

She sat, her legs apart, her head bent.

"Get up, you slut." He slapped her.

"I must go to the bathroom," she said in a quiet voice.

"Be quick."

She hobbled across the room. Guillot paced the room impatiently, then, always suspicious, went to the bathroom door.

"Hurry," he said.

"I'm coming."

He could tell from the way she spoke that something was wrong. He burst into the bathroom and found her sitting on the floor with blood pouring from her wrists. "Silly bitch," he said.

He took a towel, ripped it in two, and crudely bandaged her wrists.

"Let me die."

"No."

"I shall die anyway in Spain."

"I need you here in France."

"For what?"

"I have friends who can use you."

"Use me?"

"As the whore that you are."

"Never!"

"Never!" he mimicked her, laughing, and dragged her from the bathroom. "Never, never, never. They all say never, when whores are what they are and whores are what they've always been. Stinking, loathsome whores. . . . Now pack." He flung her on the floor, and Lucía, with the blood-soaked strips of towel around her wrists, crawled across the floor to drag a suitcase out from beneath her bed.

From the corner of the Place de l'Opéra where the Burzios' prostitutes plied their trade it was possible to see high above the city the floodlit statue of Our Lady of Lourdes. It was not as large as the statue on Notre Dame de la Garde in Marseilles, since Marseilles was a larger city, but it dominated Coustiers in the same way and at night made the Virgin's halo seem as bright and inaccessible as the moon.

At the same time, from the point of view of the statue, the thousands of human beings in the city below seemed like teeming ants, all constantly busy with their material tasks. The statue, of course, had no eyes to see the city, nor brain to compare its inhabitants to ants, but behind the statue was the cathedral and next to the cathedral the bishop's palace with a balcony from which the bishop sometimes blessed pilgrims but more often looked down upon the city below, reflecting upon the condition of his flock as if the view from this great height made it easier to see it *sub specie aeternitatis*.

One evening in the early autumn of 1941, the bishop of Coustiers, Monsignor Cartelin, was called in from his reflections on the balcony to greet his guest for dinner, his brother in Christ the bishop of Langeais, Monsignor Ravanel. The two old men passed into the large dining room, where their food was served on silver plates by a still older manservant.

They talked mostly in French, but occasionally, when a topic seemed to demand a holy discretion, broke into Latin. It was in Latin, for example, that Monsignor Cartelin, with a sigh, raised the subject of the restless young Dominican Antoine Dubec.

"What is he up to now?" asked Charles Ravanel with a sigh.

"He has taken a job as a laborer," said the bishop of Coustiers.

"Like Father Loew in Marseilles."

"Indeed. I am sure it is Father Loew who inspired him, but I am not convinced that Antoine has Father Loew's maturity."

"He was always a restless young man."

"No longer young," said Monsignor Cartelin.

"I am afraid, my dear friend, that he will always be young."

"I daresay."

"He is convinced he has a direct inspiration from above."

The bishop of Coustiers took a sip of wine from his crystal glass. "It upsets the employers."

"Of course."

"And it embarrasses many of the workers."

"They prefer their priests in a church?"

"Precisely."

"But he makes the point, which of course is a valid one, that many of the workers are quite lost to the Church, and that the workplace is where we can reach them."

Monsignor Cartelin nodded. "And the Dominicans are a preaching order."

"So perhaps one should not interfere?"

Monsignor Cartelin patted his lips with his white linen napkin. "Cardinal Rimini has come to hear of it."

"Ah. And he is unhappy?"

"He is afraid of political contamination."

"It is certainly a danger."

"The friar Antoine has been preaching some provocative sermons."

"Socialistic?"

"Almost Marxist."

"Was he corrected?"

"Yes. By his prior. But he takes correction badly."

"I can quite believe it," said Charles Ravanel.

"Should I ask the prior to send him elsewhere?"

"Yes," said Charles Ravanel, "but perhaps . . . not yet?" He raised his eyebrows and opened his face as if asking a question, not delivering a judgment. "After all, it is always possible that the grace of God will prove stronger than the allure of Karl Marx."

"In which case he might do good work."

"Indeed. It is very important, don't you think, that the Church show itself sympathetic to different tendencies?"

Monsignor Cartelin looked surprised. "But you yourself preached in favor of the regime."

Charles Ravanel was unperturbed by this rejoinder. "Of course," he said, "because at that time it seemed clear to me that the best course was to rally around the Marshal."

"And now?"

"Now too, though . . ." He hesitated. "One has to acknowledge that certain decrees make one unhappy. This resettlement of the Jews, for example. It leads one to suspect . . ." He did not finish this sentence but started another. "I have grave suspicions about Monsieur Laval."

"Yes," said Monsignor Cartelin, "but then so too, I think, does the Marshal."

"My brother-in-law, Colonel de Roujay, sees him as a sly old fox who will outwit the Germans."

"Satan, too, is a sly old fox."

"That is precisely the problem," said Charles Ravanel. "If we were monks, our life would be simpler. We could shut out the world behind ten-foot walls. But we are not monks, my dear Cartelin. We must live in the world and treat with the Prince of This World."

The bishop of Coustiers nodded. "But did you know—I have only just heard—that the Carmelite Thierry d'Argenlieu has joined de Gaulle in London?"

The bishop of Langeais shook his head—whether in sorrow or astonishment it was hard to say.

"It was he who chose the Cross of Lorraine," Monsignor Cartelin went on, "giving the whole Gaullist enterprise the air of a crusade, and he was one of the commanders of that lamentable expedition which set out to capture Dakar."

"A monk!" said Charles Ravanel.

"And the de Chabanais boy, Alain, who they always thought would choose holy orders, has also gone to London to join de Gaulle."

"And my nephew, after all," said Charles Ravanel. "An unhappy man, and perhaps a misguided man, but a good Catholic."

"Indeed," said the bishop of Coustiers, "we were all astonished when we heard that he had departed."

"But he acted from conscience, Cartelin, just as I acted from conscience when I preached my sermon in support of the Marshal, and just as Antoine, no doubt, acts from conscience as he works in a factory. The truth we must acknowledge is that Almighty God sends each of us on a separate mission so that holy and sincere men may in fact face each other in battle."

"I fear that is true," said the bishop of Coustiers with a sigh.

"We have the Commandments of God, and the commandments of the Church, but when we move outside the scope of the law, each of us, I fear, is alone with his Creator."

On the other side of the city the prefect of Coustiers, Marcel Charrier, sat at his desk working late.

He had grown thinner since the departure of Bertrand de Roujay; indeed, his subprefect's defection had cost him several pounds in weight and nearly his job. It was a tribute to Charrier's dedication and professionalism that he remained in office at all, because in most ways he was a likely candidate for the purge of the corps of prefects which had accompanied Pétain's National Revolution. What had saved him was his energy and ability and the manner in which he had devoted it to the new regime. He was punctilious in enforcing the decrees which came from Vichy, even when it came to dismissing magistrates like Pierre Moreau for whom he himself had the highest regard.

The only price Charrier had to pay to stay in place was a bad conscience. It was not that he felt that he was doing wrong, because his judgment followed an unbreakable logic. The duty of the state was the welfare of its citizens; the welfare of the French required accommodation with the power that had defeated them. The only principle which could lie behind democratic government was the greatest happiness for the greatest number, and distasteful though it might be to enforce decrees against Jews, the alternative was to see them enforced by the Gestapo.

What enraged and exasperated Charrier, when he occasionally listened to "the French speaking to the French" from London, was the Gaullists' assumption that the government in Vichy had any choice but to collaborate with the Germans. There were a million prisoners of war in Germany held as hostages against the good behavior of their fellow citizens at home. How could a man like de Roujay not see that now, as always, politics was the art of the possible, and that since it was impossible for the whole population of France to move to England, they must face the consequences of their defeat? The traitors, if the term was to be used for anyone, were those who abandoned their responsibilities to strike patriotic attitudes from a safe distance on the other side of the Channel.

Charrier's sympathies were not neutral. There were a thousand small ways in which he had been able to check the influence of the more enthusiastic collaborators within his department. He had vetoed several appointments of Fascist sympathizers to replace those purged from the municipal administrations. Though already compromised by Bertrand's defection, he had advised his colleague in the neighboring department to appoint Edmond de Roujay as mayor of Pévier.

What worried Charrier at those moments when he was tired and defenseless was the realization that while his reasoning was right, the conclusions it led to depended upon a stable reality, a constant perception of what was or was not possible, and reality he knew to be fickle. Already certain presumptions had proved false. The war had not ended as he had it assumed it would in the summer of 1940. The Germans were now fighting on two fronts, and though their advance into Russia had been spectacular, the Russians were not yet defeated. They had huge human resources at their disposal, and access to the mass-produced weaponry of the United States. For the first time since the war had started, Charrier thought its outcome uncertain.

He was also alarmed by developments in France. For a year after the armistice the population had been grateful for peace, but then the German exactions had started—first of food, now of labor. The official ration was officially acknowledged to lead to slow starvation. The population could survive only through illegality; its first and most fundamental compact with the state was broken. Then there was the shooting of hostages by the Germans in retaliation for attacks on their military personnel. The assassins in the Resistance might be criminals, but it was equally criminal to execute surrogates merely because one could not lay hands on the culprits themselves. The state could no longer ensure justice, and now the prospect that conscripted laborers would be sent to the Reich to work in German factories meant that it could no longer guarantee liberty for the innocent either.

Charrier sighed. What pleasure could there be in practicing the art of the possible, he asked himself, when the possible presented only a choice of evils, and the greatest happiness of the greatest number became only a lesser misery? That the plight of the French might be worse he did not doubt, for the cunning of Pétain, Darlan and Laval had saved them from the fate of Poland. Their policy remained correct as long as the Germans remained the conquerors of France. Only if the

Americans entered the war might the balance tilt, but even if that should happen, the Allied victory would be some years off. By that time the Marshal would be dead and he would have retired.

With this thought, Charrier sat back in his chair with an involuntary sigh of relief, for whatever regime came to power then would be sure to pay a prefect's pension.

Chapter 8

*I*N the course of the first year of her marriage, it occurred to Jenny de Roujay that the tact and tenderness of her husband, which had brought her such happiness, were not just the natural attributes of an older man but also the fruits of his experience with other women in France.

Bertrand never talked about his first marriage, and Jenny never asked about it. His past seemed to her as inaccessible as France itself. Only once, when they were dining with some of Bertrand's French friends, did the suave one called Etlin lean across the table and say to Bertrand, in English, "They say that one of the leaders of the Fortitude group, known as Hérisson, is in fact your father-in-law, Michel Bonnet."

Bertrand blushed. "He is no longer my father-in-law."

"No, of course not," Etlin said, smiling apologetically at Jenny. "I should have said your *former* father-in-law."

In the taxi going back to their flat in South Kensington, Jenny asked, "What does Hérisson mean?"

"Hedgehog."

"And was he prickly?"

"Who?"

"Your father-in-law."

"Yes."

From the way Bertrand answered, Jenny realized that he did not want to discuss the matter further. This disappointed her, because the reference to Michel Bonnet was the only thing which had interested her in the chatter about French politics that evening.

The nature of their social life gave rise to the first difficulty in their life together. For the first six months or so they were happy to spend their evenings and weekends alone together. There were never any silences between them, because Bertrand never tired of describing his home at Saint Théodore and his life in Provence, or delivering impromptu dissertations on the political significance of the day's events. By the autumn of 1941, however, Jenny felt sure enough of her husband's affection to show in her expression when she was bored, and in one of those frank discussions which married couples sometimes have together, and which often deepen the love they feel for one another, they both agreed that the honeymoon was over.

At first their sorties into society were only among Bertrand's friends, because Jenny was so much younger and naturally fell under his sway. Here she immediately encountered the difficulty of language. She could speak little French, and most of Bertrand's friends spoke little English. Whenever she was introduced to them they made some polite conversation in halting English and she made some token remarks in French, but as the evening proceeded they invariably reverted to their own language, and as they became impassioned and agitated in the course of their conversation, lapsed into such a fast babble that she understood nothing and became isolated and bored.

Every now and then Bertrand would remember that his wife could not understand French and would break off from some heated discussion to explain the issues in dispute. This often irritated Jenny more than being left in the dark, because Bertrand and his friends seemed to see everything only in terms of how it affected France. The bombing of Pearl Harbor, for example, which brought the United States into the war, was welcomed with misgivings because of Roosevelt's known dislike of de Gaulle, and the desert war in which Percy and Eddie were risking their lives seemed to have started and finished at Bir Hacheim, where the Free French division under General Koenig had held off the Germans while the British dug in at El Alamein.

Even when Bertrand and his friends were not arguing about the war —at the quieter, more civilized suppers, for instance, given by the Garys in Hampstead—Jenny felt out of place. She did not know any of the French folk songs that they sang around the piano, and when she saw Bertrand singing "Au Clair de la Lune" she felt a spasm of the hot embarrassment which lovers feel when the beloved is doing something to mar the image they treasure in their hearts.

What Jenny liked, of course, was evenings out with jolly groups of her own friends—to nightclubs, tea dances or parties held in one another's flats. The dangers and the excitements caused by the war, with men and women thrown together for what might be the last night of their lives, seemed to do away with the usual constraints and conventions and led to a frenzied gaity like the wild cavorting of a mardi gras.

In this company it was Bertrand who seemed out of place—always earnest, often exhausted and conspicuously middle-aged. Unlike his friend Etlin, Bertrand seemed unable to let go and enjoy himself. He never flirted with any of Jenny's friends from the ATS or from her debutante days, but hung around his young wife from the moment they arrived at a party, as if always ready to go home. Jenny, on the other hand, was always determined to have fun, and with a glass or two of gin in her blood sometimes found herself envying the grass widows whose husbands were serving abroad.

She was ashamed of these thoughts the next morning, and when she remembered that sooner or later Bertrand would return to France on a mission she was filled with panic and dread. When she was sober, there was no question that she loved him, and to put up with his dull French friends seemed a small price to pay for her happiness.

A second difference which arose between the de Roujays was over Ascombe Abbey. Jenny adored her childhood home, and whenever she could get leave would take the train from Kings Cross to spend it in Yorkshire. At first Bertrand, if he too could get leave, would go with her; but his marrying their daughter had not endeared him to the older Trents, who did not try to conceal their antipathy whenever Bertrand came to stay. Jenny ignored this and told Bertrand to do the same, but she remained close enough to her parents to see, through a chink in her passion for her husband, the way he must look in their eyes. He was bored at Ascombe and showed it. Nor did he conceal that he found his father-in-law a philistine and his mother-in-law a bore. He made no attempt to avoid irritating them by criticizing Churchill's treatment of the Free French over Saint Pierre and Miquelon.

Having used his parents-in-law's car and ration of fuel to drive to mass on Easter Sunday, leaving them to walk through the icy, horizontal rain to the village church, he ridiculed the Anglican religion at lunch as an absurd compromise between Catholicism and Protestantism which proved by its widespread acceptance that the English had no faith at all. "Which is hardly surprising," he added, waving toward the windows spattered by rain. "In France, after all, Easter marks the start of spring. It is easy to believe in a Resurrection. But here"—he shrugged his shoulders—"one doubts if anything will ever come out of the ground."

Jenny blushed, because it seemed improper to talk about religion and impolite to criticize the climate. She had noticed, too, that her father's mood, which was never good when Bertrand was staying, was worsened by the food served at lunch. Two weeks earlier their cook had become patriotic and gone off to do war work. They had had to engage the gardener's wife to replace her, a woman who previously had cooked only for her husband. That Sunday she surpassed herself, for not only was she a bad cook, but she had prepared the Trents' lunch the day before. The hurriedly mashed potatoes and the cauliflower with lumpy white sauce were cooked, cooled, and reheated a little too late, so that they were served both dry and tepid in the Trents' morguelike dining room. The meat was worse. It too had been well cooked the night before, and then carved in advance and left in the larder. The next day the slices had been placed in a slow oven of the old stove; as they had warmed they had dried, and as they had dried they had curled at the edges. The well-meaning lady had covered them all with a floury gravy, but she could do nothing to prevent the brittle edges of the slices from rising above the surface like the tip of a coral reef.

None of the Trents remarked upon the nastiness of this Easter lunch, because they had all been brought up to consider that form was more important than content. They were sitting at their own table under portraits of their ancestors, eating with forks marked with the family crest. To complain to the cook about the food would have been like complaining to the stationmaster because the trains were late. If these inconveniences occurred, there must be a good reason.

As a Frenchman, Bertrand had not had this stoic approach bred into him, and after the first mouthful of meat, which he ate with difficulty, he looked across at his wife as if to ask if he really must finish what was on his plate. Jenny blushed and avoided his eyes. It seemed as uncouth to complain about the food as about the weather.

When Jenny went north again in May, Bertrand did not go with her. It was only in August of 1942, when London had become intolerably stuffy and both had a fortnight's leave, that she persuaded him to go to Ascombe because Percy and Eddie would be there on leave. Eddie had been wounded in the shoulder while fighting Rommel in Libya, and it was thought that he would be given a medal, probably an MC.

Percy Trent had also been in the desert, and both he and Eddie had the sunburned skin and sangfroid of young men who had seen action. Jenny wept when she saw them, and embraced them both.

That night, as they got ready for bed, Bertrand asked Jenny what she thought of her brother's friend.

"Of Eddie?"

"Yes."

"I don't know. I don't really think about him."

"Why not?"

"I've known him for so long."

"He seems to like you."

She blushed. "He's more or less another brother."

"An incestuous one."

"Don't be disgusting."

"He isn't in love with you?"

"Of course not."

"He's never kissed you?"

"No. At least not seriously."

"What is an unserious kiss?"

"You know. At Pony Club dances."

"Like this?" He pecked at her cheek.

"A bit more."

He brushed his lips against hers. "Like this?"

"More or less."

"And what is a serious kiss?"

She looked into his eyes. "You should know."

He embraced her and moved toward her across the bed, but a moment later she drew back and said, "Not now. Not here."

"Why not?"

"I don't know. It just doesn't feel right, with Mother and Father down the corridor and Percy and Eddie probably looking through the keyhole."

This was the first time Jenny had rebuffed Bertrand, and she could see by the expression on his face that he was upset, but since women's asexual moods are often as mysterious to them as they are to their husbands, she could think of nothing to say to reassure him. However, she noticed the next morning that he was aloof, almost sulky, and retired into the library after breakfast to work on papers he had brought from London.

He was silent throughout lunch, and while Jenny knew that her cheerfulness in the presence of her brother and his friend only exacerbated his gloom, she could see no reason to pretend to be anything but happy. Both Percy and Eddie made her laugh because they knew her so well, and they teased her in the same way they had as children. They also knew the form, and ate up their beige "bangers in battle dress" as if they were the sizzling sausages of before the war, while Bertrand chewed and swallowed the tubes of grease and breadcrumbs as if forcing himself to do so to stay alive.

After lunch they went to the drawing room, where the gardener's wife brought a tray of coffee. Jenny avoided her husband's eye as he was given one of the elegant coffee cups by her mother, because even before the war the Trents had succumbed to the convenience of coffee concentrate, a treacly essence to which the cook needed only to add hot water. He grimaced as he sipped it, then put down the cup unfinished and fixed a melancholy gaze on one of the long sash windows, staring out through the drizzle at the dank, dark landscape of a Yorkshire summer's day.

Percy Trent looked up from reading the *Times* and said, "The snoopers are at it again."

"At what?" asked Eddie.

"Hotting up against the black market."

"Convictions?"

"I'll say. Another Jew by the sound of it, too."

"An Anglo-Jew or a refujew?"

"Doesn't say. Cohen. Could be either."

"You'd think they'd be grateful, now that we're knocking the Nazis."

"They can't help it," said Percy. "It's in their blood."

"What is?" asked Jenny.

"Spivving."

"It's not just the Jews. Everyone does it."

"Read the list of convictions," said Percy. "Gould, Blum, Cohen. They're all Jew names, aren't they?"

"And they're cowards, too," said Eddie. "They hogged all the shelters during the Blitz."

"I don't believe it," said Jenny.

"I swear it," said Eddie. "A chap in the regiment told me. Able-bodied Jew-boys pushed in front of women and children. He saw it."

"You get good and bad in every race," said Bertrand.

"More good in some and more bad in others," said Percy. "How many Jews do you know?"

"How many?"

"Yes. How many of your friends are Jews?"

"None," Percy said with some satisfaction.

"And how many of yours?" Eddie asked Bertrand.

"My closest friend in France is a Jew."

"The question I asked," said Eddie in a drawl, "was not whether you had Jewish friends, but *how many* of your friends were Jews."

"Two or three. Half a dozen. I don't know," said Bertrand, blushing at his exaggeration. "I've never counted them."

"But are they real Jews?" asked Jenny.

"How do you mean?"

"Well, with curly black hair and thick lips and hooked noses."

He frowned. "Some of them."

"But your friend Pierre?"

"No. He looks like . . . anyone else."

She sighed with relief and leaned forward to pick up a magazine. "I suppose it's different in France because a lot of French are dark anyway. In England they stand out so."

Bertrand made no reply but rose and went to the window, then turned back to Jenny. "What about a walk?"

She did not look up from *Country Life*. "Isn't it raining?"

"It's stopped."

She raised her head and turned to look out the window. "It still looks horribly wet."

"I know, but I need some fresh air."

She looked at him and smiled. "Do you mind if I don't?"

He frowned. "No, of course not." He turned toward his brother-in-law. "How about a walk?"

Percy groaned. *"Non, merci, mon ami."*

Bertrand turned to Eddie. "And you?"

"No midday sun."

Bertrand looked baffled. "I don't understand."

"It's a song," said Jenny wearily. " 'Mad dogs and Englishmen go out in the midday sun.' "

"Of course."

"Nor the afternoon rain," said Eddie.

"Very well," said Bertrand. "I'll see you all later." He left the room.

There was a silence after he had gone; Jenny and the two young men were absorbed in their magazines. Then Percy looked up and said, "They like the wet weather."

"Who do?" asked Eddie.

"Frogs."

"Of course."

"Do shut up," said Jenny.

"Must be a bit slimy in bed, though," said Percy.

"I'd have thought so," said Eddie.

Jenny could not stop a smile. "For God's sake, Percy."

"Some people like it."

"Like what?" asked Eddie.

"The slimy sort."

"Like Rudolph Valentino?"

"Exactly."

"I don't think I'd go for all that greasy hair."

"He hasn't got greasy hair," said Jenny.

"Who hasn't?"

"Bertrand."

"We were talking about Rudolph Valentino."

"Lots of girls go for the foreign look," said Eddie.

"Yes," said Percy. "They find it romantic."

"Are they romantic?"

"I wouldn't know." He turned to his sister. *"Est-ce que les wops sont romantiques, Madame de Roujay?"*

"More romantic than twerps like you."

"It's that charming accent," said Eddie.

"Like Maurice Chevalier," said Percy.

"And the delicious aroma of garlic as they stoop to kiss you."

"Oh, do shut up," said Jenny with a giggle.

"But everyone knows that garlic is an aphrodisiac," said Percy.

"Bertrand doesn't smell of garlic," said Jenny, "and he doesn't wear a beret or play the accordion or sell onions."

"He sounds almost like an Englishman," said Percy.

"He is," said Jenny.

"Except he isn't," said Eddie.

"No, he isn't," said Percy.

"Of course he isn't," said Jenny, throwing her magazine at her brother. "How can he be English when he's French?"

Bertrand walked out of the house in a waterproof fishing jacket and a borrowed pair of gum boots, not just to fill his lungs with fresh air but also to escape from the sense of spiritual suffocation which he felt at Ascombe Abbey. He crossed the gravel driveway in front of the house, went through a gate in the cast-iron railing into the park and made toward the woods on the far side.

As his boots squeaked on the long grass he remembered the baked earth of the path which led past the vines at Saint Théodore and was immediately overwhelmed by a wave of homesickness, for being with his English wife among her family did nothing to mitigate the misery he felt at being separated from his own parents, daughter and home. The very coldness of the Trents reminded him of their affection and warmth, and the dank view of wet vegetation recalled the fragrant scent and cheerful colors of the herbs and flowers of Provence.

He reached the woods and breathed in the stench of rotting leaves and dead birds. He felt a constriction in his throat as if he was about to weep, and suddenly he felt tears trickling down his cheek. The wet weather, disgusting food and unfriendly Trents all demoralized him. Even Jenny had appeared to side with them by declining to come with him on a walk. Whenever they came to Ascombe she seemed to withdraw her affection, changing from the pretty, loving girl who had clung to his arm during the air raid into a disdainful baronet's daughter —friendlier to her father's dogs than she was to her French husband.

There were times when she seemed to be irritated by his presence, as if it prevented her from returning to an easy role as her brother's sister or her parents' child. He suspected that both Percy and Eddie disliked him and conducted a campaign of sustained derision. Perhaps the friend had had his eye on Jenny, and resented her marrying a Frenchman. Certainly Bertrand had caught a look of triumph in Eddie's eyes when she had wept in his arms the day before. Perhaps Jenny's tears had been a form of flirtation; Bertrand was old enough to know that no husband should expect his wife to abandon a former admirer, or feel jealous if by the slightest blush or flicker of her eyes she keeps that admirer's interest alive. Flirting meant nothing—Madeleine, after all, had never flirted—and if he was foolish enough to rebuke Jenny for leading the young man on, his charges would certainly be dismissed as the absurd fantasies of a silly old man, as absurd and imaginary as the smell of garlic which he seemed to inhale as he walked through the woods.

He breathed in, and again seemed to inhale the aroma of garlic, which immediately reminded him of the Provençal cooking that he missed almost as much as his people and countryside. Before leaving France, he had never thought of himself as greedy; certainly he had thought less about gastronomy than most of his friends. It was only when he had come to England that he realized how demoralized a man can become in spirit if he takes no pleasure in the food he eats. In London there were restaurants where despite the rationing and shortages it was still possible to find dishes that he had known in France, but here at Ascombe the food served up at table was worse than he had ever imagined in boarding schools, prisons or insane asylums. It depressed him more than the enmity of the Trents. He craved sauces made with cream and wine, olives, tomatoes, tarragon, rosemary and garlic. Above all he longed for garlic, which to Bertrand could transform even the bland ingredients of the Trents' kitchen into dishes with some fragrance and taste.

Again, as he thought about garlic, he seemed to smell it in the air, but imagining this to be a self-induced hallucination he did not notice for some moments that he had walked into a sheltered dell where a few foxgloves and brambles grew among other green plants with no flower. When he did, he stopped, for the clearing in the trees seemed an agreeable place to pause before returning to the house.

He felt the ground. It was wet. He saw a tree stump, and though it too was damp, and patched with green moss, he leaned against it to rest. He looked up; the sky was clearing. Still his hallucination persisted: he could smell garlic. Looking down, he saw the greenish leaves of a plant, which he stooped to pick and smell. He laughed to himself; he had not been mistaken. It was undoubtedly wild garlic, and such was his craving for its taste that he picked a stem, put it in his mouth and chewed it to a pulp.

He turned back, retracing his steps to the house. The taste of the wild garlic had improved his spirits, and he felt strong enough to endure the rest of the fortnight at Ascombe. After that they would return to London and once again all would be well. Remembering how happy they had been until that weekend, he decided, as he came in sight of the house, that he must not allow Jenny's family to persuade her that in marrying him she had "let the side down." They must accept that she was his wife; they were married now, and would be forever.

He came in through the back door, took off his boots and fishing jacket and walked across the hall to the dining room, where he could hear the sound of the family at tea. He found the Trents seated formally at table eating sandwiches and scones. Jenny, next to Eddie, smiled when she saw him and asked, "How was your walk?"

"A little damp, but I enjoyed it," he replied as he crossed to kiss her. He stooped, and as he did so she smiled and turned her face up to meet his. Then, as if the sight of his lips suddenly repulsed her, she turned sharply back to the table, scarlet in the face. Confused, Bertrand hesitated for a moment, then went to the one empty place at table and sat down.

The others were silent until Percy tittered and Sir Edward cleared his throat and passed his cup to his wife for more tea. Bertrand looked across the table at Jenny for an explanation, but she avoided his eyes and sat, still red in the face, staring at her plate.

"*Voulez-vous manger un biscuit?*" Percy asked Bertrand, pushing a plate of beige biscuits speckled with currants toward him. "*On appelle ça les 'squashed fly' biscuits. Ils sont faits avec les mouches écrasées. C'est une spécialité Anglaise, comme les grenouilles en France.*"

"Oh Percy, for God's sake shut up," Jenny screamed at her brother. She glared at him with fury, then at Bertrand with loathing, then she burst into tears and left the room.

"What did I say?" asked Percy.

"You do go on, darling," said the mother.

"Just a tease," said Percy.

"I'd better see what's wrong," said Bertrand.

"Of course," said Mary Trent coldly.

He left the room and went up the wide oak stairs to their bedroom. Jenny was lying on their bed, her face buried in the pillow.

He came and sat next to her. "What is it?"

She would not look at him. "Leave me alone," she sobbed into the pillow.

"Jenny," he said firmly, his hand on her shoulder. "You must tell me what has upset you. It would be best."

She turned and looked up at him with angry eyes from a blotched face. "You . . . you smell."

"I smell?"

"Of garlic."

"I smell of garlic?" For a moment he could not understand what she was talking about. Then he cupped his hand to his mouth and breathed into it. An aroma of wild garlic remained on his breath. He laughed. "Well, of course. I found some wild garlic in the woods."

"And you ate it?"

"Yes."

"Why?"

He shrugged his shoulders. "I love garlic. I miss it."

She sniffed. "We . . . I hate it."

"Then I'm sorry. I'll brush my teeth." He stood and went to the basin in the corner of the room. As he took the top off the toothpaste he caught sight of himself in the mirror and saw with detachment the former subprefect of Mézac as he prepared to make his breath fragrant for his English hosts.

I was mad to leave France, he thought to himself. That was purgatory, but this is hell.

There came a battering on the bedroom door. "Jenny, Bertrand." It was Percy.

"Go away," said Jenny.

"Don't you want to hear the news?"

"What news?"

"We just heard it on the radio. Our chaps have invaded France. They've landed in Dieppe."

2
———

The British attack on Dieppe in August of 1942 was not a prelude to an invasion of France—indeed, it convinced the Allies that a direct assault on the Continent was not the best way to open a second front —but it served as a pretext for Bertrand to return to London. There, among his friends in Carlton Gardens, he could forget his ordeal at Ascombe Abbey and escape from the insoluble riddle of feminine feelings.

The operation in Dieppe was a military fiasco, but as always the Free French judged it from their own perspective and were pleased when it appeared from reports from France that the attack had helped expose the out-and-out collaborators at Vichy, who used it as a pretext to move toward an alliance with Hitler. The more the Pétainists were seen as allies of the Axis, the more likely the French people were to rally to de Gaulle. Hunger had disillusioned them with the armistice, and the German demands for forced labor had driven many of the uncommitted to take to the maquis—to join the guerrillas hidden in the woods and hills.

What alarmed Bertrand and his friends in Carlton Gardens was the thought that the Resistance, as it developed, might disregard de Gaulle, for not only did the Communist cadres retain their first loyalty to Stalin, but many of the non-Communist networks were controlled by the British Special Operations Executive. The Free French knew that other groups were appearing in different parts of France, but none of them had made contact with the Gaullists in London. In October of 1941, de Gaulle had broadcast an appeal over the BBC for a two-minute silence on the last day of the month as a national protest against the German occupation. It was almost totally ignored. This suggested to the Gaullists in London that while they might win recognition from Britain and some of France's own territories overseas, they seemed to have few adherents in France itself.

In the autumn of 1941, the former prefect of Chartres, Jean Moulin, had escaped to England by Lisbon. He too had been delayed in Lisbon by the British authorities, but like Bertrand had insisted upon serving General de Gaulle. Recognizing Moulin's talents as an administrator, de Gaulle had sent him back into France on New Year's Day 1942 with orders to form a National Council of the Resistance loyal to him.

The urgency of Moulin's task was all the greater because only a few weeks before he departed, the United States had entered the war. This was of inestimable value to the Allied cause, leaving little doubt that the war would be won, but it made the French in London uneasy. However often he had quarreled with de Gaulle, Churchill had always supported him. Now, however, he was pledged to serve as the "loyal lieutenant" of his more powerful ally, President Roosevelt, who not only disliked de Gaulle but had never accepted his claim to be the legitimate representative of France. Like Stalin, Roosevelt had kept an embassy in Vichy, and had continued to supply oil to the French in North Africa. He had been enraged when the Free French had captured the French islands off the coast of Newfoundland, Saint Pierre and Miquelon, because his policy was not to provoke Pétain but to coax him away from collaboration with the Germans. The U.S. ambassador remained in Vichy even when the United States was at war with Germany, and when it finally became apparent that Pétain and Laval were inextricably involved with Hitler, and relations were finally broken between Washington and Vichy, Roosevelt did not shift his support to General de Gaulle, but instead looked for another man to lead the Free French.

In the first months of 1942, more and more Americans were seen on the streets of London. General Eisenhower and his staff were installed in Grosvenor Square, only a few minutes' walk from the Connaught Hotel, where General de Gaulle resided during the work week.

Among the officers of the American Office of Strategic Services posted to London was Bertrand's friend from Lisbon, Harry Jackson. He first telephoned Bertrand at Carlton Gardens in August of 1942, when Jenny was still in Yorkshire, and suggested they might have lunch together to talk about old times "and see if we can't get hold of a bottle of the old *vinho verde.*" Remembering how suspicious the Free French Secret Service was of American intentions, Bertrand reported this approach to the sour and sallow Lieutenant Rivière.

Jackson was no longer posing as an engineer; he wore the uniform of a colonel in the United States Army. Bertrand nonetheless recognized him at once as he entered the restaurant, and felt a sudden surge of affection for this companion of his desperate days in Lisbon. In the two years that had passed since Bertrand had last seen him, Jackson had not changed. He still laughed at his own jokes with flaring nostrils, and despite the authority of his rank and uniform still spoke with the gleeful naiveté of a considerably younger man.

"Do you know," he said to Bertrand, almost as soon as they had sat down in the restaurant, "I brought a girl to this place last week— one I'd met in a pub, and had dated once or twice. We came in here and she said, 'Look, duckie, I'd rather have the cash than a fancy meal, so why don't we go back to my place and stop messing about.'"

"You should have chosen a cheaper restaurant," said Bertrand.

"Don't worry," said Jackson. "She settled for a carton of Camels. But I tell you, Bertrand, she wasn't up to any of those girls in Lisbon."

"I'm sorry."

"They're a dowdy lot, these English girls, and they make love as if it's an unpleasant necessity, like going to the john."

"That's not my experience," said Bertrand curtly.

"Oh, I'll grant you there are exceptions. The young wives whose husbands are abroad feel so guilty that they go at it as if there's no tomorrow."

"I'm married to an English girl," said Bertrand.

"Well, good for you," said Harry, laughing to conceal his confusion, and then rapidly changed the subject to the war. "Listen," he said. "Bir Hacheim did you a lot of good in the States. Before that, most Americans didn't know that there were any Frenchmen fighting in this war. Now, well, now they respect you."

"You may respect us," said Bertrand, "but you don't recognize us as France."

"I recognize *you* as France," said Jackson, "but I'm not so sure about General de Gaulle."

"What have you got against him?"

"To tell the truth, Bertrand, I think he's a crackpot."

Bertrand smiled. "Perhaps, but then great men often are."

"Is he a great man?"

"I think so."

"Or is he a mediocre man who thinks greatness consists of throwing your weight around?"

"Perhaps that is just what greatness is."

"Greatness demands genius, Bertrand, and genius requires an animal sense of limitation. He has none. He behaves as if he's a heavyweight in the ring with heavyweights, but in fact he's a featherweight with no support at all in France itself, outside France only a bunch of refugees here in London, and a few colonial officials scattered around the globe."

"We have another saying," said Bertrand. " 'Genius is only a greater aptitude for patience.' "

"La Rochefoucauld?"

"De Buffon."

"And would you say that your general is a patient man?"

"He may not seem so, but he is, because he knows that in the end—"

"In the end what? Who will *ever* support him? The decent, conservative, middle-class majority in France, who honestly thought they were doing the right thing in going for Pétain, will never forgive de Gaulle for deserting him. His only chance of power is to ride in on the backs of the Communists, who will use him while they have to and then throw him aside."

Bertrand frowned. "There is no alternative to de Gaulle," he said irritably. "He may not be ideal, but he did the right thing at the right time, and now there is no one else."

Jackson hesitated, as if considering how much he should reveal of what he knew. "Think about North Africa," he said quietly.

"What about it?"

"There are one hundred and fifty thousand French troops there who only need new equipment to become a formidable fighting force."

"But they are loyal to Pétain."

"As of now."

"How could that change?"

Again Harry hesitated. "There are several ways—"

"If you invaded North Africa," Bertrand interrupted, following his train of thought, "they might or might not fight against you, but they would never fight *for* you *against* Pétain."

"Unless under orders."

"From whom?"

"From whom! Precisely! It would have to be from the right man."

"Besides Pétain, only Darlan or Weygand would have a chance, and they're both loyal to Pétain."

Now Jackson leaned across the table and whispered to Bertrand, "What about Giraud?"

"Giraud?"

"A distinguished general who far outranks de Gaulle, a commander in the field, taken prisoner by the Germans, who then escapes from a fortress and returns to France."

"But . . ." Bertrand raised his hand in a Gallic gesture to denote futility.

"But what?"

"No one here would desert de Gaulle to follow Giraud."

"They might if they were given a lead."

Bertrand shook his head. "We are committed to de Gaulle."

Jackson sat back in his chair. "Giraud could unite your nation, Bertrand, in a way that de Gaulle never can."

Bertrand shook his head. "The Resistance would never accept him."

"Because the Communists control it."

"No one here would accept him."

"They might if a man like you gave a lead."

"It would be dishonorable."

"It would be patriotic."

"It can never be patriotic to be dishonorable."

"Fiddlesticks. Nations only exist because of dishonorable statesmen, Bertrand. Where would France be if it weren't for the unscrupulousness of Cardinal Richelieu or Catherine de Medici? *Raison d'état*, Bertrand. You Frenchmen invented the phrase, but now you shy away from it."

Bertrand left the restaurant in a somber mood, because he was obliged to recognize the truth in much of what Jackson had said. He feared that despite his military and diplomatic successes in different corners of the world, de Gaulle had yet to establish himself among the French people. His natural constituency, the army, remained loyal to Pétain; in Syria only one in ten of the defeated Vichy forces had volunteered to join the Free French. Nor had he any significant support among civilians in France itself. His appeal in October had been ignored, and Moulin's mission had little chance of success. With its ruthless and efficient clandestine organization, the Communist Party would undoubtedly form the most effective fighting force within France. Overtly or covertly it would dominate and control the Resistance, and with its disciplined cadres would exploit the decay of the Vichy regime to impose its own administration at the time of the liberation.

The prospect of a Communist France filled Bertrand with dismay. To exchange one tyranny for another seemed a wretched prospect for his country. Moreover, as was true of most of the Free French working in Carlton Gardens, his patriotism was mixed with a certain measure of personal ambition. He could not conceive of returning to France except as a member of a liberating army. In his worst moments of loneliness and despair he had consoled himself by imagining the look on Charrier's face when he ousted him from office. It was inconceivable that by the time he reached Coustiers some Red commissaire might be sitting in Charrier's chair.

But what could prevent it? Only the power of the liberating forces. It seemed certain that these would be Anglo-Saxon, for unless there was a sudden collapse on the eastern front which let the Soviets run across Europe like a Tartar horde, the British and the Americans would liberate France and impose an administration of their choice.

As far as Churchill was concerned, this could be led by de Gaulle. It was only the Americans who were looking for someone more amenable to their influence; thus from strict self-interest Bertrand would have been well advised to ally himself with them, because they were the more powerful partner in the alliance. But he not only felt gratitude and affection for his cold and cantankerous leader, he also knew that if the Americans were stupid enough to try to impose on his country a conservative General like Giraud, who was acceptable neither to the Communists in France, nor the Gaullists in London, then France would be faced with a civil war. If only to prevent a catastrophe of this kind, Bertrand was determined to remain loyal to de Gaulle.

At the beginning of September, Jenny returned to London, flushed and pretty from the country air. When Bertrand met her at the station she flew into his arms like a child who had been away on holiday.

Three weeks later, Harry Jackson telephoned to ask Bertrand and Jenny to dinner at the Savoy. Jenny showed little interest in meeting the American, but was delighted by the idea of a night on the town. She became flustered about what clothes to wear, and went to some trouble to borrow some nylon stockings from an old school friend who, although the daughter of a major general, had taken up with an American GI. She had also got hold of a length of white silk, which she had had made into a blouse; cut in the new utility fashion, it clung to her body and showed through its diaphanous texture the rococo lacework of her brassiere and the pink shadows of her breasts.

Bertrand remarked as they dressed, "Isn't that a bit transparent?"

Studying her appearance in their cheval mirror with a serious expression on her face, Jenny laughed and said, "Do you think so? Well, too bad."

Both their opinions of the blouse—immodest, attractive—were confirmed by the surprise and delight shown by Harry Jackson when he met them in the Savoy.

"This calls for champagne," he said, flicking his fingers for the waiters, who, sniffing a big-spending American, were quickly at his side. "Champagne," said Harry. "One bottle at once, and another on ice."

Bertrand sat down and turned to Harry's date, a raddled English girl named Marjorie who he later discovered was working as a typist for the OSS. He could see from the frown on her face as she talked to him that she was annoyed to be overshadowed by the prettier girl across the table. They made conversation for form's sake until later in the evening, when the cabaret was over and the stage in the center of the room subsided into the floor, and Harry asked Jenny to dance. Bertrand followed with Marjorie, but soon returned to sit silently beside her at the table.

He kept catching glimpses of his wife and his friend, and as he saw their animated faces and smiling eyes, the sour bile of jealousy filled his stomach and his mood changed to angry despair. The whole of human society, which allowed a man to hold another man's wife in such a lascivious way, with his loins pressed to her thighs, simply because there was music playing and they were under the public gaze, suddenly seemed corrupt. He loathed Harry's cheerful vigor, and despised Jenny for the smile on her face. He remembered her attention to her appearance—the transparency of her blouse, and the way she had left just one button too many undone so that the fold of the cloth at the collar opened like the petals of a flower to show the stamen of her pretty breasts to the greedy eyes of the predatory bee—and inwardly castigated her for her faithlessness.

Then he felt a hand on his shoulder and heard a voice saying, "What on earth are you doing here?"

He turned to see Etlin. "Having fun, as you can see."

"You have the face of a man at his own funeral," said Etlin, speaking fast in French so that Marjorie could not understand.

"One cannot summon up fun like a genie out of a bottle."

"Particularly not when one's wife is dancing with a handsome American."

"That may have something to do with it." Bertrand smiled sourly.

As he did so, Harry and Jenny came off the dance floor. Jenny, who was flushed, glanced at her husband with a puzzled look as if wondering what had put him in such a gloomy mood.

Bertrand introduced Etlin to Harry Jackson and Marjorie, whereupon Etlin turned to Jenny and said, "What about a dance with one of your French friends?"

"Of course." She smiled, delighted at this extra ration of attention from another handsome man. She quickly drank down her glass of champagne and went back onto the dance floor with Etlin.

Harry sat down next to Bertrand. "Isn't he one of Passy's men from Duke Street?" he asked, nodding in the direction of Etlin.

"If he was," said Bertrand, "I would hardly be allowed to say so."

"You still don't trust me?"

"I trust you to act in your country's interests." He spoke coldly, because in his mind Roosevelt's flirtation with Giraud was like Harry's flirtation with his wife.

"Aren't our interests the same?" asked Harry.

"Similar, but not the same."

"We want to win the war."

"Yes."

"And liberate France."

"Yes."

"And keep the Communists out."

"Yes."

"Then where's the difference?"

"Not in the end we pursue, but in the means to that end," said Bertrand. "You may be powerful, and you may win the war for us, but you don't know France or the French. We are an impossible people, not courteous and correct like Giraud, but arrogant, quarrelsome and gauche like de Gaulle. If few of us follow de Gaulle now, it is because we pursue a chimera to the left or to the right of what we would like France to be—but in the end we will all follow him, because in the end we will all recognize in him our own reflection."

"So it's no potatoes?" said Harry.

Bertrand shook his head. "I'm sorry."

"It was worth a try."

"Of course."

"Now let's drop business and have a good time." He turned to Marjorie. "What about a dance?"

Sourly she accepted, and Bertrand was left alone at his table. For a moment while talking to Jackson, he had been distracted from his jealousy, but now that his attention returned to the dance floor and he caught a glimpse of Jenny dancing with Etlin, her cheek against his chest, his hand on her buttocks, it returned like a fierce fever. He felt outraged that Jenny should cling to another man in this way, and thought it treacherous of Etlin, who was supposedly his friend, to use the pretext of dancing to lewdly caress his wife.

When Etlin delivered her back to the table he bowed to Bertrand, and with the faintly mocking smile that the experienced seducer always directs at the husband of a weak wife, thanked him for lending him Jenny.

"Anything for a friend," said Bertrand sarcastically.

Etlin laughed out loud. "I'll remember that." He turned and with a kiss of Jenny's hand took his leave.

"He's a bit oily, isn't he?" she said.

"You didn't seem to mind his greasing."

She blushed. "How do you mean?"

"You hardly kept him at arm's length."

"There wasn't room."

Bertrand snorted.

"Oh, don't be a bore, darling," said Jenny.

"It's time to go home."

"It's only eleven."

"I have to work in the morning."

"Don't be a spoilsport."

"What sport have you in mind that I might spoil?"

"You know what I mean."

"If you call smooching a sport."

"I wasn't smooching."

"You were dancing like a tart."

"God, you're a bore!" She turned scarlet and scowled.

"Hey, what's going on?" asked Harry, escorting Marjorie back from the floor.

"I'm afraid we have to leave," said Bertrand.

"Leave? So early?"

"I have a meeting in the morning."

Harry turned to Jenny. "Does that mean you have to go too?"

"I'm afraid so," she said acidly. "Bertrand doesn't trust me on my own."

Harry laughed a cuckold-mocking laugh, like Etlin's. "Well, I quite understand. If you were my girl, I guess I'd feel the same."

In the taxi going home, Jenny faced away from Bertrand and looked out of the window. He said nothing, but as they crossed Trafalgar Square and drove down the Mall, his anger gradually subsided, leaving only his corrosive jealousy.

When they reached South Kensington he paid off the driver and followed Jenny into the flat. Her diaphanous blouse now looked tawdry, and tears had left streaks of mascara running down her cheeks.

"I'm sorry," he said.

She sniffed and went into the bedroom.

"I know jealousy is horrible," he said, coming in behind her, "but there it is . . . You're so pretty. Other men want you and . . . I can't help what I feel."

"But it's so silly."

He took hold of her gently by the shoulders. "Is it?"

"Of course it is." She allowed him to turn her to face him, but she did not look into his eyes.

"I'm only jealous because I love you."

"If you loved me, you'd trust me, but you don't trust me because of *her*."

"Who?"

"Madeleine. It isn't my fault that she ran off."

"Who told you that?"

She sniffed. "Etlin."

"It's men like Etlin whom I mistrust."

"Well, they soon won't fancy me anyway."

"Why not?"

"Because I'm pregnant."

Bertrand was dumbfounded. "How can you be pregnant?"

She shrugged her shoulders. "Those Volpar Gels can't work as well as they're meant to." She looked up at him almost furtively. "Do you mind?"

He answered her by kissing her on her lips, her cheeks, her nose, her eyelids, then clasping her body in a strong embrace as if both absorbing and protecting the bodies of his wife and his unborn son.

The next morning Bertrand was exuberant, and he brought Jenny her breakfast in bed. The flirt of the night before had been transformed in his mind into a madonna by the knowledge that she carried his child. He sat down at the foot of the bed as she ate toast and drank tea, describing once again what he had so many times before—the house, garden, vines, woods and river at Saint Théodore—and repeating his dearest dream of a return in triumph with his English wife to his waiting family in France. As he reached the end of this reverie, he noticed that Jenny appeared pale and anxious.

"Do you feel sick?" he asked.

"A little."

He stood. "I'll call the office and tell them that I can't come in."

"No, no." She sat up in bed. "I'll be all right. I'll go to the doctor."

"I'll take you there."

"No, Bertrand, please. I'd rather go on my own." She smiled. He kissed her, then left the flat to take a bus to Piccadilly.

That very morning, as he sat in his office in Carlton Gardens, still dizzy with the idea that Jenny was to have his child, Bertrand was summoned up to see General de Gaulle.

De Gaulle had recently returned from the Middle East, where the sun had browned his normally sallow skin, but Bertrand saw at once from the frozen way in which the general pointed to a chair, then lit a cigarette and looked away as he smoked it that the leader of the Free French was in an agitated frame of mind. "I've read Rivière's report on the approach by the Americans," he said. "You were quite right to listen. Any straw in the wind helps tell us what they are up to."

"Thank you, General."

"I tell you, de Roujay, we are at a critical moment in our fortunes.

I saw Churchill yesterday and he said to my face, 'You claim to be France. You are not France. I do not recognize you as France.' "

"One might have expected that from Roosevelt," said Bertrand, "but not from Churchill."

"Oh, he didn't mean it. If he had, why would he have been talking to me about French interests? No, he was angry, and angry because he felt ashamed, and he felt ashamed because he is no longer his own master. He must dance to the American's tune. And they are up to something. They don't want Stalin to win the war. They want a second front. They're not ready to land on the Continent, so I suspect that they plan to land troops in our territory in North Africa to finish off Rommel and attack Europe from the south."

"Would they do that without consulting us?"

"Of course! Look at the British in Madagascar! They use us when it suits them, but at present it doesn't seem to suit them." He stubbed out his cigarette, then immediately lit another. "The danger to us is this: that to smooth their path in North Africa, they will try to neutralize the army there by leaving well enough alone. As far as Roosevelt is concerned, the only enemy is Hitler. Pétain and Laval can stay where they are, or if not Pétain and Laval, then some compromise figure like Weygand or Giraud."

"The Resistance will never accept it."

"The Communists would never accept it, but what about groups like Libération and Fortitude?"

Bertrand shook his head. "I would doubt it."

"The Americans have already started bribing the non-Communist Resistance with offers of money and arms. Once they are established in Algiers, it may be tempting for those groups in the south of France to forget about us in London and work directly with those who are near at hand."

"We must hope that Moulin acts in time to prevent it."

"Yes. But Moulin may not be enough, which is why I want you to go back to France, for when it comes to the department of Basse-Provence, you are in an unrivaled position to establish our authority."

"Of course."

"There is another thing, de Roujay. If we return to France under the skirts of the Americans, no one will accept us. If we want to govern France at her liberation, we must establish our credentials by risking our lives!"

. . .

Bertrand left de Gaulle racked by conflicting emotions. On the one hand the mission for which he had been waiting for the past two years had finally arrived; on the other the thought that he was about to have a child made him suddenly loath to leave his wife in London.

He was reassured when at lunch with Colonel Passy, whose Secret Service was to organize his drop into France, he was told that he would not leave until November, and his mission would not be of long duration. "It is a question of making personal contact with those leaders we know only by their code names—Hérisson and Sabot of Fortitude, Platane and Homard in the army group, Bouclier and Riquin in the Francs Tireurs et Partisans. Moulin, whom you must now call Rex, will brief you in Paris, but once you are in Coustiers you must make contact with the different groups, all of which are expecting you under your code name, Montrouge. Impress upon them the importance of a single French Resistance loyal to General de Gaulle, and establish your own authority under Rex as the general's representative in your area. Then come home."

"Home?"

"Back to London."

Bertrand returned that evening under orders to keep his mission secret even from his wife. He kissed Jenny as he came in with a melancholy sweetness. She had just returned herself, and still wore her ATS uniform. He unbuttoned her tunic to hold his hands against her skin, and breathed in the faint aroma of warmth and sweat like a man about to go underwater.

"Did you see the doctor?"

"Yes. He's pretty sure it's a baby, but we'll have to wait for the result of the test to be absolutely sure."

"When is it due?"

"Oh, in the spring sometime. He wasn't quite sure."

Bertrand sighed with relief. If he left in November, he should be back by Christmas, and even if there was trouble in getting out of France, he would certainly be back by the time the baby was born.

"Listen," he said to Jenny as he poured her a drink, "there are all sorts of rumors at the office since de Gaulle got back. He thinks we've all gotten fat and idle, so he's ordered us to toughen up and do some training."

"What sort of training?"

"Parachute, mainly, at Ringway."

"Was that where Etlin and Alain had been when they came back and caught us in the kitchen?"

"Yes."

"It seems odd to send you to do that sort of thing."

"Why?"

"Well, aren't you too senior to jump out of airplanes?"

"You mean too old?"

"No, darling." She laughed and came and sat next to him. "Not too old. Too grand, too high up."

"It's those high up who need parachutes."

She laughed politely at his feeble joke and lay back against him.

Bertrand laid his hand on her stomach as if it had already swollen with the child. "It will only mean an occasional weekend."

She smiled. "Are you sure it isn't a cover for some love affair with a girl from Carlton Gardens?"

"My only love affair is with my wife."

She laughed, and looked up into his eyes.

"Don't worry," said Bertrand, so relieved that his jealousy had vanished that he felt he could joke about it. "I shall tell you exactly when I'm going and when I'm coming, so you'll have time to give your lovers an early breakfast."

At the end of October, Alain de Chabanais was parachuted back into France and was met not by the Resistance but by the Gestapo. His mission had been betrayed in advance. The message reached London a few days before Bertrand was due to leave for Provence that he had died under torture at Gestapo headquarters in Rennes.

Bertrand did not tell Jenny for fear of adding to her anxiety when he broke the news to her of his own mission. Indeed, on the evening he heard of Alain's death he had agreed to take her to Claridge's with a group of the Trents—Jenny's parents, her brother and her Uncle Martin—to celebrate the victory of El Alamein and to say farewell to Percy and Eddie Macleish, who were due to return to their regiment in Egypt.

Bertrand did what he could to enter into the spirit of their celebration, but the news of Alain's death grieved him greatly. It was not just that it made him realize that his own mission was dangerous, and that his easy expectation that he would be back in London for the birth of his baby might well not be met. It was also that he had loved Alain for his clear spirit and noble soul, and the thought that his life should have ended so abruptly and ignominiously threw him into despondency. At the back of his mind there had always been the conviction that the struggle against the Germans was the battle of good against evil, in which God would inevitably take the side of good. Yet here was the gentlest and most pious among these Free French crusaders, whom God, if he loved any of them, must have loved most of all, lost to the forces of evil. What had happened to the strong arm of the Lord? Why had the devil found Alain such easy prey?

Bertrand could neither answer these questions nor shut them out of his mind; at the same time he felt ashamed that he could not bring himself to be cheerful on one of the last evenings out with his wife. Nor could he tell her why he was so glum. For once he felt glad that Eddie and Percy were there to give her a good time.

When the younger members of the party were on the dance floor and Jenny's parents were talking to acquaintances at another table, Martin Trent leaned forward and said to Bertrand, "I'm sorry about de Chabanais."

"You heard?"

"Yes, from one of our men."

"How did it happen?"

"The Gestapo arrested one of your people in Rennes. He knew the time of the drop. They tortured him, and he gave the whole thing away."

Bertrand shook his head. "We needed men like Alain."

"Yes," said Martin. "I know that he was a friend of yours. We are all very sorry."

"I haven't told Jenny," said Bertrand.

"No. It would only add to her worries while you're away."

"You know about that?"

"You're on one of our planes."

"Do you know when?"

"Tomorrow, if the weather's clear."

The next morning in Carlton Gardens it was confirmed that Bertrand was to leave that night. He found Jenny in the flat when he returned at six, and told her at once that he was leaving on a mission to France.

She looked astonished. "When?"

"Tonight."

She fell into his arms and burst into tears.

"Be brave," he said.

"Yes. I'm sorry." She pulled herself away and wiped her nose. "I mustn't be feeble. It's just that I have the feeling you might never come back."

"Nonsense."

"I don't just mean that you might get killed; all wives know that. But that once you find yourself in France, at Saint Théodore, you won't want to come back to England."

"I won't go to Saint Théodore. It would be too dangerous."

"You won't see your daughter?"

"No."

"Oh, darling, I am sorry." She fell into his arms once again. "I'm being so selfish, only thinking of myself. It will be horrible for you, being close to her and yet not seeing her."

"It will be worse not seeing you."

"When will you be back?"

"In a month or six weeks—two months at most."

"You must be back for the baby."

"I will. Of course I will."

"You promise?"

"Yes."

At eight a car came to the apartment to take Bertrand to Duke Street, now the headquarters of the Gaullist Secret Service, where he changed into the clothes of a French engineer and took the passport and papers of his alter ego, an engineer named Albert Ferlin traveling to work in a factory in Coustiers. Then he was given a final briefing by one of Passy's officers from Duke Street.

"You will go out on a Whitley," the major said, "and will be dropped near Tours. There will be a party at the drop to meet you and take you to a safe house. From there you will go by train to Paris. In Paris, with any luck, you will see Rex. You will be told how to cross into the unoccupied zone, and once there will proceed to Coustiers.

"In Coustiers, keep what you learn to yourself. There is no need

for one group to know what you have learned about the others. No
one can betray what he does not know, and only you and Rex will
have an overall view of the Resistance in your area. If you are
captured, I advise you to take one of these." He lifted the lid of a
small brown box and showed Bertrand some white pills which
looked like saccharine tablets. "Keep one of these in your pocket. It
does the trick in twenty or thirty seconds. Remember not to lick
your fingers after handling them. I know someone who did, and he
was sick for a week."

The Whitley took off at midnight and flew toward the south coast
and France. There was little conversation with the air crew over the
roar of the engines, but after they crossed the Channel the navigator
pointed down to the dark mass that was Bertrand's native land.

Every half hour or so after that, Bertrand looked down at the little
points of light of a French farm or village. Then, to his dismay, as they
flew farther inland, the little points of light became partially obscured
by wisps of mist, which at first he took to be condensation from the
engine, but which became thicker as they went farther until they
turned into banks of cloud.

"The weather's changing," the navigator shouted over the sound of
the engine.

Bertrand nodded and sat in silence for another half hour, peering
down with growing despair at the now impenetrable cloud.

"We're over target," the pilot shouted. "Can you see any lights?"

The navigator shook his head. "Not a glimmer."

"Can I jump blind?" Bertrand shouted.

Now the pilot shook his head. "Not on, old chap. I'm sorry."

"What do we do?"

"I'll make another run, but unless there's a hole in the cloud we'll
have to take you home."

The drone of the engines grew shriller as the plane circled to return
over the rendezvous, but the cloud was opaque and there was no sign
of their lights.

"The poor devils can hear us," said the navigator, "but it's no good
if we can't see them."

"Let me jump blind," said Bertrand emphatically, gripping the strap
of his parachute.

The pilot shook his head. "Sorry, old chap. Orders are orders, and orders are to bring you home."

They landed back at Tempsford at four in the morning. The same officer who had seen him off had been alerted by radio and was there to meet him, his eyes bleary after a sleepless night.

"Bad luck," he said to Bertrand.

"When can I go again?"

"Not for a while," he said. "All missions have been canceled."

"Why?"

"The Americans and the British have landed in North Africa. All officers are to stand by for a move to Algiers."

Exhausted, and torn by opposite emotions of disappointment and relief, Bertrand was driven back to Duke Street, where he changed out of the clothes of the engineer and back into his uniform as a Free French officer. The same car then took him on to his apartment in South Kensington.

There he let himself in quietly, hoping to slip into the bed with Jenny while she remained asleep, so that she would wake in the morning to find him at her side. He undressed in the bathroom, washed and brushed his teeth, then crept into the bedroom, which because of the blackout was still pitch-dark. He heard Jenny breathing—heavily now that she was pregnant—and whispered her name quietly so that if she was awake she would not be afraid. There was no answer. He groped for his pajamas under his pillow, but instead found his hand touching a stubbly chin.

A man's voice muttered, "Oh, God." For a moment Bertrand thought that he must have entered the wrong apartment, but when he stretched out his hand for the lamp he found it just where he had expected it to be, and when he switched it on, his bedroom was familiar, with everything just as he had left it, except for the naked body of Eddie Macleish lying next to his wife.

Chapter 9

1

WHEN the first statutes against the Jews were published by the government in Vichy, Charles Ravanel, the bishop of Langeais, was not unduly concerned. Indeed, he read with approval how Cardinal Gerlier in Lyons told the Jewish community in the city that their suffering should be seen as expiation for the calamities brought about by Léon Blum.

It was only some months later, when the French police, following new decrees, started to round up Jews in Paris, dragging them from their homes at four in the morning, confiscating their property, collecting them in the gymnasium at Japy and the Vélodrome d'Hiver before sending them on to an unknown fate at an unknown destination, that his conscience became troubled. In the spring of 1942 all the Jews in the occupied zone were ordered to wear the yellow star. In July a further hundred thousand Jews—men, women and children—were rounded up in Paris and sent to Drancy, where wives were separated from their husbands and children dragged from their parents' arms.

He heard, and applauded, the protests that the cardinals and archbishops of the occupied zone made to Marshal Pétain, but he feared that the Marshal had little influence over what happened in territory controlled by the Germans. Then to his horror the same roundup of Jews, carried out with the same brutality, started in the Free Zone.

In August a brother bishop, the archbishop of Toulouse, wrote an anguished denunciation of the horrifying scenes taking place in the camps in his diocese, which was read from the pulpit from every parish church. "There is a Christian morality," he wrote, "there is a human morality, which imposes rights and duties. These rights and duties belong to the nature of man. They come from God. One can violate them ... but no mortal man can suppress them. ... The Jews are men, the Jews are women . . . they form part of the human race; they are our brothers like so many others. A Christian cannot forget it."

Similar protests followed from the bishops of Montauban, Albi and Lyons, and Charles Ravanel thought and prayed hard before deciding what action he should take against this inhumanity toward the Jews. He too could write a letter and order his priests to read it from their pulpits; but since the protests by his brother bishops seemed to have had no effect, he thought it might be more prudent to try an indirect approach. He therefore instructed his secretary, Father Alifert, to ask for an interview with the prefect, Charrier.

Their meeting was arranged with great discretion. The bishop had no wish to embarrass Charrier by a public demonstration of his concern, and he entered the prefecture in Coustiers through a back door. His experience in the Curia had taught him that humility often mollified an adversary, and he was somewhat dismayed as he entered the prefect's office to see that Charrier was clearly in an exasperated mood.

"Ah, My Lord Bishop," he said in an ironic tone of voice. "Please sit down." He pointed to a chair, but then looked at his watch as if he had already decided how long the interview should last.

"I have come," said Charles Ravanel meekly, "upon a most painful mission—"

"Yes, the Jews," snapped Charrier. "Father Alifert told me that you were upset by the measures we have been obliged to take."

"It is appalling, Monsieur Charrier, that the agents of justice of the French nation should take innocent people from their homes, separate families—tear children from their mothers' arms—and herd them like cattle into wagons to send them we don't know where."

"It is an unfortunate necessity," said Charrier sharply.

"A necessity? No. Evil can never be a necessity."

"Perhaps not in a cloister," said Charrier acidly, "but in government we are constantly presented with a choice of evils."

"But what can be worse than what is happening to the Jews?" asked the bishop.

"What can be worse?" Charrier did not raise his voice, but his pent-up frustration had the effect of a shout. "You have no idea, Monsignor Ravanel, just what it is like to try to govern France under the heel of the Germans. We are like the little pig with the wolf at the door huffing and puffing at our house of straw. He huffs, he puffs, he bares his teeth, he licks his lips. They demand this, they demand that, and send oafish gauleiters like Sauckel to demand hundreds of thousands of our people to work in their factories. And if we do not comply? We become another Poland! Sauckel takes the place of Pétain, and they enslave not just a few Jews but millions of Frenchmen too!"

"But the Jews are Frenchmen," said the bishop of Langeais quietly.

"Ah, thank you, it's interesting that you should say so," said Charrier in a tone of exasperated irony, "because for centuries now it is precisely the Catholic Church that has told us to hate the Jews. It was Origen, was it not, who taught that all Jews for all time were guilty of deicide? It was your Church, I seem to remember, which first made the Jews wear the yellow star as a badge of shame. And in the sixteenth century, wasn't it a Council of the Church which first forced the Jews into ghettos, and forbade them to employ Christian servants, just as the Nazis do now? I tell you, Monsignor Ravanel, it comes as no surprise to me that the cruelest and most fanatic anti-Semites among the Nazis—Himmler, Heydrich and Hitler himself—all come from a Catholic culture, because for centuries now the Catholic Church has oppressed the Jews, denied the right of dissent and repudiated the rights of man."

"Undoubtedly," said the bishop with as much dignity as he could muster, "the Church must accept some responsibility for what has happened in the past, but now—"

"Now?" Charrier interrupted. "Now the government has no choice. We are reduced to a mathematical equation: the greatest happiness for the greatest number—or, more accurately, the least misery for the most. If a million Frenchmen can be saved at the cost of a hundred thousand Jews, then the Jews must go. That's all there is to it."

"That may pass as a justification in Vichy," said Charles Ravanel, "but it will not be enough at the gates of heaven."

"Then it is fortunate," said Charrier, "that I shall not need it because I shall not be there."

When the bishop and his secretary left the prefecture, the prefect's assistant apologized for his chief's ill humor. "He doesn't like what is going on," he said. "None of us do. We only want to avoid something worse."

In the train going back to Langeais—the bishop now had no fuel for his fine limousine—Charles Ravanel sat in silence, shaken by the diatribe of the prefect. For the first time he began to see how the injustice done to the Jews by the pagan Nazis could be blamed on the Christian tradition, and this alarmed him as much as the crime itself. He had a great affection for the Catholic Church, which he had served all his life—not just as an institution in whose temples and palaces he felt at home, but also as the mystical vehicle for man's salvation. Now he saw to his horror that if the evil perpetrated against the Jews was in the name of Marshal Pétain, then all those who supported the Marshal would be implicated too.

Some days later a secretary to the papal legate, Monsignor Tucci, an old friend from his days in the Curia, returning from Rome to Vichy, broke his journey in the bishop's palace of Langeais. It was a welcome opportunity for Charles Ravanel to bring up the questions which tormented him, and he was reassured when Monsignor Tucci told him that Marshal Pétain could not be blamed.

"I am quite sure," said the legate's secretary, "that the Marshal detests these measures as much as we do, but he is no longer a free agent. It is Monsieur Laval who holds the reins of power, and he is under constant pressure from Abetz in Paris."

"Could not the Marshal protest?"

"He has protested, but it makes no difference. He even offered to present himself as a hostage, but his colleagues wouldn't allow it. He is too valuable alive."

"It is an excruciating dilemma," said Charles Ravanel, "but these deportations . . ." He raised his hands in despair.

"And there is worse," said Monsignor Tucci darkly.

"Worse?"

The secretary to the legate drew closer to his friend and whispered, "What do you imagine happens to those wretches when they reach their destination?"

"Our brother of Montauban suggested that perhaps the Israelites were being sent to their death, but surely he exaggerated?"

"We are told," said Monsignor Tucci, "that there are camps in central Europe where these unfortunate people are exterminated."

Charles Ravanel turned pale. "But that is English propaganda."

"I fear not."

"But then the need to protest becomes more urgent!"

"Of course."

"Cannot the Holy Father condemn these barbarities?"

"He is in a most delicate position," said Monsignor Tucci with the assurance of a man fresh from Rome, "for if he appears to take sides against the Axis powers it could unleash the most fearful revenge, which would do nothing to save the Jews but merely ensure that German Catholics shared their fate."

"He could excommunicate Hitler."

"Pius V excommunicated Napoleon. What effect did that have?"

"None at all," the bishop conceded.

"Let me tell you what happened in Holland," said Monsignor Tucci. "Last July our Church, together with the Dutch Reformed Church, protested in a telegram to the Reichskommissar against the deportation of Dutch Jews, and said that they would publicize their protests if the deportations did not stop. The Reichskommissar replied that if these protests were made public, then all baptized Jews, who until then had been exempt, would be included in the deportations. The Reformed Church backed down. Our archbishop of Utrecht did not. He wrote a pastoral letter denouncing the deportations, whereupon the Germans arrested all the Catholic Jews and deported them to concentration camps. The baptized Protestants were left in peace."

The bishop of Langeais shook his head. "Even in the cloister, then, there is a choice of evils?"

"No," said Monsignor Tucci, "because evil is not only in what is done to men, but also in the disposition of those who do it, and though our two Christian leaders acted in different ways, each acted from conscience and so did good."

Before leaving Langeais for Vichy, Monsignor Tucci confided to Charles Ravanel that despite the risks involved, the Holy Father did intend to protest, on behalf of the whole Catholic Church, against the Nazi persecution of the Jews. "Listen to his Christmas broadcast," he said. "I think you will not be disappointed by what he says."

He also advised Charles Ravanel to have a rest. "You look exhausted," he said. "Your anguish is taking a toll on your health, and I daresay that you don't eat well."

"One cannot eat well when others are starving."

"You cannot help others if you are sick yourself. I strongly advise you to leave your diocese for a week or two. Take a holiday. Stay with your sister. Have some rest. Build up your health. You will need it, I think, in the months to come."

At the end of October, Charles Ravanel took Tucci's advice and went to stay at Saint Théodore, where there was peace, quiet and plenty of food. The repose was not as complete as the legate's secretary had imagined. The bishop saw at once that the war had left its mark on all the de Roujays. Although Edmond, as mayor of Pévier, went about his civic duties in his habitual manner, the bishop saw that his misgivings had demoralized him, and that Alice was saddened by the absence of her elder son and the fanaticism of the younger one. It was the change in Louis which shocked him most of all. His ebullience had gone. His eyes had sunk into his sockets, and though he had nothing to do he hardly slept at night, but pored over maps of the eastern front and listened on the hour to every radio bulletin to plot the positions of the different armies.

On the face of Hélène de Roujay the bishop saw the baffled look of a woman who cannot comprehend her husband's torment. One afternoon she took the bishop aside and begged him to persuade Louis that God had saved him to care for his family. The bishop tried, later that day, but only provoked from his nephew a long diatribe against the Soviets in the east and the Jews in the west.

"And what do they have in common, Uncle," he exclaimed with bloodshot eyes, "but their hatred for the Christian religion? The Jews crucified Jesus, after all, because he claimed to be their Messiah, and have done all they can over the ages to destroy his Church. Marx, Trotsky, Freud, Blum—they all have the same ambition to undermine our faith in Christ and destroy the nations which are the bastions of Christianity."

"But neither Churchill, Stalin nor Roosevelt is a Jew," said the bishop.

"But they are used by the Jews," said Louis, "and I am astonished that you cannot see it, Uncle."

"When it comes to the Israelites, my dear Louis, I think it is time we Catholics began to look at the beam in our own eye rather than the mote in theirs."

"Then let us agree to differ," said Louis, "and although I know you have never felt the same respect for me as you did for Bertrand, who went to fight for his cause, I trust you will allow me to fight for mine!"

It did not occur to Charles Ravanel that Louis had more in mind than taking sides in an argument over lunch. If he had done so he might have argued more vehemently against him, but since he had come to Saint Théodore for a rest, and since his mind was already burdened by his own conflict of conscience, he avoided any further discussion with his nephew—and also the reproachful eyes of the melancholy Hélène.

The bishop turned instead to the children, above all to Titine, who had now reached the age of ten. She was delighted by the visit of her great-uncle, partly because he was a bishop, partly because he was a Ravanel. As a little girl she had heard so many scraps of conversation which identified her father as a Ravanel too that she thought that by being with her great-uncle Charles she might absorb and study some of the qualities which she must share with her absent parent.

Thus by the third or fourth day of his visit it had become an established tradition for Titine and Titine alone to accompany the bishop on his afternoon stroll. Since exercise as well as rest was part of his regime, he took this walk seriously and went quite far afield. He was dressed on these occasions as informally as he ever was, in the simple garb of a priest, while Titine, fastidiously neat in her appearance, wore a skirt, jumper and brown tweed coat which Marthe had refashioned for her from one worn by Alice before the Great War.

On the last day of the bishop's visit they went off together into the bright cold air. The sun, low on the horizon, infused the landscape with a silver light. Already, when they set out, a dew had settled on the ground, giving a moist smell to the air and a glistening look to the tawny vegetation. They started as usual down the track to the river, but then, instead of continuing along the path around the vines which would have brought them back to Saint Théodore, they turned left and walked along the back of the river until they reached the small road which ran from Pévier to the Route Nationale.

There they might have retraced their steps, but since the afternoon was so fine and the bishop felt so invigorated by his week of country air, they decided to return by the village, and they set off for Pévier along the road. The bishop took wide steps under his soutane; Titine skipped along beside him, chattering all the time about her school, her homework, the pony, the dogs, and asking him every now and then what her father had been like as a boy.

"He was always the serious one, dear child," said the bishop, "and Louis was the joker."

"He doesn't joke much these days," said Titine.

"Alas, there isn't much to joke about."

"Is it true that people in the cities don't have enough to eat?"

"Yes, indeed."

"Do you think Papa has enough to eat?"

"In London, yes, I am sure he does."

"They have more food?"

"I believe so."

"When I go to see Maman, I take some food in a basket."

"Do you see her often?"

"Not now, no. Grandpapa says it would be dangerous."

"You must always love your mother," said the bishop.

"I do," said Titine without conviction.

"She too was always serious."

"Is that why they divorced?"

He laughed. "In a way."

"I think it must be best," said the girl, "if a serious person marries a joker, and a sad person a happy one."

"I agree."

"Why do bishops not marry?"

"Because they are priests."

"And why don't priests marry?"

"So that they can dedicate their lives to God."

"And nuns?"

"The same."

"I have an aunt who is a nun, and I have never seen her."

"I know. Your Aunt Dominique."

"Uncle Louis says that she spends her time singing, praying and digging vegetables."

"The singing and the praying are very important."

"Why?"

"Because God wants to know that we love him."

"But God knows everything, so he knows that we love him without us having to say so."

"Not everyone, alas, loves God, and even those who do are often distracted from their love by other things. By singing and praying, you see, your aunt is loving God, because words are thoughts and they reach up to heaven."

"And is that all God wants of us? A song and a prayer?"

"Ah no, my dear, he wants much more."

"What else?"

The light was fading. In the distance a cyclist approached along the narrow country road.

"He wants us to love our neighbor," said the bishop.

"Like the Astrans?"

"Yes, but also any fellow human being, especially those in trouble. Don't you remember the story in the Bible of the man who was robbed and left by the side of the road, and how he was helped by the Good Samaritan?"

"Yes." She sighed. "But there are so many sad people, and it is so difficult to know how to help them."

"Indeed," said the bishop. As he spoke, the bicycle came closer, and he saw that it was a *vélo-taxi* ridden by a sallow man of about thirty. Behind the bicycle on the passenger seat was a battered suitcase and, sitting on top of the suitcase, a boy four or five years old. The weight of the trailer and the child, and the slight incline in the road, demanded some effort from the bicyclist, who despite the coolness of the evening was sweating and gasping for air.

When the bicycle drew level with Titine and the bishop, the man looked shiftily at them, then down at the priest's cassock, then quickly away; but the child, who had the dark eyes, sallow skin and black hair of his father, stared at them as he rode past with tired, pitiful eyes.

In a moment they had passed. Titine looked around to watch them as they reached the top of the hill and then coasted down toward the river and the Route Nationale.

"Who were they, I wonder?" she asked her great-uncle.

"Poor Jews," said the bishop.

"Were they really Jews?" she asked. "How do you know?"

"You can tell," said the bishop.

"What were they doing here, I wonder?"

The bishop said nothing.

"Looking for food, perhaps," said the child in a matter-of-fact voice. "Monsieur Astran says that several people from the cities have come around looking for food."

"Yes," said the bishop. "For food, or for somewhere to stay."

"They could have stayed at Saint Théodore," said Titine, turning as if she might call them back.

"Too late, I am afraid," said the bishop, "but perhaps they will return."

Soon after the bishop returned to Langeais, on November 7, 1942, the Allies landed in North Africa, and a few days after that the Germans invaded the unoccupied zone of France. The Catholic college was requisitioned by the German army as its regimental headquarters. The bishop immediately decided to house the college in the episcopal palace, and moved himself into an upstairs room.

These dramatic and chaotic changes distracted him from the question of the Jews. It was not that he forgot them, but that his own flock was endangered now, and if the Pope himself was going to protest, anything the bishop of Langeais might say would be superfluous. Such were his thoughts as he stood at the altar of his cathedral celebrating the first mass of Christmas. It was an enchanting ceremony, with none of the horrors of the Passion that went with midnight mass at Easter, but only the charm and innocence of Christ's nativity. In particular, Charles Ravanel always loved the moment when, after distributing holy communion to the faithful, he would stand at the altar and conjure up in his mind the image of his Savior in the crib. He had been to the Holy Land; he could imagine the kind of cave where the Blessed Virgin must have given birth to the child. He thought of her always as his sister had been before she married, and Saint Joseph as the kindly gardener employed in their house in Valenciennes. And the child Jesus, of course, he saw as a smiling, gurgling, blue-eyed child like Bertrand or Louis when they were babies. But now, suddenly, as he conjured up this traditional image in his mind, the face which stared at him from the crib was not that of a smiling, blue-eyed baby but of the dark-eyed, frightened little Jew on the road from Pévier, clinging to his father's suitcase behind the bicycle.

The bishop uttered a cry and staggered back from the altar with Christ's words from the gospel of Saint Luke ringing in his ears: "If you do it to the least one of these, you do it to me." He stood paralyzed with horror at his own passivity. For a moment the deacons, subdeacons and other acolytes thought that he had suffered a stroke. They rushed forward to catch him, but the old man had not fallen. He simply stood for a moment staring into the middle distance at his vision of Christ as a Jew. Then, regaining possession of his senses, he remembered where he was, returned to the altar, and stumbled through the rest of the mass.

The next day the Pope broadcast from Rome. In his thin voice he told of his concern for "the hundreds of thousands who, through no fault of their own, and solely because of their nationality or race, have been condemned to death or progressive extinction," but there was no specific denunciation of the Germans or reference to the Jews.

"It is not enough," said Charles Ravanel to his secretary, Father Alifert, with the calm mien of a man who has finally decided what has to be done.

"No, Monsignor," said the cleric, astonished that the bishop should criticize the Pope.

"Words are not enough," Charles Ravanel went on. "It is by our deeds that they shall know us."

"Certainly, Monsignor."

"Christ was a Jew, Alifert."

"Yes, Monsignor."

"And so it is especially in each one of them that we should recognize his likeness. We must now do all we can to help them."

"But how?"

"I am told," said the bishop, crossing the room to a map of his diocese which hung on the wall, "that they are safe from the edicts in the Italian zone." He paused. "What shame that the godless followers of Mussolini should prove more humane than we French." He raised his hand and pointed at the map. "We can hide them here at Langeais in the Benedictine convent, or in the Hospital of Saint Sulpice. Then we can take them to the monks at Chambourg, and they can guide them over the mountains to the convent at Saint Brès." He turned back into the room. "We must start at once, Alifert, but confide only in those we can trust. There are still among us, alas, those who remain convinced that though Jesus may have been a Jew, God the Father is a Frenchman."

At Saint Théodore, Alice de Roujay heard the news of the American and British invasion of North Africa on the French service of the BBC.

She hurried to tell Edmond and Louis, who, though still reluctant to listen to broadcasts from London and always ready to dismiss what they heard as Allied propaganda, were driven by curiosity to tune the radio in the library to the forbidden wavelength. The next day they heard how the Germans had moved into the Free Zone, how the French army around Toulouse under General de Lattre de Tassigny had put up a token resistance, and how the French fleet in Toulon had been scuttled, on Darlan's orders, to prevent it from falling into German hands.

Four days later a detachment of the German army arrived at Pévier, and for the next five months its commander was billeted at Saint Théodore. Hauptmann Hildebrand was a plump middle-aged Bavarian who, far from demanding the *piano nobile* occupied by the de Roujays themselves, was content with two of the smaller spare rooms at the rear of the house. An old batman slept in one of the attics and served his master's meals in his own quarters.

On Christmas Eve, Hauptmann Hildebrand and two of his officers were seen at midnight mass in the parish church at Pévier, not in the front row of seats occupied by the de Roujays, but modestly in the rear. He was driven back in his staff car to Saint Théodore, while the de Roujays, who had no fuel, followed in their pony and trap.

They gathered with the children around the Christmas tree, lit the candles and prepared to open their presents. Titine, as always, had the largest pile, including a scarlet dressing gown "from Papa." Louis opened a bottle of champagne and filled glasses for his mother, father, Hélène and Marthe, the old servant. Then Edmond de Roujay said to his wife, "Perhaps we should ask the Hauptmann if he would like to join us?"

"But he is one of the enemy," said Alice.

"And are we not told to love our enemies?" asked Edmond.

He nodded to Louis, who went up the stairs and knocked on the door of the Hauptmann's room. It was opened by the batman to reveal the German officer, his tunic unbuttoned, sitting by a tiny fir tree on which he had stuck some homemade decorations. On the table was a single candle. In Hauptmann's hand was a half-empty glass of cognac, and there were tears on his plump cheeks.

"We would like to invite you downstairs," said Louis, "to take a glass of champagne with my parents."

It took a moment for the German to understand what had been said. The batman, however, who seemed to speak better French than his commander, explained what Louis had suggested.

"Yes, thank you, just a moment," said Hauptmann Hildebrand with a sniff. He stood and buttoned up his tunic.

At Louis's suggestion the batman came too, and a moment later all those staying under the roof of Edmond de Roujay were gathered around his tree singing Christmas carols in their native language. As they did so, the Hauptmann could not control his tears. His eldest son, he explained, was in the Sixth Army, surrounded by the Russians at Stalingrad, and his wife and children were in Cologne, which had recently been bombed by a thousand Allied planes. "This is a terrible war," he said, "and how will it end? How will it end?"

It was apparent to them all that the war had entered a decisive phase. It was not so much that the Americans were now established at one end of North Africa while Rommel was retreating from the English at the other, but rather that for the first time the Soviets seemed to have checked the advance of the Germans in the east. To both Edmond and Louis de Roujay, this was the critical front, for if the Russians could turn back the Germans there was no natural barrier to stop them from reaching France. They remembered what had happened after Napoleon's retreat from Moscow, when Cossack cavalry had ridden into Paris; but the Russians today were not commanded by the courteous Francophile officers from the court of Alexander I, but by the sinister commissars of the Third International, and they would come not to free the French of foreign occupation but to replace the German yoke with Bolshevik tyranny.

Alice de Roujay argued that the Americans and the British would reach France before the Russians, but to Louis—and to some extent Edmond too—their presence would not alter the outcome. To them the gangs of terrorists who called themselves the Resistance were merely the fifth column of the Third International, and the fact that the Allies armed and financed them proved that they had abandoned France as a sop to Stalin. When Alice suggested tentatively that there must be in the Resistance many like Bertrand who were implacably opposed to Communism, Louis asked, if that was the case, why had no shot been fired at the Germans in France until Russia had entered the war?

Alice de Roujay would not answer, partly because she still thought it wrong to argue against her husband's point of view, and partly because Louis became so agitated that she feared for the balance of his mind. She could see how his enforced idleness was poisoning his family life—how he saw too much of the placid Hélène and as a result had become intolerably irritated by her, and how he had lost faith in his own role as a man because he fought in no battles and did no work. She suspected that they no longer slept together; she could read the baffled look on Hélène's face.

Edmond too could see how this idleness and impotence at this critical time in history bored and frustrated his younger son. The crusader's conscience, which appeared to have descended through ten generations to both his sons, seemed to urge him on to some action. And the moment Edmond had dreaded came this Christmas, when after the Hauptmann had returned to his quarters and the women and children had gone to bed, Louis told his father that he planned to volunteer to fight on the German side.

"But the children . . ." murmured Edmond.

"I am not a nursemaid," said Louis at once as if he had been prepared for this objection. "And they do not need a father who at the most decisive moment in history stays at home to trim vines!"

It was two o'clock in the morning, and Louis had already drunk several glasses of champagne, but he opened another bottle and filled his father's glass. "Why, only yesterday," he went on, "my oldest asked me if he could join this *Milice* they mean to form in the New Year —Thierry, who is fifteen years old!"

"Did you forbid him?" asked Edmond.

"How could I forbid him to do what I know is right?"

"The Germans' dirty work . . ."

"Law and order is sometimes dirty work."

"With the Gestapo, certainly."

"I grant you, Papa, there may be some unsavory characters in the Gestapo, and they sometimes take harsh action against the terrorists, but they don't burn churches or murder priests or overthrow the social order that has existed in France since France began."

"I know, I know," said Edmond, "but sometimes I suspect that we judge these things too much from our point of view."

"From what other point of view should we judge them?"

"I don't know, I don't know." The old man shook his head. "If only we could discover what the good God thought about it all."

"He must want us to defend his Church," said Louis.

"Yes," said the colonel doubtfully, "but these deportations . . ."

"Only of Jews."

"But Jews are human beings, Louis, and to separate mothers from children . . ." He raised his hand in a gesture of horror.

"I agree," said Louis. "There are things done on our side which are wrong, even inhuman. But all the same, Papa, it *is* our side. The battle on the Don is not just for Fascism in Germany, but also for Christian civilization in the west. If the Russians overrun the Germans, they will not stop at the Elbe or the Rhine or the Rhône or the Pyrenees, and wherever the Red Army conquers, the homegrown Bolsheviks will creep out of the gutter and welcome them with open arms. They're waiting already in the Resistance, and when the Soviet tanks roll into Coustiers or Pévier, they are the ones who will take power. The collaboration of Laval and Doriot will be nothing compared to the collaboration of Thorez and Duclos, and they will destroy Christian civilization in France just as effectively as Lenin, Trotsky and Stalin have destroyed the Christian culture of Holy Russia!"

Edmond shook his head, not to signify that he disagreed with what Louis had said, but to express a general bafflement with the way things were turning out. "So you are determined to go?" he asked.

"It is my duty."

"Will you join the Legion of Volunteers?"

"Yes."

"If the Germans lose the war, you will never be able to return to France."

"And if they win the war, neither will Bertrand. So whichever way it goes, Papa, there will be one of us to look after you in your old age." And for the first time in many months Louis laughed, and then drained his glass of champagne.

2

When the Germans occupied Coustiers in November 1942, Oskar Lutze was appointed chief of the Gestapo by his patron, Kluge, who was SS and police leader for the region. Though there were some within the main office of Reich Security who thought that Lutze had only an opportunistic commitment to Nazi ideology, Kluge could point out that he was able, intelligent, spoke fluent French and already had a network of spies in the city.

Lutze immediately requisitioned the Hôtel de la Poste as his head-quarters and built up a staff of three hundred men, of whom only fifteen were fellow Germans. The rest were French—some fanatic collaborators from Doriot's Parti Populaire Français or Deloncle's Mouvement Social Révolutionnaire, others part-time members of the *milice* and the Service d'Ordre Légionnaire, but most of them thieves, felons, swindlers and would-be racketeers seconded to the Gestapo by the Burzios.

For the first time in his life, Lutze wore clothes which seemed to fit him—the smart black uniform and shiny boots of the SS. He also spoke and behaved as if convinced that the Germans were indeed a master race with the historic mission of cleansing the world of the Judeo-Masonic-Marxist-Cosmopolitans, who whether as Soviet com-missars or Wall Street bankers were out to corrupt the world with their materialist ideologies. The setback at Stalingrad in January 1943 did not appear to weaken his resolve. Like any disease, he told his subordinates, Bolshevism raged fiercest as it succumbed to the on-slaught of the healthy antibodies of the human race. It required only a core of dedicated Germans to marshal the resources of their faint-hearted allies and finish the enemy once and for all.

Lutze worked closely with Commissaire Guillot, but like the doubt-ers in the main office of Reich Security, Guillot was unconvinced by Lutze's pose as a dedicated Nazi. He spoke his lines too well, and played his role with a thespian detachment, as if the following season might bring a different play. Still, Guillot was too cautious to call Lutze's bluff. He knew it was an error ever to assume that a tongue is either in a cheek or out of it, because many men hold irony in reserve. He therefore accepted at face value Lutze's Nazi convictions.

To Guillot himself, Lutze's vision of society as a troop of athletes, marching in serried ranks with uniform clothes and faces toward a racial nirvana, was as fatuous as the Christian vision of a new Jerusalem or the Marxist rhetoric about a classless society. To him society was like an ants' nest which one could prod with a stick or poison with strychnine but never mold like sculptor's clay. Certainly Guillot disliked Jews as much as Lutze, but he loathed blacks and Arabs too, and his prejudice did not spring from any ideological conviction; it came from an animal aversion to any beast of a different breed. Guillot disliked Bertrand de Roujay quite as much as Pierre Moreau, and felt no affection for Lutze either, but circumstances dictated that he work with the German, because the paramount need for order meant that the devil of the day must be given his due.

But though Guillot cooperated with Lutze, their different convictions led them at times to work at cross-purposes. Lutze knew, for example, that the Jacopozzis were working hand in glove with certain sections of the Resistance and therefore planned to seize them in their known haunts on the west side of the river. He instigated such raids on the Bar Fénelon in January of 1943, but Guillot had warned the Jacopozzis, so the net drew in only minnows. Next Lutze sent squads at four in the morning to the houses of Stefano and Jaco Jacopozzi with orders to arrest the two men, but again Guillot had heard of the plan through the French auxiliaries who worked for the Gestapo, and when the doors were smashed open the houses were empty; the Jacopozzis had gone into hiding.

It was then that Lutze realized that nothing could be accomplished without Guillot. He therefore summoned him to his office at the Hôtel de la Poste and asked him point-blank why he had not arrested the Jacopozzis.

"It would not be prudent," said Guillot with his usual lack of expression.

"But they are criminals," said Lutze, his voice rising, "and it is quite clear from all interrogations that they form part of the group of terrorists that publish *Fortitude.*"

"I know the Jacopozzis, sir," said Guillot. "They follow their advantage, that is all."

"Follow their advantage? What advantage can they gain from helping the enemy?"

"Money," said Guillot simply.

"But that does not excuse it," said Lutze, "that they do it for money."

"It explains it," said Guillot.

"It does not explain to me why they are allowed to get away with it," said Lutze angrily.

Guillot was silent. His cunning lay in the manipulation of people, not words, and while he sensed that it would not be wise to explain to Lutze how the Jacopozzis were a necessary check on the power of the Burzios, he found it hard to conjure up another argument to defend his determination that the Jacopozzis be protected.

"You see," he mumbled to Lutze, "if we know that the Jacopozzis only follow their advantage, then, when the time comes, we can make it worth their while to hand over their friends in Fortitude on a plate."

Now it was the turn of Lutze to pause and ponder. "Yes," he said, "I can see some sense in that."

"For example," said Guillot, "if the Americans were to land here in Provence—"

"Impossible," Lutze interrupted.

"Of course," said Guillot, "but say they tried something, as the English did in Dieppe—that might be the moment to offer the Jacopozzis some incentive to turn in their friends in the Resistance."

Lutze looked at Guillot with the piercing stare of an *Übermensch,* but even this all-commanding glance, which he had copied from photographs of the Führer and had practiced many times in front of his bedroom mirror, failed to penetrate Guillot's expressionless gray eyes.

"If you are right," said Lutze, "then prove it to me."

"How?"

"Some small payment on account, which will not upset their friends but would satisfy me and my superiors that when the time comes they will sell to the highest bidder."

Guillot thought for a moment. "What have you in mind?"

"They have boats."

"Yes."

"Which smuggle spies and Jews to Algiers."

"Possibly," said Guillot.

"Not possibly, certainly!" shouted Lutze, exasperated by the commissaire's prevarication.

"Do you want them stopped?"

"No, not if it will jeopardize their standing. But every now and then perhaps a boat might be diverted and its cargo handed over to us."

"It might be arranged—at a price."

"The price doesn't matter. What I want to know is whether the Jacopozzis are willing to sell."

Though he played the role of an officer in the SS with some style and conviction, Lutze still retained certain modes of thought from previous performances—in particular his longing for the elusive French "countess" whom he had encountered so catastrophically seven years before at Saint Théodore. There were many attractive women in Coustiers, but those Lutze met were mostly demimondaines whom he could never introduce to the French wives of his colleague Dr. Rappert in Nantes and of the German ambassador, Otto Abetz. It was not until the spring of 1943 that Lutze met the embodiment of his romantic fantasy at a reception given at the Coustiers Chamber of Commerce. She was plump and past her prime, but she had beautiful blond hair, a pretty, sensuous face and, above all, an air of disdain for all the bourgeois around her.

"Who is that lady?" he asked his host as he entered the room.

"Madame le Fresne, the daughter of Emile Planchet."

"And where is Monsieur le Fresne?"

"They are divorced."

The host, the president of the Chamber of Commerce, was desperate for a permit to continue trading with Algiers. He was therefore delighted to satisfy the interest of the chief of the Gestapo by presenting him at once to Nellie le Fresne. He turned pale, however, when he realized that Nellie was drunk and heard her say in a loud voice, "Oh my God, a lousy Nazi." To his relief, however, Lutze only smiled, bowed and clicked his heels. Her disdain only confirmed that Nellie was just what he had been seeking.

"Is it against your principles, madame," he asked, "to drink with an officer of the occupying power?"

"A drink is never against my principles," said Nellie, whereupon Lutze flicked his fingers and a waiter came to fill their glasses with champagne.

It was an alluring evening for the German. The large nineteenth-century room, built by the merchants of Coustiers, was hardly the Hall of Mirrors at Versailles, but the liveried servants and low-cut gowns, the glitter of candlelight on glasses and jewels, came nearer to his fantasy than anything he had experienced before. There were other Germans among the guests, including officers of higher rank, but it was known that Lutze headed the Gestapo, and wherever he walked guests turned toward him, ready with fawning smiles. Only Nellie le Fresne behaved as if she despised him, and this, of course, brought Lutze back to her again and again.

"I wonder," he said as it grew late, "if you would do me the honor of dining with me one evening."

"Where?" she asked insolently. "In one of your torture chambers?"

Lutze smiled. "I can think of more congenial surroundings. The restaurant in Vieux Clocher, for example?"

"Typical of a tourist," said Nellie, "to choose a place like that." Her speech was slurred with drink.

"Perhaps you can recommend somewhere better?"

"Come to my house," she said. "The Villa Acacia. I'll see if I can buy a chicken on the black market."

The next morning Nellie le Fresne went to a small bookshop on the Rue Colbert. There, browsing among the secondhand books, stood Pierre. For a time they pretended not to notice one another. Nellie took out a volume, glanced at it, then put it back with an envelope containing banknotes concealed within its cover and moved away. A moment later Pierre took out the same volume, removed the envelope, and put it back. Then, since Nellie remained in the shop and he saw that they were alone, he came up to her and said, "Please thank your father."

"There's no need."

Pierre nodded as if acknowledging the Planchets' patriotism.

"I have something else for you," said Nellie.

"What?"

"You know Lutze?"

"Of course."

"He's coming to dine with me on Tuesday at eight."

Pierre raised his brows to register surprise. "A new friend?" he asked.

"A new admirer."

"Such good taste in a Nazi!"

She smiled. "Can you deal with him?"

"If you like."

"Preferably before dinner. It would save me an ordeal."

Pierre hesitated. As if they were being watched, he put a book back on the shelf and took out another. "You think we should assassinate him?"

"Yes," she said vehemently.

"It might be dangerous for you."

"I don't care."

"And it would lead to reprisals—terrible reprisals for a man of that rank."

She moved close to him and whispered, "But you need something like this, Pierre. It would show that Fortitude has a bite as well as a bark."

"I know," said Pierre, "but it might be infinitely more valuable to use Monsieur Lutze rather than kill him."

"Use him? How?"

"As a source of information."

She hesitated, then said, "You mean you want me to befriend him?"

"Is he a brute?"

"He is very, very vulgar. You should have seen him playing the gentleman!" She laughed. "I was unspeakably rude to him."

"He didn't mind?"

"He seemed to love it."

"If he came to love you . . ." Pierre began.

Nellie made the face of a seasick sailor.

Pierre blushed. "Of course, no one would expect you . . ."

"Ah," said Nellie, "it is a time to make sacrifices."

"Within limits," said Pierre.

"Without limits," said Nellie, returning the book she was holding to the bookshelf and kissing her friend goodbye. "I'll see what I can do if you promise . . ."

"What?"

"To put on my tomb, 'She fucked for France.' "

The dinner Nellie offered Oskar Lutze was as seductive as the clothes she had chosen for the evening. Not only was food sent in from her father's estates, but she was also rich enough to buy what she wanted on the black market, and she had a cellar of wine still largely intact from before the war. When Lutze arrived he was offered a glass of champagne which, having sampled many plundered cellars since the war began, he realized at once was one of the finest in France. Nellie's servants, who were all members of the Resistance, greeted the German officer with a grave formality and invited his driver and escort to supper in the kitchen.

Lutze was overwhelmed. Though he had long since graduated from rented rooms and SS barracks to the looted splendor of French chateaux, and now the prime suite at the Hôtel de la Poste, he sensed at once that the Villa Acacia was the acme of comfort and taste. The fabric of the furnishing had been chosen for both color and texture, so that when he sat on the deep beige sofa it was as if it were a background for an artist to paint in its center the strong black figure of a handsome man.

But nothing in the house equaled Nellie herself, who had prepared her appearance with meticulous care. She had soaked her body in a hot bath laced with sweet-smelling oil, then had sat at her dressing table looking vacantly at her reflection in the looking glass while she brushed her fair hair. After that she had made up her face, a delicate enterprise lasting almost an hour which succeeded in subtly heightening her color and camouflaging the wrinkles around her mouth and eyes. Only then, when she was ready above the neck, did she take off her dressing gown and put on the white lace underclothes which held her hips and breasts in place and then the loose dress of red silk which had been cut by a skilled couturier to show what was best and hide what was worst in her fattening, middle-aged figure.

While Nellie was brushing her hair and staring at her own reflection, a faint smile came onto the corner of her mouth as a voice within accused her of taking a certain pleasure in playing the role of Mata Hari for the Resistance. Since her divorce from Michel le Fresne, Nellie had slept with many men, none of whom she had loved, few of whom she had thought she loved, and many of whom she had consciously despised. Her desires had become detached from her affections, and it was only the innocent Pierre who could imagine that to sleep with a German would be a sacrifice equal to death itself. She did not like the Germans, but she felt a certain curiosity, which amounted to a species of lust, to see the Sturmbannführer without his breeches. However drunk she became, and however apparently uncontrolled, Nellie always watched the antics of her lovers with a cold inner eye. To her, naked men were an absurd and pitiful sight, and in planning the seduction of Lutze she envisaged not her dishonor but his humiliation.

The evening began well, because both were animated by the adrenaline which always stimulates actors on their first night. They also became quickly drunk, first on the champagne, then on an equally notable bordeaux. Nellie laughed as she drank, amused by the banality of their stilted conversation and amazed at the success of her counterfeit role. She continued to tease Lutze with a patrician disdain, but because she laughed and pampered him at her servants' hands with first a *feuilleté* of sweetbreads, then a *gigot* of lamb, he imagined that he amused her and that her offhand manner was a form of perverse flirtation.

Having served a sorbet, the servants withdrew, leaving a pot of coffee by the fire which gave off the rare and exquisite aroma of the real thing. Nellie came from the table to fill two white cups, then sat on the carpeted floor. Lutze sat back in an armchair, his shining black boots only inches from the plump pink skin of Nellie's shoulders and bosom. He had a glass of brandy, pale with age and distinction, which he sipped along with his coffee. A log fell from the fire and rolled toward the carpet. Lutze stood and kicked it back into the grate, then turned and stood above her. She looked up and smiled.

"Come on, then," she said, holding up her hand.

He knelt, and started to bombard her with kisses, as lovers do in sentimental films. First her hands, her arms, her neck were treated to the touch of his thick Teutonic lips; then suddenly, with breathless exclamations about his love and her beauty, he clasped her in his arms and crushed her mouth against his.

"Steady," she said with a low laugh. "Steady. There's no hurry."

Lutze kissed her lips and neck again, then with a moan plunged his face into the cleft between her breasts.

"Steady," Nellie said again, but in a more languorous voice. "What's the hurry, my little Fritz, what's the hurry?" As she spoke her arms began to wander over the hard black boots and breeches, sampling the strong thighs and feeling for the buckle of his belt.

Outside Coustiers, to the west, was a small suburb called the Hameau de Braulhet, where in the 1860s and 1870s some of the merchants of the city had built large villas in which to live in comfort and demonstrate their wealth. Toward the end of the nineteenth century, however, when the railway had been built close to the village, it had attracted new industry to the west of the city, including the Planchets' textile mills and, after the First World War, the petrochemical works at Castelnau.

To escape as far as they could from the grime which gave them their money, the bourgeois of Coustiers deserted the Hameau de Braulhet for the wooded hills to the north and east. Their villas were left to crumble; their railings rusted, the gardens became overgrown. Most of them remained in this condition, one serving as a barracks for the immigrants who worked in the factories, another as a warehouse for gravestones and memorials which were imported from Carrara and stacked in the garden until carved and polished in the house itself.

Behind these derelict houses, set back from the road at the end of a long drive, was one large villa which showed signs of human habitation. The tall wall around the property was in good order, and the wrought-iron gates were painted. The points on these gates were sharp, and the hinges were oiled. Night and day two men were at hand to open them whenever a car approached, and close them afterward when the car had passed through.

The garden of the Villa Fleurie also showed signs of being tended. There was no water in the fountain, weeds still grew over the gravel paths, and the five or six men who wandered around its perimeter were never seen to busy themselves with rakes and hoes, but a terrace in front of the house had been cleared, flowers grew in pots on the balustrades, and when the sun came out in the summer of 1943 a small child a year old could be seen toddling over the lichen-covered paving stones.

This boy was Antonio Jacopozzi, and the woman who watched him from a straw chair placed beneath a parasol was his mother, Isabelle. She observed him and at the same time read a book hidden in a fold of her skirt. Her large brown eyes followed the words to the bottom of a page, then were raised to see that the boy was safe. There was no expression of anxiety as she looked at her son, but there was always a flicker of apprehension if she looked beyond him toward the gate.

Isabelle had changed since bearing a child. She had lost the wiriness of an adolescent girl—her figure was almost plump—and her formerly impudent face now had a natural expression of gentle melancholy. Unlike most other women in France at this time, she showed no sign of famine or bad diet. Her skin was smooth and brown, her hair bright and strong. Nor were her clothes shabby and worn; they were more elegantly cut and brightly colored than any she had worn before.

All that she had become stemmed from her marriage to Jaco Jacopozzi. When they had returned from their honeymoon in Corsica she had imagined that she would begin teaching again at the Lycée René le Bon, but when it was discovered that she was pregnant she had accepted Jaco's strict injunction that she must give up her work and remain at home.

At this time she was still so deeply in love with her "Napoleon" that any admonition was accepted with a dazed delight. Having been a rebel toward her parents in her childhood home, she was now as obedient and devoted to her husband as Shakespeare's tamed shrew. Though she hankered after the excitement of work in the Resistance, and felt embarrassed that she lived in such comfort and luxury amid the suffering of the general population, she accepted her position as proper for that of Jaco Jacopozzi's wife. Even Jaco's mother and sister, who now lived with her at the Villa Fleurie, treated her like a princess. She was not allowed to cook or clean, and had only to step out of her clothes to have them whisked away, washed, ironed and returned fragrant and clean to her wardrobe. The baby, Tonio, once he was born, was whisked away in the same manner; she had never once had to change his diapers.

At first Isabelle had accepted this service as if she were indeed the Empress Josephine, because it seemed to make her husband happy and was a marked contrast to her previous life, but even before the child was born, her idleness had made her bored—a boredom that was exacerbated by the move to the Villa Fleurie.

It was not just that she had nothing to do, but also that she had no one to talk to. Her mother-in-law and sister-in-law and her husband's aunts were all women of good heart but little culture whose animated jabber in Corsican dialect was all gossip about their friends in Pervaccio. The men's activities were forbidden as a topic of conversation, and when Isabelle tried to engage them on subjects such as the war or the German occupation, they came out with some irrelevant banality. Once when Isabelle had asked her mother-in-law whether she thought Bismarck or Nietzsche bore a greater responsibility for German aggression, the old woman answered that the Germans were aggressive because they were constipated, and they were constipated because they did not use olive oil.

At first Isabelle was amused by life among such different people, and she conceived a real liking for the family she had married into—all, that is, except Stefano Jacopozzi, who was and always would be an oaf. In time, however, their company palled and Isabelle grew restless. With the baby growing in her belly she felt claustrophobic, and before the move to the Villa Fleurie she escaped more and more often to visit her father and mother. This Jaco could hardly forbid, but he insisted that Isabelle always go there with an escort of two of his men, who waited for her in the street.

Her parents, who were now old, had been shaken by what had happened in France—not only by public events like the defeat and the German occupation, but also by the changes it had effected first in their son and now in their daughter. They were baffled by her love for a gangster, and while grateful for the food she brought when she called, they suffered at the thought of how and where it had been obtained. They had never practiced the external observances of the Jewish religion, but they still respected the Law of Moses in their hearts, and the affluence and elegance of their daughter, which she almost flaunted in those first months as if to show that she was now grown-up, pained them because of its criminal provenance.

The old Moreaus never called on the other Jacopozzis, and the other Jacopozzis never called on the old Moreaus. During the first year of his marriage, Jaco behaved correctly, but it was apparent that he was embarrassed by the bohemian old couple in their dark apartment with books stacked to the ceiling and fine old furniture on threadbare carpets. It did not occur to him to connect the culture which he admired in his wife with the unworldly shabbiness of her parents' flat. Indeed, the culture itself seemed less admirable when studied close at hand. Jaco was as little able to compare Bismarck and Nietzsche as were his mother and sister, and as Isabelle became bored, and complained to him about his family's limitations, he inevitably felt that her strictures must also apply to him. In any case, he was ill at ease with women,

and though he supposedly revered his mother and sister he spoke to
them only about the logistics of the household. Since Isabelle did not
cook or clean, this subject was closed to them. When alone, they were
often at a loss for a topic of conversation. He sensed that she was bored
in his presence; he became ashamed of his lack of education and tried
to conceal this shame by belittling the very erudition he had once seen
as his wife's greatest accomplishment.

The intellectual incompatibility of Jaco and Isabelle might not have
mattered if the sexual bond between them had remained strong, but
here again the prejudices of the bridegroom turned small difficulties
that are encountered by any married couple into a fatal crisis. On their
honeymoon in Corsica, Isabelle had been overwhelmed by the emotion
rather than the sensation of their first encounters, but as time had passed
and her sensual nature had been drawn out of her, she had responded
with increasing fervor to his caresses. At first Jaco had been flattered
by the passion he aroused, but the greater her enthusiasm, the further
she grew from the chaste madonna whom he respected and the closer
to the whores whom he despised. He became astonished, then intimidated, by the power and impetuousness of Isabelle's physical
desires. At times he became almost repelled by her candid lusts; particularly when she became pregnant, and he became conscious of the child
in her belly, he began to think of excuses for avoiding what to her
was the sole consolation for an otherwise tedious day.

Then, suddenly, their roles were reversed. The child was born,
Isabelle regained her figure, and Jaco was drawn to her once again, but
now it was Isabelle who was indifferent. So absorbed was she in the
tiny creature sucking at her breast that the man who had engendered
it seemed superfluous. She did not consciously reject him but reacted
to his advances with a bored surprise, as if astonished that he should
want to make love to her now that a child had been born.

To be endured, not enjoyed, is the sad lot of many husbands at
certain phases of their lives, but few were as proud or jealous as Jaco
Jacopozzi. If his wife did not want him, then there were other women
who did. He took a girl from among the sluts in the bar and returned
home late at night, hoping to inspire passion in his wife by making
her jealous. Absorbed with the baby, Isabelle hardly noticed that he no
longer made love to her. If he was silent and remote in her presence,
she assumed that it was because he was preoccupied with his complica-

ted life in the Resistance and as a racketeer. He never talked to her about business—not even, since she had become his wife, about his services for her brother. All they had in common, therefore, was the child, and that, for the time being, was enough.

But Jaco remembered how Isabelle had loved him before, and without the experience or perception to know how the birth of a child can affect a woman's libido, he became tormented with the thought that like an underground river it would surface in the arms of another man. He was too proud to voice his suspicions; he knew, moreover, that Isabelle had no opportunity to see anyone but his family and the men who guarded the house. First he became suspicious of them, and made sure that only the old and ugly were given this particular duty. Then, when he realized that Isabelle would never deign to address the hoodlums who protected her, he became jealous of the men whom he was convinced she loved in her fantasies.

Unaware of what was going on in her husband's mind, Isabelle took his moodiness as part of his Corsican character. Even before the baby was born she had begun to suspect that the real Napoleon had perhaps possessed certain qualities that Jaco Jacopozzi lacked; and while she encouraged his ambition—in the sense that she urged him to devote himself to the struggle against Vichy and the Germans—she quickly realized that he had no more understanding of the great issues involved than his mother, who explained the war by a lack of olive oil in the German diet.

This life of mutual incomprehension might have continued happily enough had not the Germans occupied the zone. It then quickly became apparent that the phony war between the police and the Burzios on the one hand and the Jacopozzis on the other would be changed into a real one by the heavy hand of the Gestapo. Word reached the Jacopozzis that their haunts by the river were no longer safe. They therefore moved out to the Villa Fleurie, where mother, sister and aunts lived in the house and a dozen men slept in the servants' quarters. It was an armed camp where they were reasonably safe, but for Isabelle it became a prison. Jaco left strict orders that no one was to go out without his permission, and when she asked for this permission it was always refused. He would say that it was too dangerous, that he could not spare the men to escort her, that they were engaged on more important business for her brother.

By the summer, when Isabelle sat under the parasol watching Tonio on the terrace, her isolation had become acute. She was driven mad not only by the Jacopozzi women, but now also by the incessant demands of her son. The sweet, sucking baby had become an exacting tyrant, an uncontrolled replica of his father. He constantly insisted upon his mother's attention, and became enraged if he caught her reading a book, which was why she had to hide it in the folds of her skirt.

Now, as he tottered around the terrace, Isabelle heard a car draw up at the gates and saw them open. The black Citroën which Jaco always used proceeded up the drive to the house. She did not move; she no longer stood to greet her husband. She knew that in due course he would come out onto the terrace, would crouch and kiss the child, would then stand and turn with the smile fading from his face to fix her with his kestrel eyes.

It happened as she expected, but on this afternoon as he turned toward her she said, in an emphatic voice which trembled all the same with a certain nervousness, "Jaco, I must talk to you."

"Later."

"No. You always say later."

"There are always things to do. Stefano is waiting."

"Please."

"Tonight."

"You are never here at night."

"I work at night."

"Then please talk to me now."

He remained standing but looked down at her flushed face with an expression of wretchedly mingled emotions.

"Very well. Be quick." He went to the stone balustrade which ran along the terrace and rested his body against it.

"I want to go to Coustiers," she said.

"Impossible."

"Then bring Pierre out here."

"No."

"Why not?"

"No one must know about the villa who does not need to know. That is the rule."

"But surely it is necessary for him to see his sister?"

"He has news of you from me."

"Doesn't he ask to see me?"

"He knows it would be dangerous."

"But I want to see him, and my mother and father."

He paused. "They are leaving Coustiers."

"Leaving?"

"They are hunting down all the Jews."

"The Germans?"

"Yes. Now you see why it is dangerous."

"But where are they going?"

"To Algiers. Your brother asked me to arrange it."

"Is he going?"

"No, but he is sending his wife and children."

"Bérénice and Turco? But I must see them, I must, and perhaps . . ." She hesitated, then blushed.

"Perhaps?"

"Perhaps if it's so dangerous Tonio and I should go with them."

"On a boatload of Jews?" He spoke contemptuously.

"I am a Jew," Isabelle said.

"Not anymore. You are a Jacopozzi."

"But here, Jaco, really, I cannot bear it."

"You cannot bear it?" He snorted. "Here you have everything— butter, coffee, bread, meat . . ."

"Oh, Jaco!" She stood, crossed to him and put her arms on his shoulders. "I know how lucky I am, and how kind you are to me, but I need my family and friends."

He brushed off her embrace. "You have my family," he said.

"I know." She spoke delicately. "And I love them as your family, as I love you, but I would dearly like to see my own family, and some of my old friends."

"What friends?"

"Oh, no one in particular. But when I was at the lycée or at the university, there were people who shared my interests . . ."

"Men?"

"Some of them men, some of them women."

His eyes contracted as if light had dilated the pupils. "Men like that friend of your brother's, Guy Serot?"

"Guy was one of them."

"Would you like to see him?"

"Among others."

"Why do you want to see him?"

"To talk."

"You can talk to me."

"To hear what is going on."

"I tell you what is going on."

"You don't," she said, despair and exasperation entering her voice. "You don't tell me anything at all."

"You aren't interested when I tell you."

"I am."

"Because you think me a fool."

"I don't."

"Well, I am not such a fool that I'll let you loose in a city swarming with Germans, and see you shipped off in a cattle truck with a child that is my son."

"Oh Jaco, please . . ." She was weeping.

"Stop crying. Think of Tonio."

"Oh, damn Tonio."

He raised his hand to strike her. She flinched. The hand remained hovering in the air. Then Jaco turned, took Tonio in his arms and carried him into the house.

Leaving his son with his mother and his wife in tears, Jaco returned to Coustiers. His black Citroën sped in the fading light along the Avenue Marengo before turning down past the abattoir to the industrial zone of Castelnau. There it crossed the railway line which ran from the freight station to the wharves by the canal and stopped outside an isolated café. This unnamed bar which stood at the entrance to one of the factories now served as his new headquarters. It was deep in Jacopozzi territory and was protected by a network of lookouts and informers to warn of the arrival of the *milice* or the Gestapo.

Here Jaco sat down in the back room with Stefano and two or three of his gang, among them Angelo Bartelli, the wrinkled captain of the Jacopozzis' felucca. He had been a friend of the Jacopozzis' father, and was perhaps the only one who saw through Jaco's brooding bravado to his present confused state of mind. It was he who had told Jaco of the grumbling among his followers at his links with the Resistance, warning him on his return from his last run to Algiers how the discontent had spread. He was devoted to Jaco but he also feared him, knowing that it was his ruthlessness as well as his cunning which had made him the leader of their criminal confederation.

Certainly before the war the Jacopozzis had dabbled in politics, providing bodyguards for Socialist politicians and trade unionists and disrupting the meetings of the right-wing parties which patronized the Burzios, but in those days politics had been just another racket, with palpable gains for the friends of the party in power. Now, though there was money to be had from the Resistance, the risk was disproportionate to the gain, and Stefano had voiced the opinion that the Fortitude connection should be abandoned.

What old Angelo perceived in Jaco was that he alone was drawn to these idealists. He had watched him with the magistrate, Pierre Moreau, and the young lawyer, Serot. He had caught the same look of proud longing to be accepted by those above him that the six-year-old Jaco had shown in the company of his father. He seemed to be both perplexed and impressed by this group who risked their lives to stick posters on walls; and while to Stefano this only confirmed that education made men fools, Jaco had an inkling that from it came a superior understanding of what was important in life.

Jaco had hoped, Angelo supposed, that by marrying the magistrate's sister he would instantly possess this secret, but now he had come to realize that possession of a body does not necessarily deliver the soul, and that far from understanding through Isabelle the mysteries of culture and learning, he had only discovered that they would always be out of his reach.

Stefano joked and gossiped while Jaco sat in silence. Through the bead curtain which separated the room where they were sitting from the back of the bar in the café they could hear the hubbub of voices as the day shift ended and thirsty workers filed in. Then the barman put his head through the curtain and said, "Jaco, there's someone for you."

"Who?"

The man looked confused. "I don't know. It could be the commissaire."

Stefano reached toward the gun in his pocket, but Jaco laid his hand on his brother's arm to caution him. He was suddenly tense, his hackles rising like those of a dog. The adrenaline in his blood washed out all gloomy confusion as he exchanged the clumsy thoughts of a human being for the sharp instincts of a beast.

"Is he alone?" he asked the barman.

"I can't see anyone else."

Stefano tried to draw his gun. "Let's shoot our way out."

"No," said Jaco. "Guillot isn't here to take us in."

"Why else?"

"I don't know, but if he wanted to arrest us he would have let the Germans do it for him." Slowly, with his hand still held out to calm his brother, Jaco got to his feet, crossed to the bead curtain and peered through into the bar; there stood the seedy, nonchalant commissioner of police.

"Yes, it's him," said Jaco. He stepped back and went toward the door which led into the café. Stefano rose as if to accompany him.

"No," said Jaco. "I'll go alone."

Such was the authority of the younger brother that the older one obeyed him.

The café was smoky and crowded. None of the factory workers with their glasses of pastis and beer seemed to notice that the shabby man at the bar was a policeman. Jaco was known to them, and when he entered one or two stepped aside or looked away, but Jaco barely noticed the deference paid to him, because his eyes were on the broad shoulders of Guillot at the bar. A quick look around the room told him that there were no other policemen present, so he came up beside the commissaire and without a word stood next to him.

"We must talk," said Guillot sharply.

"Come inside," said Jaco.

"I would prefer to go outside."

Jaco darted a quick, suspicious look at the commissaire.

"It's still warm," said Guillot.

"Perhaps too warm."

Guillot laughed. "Bring your infantry if you like." He held out his arms as if asking to be frisked. "I'm clean, and outside there isn't even a car with a driver."

"It's unusual," said Jaco ironically, "for the commissaire to travel alone."

"But you see, Jaco, I am followed these days, and I didn't want to lead the Gestapo to your new lair."

Jaco was convinced. "Very well, then," he said. "Let's take some air."

They walked out onto the cobbles and away from the café along the wire-mesh fence which surrounded the factory. Guillot said nothing until they reached the end of this fence. Then he stopped and raised his foot onto one of the huge steel bollards which grew like mushrooms from the concrete on the edge of the canal. He drew a packet of cigarettes from his trouser pocket, lit one while resting his elbow on his knee, then flicked the match down past the tarred timbers which lined the sides above the oily water.

"You don't smoke?" he said to Jaco, as if to show that he had not been impolite in not offering him a cigarette and at the same time to confirm that he was familiar with his habits.

"No."

Guillot drew in the smoke of his cigarette. "I'm here because things are getting tricky," he said.

Jaco said nothing.

"The Germans are like jokers in the pack."

"Dealt in your hand."

"Yes, but I can tell you they don't make my life easy."

"No."

"That raid on the Fénelon, for example . . ."

"Yes."

"You got word?"

"Yes."

"I sent it."

"Should I thank you?" asked Jaco ironically.

"No. I do nothing for nothing."

"What do you want?"

"A little order, that's all."

"How can I help?"

"Your friends in the Resistance . . ."

"What about them?"

"Do they pay well?"

"Not as well as the Germans, but . . ." He shrugged his shoulders. "It's better than nothing."

"Yes," said Guillot, "and perhaps a shrewd investment in the future."

"You think so?"

"Yes."

"The Germans will lose?"

"In the end."

Jaco smiled. "Then others will go down with them."

"Certainly."

"My condolences," said Jaco.

"Save your sympathy," said Guillot. "It's some time away."

"I can wait."

"I am sure you can, but the Germans are impatient."

"For what?"

"You."

Jaco laughed. "They don't like me?"

"They don't like your friends."

"What friends?"

"Perhaps I should have said your relations."

Jaco blushed. "I'm a businessman, Commissaire. I do business, that's all—sometimes with friends, sometimes with relations, and sometimes with people who are neither."

"That's what I told them. You're a businessman. But they want to be convinced."

"Convinced of what?"

"That you're not in it for honor or glory or any shit like that."

Jaco frowned. "What do you take me for?"

"It's not what I take you for that matters."

"Then tell them."

"I have, but they want some sign of . . . goodwill."

Jaco cocked his head like a chicken. "And then?"

Guillot shrugged. "If they know you'll do business if the price is right, they'll leave you alone until they're ready to make an offer."

"But they want something on account?"

"Yes."

"What?"

"Your felucca . . . how often does it sail for Algiers?"

Jaco grinned. "If I had a felucca, it would go every ten days or two weeks."

"With a cargo of Jews?"

"With any cargo that pays."

"Cargoes are sometimes lost at sea."

"It gives the shipper a bad name."

"Only if it's known."

"They want me to drown some Jews?"

Guillot smiled. "No. They like doing that themselves. They want them handed over."

Jaco paused to consider. "If no one ever gets to Algiers, then the game will be up before it's started."

"They'll let some through if you make them a present of others."

"Every other trip?"

"Not even that. One in three should do."

Jaco hesitated, but only for a moment. "All right," he said. "Why not? They're only yids. And what do I owe them, anyway?"

3

In early March of 1943, General de Gaulle's plenipotentiary in France, Jean Moulin, arrived for his third and final visit to Coustiers. He departed two days later, disguised as a peasant on a horse and cart, leaving behind him a unified Committee of Liberation representing the different factions of the Resistance.

His task had not been easy, because despite a desire among the rank and file for a unified command, there had been great reluctance among the leaders of the different organizations in Coustiers to place themselves under the authority of General de Gaulle and the National Committee in London. The Communists in the Francs-Tireurs et Partisans, led in the department of Basse-Provence by Georges Auget, saw de Gaulle as Churchill's stooge, and they cooperated with him only because they were ordered to do so from Moscow; and the Communists themselves were mistrusted by the two army groups— one under Captain Ledésert (Platane), which had been active since the armistice, the other led by Colonel Bax (Homard), which had come into being only when the Germans had invaded the unoccupied zone and had dissolved the armistice army.

Ledésert in particular was angry that the contacts he had already made with the American OSS would have to be terminated, while the Communist FTP would almost certainly keep theirs with Moscow and, had it been the Russians rather that the Germans who had occupied France, would have collaborated in the same way as the *milice*. He was persuaded by Moulin, however, that it was only if the French Resistance was united under de Gaulle that the Allies would recognize his National Committee as an embryonic administration of France. The outcome of the war was not in doubt, but the future of France was entirely uncertain. If she was divided at her liberation, others would certainly rule.

Pierre Moreau also mistrusted the Communists, but he had his differences with Ledésert too. He disapproved of the funds the captain received from the OSS, and he disagreed with Ledésert's view that the only useful work the Resistance could do was gather intelligence for use by the Allied armies. For Pierre and his followers, who came largely from academic circles and the professions, the struggle was not so much to defeat the German army—the Allies would see to that— as to rouse the French people from their craven defeatism. They should do this, however, by propaganda and persuasion and avoid dramatic attacks and assassinations, which made no difference to the final outcome of the war but led inevitably to such sanguinary reprisals as the destruction of the Vieux Port in Marseilles, and the deportation of its twenty thousand inhabitants to concentration camps.

It was the Communists, under George Auget and Michel le Fresne, who insisted that the Resistance should strike at the Germans whenever the opportunity arose. It did not matter that for every German they killed, ten Frenchmen were shot in reprisal, because the horror and indignation such brutality inspired brought a hundred recruits into their ranks. The more savage the assaults on the occupying power, the more the Francs-Tireurs et Partisans would be seen as the leading faction in the Resistance, so that at the liberation they would be well placed for the seizure of power.

Le Fresne, in particular, considered that the liberation of France would provide a historic opportunity to achieve a proletarian revolution. The bourgeoisie, he argued, had been compromised and demoralized by Pétain's policy of collaboration. Even the Socialists had been compromised; Blum himself had voted for Pétain. Moreover, as long as the British and Americans hovered on the edges of the war in

Europe, it was the Soviet soldiers in the east who took the credit for the defeat of the German army. Their prestige cast a glow of reflected glory on the Communist partisans, and many a brave comrade was inspired to take horrifying risks to harass the Germans by the thought of Russian tanks at the prefecture in Coustiers.

Georges Auget was less certain that events would develop as Michel le Fresne supposed. In Moscow, Thorez had issued no order for a general insurrection, and it seemed to Auget more likely that it would be the English and the Americans who would drive the Germans out of France. He was willing, however, to prepare to take advantage of the political vacuum that would arise between the departure of the Teutons and the arrival of the Anglo-Saxons, and would perhaps present the Allies with a *fait accompli* of Communist power which they could reverse only by force.

To this end Auget decided to broaden the appeal of the National Front, the political wing of the FTP, by recruiting sympathizers from outside the Party. An eminent professor of law at the university of Coustiers, who had had no difficulty in swearing loyalty to Marshal Pétain in 1941 but now saw a way to become rector at the liberation, was co-opted onto the National Committee; so too was a former Radical mayor of the city who as a Freemason had lain low in the early years of the war but was now inspired by the prospect of an Allied victory to revive his ambition to be a government minister. Auget also looked for a Catholic priest, but since the Church was still implacably opposed to Communism, and since it was widely known that the National Front was a Communist organization, this presented some difficulty. It was only in the summer of 1943 that he heard of the Dominican friar Antoine Dubec, who at the armistice had exchanged his friar's robes for the blue overalls of a factory worker.

In search, as always, for a role that would bring some dramatic accomplishment to his life as a member of his celebrated preaching order, Antoine had now been working in a textile factory for two years beside tough and often brutal men, not just sharing their working lives but living with the poorest among them during the week in squalid lodgings in Castelnau. He had not preached to them in the canteen, nor had he said mass at the factory gates, but had quietly let it be known that he was a priest and that he was there if they needed him. Every Friday night he took a bus into the center of the city to the Dominican monastery on the Rue de la Paix, for it was a condition imposed by his prior that he return each weekend to his conventional duties as a priest, hearing confessions in church on Saturday morning and saying mass with his brothers on Sunday.

Antoine accepted these obligations with suppressed impatience; the petty sins of old ladies seemed of no significance beside the gigantic evils of social injustice, and the peace, spaciousness, cleanliness and scholarly atmosphere in the monastery itself offended him. He thought that priests had no right to live in comfortable seclusion while the poor struggled in cramped squalor.

Antoine's early experience in the factory had been disappointing. He had been prepared for persecution by those who resented his choice of a life which had been imposed upon them by circumstance, but perhaps because he was tough and swarthy in appearance and spoke with a Marseilles accent, at first no one seemed to have noticed that he was different. Even when it became known that he was a priest in mufti, the men who worked beside him had accepted the fact with indifference, as if they had been told that he was a diabetic or had Romanian grandparents.

The only workers who did show an interest once his ministry became known were the stewards of the clandestine Communist trades union—the CGT. Once again Antoine had expected antagonism, but was met only with an amused curiosity. One or two would engage him in polemics, attacking the Church for its political conservatism, but on such issues they found no contender in Antoine, who outdid their denunciations of prosperous and reactionary prelates.

If during those two years the Communists learned to respect the swarthy friar, Antoine came to admire the Communists. They were selfless, disciplined and courageous men who alone stood up for the workers not just against the harshness of their employers but also against the bullying and racketeering of the Burzio and Jacopozzi gangs.

What became clear to Antoine was that the men who worked in the factories had no time to consider their souls when it was all they could do to keep their bodies alive. He found it quite impossible to tell them, as Christ had told his disciples, that they should not worry about their lives or what they were to eat, when after long hours of backbreaking labor they returned to a supper of thin soup and a crust of bread. No one could survive on the official rations, but the workers had no time to forage in the countryside, and their wages were too low to enable them to buy food on the black market. Antoine had seen men in tears not because they themselves were hungry but because their wives and children were starving too.

How could he console them? "Look at the birds in the sky. They do not sow or reap or gather into barns, yet your Heavenly Father feeds them." The words rang hollow in the slums around the industrial zone of Castelnau, and Antoine discovered that they died on his lips. It was time not for words, but for deeds, for as Saint James had said, what was faith without good works? And as Christ had said, it was by his action that one could tell the true prophet from the false one.

But what good works were called for? What was to be done? To scrounge a few potatoes from Catholic peasants to thicken the workers' soup was not the answer, because they hungered not just for food but for justice too. The exactions of the war might have exacerbated their suffering, but even in peacetime they had struggled with poverty and privation—seeing the bourgeois in their sleek cars, with pretty girls on their arms, going into elegant restaurants whose extravagant menus mocked them from the little glass cases fixed to the wall by the door. Such wrongs would never be put right without a social revolution. The kind of democracy that had existed before the war had manifestly failed; it had been a racket to end all rackets. Only a government of selfless and disciplined men—men like the Communist trade unionists —could put right the injustice endemic in a capitalist society.

These men had become Antoine's friends. They not only shared his aspirations, but were frequently self-educated and made good company too. He went to their homes and once again was overwhelmed by the ascetic simplicity of their lives and their comradely selflessness. He could feel the grace of God working through them much more strongly than it did through the fastidious scholars of the Dominican convent on the Rue de la Paix or the well-bred bishop in his episcopal palace.

In the summer of 1943, Antoine Dubec faced a crisis, not one of faith but of conscience. The curé of the parish of the Hameau de Braulhet, which took in the industrial zone of Castelnau, had been inveighing from the pulpit against the influence of atheist Marxism for two decades. Certainly he rarely left the pulpit, and though he went from time to time to visit Catholic workers in their homes, he never went through the gates into the factories. He had been told, however, about the Dominican worker-priest—indeed, he had given his permission for Antoine to come into his parish—but when the news came out that Antoine had not only befriended the stewards of the CGT but appeared to make common cause with them, this unimaginative curé had complained to the bishop of Coustiers and had demanded that the friar be withdrawn.

The bishop dithered. He saw some value in the work done by Antoine, but word of the experiment had also reached the Vatican, and with a demand from Rome as well as from the curé of the Hameau de Braulhet, the bishop felt obliged to act. He summoned Antoine's superior, the prior of the Dominicans, to his palace and asked him to order the priest out of the factories and back to the convent.

The prior reluctantly agreed. He and his colleagues had enjoyed the two years' respite from the prickly presence of their fellow friar, but he too saw the danger of undermining the Church's struggle against Marxism. When Antoine next came to the convent the prior called him into his study and told him that at the end of the month he must leave his job and lodgings and return to live in the convent on the Rue de la Paix.

Antoine nodded, said nothing and kept his rage to himself. He knew quite well that his prior was only acting under pressure from the bishop and the bishop under pressure from Rome. He returned to the factory determined to ignore them all and remain where he was, although when he had become a Dominican he had taken a vow of obedience, and to break it now would amount to a rejection of the Catholic Church itself.

His Communist friends heard his news with a tactful sympathy. They too in their way had taken a vow of obedience, and on occasions had been forced to choose between their consciences and the Party line. They discouraged him, however, from defying his prior, arguing, as no doubt they had argued to themselves, that it was always better to fight for reform from within.

With one week left of his life as a worker-priest, Antoine Dubec returned as always to his priory for the weekend. There waiting for him was a note from Madeleine Bonnet asking if she could visit him. He telephoned at once, an arrangement was made, and he received her at three on Sunday afternoon in a room which had portraits of Saint Dominic and Saint Thomas Aquinas like those in that room in Montpellier where he had first met her a dozen years before.

He was surprised by how much Madeleine had changed; though she was only in her early thirties the hard life and bad diet of the past two years had exaggerated the marks of age. Her face seemed tired and melancholy, and her hair, which she left unkempt, had started to turn gray. There was a certain Bohemian *déshabillé* about her appearance which, though it was more in accord with Antoine's unworldly values, disappointed him because he remembered her youthful elegance.

She smiled as he closed the door. "I am most grateful to you for seeing me."

"I trust you are not about to marry another Catholic," he said, laughing and pointing to a chair.

"Not at all." She laughed too and sat down. "I am never likely to marry again; indeed, according to your Church, I have never been married at all."

"A virgin and martyr," said Antoine, sitting opposite her.

"No longer a virgin," said Madeleine, "and not yet a martyr."

"I trust never."

"Oh . . ." She shrugged her shoulders. "We may all be martyrs before long."

"For one cause or another."

She fixed him with a searching look and said, "I think, from what I hear, that our cause would be the same."

"My cause is still God."

"And your neighbor, perhaps, for his sake?"

"Of course."

" 'Who, Lord, is my neighbor?' "

He laughed again. "You remember your Bible."

"Especially the parable of the Good Samaritan."

"He would have had his hands full in France today."

"What would he do, do you think?" asked Madeleine.

"Help the poor, the oppressed, the imprisoned . . ."

"Precisely," said Madeleine. "That's what I meant when I said that our cause is the same."

Antoine nodded. "I have been working in a factory."

"I know."

"I have been told to stop."

"I know that too."

"I am of half a mind to disobey."

Madeleine hesitated, as if searching for words to put a delicate proposition. "Michel heard from our friends in the Party that you were faced with an awkward choice, and what I came here to say, on behalf of those friends, is that in their opinion the struggle of the workers for justice, which I think you support, is now subsumed by the struggle for national liberation."

"I know."

"If . . ." Again she hesitated. "If you felt . . . if, that is, you decided not to defy your prior, they feel sure that there are other ways in which you could assist the struggle of the working class."

"What other ways?"

"Resistance."

"Yes. There are already friars who resist in Témoignage Chrétien. I could always join them. But it would not help the working class in particular."

"What we had hoped," said Madeleine, "is that you might join us."

"The Communist Party?"

"Oh, no. I think that would hardly endear you to your prior. We had in mind a position on the Committee of the National Front."

Antoine looked away to hide the excitement in his eyes. "It is kind of them to consider me," he said.

"More and more people are rallying to the Resistance," said Madeleine. "The struggle has started, and sooner or later it will be won, but what kind of France comes out of that struggle will depend very much on what is prepared in advance. We are determined, as I think you are, not to sink back into the corruption and injustice of the Third Republic."

"I agree one hundred times over."

"Then join us," said Madeleine. "Help us prepare for a progressive future."

"Gladly," said Antoine. "Tell your friends that they can rely on me."

. . .

Every ten days or so a battered van with a canvas flap at the back would call at one or two of the safe houses in Coustiers to collect the fugitives gathered by Fortitude for passage to Algiers.

The Jacopozzis' felucca could take up to thirty, and while most of the passengers were Jews, there were also members of the Resistance whose cover had been blown, and Allied airmen whose planes had been shot down over France.

When full, the van would drive out of Coustiers on an unpredictable route to one of the small fishing ports along the coast. The embarkation of the passengers had to take place at night, and part of the exorbitant sum charged by the Jacopozzis for each passenger went to bribe the local gendarmes to look the other way.

The usual pattern was for one of the Fortitude group to drive the van as far as the outskirts of the city, where, at a prearranged place, one of the Jacopozzis' men would take over. On the night of June 23, however, Pierre Moreau himself was at the wheel, and when he picked up the Jacopozzis' contact he insisted on remaining in the van and traveling all the way to the felucca. The reason was that on this evening a group of fugitives who had been expected from Mézac had not arrived, so he had decided to send his family instead: his father, mother, wife and son, as well as his cousin Max with his wife and two children. There were other Jews in the party, as well as two wounded members of the Resistance and a British airman called Masters, but fully half the passengers were in one way or another relations of Pierre.

They drove for two hours on small roads until eventually they reached the tiny village of Port Rigaud. Here there were only one or two lights from the houses on the shore and a light from the felucca, which was tied to the side of the jetty. All the fishing boats had gone out to sea, and their lamps could be seen bobbing on the water about half a mile out.

The van stopped and the fugitives climbed out. Pierre embraced those he loved best in the world, and then walked to the jetty carrying Turco in one arm while the other was around the shoulder of his wife. All the women were weeping, and the face of little Turco wobbled as he tried to keep his tears back like his Papa, but the task was beyond him, and before going down the gangplank he too began to wail with despair.

"Remember to look for Bertrand when you get to Algiers," said Pierre to Bérénice. "He will almost certainly be there."

"Of course."

"He will take care of you until the war is over." He kissed her softly, tasting the salt of her tears. "It won't be long now."

"Be careful," said Bérénice, choking on her tears.

"I intend to survive," said Pierre, and the fierce determination with which he said it reassured her.

"Hurry," shouted the captain, Angelo Bartelli, in the slurred voice of someone who is drunk. "Hurry. We must go."

Pierre gave his family a last embrace, then watched them walk down the gangplank onto the boat, Turco in the arms of the British airman, Masters. It was a fine night; the sea was calm. They busied themselves stowing their luggage and provisions.

Pierre helped the crew cast off. He saw Angelo fumbling with the wheel of the boat and wondered if a man so drunk could navigate a boat to Algiers, but soon the sail was raised and the felucca glided silently out to sea. Pierre remained standing on the quai, watching its lamp shining in the darkness until it became just another point of light along with the fishing boats on the horizon.

He turned back toward the van, where the driver waited to return to Coustiers, but as he did so he heard the roar of a car as it approached the village at high speed. Immediately he drew his revolver and ran for the rocks beside the jetty, for he was constantly aware that at any moment the *milice* or the Gestapo might be upon him.

The car which stopped at the jetty, however, was a sleek black Citroën he recognized at once as Jaco Jacopozzi's, and seeing his young brother-in-law get out of the car and run down the jetty, he left the cover of the rocks and went to meet him.

"Have they gone?" asked Jaco.

"Yes."

"With your family on board?"

"Yes."

"They weren't due to leave tonight."

"A group from Mézac was delayed. I sent them to make up the number."

Jaco turned, his eyes glinting in the dark. "You should have told me."

"Why? What difference does it make?"

"I would have made other arrangements."

"They don't mind a little discomfort," said Pierre, imagining that Jaco had envisaged a picnic and some cushions.

"I would have made other arrangements," said Jaco again. "They should not have gone tonight."

Chapter 10

*I*T was not until six months after the Allied invasion of North Africa that General de Gaulle arrived in Algiers. The delay of half a year before the man who believed he represented France could lay claim to French territory was due to the determination of President Roosevelt to see de Gaulle supplanted by another leader.

Concealing from the Free French their plans to land in North Africa, and insisting that the English do the same, the Americans had brought General Giraud out of France on a British submarine and had him waiting in the wings to form a French administration in the captured colonies. As it happened, however, Admiral Darlan, the heir apparent to Marshal Pétain, was in Algiers at the time of the invasion visiting his sick son. Since Pétainist resistance continued and Allied lives were being lost, the Americans gave full powers to Darlan in exchange for an immediate cease-fire.

Although Darlan then protested that he would do everything in his power "to promote, in agreement with our American and British allies, this Christian order which opposes materialistic and pagan utopias," he could not escape his past as one of the most prominent collaborators with Hitler. It was Darlan, after all, who had allowed the Germans to use French air bases in Syria and the French naval base in Bizerte. There was therefore an outraged protest at his appointment not just by the Free French in London, but also by the press in both Britain and America.

Darlan appeared to confirm their misgivings by keeping the prefects and governors appointed by Pétain, including the notorious Boisson, who had fought so stubbornly against the Gaullists at Dakar, and he did nothing to dismantle the legal or administrative apparatus of the Vichy regime. Portraits of Marshal Pétain remained hanging in public buildings; laws against Jews and Freemasons remained on the statute book. Certainly Darlan sent secret directives to his subordinates to suggest that these laws be allowed to fall into disuse, but the Spanish Republicans, for example, who before the war had enrolled in the Foreign Legion to fight the Nazis and then at the armistice had been imprisoned in camps in the Sahara, remained incarcerated behind barbed wire.

Darlan's regime did not last long. On Christmas Eve of 1942 he was assassinated by a young royalist, Fernand Bonnier de la Chapelle. Bonnier was quickly arrested, tried and shot, but not before he had implicated two Gaullist leaders in the city—one the brother of a Resistance leader in France, the other a Catholic priest. Both were arrested for complicity in his crime. Moreover, the police investigating the assassination of Darlan concluded that there was a further plot to kill Giraud, and so detained twelve Gaullist leaders in the city under an administrative order.

Since these fourteen men were precisely those who had helped the Allied landing in Algiers, and since nine of them were Jews, it seemed to the outside world that Giraud, who had replaced Darlan and was sustained in power by the Americans, was continuing the totalitarian tradition of Pétain's government in Vichy. Giraud himself still protested his loyalty to the Marshal and insisted that he was acting in his name; to him the Vichy regime might be weak, but it was not evil, and if freed from the intolerable pressures of the German occupation, it would govern France along sound, conservative lines.

Giraud saw the Gaullists as sectarian fanatics—the same Communists and Socialists who had formed the National Front government under Léon Blum which had so weakened and demoralized France that the defeat of 1940 had become inevitable. If de Gaulle himself was not one of these men, he was certainly playing into their hands by castigating as traitors every politician and functionary who in the agonizing days of 1940 had rallied to Marshal Pétain. To Giraud it was absurd for his fellow general to talk of the war not just as a battle between armies, but as "a struggle of lies against truth, dark against light, evil against good," and at the same time to appoint himself the infallible judge of who was the patriot and who the traitor.

Since Giraud had the support of the Americans and of the French army and administration in North Africa, he might well have expected to administer the territory until the end of the war and to land in France as the natural leader of a provisional government, but since both his allies were democracies they had to take into account public opinion in Britain and the United States. Since the start of the war, de Gaulle had been the symbol of French resistance in these two countries. Moreover, the Resistance groups in France itself, which had suffered so atrociously not just from the brutality of the Gestapo but from the cruelty of their fellow Frenchmen in the *milice,* the Service d'Ordre Légionnaire and the French police, now clamored for vengeance against the government in Vichy and all those who had administered its policies outside metropolitan France.

It therefore seemed imperative to the Allies that Giraud and de Gaulle join forces. As soon as Giraud took power, de Gaulle himself had proposed a meeting between them, but it was not until the Casablanca conference between Roosevelt and Churchill in January 1943 that he was summoned from London and met, for the first time since 1940, his rival for power.

From Giraud's point of view, the meeting was a disaster. De Gaulle was incensed that they were conferring under American guard on French soil. He dismissed the Allied plans presented by Harold Macmillan for an alliance with Giraud as an unconscionable interference in France's internal affairs. He made his own conditions for a partnership between them: that the armistice of 1940 be declared null and void, that all the Vichy governors be dismissed, and that a committee be formed with all the prerogatives of a government in exile, including the power to appoint and dismiss the commander-in-chief of the French army.

These terms were unacceptable to Giraud and the Americans. Pressure was put on de Gaulle by Churchill, but the Frenchman remained intransigent and returned to London from Casablanca without reaching any agreement at all. The Americans and the British were outraged; Churchill was prepared to abandon de Gaulle, but both the British War Cabinet and King George VI restrained him.

For a time Giraud wielded power alone in Algiers, but now not only had public opinion in the democracies and among the Resistance groups in metropolitan France turned against him, but also the Gaullists were taking the offensive in North Africa itself. The Cross of Lorraine was daubed on every wall, and as the Free French forces fighting with the British in the western desert approached Tunisia, resplendent with the laurels of their celebrated stand at Bir Hacheim, there were desertions from Giraud's forces to those under Leclerc and de Larminat.

What finally tipped the scales in favor of de Gaulle, however, was developments in France itself. By the middle of May 1943, his plenipotentiary in France, Jean Moulin, had finally formed a National Council of the Resistance which pledged its allegiance to General de Gaulle. Though Moulin was himself to be arrested, tortured and killed by the Gestapo a month later, his task had been completed in the nick of time. On May 17, Giraud capitulated; he invited de Gaulle to come to Algiers without preconditions to form a unified French command. On May 30, de Gaulle arrived in North Africa, and three days later Giraud formally proclaimed a new French Committee of National Liberation, with himself and de Gaulle as copresidents. There were five other members on the committee, and only one, General Georges, could be counted a firm ally of Giraud.

In the months which followed, the tension between the two leaders was nothing compared to the open loathing of the different groups of exiled Frenchmen in the city of Algiers—the Pétainists, Giraudists and Gaullists—who all denounced one another as traitors and hurled anathemas through the press. Each had its own set of laws and its own intelligence service which intrigued not just against the others but against the British and American services too. The two French armies —the one which had remained in Algiers and was under the command of Giraud, the other which had fought with the British under Leclerc and de Larminat—openly despised one another. The regular officers in Algiers refused to acknowledge the promotions of officers who had fought under the Cross of Lorraine, and Gaullist soldiers on leave in Algiers were mocked in the barracks and ostracized in the mess.

Among the most vociferous of these anti-Gaullist officers was Captain Raymond Blaise de la Vallée, Bertrand's cousin who had been wounded during the Stavisky riots on the Place de la Concorde in 1934 and nursed back to health in the de Roujays' apartment on the Rue Marbeuf. At the time of the fall of France, Raymond had been serving in Syria. Like most of his fellow officers, he had been delighted by the rise of Marshal Pétain. Next to a king, the Marshal had seemed to him the most suitable leader for the French people, and the "National

Revolution" which had been promulgated by the government in Vichy looked liked the fruit of the seeds sown by Maurras and his followers in Action Française.

In Damascus, Raymond had corresponded with his cousin, Louis de Roujay, and the two career officers had seen eye to eye on the issues which faced France. When the British, aided by the Free French, had invaded Syria, Raymond had fought fiercely against them. Several of his friends had been killed by the bullets of the British and Gaullists, and when the armies of General Dentz were finally defeated, Raymond, along with eight out of ten of his fellow Frenchmen, chose to return to Vichy France rather than join the Free French.

He was transferred to Algiers, where, while the war raged around them, he and his fellow officers grappled with the tedium of empty maneuvers and futile parades. Then came the Allied invasion, and once again, obeying orders, Raymond fought bravely to drive the Americans back into the sea. He was wounded in the arm by shrapnel and was decorated for his courage by Admiral Darlan. He then returned to barracks, where he preferred to spend his time, for though he had a wife and children he felt more at home in the company of men.

With his friends in the mess Raymond followed with dismay the gradual erosion of Giraud's power. De Gaulle, who had acquired considerable political cunning since 1940, quickly outwitted his bumbling rival, who boasted of his political innocence. In September 1943, when Italy surrendered and the island of Corsica was liberated by Free French forces, Giraud was outmaneuvered on the Committee of National Liberation and fell from power. For a further six months he remained the titular commander in chief of the French army, and only in the spring of 1944 did this American candidate for the leadership of France retreat into obscurity.

Giraud's fall caused dismay among the officers loyal to Pétain. It was not just the Gaullists' unscrupulous pursuit of power that irritated men like Raymond Blaise de la Vallée, or the bloodcurdling rhetoric of their Communist friends in the Consultative Assembly that was convoked in Algiers from members of the Resistance; it was the way in which these newcomers had cluttered up the city, making it quite impossible to find a seat in a café or a table in a restaurant. What had not been requisitioned by the Americans had been commandeered by the Gaullists. It was well known that the best food in the city was reserved for the members of the Consultative Assembly and for the Gaullist government officials at the Lycée Fromentin. Raymond and his fellow officers were sometimes driven to eat couscous in the casbah.

One evening soon after the fall of Giraud, Raymond put his head through the door of a small restaurant called Chez Félix off the Boulevard Baudin where he had hoped to eat with a brother officer if there was an empty table. All were occupied, but his eyes alighted on two uniformed officers—one French, one American—who seemed to have finished and were about to leave. Indeed, just as he spotted them they called for their bill, so Raymond went over to their table and in as courteous a tone as he could manage to a man whose markings distinguished him as a Gaullist, asked the French officer if he could possibly take over their table.

The man turned, and at once Raymond recognized his cousin, Bertrand de Roujay.

"Ah, Bertrand," he said, "it's you. I thought you were in London."

The two cousins embraced, and Bertrand introduced his cousin to his American companion. "This is Colonel Jackson," he said, "who's been put in charge of our part of the world."

"Algiers?"

"Basse-Provence."

"Ah," said Raymond. "Then he will have his hands full."

"Why?" asked Jackson in excellent French. "Are they a difficult lot down there?"

"If you were dealing with my native province of Brittany," said Raymond, "you would have a far easier time."

Since Raymond's friend had not arrived, and since Bertrand and Harry were in no hurry, the three men sat down and ordered cognac from the harassed waiter.

"You have changed," said Raymond to his cousin with his usual bluff naiveté.

"In what way?"

"You look more serious. Even more serious! I daresay that it was the fog in London."

"War is a serious business."

Raymond shrugged his shoulders. "Oh, here the main problem has been boredom."

Bertrand gave a thin smile. "I could find something for you to do," he said.

"For de Gaulle?"

"Yes."

Raymond blushed. "You know, Bertrand, I have always considered myself a man of honor, and since I have taken a vow of loyalty to Marshal Pétain . . ."

"Pétain is a prisoner of the Germans. All oaths of loyalty are null and void."

"If I could believe that . . ."

"You should talk to the Abbé Cordier. He could release you from your vow."

Raymond continued to look perplexed. "It's not just the vow. It's also that I've always thought that you Gaullists were all Bolsheviks under the skin."

Harry laughed. "Bertrand a Bolshevik?"

Raymond frowned. "No, well, not Bertrand, of course, but the others . . ."

The American laughed again. "Like Philippe de Hauteclocque?" he asked. "Who, thank God, calls himself Leclerc. Jean de Lattre de Tassigny? Edgar de Larminat? To us Americans there are so many prefixes among the Free French generals that the staff list reads like the *Almanack de Gotha.*"

"We are not Bolsheviks," said Bertrand to his cousin. "Quite the contrary. But just as Churchill and Roosevelt work with Stalin, so we must work with the Communists in France."

"They will use you," said Raymond.

"No," said Bertrand. "We will use them—or try to—and the more units of the regular army that there are at our disposal, the more likely it is that we will succeed."

As Bertrand spoke, a tall, gangling officer entered the restaurant. Recognizing his friend, Raymond waved his hand to attract his attention, and when he reached the table introduced him as Lieutenant Alphonse de Porterre. "My cousin, Bertrand de Roujay," he said, "and an American gentleman . . . I am sorry, I did not catch your name."

"Harry Jackson."

"Colonel Jackson, of course. And both these gentlemen, my dear Alphonse, advise us to join Leclerc or de Lattre de Tassigny; otherwise, as we are told by their Bolshevik friends, we shall be consigned to the dustbin of history."

Since there was not room at the table for the four men, Bertrand and Harry Jackson left the restaurant and wandered down the Boulevard Baudin toward the port.

"Is that buffoon really your cousin?" asked Harry.

Bertrand laughed. "Yes. The son of my father's sister."

"Well, you may get yourself a new recruit, but if you do, you may live to regret it."

"He's a fool," said Bertrand, "but he's a good soldier and could kill Germans as well as anyone."

"He would be on your side already if you had Giraud as your leader instead of de Gaulle."

Bertrand shook his head. "It would never have worked."

"And now, I guess, all the glory will go to de Gaulle, and the avenues and boulevards will be named after him."

"Is that all glory is?" asked Bertrand, looking up at the street sign with a melancholy expression on his face.

"What else?"

Bertrand shrugged his shoulders. "I don't know. I used to think it was something more."

"Look," said Harry, taking Bertrand by the arm, "how about sampling some of the local fleshpots?"

"No." He smiled as he shook his head.

"Still brooding about that English girl of yours?"

"It's not just that."

"A woman would do you good."

"It's your solution to every problem."

"It usually works."

"I have to go back to my office. There is a message I must send to France."

"Please yourself," said Harry, who then patted his friend on the shoulder and set off for the casbah.

Bertrand walked slowly back toward the Lycée Fromentin. Since that miserable morning almost two years before when he had returned to his flat in London to find his wife in his bed with her brother's friend, he had been immune not just to love but to desire. It was as if the shock he had suffered at this second deception had paralyzed the part of the brain that controls the sexual senses. No real or fancied image of a woman's face or body could arouse him from a neuter indifference to the thought of sexual love. In London, and now in Algiers, he lived a life of celibate companionship among his fellow officers in the Free French forces.

Although Bertrand's general mood was, as Raymond had noticed, even more serious than before, he was not an embittered man. He had not seen Jenny after surprising her in the flat, because she had fled to Ascombe and had remained there until the baby was born, but he had felt no rancor toward her; he blamed himself for hurrying her into a marriage which in retrospect he realized she had not desired. When he had been told by Martin Trent, at an awkward lunch in his club, that the child had almost certainly been conceived at Ascombe that summer when the affair with Eddie had begun, Bertrand had felt relieved. It meant that when he finally went to Algiers in the spring of 1944, he could shake the dust from his feet and leave nothing of himself behind in England.

Once in North Africa he had devoted himself to the struggle for Gaullist ascendancy with the dedication of a Jesuit. The need at the time was for determined men, and Bertrand, because of the circumstances of his life, let no scruples or feelings distract him from the pursuit of victory. He never showed in his face or manner the longing he still felt, despite his disappointments, for human love and affection, and all his hopes in that regard were now directed toward those who awaited him in France. His family and friends were never out of his thoughts, and the very austerity of his present life gave added strength to these old affections.

It was for this reason that upon reaching the Lycée Fromentin he went to his office, bent with a sense of anguish that had burdened him all evening. The building was deserted, and for some time he sat at his desk trying to compose a message in terms that would mitigate the pain it would inevitably cause. He worked on different drafts until he realized that nothing he could say would soften the blow. Stooping not just from tiredness but from sorrow, he took his message down to the radio room and handed it in for coding and transmission. "To Sabot, Coustiers. Regret Red Cross inform British Flight Sergeant Masters prisoner-of-war in Germany. Fear for your family. No trace of them here. Advise reappraise chain for weak link. Montrouge, Algiers."

2

Two days after the Allied invasion of Normandy in June 1944, two German soldiers were shot down outside the Café de la Gare in Pévier. Edmond de Roujay immediately summoned the commander of the gendarmerie to ask who he thought was responsible, and was told that it was thought to be a detachment of the maquis composed of Spanish Republican refugees.

"They do the killing, we pay the price," said Edmond de Roujay, whose tenant, Astran, had disappeared with his son three months before. He looked gloomily out the window of his office in the *mairie*, watching as the staff car of Hauptmann Hildebrand approached across the square.

Hildebrand entered his office like an understudy playing an ill-rehearsed role. For the sake of security he had left his billet at Saint Théodore, but he remained on courteous terms with Edmond de Roujay, and he loathed painful missions of this kind.

"Monsieur le Maire," he said, speaking in a halting, pompous German which he knew Edmond could understand, "it is my duty to inform you that as punishment for the assassination of two of my men last night, ten hostages are to be taken and executed."

Edmond sighed. "Men, women or children?" he asked sardonically.

Hildebrand blushed. "Men, naturally. Ten men."

"There are barely ten men left in the village," said Edmond.

"I am sorry," said Hildebrand, "but I have my orders. You will produce, at dawn, ten men, or we shall be obliged to seize them ourselves." He saluted, clicked his heels and left the room.

Edmond de Roujay did nothing. He returned home at lunch, had an amusing conversation with Titine, snoozed as usual under the chestnut trees, and returned to Pévier in the late afternoon.

"Monsieur le Maire," said the chief councillor, "we must prepare a list for the Kommandant."

"Are you volunteering?" asked Edmond.

The old man turned pale. "I . . . not, that is, unless . . . well, perhaps we should draw lots."

"We shall see," said Edmond.

He walked out into the street and toward the parish church. There the service of benediction was coming to an end, and the old colonel sat nonchalantly at the back of the church until it was finished. Then, fanning the air with a hymn book to dispel the suffocating smell of incense, he went out of the church and around to the priest's house to see the old curé who had been his friend for thirty years.

The two old men sat down in the parlor.

"This shooting . . ." said Edmond.

"A terrible business," said the curé. "What is the use of it? It hardly changes the course of the war, yet the Germans exact a most terrible revenge."

"Precisely," said Edmond. "That is why I am here."

"They demand hostages?"

"Ten."

"Ten! But all the men are away, either working in Germany . . ."

"Or hunting Germans in the hills. Yes. There are hardly ten able-bodied men to choose from, and if all those are shot there will be none."

"None." The priest repeated the word with a gloomy nod of his head.

"You can imagine what that will mean when it comes to harvesting the grapes and olives."

"I suppose the women can do it."

"There's always some work that has to be done by the men."

"Yes," said the priest. "I suppose there is."

"Therefore what I propose is this," said Edmond, "that instead of quantity, we offer them quality—not ten peasants for two soldiers but two men whose dignity makes each worth five of the other."

"Would they accept that?"

"We could try."

"But are there two such men?"

"I had two in mind."

"Mercier, the butcher, perhaps, and Bonastier? He owns the olive press and was a Freemason."

"No. Two others."

"Who, then?"

"You and me."

The priest turned pale. "You?"

"Yes."

"And me?"

"Yes." Edmond sighed. "The truth is, my dear curé, that we're both getting old. Our lives are almost over anyway. What use are we when it comes to the harvest? None at all. Have we families who rely on us? I have a wife, but she's more than able to look after herself, and you have no one. We're the obvious choice."

The priest had not recovered from shock. "But . . . but we must not just think of the harvest of grapes and olives. There is also the harvest of souls, and though I may have no natural children, I have spiritual children, a whole parish who, particularly in times like these . . ."

Edmond de Roujay raised his hand. "I have no wish to conscript you, my dear curé. In times like these, as you say, it is a foolhardy man who imposes his conscience on anyone else. Sleep on it. Think it over. I'll look in tomorrow morning on my way to the *Kommandantur,* and if you feel up to it, come with me. If not . . ." He shrugged his shoulders. "You never know. Perhaps they'll be satisfied with me. But if you don't mind, to prepare for the worst I'd be grateful if you would hear my confession."

Having been absolved of his sins, Edmond de Roujay took his leave of the curé as if what he had proposed was a morning shooting snipe, and sauntered back to the *mairie* with the same insouciance. There the rump of the town council was waiting for him, but he brushed the old men aside, saying that the question of the hostages should be left to him.

That evening at supper, he was again unusually spirited, joking with Alice, Hélène and the children. Thierry, the eldest, who was now a member of the *milice* and, since Louis's departure for Germany, infuriated the whole household by assuming his role, asked his grandfather in a croaky, newly broken voice what was going to happen about the hostages. Only then did the old colonel look severe. "Don't speak about that at table," he said. "There is enough death all around us without bringing it into the home."

When supper was finished the children dispersed, and Alice as always went to her room to listen to the BBC. Departing from routine, Edmond came in behind her; together they heard that the Americans in Normandy had now cut off the Cherbourg peninsula, and that the Russians in the east had broken through the Mannerheim Line.

When she had switched off the radio, Edmond leaned his body against the edge of his marriage bed. "The die is cast," he said. "Nothing will stop them now."

"It will be the Americans and the English who will liberate us," said Alice, "not the Bolsheviks as you feared."

"Yes," said Edmond, "and Bertrand will be home again."

"And, God willing, Louis too."

"I fear he is lost," said Edmond sadly.

"One must always hope," said Alice.

"I haven't lost hope," said Edmond. He stood, and in the stance he always adopted when he had something awkward to say, he went to the window and stood looking out at the dusk with both his hands plunged in his trouser pockets.

"Did you hear about the assassinations and the demand for hostages?" he asked after a moment.

"Yes."

"A bad business."

"Was it Astran and his friends?"

"I fear so."

"What are you going to do?"

"I have asked the curé to come with me tomorrow morning."

"Where?"

"To the *Kommandantur*. As a hostage."

"You?"

"The two of us."

"No, Edmond . . ."

Now he turned to face his wife. "We can't let all the young men die."

"We need you."

He smiled. "I've had my spell. God could take me any day."

"Edmond . . ."

"And soon Bertrand will be back to take care of things."

"Edmond . . ." she said again.

He came forward from the window and embraced her—a gentle, kind embrace which told her that his mind was made up.

Edmond de Roujay slept well that night in bed next to his wife. He rose early the next morning and dressed in a suit as if it were Sunday.

Marthe had risen early too, and had prepared his coffee, but Hélène, Titine and the other children were bleary-eyed when he came to kiss them goodbye.

"Where are you going, Grandpapa?" asked Titine.

"On a journey."

"Will you be long?"

"Wait and see."

In her dressing gown, Alice went with him to the door.

"Pray for me," he said.

She inclined her head.

"And don't despair."

"No."

"I may be back."

"Of course."

"And if not . . . well, whatever happens, we shall see each other soon."

Edmond was driven as always into Pévier by the one-legged old soldier in the pony and trap, but on this occasion was dropped at the church. The morning mass had begun, and Edmond knelt quietly at the back. He took communion and after mass waited while the curé removed his vestments. He heard a click of the catch on the presbytery door. Concluding that the curé had preferred his breakfast to his death, he left the church and started to walk toward the *Kommandantur*. Suddenly he heard a wheezing and panting behind him and turned to see the curé coming after him. Neither man spoke as they walked side by side down the street. The priest clutched his breviary, and his normal expression of jovial holiness had been replaced by one of earnest determination.

At the *Kommandantur* they were shown into the Hauptmann's office. Hildebrand was at his desk.

"I have your hostages, Heinrich," said Edmond de Roujay.

"Where?"

"Here."

"You?"

"Only two, I am afraid, but in our offices we represent many more."

"But that is impossible," said Hildebrand.

"Take others if you must," said Edmond. "But first you must dispose of us two."

The curé muttered a prayer. The Hauptmann dropped his mask. "Edmond, I beg you, find some others."

"No," said Edmond. "If anyone in Pévier is to be executed, you must start with the mayor and the curé."

Hauptmann Hildebrand stood for a moment, trembling with confusion. Then he turned to the two Frenchmen and said, "Wait."

Edmond and the curé were led outside. They sat on a bench under the empty eyes of two German soldiers. From the office they could hear Hildebrand shouting into the telephone. Edmond's German was good enough to follow what he was saying: that the assassinations were undoubtedly the work of the Spaniards, that the only men left in the village were the Germans' friends. He made a second, then a third call as responsibility was shifted higher up the hierarchy of the German command. Hildebrand's tone became more circumspect as he graduated from a "Herr Major" to a "Herr Oberst" and from a "Herr Oberst" to a "Herr Generalmajor" but he stubbornly persisted in his line of argument. Finally Edmond heard him argue with a "Herr Standartenführer" and knew that he had been referred to the S.S. Now Hildebrand was risking his own comfortable posting in Pévier, for recalcitrant German officers were quickly transferred to the Russian front, but his stubborn Bavarian voice continued to insist upon the futility of reprisals in the area under his command.

Finally he came out of his office with a wide smile on his exhausted face. "Thank God," he said, "I have convinced them. It was the Spaniards, not the French, so on this occasion there will be no reprisals. Thank God, oh God, thank God."

Out in the street Edmond turned to the curé. "I am sorry, Father, if I did you a bad turn."

"No, Colonel," said the curé. "You did me a good turn, a good turn. It is always salutary to prepare oneself for death." He shook his hand and then waddled back toward the church.

Edmond walked on to the *mairie*. There the one-legged veteran from Saint Théodore was waiting with the trap.

"Go back to the house," said Edmond, "and tell Madame de Roujay that I shall be back for lunch after all."

"May I report that all is well?" asked the old soldier.

"Yes," said the colonel as he climbed the steps of the *mairie*, "you may report that all is well."

One evening in the early summer of 1944, Pierre Moreau and Guy Serot sailed out of the village of Saint Justin with the fishing fleet on the small trawler *Elise*. Two miles from the coast the *Elise* separated from the other boats and sailed toward Fréjus.

It was a warm, clear night. There was only half a moon, but it gave light enough to throw back a reflection from the lapping seawater and reveal the black line of the distant coast against the dark blue sky. The two leaders of Fortitude stood silently looking out to sea while behind them the captain issued quiet commands to his crew. Three of the sailors had British sten guns slung across their shoulders. An hour out of Saint Justin, the engines stopped and the sailors lowered the anchor.

They waited in silence for almost forty minutes until suddenly, only a hundred yards or so from where they were anchored, there was a sucking and a swirling of the water, and slowly the huge shape of the submarine *Casabianca* rose from beneath the sea. Even before she was fully on the surface, a sailor had jumped from the conning tower and snapped a message at the *Elise* with a lamp. With a torch, the captain gave a coded reply. Then, as two of the crew of the *Elise* jumped into a dinghy which was in tow behind the boat and started to row toward the submarine, three more men emerged from its conning tower, one of whom, after taking leave of the others, climbed down a steel ladder and prepared to board the dinghy.

"There is our commissioner of the Republic," said Guy Serot.

The dinghy came alongside the submarine, and the man leaped on board. A moment later, after another wave to the officers on the *Casabianca,* he turned his face toward the *Elise*. In the gloom it was impossible to make out his features, although Guy Serot strained his eyes to do so, because here was the man sent from Algiers by General de Gaulle to govern the department of Basse-Provence at the liberation. As the dinghy came closer he could see that the commissioner was a tall, middle-aged man, thin and earnest, with the air of a civil servant.

"Well, he looks the part all right," he said to Pierre, turning toward his chief.

"Yes," said Pierre. "They've sent us the right man."

In the moonlight Guy saw that there were tears on his friend's cheeks. "Do you know him, this Montrouge?"

"Yes. I've known him for some years."

The dinghy bumped against the side of the boat. The three armed sailors stood upright in a row, and the commissioner came aboard as if the *Elise* were a warship of the French navy.

Pierre stepped forward. "Welcome home," he said simply, and then, to the astonishment of Serot and the crew of the *Elise,* the two men fell into each other's arms.

When they drew back, Pierre led the commissioner to greet Serot and the captain and to inspect the impromptu guard of honor. "Gentlemen," he said, "let me present the commissioner of the Republic, Montrouge."

Bertrand shook their hands with patent emotion. "Gentlemen, I thank you in the name of General de Gaulle, and of the Provisional Government in Algiers, for coming to meet me tonight. Now, if you please, take me ashore, because I am impatient to set foot in France."

On the last day of the summer term of 1944, Madeleine Bonnet left the Lycée René le Bon carrying a leather briefcase in one hand and a string bag in the other. Both were bulging with books she was taking home. After passing through the gates and walking for fifty yards or so through the jostling crowd of teachers and children, she felt a hand relieving her of her load, and heard the familiar voice of Pierre Moreau ask if he might carry her bags.

"Ah, Pierre," she said. "You made me think that I was back in Montpellier." Then she added in a quieter voice, "You must take care. I may be followed."

"I know," he said. "I have taken precautions."

"They have turned very nasty."

"Yes," he replied bitterly, "like cornered rats."

She glanced at Pierre with a look of compassion as she walked beside him, because of all her friends he had been most changed by the war, not just in appearance but in temperament as well. His face and his body were thin from meager rations, and his hair had retreated a good inch from his brow to reveal a domelike forehead on which wrinkles of anger, anxiety and melancholy played like ripples on the surface of a pond. Gone was the look of kindly skepticism which had once made him so endearing. It had endured far into the war, particularly when he was in Madeleine's company, but five months after the departure of his family to Algiers, when he had heard that the British airman who had gone with them was in a German camp, his anxiety on their behalf had finally degenerated into despair.

Now, as she always did on the rare occasions when she saw him, Madeleine asked if there was news of them.

He gave a slight snort. "No, there is no news, and I have ceased to expect it."

"Were they betrayed?"

"Almost certainly."

"But the boatman? What did he say?"

"Nothing. He had been dealt with before we got to him."

"By Jaco?"

"Yes. He said the old man had sold out to the Germans."

"Was it true?"

Pierre shrugged his shoulders. "I don't know."

"I am sorry."

He gave another snort—half a sob, half a snarl. "The great advantage of being a Jew, Madeleine, is that you are not expected to forgive your enemies, but in all good conscience can take your revenge."

"Of course."

"Nor is suicide a sin," he added.

"Don't speak of that," she said. "There's always hope."

"Of what?"

"That they may be alive."

"I hope they are dead."

"But where there is life . . ."

"Where there is life there is suffering, whereas where there is death there is oblivion."

They reached the junction of the Rue de la Motte and the Avenue de la République, where if Madeleine had been returning to her apartment she would have turned right. Pierre, however, still holding her bags, stopped at the street corner and, facing in the opposite direction, waited for the traffic lights to change before crossing to turn left up the avenue.

"Where are you going?" she asked.

He smiled, as if surprised. "To the Jardin des Plantes. I have to meet someone there."

"Then you'd better give me back my books."

"You wouldn't like to come too?"

She frowned, thinking of the queue at the baker's shop. "If you like, but I am off tomorrow and there's a lot to do."

"It won't take a minute."

"Very well."

The lights changed and they crossed the street.

"Who are you meeting?" she asked as they walked up the section of the Avenue de la République where the shops gave place to the ornate apartment buildings of the Second Empire.

"A man called Montrouge."

She stopped. "So he's here?"

"Yes."

"Who is he?"

Pierre smiled. "He'll introduce himself."

They turned left through the gates of the Jardin des Plantes and walked along the gravel path between the well-mown lawns.

"But what if I'm followed?" asked Madeleine. "We will lead them to Montrouge."

"There are five of my men behind us," said Pierre. "If anyone is following us they'll cut his throat."

"Michel is very dubious about this Montrouge," she said. "He says he's sure to be some old army officer who's been sitting out the war in London and Algiers."

"You must tell him that," said Pierre with a smile.

"No," said Madeleine, suddenly overcome by an unusual modesty. "I'm curious to meet him, but after that I must go home."

"Well, there he is," said Pierre, nodding ahead to a man sitting on a bench in front of a Japanese pine.

Madeleine screwed up her eyes, which in middle age had become nearsighted. She could tell at once that he was tall, thin and somehow familiar, and a moment later, as he looked up from the newspaper on his knee, she saw that it was Bertrand. She stopped, though they were still some ten feet from the bench.

"Take care," said Pierre. "It's very important to behave naturally."

She walked forward again, nodded to Bertrand as if he were a casual acquaintance, and like Pierre sat down beside him on the bench.

"You've come back," she said.

"As I promised," he said. He spoke kindly, as if he had forgotten

—or had chosen to forget—their last meeting, when she had ridiculed his plan to leave for London.

"And you are Montrouge?"

"Yes."

"I should have known. It was to be expected."

"I know this corner of France."

"Yes," she said, then added, "But it has changed."

"We have all changed," said Bertrand, looking at her with calm eyes, and as he spoke she could see that this man was certainly quite different from the one she had married. His hair, though still thick, had turned partly gray, there were lines of a certain stoic sadness on his face, and the look he directed at her had no trace of the rebuke which had always lurked in his eyes in the years following their separation.

"Tell me," Bertrand said quietly, "how is Titine?"

Now she understood why she was there, and with that inevitable feeling of affront which we all feel when we realize that we are being used as a means to an end, she frowned and looked away. Bertrand, who seemed to take the gesture to mean that she had bad news to hide, leaned toward her and repeated in a more agitated tone of voice, "She is all right, I hope? Nothing has happened to her?"

Madeleine quickly recovered her composure. "Of course. She is fine. I am fetching her tomorrow to go on holiday."

"From Saint Théodore?"

"From Mézac. Your mother is bringing her to the station."

Bertrand turned to Pierre. "Could I see her at the station?"

Pierre shook his head. "Every porter and ticket collector would recognize you."

Bertrand turned back to Madeleine. "I can't go to Saint Théodore; it would be too dangerous."

"Of course."

"But I would love to see Titine."

"I'm taking her to the mountains."

"To your parents?"

"To their house, yes, but they themselves are in hiding nearby."

"Hérisson is burned," said Pierre. "They are hiding with peasants near Cressac."

"I would also like to see Bonnet," said Bertrand.

Pierre now leaned across Bertrand to Madeleine. "Do you know the Hôtellerie de la Forêt in Cressac?"

"Of course."

"We could meet there for lunch on Sunday."

"There are Germans in Le Tréfort."

"I know, but not in Cressac, and Parigny, at the hostelry, is one of us. We can trust him absolutely, and with the three generations it will look like any other family at lunch."

"As indeed we shall be," said Madeleine with a quick sideways glance at her former husband.

Once this arrangement had been made, Pierre became impatient to disperse. Bertrand and Madeleine hesitated before parting, as if each had seen changes in the other which, like an arresting book jacket, tempted them to read what was within; but seeing this, Pierre gave the briefcase and the string bag back to Madeleine and said with a laugh, "I am sorry, but we are going in a different direction."

"Don't worry," said Madeleine with a smile. "It was worth a detour." She shook hands with Bertrand. "Until Sunday." Then she turned back to Pierre. "May I tell Michel that Montrouge has arrived, and who he is?"

"Of course. He'll find out soon enough."

When Madeleine got back to her apartment, the concierge, who could be trusted, handed her a note which, although not written in Michel's hand, came from him. It gave two numbers which, following a prear-ranged code, referred to a time and a place. She took the books up to her study and then lay down for a moment on her bed, for when there was no food in the kitchen she often took a rest instead of an evening meal.

On this occasion, however, she knew she could look forward to eating something later, because the meeting place given by Michel was a restaurant where it was possible to eat well at black-market prices. She did not sleep, but simply lay staring at the ceiling, thinking of how age had reduced in her passion of any kind, for that afternoon she had been surprised by how fond she had felt of the husband she had once despised, and now the prospect of a night with her lover provoked neither excitement nor pleasure. Without making much of it, she even wished that she could have supper with Bertrand rather than Michel, because she was curious about his years in London and wondered what had made him so sad.

She felt no physical yearning for either, or for any other man, and though she knew that Michel would take her back to wherever he was staying that night and would make love to her as a reward for the clean shirts and underclothes, she felt less pleasure in anticipating these sexual attentions than at the thought of the food in the black-market restaurant.

At eight she rose from her bed, collected the clean clothes for Michel from a drawer, changed from her skirt and blouse into a dress and set out once again into the streets. By now she was experienced in the clandestine life; she took three different buses to make sure she was not followed before reaching her destination. She no longer felt excited by these contrived deceptions, because she could no longer pretend to herself that she had any substantial role to play in the Resistance; though she was used on occasions by Michel's friends—to recruit the friar, for example—she was mistrusted by the Communists as the daughter of Bonnet and by the Fortitude group as the mistress of Michel le Fresne.

This isolation saddened her, because she would have liked to play a more important role, but there were compensations in living alone. She no longer had to face Michel's unspoken rebuke that the supper she had cooked from scrounged scraps of food was inadequate, but could share with some relish the black-market meals in restaurants which came, as Michel put it, "with the compliments of Churchill." Nor had she to endure his love affairs going on under her nose. She did not doubt that he had liaisons with the girls of the FTP, but during their hasty, clandestine meetings he had no time to discuss his personal affairs; unlike his comrades in the Party, Michel did not mistrust Madeleine, but used her as a sounding board for his own restless thoughts, and relied upon her to keep him informed about what was going on in the Fortitude group.

This evening, for example, in the restaurant he asked her if she had discovered how Pierre could be so certain that while he was hunted she was safe.

"I don't know," said Madeleine. "They must have someone with the Gestapo at the Hôtel de la Poste."

"Who?"

"I don't know."

"A pity. We could use him."

"It may be one of the Jacopozzis' men."

Michel nodded. "The links between the two are still strong?"

"Yes," said Madeleine. "They are forged by a marriage, after all."

"But does the alliance go deeper than the bond between Jaco and Pierre?"

"I doubt it. Jaco's men remain gangsters. One of them—the captain of their felucca—sold a boatload of Jews to the Gestapo."

"When?"

"Last year. It has only come out now, and the worst of it is that Pierre's whole family were on that boat."

Michel looked less sorry than curious. "That can't have pleased Pierre."

"Nor Jaco, since they were his family too. He dealt with the captain."

"Executed?"

"Yes."

Michel lit a cigarette and sat back on his chair with a sigh. "So if it wasn't for Jaco, his men might be suborned by the Fascists?"

"By whoever paid the highest price."

After supper, Michel took Madeleine back through the narrow streets of the old quarter of Coustiers where they had dined to the studio of a fellow-traveling painter who had left the city for the summer. There he made love to her like a diligent rooster reaffirming his rights over an old hen. Madeleine lay beneath him, looking aside to avoid the smell of garlic and nicotine on his grunting breath, her mind detached and at times almost disgusted by the sensations her body enjoyed.

When they had finished, and Michel sat back against the headboard smoking a cigarette, she lay staring at the thick gray hair on his chest, wondering at the mixture of attraction and repulsion which it aroused in her, while he returned to the subject which obsessed him—the rival factions in the supposedly unified Resistance—because already the Party was preparing to seize power.

"The army groups are not strong," Michel said, "and some of them are with us already. They see which way things are going. The Ursus group isn't interested; they take their orders from England, and the

English won't interfere. That only leaves the Fortitude group who might oppose us, and they're mostly just students, teachers, lawyers— the idealistic froth of the bourgeoisie. Their only strength is their alliance with the lumpenproletariat, and that's what we have to break."

Madeleine laughed. Michel's plans for revolution always reminded her of her adolescent pupils. "I don't think that Jaco Jacopozzi would like that label," she said.

"He wouldn't understand it. He's a fool."

"Fools can be dangerous."

"They can also be bullied and bribed."

"To do what?"

"Abandon their friends in Fortitude."

"You'll find it hard to drive a wedge between Pierre and Jaco while Jaco remains married to Isabelle."

"I know." Michel drew the precious smoke from his cigarette into his lungs. "There's also the problem of Montrouge."

"Ah, Montrouge," said Madeleine with the mysterious smile of someone with a secret.

Michel did not notice either her smile or her enticing tone of voice. "He's due here any day, with full powers as commissioner of the Republic. Now while he may be sympathetic to our point of view, we can't be sure of it, and if he should side with Fortitude . . ."

"He will," said Madeleine.

"How can you be so sure?"

"Because I've met him."

"What?" Michel took the cigarette from his mouth and turned sharply toward Madeleine, as if realizing for the first time that he was not thinking aloud but had a distinct and separate person lying next to him on the bed. "When did you meet him?"

"This afternoon."

"Where?"

"In the Jardin des Plantes. With Pierre."

"But . . . how?"

"Pierre met me outside the school. He took me to see him."

"*You?* To see Montrouge? But why?"

"Montrouge wanted me to arrange for him to see his daughter."

"His daughter?" For a moment Michel's fleshy face puckered in bafflement, but then the look on her face, together with the words she had spoken, suddenly enlightened him. "Of course," he said. "It had to be him."

"He was the obvious choice."

Michel drew on his cigarette with a frown on his face. "As you say, he will certainly side with Fortitude."

"Unless he has changed his opinions in exile."

"A man like that never changes." He stubbed out his cigarette. "Is he going to see Titine?"

"Yes."

"Isn't it dangerous?"

"It would be if he went to Mézac or Saint Théodore, but I'm taking her to the mountains tomorrow, and Bertrand and Pierre will come up to Cressac for lunch on Sunday."

"Aren't there Germans at Cressac?"

"No."

Michel shook his head as if still shaken by the news. "It's a cunning choice, of course. He'll draw support from the left and the right, and he'll have all the prestige of someone who took up with de Gaulle at the start of the war."

"I am afraid the revolution may not be as imminent as you think," said Madeleine with a trace of mockery in her voice.

"On the contrary," said Michel in a hard voice. "One man like Bertrand cannot stop the tide of history. We may have botched it in 1871 and in 1936, but this time, I promise you, we'll bring it off." And as if to prove his point by a demonstration of his prowess, he rolled over and made love to her again.

The little village of Cressac to which Madeleine brought both Titine and her parents to meet Pierre and Bertrand that Sunday was perched on the side of Mont Pezat. There was hardly the space between the side of the mountain and the ravine below for two rows of houses to line the street, and in the center of the village, where the road widened to form a small square, the houses on the south side—among them the Hôtellerie de la Forêt—were built on tall foundations from the rocks below. Next to the hostelry, forming one side of the square, was a large terrace built out like a balcony over the valley. In its center was a memorial to those who had died in the First World War, and behind the memorial were two benches facing out over green railings to the magnificent view down the valley.

Behind the hostelry there was also a terrace with the same sheer drop and fine view. It was shaded by a vine which had been trained over many decades to grow up the two pillars at the edge of the terrace and lie on a bed of trellises, and it was on this terrace that the owner of the hostelry, Monsieur Parigny, served lunch for the Bonnets and their friends.

In a sense, of course, it was a dangerous place for fugitives to have lunch, because there was no way off the terrace except through the door into the dining room of the restaurant. Even at this altitude, however, it was hot at midday, and Parigny, who was a member of the local maquis, knew that the Germans had their hands full guarding their own installations and centers of communications. Since the invasion of Normandy the maquis had moved about the mountains almost at will. When in Cressac they behaved as if the liberation had already taken place, and they withdrew only when a sizable contingent of the German army or the SS was spotted on one of the hairpin bends far above or below the village.

Parigny had known Michel and Françoise Bonnet for many years. Their cottage was half a mile down the valley, and when it became dangerous for them to stay there it was Parigny who had arranged to hide them in different peasant dwellings. He also knew Madeleine and Titine from their visits to the Bonnets in the summer, and he had met Pierre before the war and knew that he was a leader of the Resistance in Coustiers.

The third man who made up the party was a stranger to him, but from the way in which the young girl clung to his arm as she entered the restaurant and never moved her gaze of smiling delight from his face, he guessed that he must be her father, the Gaullist Bertrand de Roujay. Only then, when he realized that this family gathering was also a gathering of Resistance leaders, did he wish that he had brought down a contingent of the maquis from the hills.

In the mountains food was easier to obtain than in the cities, but even so it had not been easy to find the leg of lamb and the potatoes which he served these guests, or the cream to go with the strawberries he had bought for an exorbitant price. But to Parigny profit was not the point on this day. Nor were the grumbles of the other customers in the restaurant who were not being offered the same fare. There was honor as well as prestige in providing a good spread to a distinguished party of this kind.

When the maid had cleared away the empty plates from which the Bonnets and their friends had eaten the strawberries, Parigny himself brought the luxury of four cups of coffee, together with a bottle of framboise, which he offered on the house. They invited him to join them, which he did, dragging forward an empty chair from a neighboring table whose occupants had departed.

"Isn't it nice to see my father, Monsieur Parigny?" Titine said to him excitedly. "He's been away for such a long, long time."

"That's certainly the reason," said Parigny, "why I've never met him before."

"Then you should know," said Professor Bonnet, his face a little flushed with pride, and from the wine he had drunk at lunch, "that my son-in-law has just come from Algiers as the plenipotentiary in this department of General de Gaulle."

"I beg you, Professor," said Pierre, "to remain discreet."

Bonnet looked around. "But there's no one else here, my dear Pierre."

"Even so, such information should not echo down the valley."

Françoise Bonnet gave one of her whinnies; they had survived intact into her old age.

Parigny shook Bertrand by the hand. "If I had known," he said, "I would have arranged a guard of honor of our maquis."

"I am sure they have better things to do," said Bertrand.

"But there *is* a guard of honor," said Titine, pointing toward the door. "There are soldiers in the square. I saw them."

Parigny leaped from his seat and ran into the restaurant. Through the glass panes of the door he could see four or five uniformed men with submachine guns on the opposite side of the square. He ran back to the terrace.

Pierre had drawn a revolver. "The *milice?*" he asked Parigny.

"No, the Germans."

Françoise laughed.

"Is there any other way out?" asked Pierre.

Parigny said nothing, but the look of despair on his face told them all that they were trapped.

"Here they come," said Parigny as he saw a heavy German with a submachine gun approach the door of the restaurant.

Pierre turned to Bertrand. "I am sorry," he said. "Someone has betrayed us."

"But who?"

"I don't know, but if I live I shall find out." He went to the edge of the terrace and looked over into the ravine, then up at the vines as if to see if it would be possible to climb onto the roof.

"There's no way out," said Bertrand. "Our best hope is to bluff it out."

"No," said Pierre. "If they know we're here, they know who we are."

He looked again at the vine, then across toward the war memorial on the esplanade, which was only some twelve feet from where he stood.

Bertrand followed his glance. "It's impossible," he said. "It would be suicide."

Pierre laughed. "It's worth a try," he said, putting his revolver back into his pocket. In a moment he was over the railing, standing on a ledge high over the ravine.

"Please, Pierre," muttered Madeleine.

"Papa!" shouted Titine, burying her face in her father's shoulder.

The Germans burst through the door. "Halt!" the first shouted.

Pierre laughed, leaped, and with extraordinary agility landed on the ledge on the other side.

"Halt!" the German shouted again, raising his gun to shoot at the fugitive, but Pierre jumped over the railing, and as the German pulled the trigger Bertrand swung around and jogged his gun so that the bullets went up into the air.

At this point Pierre might have escaped had not three other Germans, alerted by the shooting, come around the side of the hostelry and, seeing him between the war memorial and the railing, moved toward him with their guns ready to fire.

For a moment Pierre sidled along the railing as if he might outflank them, but suddenly it became clear to them all that he was trapped between the ravine and the advancing soldiers. Pierre stopped, looked back toward his friends on the restaurant terrace, raised his hand and waved, as if greeting them from a distance, and then with the same unexpected agility vaulted over the side and fell without a sound onto the rocks below.

3

On the wall of his office on the first floor of the Hôtel de la Poste, Sturmbannführer Lutze had a chart on which the strength and disposition of his enemy, the Resistance, was diagrammatically displayed. Each group was represented by a different-colored box, and in each box was written the name of the leader—his code name and, where it was known, his true identity.

Above these boxes, but attached to them by lines like the patriarch at the top of a family tree, was the name "Montrouge" followed by a question mark, for by the judicious admixture of torture and bribery Lutze had established that the Gaullists in Algiers had sent, or were about to send, a plenipotentiary to represent them when the German army withdrew.

That the German army would withdraw from France now seemed certain. Lutze, once so comfortable in his SS uniform, was already window-shopping for the lightweight suit of a Paraguayan businessman. To his colleagues he still spoke of the inevitability of a rupture between the Americans and Soviets, and how the V-1 would bring the British to their knees; but once the Russians had defeated the German panzer corps at Kursk and the Americans had broken through at Avranches, he knew that the final outcome of the war was not in doubt. It would end with unconditional surrender.

This did not prevent him from doing his duty with his habitual dispatch, for there is in every German an innate professionalism which drives him against reason to do anything well. Lutze saw no reason to give up his role simply because the audience had left the theater and the run was scheduled to end. Thus when he received the information from an anonymous source that three leaders of the Resistance would be lunching in the village of Cressac, he went to his map with the excitement of a huntsman who kills not for food but for sport.

He saw at once that Cressac had been well chosen, because it was isolated and well protected by natural defenses. If his men approached by the road they would be seen and heard half an hour before they got there, and if he sent them in plainclothes they would be as conspicuous to the villagers as uniformed soldiers. He therefore decided to request that a detachment of paratroopers be sent over the mountains from their base at Le Tréport.

The lieutenant to whom this task was entrusted returned to Coustiers with three men—two living, one dead. To Lutze's irritation he reported that the three women who had formed part of the group had been released because the request had only spoken of "wanted men."

"You will also notice, Lieutenant," said Lutze, "that your orders were to take the wanted men alive."

"That was impossible, Herr Sturmbannführer. The third man took his own life. There was nothing we could do to stop him."

Lutze had the living prisoners shut up in the cellars of the Hôtel de la Poste and the dead man laid out on a table in a room on the ground floor. He then sent for Guillot to identify the fish that he had landed in his net.

As Guillot drew back the blanket which covered the mutilated body of Pierre Moreau, he said nothing, but Lutze noticed a movement on the muscles on his face which almost amounted to a smile of satisfaction.

"You know him?"

"It's the man they call Sabot."

"His real name?"

"Pierre Moreau."

"He killed himself."

"He was a Jew."

They left the temporary morgue, and Lutze gave orders for the other prisoners to be brought to his office.

"No," said Guillot. "It is better that they should not see me."

Lutze laughed. "Don't worry, Commissaire. They won't live to tell tales."

If Guillot was embarrassed by this jibe, he did not show it. "Let me see them in their cells," he said. "That should be enough."

In the cellar Guillot peered through the small spyholes that had been cut into the doors.

"Who is the old man?" asked Lutze.

"The man they call Hérisson."

"Professor Bonnet?"

"Yes."

"Excellent."

They moved on to the next cell.

"And this one?" asked Lutze.

Guillot looked for some time before speaking, but the tip of his tongue came out of his mouth, and slowly he moistened his lips. "You've landed a prize one here," he said to Lutze.

"Requin? Bouclier?"

"No. This must be the one they call Montrouge."

Now Lutze looked through the spyhole to see this prisoner for the first time. "Do you know the real name of this Montrouge?" he asked Guillot.

"De Roujay. Bertrand de Roujay."

Lutze gave a second look through the spyhole, then turned and walked toward the stairs.

"Tell me," asked Guillot, "how did you come by such accurate information?"

"An anonymous denunciation," said Lutze. "We get them every day."

"Probably from someone who wanted them out of the way," said Guillot.

"What use is the professor?" asked Lutze. "How much will he know?"

"Nothing," said Guillot. "He was a figurehead, nothing more. Don't waste your time on him." He glanced toward the room where Pierre's body lay on the table. "He would have been the most useful, but Montrouge, too, must know about all the networks. If you can persuade him to talk, you should learn a lot."

After Guillot had gone, Lutze returned to his office. He crossed to the chart on the wall and with a red crayon put a line through the names of Sabot, Hérisson and Montrouge. He stood for a moment, seeing how the work of a single day had decapitated the Resistance in his area; then he went to sit at his desk, wondering why he felt no elation at the successful outcome of this operation.

An adjutant came in to say that there was no cell available for a new suspect who had been brought in from the city. Lutze looked at the list of those held in the cellars of the Hôtel de la Poste, and seeing the name of Professor Bonnet, whom Guillot had said would know nothing of importance, he gave orders for his transfer to the city jail. The adjutant left the room, and once again Lutze was free to mull over his feelings, gently probing his melancholy mind as a doctor prods the stomach of a patient.

Suddenly he touched the source of pain; he remembered where he had met Bertrand de Roujay before. He was the man who had treated him so courteously when he had visited his estate eight years before. Lutze smiled as he remembered that evening—the disdainful chatelaine, and her humiliation when her husband had asked him to stay to dinner. He remembered their conversation at table, a free-ranging discussion about the issues of the day.

Like any man fighting a war, Lutze had formed an image of his enemy as treacherous, cowardly and subhuman. Now, faced with a man he remembered with respect, he felt confused. It was not that he was a sentimentalist who thought that one good turn deserved another, but rather that if Bertrand de Roujay were to be reduced through pain to the abject condition of all the others who had passed through his hands, then Lutze would have no peers and the world became a lonely place.

Perhaps there would be no need to torture him. Lutze took pride in his ability to assess the particular points of psychological vulnerability in his prisoners by talking to them informally in the civilized atmosphere of his office. Remembering their conversation at Saint Théodore, he even thought that de Roujay might be open to persuasion to alter his allegiance from the Free French to the Third Reich. He therefore sent for him, and while waiting stood at the window of his office to compose his thoughts.

When he heard the guards bring in the prisoner behind him, Lutze turned and said, "Ah, de Roujay. Or would you rather I called you Montrouge?"

Bertrand de Roujay shrugged his shoulders as if it did not matter. It was clear that he did not remember the salesman from Ludwig and Kummerly.

Lutze dismissed the guards, then pointed to a chair in front of his desk and said to Bertrand, "Please sit down."

Bertrand did as he was told. His face was pale, his manner indifferent.

"A cigarette?" asked Lutze, holding out his pack.

"Thank you." Bertrand took a cigarette, but not with the alacrity which Lutze had expected.

Lutze, too, lit up and began to pace up and down the room. "We have established," he said to Bertrand, "that you are Bertrand de Roujay, otherwise known as Montrouge." He paused. Bertrand said nothing. "You went to London in 1940, then to Algiers, and returned here some weeks ago as so-called commissioner of the Republic."

Again Bertrand said nothing.

"I think you know," said Lutze, "that you will be shot."

"It was always a possibility."

"I would be delighted, of course, if it could be avoided."

"So would I," said Bertrand, "but I fear that it cannot."

"Since we know who you are, we also know what you must know. You have a simple choice: either to tell us, or to oblige us to try to extract it from you." He shrugged his shoulders. "In the end, I think you should know, people always either talk or they die."

"As I have said," said Bertrand, "it was always a possibility."

"Even if I were to hand you over to your own people," said Lutze, "you would be executed because you have been condemned to death *in absentia* as a traitor."

"That too was in the cards."

"You concede that you are a traitor?"

"To whom?"

"To France."

"No."

"But it is your own government which calls you one."

"My government is that of General de Gaulle, not Marshal Pétain."

"Then you are no democrat, Monsieur de Roujay, because Marshal Pétain was given his powers under your Republican constitution, whereas de Gaulle was appointed either by himself or by Mr. Churchill —but not, in any case, by the French people."

"Pétain was elected under duress."

"Only the duress of a defeat in a war you brought upon yourself."

"It was you who invaded France."

"It was France who declared war on Germany."

"To assist Poland."

"What was Poland to you?"

"An ally."

"And why was an undemocratic and, incidentally, an anti-Semitic nation like Poland an ally of the western democracies?"

Bertrand frowned; he seemed bored by this discussion. "We had a treaty of mutual assistance."

"But why?"

"To protect ourselves against Germany."

"Precisely. The alliance with Poland, like the Treaty of Versailles, was a contrivance to restrain the German people within limits prescribed by the western powers."

"Your government accepted them."

"Under duress," said Lutze with a mocking smile.

"We gave you the Rhineland, the Sudetenland—"

"We took the Rhineland and the Sudetenland."

"You would not stop—"

"Until we had recovered what was historically ours."

"Prague?"

"A Hapsburg city."

"And the Czechs?"

"A minority, like the Bretons or the Basques."

"But even then," said Bertrand, his curiosity slowly aroused by the argument, "you had your eyes to the east. You were determined to conquer and colonize the Slavs."

"Of course," said Lutze. "You must understand, my dear de Roujay, that we Germans are a straightforward and slightly naive people. Like the Italians, we only belatedly formed a nation-state, and upon graduating, as it were, into the adult world we looked to our older and more sophisticated neighbors, France and Great Britain, and decided to emulate them. What did they have that we did not have? Empires. Where could we find an empire? Not in Africa, certainly; that had already been taken. Not in India, either; the British had that. In Asia? You and the Japanese had already staked your claim, and the British ruled the seas. So what was left? Only the wastes of eastern Europe —quite as primitive and underdeveloped, for the most part, as those Arab and Asiatic nations which you French and the British had seized in the recent past.

"You see, my dear de Roujay, it was really not quite 'fair play,' as the English say, to invent new rules of the game like 'self-determination' for others, and not apply them to yourselves. What the Italians tried to do in Ethiopia, and what we have tried to do in the east, is only what you, the British, the Spanish and the Portuguese have done all over the world—with the additional benefit that had we succeeded we would have extirpated once and for all the malign ideology of Karl Marx."

"It is not the same," said Bertrand. "Russia, after all, is an ancient nation."

"Ancient?" Lutze laughed. "Is the Muscovite civilization older than the Mongol principalities of Rajasthan? Or the sultanates of Morocco? Or the Annamite Kingdom in Tonkin?"

"But the Russians are European. They are . . ." He hesitated.

"White?" Lutze laughed. "Is that what you meant to say? No, de Roujay, you French and British, with all your self-righteous indignation, have no principles at all in international affairs except self-interest. You took what you wanted of the world by force, then drew a line in history and said that from 1919 new rules of morality would apply."

"Never," said Bertrand darkly, "have either France or Britain conquered weaker nations with such barbarous savagery as you have shown."

"Never?" asked Lutze. "I seem to remember some rather fine sketches by Goya depicting the atrocities of the French in Spain."

"The scale was not the same."

"Of course not. We live in the modern age, when everything is done on a large scale, but morality, I suggest, is not just a matter of scale. You therefore cannot condemn us for our *Realpolitik* if you do not at the same time condemn your Emperor Napoleon."

"Undoubtedly," said Bertrand, "all nations have their sins to answer for, but those of the Germans—"

"Will go down in history as the worst of all?" Lutze interrupted. "Yes. There we can agree. Ours will go down as the most infamous because we will lose the war, and it is the winner who writes history and educates subsequent generations. The uniforms of our Waffen SS will be portrayed as the costumes of Satan, whereas the kepis of your Foreign Legion will be romanticized and regarded with affection. Your venerable Marshal Pétain, who, when all is said and done, has performed just the duty that was asked of him by the French people four years ago by preserving them by and large from the worst ravages of a world war, will be condemned as a traitor by you eccentrics and adventurers who disobeyed your leaders and deserted your country at its hour of need."

"We have been vindicated," said Bertrand.

"Vindicated? By what?"

"By history."

"What is history? It is nothing but the retrospective propaganda of those in power."

"Totalitarianism can never triumph," said Bertrand, "because it is inimical to the human spirit. Freedom will always triumph in the end."

"It is not freedom that has triumphed in this war," said Lutze. "It is the methods of mass production in the United States and the Russian winter. Whose freedom are the British fighting for in the Far East? What freedom will follow in the wake of the victorious Russians? Do you imagine that Stalin will restore democracy where the Red Army has triumphed? And your own Resistance—do they really believe in liberty as you pretend? Will they have the courage to let the Marshal stand for election against General de Gaulle?"

Bertrand did not answer.

"I hardly think so," said Lutze. "Why, only last month, when Pétain went to Paris, a vast crowd turned out to cheer him at Notre Dame. But Pétain is on the losing side, and the loser pays heavily in France. Those who have fought for us will be branded as traitors, even though they have done so legitimately, whereas you renegades who have fought with the British and the Americans will be called patriots."

"We have never taken orders from a foreign power," said Bertrand vehemently.

"Oh, certainly," scoffed Lutze, "your General de Gaulle has put up a most convincing charade of independence, and has even, I daresay, kept the British and American jackals off the carcass of the French empire. But can you honestly pretend, my dear de Roujay, that the Communist cadres of your Resistance are any less in the service of a foreign power than are the Frenchmen who are fighting for us in the Legion of French Volunteers or the Waffen SS?"

"They do not wear the uniform of the Red Army," said Bertrand.

"So that is how it will be decided, is it?" asked Lutze. "The traitor will be distinguished from the patriot by the cut of his clothes? Well, if you sincerely believe that it is as simple as that, you are a lucky man."

Later that evening, Lutze was driven to the Villa Acacia. The servants admitted him without question, and he walked into the house with the familiarity of a husband returning from work. Nellie was usually waiting for him in the drawing room, but on this particular evening it was empty. Seeing that the doors leading to the garden were open, Lutze went out onto the terrace expecting to find her there, but there too there was no sign of her, so he returned to the house and climbed the stairs to her bedroom.

She was lying on her bed wearing a dressing gown. She seemed to be asleep, and for a moment Lutze felt annoyed that she had not been waiting for him as usual, dressed with an elegance which confounded the austerity of the times, but the sight of her heavy, disheveled hair, and the white stretch of her legs where the dressing gown had fallen away, filled him suddenly with both compassion and desire. Though Lutze was formal even in affairs of the heart, he was fond enough of Nellie to soften when he saw her in such vulnerable disorder.

He came and sat beside her on the bed. "Good morning," he said quietly in a jocular tone of voice.

She awoke, startled. "Morning?"

"No, evening."

"Ah." She looked quickly around the room. "Of course. I'm sorry."

He saw at once that the skin around her eyes was red. "Have you been crying?" he asked.

"Yes." She sat up and covered her legs.

"Why?"

"A friend has been killed. I have just heard."

"On the eastern front?" He asked it automatically, because that was where most men died.

"No," she said coldly. "On the western front." She got off the bed and went to her dressing table to powder her face.

Once again Lutze's unimaginative mind went to the second most common cause of death. "The Americans annihilate everything that lies in their path," he said.

"He was not killed by the Americans," she said.

"How, then?"

She took an eye pencil and delicately darkened the edges of her eyelids. "He killed himself."

"I see. I thought you meant . . ." Lutze stopped.

She turned. "That he had been killed in the war?"

"Yes." He had turned pale.

"One can die, like that, for one's country." She looked back at her reflection in the mirror.

For a moment Lutze said nothing. He wanted to change the subject, but then caught a glance of provocative disdain from her eye in the mirror, as if she was daring him to speak about what he knew.

"So you knew Moreau?" he said coldly.

"He was my closest friend," she said defiantly.

Lutze was afraid, as all men are when they sense that a woman's feelings are out of control. "I am sorry," he said abruptly, "but he was playing a dangerous game. He knew the risks."

Tears came into her eyes. "You bastard." She sobbed.

Lutze stiffened for a moment, but the sight of her shaking shoulders made his pity outweigh his anger—not just pity for Nellie but for himself too, because the only person he loved suddenly seemed to loathe him.

"I am sorry," he said again in a tone of far greater sincerity. "This is a wretched war. Nothing is left now that is not ugly."

"All the best men die," she said.

"I know. Moreau was undoubtedly a brave man."

"But you would have tortured him," she cried, struggling to buttress her hatred of a man she involuntarily loved.

"Yes."

"It is horrible."

"The whole war is horrible," said Lutze. "In Germany now, tens of thousands of women and children are burned alive by the Allies' bombs. On the eastern front men fight to the death from street to street, and from house to house. You cannot expect us to wear gloves in Coustiers when everywhere else they fight with bleeding knuckles."

She turned to face him, her eyes wide with the torment of her conflicting feelings. "And will you torture Professor Bonnet and Bertrand de Roujay?"

Again Lutze turned pale as he realized for the first time how close Nellie was to the Resistance. "Are they too your friends?"

"My oldest friends."

"Bonnet has gone. He won't be tortured."

"Will he be sent to Germany?"

"I daresay."

"To a concentration camp?"

"He knew the risks."

"We all know the risks," she said savagely.

"You?" His voice was hoarse.

"Of course."

His eyes dropped pathetically to look at the floor. "Then I was always an intelligence operation?"

She did not answer.

"You can tell me. *You* run no risks."

She turned and said with a subsiding anger, "I'm not afraid to die."

"Then tell me."

"What?"

"Whether you have ever loved me."

"Love!" She shrugged her shoulders and snorted. "What is love? I don't know."

"That is no answer."

"I would like to loathe you."

"But you don't?"

"I'm still trying."

Lutze smiled, and Nellie involuntarily smiled back. "Come here," he said.

She rose and came to sit next to him on the bed.

"I cannot believe . . ." Lutze began.

"What?" She kissed him softly on the lips, then drew back. "That I could play the whore with such conviction?"

"I cannot believe it," he muttered.

"It's astonishing what people will do for their country," Nellie said.

Now that she was mocking him, Lutze felt reassured. "I love you," he said, taking her hand and holding it on his knee.

"Then please don't torture my friends."

"Bonnet is now out of my hands, and de Roujay . . . I shall have to ask him what he knows."

"He will die before he tells you."

"I have no choice."

"You know the war is lost, Oskar."

"I know that, yes."

"Then let him live. We will need him when it is over."

"Why should I care what happens after the war?"

"Because I care."

"And if I did," said Lutze, his mind now flying to a world where the Third Reich no longer existed, "if I were to let him go, and, when the time came, leave France . . ."

"For where?"

"South America."

"Yes."

"Would you come with me?"

She hesitated for a moment, then said, "Yes."

"As my wife?"

"Yes."

He turned to look at his prize. For a moment he saw the confusion in her mind expressed in her eyes, but then the fear and resentment gave way to the drugged look of desire. She moved toward him and he embraced her. The dressing gown fell away from her legs.

"And your father would not let you starve?" murmured the former salesman of Ludwig and Kummerly.

"No."

"He would look after us?"

"Of course."

"And you would love me?"

"Of course, of course I would love you," she murmured, drawing him closer and feeling once again for the buckle of his belt.

For the next six weeks, Bertrand de Roujay remained a prisoner in the cellars of the Hôtel de la Poste. Every other day he was taken up to the office of the Sturmbannführer, where he was questioned by Lutze for an hour or so, and then was returned to his cell. Besides Lutze, he saw only the French auxiliaries who brought food to his cell.

The long hours of solitude and silence in the musty air under an electric light might have lowered his spirits had they not reached a nadir in the village of Cressac when he had seen Titine pulled from his arms by a German soldier and Pierre fall to his death. During his last months in London, and throughout the year in Algiers, the pessimism which had overwhelmed him after the infidelity of Jenny and the celibate solitude which he had chosen after the divorce had been made palatable only by the promise of a reunion after the war with those of whose love he could be sure.

Certainly in Algiers he had been sustained by the urgent work of preparing for the liberation of France, and the very fact that like a priest he was free of all personal encumbrance enabled him to devote himself to the Gaullist cause. But the acrimony and intrigue among the Frenchmen in the city had tempered the heady patriotism which had taken him to London, and by the time he had landed in metropolitan France he was driven only by a determination to finish what he had begun.

Like Pierre, Bertrand had realized at once that the ambush in Cressac meant that they had been betrayed. This again demoralized him, because besides the Bonnets only two or three of Pierre's closest collaborators had known where he was to be. It therefore seemed certain that there was a traitor in the inner circles of Fortitude. Since it was upon Fortitude that he had relied for the personnel to administer the liberated department, this discovery that it too was rotten exacerbated his depression. He knew that he would be tortured, he expected to die, but he would have liked to know that good men, not traitors, would survive him.

Concealed under a small patch of false hair were the two cyanide tablets that had been issued to him upon his departure from Algiers. Bertrand considered taking them as he moldered in prison, but where Pierre in killing himself had been true to the tradition of Masada in the first century, or of York in the eleventh, when his fellow Jews had preferred suicide to defeat, Bertrand was inhibited by his Christian belief that a man may not take his own life. There was a sense, too, in which the prospect of torture kept the spirit of revolt alive within him. He was determined to atone for the tragedy that had followed his return to France by enduring whatever pain the Germans would inflict.

As the weeks passed, however, and Bertrand was not tortured despite his refusal to divulge what he knew of the Resistance, he could not sustain this spirit of defiance and relapsed into apathy. He began to forget what it was that had inspired him before his capture. The imperatives of the outside world faded from his mind, and he became obsessed with the minutiae of life in the institution itself—the personalities of the warders, the nastiness of the food.

Suddenly, one day in late July, instead of being taken up to Lutze's office, Bertrand was shown to the door of the Hôtel de la Poste and was told that he was free. Finding himself in the midst of a crowd on the Avenue de la République, he became a prey to complete confusion. Having spent so many weeks alone in a dark and airless cell, preparing himself daily for torture and death, he could not now imagine that his release was not some hideous trick played by Lutze to undermine his resolve. As he walked toward the river and was not dragged back, he regained some confidence in his liberty of action, but then became certain that he must be being followed, and had only been released to lead the Germans to other members of the Resistance. He therefore walked for an hour through the back streets of the city, entering shops by one door and leaving by the other, and taking odd buses, until he became certain that he had shaken off anyone on his tail.

At last he went into a small bar, where he sat over a cup of ersatz coffee to consider what he should do. He must make contact again with the Resistance, but which branch could he trust? In prison he had gone over and over the possibilities of who the traitor might be, and decided that it could have been almost any of the leaders of the different groups who for one reason or another might have wanted him out of the way. Ledésert, the leader of the army group, worked hand in glove with the Americans, who still at this late hour hoped to liberate France without de Gaulle. Guy Serot seemed an unlikely candidate, because he so clearly had been devoted to Pierre, but although Bertrand had liked the young lawyer when he had met him, he had also sensed in him a strong and perhaps unscrupulous ambition to play a leading role in Coustiers after the war. Had he perhaps seen a chance to get rid of the leader of Fortitude so that he could take charge of a nascent political party?

The dilemma faced by Bertrand as he sat in the café was acute, because if he could trust neither the officers of Ledésert's army group, nor the Communists in the FTP, nor the Socialists and Freemasons of Fortitude, he was in a poor position to represent and assert the authority of General de Gaulle, because these three movements among them made up the greater part of the Resistance in the department of Basse-Provence.

To be sure, if he could survive until the liberation of Provence, he could call upon units of the French army to support him, but it was precisely to avoid this semblance of a Gaullist coup d'état, which would tie down troops in France itself, that he had been sent ahead to establish an administration. If the Communists were to be thwarted, it must never be possible for them to say that General de Gaulle had used an army of Moroccan mercenaries and former Pétainists to frustrate the will of the French people as expressed through the civilian Resistance.

Only one group remained which was strong, civilian and immune to any ideological bacillus: the wing of Fortitude in the pay of the Jacopozzis. Galling though it was for Bertrand to have to go cap in hand to the gangster whom he had once been so determined to imprison, he could see no alternative, and knowing that Jaco was now married to Isabelle, and had already served the Resistance well, he felt he could justify what he proposed to do on the grounds that Jaco's services to his country merited a pardon for his crimes.

Early each evening, Isabelle Jacopozzi went to her room in the Villa Fleurie. After a day in the company of her Corsican relatives and the children, she was always relieved to find herself alone in her own domain. As Jaco's wife she had the finest room in the house, with a balcony which overlooked the garden. In summer the double doors which led onto the balcony were left wide open to admit the sound of crickets and the pine-scented air.

Isabelle had as little to do in her room as she had downstairs. The few books she had brought with her when she had first married had been read and reread a dozen times until too great a familiarity had spoiled them. Her timid requests for a new stock had been peremptorily refused. Jaco had told her that the books she wanted were unobtainable because of the war. She knew quite well that this was not true, and that it was because Jaco was as jealous of her favorite authors as he was of her old friends that he would not allow her to restock her library.

One of the ways in which she spun out the time between coming up to her room and lying down to sleep was to take an inordinate amount of time getting ready for bed. First she took a bath, lying for a good half hour to let the fragrant oil which she had added to the water permeate her skin. Then she dressed in a white cotton nightdress, returned to her bedroom and spent another half hour at her dressing table brushing her long black hair. She liked to make the tresses glisten, and to stare sadly into her own large eyes, glancing wistfully every now and then at the soft brown skin of her body, which glowed through the netting of lace.

Her most agreeable companion thus became her own reflection in the glass, for it was the only one without a trace of the rough Corsican physiognomy which she had now come to hate. She admired her own beauty, which had become outstanding over the months of languorous idleness. While women in the world outside the villa had starved, Isabelle had eaten her fill. While they had slaved and scrounged to get through the day, she had played tennis or splashed in the swimming pool in the grounds, so that the almost gawky body of the girl who had married Jaco Jacopozzi had grown into that of a healthy and handsome woman.

None of this was of much benefit to Jaco, who never now shared her bed. For the sake of appearances he retired behind the door of their room, but behind it he remained aloof and slept on a bed in an annex. Not since she had repulsed him after the birth of Tonio had Jaco claimed his rights to her body, and not since then had Isabelle felt inclined to acknowledge them. Yet each remembered the passion of the first year of their marriage, and so hated the other for the pain of their present unsatisfied desire.

It was part of Isabelle's vengeance to make herself at once both indifferent and alluring. The more care she took of her long brown body and the more tantalizing the way in which she presented it, the colder became the look that she gave to her husband when she saw him. Her beauty was the weapon with which she could punish him for her incarceration.

By now she had abandoned any idea of leaving the Villa Fleurie. Her earlier life had taken on the unreality of someone else's biography, and even where it forced itself into the reality of life in the villa, it was only as a postscript to the story. First of all she had heard from Pierre that their parents had disappeared; then that they had been captured by the Gestapo and deported to Germany; and finally the news had come from Jaco that Pierre himself was dead.

This finally defeated any hope of flight, for it meant that even if she could have climbed the walls there was nowhere to go. Therefore the dream of escaping from the Jacopozzis which had once preoccupied her gave way to girlish fantasies of rescue by a strong and handsome man—at times resembling Guy Serot, but later, as his memory faded, becoming an amalgam of all the heroes in the novels which she had read and reread in her room.

One evening in early August she had taken her bath and was sitting at her dressing table brushing her hair when she heard through the open doors which led onto the balcony the sound of cars on the gravel. She laid down her brush, pursed her lips together to make them pink, and then went to her bed so that Jaco should find her there defiantly reading *Le Rouge et le Noir*.

She heard his voice in the hall, then other voices, which was not unusual, since Jaco often returned with some of his men. It was some twenty minutes before she heard Jaco's step on the landing and saw him come through the door.

As always, neither greeted the other. Jaco merely glanced at her as if to make sure that his property was as he had left it, then went to the balcony and closed the shutters.

"You shouldn't leave them open like that."

"It lets in the air."

"People can see in."

"Who?"

"The men at the wall."

"So much the better. It gives them something to do."

Jaco turned and glared at her; he did not like such jokes. "In future close the shutters."

"Whatever you say." She spoke to him with an irony which infuriated him.

"Particularly now."

"Why?"

"We have a guest."

She smiled. "You honor your thugs by calling them guests?"

"He is not one of the men."

"Who is he, then?"

"The commissioner of the Republic." As he said this he raised his head and looked at her with an expression of triumph.

The words and his look had their effect. Isabelle dropped her mask of mockery. "What is he doing here?"

Normally Jaco would not have answered a question of this kind, but now he hesitated as if he himself was somewhat confused about what to do.

"He's on the run."

"From the Germans?"

"Yes. No, not from the Germans. From your friends."

"I have no friends," said Isabelle curtly.

Jaco frowned. "Your brother's friends, then."

"Why should he run from them?"

"Because one of those bastards ratted on him, didn't they? On your brother too."

"He was with Pierre?"

"Yes. He and the old man were taken."

"How did he escape from the Germans?"

"He was released."

"Why?"

"I don't know."

"Why did he come to you?"

"Because he doesn't trust the others."

Isabelle sat up in bed. "What is his mission?"

"To take over."

"Where?"

"Here in Coustiers. When the city is liberated, he'll be the prefect —except now it's called commissioner of the Republic."

"Ah," said Isabelle, with a trace of scorn returning. "Then you'd better treat him with care."

"Or cut his throat," said Jaco.

"But remember your plans, Jaco."

"What plans?"

"Why, to pick up the crown of the Burzios, which will be rolling in the gutter."

"If he ends up owing me—"

"His life. His position. Why, Jaco, you'll be able to do in Guillot and the Burzios with the blessing of the law."

"I don't need you to tell me that," said Jaco gruffly, relieved to be told by Isabelle that he had done the right thing, but unwilling to acknowledge that he valued her advice.

"Of course not," she said acidly. "You don't need me for anything."

She picked up her book while Jaco, with a lizardlike lick of his lips, stole a glance at the bodice of her nightdress, then looked away and went through to the dressing room to sleep on the single bed.

The next morning Isabelle rose early and went to the pool to swim. As the water lapped around her body she heard the sound of the cars starting; Jaco was leaving for Coustiers. She went back to the house, dressed, and came down to find the other women and her son Tonio sitting at breakfast.

After breakfast she went out onto the terrace to lie in the sun before it became too hot. She closed her eyes and was dazzled by the bright pink light which shone through her eyelids. In the background she could hear the cries of the children, the squealing singsong voices of the Corsican women in the house, and then, close to her, a man's voice speaking her name.

She opened her eyes. For a moment, still dazzled, she saw nothing.

"Don't you remember me?" the voice said.

She shielded her eyes from the sun and saw Bertrand.

"It is only four years," he said with a smile, "since you kissed me goodbye in Céret."

"Bertrand?"

"Yes."

She stood up, astonished and uncertain how to behave; then he held open his arms to embrace her, and because he was a friend of Pierre's she clung to him and wept with an abandon that she had not shown since she was a child.

They were unobserved, and when some moments later she had stopped sobbing they left the terrace and walked in the garden to give time for her tears to dry.

"Of all the tragedies in this terrible war," Bertrand said to her gently, "Pierre's death was the worst. As I lay in my cell expecting to die, I felt almost an urgency to join him."

"Did he really fall," asked Isabelle, "or was he shot?"

"He was cornered up there at Cressac, so he threw himself down the mountain."

She stopped under the shadow of an umbrella pine and hid her face in her hands.

"But I saw his face, Isabelle. He was radiant, triumphant, possessed by a defiant courage. He had sworn to himself that they would not take him; moreover, he knew too much to run the risk of betraying those secrets under torture. It was not despair, Isabelle, but the joy of a willing martyr that we all saw on his face."

She looked up. Once again she had composed herself, and they continued their walk around the garden.

"The practical problems posed by his death are immense," said Bertrand, speaking quietly but also with urgency, as if uncertain for how long he would have the company of someone he could trust. "You see, we were betrayed by someone at the heart of the Resistance in Coustiers, and until I know who it was I can trust no one."

"But you trust Jaco."

"I thought that because of you . . ."

"Because of me, no," she said grimly. "He would sooner kill a friend of mine than save him. But he has high hopes of the pickings after the war, and if he can pocket the prefect in advance . . ."

"I always felt skeptical about his patriotism."

"He is a patriot, all right, but his nation is his family, the Jacopozzis. As long as their interests and yours coincide, you can trust him."

They sat on a stone bench at the far end of the garden, a pink tinge of sunburn slowly appearing on the gray skin of Bertrand's face. "Have you any idea," he asked Isabelle, "who might have given us away?"

She shook her head. "I know nothing. I have been imprisoned here for so long."

"Imprisoned?"

"Jaco won't let me out."

"He wants to protect you."

She laughed. "Yes. From phantom lovers."

Bertrand thought for a moment, then said, "You cannot realize how complex and chaotic it has become now that the end draws near. The Resistance has become an insurrection, the struggle against the Germans a civil war."

"But that's good, isn't it?" asked Isabelle. "The Vichy regime must be overthrown."

"It will go," said Bertrand gravely, "there is no question of that. But what will replace it? A democratic republic or a dictatorship of the proletariat?"

"The Communists mean to seize power?"

"They mean to try."

"Will the Americans allow it?"

"They may not be able to prevent it."

Isabelle shook her head. "It will be horrible," she said, "if Pierre died only to replace Hitler with Stalin."

"I am determined," said Bertrand, "that here in Coustiers, at any rate, we will frustrate them, but they are well organized and cunning. With Pierre gone, the Fortitude group will be in confusion."

"Guy will take it on."

"You know him?"

"Yes."

"Could it have been him?"

"Who betrayed you? No. Not unless he has changed beyond recognition."

"When did you last see him?"

"Nearly two years ago."

"You have been here all that time?" Only now did Bertrand seem to appreciate what she had told him earlier—that she was a prisoner in the Villa Fleurie.

"Jaco is a simple, not to say primitive, man," said Isabelle bitterly. "I did not realize when I married him that I would be kept in a seraglio."

"But Pierre, before he died? Couldn't he have helped you escape?"

She laughed. "Pierre lived only for Fortitude, and Fortitude needed the Jacopozzis. He had to take great care not to offend Jaco."

"You were sacrificed?"

"I don't think he saw it that way. After all, I chose to marry Jaco. I did it of my own free will."

A fleeting look of sadness came onto Bertrand's face. "One can make mistakes of that kind," he said.

"Yes," said Isabelle. "You and Madeleine, after all."

"And again in England."

"You married?"

"And divorced."

She glanced at him solicitously. "Were there children?" she asked.

Again he looked pained. "A boy, but not mine." He hesitated, then added, "Almost certainly not mine."

"Poor Bertrand. You've had hard luck with women."

"And you with men."

"With one man. But after the war . . ." She laughed. "Wait and see."

"You'll leave him?"

"Oh, yes. I'd have left him by now if I had anywhere to go." Then she added, with a slight blush, "Or anyone to go to." And having said it she looked away, so that when Bertrand glanced at her he saw not her eyes but her body, and noticed for the first time how the child he had left at Céret had grown into a woman.

At midday Jaco returned with half a dozen men. From the garden Isabelle saw that one of them was Guy Serot. A week before—a day before—she might have run to him, but now, as she watched him walk from the car to the house, she suddenly remembered all the reasons why she had resisted his advances before.

At four that afternoon the cars drove out again and Bertrand came out onto the terrace.

"Serot sent his regards," he said.

"I am glad he remembered me."

"He wanted to see you, but your husband put him off."

"He doesn't like me to meet other men."

"Then it's fortunate," said Bertrand, "that he sees me as something less than a man."

"I'm sure it's not that," Isabelle said with a blush.

"He thinks I'm too old?" asked Bertrand.

"Perhaps." She blushed again. "But that only shows how little he knows about women."

After the death of Pierre Moreau and the arrest of the others at the Hôtellerie de la Forêt, Madeleine Bonnet had found herself left in the restaurant with her mother, daughter and the restaurateur, Monsieur Parigny. The horror of what they had witnessed stunned the three women, and they were only brought to their senses by Parigny, who thought at first that their liberty was an oversight, and that the Gestapo would soon return to arrest them too.

They therefore fled up the valley to the peasant's dwelling where Françoise and Michel Bonnet had been hiding. Here they were safe, but here, on reflection, Madeleine realized the true significance of the apparent oversight of letting Parigny and herself go free. It showed not only that the Germans had come hunting for a specific quarry, but that this quarry had been identified and betrayed by someone in Coustiers, because if it had been a traitor in the maquis, Parigny himself would certainly have been arrested.

Who had known that they would be there? She herself had told Titine only when they were already in the mountains, so the secret could not have slipped out at Saint Théodore. Michel had known, but it was unlikely that he would have told anyone else, and inconceivable, even if he had, that his friends in the Resistance would have passed such a secret on to the Gestapo, unless under torture. But there had not been time enough for that to have happened.

The only alternative explanation was that someone in Fortitude had wanted to dispose of Pierre. Though not a member of the group, she knew more about it from Pierre and her father than many of those who were, and her suspicions at once settled not on Serot, who she knew would have died for Pierre, but on Bertrand's former colleague at the subprefecture of Mézac, André Pidner. He was on the committee of Fortitude, he might well have known about the meeting, and he was likely to resent Bertrand's return to power as commissioner of the Republic.

Although this antipathy itself might not have been enough to betray them—Bonnet, after all, had been a fellow Mason—she also knew that some weeks earlier Pidner's daughter had been arrested by the police for distributing issues of *Fortitude;* and she knew from experience that nothing makes a man more vulnerable to blackmail than the threat of torture of someone he loves.

In the solitary vastness of the mountains, Madeleine's hunch grew in her mind into a certainty, and she became convinced that it was her duty to return to Coustiers to warn Guy Serot that Pidner was not to be trusted. She therefore left Titine and Françoise in the care of Parigny and the maquis and made her way back to Coustiers.

Her first frustration when she reached the city was the difficulty she faced in making contact with any of the Resistance leaders. As the end approached, the battle between the Resistance and different units loyal to Vichy—the *milice,* the Service d'Ordre Légionnaire and certain units of the Sûreté—had degenerated into an open civil war, with skirmishes in the streets and atrocious vengeance taken on both sides by peremptory revolutionary tribunals or courts-martial. As a result, men like Guy Serot, Georges Auget and Michel le Fresne never spent two nights at the same address, and Madeleine had no way of knowing where they might be.

There was only one man she could trust, who she knew was in constant contact through the National Front with the FTP, and that was the Dominican, Antoine Dubec. She went unannounced to the monastery on the Rue de la Paix, where he received her as before in the room with the portraits of the Dominican saints.

"Madeleine," he said, "thank God you are free."

"You heard about Pierre and my father?"

"Yes. It is terrible. How did it happen?"

"I don't know. There must be a traitor in Fortitude."

"But who?"

"I have my suspicions, but my only contact with Fortitude was through Pierre and my father, and anyway, I wouldn't know whom to trust."

"Have you told Michel?"

"That's why I'm here. I don't know how to get hold of him."

"I can send a message."

"Please do. As soon as possible. It is a matter of life and death."

That night Madeleine received a note from the concierge with another coded message giving a time and a place to meet Michel le Fresne. Once again she set off in good time to shake off any possible pursuer, and at eight arrived at the newsstand on the corner of the Rue de Grenelle.

"Do you sell *La Chronique du Passé*?" she asked.

"No," answered the vendor.

"And *La Chronique de l'Avenir*?"

He looked at her without answering, then nodded over his shoulder. "The bar across the road," he said. "He's waiting."

She turned and crossed the street. As she entered the bar she saw not just Michel but Georges Auget too. Both expressed their regrets at what had happened in Cressac.

"They were betrayed," said Madeleine immediately.

"Are you sure?" asked Auget.

"How else could they have known that we'd be there?"

"It certainly looks fishy."

"I think I know who did it."

Michel looked up. "Who?"

"Pidner."

"Why Pidner?"

"He's always hated Bertrand, from the old days in Mézac, and his daughter's in the hands of the *milice*."

"Did he know you were there?"

"I don't know, but it's possible. And there is no one else, unless Serot is not to be trusted."

"It's more likely Serot," said Auget. "Pierre was in his way."

"He loved Pierre," said Madeleine.

"Love," said Michel, "is a salable commodity."

Madeleine blushed at her lover's cynicism. She could not understand why Michel seemed so nonchalant and Georges Auget so detached, as if the treachery of Pidner were a matter of small importance. "Doesn't it matter," she asked vehemently, "who betrayed them?"

"Keep calm," said Michel. "You will attract attention."

"Subjectively," said Auget in the same pedantic tone he had used to discuss politics when dining at their house, "it matters very much that those three men were taken at Cressac, because Bonnet is your father, Pierre your friend and Bertrand de Roujay your former husband. But at this juncture in history, Madeleine, it is our duty to see through the dust raised by our feelings to the objective significance of these events. First, we must consider what damage has been done. To our morale, some damage, undoubtedly. To our efficacy, little harm is done. Pierre, who knew all, had the courage to cheat the Germans by taking his own life. Your father, a magnificent symbol, knows nothing concrete, and they realize it, because otherwise they would not have sent him straight to Germany. De Roujay, our commissioner, knows a certain amount, and I daresay, poor man, that they will extract it from him in due course, but he knows nothing about our own organization, only about what stems from Algiers. Now Pidner, if he betrayed them, will already have told the Gestapo what he knows of the Fortitude organization. We can therefore deal with him at our leisure, and perhaps even use him to give false information to the enemy."

"In this sense," said Michel, "what happened in Cressac, though subjectively a tragedy, may turn out objectively to our advantage."

Madeleine was dumbfounded. Only a fear of drawing the attention of others in the café prevented an angry outburst at this calculating indifference to the three men's fate. "Really," she said with a fierce hiss of irony in her voice, "you seem to have everything well under control. I could have stayed in the mountains."

"You are a woman, Madeleine," said Michel. "You are inevitably upset by what has happened. But we are men, and we cannot afford to be governed by our emotions."

"It's true, Madeleine," said Georges. "Circumstances have put us at the helm of history. Our course is clear. It is our duty to mankind to follow it. We must be strong and dispassionate, because the coming weeks are critical not just for the prosecution of the war but for the whole future of France."

4

On August 16 the news reached Coustiers that American and French forces had landed near Saint Tropez. A day later they had broken through the German defenses and were over the Massif des Maures into the valley of the Aille. From here the U.S. Seventh Army under General Patch pursued the Germans north over the Alps toward Grenoble, while the French First Army under General Jean de Lattre de Tassigny fought its way west to encircle the ports of Toulon and Marseilles. On August 27, four days after General Leclerc had liberated Paris in the north, the Germans surrendered to General Montsabert in Marseilles.

Bertrand, who had established his temporary headquarters at the Villa Fleurie, had been forewarned of the invasion by the government in Algiers, with which he had now made contact by radio. What he had not anticipated, however, was the speed with which the French forces would penetrate the German lines, or the chaos that would ensue in the cities under his nominal jurisdiction.

In Coustiers the Germans had disappeared from the streets, either to reinforce the new front to the north or to blow up the installations which if captured intact could be used to supply the Allied armies. As a result, the secret skirmishes between the Resistance and the various paramilitary forces loyal to the Vichy regime had come out into the open. While the gendarmes and the police stood aside, the units of the *milice* and SOL vied with squads of partisans in inflicting summary justice on their political opponents.

The moment drew near for Bertrand to leave the Villa Fleurie and move to the prefecture. He hesitated for two reasons. He still had few men under his direct command. He had made contact with Captain Ledésert, who headed the Coustiers section of the Army Resistance Organization, and Guy Serot, who headed the Fortitude group, but both these networks remained insignificant beside the hardened cadres of partisans in the Communist FTP. Moreover, these in their turn had now been joined by a horde of murderous riffraff—many of them defectors from the Burzios' organization—who, by calling themselves Resistants, sought to take advantage of the chaos to indulge in looting and revenge.

The only armed men upon whom Bertrand could depend to counterbalance the power of the partisans remained those units loyal to the Jacopozzis, and it was his intention to use them, when the moment came, to establish his authority in the prefecture. But there was a second factor which made him hesitate before moving his headquarters from the Villa Fleurie, and that was his attachment to Isabelle.

At first he did not realize that he was drawn to her by anything other than the affection that any man would feel for the sister of his closest friend. Sexual love did not suggest itself, not only because she was so much younger than he was, and another man's wife, but because since his divorce Bertrand had put love aside for the duration of the war. In his solitude, he had consoled himself with his memories of those he loved in France. Without his realizing it, however, those memories became expectations, and no sooner had he returned to France than his appetite for human love had become ravenous, as if craving the replenishment it had been denied over the past two years. In particular he had longed for Titine—the cause, in a sense, of his self-exile, and the justification of all that he had suffered. It was for this reason that he had ignored Pierre's sound advice to wait a few more months until the war was over before seeing her, and had insisted upon the meeting at Cressac. The trap which had been set, and which had led to Pierre's heroic but horrible death before his eyes, Bertrand now blamed upon his own folly. He had therefore gone to the airless cell in the Hôtel de la Poste almost grateful that he would suffer for his sins and soon follow his friend to the grave.

The weeks Bertrand had spent in the cellar of the Hôtel de la Poste in daily expectation of torture and death had exacerbated the fragility of his frame of mind. He had therefore arrived at the Villa Fleurie in a confused condition, and though quite able, after his years as a civil servant, to present a controlled, even imposing facade, he was unusually vulnerable within. When he had seen Isabelle he had not at first remarked on her beauty, but had embraced her as the sister of Pierre. Even when he realized that she was trapped and unhappy in her marriage to Jaco Jacopozzi, he saw his role ahead as a fraternal, even paternal, protector.

Isabelle, however, who for so long had imagined this knight errant who would come to save her, recognized him at once in Bertrand de Roujay, and unleashed upon him all the power of her frustrated sexual allure. It had its effect. The instinct which Bertrand had thought not just dormant but dead awoke with a start, and suddenly he found himself overwhelmed by an acute desire for the sexual possession of Isabelle Jacopozzi. While the shell of his body and mind continued to be preoccupied with the progress of the war and the administration of the liberated department of Basse-Provence, the pulp of both was inflamed with this obsessive passion. If he could have fled from the villa he might have been able to subdue these feelings, but he was obliged by circumstance to remain there, so while Jaco and his men shuttled between the villa and the city, Bertrand and Isabelle found themselves alone.

At first, they talked like brother and sister, but from the first day it was plain from the glances they exchanged that both felt and recognized the love they felt for each other. Of the two affections, Bertrand's was the more timid, Isabelle's the more demanding, for while he was racked not just by his religious scruples but also by the thought that to seduce her would be a reckless and dishonorable abuse of Jaco Jacopozzi's hospitality, she was goaded on and felt justified by the contempt she felt for her husband.

The end was not in doubt, for when sexual desire is aroused in this way it has the power of the instinct for life itself. Their first kiss was behind a tree in the garden, a hurried, dreadful brush of the lips. Their second, the next day, was in the pavilion by the tennis court, where he clasped her body, glistening and scented by her sweat after her exertion, and savored for longer the taste of her lips and felt for the first time the bulge of her breasts. There were two more fumbling encounters in the pavilion, each pushing back the frontiers of discretion. Then, during the siesta, when the men were in Coustiers and the whole household was asleep, Isabelle came to his room on tiptoe and they made love in silence behind the closed shutters.

At around the same time, on the other side of the city, another couple made love on a bed; but while the actions of their bodies were much the same, their hearts were as empty of passion as those of the first two were full. Madeleine, who had met Michel to deliver some clean clothes, had her mind not on her body but on the conversation they had had at lunch.

Michel had been in an irritable mood, and at first would not say why, but toward the end of the meal he had let drop that the Party's plans for an insurrection in Coustiers were being frustrated by the unlikely alliance of Bertrand de Roujay and Jaco Jacopozzi.

"But you said it was impossible," she said mockingly, "for history to be thwarted by historically irrelevant forces."

"And so it is," said Michel.

"Then don't you find it paradoxical," she said, "that it is the capitalist Americans and our own colonial troops who are chasing out the Germans?"

"Only when they have been routed by the Red Army."

"But then the Gaullists, too, may take advantage of the Soviets' sacrifices."

"We must stop them."

"How?"

"By eliminating them."

"But my dear Michel," Madeleine said with the same touch of mockery which always goaded her lover into saying more than he intended, "if one half of the Resistance tries to eliminate the other, it will start a civil war which would almost certainly end in the same way as it did in Spain."

"There's no question of a conflict at the grass roots," said Michel. "The great majority of the Resistance is with us."

"But they are misled?"

"Yes."

"Then get rid of the leaders."

"It isn't so easy."

"They are too cunning?"

"They are too lucky."

"But really," she said, laughing, "if history is *inevitable,* it can hardly depend on luck."

Michel scowled. "It cannot last."

"Their luck?"

"The alliance between Bertrand and the Jacopozzis. It is too improbable, too absurd."

"Don't be so sure," said Madeleine, still smiling at his discomfiture. "The Jacopozzis can smell dollars and a fat black market. What interest do they have in a Communist France?"

"The interest of being on the winning side."

"Perhaps they think they are already on it."

"We shall see."

After a good lunch "on Churchill" they went back to the room in the tenement where Michel was hiding.

"What did you mean," she asked as they climbed the dark stairs in a sudden spiral of coolness in the great heat of the city, "that it isn't easy to get rid of their leaders? Have you tried?"

"Not really." He sounded uneasy.

"Then why did you say that they were lucky?"

They came into the small apartment, and Madeleine followed Michel into the bedroom.

"I don't know," said Michel. "They just seem to be lucky." He started to remove his clothes.

"Not Pierre," she said, lifting her dress over her shoulders as if preparing for a medical inspection.

"But Bertrand," said Michel. "Who could imagine that the Gestapo would let him go?"

"Yes, that, I agree, does seem a miracle."

As Michel climbed over her and went to work, Madeleine lay back on the bed, listening to his grunts in her ear and wondering why he had been uneasy when she had asked him if he had tried to get rid of his opponents in the Resistance. He had said that it was not easy, which seemed to imply that he had tried. He had said they had been lucky. Who had been lucky? Bertrand, to have been released for no reason. Who had been unlucky? Her father and Pierre. Who had known that they would be at Cressac? Michel! Suddenly she knew, and gave a cry of anguish. As she did so, Michel ejaculated and collapsed onto her with a sigh.

As he heaved himself off her body he gave her a wink of male self-satisfaction. "You really like it, don't you?" he said. "They say women do as they get older." He patted her on the stomach, then leaned across her body to reach for a cigarette.

Chapter 11

1

WHEN de Lattre de Tassigny's troops were only ten miles from Coustiers, Oskar Lutze prepared to depart not just from the city he had terrorized for two years but from the skin of a member of the master race. He had Panamanian passports for himself and for Nellie under the name Sternheim, and tincture to darken both his hair and his complexion. He had packed a suitcase with tailor-made tropical suits and had fitted it with a false lid to conceal the gold coins he had collected during his tenure at the Hôtel de la Poste. These would see to their immediate expenses, and for the long term he felt confident that he would be provided for by his father-in-law, Emile Planchet.

For some weeks he had been anxious that Nellie might not keep her part of the bargain, because he recognized that he inspired in her ferocious emotions of both love and loathing. He had kept Bertrand de Roujay in custody not just to reassure his superiors that he was making full use of this valuable captive but also as insurance against Nellie changing her mind. It was only after she had married him in front of her father at the *mairie* that Bertrand was finally released.

To explain this course of action to his superiors in the SS he persuaded them that Bertrand had been "turned" and was now working for the Gestapo. He knew that Delage in Marseilles suspected him of striking a private bargain, but since at this stage most of his colleagues were doing the same thing, these suspicions led to nothing and the path was clear for Lutze's escape.

The actual traveling arrangements had been made, through Guillot, by Andréas Burzio, who was himself preparing to leave for South America. They were to be taken by car to the coast; there a felucca would carry them to Genoa, where berths had been reserved on a freighter sailing to Montevideo. Lutze had a letter confirming the reservations, and though he trusted neither Guillot nor the Burzios, he relied upon their greed and had kept back the final payment of the exorbitant cost of these arrangements until he was safely away.

The plan went into effect on August 25. Lutze left his office, where half the personnel had disappeared, and was driven as usual to the Villa Acacia. There Nellie was waiting in a green linen suit, her suitcases ready in the hall.

"You can only take one," said Lutze.

Her face fell. "But what shall I wear?"

"The clothes on your back."

He went upstairs, took off his uniform for the last time, and twenty minutes later returned as Ignatius Sternheim, a Panamanian businessman.

Nellie smiled when she saw him. "No one will recognize you," she said. "You are more convincing as a salesman than you were as a policeman."

At six, Guillot arrived with two cars. "Quick," he said. "We must leave at once."

His cold eyes watched as Nellie's servants loaded the luggage into the second car. He noticed that Lutze carried his brown suitcase himself and placed it in the trunk with particular care.

"Follow," he said to the driver of the second car; then, leading the way in his own car, he set off through the gates. They took side streets into the city, avoiding the Avenue de la République, but they had to cross the river, and as they turned onto the Pont Neuf they suddenly found their way blocked by two Citroëns whose doors had been removed to give a free field of fire to the machine guns held by their passengers.

"Halt, in the name of the Republic," shouted a gun-toting youth wearing a checked shirt and a tricolor armband as he leaped from his car with his gun pointed at Guillot. Others tumbled out behind him, so that the first car was surrounded.

"Drive around them," Lutze hissed to the driver of the second.

The man shrugged his shoulders and did nothing.

The swarthy face of the young man wearing the checked shirt, who had the air of a brigand, looked through the window at Lutze and Nellie. "Out," he said.

Lutze, Nellie and the driver got out of the car. Guillot and his driver were already standing on the road.

"Papers," shouted the young man.

Guillot and the drivers took out their frayed identity cards, Lutze the shining new Panamanian passports, but before the leader could look at them a still younger man, whom Lutze recognized at once as one of those who had run errands at the Hôtel de la Poste, came forward shouting in a croaky voice, "It's him, it's Lutze." He reached up and touched his hair. "Look, it's polish, that's all."

The youth holding the passports looked up, and Lutze met his eyes. The boy grinned. Suddenly Lutze realized that it was all a charade. He turned to Guillot, who looked away.

"You swine," Lutze whispered, and with a sudden lunge reached for the revolver in his pocket, but before he could draw it out a third man from the group of supposed Resistants shot him in the stomach with his machine gun.

Nellie screamed; the drivers cowered. For a moment the group stood watching as the German writhed on the cobbles, coughing, spluttering and crying with pain. Then the young man fired a second burst into his body, and after a few more spasms Lutze lay still.

There was a cackle from the killers, a moan from Nellie Planchet. This reminded them of her presence, and three of them grabbed her roughly by the arms and dragged her to their car. She turned for help to Guillot, but already the commissaire, accompanied by the young man wearing the checked shirt, had gone to the second car to recover Lutze's brown suitcase.

As the car set off down the boulevard, Nellie was held tightly by two coarse and evil-smelling men, one holding her arm, the other with his elbow around her neck. The driver accelerated, then braked, then accelerated again, swerving around corners and scraping the exhaust on cobbles, until finally the car stopped outside a school in the industrial suburb of Piron. The place appeared to have been requisitioned by a gang of demented youths, some of whom might recently have been pupils there, as part barracks, part prison, part palace of justice. There was a lavish display of the tricolor armbands, but the leader here was an older, sallow, ill-shaven man who sat on a podium in the school hall and was addressed as the commissioner of the people.

As Nellie was dragged in by a crowd of men and women, the men prodding her and tearing at her clothes, the women shouting obscenities at her in hoarse voices, the commissioner of the people hammered on the table and called for order.

"Who is the accused?" he shouted.

"A tart," someone shouted, and all the others guffawed.

"She was skipping with the Nazi," said the youth who had arrested her.

"She's been fucking him for months," said another.

"She married him!" shouted a third.

The older man looked at the passports, then threw them aside. "Then give her what she deserves," he said.

"But wait, please," shouted Nellie. "I worked for the Resistance. I saved the life of the commissioner."

"What commissioner?" asked the sallow man.

"The commissioner of the Republic, Bertrand de Roujay."

"There's only one commissioner here," he said savagely, "the commissioner of the people, and that's me." He turned to the others. "Now get on with it. Deal with her."

"Yes, deal with her," the cry went up.

Two men grabbed Nellie's arms, two her legs, and she was laid on her back on the floor. Then, while a fat middle-aged woman grabbed her hair and started to cut it off close to the scalp, the commissioner of the people stood over her, tore back the bodice of her dress, and with a quick slash of a knife cut a swastika on the skin between her breasts.

"So that you won't forget your lover," he said with a leer; then, with another deft gesture, he leaned down and gripped an ear on the side of her half-shaved head.

"And so that I won't forget you," he said, brandishing his knife above her.

The crowd howled and Nellie screamed as he cut off her ear.

"A souvenir!" the commissioner shouted to his followers, holding up the bleeding flap of skin. He turned back to Nellie, spat in her face, and said, "Take her out."

She was pulled to her feet, and with blood streaming down the side of her bald head onto her uncovered shoulders, she was led out of the school into the street to be scoffed and spat at by the jeering, jubilant crowd of liberated Frenchmen.

The moment had arrived for the transfer of power. Dressed in a light gray suit which he had brought from Algiers for the occasion, Bertrand de Roujay came down from his room in the Villa Fleurie and with dignified formality inspected a guard of honor made up of the ruffians who had protected him for the past two weeks. Then he turned to Isabelle and took his leave with the same formality and reserve, as if she were his hostess in a country house where he had been staying the weekend.

"I trust we shall meet again soon," he said, "in easier circumstances."

"Indeed," she replied, and in that one word, and the look in her eyes that went with it, were all the plans and promises they had made in secret to be united after the war.

Bertrand set off in a cavalcade of two cars and two trucks. The first car, sporting a tricolor, had also had its doors removed and contained four armed men who had been assigned as the commissioner's body-guard. The driver was one of Jaco's men, called Vittorio; beside him, with a submachine gun on his knee, was another of the gang, known as Charlot-le-Chinois because of the Asiatic look given to his face by ten years as a boxer. Behind them sat two students from the Fortitude group, André and Jean-Christophe, also with submachine guns. In the second car, next to the driver, sat Jaco Jacopozzi himself, and on the backseat were Bertrand de Roujay and Guy Serot. The first of the two trucks was driven by Stefano Jacopozzi and contained more of his men; the second held an equal contingent drawn from Fortitude.

They set off for the city. At various junctions small groups of Resistants cheered, waved flags or showed their enthusiasm by firing their guns into the air. By the time they had reached the Avenue de la République the group of two cars and two trucks had grown into a convoy of twenty or thirty vehicles, all crammed with gun-toting Resistants, some waving the red flag, others tricolors daubed with the Cross of Lorraine.

Two armed gendarmes stood at the entrance to the prefecture. As the column drew up and the wild band of armed men leaped out of their vehicles, these guardians of Republican order looked uneasily at one another as if wondering whether to fight or flee, but then the older of the two recognized the former subprefect of Mézac. He therefore stood at attention and with his companion saluted as Bertrand approached.

Bertrand acknowledged this salute as he passed them and entered the hall of the prefecture. Here again the duty officer recognized Bertrand, and at once stood to his feet and saluted. Other officials, scurrying to and fro, hesitated as they saw the group enter, but then deciding that whatever was happening was none of their business, continued with whatever they were doing.

With Guy Serot a few paces behind, Bertrand climbed the wide stone steps toward Charrier's office. For the first time in many days his passion for Isabelle was replaced by the intoxicating excitement of this moment of vindication. He remembered vividly the many meetings he had attended here before the war, and his last visit to the same building when he had sneaked out with a sheet of the prefect's letterhead.

Now, as he entered the anteroom, he was astonished to see that nothing whatsoever had changed. The desk, the telephones, the secretary herself were just as he had left them four years before. She too recognized him immediately, and showed only mild surprise at seeing him there; it was as if he had returned earlier than expected from his holiday. "Why, Monsieur de Roujay," she said. "We thought that you were in London."

"I have come back."

"Of course. I'll just see if Monsieur Charrier can see you." She went to the door of the prefect's office. "Monsieur de Roujay," she said, before standing aside to let Bertrand by.

As Bertrand entered, Charrier looked up from his desk. He seemed sad and exhausted. "Ah, good, yes, I was expecting you."

"Monsieur le Préfet," said Bertrand in a severe and formal tone of voice, "by the authority invested in me by General de Gaulle and the Provisional Government in Algiers, I hereby assume your powers as prefect in the department of Basse-Provence.

Charrier hesitated for only a moment, then put down his pen, rose from his chair and said: "So much the better. Perhaps you will have better luck than I have had." He moved away from his desk and pointed to his chair as if inviting Bertrand to sit in it. "There's no food in the city. The electricity supply is spasmodic, and the water main has been broken somewhere between Coustiers and La Motte."

"Thank you," said Bertrand. "I shall refer to you, if I may, for advice."

"I am at your disposal," said Charrier.

"In the meantime, I am afraid, I must place you under arrest."

"On what charge?"

"Treason."

"I only did my duty."

"I daresay." Bertrand turned to Guy Serot. "You are responsible for the safety of Monsieur Charrier."

"Very well." Serot gestured to two of his own men to lead Charrier away.

Bertrand went to the wall behind the prefect's desk, but before sitting down reached up to remove the portrait of Pétain. "Take this," he said to Serot, "and throw it away."

"Willingly," said Serot. "Into the dustbin of history."

Now Bertrand took his place at the prefect's desk. The seat of the chair was still warm.

For the rest of that day Bertrand did what he could to restore some semblance of an administration. The front line of the French army was still eight miles from the city, and had encountered some unexpected resistance from the German 11th Panzer Division. In Coustiers itself the German army had withdrawn to a few fortified positions overlooking the city. In the area between the two armies there was anarchy, and the breakdown of the most elementary requirements of everyday life.

What hampered all Bertrand's efforts was the lack of a trustworthy chain of command. In theory he now had at his disposal the whole administrative apparatus of the department, because all the prefect's subordinates accepted his authority without demur; but outside the actual building it was a different story, for while the principal vengeance of the Resistance was taken against the *milice* or the Service d'Ordre Légionnaire, there were also attacks on the uniformed police and gendarmes as agents of the government of Vichy. These guardians of law and order therefore lay low, the gendarmes skulking in their barracks, the police in the stations of their arrondissement. Not a single uniform was to be seen in the streets, only tricolor armbands, sometimes marked with the Cross of Lorraine, worn by armed bands of self-styled partisans. The few disciplined cadres of the Francs-Tireurs et Partisans were preoccupied with containing what remained of the German garrison in the city. If they belonged to the Resistance at all, the gangsters and delinquents who roamed the streets, executing *miliciens* and shaving the heads of collaborating women, had joined a week or a day before. Most were using the liberation as a pretext to settle old personal scores.

Certainly Jaco and Stefano Jacopozzi saw that the time had come to settle once and for all their feud with the Burzios, and in their doorless Citroëns they raced up the Esplanade de la Roseraie to the Burzios' villa. They arrived too late. Their work had been done for them by some of the Burzios' own men, who, seeing which way the wind was blowing, had thought to curry favor with the Jacopozzis by murdering their former employers. The old man, Bruno Burzio, was dead, shot as he sat at the table. Andréas Burzio had disappeared.

There were a dozen or so more executions of those among the Burzios' men against whom the Jacopozzis had a personal grudge; but in general they were happy to accept their rivals as new recruits into their own army, and some of the auxiliaries of the Gestapo from the Hôtel de la Poste were later to be seen wearing the armbands of the Resistance.

Bertrand and Guy Serot despaired of imposing any discipline on these criminal bands until the arrival of de Lattre de Tassigny's troops. Colonel Bax, who had been appointed the regional military delegate, came to the prefecture later that evening to offer what support he could, but most of his units, like those of the FTP, were heavily engaged in harassing the German lines of communication, and since the prosecution of the war took priority they could not be withdrawn to restore order in Coustiers.

Food was the most urgent requirement, for if Bertrand as the commissioner of the Republic could not assure a supply to the civilian population, his official title was worthless. The key to the supply of food, however, lay with the Americans, who not only had the food itself but also the ships to bring it to the coast. Bertrand therefore made it a priority to make contact with Harry Jackson, who he had heard was already in the city, to impress upon him the urgency of the predicament, and to make the point that the area could be saved from Communist control only if he could feed people.

It was Bertrand's good fortune that he had a long-standing friendship with this American. In Algiers, Jackson had been assigned to oversee the department of Basse-Provence, and had landed in the south of France a few weeks before the American invasion. Since President Roosevelt still refused to recognize de Gaulle or his provisional government in Algiers, Jackson had established contact with the most Giraudist sections of the Resistance, particularly the army group led by Captain Ledésert.

Bertrand heard from one of Ledésert's officers that Jackson had already established himself in a suite on the top floor of the Hôtel du Pavillon, from where he had a radio link with General Patch's headquarters and the American fleet off the Mediterranean coast. Bertrand's first instinct was to go to the Pavillon himself to ask for food supplies, but then, remembering his new role as the commissioner of the Republic, thought that he would send Serot instead. Then he again changed his mind, and decided to invite Harry to visit him; if the American could see him at the prefect's desk in the prefect's office it might convince him that the Gaullists were already in power.

He therefore sent a message to the Hôtel du Pavillon on the letterhead stationery of the prefecture inviting his friend to call as soon as he could, and at six that evening Jackson appeared at the door with the same genial smile that he had worn at the Savoy in London and the Avenida Palace in Lisbon.

"Why, Bertrand," he said. "It sure is a fine sight to see you sitting in that chair. You've really made it. It's your dream come true."

"So far," said Bertrand, rising to greet his friend with a cordiality that only a sense of advantage could afford him, "the dream is more like a nightmare."

"Things seem a little out of control out there."

"It is chaos," said Bertrand, showing his friend to a chair and offering him a glass of cognac from a bottle that Charrier had left behind.

"Well," said Harry cheerfully, "you can't stir people up to fight the Germans and then expect them to settle down without buzzing around a bit."

"There are more serious problems than the buzzing," said Bertrand.

"I noticed that the electric lights go on and off."

"Power, water and above all food are in short supply."

"That's bad."

"If we can't feed the people, we can't hope to govern them."

"As Caesar said, an army marches on its stomach."

"I think it was Napoleon," said Bertrand.

Harry laughed. "You think everything clever was said by a Frenchman."

"It doesn't really matter," said Bertrand. "The point it makes is true. I can only regain control of the city if I can feed the population, and I can only feed them if General Patch can be persuaded to send in supplies."

Harry frowned. "It will be difficult," he said. "The war takes priority, and all available transports are earmarked for the army. And even if we could direct a shipment of food to Coustiers, how could we get it upstream?"

"I have spoken to Emile Planchet," said Bertrand. "He thinks that if food can be brought to the mouth of the river, it can be loaded onto barges and brought here."

"Okay," said Harry, "I'll do what I can, but I don't hold out much chance of success. Your General de Gaulle is not exactly our favorite person right now."

"He never was," said Bertrand, "but bear in mind that without food my administration will fail, and if that happens it is not Giraud but the Communists who will replace me."

"I get your point," said Harry. "I've seen what's going on out there, and I'm inclined to agree with you. I'll get on to General Patch tonight. If you'd care to look in for breakfast in the morning, I should have an answer by then."

That night Bertrand slept at the prefecture with a loaded revolver under his pillow. Outside the door of the prefect's private quarters were André and Jean-Christophe, the two young men from the Fortitude group, and below in the lobby of the prefecture were six Jacopozzis, led by Vittorio and Charlot-le-Chinois. Outside in the city all was anarchy, but the murderous bands at large in the streets were too preoccupied with settling scores with their personal and political enemies to pay any attention to the Gaullist commissioner of the Republic.

He awoke early in unfamiliar surroundings, and for a moment lay languid and warm, imagining that Isabelle was beside him. Then, like a slack rope which is suddenly drawn tight, he realized all at once where he was and became alert with the anxieties of the day before. He remembered that he was responsible for a whole department, with only a group of hoodlums and idealists at his command.

He got up and knelt to say the prayers with which he always started the day, but as he buried his face in his hands to ask God to help him he remembered Isabelle again, not with the erotic nostalgia of his semisleep, but with the conflicting emotions of passion and remorse which the thought of her aroused in his conscious mind. However earnestly he loved her, however powerful the memory of her voice, her lips and the scent of her skin, Bertrand could not forget that she was the wife of another man, and doubted his right to ask for divine assistance when he had broken one of God's ten commandments.

He abandoned his prayers and shaved, but his moral uncertainty left him in an uneasy frame of mind. As he finished dressing, Serot arrived. "The front has advanced as far as Lissanne," he said. "The city should be encircled by tomorrow."

"Good," said Bertrand. "They may not put troops at our disposal, but a parade through the city should calm things down."

"If we can only secure supplies," said Serot, "all will be well."

Leaving Guy at the prefecture with the detachment of Jacopozzi men, Bertrand, followed by André and Jean Christophe, walked out into the warm morning sunshine on the Avenue de la République, and rather than use the car waiting for him walked the four blocks to the Hôtel du Pavillon. There he was heartened to be saluted by two of Ledésert's men who were guarding the entrance, and to find Ledésert himself waiting to greet him.

"Congratulations," he said to Bertrand. "I'm delighted that everything went so well at the prefecture."

"If we can survive the next seven days," said Bertrand, "the Republic will be secure."

"Colonel Jackson suggested taking breakfast in his room," said Ledésert. "He thought you would have more privacy there than in the hotel dining room."

"Good."

Bertrand ordered André and Jean-Christophe to wait in the lobby, then entered the elevator with Ledésert.

"You knew Jackson in London, didn't you?" asked Ledésert as they were carried up to the fifth floor.

"First Lisbon, then London," said Bertrand.

"Rather a man for the ladies, I gather," said Ledésert.

"Already? Here in Coustiers?"

"He was very keen to see the sights."

"The Place de l'Opéra?"

"Certainly."

Bertrand smiled. "He always believed in sampling the local specialties."

On the fifth floor Ledésert knocked on the door to Jackson's suite, which was opened by an American sergeant. "Come on in," he said casually. "The colonel's just taking a shower, but he'll be with you in a minute."

"I shall wait downstairs," said Ledésert. He saluted Bertrand, then added in an undertone, "Good luck."

Bertrand followed the sergeant through the small lobby into a large and lavish living room. "I'm just making some breakfast," said the American. "Luckily we have our own kitchen up here, and our own supplies, because if you send any food downstairs you never see it again."

He disappeared, leaving Bertrand alone in the room. He walked across over the thick carpet and went through the open doors onto the balcony. There was a wide view over the city toward the wharves along the canal and the tangle of tilting cranes which had been crippled by the Germans before they had withdrawn to their barracks and redoubts.

He turned back into the room just as Harry came through the door from his bedroom.

"Bertrand. You're here. I'm sorry to keep you waiting." He put his arm around his friend's shoulder. "You can enjoy your breakfast. I've been on to General Patch, and your supplies are on their way."

Bertrand did not conceal his relief and delight, and as they sat down at the table he thanked Harry for all that he had done. The sergeant came in with a tray on which there was not merely a pot of real coffee, but also three glasses of orange juice and three plates loaded with bacon, sausages and scrambled eggs.

"You can eat with a good conscience," said Harry, "because soon your people will have powdered eggs too."

"You can't imagine how much this means to us," said Bertrand, glancing at the third plate and wondering if the American army was so democratic that sergeants ate breakfast at the same table as their officers. "And in the name of General de Gaulle and the Provisional Government—"

"That's enough of that," said Harry. "I did it for you and for your people, so please don't spoil my appetite by talking about General de Gaulle."

The sergeant left the room; the third place remained empty.

"Very well," said Bertrand, also smiling, and starting his breakfast with relish. "Let's keep right off politics, at least until our stomachs are full."

"That's right," said Harry, "never let yourself be distracted by a nagging appetite. Which reminds me . . ." He leaned forward and whispered, "I hope you won't mind if we're joined by a lady."

Bertrand frowned. "What kind of lady?"

"Well, she's not exactly from your social register. In fact, I don't think she's even French, but she's better than any whore I ever had in Algiers, London or Lisbon."

As he spoke, a woman came to the door of the bedroom. Seeing the visitor, she stopped and stepped back into the shadow. She was thin, with dark hair and brown eyes, which flickered restlessly as if she was accustomed to cocaine.

"Really, Harry," said Bertrand with a frown, "it's a bit much to expect me, in my present capacity, to have breakfast with a woman of that kind."

Harry laughed. Like Bertrand, he had not noticed the woman who hovered behind the jamb of the door. "Why do you French have to take yourselves so seriously?" he said.

"Try to see it from my point of view," said Bertrand, patting his mouth with a white linen napkin. "If word gets out that the commissioner of the Republic is having breakfast with a whore in the Hôtel du Pavillon . . ."

"Bang goes your reputation for probity."

"Exactly."

"I see your point," said Harry. "She'd better have her breakfast in the bedroom." He turned and called for the sergeant, but as he did so he saw the woman. "Ah, there you are, honey," he said. "Look, we've got business to discuss, so I wondered . . ."

Bertrand turned and saw Lucía. Despite her painted face and clinging clothes he recognized her at once.

She, too, had recognized him. "You came back," she murmured, her eyes fixed on him from across the room.

"So you two know each other?" asked Harry with a smirk; he had noticed that the woman had addressed his friend as *tu*.

"No," said Bertrand coldly. "We don't know each other."

Lucía stepped back as if he had struck her, with eyes like those of a frightened sheep.

"She seems to know you," said Harry.

"Don't be absurd," said Bertrand, turning back to the table.

Lucía withdrew into the bedroom, and the sergeant put her breakfast on a tray.

"You don't seem to understand," said Bertrand to Harry in an urgent, breathless voice, "that this game with the Communists is touch and go. My only power is my authority, and my authority depends upon my reputation."

"Sure," said Harry, crunching his toast, "and an honest man in a Christian country is one who only screws his wife."

"If the Communists had anything against me . . ."

"I know. I'm sorry. I should have thought of that."

The sergeant came back from the bedroom. "She ain't there," he said.

"Where's she gone?" asked Harry.

"Out the window."

"What?"

"Yep. She's five stories down in the backyard."

Bertrand turned pale. Harry leaped to his feet. "Jesus Christ," he muttered, running toward the bedroom.

Bertrand followed Harry through the door and onto the balcony outside his bedroom window. There, on the ground beneath them, lay the body of Lucía Rodríguez de Astran.

In the foyer of the Hôtel du Pavillon, Captain Ledésert waited nervously for the outcome of the meeting between Harry Jackson and

Bertrand de Roujay. It was he who had convinced Jackson that although Bertrand was a Gaullist he was the only man who could hold together a coalition of the different factions of the Resistance and so keep the Communists from power.

Suddenly Bertrand came out of the elevator alone, and without a word or a glance to anyone in the foyer strode toward the door. His face was pale, his lips pressed together, and Ledésert immediately assumed that Jackson had imposed some intolerable conditions for supplying food to the city. He started to follow Bertrand, but then thought it would be better to find out what had happened from Jackson. He waved to the two students from Fortitude to follow the commissioner and turned to take the elevator to the fifth floor.

As Bertrand walked away from the hotel, his shock at what had happened was mingled with a passionate self-disgust. His mind reeled with remorse, not just for his callousness toward Lucía but also for his seduction of Isabelle. The guilt of this adultery and the suicide of Lucía now mingled with the pain he himself had suffered from the infidelity of his two wives, so that as he made his way through the crowds in the streets he felt that sexual love was a monstrosity which led only to suffering and sin.

Worse still, his weaknesses seemed to disqualify him for the task he had undertaken as commissioner of the Republic. He remembered his conversation with Alain de Chabanais, the young Gaullist he had known in London, who had already died for France. Had they not both agreed that the righteousness of a cause was indissolubly linked to the righteousness of those who upheld it? And that if a man breaks one commandment, he breaks them all? How could he, an adulterer, battle the atheistic materialism of the Communists except as a knight without fear or blemish? His mission in France was one with his mission in life, and even while Isabelle's body delighted his memory, he knew that he could not continue unless he repudiated their passion and abjured her now before God.

Ahead of him he saw the steps of the prefecture. He stopped, hesitated, then turned to the right into the Rue de la Paix. He was unworthy, ignoble, a man with no right to uphold or represent the integrity, purity and honor of France. He could not resume his office until he had purged himself of his sin. Ahead of him he saw the stuccoed tower of a church. In the church was Christ, the Son of God, who had died so that sins could be forgiven. He had given to his disciples the power of absolution, which had been handed on to Catholic priests. He had only to hear the words *Ego te absolvo* spoken after confessing his sins, and all the wrong he had done to Lucía, Isabelle and Jaco Jacopozzi would be annulled. Then he could return to the prefecture with his moral integrity restored.

He entered the cool, dark church. Walking slowly up a side aisle, he saw two old ladies waiting to confess. He knelt down beside them, watched from the entrance by his two faithful bodyguards, and prayed for the protection of the Mother of God and his guardian angel in heaven.

The last of the two old ladies went to kneel at the ornate confessional, which, like a large rococo wardrobe, had a grille at each side while the priest sat hidden in the center. Bertrand saw that his turn had come. He knelt in front of the grille and waited until the shutter behind it was opened and from the darkness a gruff voice mumbled a Latin prayer.

It was thirteen years since Antoine Dubec had seen Bertrand de Roujay in Montpellier, but when he knelt now at the confessional he recognized him at once. Trained to maintain a silent anonymity, Antoine said nothing to make Bertrand realize that he was confessing to someone he knew; but as he listened to the account of the commissioner's sins the priest became excited, not because of the sins themselves but because of the political significance of the sinner.

From his position on the Committee of the National Front, Antoine was privy to the frustrations of his Communist friends. He knew that their plans for converting Resistance into revolution had been stymied by the unholy alliance of the bourgeois Gaullists and the Coustiers underworld. He knew too that Bertrand had taken refuge in the Villa Fleurie, so when Bertrand confessed that he had seduced the wife of a man who had taken him into his home, Antoine realized that it must be Isabelle Jacopozzi.

"Does she have a child?" he asked, as if assessing the seriousness of the sin.

"Yes. One son."

"And is she unhappy with her husband?"

"Yes. He is a brute. A criminal."

Antoine said no more; he knew enough. He mumbled some platitudes about the virtues of family life, then prescribed a decade of the
rosary as penance and absolved Bertrand of his sins. As he did so,
however, and turned his ear to listen to the next penitent, his mind
was not on the magic power of forgiveness that had been conferred
upon him by Christ, but on the political significance here on earth of
the knowledge he had obtained. Antoine realized at once that if Jaco
Jacopozzi was told that Bertrand de Roujay had slept with his wife,
the unholy alliance would be ruptured and the power of the Gaullists
destroyed.

Yet Antoine also recalled the sacred and inviolable vow he had
taken as a priest never to divulge the secrets of the confessional.
Penance was a sacrament, like the Eucharist, and one in which the priest
acted not for himself but for Christ; yet as he looked through the crack
in the curtain and saw Bertrand kneel to pray before the altar, he felt
rise within him the old smoldering dislike which he had always felt
for this smug civil servant, who would now return to the prefecture
with a clear conscience to sabotage the revolution.

He recalled the suffering which he had witnessed among the workers
of Castelnau, and the sacrifices made by the Communist partisans, the
young men and women he had known who had been shot by the
Gestapo or the *milice*. Was their martyrdom to have been only so that
France should be governed by the same ascendant class, and so that this
bourgeois bureaucrat should be restored to power?

The prospect was intolerable, not just because it cheated the martyrs
of the Resistance of the fruits of their sacrifice, but because it would
deprive future generations of a just society in which "princes were
pulled down from their thrones and the lowly exalted—the hungry
filled with good things and the rich sent empty away." He, Antoine,
could bring this about. One word in the right ear and Bertrand de
Roujay would be toppled from power. Certainly it would break a
vow, but could the scruples of one man stand in the way of God's
manifest intention for mankind? Could a rule imposed by canon law
in the Middle Ages frustrate the progress of humanity toward a true
and permanent liberation?

Such were the thoughts running through the mind of the friar as
another old lady mumbled her sins in his right ear. She lived with her

sister; her sister irritated her; she had lost her temper and had spoken sharply to her because her sister had a cat which the old lady suspected was fed with their ration of meat. She had also lost her temper at the baker's when a neighbor had tried to jump the queue. Did God expect one to stand aside if people jumped a queue? Should one turn the other cheek?

There were more sins, a long list of trivialities, which pattered on the priest's ear like light rain while the tempest of conscience raged within. Could the secrecy of the confessional be considered paramount, as a good in itself which was not to be measured against a greater good? If the divulgence of this old woman's uncharitable thoughts about her sister's cat could for some obscure reason save ten thousand lives, would God expect a priest to keep silent? But if in such a case the vow could be broken, then it could not be considered an absolute good. It became a matter of weighing the abstract evil of breaking the vow against the concrete good of the consequences, and in the case of Bertrand de Roujay it was clear which way the scales would fall.

The old lady ran out of transgressions, and Antoine imposed a penance of two Hail Marys; then, seeing that no one was waiting, and that it was close to the hour when another friar would relieve him, he lifted the stole from around his neck, laid it on the arm of the chair in the confessional, hastily walked down the aisle and left the church.

Bertrand returned to the prefecture to find everything in confusion. Even as he walked up the stairs, Charlot-le-Chinois shouted in his rasping dialect, "He's here, the commissioner is here!" When he reached the top he was met by a distraught Serot, who had come out of the prefect's office to meet him.

"At last," he said. "We thought you'd been abducted."

"What has happened?" asked Bertrand, striding into his office and going to his desk.

"The Communists have seized power in Mézac."

"In Mézac?"

"They have occupied the subprefecture and have made their head-quarters at the town hall. The police and the gendarmes are confined to barracks. They are issuing ordinances in the name of the Committee of Liberation."

"It must be stopped or it will spread," said Bertrand.

"It is spreading already. The same sort of thing is happening in Nîmes, Avignon, Montpellier, Valence . . ."

"They are not my responsibility," said Bertrand, "but I will be held to account for what happens in Mézac. What men have we at our disposal?"

"In Mézac? None. The Communists are in complete control."

Bertrand hesitated, then said, "What would happen if we moved against them with the men we have here in Coustiers?"

Serot shrugged his shoulders. "We would be outnumbered by ten to one. Anyway, the Jacopozzis would be useless outside Coustiers, and my own men would be reluctant to fire on their fellow Resistants."

"Then I must go to Mézac on my own," said Bertrand.

"Without support?"

"With a small escort and the moral support of my appointment by de Gaulle."

"And Coustiers?"

"The troops will be here tonight or tomorrow."

"Can't Mézac wait for the troops?"

Bertrand turned to the map of the department on the wall. "They won't go to Mézac. They'll pursue the Germans up the Rhône."

"It will be a gamble," said Serot, "facing submachine guns with only your moral authority."

"Is it known who is behind the rising in Mézac?"

"Bouclier."

"Who is Bouclier?"

"Georges Auget."

Bertrand nodded. "Of course. We were looking for him in '39. He is a determined man, but not a fanatic. He'll think twice before starting a civil war."

The Jacopozzis had returned to the Bar Fénelon on the west bank of the river, and it was there that the scoffing started. No one knew quite how the rumor had reached Stefano Jacopozzi that his brother had been cuckolded by the commissioner, but when he heard it he laughed with a long and loud guffaw. He had always thought that his younger brother was too clever for his own good, and now, through that imbecile marriage, he had made himself appear ridiculous to his friends and enemies alike.

For months now Stefano had thought that Jaco should get rid of his conceited wife, abandon politics and return to the family's traditional business. He knew, however, that Jaco was not only obsessed with Isabelle but also too proud not to finish something he had started. If there was to be a change in the way things were run, there would have to be a change of leader, but Stefano, though older, was afraid of the cunning and cruelty of his younger brother. He had never before dared oppose him.

Now he saw his chance. He knew that by the simple but savage standards of his Corsican friends a man who cannot keep a woman is not a man at all. Jaco the cuckold would lose face; with face, authority; and with authority, power. In the laughter which rang out in the bar as Stefano passed on the rumor, he recognized not just derision at Jaco's discomfiture but also an acclamation of himself as the rightful heir.

At nine Jaco returned, and like a beast sensing an intruder in its lair, he hesitated on the threshold of the bar. There was a momentary hush. Jaco walked toward the back of the room, his eyes flitting from man to man, searching for a clue to their altered manner. He saw Stefano, who smirked.

"Come," Jaco said. "There are things to discuss."

Stefano stood up, but as he followed his brother toward the back of the bar he held up two fingers above Jaco's head to signify the horns of a cuckold. There was an immediate roar of derisive laughter.

Jaco stalked into the room behind the bar and turned to Stefano as he entered. "Close the door," he said.

"Close it yourself," said Stefano.

Jaco's features did not move. "Very well," he said quietly. As he walked around his brother to close the door, Stefano turned to watch him, afraid that his insolence might result in a knife in his back.

"What's going on?" asked Jaco.

Stefano smirked. "The husband is always the last to know."

"Know what?"

"The commissioner fucked Isabelle. He was fucking her right under your nose. There! That's what was going on."

Jaco turned pale. "It's a lie."

"Ask her."

"I will," Jaco hissed, "and if it's a lie, I'll cut out every tongue that told it." He stood for a moment, his eyes fixed with fury on his brother, then turned and went out the back door.

In the Villa Fleurie that afternoon, Isabelle had heard the news of the Allied advance with a certain detachment as she waited for her own private liberation. Sitting in the shade of a parasol on the terrace, she found that for the first time in many months she took pleasure in the fragrant scent of pine, rosemary and eucalyptus coming from the baked garden, and she laughed girlishly as she watched her son Tonio play with the other children of the Jacopozzi family.

Out of the corner of her mind's eye, Isabelle had noticed that Jaco's mother and sister and Stefano's wife had all come to treat her with a certain mistrust; and if she had not been so intoxicated by her own happiness she might have remembered that the very simplicity of these Corsican women endowed them with an acute sensitivity to the moods of their own sex. As the sister of a magistrate, Isabelle felt confident that there was no concrete evidence of her infidelity, and she was too cerebral a woman to guard against feminine intuition or realize that Jaco's mother had noticed at once how her spirits had been raised by the arrival of Bertrand de Roujay, how the glances they had exchanged during his visit had progressed, and how the flush which had come to her cheeks after their games of tennis together signified more than bodily exertion.

It was beyond Isabelle's imagination to comprehend that the crafty old woman who thought that the war had been caused by German constipation could have remarked upon her daughter-in-law's mood of drowsy contentment one afternoon after her siesta, or that she could have intercepted a glance of languorous love as she came out into the garden and caught sight of the commissioner.

Even if Isabelle had realized that old Madame Jacopozzi had then crept in to examine the sheets on the commissioner's bed, she had such an overwhelming confidence in the power and the prestige of her lover that she was recklessly indifferent to scandal. She was quite out of touch with the realities of the Resistance. She knew that Pierre and then Bertrand had made use of Jaco, but she knew better than they that he was no Bonaparte, and it was inconceivable that Bertrand, the commissioner of the Republic, should have anything to fear from a minor crook.

That night she could hear the guns of the advancing French and the retreating Germans; she knew that in a day or two the Allied armies would have liberated Coustiers and that Bertrand would then deliver her, behind him the power of the French state. Basking in that certitude, she went up early as always to her room, and prepared herself in the same leisurely way for bed. As she brushed her black hair in front of the mirror of her dressing table, she studied her smooth skin with the pride of a curator who has custody of something precious that belongs to another. Through the open window came the sound of the crickets, and occasionally the faint rumble of gunfire. Closer to her was the rasp of the brush on her hair and the hypnotic whisper of her own breathing, which accompanied the gentle rise and fall of her smooth brown breast.

Then her eye caught a movement in the mirror, and she saw that the door behind her was being opened silently by a man's hand. She turned and saw Jaco, and was only surprised that she had not heard his car draw up on the gravel outside the house. As always she said nothing, but returned to brushing her hair; as always he walked toward the window, but there he altered his routine by closing not just the shutters but also the glass-paneled doors which led out onto the balcony. It was this irregularity which led her to glance at her husband again and notice the peculiar expression on his face.

"It will make it too hot," she said, continuing as she spoke to brush her hair.

The dim light flickered as Jaco came and stood behind her. She glanced up, and for the first time felt some alarm at the look in his kestrel eyes.

"What is it?" she asked.

"They say," he said slowly, "that the commissaire fucked you here in my own bed."

"No," she said softly, and her hands kept moving with the brushing of her hair.

"I asked Mama. She says it's true. She saw the sheets."

"Not here," she said. "Not on our bed."

"But he fucked you!" hissed Jaco between clenched teeth.

She stopped brushing her hair and laid her hands in her lap. "I love him, Jaco."

"You cannot love him."

"But I do." She turned to face him, and saw to her horror that there were tears on his cheeks.

"And you let him fuck you!" he shouted, his voice choking in rage and despair.

"When one loves someone—" she began in the firm voice of a teacher with a delinquent child.

"But you are mine!" he shouted.

"No," she replied. "One belongs to those one loves and who love one in return."

"But *I* love you," he cried.

"No," she said. "It was a mistake. We should never have married."

"But I love you," he said again, coming forward with outstretched hands as if to embrace her.

"No, Jaco, leave me alone," she shouted, her voice now trembling, her arms raised to fend him off.

"You are mine," he said, his hands gripping her neck.

"Jaco," she gurgled, trying to turn to look into his eyes, but his grip was so strong that she could neither move nor breathe. Her frail fingers went to his hands, but they were cold and strong as steel. She tried to turn to beseech him to release her, but as his grip tightened her head was pushed down toward the dressing table, and all she could see was the handle of her hairbrush and the wastepaper basket on the floor. "Bertrand," she tried to cry, but his name came from her mouth like the bleat of a sheep, and apart from the gagging and choking that convulsed her as she suffocated, it was the last sound that she uttered alive.

For some time Jaco Jacopozzi sat brooding over his wife's body. The mixture of jealousy and despair which had driven him to strangle her subsided slowly as he contemplated the victim of his revenge, and his mind returned to its normal mode of cunning and calculation. He had no fear of retribution for what he had done; quite the contrary, he would let it be known what Isabelle had suffered for her crime, because his power depended upon his authority, his authority upon his honor and his honor upon a public and dramatic revenge.

De Roujay, too, must be hunted down and killed, but his death alone would not be enough. He must suffer before he died, suffer as Jaco had suffered by seeing the life squeezed out of someone he loved.

But who? Who did de Roujay love? Jaco's inner eye searched what he knew of Bertrand's life like a hovering hawk watching for a movement on the ground below. Suddenly he remembered the daughter whom Bertrand had been with when he was captured by the Germans. He had loved her enough to take risks to see her; he would love her enough to suffer to see her die.

The room was hot, and there was a sweet smell in the air which came from Isabelle's bath oil but seemed to be that of putrefying flesh. Jaco went to the windows, opened them and went out onto the balcony. There was silence; even the crickets and guns were quiet.

"Marco," he said in a low voice to a figure standing in the shadows.

"Jaco?"

"Dig a grave."

"Where?"

"In the garden."

"Very well."

"And Marco . . ."

"What?"

"Get word to Charlot and Vittorio to bring in the commissioner."

"Dead or alive?"

"I want him alive."

"Very well."

"And Marco . . ."

"What?"

"Tell the boys to be ready. We're going for a drive in the country."

The Germans had left Pévier on August 29. Edmond de Roujay returned home for lunch, and passed on to his wife the Hauptmann's best wishes, and his sincere desire that they might meet after the war.

"I would never have thought it possible," said Alice, "but I am sorry to see him go."

"Yes," said Edmond. "He was not a bad man in himself, but he has left a mess behind him."

He then sat down to lunch with Alice, Hélène and his grandchildren, among them Titine, who had returned from the mountains.

Before lunch was over a car drew up outside the front door. A tricolor with a Cross of Lorraine had been daubed on its roof, and the

542

five young men who clambered out were armed with rifles and wore makeshift armbands.

Edmond went out onto the steps to meet them.

"In the name of the Resistance," shouted one of the youths in a voice that had hardly broken, "we demand that you hand over the gold coins that you have hidden in your house."

Edmond recognized, skulking at the back of the group, the son of a woodcutter who had been dismissed two years before for drunkenness and poaching.

"Ah, Daniel," he said to him, "was it you who told them that there was gold hidden in the house?"

The boy blushed and looked away.

Edmond turned back to the leader. "Listen, young man. The French army will be here in a day or two, and then looters will be shot on sight. So go back home and stay out of trouble, because I know who you are, and you are no more in the Resistance than I am."

With that he turned his back and walked slowly into the house. Alice, holding a shotgun at her bedroom window, saw the group of youths confer and then, after a brief dispute, get back into their car and drive away.

That night Edmond de Roujay closed all the shutters at Saint Théodore and bolted all the doors. At four in the morning he was waked by a handful of gravel thrown against the shutters in front of his bedroom window.

"Who is it?" he asked.

"It's me . . . Thierry."

He went downstairs and unbolted the door. His grandson stumbled in. He had abandoned his uniform of the *milice* and was dressed like a tramp in clothes which did not fit him.

"They're after me," he said in a terrified tone of voice.

"Who?"

"The Resistance. They shoot *miliciens* on sight."

"I'm not surprised," said the old man, leading Thierry to the kitchen to find him some food.

"But I have done nothing wrong," said Thierry with a pitiful croak.

"And your friends?"

"Ah, yes, they were hard, but with terrorists one can't be gentle."

"Well, your terrorists are now the agents of justice."

"Because they've won?"

"Yes." He put some bread and cheese on the table.

"So losing turns terrorists into policemen and policemen into terrorists?"

"Yes."

"Papa said that we were fighting for Christ."

"I know."

"So the devil has won?"

"In a war it is always the devil who wins."

Thierry gave a sob. "I don't understand," he said, crying like a child.

"It's not easy," said Edmond de Roujay. "Now have something to eat, then go down into the cellar."

When Edmond returned to his bedroom he found Alice awake.

"Was it Thierry?" she asked.

"Yes."

"Thank God he is safe."

"For the time being."

"Will they come for him?"

"I daresay. And for me too."

She sighed. "Poor Edmond. First the Germans, now the French."

"Yes," he said. "It will be an irony if after two wars against the Boches I am shot by my own people."

"It won't be long," said Alice, "before de Lattre's men reach us."

"That's true," said Edmond, watching the morning light glimmer through the slats of the shutters. "If we can get through today, I daresay we shall survive."

They lay silently side by side. Then Alice whispered, "Edmond?"

"Yes?"

"Are you asleep?"

"No."

"Do you believe . . . have you ever believed in the power of prayer to alter what would otherwise happen?"

"I don't know. I'm never sure."

"I prayed for Bertrand, and he was released by the Gestapo for no reason at all."

"I know."

"Like Saint Peter from the prison of King Herod."

"We shall have to ask him if an angel let him out."

"Don't mock me, Edmond."

"No. I don't mean to mock you. Certainly it is better to pray than to do nothing."

"But when I pray for Louis on the eastern front, I feel cold."

"But it isn't cold in August, even in Russia."

"I know, but I feel cold all the same."

He held out his hand and clasped hers. "Pray, my dear, pray for all you are worth, but remember always that there is much we cannot expect to understand."

They rose at six but left the shutters closed. Only Marthe was told that Thierry was in the cellar. Edmond himself took him some breakfast.

At seven, Edmond went out of the house to discuss the day's work with the one-legged veteran who was the only laborer left at Saint Théodore. As they stood at the door to the coach house, Edmond felt that he was being watched from the woods above, but he could see nothing through the summer foliage of the trees.

At eight the postman—the man with the three Jewish grandparents —came up the drive on his bicycle to deliver a single letter, a bill from Edmond's tailor in Mézac. "There are some men looking for your house," he said.

"Resistance?" asked Edmond.

"So they said, but they seemed like ruffians to me. I sent them off in the wrong direction."

"Thank you."

"But they may be back."

"We'll be prepared."

Having been built at a time when memories of the peasant rising of 1790 were still vivid in the minds of the landowning classes, Saint Théodore was not difficult to defend. The doors were thick with heavy bolts; so too were the shutters. All the windows on the ground floor were more than ten feet above the ground, except for the glass doors which led into the garden, but these too were protected by heavy wooden shutters which could be bolted from within.

The armory was also adequate to withstand a short siege. There were one rifle, four shotguns and the colonel's revolver from the First

World War. Edmond kept this for himself, gave the rifle to the one-legged veteran and a shotgun each to Alice, Marthe, Hélène and Thierry, who was brought up from the cellar and given a change of clothes.

While Titine and Helene's younger children were sent down to the cellar in charge of a whimpering housemaid, Edmond stationed one shotgun at a window on each side of the house and the rifle at his own bedroom window, while he himself remained in the hall both to command and stand in reserve.

At nine a column of three cars was seen approaching up the drive. Edmond watched them through the drawing-room window, and seeing that there were five or six in each car, estimated that the enemy were between fifteen and eighteen strong. He noted too, from the car registry plates, that they came from the department of Basse-Provence, and he concluded from their appearance that they were the dregs of the criminal underworld, possibly from Mézac but more likely from Coustiers. He saw that all of them were armed either with revolvers or submachine guns.

The cars stopped at the gates and the men got out. Edmond watched as the leader, a thin, swarthy man, ordered some to the back and others to the front of the house. From the way they took no cover but instead strutted around as if lounging at the corner of a city street, Edmond realized at once that they had had no military training. This might not improve the odds, but it showed that despite their armbands with the Cross of Lorraine, they were not authentic units of the Free French forces.

The leader came to the front of the house and hammered on the door with his pistol. "Open in the name of the Resistance," he shouted in a heavy Corsican accent.

"What do you want?" shouted Edmond in return.

"We have an order for the arrest of all de Roujays."

"Fiddlesticks."

"Open and I'll show you the order."

"We'll wait for the army."

"We are the army."

"Nonsense."

"Open, or we'll force our way in."

"One step over our threshold and we'll shoot you down."

Peering through the shutter from the window beside the door, Edmond could see the man's face twist with fury as, stepping back from the house onto the gravel, he fired a wild burst of bullets at the house. Taking their cue from their leader, his men did the same; without aiming at anyone in particular, they emptied their magazines at the house with a sound more like a display of fireworks than an armed assault.

Only one shot rang out in return, from the rifle in the hands of the one-legged laborer in the de Roujays' bedroom. One of the attackers gave a cry, raised his hand to his eye, then fell twitching onto the gravel and finally lay still. His companions looked stunned, then, realizing how vulnerable they were, they suddenly scuttled back from the front of the house into the garden. One turned over the garden table and hid behind it; another took up a position behind the chestnut trees; the leader, Jaco Jacopozzi, sprang back and crouched behind a huge earthenware jar.

The battle started, with all the hoodlums from Coustiers shooting at the house, but for all the effect of their fusillade they could as well have been shooting in the air, and after some minutes it became apparent that the defendants of Saint Théodore were quite safe inside. Jaco held up his arm for his men to cease fire. Slowly the shooting stopped. Then he crept around to join his men behind the house to see if there was a way in at the back. Here, clearly, they could get closer, because the outbuildings provided some cover, but the back windows and doors were equally well protected.

Scampering like a leopard from one outbuilding to another, Jaco came across the wood house, where the trunk of a pine tree was waiting to be sawn into logs. At once he saw it as a battering ram, and quickly ordered his men to bring it to the door. Then, with another leap, he returned to the front of the house to tell his men to give covering fire while he led the assault on the kitchen door.

Above was Hélène with a shotgun. She saw six men holding the log below her. Gingerly poking the barrel of the shotgun through a broken slat in the shutter, she pulled both triggers, then fell terrified to the floor.

Her shot was answered with a spattering of bullets, some of which came through the shutters and embedded themselves in the plaster of the opposite wall. Hélène was safe beneath the window, but she was so frightened that she dared not rise to shoot again, and instead crawled across the floor to tell Edmond what was happening.

Edmond ran up the stairs. He saw at once that he could not shoot down on the men attacking the door without leaning out the window, and that if he did so he would certainly be killed. He therefore ran down to the kitchen window to see if he could reach them from there, but here the shutters were solid. He could not shoot unless he opened them, and if he did so it would make a breach in their defenses which the attackers could carry by force of numbers.

There was a crack as the tree trunk hit the door for a third time. Edmond went to the kitchen, turned the kitchen table on its side, and waited behind it to shoot the first man who came through the door.

Outside, Jaco Jacopozzi was jubilant. The shot from Hélène's shotgun had gone wide, and he realized that if he and his men stayed close to the house they were out of reach of the de Roujays' guns. Moreover, the battering ram was taking its effect; one panel of the door had split. He told his men to aim the tree trunk at the central strut, which at the fourth run cracked and at the fifth splintered.

Now Jaco himself ran forward and kicked away at the remaining wood. But as he did so he he heard a cry from one of his men, and he turned to see emerging from the woods behind him a long line of twenty or thirty men, each with a rifle or a submachine gun, standing five or six feet apart.

"Wait," he shouted, and then went cautiously to meet these new arrivals.

The man who commanded them stepped forward. "What are you doing here?" he asked in a heavy Spanish accent.

"We are here to apprehend the de Roujays," said Jaco.

"On whose orders?"

"The Committee of the Resistance in Coustiers."

"That has no authority here."

"And who are you?" asked Jaco, as if the Spaniard could have no authority either.

"Astran. I command this section of the maquis."

"You have been up in the hills?"

"Fighting the Germans."

"Then you cannot have heard that the de Roujays have been denounced as collaborators and traitors."

"That's as may be," said the Spaniard impassively, "but this house is under my protection, so I advise you to be on your way."

Jaco looked shiftily to the side to see where his men were standing, then at the line of hardened Spaniards, then at the door, then back at the determined face of their commander. He spat on the ground.

"Right," he muttered, "but you'll answer for it." He turned and walked back toward the cars. His men followed. The Spaniards replaced them on each side of the house and took up well-protected positions, not to attack Saint Théodore but to defend it.

The short convoy of two cars carrying the commissioner of the Republic to Mézac was stopped at the city gates. A sour-looking man, apparently the commander of the post, approached the car. Bertrand opened his window and said in a firm and forthright voice, "Let me pass. I am the commissioner of the Republic for the department."

The man spat on the ground. "I don't give a shit who you are," he said. "No one is to enter the city."

"Consult your superiors," said Bertrand curtly, "or you will find yourself responsible for an act of insubordination that you will regret."

He waited. The partisan sauntered insolently to his post and then, after what seemed only a pretense at a conversation with his headquarters, waved the two cars through.

They drove up the Avenue Emile Zola and stopped outside the Hôtel de Ville. A cluster of partisans stood at the entrance, much like a group of the kind of soldiers of fortune who might have been there when it had been built in the seventeenth century. Conscious of the effect of a minor theatrical detail, Bertrand waited for André and Jean-Christophe to alight from the car so that they could open his door. When they had done so he got out, and followed by these two young men walked up the steps to the entrance of the Hôtel de Ville.

Again he was stopped. "Who is in command?" he asked.

"The commissioner of the people, Bouclier."

"Tell Monsieur Bouclier that the commissioner of the Republic, Montrouge, is here under the direct authority of General de Gaulle."

The partisan, a young man with a smooth, naive face, hesitated for a moment, then ran up the wide stone stairs.

Bertrand waited, flanked by André and Jean-Christophe. Vittorio and Charlot-le-Chinois waited by the cars, eyeing the group of partisans as if ready to shoot them down.

The young man returned. "You can come up," he said, "but your men must stay here."

"It is not for you to command me or my men," said Bertrand severely. "I shall go up, and they will come with me."

Without waiting for an answer, he strode into the Hôtel de Ville, and André and Jean-Christophe followed. The partisan stepped aside.

Bertrand climbed the familiar steps to the council chamber. The doors were open. A group of men and women were sitting around the table, and in the place normally occupied by the mayor sat Georges Auget. No one stood to welcome him; instead, most of those present scowled in silence as Bertrand stood at the door.

"Citizens," said Bertrand. "In the name of General de Gaulle and the Provisional Government of France, I congratulate you upon the liberation of Mézac. I am confident that from now on you will place yourself under my orders. I intend to establish my headquarters in the subprefecture, and I await your presence there, Monsieur Auget, without delay."

Then, without waiting for a reply, Bertrand turned and walked down the steps of the Hôtel de Ville and out into the square. He came out into the sunshine to discover that two further cars had drawn up next to those of the Jacopozzis. Jaco, it seemed, had sent reinforcements.

"To the subprefecture," he said to his driver.

André opened the door. Bertrand got into the car and at once felt a pistol against his neck. From reflex, he moved to escape, but as he turned he was gripped by an arm around his neck, while the pistol was jabbed into the flesh below his ear.

"What's this?" he said.

"Shut up," muttered Charlot-le-Chinois, his face close to Bertrand's ear.

Out of the corner of his eye, Bertrand could see that André and Jean-Christophe had been seized in a similar manner by the Jacopozzi men. "Have you gone mad?" he asked.

Charlot laughed and nodded to the driver to set off. "I haven't gone mad, but the boss has." He brought his face closer still. His breath smelled foul. "He didn't like you fucking his wife."

Bertrand turned pale.

"He's dealt with her," said Charlot-le-Chinois. He let go of Bertrand to hold his hands to his own neck and imitate the sound of choking. "Now it's your turn, but if you ask me it won't be so easy or so quick."

A quick succession of thoughts passed through Bertrand's mind. Jaco knew. How? Isabelle must have told him. She was dead. Now he would die. So much the better. There was no one to live for. Except his duty. And Titine.

The car stopped at the gate. Charlot-le-Chinois leaned out the window to argue with the guard. His right hand was on the seat behind him, holding a revolver pointed at his prisoner, but Bertrand took the opportunity to push down the handle of the door. The door moved. With a sudden shove of his shoulder, he pushed it open and rolled out onto the ground as he had been trained to do at Ringway. In a moment he was up again, running in a zigzag toward the corner of the square. He heard a shot, then another, but nothing hit him. Five seconds later there was a burst of machinegun fire, but by then he was in one of the narrow, medieval streets which from his years in Mézac he knew well.

He ran fast, in and out of alleys and across small squares. At first his only thought was to escape from his pursuers, but then he realized that he would soon reach one of the arterial streets which led from the Hôtel de Ville to another of the city's gates. He therefore turned up a side street and hid in a doorway to catch his breath and think of where he might hide. As he looked up, he saw that he was in the Rue des Carmélites, only fifty yards from the heavy studded door to the convent where his sister Dominique was a nun.

When Bertrand de Roujay had appeared at the door of the council chamber at the Hôtel de Ville and announced that he was taking charge, Georges Auget, the secretary of the Committee of Liberation and leader of the Communists in the department of Basse-Provence, had felt an involuntary sense of relief, because the insurrection he had instigated had already passed out of his control. In theory it was to have been a rising of the proletariat, but Mézac was not an industrial city and few of the armed insurgents had ever been industrial workers. In many cases the rising had been used to settle personal rivalries that had nothing to do with the class war. Not only had Resistants turned on the Pétainists and workers on their employers, but in every little neighborhood a hundred petty quarrels between families had been settled with guns.

Worse still, the process of revolutionary justice had gotten out of control. People were being denounced, imprisoned, condemned and executed with no evidence whatsoever that they were guilty of any crime. The Roman arena had been transformed into a makeshift prison, and a self-appointed revolutionary tribunal was in constant session in the Café des Arènes, shaving the heads of women and passing death sentences on real and supposed collaborators with nonchalant dispatch.

Even before Bertrand de Roujay had arrived in the city, some of the more conscientious members of the Committee of Liberation, in constant session in the town hall, had come to realize that their insurrection had stirred up passions that the Party could no longer control. Suggestions had been made that something should be done to restore some semblance of order without reversing the process of revolution; then, in conformity with the discipline of democratic centralism, they had waited to be told what they should do by their leader, Georges Auget.

To their consternation, Auget himself had appeared to dither. Certainly he had three or four hundred disciplined men at his disposal, but if he used them to restore order he risked alienating his supporters among the dispossessed, to whom revenge on the rich was the only point of revolution. If, on the other hand, he did nothing, the Party would become tainted by anarchy and atrocity, which in due course would provoke the forces of reaction.

Bertrand de Roujay had appeared to rescue Auget from this dilemma. While he had made his brief address, the Communist had listened in silence and had said nothing in the clamor which followed Bertrand's departure, but when quiet had been restored in the council chamber he had suggested that as a tactical measure the committee should cooperate with the commissioner, and through him bring the uprising under tighter control.

No sooner had he proposed this, however, than word came up from the entrance to the Hôtel de Ville that the commissioner had been kidnapped at gunpoint by his own supporters, and ten minutes later they heard from the Porte de Coustiers that de Roujay had escaped from his captors into the side streets of the city.

Mystified by this turn of events, Auget adjourned the meeting of the committee and retreated into the office normally occupied by the mayor. It was at this moment that Michel le Fresne arrived from Coustiers to enlighten him. It had been established beyond doubt that

Bertrand de Roujay was the traitor who had betrayed Pierre Moreau and Professor Bonnet to the Germans.

"But that is impossible," said Auget. "Moreau was his closest friend."

"It turns out that de Roujay has always been a Cagoulard," said Michel, pronouncing the name of that secret society of right wing fanatics with a dramatic resonance.

"Impossible," said Auget again, and one or two other comrades, who remembered the leniency of the subprefect of Mézac in 1939, also protested.

"You think it's impossible?" said Michel. "Then ask yourself why de Roujay was released by the Gestapo! Released, moreover, without a mark on his body!"

"It's true," said Auget. "That was never explained."

"You know that his brother, Louis de Roujay, joined the Legion of Volunteers, and is now fighting in the Waffen SS?"

Auget nodded, but the others present heard this information for the first time.

"It seems," said Michel, "that at the outset of the war the two brothers decided to back different horses so that whatever the outcome a Cagoulard would win."

"But does de Gaulle know this?" asked Auget.

"I don't know," said Michel. "It's quite possible that he does not fully appreciate the link between the de Roujays and the Germans. It is also possible, on the other hand, that because he has so often been obliged to appoint men with a progressive outlook to positions of authority, he has sought to redress the balance whenever he can with men like Bertrand de Roujay."

"It is out of the question," said Auget, "after all we have been through, to see a Cagoulard replace a Pétainist in the prefecture of Coustiers."

"Precisely," said Michel. "That is why we must find de Roujay and hold him to account for his treason."

There was a silence among the four or five men in the room.

"But we cannot liquidate the representative of General de Gaulle," said one of the members of the committee.

"We'd certainly have to consult the Central Committee before we did," said Auget.

"If we wait for that, it will be too late," said Michel. "We must act now, dispose of him, and later disown what was done."

"But how, if we try him—"

"We won't try him," said Michel le Fresne. "We'll turn him over to those anarchists at the arena and let them do it for us."

Michel le Fresne himself took charge of the search for Bertrand de Roujay, and having been told that the Jacopozzis' men had abandoned their chase in the area of the Carmelite convent, he realized at once that this was where he would be hiding. Not only was it likely that a Catholic like de Roujay would hide under the skirts of the nuns; he also remembered that Bertrand had a sister who had taken the veil in Mézac. He therefore sent a detachment of partisans to search the buildings and grounds of the convent.

They returned to say that he could not be found, but as the rumor of their fruitless search spread among the groups of partisans at the Hotel de Ville, it reached a fifteen-year-old boy who together with his parents had been hidden in the convent until the Germans had left Mézac. In his enthusiasm to prove to the Resistant that he was worthy to be one of their number, he forgot for a moment what he owed the nuns and boasted of his private knowledge. The detachment went back with the boy, who took them down to the cellar and pointed to a barrel which had been rolled in front of a door.

Under the startled eyes of the silent nuns, the door was broken open and Bertrand de Roujay was dragged out of his refuge. He was frog-marched up the steps of the cellar, out through the gates of the convent and into a Citroën which then raced off to the arena.

The nuns who had witnessed this abduction had no sooner seen the car depart that they heard the bell summoning them to vespers. Obedient to this rule, which Dominique de Roujay had obeyed now for fifteen years, they filed into the chapel and sang the praises of God in the high-pitched voices which gave a girlish sound to the chanting even of the most wizened old nuns.

To a human eye the two rows of veiled women had the same symmetrical abstraction as the architectural design of the Romanesque church, and it was only under the closest scrutiny that a tremble might have been heard in the voice of Dominique as she sang, "I cried unto thee, O Lord: Attend unto my cry; for I am brought very low; deliver me from my persecutors, for they are stronger than I. Bring my soul out of prison, that I may praise thy name."

When the service was over, the nuns filed through to their refectory and ate in silence. It was only after their supper was finished and they had retired to enjoy the only hour of leisure they were allowed during the day that Dominique went to the cell of the prioress.

"I am sorry," the older woman said at once to the younger nun, so clearly in distress. "I pray to God that no harm will come to your brother."

Dominique knelt before her superior. "I have come to ask you, Reverend Mother, for permission to leave the convent and get help."

The prioress sighed. "Of course, Dominique, but where would you go? Who is there who could help him?"

"If I could reach the French army, or the Americans . . ."

"Yes," said the prioress uncertainly. Her window was open, and from outside came the sound of a bee which in the golden light of the late evening was taking pollen from the honeysuckle growing up the wall.

"He is a good man, Reverend Mother. It would be terrible to see him killed by his enemies."

"I don't doubt it, Dominique, and I would never forbid you to save your brother from evil men. But you must consider how you can best help him, remembering always the vow you took never to leave the walls of the convent."

"I do remember, Reverend Mother, but I cannot bear to sit here doing nothing while Bertrand is in danger of death."

A brief frown came onto the face of the old nun. "But do you sit here doing nothing, Dominique? Aren't you sometimes also on your knees?"

"Of course, Reverend Mother. I only meant—"

"A figure of speech. I know. And I understand why, when the world breaks in on us as it did today, you would react at first in a worldly way. But remember the words of the psalm: 'Put not your trust in men in power, or in any mortal man. . . . Happy the man who has the God of Jacob to help him.'"

Dominique bowed her head.

"We have left this world," the prioress went on, "and have put all our trust in God. To falter now, and turn instead to the Americans!"

"Yes, Reverend Mother."

" 'God loves the virtuous and frustrates the wicked,' " Dominique. Ask him to help your brother, and I am sure your prayer will be answered."

Later that day the German garrison in Coustiers surrendered to the 3rd Algerian Division of the French First Army. An enormous crowd thronged the pavements to cheer the victorious troops as they marched down the Avenue de la République. In the absence of Bertrand de Roujay, Guy Serot took the salute at the prefecture.

The arrival of the army had a calming effect on the city. The wild militias disappeared from the streets, and an occasional uniformed gendarme reappeared—though only, as yet, to direct traffic. Serot himself had had a hectic day struggling to reestablish the administration, but as the hours passed he became gradually more intoxicated by the exercise of power and began to dread the moment when Bertrand de Roujay would return.

Throughout the afternoon, Serot's subordinates had reported that the units of the Jacopozzis' men were becoming increasingly recalcitrant, and by six they had all disappeared. It was then that the rumor reached the prefecture that Bertrand was said to have seduced Isabelle Jacopozzi and that Jaco Jacopozzi was hunting him down. Serot's first reaction was to disbelieve it, but the defection of the Jacopozzis indicated that at least they considered it true. Serot then flew into a rage. At the back of his mind he had always thought that he would be the knight to deliver Isabelle from her odious husband, but he justified his exasperation by lambasting the absent commissioner for jeopardizing his mission by amorous intrigue.

It was in this frame of mind that in the early evening he received a message from Mézac that Bertrand de Roujay had been arrested and charged with the betrayal of Pierre Moreau and Professor Bonnet. Again Serot's first reaction was to laugh at the idea, but this was the last spasm of his conscience before it was anesthetized by his passion for power. Realizing at once just what political prestige he could win for himself by remaining in charge of the department, he quickly found reasons why no precipitate actions should be taken to free the commissioner of the Republic. Certainly such an operation would not be easy where the Communists held power. It might unleash the civil war which everyone dreaded, and since Bertrand was clearly in no immediate danger, because no one would dare harm the man appointed by General de Gaulle, there was something to be said for waiting until order in the department had been restored.

The news of de Roujay's arrest also reached Harry Jackson and Captain Ledésert at the Hôtel du Pavillon. Harry's first reaction was to smile.

"So much for the prestige of his office," he said to Ledésert. "It seems the wild men of Mézac don't give a fig for General de Gaulle."

Ledésert frowned. "Our men report complete anarchy. Even the Communists have lost control."

"That's what happens when you open up a can of worms."

"It is unlikely," said Ledésert, "that de Roujay is in any danger."

"Even so," said Harry, "there must be something we can do."

"What do you think we should do?"

"We could send regular troops to rescue him."

"Would General Chevalier release them?"

"I don't know. In theory the troops are not to intervene, but if de Gaulle's own representative, the commissioner of the Republic, is in trouble . . ."

Harry nodded thoughtfully. "You're sure they won't kill him?"

"The Communists? No. Nor the men holding Bertrand, if they know that he is the commissioner of the Republic."

"And if Bertrand is imprisoned in Mézac," said Harry, "won't it be the Communists who will be blamed?"

"They may disown those who hold him."

"But they are supposed to be in power."

"Certainly they will bear some responsibility for what happens to him," said Ledésert.

"It will be an affront to all decent opinion."

"Undoubtedly."

"It could turn the public against them."

"Of course, but you surely don't mean to suggest that we abandon de Roujay for some anti-Communist propaganda."

Jackson smiled. "He's been in prison before, Ledésert. Another day or two won't hurt him."

Ledésert looked perplexed.

"You're a soldier," Harry went on. "You like to fight clean. But I tell you, Captain, when you're fighting the Communists you can't fight clean, because they certainly don't. But now, in playing a little too dirty, they have given us a chance to show them up which may never come again."

"But de Roujay is your friend!" said Ledésert.

"Sure," said Harry, "but if he had the chance, don't you think he'd use me in the same way?"

The third faction in the Resistance whose men were mingling among the crowds of partisans in the streets of Mézac, and who therefore heard of the arrest of Bertrand de Roujay, was the Ursus group, which had always worked directly for the British Special Operations Executive. Since the spring of 1943 it had had a British liaison officer in joint command, and this Englishman, hearing that Bertrand had been arrested, immediately drew up a plan to rescue him from the makeshift prison in the arena. But before embarking upon a mission with such delicate political ramifications, he radioed to London for the authority to put it into effect.

The message reached Bletchley at five in the afternoon, and having been decrypted was passed on to London, where it landed on the desk of Martin Trent just as he was about to leave for the day. "Montrouge menaced by Tartars," the message read. "Serious danger of death. Request authority to intervene. Ursus."

Without discussing the matter with any of his colleagues, Martin Trent put the message in his pocket and took a cab to White's Club in Saint James's Street, where he had arranged to dine with his brother. Since the baronet rarely came to London, Martin felt flattered that he had chosen to spend an evening with him and took it as a sign that he was forgiven for the fiasco of Jenny's marriage to the Frenchman.

It was only after dinner, when Sir Geoffrey offered his brother one of the rare cigars which his merchants in Jermyn Street had managed to procure for him, that Martin asked after Jenny.

"She's up at Ascombe with the little boy. They both seem fine."

"And Eddie?"

"In Italy with the Guards."

"I hear that he was promoted."

"That's right. He's Captain Macleish now."

"Excellent," said Martin. He puffed at his cigar. "And the boy . . ." He hesitated.

"Sweet little chap."

"Is he fond of Eddie?"

"Hardly seen him, of course, but when he does he thinks he's his father."

"The other . . . the Frenchman . . . never made any claims?"

Geoffrey Trent sucked in the thick smoke of his cigar while envious fellow members eyed him from across the room. "To the child? No."

"Did he intimate that he would?"

"He went off to Algiers before the boy was born."

"Before he left, I led him to understand that Eddie was probably the father."

"I'm certain he was. They were at it like rabbits that summer. But she was still married to the frog, and so legally he's the father."

"I know."

"He could claim the child after the war."

"Indeed."

"Jenny's worried that he will."

"It's always possible that he won't survive the war," said Martin.

"He'll survive, all right," said Sir Geoffrey with a scowl. "That's one of the things I didn't like about him. A lot of talk but no fight. Don't imagine the fellow will face the Hun from start to finish!"

Martin Trent said nothing more on the subject of Bertrand de Roujay, but later, after he had finished his cigar and taken leave of his brother, he returned to his office and sent a message to be transmitted to the Ursus group in France: "Plight of Montrouge domestic French affair. Do not in any circumstances intervene."

When Michel le Fresne drove to Mézac, he was accompanied by Madeleine Bonnet. She no longer had any illusions about her lover, but contempt is often an insufficient reason for long-standing couples to part. Moreover, the suspicion she entertained that it was he who had betrayed her father had yet to be substantiated, and it was only by remaining close to him that she might expose his treachery and limit its effect. She could also use the power he now wielded for the practical advantage of her friends. When Nellie Planchet had been traced to an unofficial prison in the suburb of Piron by her own domestic servants,

it was only through Madeleine's intercession with Michel that an order
to release her had been issued—an order, moreover, which was carried
out.

Madeleine had seen Nellie in the Villa Acacia, and had heard from
her why Bertrand had been released. She relayed this information to
Michel in the car on the way to Mézac, and he in turn told her about
Bertrand's liaison with Isabelle Jacopozzi.

"Isabelle?" she exclaimed. "I don't believe it."

"He always had a weakness for women."

"But she's too young," she said with a frown.

"And married," said Michel.

"Who told you this?"

"I heard."

"Does Jaco know?"

"So it seems."

"What has he done?"

"I don't know, but the honeymoon is over."

"How convenient."

"Do you think I arranged it?" he asked with a smirk.

"No," she said uncertainly.

"He was a fool to play around with one of the Jacopozzis' women."

"She is Pierre's sister," said Madeleine, as if to explain rather than
justify what her former husband had done.

"All the same . . ."

"Where is he now?"

"Bertrand?"

"Yes."

"In Mézac."

"Is he in danger?"

"From whom?"

"The Jacopozzis."

Michel laughed. "He's the commissioner of the Republic, isn't he?"

When they reached Mézac, Michel left her with their luggage at
the Hôtel des Capucins. There a suite had been reserved for them by
the Party, and since no one is more sensitive than the staff of a hotel
to shifts in power, she was treated with groveling deference by the
manager. His very unctuousness, however, and the luxury of the suite
irritated Madeleine and exacerbated her pessimism, as if it showed that

there was no more to a proletarian revolution than a change in clientele.

Once in her room, she turned to tip the porter who had brought up the suitcases and recognized him as a man whose daughter had once worked as a housemaid at Saint Théodore.

"What's happening in the town?" she asked as she looked into her purse for a coin.

He was an old man, and he glanced at her suspiciously as if uncertain how to answer.

Madeleine saw his hesitation. "Do you remember me?" she asked.

"Yes, madame," he said. "You are the wife of Monsieur de Roujay."

"That's right. Now tell me, do you know if my husband, the subprefect, is in Mézac?"

Again the old man looked confused. "They say he is here, yes. They say he arrived at midday."

"Where is he now?"

The man did not answer.

"Is he at the Hôtel de Ville? Or the subprefecture?"

"They say he is hiding, madame."

"Ah." She paused, then took a fifty-franc note from her bag. "Listen," she said to the porter. "Find out all you can. Keep me informed."

He nodded, but refused the tip. "I would rather not take the money," he said, "because I remember Monsieur de Roujay, and he is a good man."

Madeleine took a tepid bath, then rested. She did not know when Michel would return, but assumed that she would meet him for supper. She had with her a bundle of newspapers and magazines which had been printed in Coustiers since the liberation, and she read them as she lay on the bed, with a growing dismay at their vengeful tone.

At six there was a knock on the door. It was the old porter in his frayed uniform, carrying a tray on which was a cup and a pot of tea.

"I thought," he said quietly, "that Madame de Roujay might like some refreshment."

Madeleine got up off the bed. The porter closed the door and carried the tray to a table in the middle of the room. "I regret to say," he whispered, "that Monsieur de Roujay has been taken."

"Taken?"

"He was hiding in the Carmelite convent. He has been apprehended and is held in the arena."

"The arena?"

"They are using it to detain suspects."

"But he is the commissioner of the Republic."

"They say he was a collaborator."

"But that's absurd. He was in London."

"I know, madame, but the people at the arena like the English no better than the Germans."

"Who are they, these people at the arena?"

"They call themselves the Resistance, Madame, but truly . . ." He lowered his voice. "They are rats who have escaped from the sewers."

Madeleine left the hotel shortly before seven and walked through the narrow streets of the town which she had always despised to the Hôtel de Ville. There a group of partisans stood guard. She told them that she was the wife of Comrade Requin, and was allowed to pass. Some members of the Committee of Liberation greeted her as she passed them on the steps, and when she reached the landing a comrade from before the war directed her toward the mayor's office.

She opened the door and saw Michel and Georges Auget sitting alone in the room.

"Madeleine!" said Michel, a look of surprise on his face. "What are you doing here?"

"I want a word," she said.

"Later," said Michel, but Georges Auget, from a reflex politeness toward the woman who had fed him so often in the past, got to his feet and offered her a chair.

"I am glad you are here," he said. "You deserve to be a witness when history is made."

Madeleine did not sit down. "Where is Bertrand?" she asked.

"Bertrand?" For a moment Auget looked puzzled. "Ah, de Roujay. Of course, he was your husband."

"Is it true that he has been arrested?"

Auget looked anxiously towards Michel le Fresne.

"I explained to you," Michel said, "that Bertrand has fallen out with the Jacopozzis."

"Are they arresting all adulterers?" she asked sharply.

Auget laughed. "Of course not. The charge is not adultery."

"Then what?" asked Madeleine.

"Collaboration."

"That's absurd. He was with de Gaulle from the start."

"Many Fascists went to London."

"Bertrand has faults," said Madeleine, "but he was never a Fascist."

"But a Cagoulard," said Michel.

She turned to her lover. "You can't believe that."

"I am sure of it," said Michel without a blush.

"Madeleine," said Auget kindly, "it may be hard for you to accept it, and I can understand why Michel may have spared you the knowledge until now, but we are certain that it was de Roujay who betrayed your father and Pierre Moreau to the Germans."

She looked back at Georges Auget. "And what makes you so certain?" she asked derisively.

"Why else was he released by the Germans?"

"Don't you know? Didn't Michel tell you? Or did he want to spare you the knowledge?"

"Know what?" asked Auget, glancing uneasily at Michel le Fresne.

"That Nellie, *his* former wife, made a bargain with Lutze."

"What kind of bargain?"

"Bertrand's life for a comfortable exile."

Georges Auget looked confused. "What is this?" he muttered to Michel.

"It's true," said Michel nonchalantly, "that Nellie now makes out that she did this and that for the Resistance, but it is common enough for collaborators to pretend they were playing a double game."

"You might have mentioned it," said Auget.

"Quite honestly, Georges, it would only have confused the issue. I know my former wife. She was always a liar and a slut."

"And I know my former husband," said Madeleine, "and he was never a collaborator or a Cagoulard."

Georges Auget sat down and thought for a moment with his face hidden in his hands. "It is not really for me to decide these things," he said. "There is a revolutionary tribunal . . ."

"But Georges," said Madeleine, "you know as well as I do that they are all ruffians down there who are shaving heads, cutting off ears and shooting people in the back of the neck for no other reason than that they don't like the look of them. They'll condemn Bertrand for the sound of his voice and the cut of his clothes."

Auget looked up, his eyes troubled and undecided. He opened his mouth to speak, but before he did so he was interrupted by his mentor, Michel le Fresne.

"You must understand, Madeleine," said Michel calmly, "that revolutionary justice and bourgeois justice are not the same things at all. The bourgeois believes in the letter of the law, the revolutionary in the spirit of the law. Perhaps Bertrand did not betray Pierre and your father, but his technical innocence or guilt of a single act is not at issue. Bertrand now represents his class, and his class is guilty before the tribunal of history."

"But he fought for France," she said, pleading not with Michel but with Georges Auget. "He fought for France against the Nazis before you, before me, before anyone else."

"But that's just the point," said Michel, lowering his voice to a whisper and speaking as if to Madeleine but in fact addressing himself to the other man. "If Bertrand is innocent, then the Party is guilty, because he was the first to take up arms against the invader. He claims the spoils of victory. He turns his prestige into power, and with that power mounts a counterrevolution. Everything we have fought for, all the suffering and sacrifice, will come to nothing."

"You are right," said Georges Auget, hitting the desk with his clenched fist. "By bourgeois criteria he may be innocent, but from the standpoint of history he is guilty. The well-being of the masses and the future of France are at stake, and in such circumstances it is better for one man to die for the people."

The partisans who had apprehended Bertrand de Roujay had taken him straight to the Roman amphitheater. There he had been penned in the arena under the hot sun with a herd of dejected suspects. Among them were some officials from the subprefecture who immediately recognized their old chief, and the entire family of Hélène de Roujay's de Sourcy cousins, who had been prominent supporters of Deloncle's Mouvement Social Revolutionnaire which had collaborated with the Germans. They immediately clustered around the former subprefect, because they knew of his connection with de Gaulle; but after listening to their stories Bertrand was obliged to point out that if he had been in a position to help them, he would not be with them in the arena.

Only an hour after his arrest, at seven in the evening, around the time when Madeleine was pleading for his life at the Hôtel de Ville, Bertrand was summoned from the crowd of thirsty, sweating detainees, was dragged from the compound and was frog-marched under the huge arch of the amphitheater across the cobbled pavement to the Café des Arènes, where a revolutionary court-martial was in session.

"You are accused," said the snarling prosecutor, "of collaboration and treason."

"By whom?" asked Bertrand.

"The people."

"That's absurd. I am Bertrand de Roujay, appointed by General de Gaulle as commissioner of the Republic—"

"There's no republic here," said the prosecutor, "only the revolution."

Bertrand looked around; nowhere could he discern an honest or even a dispassionate face. There seemed to be no men from Fortitude, nor even the conscientious Communists who had sacrificed so much over the past three years. All he could see was the twisted, jeering expressions of loathing, envy and malice, the image of evil anarchy that had shown itself so often in France when misery was uncorked by chaos. If their costumes had been different, they might have been living in 1790; all that was missing was the guillotine.

He defended himself as a formality, realizing as he did so that his judges were not only imbecilic but also drunk. Yet they had been furnished with well-chosen facts, and he was obliged to acknowledge that he had been released by the Gestapo unharmed. He could understand that to his judges only treachery could explain a miracle of this kind. He could also understand why his credentials as a Gaullist did not impress them: "If you are not a German spy," said the prosecutor, "then you are an English one, and for that you deserve to die."

At this there were shouts of approbation from the crowd, gathered around the tables and chairs as if watching a cockfight. The judge grinned at their applause, then pronounced sentence: Bertrand de Roujay was a traitor and would be shot at dawn.

Bertrand was led back across the cobbles to the Roman amphitheater, but instead of throwing him back among the other prisoners in the arena, his captors took him down dark steps into a labyrinth of passages below. There they locked him in a room lit only by a narrow slit at the top of one wall like the opening of a letter box.

He was tired. It seemed a week, not a day, since he had slept at the prefecture in Coustiers, and his fatigue made it difficult for him to organize the images and thoughts clamoring for attention in his mind. The memory of Lucía's corpse mingled with horrified speculations about what had happened to Isabelle. Both filled him with such remorse that if it had not been for the thought of Titine he would have welcomed the ignominious death which awaited him.

He remembered the passion he had felt for each of the women, and the love he had felt for both Madeleine and Jenny, but only as remote episodes in his life. His immediate longing was for the serenity which he had encountered that day while taking refuge in the Carmelite convent. The madness he had ascribed to Dominique when she had become a nun now seemed like the only sense, because the world outside the convent walls was the principality of Satan, and it was impossible to live in it without giving the devil his due.

In the fading light Bertrand could see farewell messages that had been scratched by former prisoners in this condemned cell. "A kiss for Elise and the children," one had written; a second, undoubtedly a defiant *milicien*, "Long live Christ the King." How wretched the illusions of those who imagined that it could ever be right to kill for Christ. How mistaken the example of the crusaders; for evil could only be answered with evil, the bombardment of London with the obliteration of Berlin. God took no sides in wars, because as Christ himself had said, his kingdom was not of this world, and no legions of angels were ever summoned to battle for his cause.

Then what had Bertrand fought for? For France—but what was France but a collection of the very vermin who had condemned him, their souls, like their faces, twisted with hatred and envy? For democracy? Yet had he not denied democracy when he had deserted Pétain and joined de Gaulle? For liberty? Yet now those who had been liberated had imprisoned him.

He remembered his meeting with Madeleine on the eve of his departure from France, and her scoffing jibe that it was only boredom and disappointed ambition that was leading him to join de Gaulle. But he also remembered his own high-flown conviction that he must risk his life for the future of his child. Had that aspiration been an illusion?

Were all ideals simply the masks of self-interest, as Lutze had suggested, just as love was a veneer over lust?

He watched a fly as it landed on the scratched inscription "Long live Christ the King." It nibbled at the letter C of "Christ." What did that crevice mean to the fly? A trough in which some sweat from the condemned man's hand had collected, which the fly was sampling for its supper? Did man know as little about God, and the true nature of his creation, as the fly knew about the alphabet? Tomorrow, no doubt, he would have the answer, and would receive his judgment too. To prepare himself for that judgment, Bertrand now knelt to pray on the earth floor, for though he might not have been good, he had aspired to what was good, and he earnestly besought his Christian God to protect those whom he loved, and to forgive him for what he had done wrong.

That night in Coustiers, soldiers from the French First Army roamed the streets to enjoy a brief respite before moving on against the Germans. The crowds on the pavements were jubilant; the drinks in the cafés were on the house. So too were the attentions of all the young women who from patriotic fervor gave the young French soldiers their second surrender of the day, and obliged the girls around the Opéra to emulate the proprietors of the cafés and provide their services free as well.

On the Quai du Fleuve, the Jacopozzis were back in the Bar Fénelon, but Jaco was yet to be seen. The men who had been with him at Saint Théodore had told their friends how they had been frustrated by the Spaniards; then the party from Mézac had returned with the news that Bertrand de Roujay had eluded them. Stefano laughed at the news of these fiascos, which only confirmed that his brother had lost his touch. A brief glance around the bar convinced him that everyone now looked to him to lead them.

On the other side of the city, in the Hameau de Braulhet, Jaco Jacopozzi returned alone to the Villa Fleurie. He had sent his men back to Coustiers because he knew that had he not done so they would have deserted him. His humiliation at Saint Théodore had destroyed the last vestige of their respect. No one would follow a cuckold who had run from some Spaniards.

The villa was now empty; the women had returned to Coustiers, and with them Tonio and the men who had guarded the house. For a moment he thought of his son, and how the little boy used to rush to hug him when he returned. Involuntarily he looked up for a light in the bedroom window where Isabelle was always waiting, but behind the shutters all was dark.

He stopped as if he did not believe his memory, and then instead of entering the house he turned down the path which led across the garden to the spot where his men had dug a shallow grave. There, sure enough, was the mound of fresh earth, and as he looked at it he sobbed, and then fell to his knees and wept.

Then he heard the sound of footsteps on the gravel. He looked up, but could see no one. Afraid that he might be caught in this ignominious position by one of his men, he stood, wiped his eyes on the sleeve of his jacket, then brushed off the earth and pine needles that had stuck to his trousers.

He walked toward the house. In the dark he could see the figure of a man walking quietly from the front door to the terrace. His shape was familiar, but it was only when he came close and the man suddenly turned to face him that Jaco saw that it was Guillot.

"What do you want?" asked Jaco, confident that in the dark the policeman could not see the traces of his tears.

Guillot turned. Though he must have been startled, he showed no surprise. "Ah, Jaco," he said. "I was looking for you."

"Well, here I am."

"I thought we might have a little chat."

Jaco shrugged his shoulders and sat on the garden chair where Isabelle had so often waited for his return from Coustiers. "What about?"

Guillot sat on the arm of a wooden bench. "This and that," he said, lighting a cigarette.

"I daresay you're on the run," said Jaco.

"Not at all," said Guillot calmly.

"They'll do you in."

"For what?"

Jaco laughed; the list was so long he would not know where to start. "For everything," he said.

"I did my duty," said Guillot.

"And more."

Guillot drew on his cigarette and looked at Jaco with expressionless eyes. "More?" he asked.

Jaco chuckled. "Remember the deal about the Jews?"

"Yes."

"They won't like that."

"They won't know about it."

"Lutze will blab if they catch him."

"Lutze is dead."

Suddenly Jaco realized why Guillot was there. His hand moved toward his pocket for his gun, but then stopped; Guillot's revolver already rested on his knee.

"You're a fool," he said quickly, but with the panic evident in his voice.

"Why?"

"They'll know you did it, and ask why."

"No," said Guillot, finishing his cigarette and crushing it under his heel. "There are too many bodies already for anyone to worry about the corpse of a crook."

Jaco snarled and sprang at him, but Guillot pulled the trigger of his revolver. Jaco fell gasping on the paving stones. He turned for a moment, his face taut with shock and pain. The light from the stars caught the flickering lids of his kestrel eyes. They opened for a moment with a look of loathing; then Guillot stooped and dispassionately fired a second shot into his ear.

Among the officers of the 3rd Algerian Division in Coustiers was Raymond Blaise de la Vallée, who on the night of the city's liberation was celebrating the surrender of the German garrison with General Chevalier and his staff.

Raymond was in high spirits, because having joined de Lattre's army in Algiers, he was at last fighting on the winning side in the war. He was quite untroubled by the paradox that within the past three years he had killed Englishmen, Americans and Free French with the same patriotic enthusiasm as he now killed Germans. When his tanks had rolled into Coustiers that day and the delirious crowds had shrieked and cheered with joy, when girls wearing flimsy dresses from the working-class districts of Piron had clambered onto his Sherman to garland him with flowers, Raymond had been unable to prevent tears of manly patriotism from flowing down his cheeks. Now he sat with his commander and five or six fellow officers with an open bottle of Calvados, proud and happy that they had come so far, and eager the next day to press on to join the rest of the army.

Their modest celebration was suddenly interrupted by the intrusion of the duty officer, a young lieutenant, who crossed the room and whispered in the general's ear. The general frowned as the lieutenant stood back, waiting for an answer. The general looked across to his adjutant. "What's going on in Mézac?"

The adjutant looked blank. "In Mézac? No idea."

The general turned to the lieutenant. "You'd better show her in."

The lieutenant left the room, and the general turned to his officers. "Apparently there's a woman at the gate who says that the commissioner, de Roujay, is a prisoner in Mézac, and that he's to be shot at dawn."

"By the Germans?" asked the adjutant.

"No, damm it, by the Bolsheviks!"

"But that's ridiculous," said Raymond, "because I know the commissioner. He's my cousin."

"Then perhaps you know his wife," said the general.

As he spoke, the door opened and Madeleine Bonnet was ushered in by the lieutenant.

"Why, yes," said Raymond. "It's Madeleine."

She blinked in the bright light, and the officers, though it was immediately apparent from her bohemian appearance that she was not their type, rose to their feet and offered her a chair.

"Now, madame," said the general courteously, "what is this news you bring us from Mézac?"

"The commissioner, Bertrand de Roujay"—she glanced at Raymond—"who was my husband—"

"Is a prisoner?"

"Yes. They mean to kill him."

"Who?"

Her voice was low. "His enemies."

"The Resistance?"

"No . . . yes. I don't know. They call themselves the Resistance, but they are being used . . ."

"By whom?"

"By the Communists."

The adjutant leaned forward. "But would they dare kill the commissioner?"

"When it is done they will blame it on the chaos, the anarchy, the riffraff. But they want him dead."

"Why?"

"They think that without him they can take power."

The general turned to his adjutant. "We should do something," he said, but more as a question than as a statement of intent.

The adjutant, who had more knowledge of the political niceties, shook his head doubtfully. "This is more a question for the prefecture."

"They have no power," said Madeleine. "Moreover, no one—*no one* can be trusted."

"Then the Free French Forces of the Interior. We must call Captain Ledésert."

"It will be too late," said Madeleine. "All the Free French Forces in Mézac are controlled by the Communists. By the time they send in other men, Bertrand will be dead."

The general drummed his fingers on the table. "De Roujay was handpicked by de Gaulle," he said to his adjutant. "It's surely our duty to save him."

The adjutant lowered his voice. "Of course," he said, "but our orders are to fight the Germans and only the Germans, and not to become embroiled in civil disturbances."

The general looked uncertain. "I know, I know . . ."

Now Raymond Blaise de la Vallée spoke up. "General," he said, "Bertrand de Roujay is not just my cousin. He also saved my life!"

"In battle?"

"Place de la Concorde, General, in '34."

The general went pink in the face, drew himself up to his full height, turned to Raymond and said, "What will you need?"

"Six tanks, transporters, and a company of spahis."

"Your intentions?"

"To leave now, and enter the city at first light."

The general slammed his fist down on the table. "Very well. Damn the risk. Didn't de Gaulle himself disobey? But take care, la Vallée. Political minefields are more dangerous than those on the field of battle."

·   ·   ·

Bertrand awoke when the first dim light of the approaching dawn could be seen through the slot in the stone ceiling. For a moment he was confused, and feeling the hard earth floor, thought that he had fallen out of bed. Then he remembered, and all at once a terrible dread came over him, a despair which ran from his brain throughout his frame to numb the tips of his body; but a moment later, like a second wave breaking on the beach which overwhelms the first, he remembered the God who was waiting to receive him, and fell on his knees to pray.

It was not long before they came to fetch him, and as he was led up into the arena he felt glad of a chance to see the sky again before he died. He stood for a moment to breathe in the cool air and admire the pink-and-blue light of the dawn. It seemed like a foretaste of the beauty that was awaiting him. The grumpy, sullen partisans who were guarding him prodded him forward with their submachine guns beneath the arch which led out of the arena.

A truck was waiting to take Bertrand and five others to the city prison where they were to be shot. His hands were tied; then he was lifted onto the back. One prisoner was still to come. They waited silently. A man next to Bertrand shivered from the dew. "It's cold," he said.

"It will be colder in your grave," said the partisan who was guarding them. Then he cursed quietly at the delay, took out a cigarette and struck a match to light it.

The match gave a hiss, and it was when this sound stopped that Bertrand heard a quiet rumble from the town. In the distance there was a faint cry, then more cries and a louder rumble.

The partisan drew on his cigarette and walked around the truck to see what was happening. It sounded as if a tractor was approaching, perhaps two, but there was shouting, too, with cries of *"Vive la France"* and "Hurrah," as around the corner came a group of girls in white tunics smudged with flour who seemed to have left a baker's shop. As they skipped into view they looked back over their shoulders at the approaching cavalcade, which as it drew closer made the ground tremble. Suddenly Bertrand saw, as it turned the corner, the gun barrel of a Sherman tank. It rolled forward with a deafening roar and a rattle of its tracks on the cobbles, which echoed off the huge walls of the ancient amphitheater. Sitting in the turret, his head covered by a leather cap, was the commander, and beside him on the street beside the tank were the fierce, dark faces of Algerian soldiers.

"Shit," said the partisan who was guarding the truck. He glanced at his half-smoked cigarette, as if wondering if he had time to finish it. He looked up again at the tank, whose huge cannon seemed to be pointing at him. He threw away his cigarette, slipped the sling of his submachine gun off his shoulder, dropped the weapon on the cobbles, and ran.

The tank stopped outside the amphitheater. The commander removed his cap and waved at Bertrand, who recognized him at once as his inane cousin.

When the Committee of Liberation in Mézac arrived that morning at the Hôtel de Ville they found that a delirious crowd had already gathered around three formidable Shermans of the French First Army and a dour guard of spahis. Faced with this force of American tanks and African mercenaries, with a Breton count in command, the small group of Communists who as the midwives of history had until this moment controlled the city made a tactical retreat into the side streets. A hurried meeting of the leadership gathered in a small café and decided that Mézac, which had no proper proletariat, should be regarded as "tangential," and that the energies of the Party should henceforth be concentrated on Coustiers. Georges Auget and Michel le Fresne then departed for the larger city, leaving it to the local leaders to explain how anarchists had abducted the commissioner of the Republic.

By noon that day, Bertrand de Roujay was back in his office in the prefecture at Coustiers. Though he had learned from Raymond of the role the Communists had played in his ordeal, the political realities were such that he had no choice but to appoint Georges Auget president of the Departmental Committee. Guy Serot, whose outrage at what had happened in Mézac was almost convincing, asked for and was given the presidency of the Regional Council, and Emile Planchet was appointed the president of the Chamber of Commerce.

It was to Planchet, that evening, that Bertrand confided his misgivings about his own competence for the office he now held. "To prepare yourself for death," he said, "you have to detach yourself from life. I find myself almost indifferent to what happens here in Coustiers."

"So much the better," said Planchet. "There is too much passion and not enough detachment."

"But I am the wrong man for the job," said Bertrand. "As you have seen, I have just had to appoint a man who tried to murder me. I have no real power in the city, and my impotence discredits de Gaulle."

Planchet shook his head. "You must be patient," he said. "You are the only man with the experience and prestige to govern the department."

"But one cannot govern without some force to impose one's authority."

"There are the troops."

"They are reserved for the war."

"The police?"

"Disorganized, demoralized, terrified of the crowd."

"It will burn itself out," said Planchet. "It is always the same in France. These insurrections are like earthquakes which bring down a few old buildings, but then, when the dust settles, we build them up again in much the same style as before. That is what happened in 1789, 1830, 1848, 1871. It is only a matter of waiting."

"You may be right," said Bertrand, "but even Napoleon had a Fouché to tell him when the tremors had stopped."

"And you have your Fouché," said Planchet. "I saw him waiting in the corridor as I came in."

"Who?" asked Bertrand.

"Commissaire Guillot."

Guillot entered when Planchet left, and as he did so there was a hiccup in the power supply and the light dimmed. The eyes of the two men met, and Bertrand recognized in the fleshy, impassive features of the policeman the face he had seen through the window of the train in Toulouse.

He made no allusion to their last encounter but looked up from his desk as if it were only a day since he had last received Guillot in his office in Mézac.

"Guillot. Good. What have you to report?"

Guillot understood at once how he was to behave. "Things are settling down," he said.

"I am told that some of the police won't leave their barracks."

"They are more confident now that the army is around."

"Can you deploy them to control the militias?"

"It can be done if some of them are in plainclothes."

"As you like. Our objective is to put a stop to all arbitrary trials and executions, and to restore the due process of law."

"Of course, Commissioner." Guillot glanced at the pen on Bertrand's desk. "I only thought, if you don't mind, that it might be useful if I had some document confirming my appointment. There are many who might question it."

"Very well," said Bertrand. He called in his secretary, the same woman who had served Charrier. "Please draw up a document confirming Monsieur Guillot as commissaire of the Coustiers police."

She looked surprised. "Of course," she said, and left the room.

"There is a further matter," said Bertrand to Guillot in a quieter tone of voice. "I want you to send a man to the Villa Fleurie to find out just what happened to Isabelle Jacopozzi."

"That has been done," said Guillot simply.

"And?"

"We found her body in a grave in the garden. She had been strangled."

"Ah. And Jaco?"

"He is dead."

"I see."

"You may not have heard, Commissioner, but there were rumors about you and Madame Jacopozzi."

"So I gather."

"They have been traced to the Communists. It was to discredit you."

"But Jaco believed them."

"Yes. He was rather unstable. But Stefano is more practical. We can count on him."

"Good."

"He tells me that Jaco went out to the house of Colonel de Roujay, your father, but that he was turned back by the local Resistance."

"Are they safe?"

"Yes."

Bertrand looked toward the window. "What else?"

"Many unexplained deaths," said Guillot. "Bodies floating in the river, on derelict sites. A girl dead in the courtyard of the Hôtel du Pavillon."

"A suicide?"

"Undoubtedly." Guillot paused. "Or some quarrel with a pimp. Many are settling old scores under the pretext of the political purge."

"Clearly," said Bertrand, turning to face the commissioner just as the secretary came back into the room. "And that is just what must stop. We must regain control, reestablish justice . . ." He took the piece of paper, read it cursorily, then signed it and stamped it with his seal of office.

"There, Guillot," he said, handing it to the policeman. "You have my full authority to take what measures are necessary. I count on you, just as General de Gaulle counts on me."

At the beginning of September the schools reopened in Coustiers, and it was only then that Bertrand found Madeleine, by waiting for her, just as Pierre once had, as she came out through the gates of the Lycée René le Bon.

"Where have you been?" he asked.

"In the mountains with Maman."

They walked down toward the Avenue de la République as Madeleine described in detail the events which had led her to call for the help of Raymond Blaise de la Vallée. Upon reaching the avenue they turned left and returned to the Jardin des Plantes, where Pierre had arranged their meeting in July. The memory of their friend was so powerful that they sat for a moment in silence, too careful of one another's feelings to risk an inappropriate word.

Then Madeleine turned, and blinking into the weakening light of the sinking sun, asked if there was news of her father.

Bertrand shook his head. "I am sorry."

"And Bérénice?"

"No."

"It is so easy to forget," Madeleine said, "now that we are free, that the war goes on in the rest of France."

He nodded. "It was always our weakness, to see it only from our own point of view."

"Not you." She smiled. "When I remember how I scoffed at you the day you told me that you were going to London."

"You have made up for that by saving my life."

"I realized just in time that it was a life worth saving."

"I am grateful," he said, "and I would like to tell Titine what you did."

"If you like. It might make her approve of me at last."

"I haven't seen her yet. I couldn't leave Coustiers. But I thought that this weekend I would go to Saint Théodore, and I am sure she would be delighted if you came too."

Madeleine wrinkled her nose. "I can't believe that your mother would share her delight."

"She knows that you saved my life."

Madeleine looked wistfully into the air. "They were carried away," she said. "I wanted to save you, but also to save them from themselves."

"And are they grateful?"

She focused on his face, and then smiled. "No. I have lost a few friends—and a lover too, for that matter."

"I am sorry."

"Don't be sorry. My second divorce, if you can call it that, has left me much happier than the first one ever did."

That Sunday, at Saint Théodore, it was thought cool enough to eat lunch under the shade of the chestnut trees. Never short of food like their compatriots in the city, the de Roujays had slaughtered a suckling pig to celebrate their son's return.

With Bertrand and Madeleine in the commissioner's official car came Françoise Bonnet, laughing almost constantly under the pressure of conflicting emotions, and Nellie Planchet, her head swathed stylishly in a scarlet turban. Soon afterwards, Harry Jackson arrived in a staff car of the U.S. Army. From the other direction, in a decrepit little Renault, came Charles Ravanel, the bishop of Langeais. Alice had ordered that the Sèvres china was to be laid on a white linen tablecloth, as well as the silver cutlery with the de Roujays' coat of arms. When they were all seated at the table, Hélène helped Marthe serve the food while her children stared with wide eyes at their tall Uncle Bertrand, wishing without saying so that it was their father who had returned.

The thought of those who were dead, or still lost in the devastated wastes of central Europe, constrained their joy. Louis, Pierre, Bérénice, Turco, Isabelle, Lucía and Professor Bonnet stood like stone statues in the hearts of them all. But if this one small group of a family and their friends still bore the wounds and weals which all the French had suffered over the past four years, either from the assault of an enemy or inflicted upon themselves, there was also in their gentle and tolerant manner, as there was in the soft autumn sun and the breeze which rustled the chestnut trees, the promise that these wounds would heal and enmity be forgotten.

Astran and his wife had been invited to come to lunch, but the Spaniard had courteously refused. Already his group of Resistants had been disbanded, some like his son joining de Lattre de Tassigny's army as it fought its way into Germany, others going west toward Toulouse, pursuing a rumor that a legion of Republican Resistants would soon march against Franco across the Pyrenees.

Astran himself, however, had returned to prepare the grapes for harvest. He could be seen from the garden, bent over the vines by the river, working on Sunday as he had always done to show his disdain for religion. When lunch was over, and the bishop slept in the sun, Bertrand decided that he would walk down to see him to express what he could of both his gratitude and his regret. Madeleine, who had heard how her daughter had been saved by the Spaniards, decided to go with him; and it was perhaps only in the heart of Titine, as she saw her mother and father walk side by side down the familiar path to the river, that both happiness and joy were unalloyed.

Postscript

O_F the two hundred thousand men and women deported from France during the German occupation, only fifty thousand returned. As soon as the war was over, a search was made for the parents, wife and children of Pierre Moreau. They were traced from Coustiers to Drancy, and from Drancy to Auschwitz, where, it was assumed, they suffered the fate of so many millions of their fellow Jews.

Michel Bonnet died in Buchenwald. A French priest, Yves Coulet, who had befriended him there, told Madeleine after the war how her father had frequently given his paltry rations to younger men, which had led inevitably to his death. "I tried to persuade him," said the priest, "that it was an unreasonable thing to do, but he would not agree. He said that his life had served its purpose, and that he was quite ready to die."

Louis de Roujay was killed in Berlin in the last weeks of the war. He was among the three hundred Frenchman of the Charlemagne Division of the Waffen SS who, when the Russians were only two streets away from the Chancellery, were sent to reinforce General Mummert's army corps, which was defending it. As Hitler prepared his suicide, they fought fanatically to defend him, many leaping from the rubble to attack tanks with grenades, shouting "Long live Christ the King!"

On October 28, 1944, the militias of the Resistance were dissolved. Where there had been a Communist conspiracy to seize power in France, it had been frustrated by de Gaulle and his commissioners. In the municipal elections of May 1945, Guy Serot, standing for the Socialist Party, was elected mayor of Coustiers. In the election for a

Constituent Assembly six months later, Georges Auget was returned as a representative of the Communist Party. Michel le Fresne was made head of the hospital in Coustiers.

After the obliteration of Hiroshima and Nagasaki, and the surrender of the Japanese in the Far East, Raymond Blaise de la Vallée was sent to Hanoi on the staff of the military commander, General Leclerc. The former Carmelite monk Thierry d'Argenlieu, who had chosen the emblem of the Cross of Lorraine for the Gaullist crusade, was appointed high commissioner and sternly reimposed French rule over the Vietnamese.

At the instigation of Ho Chi Minh, who had led the local resistance to the Japanese, the Emperor of the Annamite Kingdom, Bao Dai, wrote to de Gaulle asking for Vietnamese independence. "You have suffered too much," he wrote, "during four deadly years not to understand that the Vietnamese people, who have a history of twenty centuries and an often glorious past, no longer wish, can no longer support, any foreign domination."

De Gaulle did not reply to this letter, and the war which followed took the life not only of Raymond Blaise de la Vallée but also of Etlin, Bertrand's friend from his days in London, who was murdered while gathering intelligence on the Vietminh in a brothel in the Chinese suburb of Saigon.

In the winter of 1944, the French army became bogged down in the war against Germany, which, though it continued with great ferocity, seemed to have been forgotten in France. While some of the Resistants from the disbanded militias went on to fight in the regular army, others had lost interest in the conflict when it ceased to hold out promise of political power. De Gaulle therefore felt obliged to issue an appeal to the French to remember that the war was not over, and among those who volunteered as a result of this call was young Thierry de Roujay. Eager to expunge the guilt he felt at his role in the *milice,* and to earn the approbation of his absent father, even by fighting on the opposite side, he was given his training on the battlefield, crossed the Rhine with de Lattre de Tassigny, was grazed by shrapnel at the taking of Stuttgart, but fought on to witness the raising of the tricolor over Hitler's mountain retreat at Berchtesgaden.

After the war he went to Saint Cyr, and like his father made a career in the army. He fought at Dien Bien Phu and in Algiers, but in 1957 was released from the army because of "nervous disorders." Only later did it emerge that he had suffered some kind of collapse when witnessing the torture of FLN suspects during the Algerian war. His commanding officer, Colonel Rivière, who was directing the interrogations, was the same Rivière who had questioned Bertrand at the headquarters of the Gaullist Secret Service in Saint James's Square.

On January 20, 1946, exasperated by the determination of the Constituent Assembly to bring back the kind of constitution that in his view had enfeebled France before the war, General de Gaulle resigned as the provisional President of France. In Coustiers, Bertrand de Roujay felt released from his duty and resigned too. Though under his administration the recovery of the department had been remarkably successful—by the end of 1945 the economic output had returned to the level of 1939—he had never accustomed himself to the bickering of the different political factions or the antagonism of the Communists, who continued to wield considerable power.

He returned to Saint Théodore to live quietly with his family and manage the vineyard with the help of Astran. Madeleine Bonnet spent her holidays there, and, in 1952, when her mother died, she gave up her post at the Lycée René le Bon and came to live there altogether. By then the senior de Roujays were both dead—first Edmond, followed by Alice only two weeks later—and Hélène de Roujay had remarried a widowed officer from Louis de Roujay's regiment in the French army. Bertrand and Madeleine never remarried, but they remained together at Saint Théodore for the rest of their lives.

Nellie Planchet returned to live at the Villa Acacia in the same style as before, with the same devoted servants. As she grew older her lovers grew younger, but with the loss of the French empire, Coustiers went into a relative decline, and with it the fortunes of the Planchets. At the age of fifty, Nellie discovered that she was in debt and that her father could do nothing to help her. She therefore dismissed her current lover, a German student at the university, gave up drinking and opened a boutique on the Avenue de la République. The boutique prospered —she knew just what the young wanted to wear—and in time became a chain of shops which, when floated as a public company, made Nellie once again a millionaire.

Charles Ravanel died in Rome in 1953. His speech supporting Pétain had been remembered more vividly than his assistance to fugitive Jews, and after the war he had been transferred from his diocese in Langeais to a post in the Vatican.

Antoine Dubec, the Dominican friar, became prominent in the worker-priest movement of the 1950s, and when it was suppressed by Pope Pius XII he abandoned his calling and became a full-time official of the Communist Tracks Union, the CGT.

Charrier, the former prefect of Basse-Provence, was tried for the part he had played in enforcing the policies of Vichy. He prepared a vigorous and detailed defense, proving that thanks to the policies of Darlan and Laval the French had suffered significantly less than comparable nations like Belgium or the Netherlands. The sixty thousand executions he blamed upon the Resistance, which for its own political purposes had unscrupulously provoked the occupying power without affecting by one jot the final outcome of the war. When attacked for his role in the deportation of Jews, he proved with a masterly display of statistics that just as King Aegeus had sent seven youths and seven maidens to be devoured by the Minotaur for the greatest good of the greatest number of Athenians, so the sacrifice of the Jews had been necessary for the greatest good of the greatest number of the French. His defense fell on deaf ears. He was sentenced to ten years in prison, but was released under the general amnesty in 1952.

Guillot remained commissaire of the police in Coustiers until 1948. He then became compromised by a scheme to cheat the American CIA by pretending to employ the Jacopozzi gang to break the Communist general strike. The American behind the plan, Harry Jackson, complained to the mayor, Guy Serot, and Guillot was obliged to resign from the police. For a time he ran a brothel for the Jacopozzis near the Place de l'Opéra, but a year later he was found dead in a back street of Coustiers. It was said that he had tried to take over from Stefano Jacopozzi. Stefano Jacopozzi himself was shot dead in a bar in Marseilles in 1952, apparently the victim of a dispute with the Guerinis.

In 1947, when the alliance formed during the Resistance between the Communists and the Socialists was finally ruptured and when the prime minister, Ramadier, got rid of his Communist ministers in Paris,

Serot undertook a purge of a similar kind in Coustiers. Among those he dismissed was the director of the hospital, Michel le Fresne. No reason was given for this firing, but rumors were put about that he had sold penicillin from the hospital on the black market and had performed abortions for the nurses he had seduced and made pregnant.

Worse still, it was now said that it was le Fresne who had betrayed Pierre Moreau to the Gestapo. He was shunned by his former friends from the Resistance. Only the Communists stood by him, ascribing all the charges to capitalist slander, and for want of any other friends Michel stood by them, linking arms with the Party leaders of Basse-Provence during the demonstrations they organized in Coustiers during the general strike. A blow from a truncheon of the police during one of these riots cracked his skull and damaged his brain. His former colleagues at the hospital operated at once but could do nothing to save him from a semivegetable existence. The Communists in Coustiers wanted to exploit his misfortune and canonize le Fresne as a martyr for their cause, but to their astonishment this was forbidden by their local leader, Georges Auget. He arranged instead for Michel le Fresne to end his days in a Soviet sanatorium.

Eddie Macleish was demobilized after the war with the rank of major and two decorations, the Distinguished Service Order and the Military Cross. He returned to Glengoyle, his estate in Scotland, with Jenny, his wife, and Henry, his son. There he raged against the rates of taxation introduced by the Labour government and entertained his neighbors with his invective against the buggers and bolshies in London.

Though Jenny hankered for the metropolis, Eddie would never go farther south than Addington Abbey in Yorkshire. She consoled herself with gardening during the long, light summers, and with malt whiskey in the winter. In 1947 she gave birth to a second son, who, Eddie told her, would be heir to Glengoyle.

"But Henry is your eldest son," she said.

"Take a good look at him," Eddie snapped. "He's no more my son than you are."

Early in 1949, on his way to Saigon, Bertrand's friend Etlin came to stay at Saint Théodore, where he confided to Titine, now sixteen, that her father had married in England and that there was a son, Henry, who bore his name.

When Etlin departed, Titine asked Bertrand about this wife and child. A look of anguish and perplexity passed over his face. "That is not something I want to remember," he said. "I would be grateful if you would never mention it again."

A year later, however, a letter arrived from England which Madeleine told Titine was from Bertrand's English wife. At the end of June she arrived at Saint Théodore with a seven-year-old boy wearing gray knee-length shorts. When Titine saw him she burst out laughing, because he was a miniature replica of her father.

The English wife only stayed for lunch, but the boy remained for the summer. Bertrand and Titine taught him to ride and swim, and when Titine was married the following year to a young architect from Aix-en-Provence, Harry came out from England for her wedding. By the end of that summer he could speak French—well enough, at any rate, to sing the "Marseillaise" when he stood next to his father at the opening of the new airport for Basse-Provence named Coustiers–Pierre Moreau.

PIERS PAUL READ was born in 1941, brought up in Yorkshire and educated at Cambridge. In addition to two years spent in Germany and one in the United States, he has traveled extensively in the Far East and South America. He is married with four children and lives in London.